MUSIC
BUSINESS

IMMEDIA Music Business Books
20 Hordern St. Newtown 2042
Australia (02) 9557 7766
www.immedia.com.au/books

Music Business first published in 1994 by Warner Bros Music

Second edition published 2002 by Omnibus Press
Revised edition published 2003 by Omnibus Press
This Third edition published 2006 by Omnibus Press

Cover Design: Chloe Alexander
Text Design: Campbell Murray Creating
Index: Puddingburn Publishing Services

ISBN 1 921029 315
Order Number: OP51315

Exclusive Distributors:

Music Sales Limited,
14/15 Berners Street,
London W1T 3LJ, UK

Music Sales Corporation,
257 Park Avenue South,
New York, NY 10010, USA

Macmillan Distribution Services,
56 Parkwest Drive
Derrimut Victoria 3030 Australia

To The Music Trade only:

Music Sales Limited,
14/15 Berners Street,
London W1T 3LJ, UK

Music Sales Pty Limited,
20 Resolution Drive,
Caringbah NSW 2229
Australia

Printed by McPherson's Printing Group,
Maryborough Victoria.

www.omnibuspress.com

MUSIC BUSINESS

A MUSICIAN'S GUIDE TO THE AUSTRALIAN MUSIC INDUSTRY
BY TOP AUSTRALIAN LAWYER AND DEALMAKER

SHANE SIMPSON

OMNIBUS PRESS

LONDON/NEW YORK/PARIS/SYDNEY/COPENHAGEN/MADRID/TOKYO

To those who write the music and those who perform it

CONTENTS

PREFACE   18

ACKNOWLEDGMENTS   20

1 SELECTING AND PROTECTING A NAME   21

THE NAME SEARCH   22

PROTECTING THE NAME?   23
Business Name Registration • Trademark

BAND STRUCTURES WHICH PROTECT THE NAME   24
Partnerships • Companies And Shareholder Agreements

WHAT'S IN A NAME?   25
Pop Mechanix • Fleetwood Mac • The Five Platters Inc •
The On-going Story

SOUND-ALIKES   27
Protection From Sound-alikes

2 BUSINESS STRUCTURES   30

WORKING SOLO   30

WORKING WITH OTHERS   32

Starting Out

THE OPTIONS   32
Partnership • Companies • Trusts

3 NOT-FOR-PROFIT ORGANISATIONS   40

PRELIMINARY ISSUES   41
What Does 'Non-Profit' Mean? • What Will the Primary Sources of
Funding Be?

ESTABLISHING A MUSIC ORGANISATION   43
Defining the Objects • Defining the Implementation Strategy
• Selecting the First Board

SELECTING THE STRUCTURE   45
Unincorporated Non-Profit Groups • The Incorporated Association
• Co-operatives • The Company Limited by Guarantee • Trusts

REGISTER OF CULTURAL ORGANISATIONS   52

MANAGING A NON-PROFIT ARTS ORGANISATION   53
Purpose of the Board • Selecting the Board •Skills Matrix • Assignment
of Responsibilites • Decision Making, Defining Policy and Setting
Strategy • Setting Limits and Creating Communication Channels
• Delegation

DEALING WITH PROBLEM BOARD MEMBERS   61
Ghosts • Back Slappers • Celebrities and Socialites • Sleepers • Bullies • Lifers • Martyrs • Secret Agents • Talkers • The Diary Afflicted • The Conflicted

LEGAL RESPONSIBILITIES OF PEOPLE IN AUTHORITY   65
Statutory Bodies • Duties of Committee Members of Unincorporated Associations • Duties of Management Committee Members of Incorporated Associations • Duties of Directors of Companies Limited by Guarantee • Liability of Directors and Employees to Pay Company Debts • People Forbidden to be Involved with Management of the Organisation

CHECKLIST FOR BOARDS AND MANAGERS OF NON-PROFIT ARTS ORGANISATIONS IN AUSTRALIA   73

4   AGENTS   **78**

THE FUNCTION OF AGENTS   79

THE POWERS AND AUTHORITIES OF AGENTS   80
The Authority to Represent • The Authority to Receive and Negotiate Offers of Employment • The Authority to Sign Booking Agreements on the Musician's Behalf • The Authority to Collect Deposits and Performance Fees

AGENTS' FEES AND COMMISSIONS   82

WRITTEN AGENCY AGREEMENTS   82

BOOKING AGREEMENTS AND ENGAGEMENT CONFIRMATIONS   85

VENUE CONSULTANTS   87
Payroll Services

5   THE MANAGER   **89**

QUALIFICATIONS   90

WHEN DO YOU NEED MANAGEMENT?   91

THE LEGAL RELATIONSHIP BETWEEN MANAGER AND ARTIST   92

THE FINANCIAL RELATIONSHIP BETWEEN MANAGER AND ARTIST   93

SCOPE OF MANAGEMENT   94

EXCLUSIVITY   96

CO-MANAGERS   96

PERSONAL MANAGERS   97

TERRITORY   97

LENGTH OF THE MANAGEMENT CONTRACT   98

THE FUNCTIONS OF THE MANAGER   99
Finding Work • Business Management • Confidentiality, Integrity and Hard Work

THE MANAGER'S REMUNERATION   103
Commission • Advances • Exclusions • The Right to Payment After Termination

THE MANAGER'S POWERS   109

ENFORCEMENT   110

ENDING THE MANAGEMENT RELATIONSHIP   111

CONCLUSION   112
Management Agreement Checklist

**6 CONTROLLING MANAGERS, AGENTS
AND VENUE CONSULTANTS BY LEGISLATION**   **114**
THE NEW SOUTH WALES MODEL

PURPOSE   115

THE ENTERTAINMENT INDUSTRY INTERIM COUNCIL   115

ENTERTAINMENT INDUSTRY REPRESENTATIVES   116
'Entertainment Industry Agent' • 'Manager' • 'Venue Consultant'

LICENCES   118

REGULATION OF FEES   119
Agents • Managers • Venue Consultants

TRUST ACCOUNTS   120

RECORDS   121

BONDS   122

COMPLAINTS COMMITTEE   122

INTERSTATE REPRESENTATIVES   123

CONCLUSION   123

7 PERFORMING LIVE   **125**

STARTING OUT ON THE ROAD   125
Bargaining Power • Dealing with Potential Employers • Basic Terms •
Enforcement of the Deal • Tax • The Role of the Agent

TOURING   131

DOING IT YOURSELF   132
Planning the Tour • Budget Preparation • Funding the Tour •
Contracting the Performances

DOING IT WITH AN AGENT OR A PROMOTER   134
Promoter Attitudes • The Letter of Intent

REMUNERATION   137
The Set Performance Fee • The Percentage of Gross or Net • Fee Against
Percentage of the Gross or Net • Fee Against Staggered Percentage of
the Gross • Net Participation Deals • The Four Walls Deal

PAYMENT   140

AUDIENCE NUMBERS   141

TICKET PRICES   141

TICKET SALES   142

COMPLIMENTARY TICKETS   142

SUPPORT ACTS   143
Buying In

FESTIVALS AND EVENTS   145

PUBLICITY   145
Interviews • Promotional Materials • Press Releases • Using the Record
Company • Other Uses of the Artist's Name and Reputation

MERCHANDISING   147

PRACTICAL CONSIDERATIONS   147
Set Up • Performance Details • Security Arrangements • Staging • Power
Requirements • Dressing Rooms • Catering • Recording the
Performance • Photographers • Permits and Consents • Insurance
• Accommodation • Termination

8	**MUSIC COPYRIGHT – THE BASICS**	**153**
	WHY IS COPYRIGHT IMPORTANT?	153
	WHAT IS THE SOURCE OF COPYRIGHT?	154
	WHAT IS COVERED BY COPYRIGHT?	155
	WHAT RIGHTS DOES COPYRIGHT INCLUDE?	155
	COMMUNICATION TO THE PUBLIC	155
	USA FREE TRADE AGREEMENT	156
	REPRODUCTION	157
	PUBLICATION	157
	WHAT FORMALITIES ARE NECESSARY?	157
	WHO OWNS THE COPYRIGHT?	159

Musical Works • Sound Recordings • Special Rules Appling To Sound Recordings Made Prior to 1 January 2005 • Limits on Rights Given To Performers • Published Editions

| | HOW LONG DOES COPYRIGHT LAST? | 164 |

Musical Works and Literary Works • Sound Recordings Made Before 1 May 1969 • Recordings Made After 1 May 1969 • Published Editions • Anonymous or Pseudonymous Works • Works of Joint Authorship • Films

| | COPYRIGHT TRANSACTIONS | 165 |

The Assignment of Copyright • Licensing the Rights • Basic Terms

| | IS ALL USE OF COPYRIGHT MATERIAL FORBIDDEN UNLESS YOU HAVE A LICENCE? | 168 |

Fair Dealing • Use of an Insubstantial Portion • Home Copying

	PROTECTION OF NON-COPYRIGHT RIGHTS OF PERFORMERS AND THEIR PERFORMANCE	170
	PERFORMERS' COPYRIGHT?	171
	MORAL RIGHTS	172

The Right of Attribution • The Right Not To Be Falsely Attributed • The Right of Integrity • Duration • Remedies for Infringements • Defences to Infringements • No Cause for Alarm

| | SAMPLING | 176 |

Who Pays and Gets Paid for the Sample?

| | PARALLEL IMPORTING | 180 |

Importing Sound Recordings • How Parallel Import of Sound Recordings Works • Competition Policy • Geting Used To Parallel Importing

| | CONCLUSION | 185 |
| | FURTHER INFORMATION | 185 |

9	**MUSIC PUBLISHING**	**186**
	WHAT A PUBLISHER DOES	187
	PUBLISHING INCOME AND COPYRIGHT	187
	RIGHTS USES AND MONEY	188

The Right to Publish • The Right to Reproduce • The Right to Comunicate to the Public • The Right to make an Adaptation • Combination of Rights

| | SOURCES OF PUBLISHING INCOME | 189 |

Sheet Music • Mechanical Rights Income • Synchronisation in Film or Television • The Promotion of Third Party Goods and Services • Communication to the Public • Sundry Income

COLLECTION, CALCULATION AND DISTRIBUTION OF 198
PUBLISHING INCOME
Sheet Music • Mechanical Income From Records • Mechanical Income
Payable in Other Situations

THE MECHANICAL LICENCE PROCESS 200
Reportin The Use • Claiming the Work and the Royalty • Issuing the
Prescribed Notice • Payment • Accounting • Returns and Retentions
• The Financial Results • United Kingdom Practice • United States Practice
• Controlled Composition Clauses

SYNCHRONISATION WITH FILM OR TELEVISION 204
Production Music • Commissioned Material • Pre-Recorded and Released
Material • The Promotion of Third Party Goods and Services

COMMUNICATION TO THE PUBLIC 206
Licensing of Users • Overseas Income

10 **ANATOMY OF A MUSIC PUBLISHER** 210

THE MANAGING DIRECTOR 211

THE CREATIVE SERVICES MANAGER 211

LICENSING MANAGER 212

TRANSCRIBERS 212

PRINT MUSIC 213

PRINT MUSIC SALES 213

PLUGGERS 214

BUSINESS AFFAIRS 214

COPYRIGHT AND ACCOUNTS 215

WAREHOUSE 216

11 **COMPOSING AND WRITING WITH OTHERS** 217

DOCUMENTING THE RELATIONSHIP 218

PARTNERSHIPS 219

COPYRIGHT OWNERSHIP - JOINT AND COLLECTIVE WORKS 219
Collective Work • Joint Works • Control

CONTROL 221

THE ROYALTY SPLITS 222

APRA REGISTRATION 222

CONTRACTUAL OBLIGATIONS 222

ARRANGERS AND TRANSLATORS 223

RECORD PRODUCERS 225

ADDITIONAL WRITERS 225

ACCIDENTAL CO-WRITERS 226

12 **TYPES OF PUBLISHING CONTRACTS** 227

WRITER-FOR-HIRE AGREEMENTS 227

SINGLE-SONG ASSIGNMENT 228
The Rights Period • The Advance • Royalties

OTHER SPECIFIC-WORKS AGREEMENTS 229

TERM PUBLISHING AGREEMENTS 235
Duration • The Advance • Split Publishing Deals • Recoupment
• Productivity Commitment

SELF PUBLISHING 252

ADMINISTRATION DEALS 253
Length of Contract • Copyright Ownership • Advances • Income Splits
• Covers

13	**COMMON CLAUSES IN PUBLISHING DEALS**	**256**
	ASSIGNMENTS AND LICENCES	256
	PUBLISHER'S OBLIGATION TO EXPLOIT	257
	ROYALTY SPLITS	258
	General • Synchronisations and Covers • Sheet Music Income • Public Performance and Communication Income	
	OVERSEAS INCOME	260
	The Sub-Publisher's Commission • Net Receipts v. At Source	
	MECHANICAL ROYALTY REDUCTIONS IN THE UNITED STATES AND CANADA	263
	GST	264
	ACCOUNTING	265
	CREATIVE CONTROL	266
	WRITER'S WARRANTIES	267
	PUBLISHER WARRANTIES	268
	REVERSION OF COPYRIGHT	268
14	**TECHNOLOGY AND MUSIC: EVOLUTION TO REVOLUTION**	**269**
	THE MECHANICAL AGE	270
	Early Recordings • Flat Records	
	THE ELECTRONIC AGE	272
	Electricity • Hi-Fi • The Transistor – Music on the Move • Audio and Video Tape • Portable Recording	
	DIGITAL TECHNOLOGY	275
	The Birth of the © Blues • Other Digital Formats	
	PERSONAL COMPUTERS	280
	THE INTERNET	281
	ON-LINE DELIVERY	282
	MP3	284
	WEBCASTING	284
	RINGTONES	285
	DIGITAL BROADCAST	287
	MOBILE PHONE	288
15	**DOWNLOAD DELIVERY: EVOLUTION IN BUSINESS – REVOLUTION IN THINKING**	**289**
	The Birth of Download Delivery • Napster • Post Napster •Webcasting • The Battle Won, The War Rages On • The Way Forward • Change in the Way Companies Do Business • The Slogans that Come and Go	
	NEW TECHNOLOGY AND ARTISTS' ROYALTIES	298
	ARTISTIC CONTROL IN THE DIGITAL AGE	301
	COPYRIGHT ISSUES ARISING FROM RECENT AND FUTURE	302
	TECHNOLOGICAL DEVELOPMENTS	
	Does Copyright Have a Future? • Copyright Management • Promoting Controlled Copyright Access • Policing Copyright • Collection of Copyright Income for Internet Use	
	THE FUTURE OF ON-LINE MUSIC – 'THE TIMES THEY ARE A CHANGIN'	308
	A POSSIBLE FUTURE	309
	A Story • Features of the Possible Future • Timing	
	CONCLUSION	312

16 THE GROWTH OF THE AUSTRALIAN RECORD BUSINESS   314

PROFIT – SKILL OR LUCK   318

A SHORT HISTORY   319
  Language and Geography • Covers • The 1960s • The 1970s • The 1980s
  • The 1990s • The 2000s

VERTICAL INTEGRATION   323

THE RECORD COMPANIES   325

MAJORS' STRUCTURES   326
  Head Office

MULTINATIONAL MAJORS   327
  EMI • Sony/BMG Music • Universal • Warner Music

LOCAL MAJORS   334
  ABC

THE INDEPENDENTS   335

RECORD DISTRIBUTORS   336

TELE-MARKETERS   336

BUDGET RECORD COMPANIES   337

RECORD CLUBS   337

17 ANATOMY OF A RECORD COMPANY   339

ARTIST AND REPERTOIRE (A&R)   339

BUSINESS AFFAIRS   341

ART DEPARTMENT   341

PRODUCTION DEPARTMENT AND STOCK CONTROL   342

MARKETING AND PROMOTIONS DEPARTMENT   343

SALES REPRESENTATIVES   344

ORDERS AND WAREHOUSE   344

ACCOUNTS AND ROYALTY ACCOUNTS   345

ON-LINE   345

18 CHOOSING A RECORD COMPANY   346

THE ARTIST ROSTER   346

WHO'S HOT   346

WHO'S THE BEST AT PROMOTING RECORDS?   347

CAN I WORK WITH THEM?   347

WHAT DO I WANT MY RECORD COMPANY TO DO?   348

WHO'S GIVING THE BEST DEALS?   348

19 GETTING A RECORD CONTRACT   349

DREAMS OF INSTANT SUCCESS   349

CREATING AWARENESS OF YOUR MUSIC   350
  Knowing Someone • Live Work • Publicity Stunts • Image
  • Demos • Talent Shows

STARTING NEGOTIATIONS   355

20 RECORD CONTRACTS   357

WHY HAVE A RECORD CONTRACT?   358

THE FORM OF THE RECORD CONTRACT   358
  Oral Agreements • Written Contracts

KEY ISSUES IN RECORDING CONTRACTS   360

Contract For Services • Exclusivity • The Artist's 'Services' • Working in Other Media • Internet and Website Control • Contract Definitions • The 'Term' of the Contract • Delays and Interruptions • Suspension Clauses • The 'Territory' • Overseas Releases – Release Options • Artist's Minimum Delivery Commitments • The Record Company's Recording Commitment• Artistic Control • Working with A&R • Release Commitment • Publicity and Image • Funding Recordings – Advances and Recording Costs • Secondary Exploitation of Records • Who Owns the Recordings? • Cover Art • Re-Recording Restrictions • Moral Rights and ReMixing • American Federation of Musicians • The Right to Assign the Contract • Warranties and Indemnities • Giving Notice

21   RECORD DISTRIBUTION DEALS   **386**

LABEL DEALS   386
What are Labels? • Label Ownership • Why Do a Label Deal? • Negotiating Label Deals • Artists and Label Deals

PRESSING AND DISTRIBUTING DEALS   394
Why Do P&D Deals? • P&D Versus Master Licence • Selecting a Distributor • Expenses • Funding • Who Does What? • Manufacturing • Who Owns the Records? • Stock Control • Promotion • Promotional Copies • Distribution • Trading Terms • Distribution Fees • Deductions and Accounting • Goods and Services Tax • During The Deal • At the End of the Deal

MASTER LICENCE DEALS   404
Exclusivity • Basic Elements of Master Licences

RECORD RENTAL   417

22   GROUP RECORDING CONTRACTS   **418**

GROUP CONTRACTS   419

THE DYNAMICS OF GROUPS   419

GROUP STRUCTURES   419

THE CONTRACT PROVISIONS   420
The Parties • Individual and Group Liability • The Group's Professional Name

LIASING WITH THE RECORD COMPANY   422
Who Speaks For The Group? • Who Makes Decisions? • Line-up Changes

FINANCIAL CONSEQUENCES OF LINE-UP CHANGES   425
Royalties and Accounting • Recoupment • Ill and Absentee Members

23   RECORD ROYALTIES   **427**

NON-RECOUPABLE DEALS   427

RECOUPABLE DEALS   429

'NET SALES'   429

THE ROYALTY RATE   431

THE ROYALTY BASE   431
    RRP Royalty Calculation • Dealer Price Calculation

DEDUCTIONS – CALCULATING THE ROYALTY BASE PRICE   433
    Goods and Services Tax • Delivery Charges • Packaging Deductions
    • Specific Packaging Deductions • New Technology Deductions
    • Arbitrary Deductions • Double Deductions

ROYALTIES FROM RECORDS SOLD BY UNUSUAL   438
MARKETING METHODS
    Record Clubs • TV Advertised Records • Premium Records • Budget and
    Mid-Price Records

OTHER INCOME   441
    Broadcast and Public Performance Royalties • Synchronisation Fees

ROYALTY ACCOUNTING   443

PRODUCERS' ROYALTIES   444

ALTERNATIVES TO ROYALTY PAYMENTS   444
    Lump-Sum Payments • Shares (Equity in the Record Company)
    • Being Creative

MECHANICAL ROYALTY CAPS AND REDUCTIONS   445
    Background • North American Practice • Payment of Mechanicals on
    Records Sold • Three Quarter Rate • Capping Controlled Compositions
    • Capping All Mechanical Royalty Bearing Tracks • Your Publisher
    •Practical Examples

24   RECORD PRODUCERS   454

WHO PAYS?   455

THIRD PARTY PRODUCERS   455

WRITTEN CONTRACTS   456
    The Job Description • Who Hires the Producer? • Services

SELECTING A PRODUCER   458

PRODUCER'S REMUNERATION   458
    The Fee • Timing of Fee Payment • Royalties • Royalty Rates • Advances
    and Recoupment • When Does the Producer Earn Royalties? • Timing
    of Royalty Payments • Share of Licence Fees • Video Royalties • Royalty
    Reductions • Pro-Rata Calculations • A-Side Protection

RESPONSIBILITY FOR BUDGET OVERAGES   464

COPYRIGHT OWNERSHIP   464
    The Masters • Works Composed with the Artist • Works Composed by
    Third Parties

REMIXING   465

TERMINATION   465

25   MUSIC CLIPS   467

HISTORY   468
    Clips as a Promotional Tool • Concert Films • Television

CLIPS AND RECORDING BUDGETS   469

MTV   470

OTHER USES OF CLIPS   470
>Video Juke Boxes • Sell-Through Video and DVD • Telecast

FUTURE FORMATS   472

CLIP PRODUCERS   473

COMMISSIONING YOUR OWN CLIPS   474

MUSIC COPYRIGHT IN CLIPS   474

CLIPS AND RECORDING CONTRACTS   474
>Budgetary and Creative Control • Royalties • Packaging Deductions on
>Sell-Through Videos and DVD

THE VIDEO PRODUCER'S CONTRACT   476
>The Parties • Choice of Director • Storyboard • Budgets • Factors
>Affecting the Budget • Who Owns the Rights? • Clearances •
>Delivery Dates • When Things go Wrong

THE FUTURE   479

26 COLLECTING SOCIETIES   **480**

INTERNATIONAL CONVENTIONS   481

CHARACTERISTICS OF COLLECTING SOCIETIES   481

COLLECTIVE ADMINISTRATION   481

PRIMARY FUNCTIONS OF COLLECTING SOCIETIES   482

AUSTRALIAN COLLECTION SOCIETIES   484
>APRA • AMCOS • PPCA • Screenrights • CAL • Christian Music
>Copyright Collecting Companies

COPYRIGHT SOCIETIES CODE OF CONDUCT   498

INTERNATIONAL CO-ORDINATION   499
>Public Performance • Mechanical Copyright

THE FUTURE ROLE OF COLLECTING SOCIETIES   501
>Multi-Format Licensing

27 MERCHANDISING   **503**

AREAS OF MERCHANDISING   504
>Tour Merchandising • Retail Merchandising • Mail Order
>• Marketing and Web Merchandising

SOME BASIC QUESTIONS   506
>Why Merchandise? • When to Merchandise? • Have You Got the Rights?
>• Who Negotiates? • How Do we Allocate the Rights?

MERCHANDISING AND RECORD COMPANIES   507

TOUR MERCHANDISING   509
>Territory • Length of a Tour-Merchandising Deal • Extension for
>Unrecoupment • Advances for Tour Merchandising • Timing of
>Advance Payments • Recoupable and/or Repayable Advances • The
>Splits • The Artist's Share • Quality Control • Inventory Leftovers
>• Accounting and Payment • Sales Efforts • Group Members'
>Obligations

DOING YOUR OWN TOUR MERCHANDISING   515

RETAIL MERCHANDISING   516
>The Agent's Commission • The Agent's Role • The Agents' Rights

PROTECTION   518

28 **SPONSORSHIP AND PRODUCT ENDORSEMENT** — 521

SPONSORSHIPS — 521

WHY COMPANIES BECOME SPONSORS — 522
Image Establishment • Image Definition and Brand Development • Image Improvement • Association with Excellence • Client and Staff Relations • The Relationship

WHAT TO ASK FOR — 525

A MOMENT'S REFLECTION — 526

TOUR SPONSORSHIP — 526

CONFLICT WITH VENUES — 527

SPONSORSHIP OF RECORDS — 528

DIRECT ENDORSEMENTS — 528

THE ENDORSEMENT CONTRACT — 529

ENDORSEMENT PROPOSAL — 529

29 **PHILANTHROPY** — 532

GIFT RECEIVERS — 533
Establishing Relations • Setting up an Organisation with Tax Deductible Status

MAINTAINING RELATIONSHIPS — 536

GIFT GIVERS — 537
Individuals • Companies • Workplace Giving • Volunteering • Tax Considerations for the Gift Giver • Prescribed Private Funds

30 **MUSIC IN ADVERTISING** — 542

SOURCES OF MUSIC — 543

COMMISSIONING ORIGINAL MUSIC — 543
The Rights • The Budget

PRODUCTION MUSIC — 547
How Libraries Work

LICENSING PRERECORDED AND RELEASED MATERIAL — 548

31 **MUSIC IN FILM** — 550

AND NOW TO THE PRESENT — 551

SOURCES OF MUSIC — 551
Production Music • Licensing Existing Recordings • Commissioned Music

COMPOSERS WITH PUBLISHING CONTRACTS — 557

THE COMMISSION CONTRACT — 557
Composing the Music and Making the Soundtrack • General Terms

AUSTRALIAN GUILD OF SCREEN COMPOSERS — 566

AN ENDNOTE — 586

32 **INSURANCE** — 589

INTRODUCTION — 589

HOUSEHOLD CONTENTS — 590

EQUIPMENT INSURANCE — 590

TRAVEL INSURANCE — 591

INCOME INSURANCE — 591
Income Protection Insurance • Personal Accident and Illness Insurance

PUBLIC LIABILITY INSURANCE — 592

NON-PERFORMANCE AND NON-APPEARANCE — 593

EVENT INSURANCE — 593
Common Insurance Mistakes in Event Insurance

FURTHER READING — 595

33 MUSIC LAWYERS — **596**

CHOOSING YOUR MUSIC LAWYER — 596

FINDING YOUR MUSIC LAWYER — 597

WHAT MUSIC LAWYERS DO — 598
Contract Analysis, Advice and Negotiation • Contract Drafting
• General Advice • What Lawyers Cost • The Hourly Rate • Estimates
• The Capped Fee • Success Fees • Percentages

PAYING THE BILLS — 602

COMMUNICATION — 602

CONFLICTS OF INTEREST — 603

CHANGING LAWYERS — 604

FREE LEGAL ADVICE — 604

CONTACTS — 605

34 INDUSTRY AWARDS — **606**

EMPLOYEE OR INDEPENDENT CONTRACTOR? — 606

UNIONS — 607

ENTERTAINMENT INDUSTRY AWARDS — 608

SESSION MUSICIANS — 608

MAKING 'CAST' RECORDINGS OF SHOWS — 609

35 KEEPING THE BOOKS — **611**

MANAGING THE MONEY — 612

TAXATION — 612

TOUR BUDGETS/GRANT APPLICATIONS — 612
Tour Budgets • Submissions for Subsidies or Grants

BORROWING MONEY — 613

BOOK KEEPING ESSENTIALS — 614
Cash Book • Petty Cash Book • Periodical Accounts • Filing System
• GST Paperwork – Business Activity Statements (BAS) • Role of the
Accountant

CONCLUSION — 618

36 TAXATION — **619**

INTRODUCTION TO THE TAXATION SYSTEM — 619
IN AUSTRALIA

TAXABLE INCOME AND ASSESSABLE INCOME   620
Assessable Income • Taxable Income • Taxable Income and Assessable Income for Overseas Artists • Tax Rates for Australian Residents • Tax Rates for Non-Australian Residents

LODGING YOUR TAX RETURN   623
Do I Have to Lodge a Tax Return? • Individuals • Partnerships • Companies • Trusts • Deductions • Capital Expenses and Depreciation • Recurrent Expenses

HOBBY OR BUSINESS?   631
What is a Business? • Significant Commercial Purpose or Character • Intention of the Taxpayer • Size or Scale of Activity • Examples

REGISTERING YOUR BUSINESS: GST, ABN, TAX FILE NUMBERS AND PAYG WITHHOLDING TAX   638
The ABN • Registering for an ABN • The Australian Company Number and the ABN • What is GST? • GST Paperwork • Registering for GST • What are the Benefits of GST Registration? • Obtaining a Tax File Number • Registering for PAYG Withholding • Registering for Fringe Benefits Tax

PERSONAL SERVICES INCOME   641
Does This Affect You? • Carrying Forward Losses • Abnormal Receipts • Income Averaging for Special Professionals

TAX PLANNING AND BUSINESS STRUCTURES   643
Partnerships • Companies • Trusts • Superannuation

TAX ISSUES FOR OVERSEAS ARTISTS   645
Income from Engagements • Income from Royalties • Double Tax Treaty

CHOOSING A TAX OR ACCOUNTING PROFESSIONAL   645

37   **GETTING THE INTERNATIONAL DEAL**   **646**

TALENT – THE STARTING POINT   646

CONTACTS   649
Colleagues • Lawyers • Managers • Agents

WHERE TO BASE THE BUSINESS   652

38   **THE ART OF THE DEAL**   **653**

A DEAL IS A RELATIONSHIP   653

THE BACKGROUND INTELLIGENCE   654
What are the Parties' Creative Needs and Expectations? • What are the Client's Commercial Needs? • Will the Artist have the Personal Support Necessary to be Successful? • What are the Company's Commercial Needs? • What Do Other Artists of the Same Genre and a Similar Level of Success, Receive? • Understand Negotiation Discipline

TECHNIQUES OF THE NEGOTIATION   658

CONTENT OF THE DEAL   660
The Myth of the Grand Advance • Understand how the Deal Works • Defining the Unknown • Dispute Resolution • Renegotiation

CONCLUSION   662

INDEX   663

PREFACE

This is the third edition of this book about the business of the Australian music industry. So much has changed in the five years since the last edition: Majors have merged, even disappeared entirely; business models and practices have changed to take into account the demands of new and evolving technologies; the Copyright Act has been through one its greatest periods of reform for more than a quarter of a century.

The book has not been written for lawyers. Readers who expect to get lots of case references and detailed analyses of statutes have bought the wrong book. It is meant to show how, and why, things are done as they are in the industry and what to what to watch out for when negotiating deals.

Part of the difficulty of working in the Australian music industry is that most of the available texts come from the United States. Whilst many deal structures and contract precedents used in this country derive from the United States, the Australian industry has subtly changed many of these, so that the meaning of some industry terms now vary between the United States and Australia, the legal expression of contracts differs enormously, deal points which are standard overseas are not necessarily similar to the Australian practices and so on. Because the Australian industry has taken so much from the American industry and because the language remains apparently similar, it is all too easy to assume that what is written about the U.S. industry necessarily applies to the Australian business. It does not.

One of the difficulties in undertaking a book like this is that the level of knowledge of the readership will vary so much. Many readers will be at the outset of their careers; others will have had many years in the industry - perhaps with great success and recognition. To write something that is relevant to both a novice performer and an experienced promoter, a composer and the managing director of a major publishing company, a musician entering a record agreement for the first time and one who has had international success, is the problem facing all authors who attempt this sort of book.

To the novice, I would say; there are things in this book that you may not need to know about at this early stage in your career. Don't worry. Use what is useful to you now; I hope the book will continue to act as a reference text for you as your career develops. To the experienced player; whilst there will be much in this book that you may already know, I hope that there will be material that is either new, or which causes you to reconsider or re-evaluate some aspect of your already extensive knowledge.

The other difficulty in writing a book such as this is: "How much do you tell?" As a lawyer specialising in the entertainment industry, part of my professional value and reputation is the depth of industry knowledge that I bring to my legal and commercial advice. This industry knowledge is one of the factors that separate a would-be expert from the real thing. I have taken the rather difficult decision to be detailed, to disclose figures and percentages, to reveal rather than conceal. Every chapter could have included more, (nearly every chapter could be given a book to itself), but generally the decision not to include material was made in order to achieve a reasonable balance within the book, rather than to protect trade secrets. At the end of the day, it's not how much you know, it's how you apply what you know. That goes for both musicians and for lawyers.

Finally, it is worth remembering that this book is a personal snapshot of the industry: I welcome disagreement with the subjective comments I have made; such discussion promotes an informed, thinking approach to the business of music. And that is the basic purpose of the book.

Shane Simpson
Sydney, 2006

ACKNOWLEDGMENTS

Above all, this book is a personal view. That said, I asked people who have established reputations in their particular area of the business to act as a 'brains trust' and to comment on the text prior to publication.

I am particularly grateful to my colleagues Adam Simpson, Jules Munro, Kasey Ekert and Kate Ingber for their detailed comments and generous contributions.

Many others reviewed particular chapters: Bob Aird and Norm Lurie; Performing Live and Agents: Michael Chugg; Merchandising: Geoff Stewart; Collection Societies: Brett Cottle, Richard Mallett; Music in Advertising: Ken Francis. Music in Film: Andy Stern, Jo Smith, Guy Gross, Michelle O'Donnell and Art Phillips; Insurance: Ken Killen. Ben O'Hara's comments as to structure and clarification were valued.

I should add, however, that the views expressed are not necessarily theirs. I have always listened, but have not always agreed. Similarly, my views will not necessarily accord with your own. With something as sprawling as the music business, it is important to realise that much of what is expressed as fact is really only opinion confidently asserted. I put it no stronger.

Thank you Danielle. You have been extraordinarily supportive and forbearing.

Thanks to the team at Music Sales and Pan Macmillan who have been enormous supporters of this book – in particular Norm Lurie and Melissa Whitelaw – and the production team at Campbell Murray Creating.

Oh, and Ritchie Benaud, my teacher in first grade and the members of the Academy … 'Free Tibet'. (Tears. Pause for applause.)

1
SELECTING AND PROTECTING A NAME

WITH SUCCESS, AN ARTIST'S NAME BECOMES MORE AND MORE VALUABLE. THE NAME AND REPUTATION HELPS SELL RECORDS, TICKETS AND MERCHANDISE. ACCORDINGLY IT IS IMPORTANT TO CHOOSE AND PROTECT YOUR PROFESSIONAL NAME WITH CARE.

So much of the success in the modern music industry is based on marketing and promotion that you have to pay a lot of attention to establishing, shaping and maintaining a public profile. Your name is central to that profile, although lots of bands with catchy names never surface and lots of bands with so-so names sell as many records. Quirky gimmicks may help get you noticed but, in the end, it is the quality of your music that determines long-term success.

That said, if you do have success, your name will become the most important asset of your business. The association of your name with your sound, professional reputation and popularity will be inextricable: your fans will buy tickets, records and merchandise on the strength of, and belief in, your name.

Given that your professional name can become so valuable, the last thing you want to discover is that you have selected a name that is already being used somewhere in Australia or even in a major overseas market ('Sherbet' found this out when they first tried to crack the American market). If your real name happens to be (say) 'Norah Jones' and you come from Fitzroy, there is little point going out on the road using your own name, as there is already an internationally famous performer of that name.

You must try to find a name that people will associate with you and your music. You must establish your own identity. Part of this task is to make sure that there aren't other musicians using the name that you want to use. Once you have done your checks, you should protect that name so others cannot take advantage of it.

THE NAME SEARCH

When choosing a name for your act, don't fall in love with just one name. Unless the name is very weird, the chances are that someone has got there before you. Have a list of three or four possibilities so they can all be checked at the same time. It can be cheaper that way.

There are a number of basic searches worth doing.

First, do an Internet search. This is often the quickest and cheapest way of establishing that there are already other groups in the world using the name you want to use.

Then look through the *Australasian Music Industry Directory* and even through a range of directories such as the Billboard International Talent & Touring Directory and maybe even record directories such as Phonolog Reports.

More prosaically, go on-line and check the white and yellow pages. Check not only your hometown but also the whole country. Even check the major overseas territories. All of them. You may well find that there is a restaurant in some town 2,000 kilometres away with the same name. Don't assume that you don't have a problem just because the other user of the name is in a different business or in another geographical area. They may well have the right to stop you from using the name.

Do a search at the Australian Securities and Investments Commission (ASIC) website (www.asic.gov.au) to see if there are already business names or companies registered with the same name (or one similar to the one) you want to use. ASIC has records that you can search on-line.

Then check the records at IP Australia (www.ipaustralia.gov.au). These will reveal if anyone has registered (or applied to register) a trade mark that may conflict. This is usually the domain of trade mark lawyers but anyone can get on-line and do a basic local search.

If your searches reveal that someone else is using a name identical or even similar to the one you want to use, be careful! Don't assume that 'things will be all right'. You should get expert advice. You may have to forget about the name and select another. You may be able to vary the name or you might have to get permission from the present name users, or buy the rights to use the name. Just going ahead and optimistically using the name may be very expensive in the long run. No name is worth anything before you have built a reputation around it, so don't get emotionally committed to just one, until you know it is clear to use. If there is another group already using the name anywhere in the country, or in any major territory, don't use it. Be creative. Get another name.

PROTECTING THE NAME

Generally speaking you do not 'own' a name. You may, however, acquire rights in it by using it and establishing a 'goodwill' or reputation in the name. It doesn't matter who came up with the name first. The rights go to the person who developed the reputation. The greater your reputation, the greater your claim to ownership. For example, a group that is unknown outside its local area will have little chance against a band of the same name which has toured several States, released a single nationally or which has received some reviews in the national music press and so on.

In the general law, there is an action called 'passing off', which prohibits any party from misrepresenting itself (or its goods or services) as though it was another. In other words, it prohibits the false appropriation of the other's reputation.

The Trade Practices Act (sections 52 and 53 in particular) and various States' Fair Trading legislation, provide comparable protection in that they prevent corporations and individuals from engaging in conduct that is 'misleading or deceptive'.

BUSINESS NAME REGISTRATION

If you are trading under a name other than your real name, you will have to register under the relevant State's Business Names laws. The process is simple and cheap. You can do it yourself. Contact your State's Consumer Affairs Department for details.

Registration is merely a consumer protection provision. It provides a bureaucratic way to find out the identity of the people or companies behind a fictitious name. Registration of the business name (or even a company name) does not give you any rights of ownership in the name. This is a frequent and expensive misconception. Remember that there are only two ways that you get ownership of a name - by establishing a reputation or by registering a trade mark.

TRADE MARK

Other than getting out and developing a reputation in the name, the only other way of protecting it is to register a trade mark. This is a formal process and can be quite a complicated affair. It should not usually be undertaken without expert advice. It is also quite expensive, particularly if you seek registration in all of the major international territories.

A trade mark can be a name, a logo or a combination of both. You can even trade mark a smell, a sound or a colour. Trade mark protection is given according to 45 different categories of goods and services. A band would need to take out registrations in several different categories to get optimum coverage of the monopoly which owning a trade mark can provide. This is particularly important in the protection of the value of the name for merchandising purposes: today the T-shirt, tomorrow the soft drink!

It can be difficult to get your name approved by the Trade mark Office. Because a trade mark gives you a monopoly on the use of that mark (for those categories in which it is registered), you will not be allowed to hijack bits of the language! You can't trade mark descriptive words like 'Beautiful Music' or 'Super Group'. That is why so many products have completely made-up names. (For example, Xerox, Disprin, Kleenex, Rollerblade, Microsoft.)

If you have a name such as 'Chicago', chances are you will only be able to protect the manner of its presentation. You hire an artist to design a logo incorporating your name and then register the logo as a trade mark. Remember though - registration of a logo doesn't give you a monopoly over the name; it gives you a monopoly over the logo which embodies that name.

Once registered as a trade mark, you have to make sure that whenever you use it in a visual form, you use it in the form it was registered. Don't alter it. Your record labels and packaging, letterhead, merchandise, set-design, promotional material and everything else you produce must use it without any variation. That way, as time goes by, your increased fame and reputation enhances the value of the trade mark. It becomes symbolic of the authenticity of the thing to which it is attached. It also becomes hugely valuable.

Registered trade marks are identified by the ® symbol. Unregistered trade marks are identified by the ™ symbol. Although both registered and unregistered trade marks are enforceable, the value of registering is that registered trade marks are much easier to establish in court. All you have to do is prove that the mark is registered, that you are the registered owner and that the defendant has used your mark without permission. Proving that you are the owner of an unregistered mark is a comparatively difficult and expensive exercise.

BAND STRUCTURES WHICH PROTECT THE NAME
PARTNERSHIPS

Protecting a group's name is one of the most important reasons for having a partnership agreement (or some other formal agreement) between the group's members.

There is no particular approach that will work for everyone. In some partnerships, the founder of the group retains all rights in the name and none of the group members ever get rights in the name. In other examples, the group members all share the ownership of the rights to the name. Where ownership is shared, it is sensible to include mechanisms in the partnership agreement that specify what will happen if any member wishes to leave (or is expelled from) the group. For example: How will their share of the name be valued? Will they be bought out? Over what time? Will they lose the right to use the name? What if two members of a group of four stop playing with the other two? Who is the real group? Who has the right to use the name?

A properly discussed and carefully drafted partnership agreement is a very personally shaped document. It is not something that your lawyer should just churn out of a computer. Like your shoes, your partnership agreement must fit your particular needs. Good partnership agreements are hand-made, so they are not cheap. (See next chapter.)

COMPANIES AND SHAREHOLDER AGREEMENTS

Some groups overcome the ownership problem by establishing a company and having the company own the name. Of course, just setting up a company is not enough. You need an agreement between the shareholders to make clear how the company is going to be run. As well, there should be employment (or 'services') agreements between the company and the individual group members.

This structure means that everyone's rights in the name (and all other aspects of the band's business) are defined and everyone knows their rights and responsibilities, e.g. musicians who are shareholders would be obliged to give up all rights in the name when they sell their share in the company. Where sidemen play in the group, there should be a short employment agreement in place that specifies that they would not have any rights in the group's name or reputation.

This approach permits the company to retain control of the rights in the name and provides a high level of protection.

Remember, however, that if you are going to use a company structure, you should make sure that you transfer all rights in the group's name into the company as early in your career as possible. This transfer of rights from the individuals to a company, can attract capital gains tax - so do it before you get famous and the name becomes valuable. (See next chapter.)

WHAT'S IN A NAME?

POP MECHANIX

One famous dispute over the rights to a name involved a dispute between an Australian group called 'Popular Mechanics' and a New Zealand group called 'Pop Mechanix'. The Popular Mechanics sought an injunction to stop the New Zealand band using the 'Pop Mechanix' name in Australia. Even though the

Australian band had worked principally in New South Wales, the court found that this work had created sufficient reputation in the name (throughout the country) to justify the court granting an Australia-wide injunction, preventing the New Zealand group from using its name. The fight cost a lot of money and effectively halted the New Zealand group's career.

FLEETWOOD MAC

In 1967, Mick Fleetwood and John McVie formed the group Fleetwood Mac. They were managed by CDM Ltd, a company owned by Clifford Davis. After six years of success, during a tour of North America, the band broke up. Clifford Davis promptly put a new band together to complete the tour. The new band did not contain any original members of Fleetwood Mac.

As might be expected, there were a vast number of complaints from members of the public who had bought tickets in the expectation of seeing and hearing the original members. Fleetwood and McVie went to court to stop CDM and the other musicians from using the name 'Fleetwood Mac'.

The court held that the value of the reputation in the name attached to specific musicians, i.e. those who had actually developed the reputation. If the second group were allowed to use the name, there would be confusion in the minds of the public and this amounted to a misappropriation of the reputation developed by Fleetwood and McVie. The tour was stopped.

The situation would have been different if the original group had split up and some of those members had decided to use the original name. As each member of the group equally owns the rights in the name of the group (unless there is an agreement which varies that position), it is perfectly possible for all members of a group to use the name legally. This was the argument used by various members of The Five Platters.

THE FIVE PLATTERS INC

The "Platters" was one of the most successful groups of the 50's and the first doo-wop groups inducted into the Hall of Fame. The power behind the Platters was the improbably named manager and producer, Buck Ram. He was never a performer in the group. He set up a company called 'The Five Platters Inc' and this company employed the musicians. For 25 years, the company toured a group called 'The Platters', performing the material selected and produced by Buck Ram. The membership of that group changed many times over the years. Three of the original group and two members of later formations, set up their own groups, each called 'The Platters'. At one stage there were five groups touring using the "Platters" name.

Buck Ram spent many years and a lot of money on court cases, protecting the goodwill in 'his' group's name. He had great trouble establishing his rights against the original group members, because although they were employees, their contracts had insufficiently specified that the performers could not use the name after they left the group. Given that those performers were the very people who had been so involved in developing the popularity of the Platters in the first place, the USA courts took the approach that, in the absence of formal agreements to the contrary, the performers themselves had certain rights in the name.

The Five Platters Inc had little trouble protecting its business after it started using contracts of employment that contained clauses preventing its employee musicians from using 'The Platters' name or trademark. As it happened, Buck Ram left this life to join the Choir Celestial, which settled the disputes more effectively than the court system.

THE ON-GOING STORY

In addition to these tales of woe there are many others: The Little River Band, Sam and Dave, Deep Purple, The Drifters, Pink Floyd, Genesis, The Firm (Jimmy Page) and New Edition. They have all had their careers interrupted or at the very least, interfered with, by disputes about name ownership.

SOUND-ALIKES

Because the price of reflected glory is high - from tens of thousands to several million dollars - advertisers now seek to reduce costs by using 'sound-alikes' and 'look-alikes'.

United Airlines used as its theme the song 'Up Up And Away', which was made famous by The Fifth Dimension. They had a very distinctive sound and sold many millions of records of that song throughout the world. In the advertisement, the melody is the same, the words are a little different, the arrangement is almost identical, the sound of the musicians is essentially indistinguishable from the original, but the identity of the musicians is different. Although the advertisement used the group's distinctive sound and their international reputation, The Fifth Dimension had nothing to do with the version used in advertisement.

Similarly, when Air New Zealand used Puccini's 'Nessun dorma' to promote flights to New Zealand, they used a tenor who many mistook for Pavarotti. You can bet the Australian tenor got paid a lot less than the Italian one would have demanded!

Imitation is not the most sincere form of flattery. It is merely the cheapest. It is a way of using the artist's name and reputation without paying the artist anything for that usage. If you are an advertiser it is cheaper to hire session singers to imitate, than it is to hire the original artists to perform their hits. That said, the money saved at first instance often ends up in lawyers' pockets.

And where does that leave cover bands? They undoubtedly use the name, reputation and sound of those that they imitate. That said, there has never been a case in Australia where an original act has sued a cover band. Perhaps it is because there is no doubt in the mind of the audience that they are attending "homage" rather that the real thing. There is no confusion in the mind of the consumer: Indeed attendance at the performance of a cover band might even stimulate record sales for the original act.

The latest battleground for record companies is the sound-alike ringtone market. The companies are arguing that ringtone retailers selling sound-alike recordings using the name of the original artist as a descriptor, are making a false and misleading statement and therefore breaching the Trade Practices Act. This argument is a very long bow to draw: If the site clearly describes a particular download as "Robbie Williams sound-alike" it is difficult to see how customers would imagine that Mr Williams was endorsing the product or associating himself in any way with the download. Customers in this environment are smarter than that.

PROTECTION FROM SOUND-ALIKES

The right of any celebrity to control the commercial exploitation of his or her name, image and likeness has attracted extensive litigation in the United States. There, numerous cases have conferred a common law 'right of publicity' and many States have introduced statutes conferring so-called 'Publicity Rights' and 'Celebrity Rights' that can even restrict the right to use a dead artist's likeness.

The fight for and against sound-alikes has not yet been fully waged in Australia. There is certainly no Right of Celebrity. The remedies are much more traditional: defamation, section 52 of the Trade Practices Act, passing off, and sometimes contract.

The most common tool for protecting an individual's rights in his or her name, image or likeness is the Trade Practices Act. Sections 52 and 53 of that Act prohibit corporate conduct that is false or misleading. For example, Blaupunkt was sued by a television personality named Sue Smith for use of a look-alike to advertise Blaupunkt videos (and they added insult to injury by coincidentally referring to the look-alike as Sue Smith!). In that case, the judge said that the company had improperly associated its product with the public image and reputation of the celebrity. It was held to have 'represented that the Blaupunkt video had the sponsorship and approval of Sue Smith that it did not have' and so to be in breach of section 52 of the Trade Practices Act.

In a similar case between Kieran Perkins and Telstra, Telstra published advertisements using a photo of Perkins wearing a swimming cap with the Telstra label (without the swimmer's consent), with a caption suggesting that

Perkins preferred Telstra to Optus. Perkins successfully sued Telstra. The court held that the unauthorised use of his image together with the caption suggesting his preference towards Telstra (when he had never made such statement) was deceptive and misleading.

In music, the sound is the basis of the fame and, as such, is even more identifiable with the performer than as face. The above examples were not just about the use of the celebrity's photograph: they are about the unauthorised use of the celebrity's reputation for commercial purposes in a situation in which the consumer may be misled into believing that the celebrity was endorsing the product. It is a very small step indeed between using a photograph and using the sound that is uniquely identified with a particular performer.

As Justice Greenfield said in Onassis v. Christian Dior [NY Inc] (1983) 472 NYS 2d 254 (a celebrity look-alike case): 'Let the word go forth, there is no free ride'.

2
BUSINESS STRUCTURES

GIVEN THE HUGE AMOUNTS OF MONEY THAT CAN BE GENERATED IN THE MUSIC INDUSTRY, IT IS ESSENTIAL THAT YOU STRUCTURE THE BUSINESS OF YOUR MUSIC TO MAXIMISE YOUR OPPORTUNITY FOR PROFIT AND PROTECTION. YOU HAVE MANY OPTIONS AND SHOULD CHOOSE OR MOULD ONE THAT SUITS YOUR INDIVIDUAL NEEDS. THIS CHAPTER INTRODUCES YOU TO POSSIBLE TYPES OF BUSINESS STRUCTURE.

It is only common sense to structure the commercial and legal aspects of your business in such a way that will promote your commercial and artistic aims.

If you are a solo performer or writer, your needs will be different from musicians who are working with others. After all, if you are working by yourself you are working only for yourself and have no-one else's needs to consider. If you are working with others, you must consider the other members of the group and come up with a way to satisfy everybody's needs.

As with most commercial relationships, if the deal isn't fair to everyone involved, it will not last long. Eventually the members in the group who have been hard done-by (or just think they have been) will wake up to what has been going on and start to resent the way they've been treated. That mistrust and resentment usually signals the end of the group but, in reality, the end really began right back when the unfair deal was first made.

WORKING SOLO

Most solo musicians are just 'sole traders'. They don't have any formal legal structure. Most don't need one. The sole trader is the most common, flexible and unrestricted form. To be strictly accurate it is not a structure at all; rather it is an absence of a structure. Of course, if you are a sole trader you must still obey the general law, but there are few other constraints, no formalities, essentially no supervision and you get to enjoy freedom of artistic and commercial direction.

It perhaps follows that the sole trader is also the most vulnerable: Without the protection of a company structure, the entire financial exposure of the business is the personal responsibility of the individual. There is no limit to that liability. All your money and all your assets are at risk. The only protection is bankruptcy - if you can call that 'protection'. It's more like a mattress at the bottom of a cliff.

It used to be that most solo musicians formed a company and ran their business through it. These days, because of extensive changes in the tax laws, there may be no great tax advantage in using a company to administer your finances. Generally speaking, deductions that a company can claim can also be claimed by an individual (and of course, a company pays tax from the first dollar it earns, whereas individual tax payers enjoy the first few thousand dollars tax free).

However, there still can be some advantages in a solo performer setting up a company. These include:

(a) Where you are making so much money that you need a tax-effective mechanism for income distribution or to permit the easier transfer of funds overseas, your advisers may suggest that you set up a trust. (Trusts are explained in more detail later.) Such a trust will probably have a company as trustee. The company will control the trust but you will control the company that controls the trust. Yes, this is getting complicated.

(b) When you perform live, if you contract through a company, the employer does not take the tax out of your fee. This saves the employer the headache of administration and means that you get paid the gross fee. Just make sure you provide for the tax that will have to be paid some time in the future.

(c) If you are taking on financial and legal risks (for example, the employment of staff or self-promoting your concerts or working in a manner or location that can be physically or financially dangerous) you would be well advised to form a company and enjoy the benefits of limited liability.

The general rule should always be: keep it simple, unless you have a very good reason to complicate it.

WORKING WITH OTHERS
STARTING OUT

As soon as two or more musicians decide to work together (whether long-term or just on a project-by-project basis), some thought should be given to devising a structure so that the parties will understand their mutual rights and expectations.

All too often, artists do not work out the business aspects of their relationship at an early stage. Many, quite mistakenly, seem to believe that the costs outweigh the benefits. Others simply can't be bothered, perceiving the effort as diverting their energy from the more creative aspects of their work. This is fine if the project is a failure. If the song-writing partnership is arid or the band never has success, who cares? But what if the combination works and the money starts coming in? The stresses created by the demands of success almost inevitably mean that it will be more difficult to work out a mutually satisfactory deal between the parties. Success in the music industry is hard enough to achieve at the best of times and the last thing you need is to start infighting about who gets what and why, just when you need to be concentrating on consolidating that early break. Once the physical, emotional and creative strains of success start to influence the members in various ways, reasonableness can become a rare commodity, so plan your business relationship early. It will never be easier to resolve than at the beginning.

THE OPTIONS

Most musicians do not have much money when starting out. Consequently it doesn't seem to make sense to spend a lot of money on lawyers and accountants. That said, you must plan for success. If you are successful you will be thankful that you structured the business properly at the outset.

Your basic options are: partnership, company, a trust, or some combination of these.

PARTNERSHIP

Each State has its own Partnership Act. 'Partnership' is defined as the legal relationship between people who carry on a business in common, with a view to making a profit. The parties' intention is important. If you have a group which you run as a hobby, with no intention that it will make a profit, you may not have a partnership. The expression 'business' is defined as including 'every trade, occupation or profession', so it is very wide-ranging.

If the above factors are present, a court is likely to decide that a partnership exists, whether or not the people involved considered themselves to be 'partners'. No formalities are required. Consequently, many musicians working together are actually operating a partnership without knowing it.

The legal concept of 'partnership' can be very important, because each partner is individually responsible for all of the debts or liabilities incurred in the name of the business by any of the other partners. For example, a member of the group may, without permission from the others, purchase an expensive piece of equipment, charge it to the partnership's account and then go overseas, taking the new equipment. In such a case the remaining partners would be liable for the debt, even though they had not actually approved the purchase nor had the use of the equipment. Given this, you can see the danger in having credit cards and other accounts in the name of the band! The burden upon partners can be heavy.

Also, the group must get an ABN (Australian Business Number) from ASIC. Every partnership has to have one. This can raise complications because each time a member leaves the group and a new one joins, legally, the old partnership concludes and a new one starts up - requiring a new ABN. It will create a problem for your accountants if they are unaware of your line-up changes.

When going into any sort of partnership business, the participants should discuss the basic rules that are going to control their business relationship. For example, if one of the partners is going to get a bigger share of the income, it should be confirmed in writing. In 1999 the English Court of Appeal decided that Morrissey and Marr, the dominant force of the 80's group The Smiths had been taking a greater share of the income than to which they were entitled. Partners are presumed to be equal unless otherwise agreed. Marr and Morrissey could not rebut that presumption. It wasn't in writing.

At the beginning of a business relationship, partners often decide that they will not enter a formal, written, partnership agreement because it is time-consuming, involves legal expenses and seems rather pessimistic. This is understandable, but the partners must realise that as the success of their business increases, so too will the strains.

It makes good commercial sense to go to a music lawyer to have your partnership agreement drawn up. You need someone used to doing this specialised work so that you can be sure that he or she knows the most commonly arising problems in the life of a musical partnership.

You will save a lot of your lawyer's time (and yourself a lot of money in legal fees) if you prepare for your meeting with your lawyer. The following are some suggestions for you to use in discussions, but the list is by no means exhaustive:

PARTNERSHIP CHECKLIST
1. Define exactly what the partners intend doing. Will you be performing? Writing? Producing? Who will do what? Is it just one project (like writing a musical) or will it be ongoing?

2. What work is involved in the project?
3. How many partners will there be? For example, if the group consists of a couple of key members and the others have just joined or are just hired for particular sessions, who should be in the partnership?
4. If not all the members of the group are going to be partners, how will the non-partner members be paid?
5. Will each partner have set responsibilities in the venture? How much time is each partner expected to spend on partnership business? Will it be a first priority or not. (If one member of the group has a full-time job that doesn't permit time off for touring, or another has a spouse who doesn't want their spouse to be out late at night, you have a problem. You might as well know about and deal with these issues sooner rather than later!)
6. What will be the costs incurred in setting up your musical business? Do a budget of anticipated expenses.
    (i)   Where possible, use real figures and get quotes, not guesses. Where you can't, be pessimistic. It always seems to cost more than you thought!
    (ii) How will the set-up funds and initial running costs be raised? How much will each of the partners have to contribute at the outset?
    (iii) To answer this you have to do a budget of your set-up costs. What are they?
    (iv) How much is it likely to cost to run the business? How will the running costs be met?
7. How will income or profits be distributed? There are many different ways that this can be done, e.g. take a group of four people that performs live and makes records. The lead singer put the group together. The keyboard player and the guitarist write the songs that the group performs. The drummer is a very good drummer:
    (i)   What are their various sources of income?
    (ii) Should each share in all sources?
    (iii) In what proportions should they share?
8. What decision-making process will be used? There are obvious problems in demanding that all the decisions of the group be unanimous. Just one member, who is having a bad day or who genuinely disagrees with the plan, could frustrate the wishes of the majority:
    (i)   Are there some decisions that should be unanimous?
    (ii) If so, which are they?
    (iii) What will be the quorum (i.e. the minimum number of members needed at any given meeting, to be able to make binding decisions)?
    (iv) Will minutes be kept?

9. Will leaving members promise not to use the business name of the partnership?

10. Will leaving members promise not to use information that is confidential to the partnership or the individual partners? In almost every business, and music businesses are no exception, the participants come into possession of information that is commercially significant and must be kept in confidence. What sort of information might this cover?

11. Where are the partners going to work?

12. What name will be used?

13. The group must set up accounts in the name of the group. The income of the group must never be mixed with the funds of the manager or individual group members. The reasons for this should be obvious. You have to decide:
    (i)   Where will the accounts be set up?
    (ii) What sort of accounts will the group operate?
    (iii) Who can operate them?

14. Will all partnership income be paid into the partnership account and will all partnership expenditure be paid from that account, so that a proper financial record is maintained? The old tradition of having a manager take all the musicians' income and hand out net sums to the musicians (after deduction of all expenses, fees and commissions) is, thankfully, becoming less prevalent.

15. Who will be responsible for overseeing financial affairs, including taxation obligations? Who will maintain the books of account?

    Few managers or artists have the necessary skills. Some managers get a poor reputation because they assume these important financial obligations without having sufficient skills for the task. More and more artists are appointing accountants to look after all of their financial affairs. In these cases, the manager takes a few percentage points less in return for being relieved of responsibility for financial administration. Accountants run the bank accounts, keep the books and make sure both the manager and the artist (and everyone else involved) has their proper share of the profits.

    This extra expense is more than justified by the security it gives to all parties. It also encourages everyone to get expert financial advice rather than to try to make it up as they go along (which can be expensive, e.g. if you make a mistake in not paying the right amount of tax).

16. Will all loans to the business by any partner be noted formally in the books and note taken of the terms upon which any loan is made?

17. What will be considered as being partnership income and what will be non-partnership income? Will there be different sources of income? Will all income be dealt with the same way?

18. Who will have the authority to enter contracts and incur debts in the partnership's name? Is there to be a transaction-value limit set on this authority, with any expenditure in excess of that amount needing the approval of the other partners?
19. Are the parties allowed to do work outside the partnership? What if that work competes with the partnership itself?
20. What happens if a partner dies or wishes to resign from the partnership? What is a fair and business-like way of retiring from the partnership? What notice should a retiring member have to give? What payment, if any, will leaving members receive? What will that member's responsibility be for partnership debts or unrecouped advances? What use can they make of the business name and trade marks?
21. How can a partner be expelled by the others? On what grounds?
22. How can the partnership be dissolved voluntarily? How will the assets (and liabilities) of the business be divided?
23. How can the rules of the partnership be altered?

This is not an exhaustive list.

COMPANIES

Unlike a partnership, you can't form a company without going through lots of formalities. The formalities are important because, unlike partnership, what you are doing is creating a legal entity that is quite separate from its members. A company can sue, be sued, hire, fire, buy and sell - all in its own name. With a partnership, the partners always remain individually liable whereas, with a company, the members' liability is strictly limited. It is the company itself that incurs the obligations and liabilities. If a company becomes liable for more money than its assets can meet, it may go into liquidation or be wound up, in which case the personal assets of the shareholders will remain largely intact. (For more details about directors' duties and liabilities, see Chapter 3.)

The most common form of private company is the 'company limited by shares'. You identify such companies by the "Pty Ltd" at the end of their name. ("Pty" stands for 'proprietary', in other words, they are privately owned. They are called 'limited by shares' because you acquire an interest in the company by purchasing its shares. The profits of the company will be distributed to its shareholders according to their shareholdings. (For discussion of companies 'limited by guarantee', see Chapter 3.)

Proprietary companies now only need to have one shareholder (whether a human or another company). If there is more than one, the shareholders can hold the shares in any proportion. Companies only need one director.

The shares may be of several sorts (e.g., voting or non-voting, preference or ordinary, etc.), but usually the percentage of shares held determines the degree of control over the company and the proportion of income that will be received from company dividends.

OBJECTS

In establishing a company, you must remember that it is an artificial creature and can only do the things permitted under its constitution and the Corporations Act.

A company is a highly flexible structure with an almost unlimited range of objects. Indeed, these days, it is not compulsory to nominate any purposes at all! However, there are sometimes advantages in specifying the objects of the company more closely.

LIABILITY

Members' liability is limited to the amount of any unpaid-up value of their shares. Let's say four people form a company with an issued capital of 100 shares, and each shareholder holds 25 shares. Assume that the constitution says each share has a value of $10. After trading for some years, the company incurs losses of $100,000. Its assets are only $50,000. If the company cannot pay its debts the creditors may wind the company up but the shareholders' personal liability will be limited. If the shareholders have each actually paid the full $10 per share, they pay no more money, but if they have only paid, say, $1 of the nominal value, the remaining $9 per share will be payable (i.e. $9 x 25 shares). The shareholders' other personal savings and assets will be untouchable.

In other words, if you are entering a high-risk business (and what can be more high risk than the music industry) it is a common-sense way to protect personal assets.

WHEN AND HOW TO FORM COMPANIES

The establishment of a company is something that should be discussed with your lawyer and your accountant. Since the introduction of the Fringe Benefits Tax and other taxes, the benefits have been reduced although not entirely removed. Forming a company is probably not worthwhile for tax purposes unless you are earning (or are about to earn) in excess of, say, $40,000 a year because it is only about that figure that the corporate rate of tax becomes advantageous over personal rates.

As already explained, companies are also useful for limiting personal liability and thus protecting personal assets. This is particularly so when an individual wishes to combine with others in a specific venture but does not want to be liable (as a partner) for the errors or defaults of another party. It is also possible to choose a company structure to make use of its shares as a way of defining the members' rights to control the venture and their rights to profits; e.g. you can have different classes of shares - with different rights attaching to various classes of share. You will need to discuss this with your advisers before tackling it.

Many people simply buy a 'shelf company' (so-called because it is set up in advance, ready-named, and can be purchased and established without delay). The price for these starts at about $1,100, although if you want to change its usually inelegant name, it will probably cost extra. The advantage of the shelf company is that it is operative quickly and it can be obtained readily.

These days, it is just as fast to set up a company from scratch. This is slightly more expensive but is preferable as you can tailor the creature to your own individual needs. As with so many things, the structure you choose should be moulded to your particular requirements, not vice versa. Saving a few hundred dollars here can be a very false economy in the long term.

WRITTEN AGREEMENT BETWEEN SHAREHOLDERS

All too often, groups (or their accountants) set up a company but fail to have a written agreement between the shareholders that establishes how they will operate the company. The constitution of the company sets out only the basic machinery of the company. It doesn't deal with the nitty-gritty aspects of the commercial relationship between the individuals involved.

The shareholders' agreement will cover many of the points that are contained in the *Partnership Checklist* (set out earlier in the chapter). Companies are easy to establish. The more difficult, but important, part of the process is to sculpt a shareholders' agreement so that the basic company structure really fits the needs of the individuals who will be working under the umbrella of that company.

To assist your lawyer to draft your shareholders' agreement, review the *Partnership Checklist*, work out which questions are relevant to you and try to work out some preliminary answers. The more information you can prepare for yourself, the less time it will take to draft the shareholders' agreement and the cheaper it will be.

SERVICE AGREEMENTS

Since a company has no hands and feet, let alone any musical ability, it will have to retain the services of musicians. Each musician should have a simple written agreement with the company, spelling out the terms on which they will supply those services. What services will each supply? Will the services be exclusive to the company or will they be able to do outside work? If so, what work and in what circumstances? How will they be paid? Will there be a superannuation fund set up, so savings can be put away? What rights will they own or control?

OTHER AGREEMENTS

It is important to remember that if the group forms a company, the company must become the vehicle for all aspects of the group's business. It is the company that enters all of the group's music business contracts: Record contracts, management contracts, rental contracts, car and truck hire, side player agreements, studio hire, producer agreements, and everything else that involves money and/or liabilities, should be in the name of the company.

TRUSTS

A trust may be loosely defined as being an arrangement by which someone (the trustee) holds and manages property on behalf of others (the beneficiaries).

Trusts are generally used as a device for splitting income earned by one or more persons amongst a greater number of beneficiaries. This can have considerable tax advantages, although developments in taxation laws have considerably reduced these advantages.

Trust structures used in the music industry can be divided into Discretionary Trusts (in which the beneficiaries' right to income is flexible) and Unit Trusts (in which the right to income is determined by the number of units that have been allocated to each beneficiary). Which you choose will depend on the reason you are creating the trust.

The trustee will usually be a company (generally referred to as the corporate trustee). The corporate trustee enters all the agreements, undertakes all the liabilities, collects all the money and arranges for the payment of the profits to the beneficiaries of the trust. This way, the beneficiaries can get the benefits of limited liability that the company offers while still enjoying any tax advantages that the trust may offer.

You should definitely not enter the world of trusts without very detailed expert advice.

3
NOT-FOR-PROFIT ORGANISATIONS

THE USE OF 'NON-PROFIT' STRUCTURES IS COMMON
IN THE MUSIC WORLD. THIS CHAPTER DESCRIBES THE
STEPS NECESSARY TO SET UP A NOT-FOR-PROFIT
MUSIC ORGANISATION, TO SELECT APPROPRIATE
BOARD MEMBERS AND TO STRUCTURE
THE ORGANISATION.
IT ALSO DESCRIBES THE LEGAL DUTIES OF BOARD
MEMBERS AND OF SENIOR MANAGEMENT. THESE
OBLIGATIONS APPLY TO THE DIRECTORS OF ALL
COMPANIES, NOT JUST NON-PROFIT ONES, AND
MANY OF THE ISSUES DEALT WITH HERE ALSO APPLY
TO THE ADMINISTRATION OF ORGANISATIONS AND
GROUPS GENERALLY.

'Not-for-profit' organisations are the largest employers of professional musicians and music administrators in Australia. Almost all ensembles and music organisations that receive government grants are structured in this way because most government grant schemes require that grant recipients be structured as public, not privately owned, enterprises. Moreover, if the group wants to attract tax-deductible donations, it has to have a not-for-profit structure.

The not-for-profit company is the most common legal structure in the classical music field. Nearly all orchestras, ensembles and choirs are structured this way. Examples of performance groups range from the flag-ship companies such as the symphony orchestras, the Australian Opera and major festivals (such as the Adelaide Festival, Moomba, the Sydney Festival) and hundreds of smaller performance groups such as the Philharmonia, The Song Company, Synergy, the Australian Chamber Orchestra, the Australian Brandenburg Orchestra).

Similarly, most of the support organisations that underpin the strength of the music industry are structured as not-for-profit companies. Examples include APRA, AMCOS, Musica Viva (reputed to be the largest chamber music entrepreneur in the world), CAAMA, the Music Council of Australia, the Australian Guild of Screen Composers, the Arts Law Centre of Australia and the Australian Copyright Council.

Although it is not a structure that you would consider if you want to form a band with aspirations to produce commercial, popular music, the not-for-profit structure is an essential part of the Australian music industry.

There are many non-profit distributing organisations in the Australian music world. They range from companies with budgets of millions of dollars, through to small and informal clubs with no financial resources at all. They vary in size and purpose. Some receive funding from governments, some are supported by funds from their members and some are supported by sponsorships and donations. Indeed most live off a cocktail of funding types.

When starting any not-for-profit organisation it is important to choose the optimal legal structure. The structure adopted must complement the objectives of the organisation and provide for the needs and expectations of its members. As might be expected, some forms are better than others.

Which structure should be used must be considered with care. Some legal structures suit certain purposes better than others, and those responsible for establishing the organisation must seriously consider whether they are making the best use of their options.

Every organisation should be thought of as a living creature: it grows, learns, matures, develops diverse interests, can be trained or ill trained, and eventually, many should either be put to sleep or just allowed to gracefully die. The continued existence of an organisation should never be taken for granted.

This chapter is intended to outline the various options that are available to non-profit organisations, and it may be advisable to consult an accountant or lawyer with appropriate experience, or the Arts Law Centre of Australia, when setting up a non-profit organisation. It also discusses the importance of defining the objectives, devising budgets, choosing structures and selecting personnel. It then examines the legal duties of those in positions of responsibility and discusses some of the issues relating to the management of non-profit organisations, and the management of boards.

PRELIMINARY ISSUES

There are two preliminary questions that must be resolved at the outset. Given your general aims:

- What will be done with any profits the organisation makes; and
- Will the organisation be dependent on government funding, membership fees or donations?

The answer to these two questions will usually determine whether or not you should be forming a non-profit organisation.

WHAT DOES 'NON-PROFIT' MEAN?

'**Non-profit**' does not mean that the group or organisation does not make money. 'Non-profit' means **non-profit-distributing**, not non-profit-making. A 'non-profit' organisation does not divide the profits among its members. Instead, all profits are spent on the objects of the organisation. (This is why such organisations are also called 'not for profit organisations'.)

Nor does 'non-profit' mean that the participants cannot be paid. It is not the same as 'voluntary'. For example, in a non-profit company such as the Australian Opera or the Melbourne Symphony Orchestra, the players and the staff get paid – they just don't get a share of any profits that the company may make. All profits go back into the business.

That is why it is important to ask: 'What will happen to any profits made by the organisation? Will they be distributed to the members or will they be ploughed back into the objectives of the organisation?'

If it is intended that the **profits** be split between the participants, the group should consider forming a company limited by shares (in which the profits are distributed according to the shareholding) or a partnership. (These types of organisations are considered in more detail in Chapter 2, **Business Structures**.) If the intention is to return any profits to the organisation, in order to further that organisation's objectives, then there are a number of different structures that might be suitable for setting up such a 'non-profit' organisation.

It can even be useful when a number of private enterprises want to get together to do something communally. For example, if a number of musicians wished to buy jointly and share the use of production facilities, they could form a 'non-profit' structure. This would permit them to benefit from the bulk-buying capacity of the organisation, the shared purchase and maintenance costs of the equipment, and enjoy the opportunity for discussion and stimulation of ideas and interests. However, if the organisation itself were to make any money, those profits would have be put back into the organisation – new gear, better salaries for staff and so on. Whilst all members would benefit, no individual member could receive anything in the nature of a dividend or any other form of sharing in the organisation's profits.

WHAT WILL THE PRIMARY SOURCES OF FUNDING BE?

If the organisation is likely to be funded from:
- donations,
- membership fees, or
- government grants,

it is almost certain that a non-profit structure will be required.

Most government funding bodies insist that the organisations that they fund are non-profit distributing. Most will not fund privately owned enterprises even if they are for good purposes and are unlikely to make a profit. With few exceptions, those seeking government funding are going to have to adopt one of the non-profit-distributing structures.

Similarly, all organisations that need to get tax-deductibility for donations they receive, will need to be non-profit-distributing.

ESTABLISHING A MUSIC ORGANISATION

Whether you are setting up an organisation to promote the interests of screen composers, a symphony orchestra, a medieval music ensemble, or a vehicle to present live music to under-18s who don't have access to licensed venues, a similar process applies.

DEFINING THE OBJECTS

When starting an organisation, no matter how small or large, the steering committee must clearly define the intended functions. What does it expect the organisation to do or to achieve? You need a Statement of Objectives.

Although this sounds easy, it is not. This elementary step sometimes takes several meetings because various members will have different perceptions of what should be done and why. These differences are not usually obvious until the steering committee tries to distil the aims and objects in writing. The process of describing the ideas in writing, as fully and precisely as possible, winkles out misunderstandings and ensures that the members have a common purpose.

- Meet and discuss the aims.
- Appoint one person to take notes at the meeting.
- Have that person draw up a written summary of those aims.
- Circulate the summary for further consideration.
- Meet again to refine the written aims.
- Be as precise and unambiguous as possible.
- Finalise the aims.

Let's call the resulting document the '**Statement of Objectives**'. (Even those organisations that have been in existence for many years, should as a matter of good governance, review their constitution every few years. Regular corporate and constitutional review ensures that there is harmony between the objective, purposes and powers set out in the organisation's constitution and those that are being assumed in the course of the day-to-day operation of the organisation. It is very common to find that the purposes and function of the organisation have incrementally evolved over the years but no one has thought to check whether that evolution is either permitted or even contemplated by the constitution.)

DEFINING THE IMPLEMENTATION STRATEGY

Having defined **what** it wants to do, the group must then decide **how** it wants to do it.

The committee will probably come up with several different ways of implementing the goals of the group. All of these ideas should be circulated and discussed, as sometimes the most obvious approach is not the best. If the plan is to work it must be practical. Let's call this document the '**Implementation Strategy**'.

Inextricably associated with the Implementation Strategy are two elements - money and people. Many organisations fold prematurely because they do not ensure that they have both the financial resources and the human skills necessary to achieve their goals.

FINANCIAL PLANNING

It is now essential to work out how much it is going to cost to give effect to your Implementation Strategy. This requires you to work out a '**Preliminary Budget**'. It should be detailed and conservative.

* Can the group afford to tackle the project?
* What will it cost to set up?
* What will it cost to run?
* How will these expenses be met?
* How will the budget be administered?
* If there are any profits, how will they be applied?

This is a strange process, in that it is a mixture of exactness and guesswork. For some items, such as insurance, you can get quotes whereas for others, such as projected income, you can only estimate. The cardinal rule is simple: where possible, use an exact figure. If an estimate must be made, you should err on the side of conservatism. Most organisations cost more to run, and return less, than expected.

HUMAN RESOURCES

By this stage, the steering committee has three documents: a Statement of Objectives; an Implementation Strategy; and a Preliminary Budget.

The next series of questions it must ask itself is: 'Do the present members of the group have the necessary skills and resources? What additional skills are needed? Who can provide them?'

SELECTING THE FIRST BOARD

It would be very rare that the group that first comes up with an idea will not benefit from the involvement of others with different attributes, knowledge and skills but similar interests. The people with the original ideas are not necessarily the right people to be on the board which actually runs the organisation, though often there will be substantial overlap.

The 'founder syndrome' is a dangerous one: every new organisation needs catalysts, initiators, those with a fire in their belly. That said, such people are sometimes so driven by their vision that they do not welcome advice and do not want to share control. Founder syndrome is a terminal disease caught by many organisations.

Accordingly, it should be expressly agreed by all of the members of the first committee that they are there only to steer the new organisation to an agreed stage of development. A not-for-profit company that looks to the public or the government for funding should not be seen as a private bailiwick of the founders. It is not "their" organisation; they merely have temporary stewardship of the public purpose. As an integral part of establishing the organisation, they should be planning their own, responsible, exit from it. Organisations that are dependent on their founders are very temporary indeed for it must be the public purpose that ignites the support of others with new skills and energies.

The board is an invaluable source of knowledge, wisdom, contacts, vision and experience. The American approach whereby board members are expected to be major donors, is not common in Australia or New Zealand. In the local environment, one should beware the donor that demands or expects a place on the board. The ability and preparedness to write a cheque is no guarantee of governance skills. There are almost always better ways of attracting and retaining donors than also expecting them to work as a director. Look first to the **skills** required on the board. If the organisation has the right balance of skills, the money will follow. The reverse does not apply. (This is discussed in more detail in Chapter 29, **Philanthropy**.)

SELECTING THE STRUCTURE

Once the steering committee has determined the objectives of the organisation and has decided that the organisation is going to operate on a non-profit basis, the members of the Committee must decide which non-profit structure will be the most suitable. It is important to ensure that the organisation is making the best use of available legal structures and is selecting a structure that will allow the organisation the best opportunity to fulfil its objectives. If in doubt, consult an accountant or a lawyer who is experienced in the area.

There are five non-profit organisation types:

(a) unincorporated associations;

(b) incorporated associations;

(c) co-operatives;

(d) companies limited by guarantee;

(e) trusts.

The first of these is by far the most common, though it offers few of the advantages offered by the other, more formal, structures.

UNINCORPORATED NON-PROFIT GROUPS

Any group of people that bands together for a specific not for profit purpose, but which does not incorporate as a company, an incorporated association or a co-operative, can be described as an unincorporated association. Formation is free and without formality and thereafter the association runs itself according to its own rules and settles internal disputes in its own way. It is basically a private club. It sounds ideally simple and effective, but unincorporated bodies would usually be better served by a more considered, more certain, formal structure.

ADVANTAGES

(a) Unincorporated associations are easy to set up. There are no formalities.

(b) Formation costs are minimal.

(c) The on-going administration is not regulated by government agencies and this permits a flexibility much cherished by some groups.

(d) Because of the absence of governmental supervision, the unincorporated form permits maintenance of privacy for the organisation's dealings. Its objects, minutes and accounts are not available for public scrutiny.

DISADVANTAGES

(a) Unlike incorporated bodies, an unincorporated association has no legal identity distinct from its members. It is merely a collection of individuals. This has important consequences for the members of the organisation, especially in relation to the liability of the members for the actions of the group.

(b) It cannot sue or be sued in its own name. Its members (usually the committee) must accept such responsibilities. For example, they will be liable personally for the debts of the association.

(c) An unincorporated association cannot enter into contracts in its own name so, if it is decided to lease or buy premises or goods, representatives of the group will have to accept this onerous financial responsibility.

(d) An unincorporated association cannot own property or goods in its own name. Ownership must be vested in trustees and this imposes very high personal liabilities and duties on those trustees.

(e) Problems can arise if a member, who was the signatory to a long-term contract, leaves the organisation before the term of that contract expires. This makes it very difficult (indeed often impossible) for the remaining members of the association to enforce the agreement because the person who entered the agreement is no longer around.

(f) It is usually a condition of receiving funding from government programs that the group be incorporated. This means that an unincorporated association will only be able to obtain a government grant if their application is submitted and managed by another incorporated association. (This process is referred to as "auspicing a grant".) This can cause problems with accountability and control over the funding.

(g) The members of an unincorporated organisation may be personally liable for the breach of any contract entered on behalf of the group and similarly will be personally liable if the organisation commits a tort (such as an act of negligence) that causes someone loss. Because of the difficulty caused by fluctuating memberships it is often difficult to sue all members of a group, so, plaintiffs tend to sue the committee members. This is an enormous personal liability for those committee members and is one that is all too rarely considered. (There are many court cases involving sporting clubs and the principles are identical in arts organisations.)

(h) The unincorporated association does not have limited liability. Thus, even if the association agrees to indemnify its members, if the amount owed is greater than the assets of the organisation, recourse may still be had against the members and there is no way for the members to limit their financial responsibilities. The sky's the limit.

FORMING AN UNINCORPORATED ASSOCIATION

A structure of this type is easy to set up. If, after considering its disadvantages, you still decide that it is your best option, the most important consideration is to draw up a constitution that reflects the aims of the organisation and provides an administrative structure by which these aims can be achieved. If, however, the association intends employing people, hiring or buying premises, trading, or doing other things that might expose the members to financial liabilities, seriously consider incorporation.

THE INCORPORATED ASSOCIATION

Legislation has been enacted in all jurisdictions to make the incorporation of non-profit organisations with community, artistic or sporting purposes, a fairly simple matter.

Generally, to be eligible to form an incorporated association the organisation must have more than a specified number of members (usually five or more), have a set of objects and rules and have a non-profit purpose.

ADVANTAGES

(a) The structure is ideal for many music societies, groups or organisations. It provides most of the benefits of a company limited by guarantee but without involving the association in the same initial and on-going expenses and formalities.

(b) It is easy to form. Lawyers are not needed. (Brochures and information kits are available from the relevant government department in each State, which explain how to go about forming an incorporated association and guidelines about how to draw up an appropriate constitution. Most even supply a model constitution that you can use as is, or modify according to your needs.)

(c) When the association is incorporated, the law treats it as a 'legal person', distinct from its members. Thus, an incorporated association can own property in its own name, it can hire and fire, sue and be sued. This generally relieves the members from personal liability should anything go wrong with the association. Their liability is limited. Note, however, that the members of the Management Committee (or board) of the association may be liable for debts incurred by the association in certain circumstances. (These are discussed further below in the section, **Managing an Organisation**.)

DISADVANTAGES

(a) An association cannot be incorporated if its object is to provide 'pecuniary gains' for its members. The term 'pecuniary gain' is not clearly defined in the legislation, but it certainly amounts to a requirement that the organisation be one that is non-profit-distributing.

(b) There are also restrictions on 'trading' in most States. This limitation makes the incorporated association inappropriate for music ensembles that sell tickets to their performances.

The strictness of this limitation varies from State to State, so careful attention must be paid to ensure the group's objectives are compatible with the restrictions. Often, these difficulties may be overcome quite easily. If, say, a group wishes to set up a shared production studio facility, most States would not permit it to form an incorporated association because the primary purpose would be to 'trade'. However, it would not be at all difficult to incorporate the association if its object was 'to provide facilities to assist musicians to make demonstration recordings of their own work and thus enhance the quality of their work and the opportunity of gaining contracts'. This way, the organisation would simply provide the resources, rather than it being involved in 'trading'.

(c) There are also some restrictions on who can be employed by the association. Generally, while members can receive wages for work performed for the association, the work and the payments should be incidental to the running of the association.

(d) There are annual costs associated with running an incorporated association. These include filing fees and taking out public liability insurance to cover the activities of the association. These costs will vary from State to State but are likely to be between $200 and $300 per year. These costs are much cheaper than those associated with running a company.

(e) Because an Incorporated Association is a creature of State legislation, if it is going to operate over State borders you are usually better off forming a company which will guarantee you national protection.

(f) The accounting requirements are ideal for small organisations but not generally adequate for those with large budgets. Most organisations with budgets over $200,000 should be considering a company structure instead of an incorporated association.

FORMING AN INCORPORATED ASSOCIATION

The exact procedures that govern the formation of an incorporated association will vary from State to State, and information kits should be obtained from the relevant government department. Generally, the members must hold a meeting to approve a constitution, appoint the members of the Committee to run the association and authorise a member to apply for incorporation. This member will become the first public officer of the association and will be responsible for lodging the annual statements of the association with the relevant State department. The address of the public officer will also be the address of the association for the purposes of the service of documents and correspondence with the department.

CO-OPERATIVES

Although all States have legislation that permits the forming of co-operatives, more attractive alternatives are available in all jurisdictions.

The co-operative was developed in the 19th century for the specific purpose of regulating 'friendly societies' (i.e. workers' mutual insurance funds) and later, to permit incorporation of both consumers' and producers' co-operative societies. Although the structure has since been stretched to permit their use by organisations of more general community benefit, this option is usually considered the choice of last resort for arts organisations.

The formation of a co-operative society gives the benefits of incorporation without the expense or formalities of forming a company. No stamp duty is payable, no fees are payable upon registration, and no solicitor need be retained. The Registrar of Co-operative Societies will assist interested persons in completing the formalities and drafting the co-operative's rules.

Best of all, the name has that nostalgic ring that we associate with flowers and the '60s.

There are very few successful long-term co-operatives working in the music world. Those that are successful are so because of the personal strengths and skills of key members.

Non-profit organisations seeking the benefits of incorporation would do well to bypass this mode and either form an incorporated association or a company limited by guarantee. Its cheapness is attractive and it may be ideologically alluring but, in general, the co-operative is a cumbersome way of providing services to members.

THE COMPANY LIMITED BY GUARANTEE

Although there are several different types of company, the one most suited to non-profit organisations is the 'company limited by guarantee'. This means that if, when the company is wound up, its debts exceed its assets, the liability of the members is limited to the amount that each is guaranteed. The amount of this guarantee is stated in the constitution. It is usually only a nominal amount (i.e. usually between $20 and $100).

If one of the principal purposes of the organisation is to trade (e.g. presenting concerts to a paying audience) then the company will be the most likely choice. Similarly, if the budget is large and activities extensive, the company will probably be more appropriate. Certainly if you are intending to have a national or interstate focus you should consider this structure.

ADVANTAGES

(a) The company is a separate legal entity from its members. It can sue and be sued, enter contracts in its own name, own property in its own name, and is responsible for its own debts.

(b) The potential liability of its members is limited to the amount stated in the constitution.

(c) A company limited by guarantee is more autonomous in the management of its affairs than a co-operative or an incorporated association. A company is less restricted in when, how and what it may do. Its advantage over the incorporated association is that it can 'trade' without difficulty.

(d) It is quite easy for the members of the company to change its constitution.

(e) Registration is virtually automatic, once the proper papers are filed and the fees paid.

DISADVANTAGES

(a) A company is quite expensive to set up. If the organisation has to pay for the preparation of the documents it will usually cost between $2,000 and $5,000. Some, more complicated ones can be more costly.

(b) The name of the association must contain the word 'Limited' unless the members apply to have the 'Limited' removed. However, doing this does impose restrictions on the company.

(c) The administrative requirements for running a company are generally more onerous, for example the company must keep separate books for directors' minutes and members' minutes, maintain a register of directors, secretaries and keep the financial records of the company in a prescribed manner.

(d) An annual return must be lodged. As this must be signed by an auditor, this also involves an annual expense for auditor's fees.

(e) Forming a non-profit company should not be attempted without legal advice.

FORMING A COMPANY

The Corporations Act establishes the formalities required for the incorporation of a company limited by guarantee and imposes a number of restrictions and duties upon those responsible for running a company. The Australian Securities and Investment Commission (ASIC) has an information kit and website (www.asic.gov.au) with detailed information about the various statutory obligations of a company and its directors. The information in Chapter 2, **Business Structures**, about setting up a company is also applicable to the formation of a company limited by guarantee. The section below, **Managing a non-profit organisation**, indicates the range of formalities and responsibilities, but it is no substitute for specialist advice. The process for incorporating a company is detailed and it is advisable to delegate this task to an experienced lawyer.

TRUSTS

In some respects a trust is an obligation rather than a structure. It is an obligation that rests on a person (or group of people) who is given the legal ownership of property (be that land or money or rights), either for the benefit of someone else or for a specified purpose. The structure is usually provided in the "trust deed", the written document that sets out the property, objects, powers and persons responsible for the trust.

If a trust is created and comes into effect during the lifetime of the person who sets it up, the trust is called an **intervivos trust** or a **settlement**. The person who creates such a trust is known as the **settlor**. Where the trust comes into effect upon the death of a person it is known as **testamentary trust** and the person who created it is referred to as the **testator**.

One example of the latter is the Peggy Glanville Hicks Composers' Trust. This was established when the late composer left her Sydney home to a testamentary trust for use as a composer-in-residence studio. It has a formal trust deed (in effect the constitution of the trust) and because it is registered on the Register of Cultural Organisations, it can receive tax-deductible donations.

REGISTER OF CULTURAL ORGANISATIONS

The Register of Cultural Organisations (ROCO) was established by the Federal Government in 1991 and is the principal machinery by which the Government promotes individual and corporate philanthropy: If an organisation is admitted onto the Register, gifts and donations to it will be tax-deductible. This has made it easier to attract gifts from individual donors. (Companies have always been able to get a deduction whether or not an organisation is on the Register because if they structure the transaction as promotion or marketing, it will be a deductible business expense.) The ROCO initiative is significant because it is governmental recognition that the public good that flows from philanthropic contribution to culture is every bit as real and desirable as that which flows from the expenditure of business expenses.

To be eligible for inclusion on the Register, an organisation must:

- Demonstrate that it is 'not for profit'. It does this by showing that its constitution makes it clear that its profits are not to be distributed to its members. (The Department provides recommended wording for this purpose.)
- Be constituted as a legal body (this includes a company, incorporated association, a statutory body or an organisation established under a trust or a will).
- Have as its principal purpose the promotion of one or more of the following cultural activities: literature, music, performing arts, design, crafts, film, video, television, radio, Aboriginal arts, community arts and moveable cultural heritage.
- Establish a separate bank account to receive donations from the public.

Once the organisation is registered, the requirements are not arduous. Essentially you have to report to the Department every six months and disclose all donations received from the public during that time.

Every non-profit organisation in the music sector should consider this avenue for attracting donations. If you do have benefactors, you should adopt a structure that will provide them with partial recompense for their philanthropy so that they are more likely to become long-term benefactors. (For more detailed discussion see Chapter 29, **Philanthropy.**)

MANAGING A NON-PROFIT ARTS ORGANISATION

There are several aspects to the successful management of a non-profit organisation:

- Ensuring that everyone involved has a clear idea of their expectations, roles and responsibilities in relation to the objectives and running of the organisation, and the management of its finances;
- Recognising and addressing the problems that can occur in organisations that depend heavily on the commitment and enthusiasm of a few individuals;
- Establishing and managing an effective working relationship between the individual members of the board so as to make the most of the skills and talents of its members;
- Creating and maintaining the relationship between the board, the staff and volunteers of the organisation to ensure that there are proper lines of communication, accountability and responsibility established and maintained;

The following material outlines the responsibilities of people in authority and then looks at other aspects of the successful management of a non-profit organisation, including how to manage difficult board members.

PURPOSE OF THE BOARD

The main responsibilities of the board are to:

- establish and review the structure of the organisation;
- define and review the policies and practices of the organisation. These include policies concerning the cultural objectives of the organisation but also policies relating to the employment of staff, the relationship of the organisation to other institutions and to the public, the raising of funds, and the financial management of the organisation;
- devise and review the strategies for implementation of the organisation's objectives;
- establish clearly defined lines of communication, delegation and responsibility;
- provide the organisation with a network of contacts;
- help raise money for the organisation; and
- lend their reputation to the organisation.

SELECTING THE BOARD

The board is the head of the organisation – both actually and metaphorically. Effective companies have good boards; ineffective companies have dysfunctional boards. (There is an old management maxim: "A fish rots from the head".)

When selecting a board you are creating a reservoir of wisdom and skills to assist the implementation of the organisation's objectives. The board needs to be comprised of people who will provide the organisation with managerial, financial and cultural experience and expertise. They must be people with credibility in their field and have a network of contacts that can be called upon so that the resources of the board are greater than the sum of its members.

The long-term strength of the organisation will flow from the strength of the board. For example, it can be invaluable to have a person skilled in accounting and finance to assist in budgeting, advising on fund raising strategies, reviewing expenditure and preparing financial reports. Similarly, as most organisations these days have to raise money of their own it is important to have someone who is experienced in fundraising. Similarly it can be advantageous to have a well-connected business person on the committee. Such a person will not only give sensible practical advice on finance and administration but will also be able to make personal contact with potential sponsors.

At least at the beginning, it will be useful to have a lawyer on the committee, be it to assist with the design of the organisation's legal structure or to advise on the many legal requirements, rights and responsibilities that will affect the organisation. Moreover, as one of the most important functions of any board is to determine policy, it is vital to have a strong representation of persons with relevant experience in the relevant area. Knowledge and practical experience is more important than fine intentions.

As mentioned above, one of the important contributions that board members must be expected to make is to lend actively their personal reputation to the organisation. This is often overlooked. If you are establishing an organisation of national focus, the board must contain members of national reputation and networks. If it is a local community organisation, persons with influence within the local community are more appropriate. It is horses for courses. Not only must they have the reputation, they must be prepared to use it for the benefit of the organisation. Their name alone may help, but they must also be prepared to write that letter or make that phone call; in other words, actively to use their contacts for the benefit of the organisation.

So, don't invite figureheads. Board members are workers. Famous names who won't come to meetings, won't become actively involved, won't write that letter or make that important phone call, have no place on the board. Figureheads make good patrons but can make terrible board members.

In summary, when forming the board one must keep in mind a few basic rules:

- Determine the number of people that should be on the board. Remember that big board are generally ineffective. Keep it tight. Most need no more than seven or eight members.
- Having regard to the objects of the organisation, work out the talents that are needed on the board. Selection must be skills-based. Avoid inviting friends and 'yes-people'. Write down the list of skills and allocate them against each of the board positions.
- In addition to the skills requirements, there may also be other characteristics that are desirable. For example, there should be a balance of gender representation. In some cases, it is desirable (or even essential) that the board should have particular characteristics of age, ethnicity, or geographic location.
- Make a list of all the people who have those talents and attributes and who would be appropriate for the organisation.
- Professional advice is expensive. So, unless the organisation is so rich or successful as to be able to afford professional fees, or so small-scale as not to need professional skills, the group should invite the necessary professional expertise onto its board.
- Don't invite figureheads. Board members are workers. Famous names who won't come to meetings, won't become actively involved, won't write that letter or make that important phone call, have no part on the board. Figureheads make good patrons and terrible board members.
- Don't invite someone just because they are rich. Look for people with true networks of influence: They are often more valuable and usually require less maintenance.

If you have done the above steps you will now have a document that looks something like the following table.

Now that you have identified your needs and the best people to fill those needs, **review** the potential names - quietly ask around the traps about each of them. People who have worked with them will have views about their true value and effectiveness (this may be quite different from their public persona).

Ask only the best. Don't worry if you don't know them personally. Nobody minds being invited onto a board. It is usually flattering. Get an appointment and do your pitch in person. It is much more effective than just writing a letter or talking on the phone.

If your first choice says 'no', don't be disheartened. It's not personal. Instead, ask them for names of persons that they think might be suitable. They may well come up with a suggestion that is fantastic but one that you hadn't considered or hadn't dreamed would be interested. (If the suggestion is someone you don't personally know, ask if you can use his or her name to make contact. It makes the next approach so much easier: ("... Albert Einstein suggested that I give you a call...")

SKILLS MATRIX

		Board Member				
Relationships	Access to Art Community					
	Access to Government					
	Acces to People with Business Expertise					
	Access to Funds					
Geographic Area	Marketing					
	Public Relation					
	Financial Management/ Compliance					
	Fundraising					
	Business Administration					
	Legal					
	Contemporary Art					
	Event Management					
Geographic Area Represented	Other					
	Northern Territory					
	Queensland					
	New South Wales					
	Victoria					
	South Australia					
	Western Australia					
	Asia Pacific					
Sector	Arts					
	Local Media					
	Corporate					
	Political					
	Education					
	Legal					
	Finance					
Race/Ethnicity	Other					
	Indigenous					
	Hispanic / Latino					
	Caucasian					
	Asian					
	Pacific Islands / Maori					
Gender/Age	Over 65					
	51 - 65					
	36 - 50					
	21 - 35					
	Male					
	Female					

HELPING THE BOARD TO BE EFFECTIVE

The health and success of an organisation reflects the effectiveness of the board. There just aren't any cot case companies with terrific boards. This section discusses some of the ways that an organisation can get the most out of their board and ensure that their board works as well as it should. Given that non-profit organisations are run by boards of volunteers it is important to put in place, from the outset, mechanisms that will assist them to maximise their skills and generous preparedness to contribute to the organisation and the sector.

THE CARE AND FEEDING OF BOARD MEMBERS

Board members give their time generously and without much return. Nobody accepts appointment to the board of a cultural organisation for the money! They are making a voluntary contribution to a community activity that they really care about. They are almost certainly very busy and it is important that they are made to feel welcome and involved. If they are to contribute to their maximum ability to the benefit of the organisation, there are some basic steps that every organisation should put in place.

INTRODUCTION PROCEDURES FOR NEW BOARD MEMBERS

Every organisation must ensure that there are clear handover procedures for the induction of new members onto the board. A good handover 'package' would include:

- A personal brief as to what is expected of them;
- Copies of the management plan, the financial reports and papers and minutes of the last few meetings;
- The policies of the organisation (including ethical conduct policy);
- Guidelines as to discipline and lines of communication;
- A list of key personnel; and
- Any other papers of which the new board member should be aware.

The new board member should be introduced to the staff and, if there are premises, shown around the offices. Every new board member should have a feeling of belonging.

Then, every three or four months, the Chair should contact each member individually and have a brief chat as to how they think the organisation is going, whether there are any issues that need addressing and, most importantly, how they feel they are contributing to the organisation. This gives the Chair the opportunity to hear more private views that may need to be expressed and acknowledged and also permits the Chair the opportunity to deal with any problems or issues, such as lack of performance, that may be embarrassing to discuss at the board meeting. Board members need to feel part of the organisation but they are also subject to performance review (albeit in a subtle way!)

ASSIGNMENT OF RESPONSIBILITIES

Perhaps the most important internal function of any board is the definition and assignment of individual responsibilities to directors. In all cases, because a board can only function by delegating certain tasks to individuals or subcommittees, it is important for boards to consider how to go about delegating tasks in the most effective manner. This also involves an understanding of the appropriate limits that should be placed on individual board member's actions and responsibilities.

When assigning responsibilities you must make sure that:

- The best use is being made of their expertise and contacts.
- Individual board members are being realistic about the level of responsibility they can take on. (The Chair must be careful not to overload any particular board member. They are volunteers. That generosity must not be abused or they will soon lose the fire in their belly. Jobs need to be spread around between board members. If they can't be, it may well indicate that you need to review the composition of the board.)
- The responsibility is clearly articulated so that there can be no mistake as to the commitment being undertaken.
- There is a reporting line and a time line put against each task.
- Each task should be fully minuted so that the responsibility is recorded and both the individual and the board itself knows that there will be a report on the activity at the next meeting.

DECISION MAKING, DEFINING POLICY AND SETTING STRATEGY

When looking at the policies and strategies of an organisation, board members must ask themselves:

- Does our organisation have a written Statement of Objectives that is clearly articulated, understood and accepted? Without it, the organisation has no basis for determining its actions and its priorities. Without it, the senior management of the organisation has no tiller with which to guide its day-to-day decisions.
- How long is it since the organisation's policies and priorities were reviewed? Unless these are regularly reviewed, the organisation may become stagnant or the victim of conflicting and incompatible priorities for resources.

- How are policy reviews undertaken? Is the board involving all the people who have a contribution to make in the policy development process? Is it using the best available techniques? All too often, boards make policy without sufficient involvement of their members, their staff, their funding bodies and other groups who may have real contributions to make to the process. The involvement of select outsiders may assist the board to gain a wider perspective of their own organisation. Few boards have the internal skills to carry out thorough policy reviews using only their own internal resources and the board could consider seeking the assistance of a professional facilitator to assist in the process.
- How are strategies determined? While the responsibility for determining strategy lies with the board, in most cases it is the staff, volunteers and members who will carry out the strategies and in many cases it is the staff that actually designs the strategies. It is one of the areas in which there is great potential for conflict with staff but it is important that the board oversees the development and implementation of the organisation's strategies. It is the board that must call for them, query them and, when satisfied, approve them. Later, it must evaluate and amend them. This remains an ongoing process.

SETTING LIMITS AND CREATING COMMUNICATION CHANNELS

Many board members need to understand better the nature of and limits to their relationship with employees or volunteers of the organisation, with members of the organisation and with the public. Each of these relationships is potentially complex and may give rise to difficulty, whether an organisation is large and has numerous employees and a senior management, or whether it is a small organisation that is not much larger than the board itself.

There should be clear guidelines as to what a board member may or may not do in relation to management, staff, members and volunteers. For example, in terms of dealing with staff it should provide written guidelines articulating the staff selection, instruction, reporting and review procedures. It is the board (as a whole) that has responsibility for staff and it is the responsibility of each director to ensure that the board fulfils its duties in relation to staff. It is not each director's individual duty to get the staff to do what he or she individually thinks is best. If you are a director and if you cannot persuade the board as to what needs to be done in relation to staff, do not take it upon yourself to interfere.

Linked with this, where an organisation has a substantial staff, boards should have a mechanism (e.g. holding annual or semi-annual confidential interviews with senior management) by which it can learn more about the needs and expectations of those controlling key sections of the operation.

DELEGATION

The delegation of power and authority is another form of setting limits - whether it be upon subcommittees or on individual directors who are delegated responsibilities.

If boards have one problem that is greater than almost any other it is in the delegating of power and authority. Because a corporate body can only act by a series of delegations it is necessarily and fundamentally dependent upon the quality of those delegations. Three common problems arise with delegations: invalidity, vagueness or, quite simply, they are forgotten.

- Invalidity usually arises because the delegation is outside the powers of the board, or outside the objects of the organisation, as set out in the constitution.
- Vagueness arises because the terms of the delegation have been insufficiently articulated.
- Oversight usually occurs because the delegation has not been formally or clearly recorded in a special delegations book (and not just in the Minutes Book).

When establishing a delegation of power the board needs to ensure that the constitution allows that authority to be delegated. Once that has been established, when setting out the extent of the delegation it is important that the parameters are clearly defined and that everyone knows what is expected. The board needs to:

- Make it clear whether the subcommittee is being given the power to make a decision or whether it is merely authorised to make a recommendation to the board that in turn makes the decision;
- Ensure that the nature and burden of work involved is appropriate - indiscriminate assignment of work to others is not delegating, it is dumping, and giving orders is not the same as delegating;
- Select a capable person;
- Provide a specific time frame through each of the project's phases;
- Establish specific review dates throughout the entire time frame; and
- Record the fact of the delegation and its ambit. Verbal instructions should usually be followed up in writing so that the memo can be referred to later.

Remember that while the ultimate responsibility stays with the delegator, true delegation implies that the individual, subcommittee, or subordinate is given the authority to do the job: that they can make independent decisions and have the responsibility for seeing the job done well. When a board delegates a task it should avoid unnecessary interference. If you have selected the right person and given clear instructions, let them get on with it.

"BLESSED BE THE CHAIR": DEALING WITH PROBLEM BOARD MEMBERS

The successful leadership and management of a board is a learned skill. There are many publications that deal with the proper conduct of meetings and a Chair of a board should find one that suits the organisation and use it as a resource for setting up and conducting effective meetings. However, there will also be occasions when a Chair or organisation has to deal with 'problem' board members and it is a good idea to consider how an organisation can set itself up so as to avoid difficult members becoming entrenched on an organisation's board. The 'types' described below do not form a closed list, rather they are meant to provide some 'warning signals' to members of organisations and Chairs to assist in recognising that the needs of the organisation will not be met by allowing boards to become hijacked by members who are not fully committed to the needs of the organisation.

GHOSTS

Ghosts are those who don't turn up to meetings or functions which board members would be expected to attend. A poor attendance record often indicates that a board member is not committed to the organisation, is too overcommitted to contribute as a board member, or has a problem with something within the board, but is unable to express it. It is the job of the Chair to keep an eye out for this pattern, make contact with the member and find out what is happening. This must be non-confrontational but direct. Handled properly, this will have the effect of either facilitating the board member's return to the flock as a positive, contributing member or will facilitate an early resignation. Either result is good.

If this does not work, rather than moving to expel an individual board member, it may be less contentious to move an amendment to the constitution tightening up the attendance requirements. Then, failure to attend a prescribed number of meetings without leave of the board will mean that the member is automatically deemed to have resigned.

Sometimes, for reasons of board politics, certain members will stay away from meetings thus causing paralysis of the affairs of the organisation by denying the board a quorum. If this cannot be dealt with through negotiation, the Chair (or the requisite number of directors/members) should call a general meeting of members. Failure to act, refusal to act, deadlock, repeated failure of quorum, are all matters that the membership has a right to consider and in which they have a right to intervene. Although the general meeting of members cannot overrule or interfere with an exercise of conferred powers by the directors, it can interfere to exercise power where the directors are unable or unwilling to do so. Accordingly, if the membership is dissatisfied with the attendance of its board members it can call a general meeting and vote upon the removal of those directors.

BACK SLAPPERS

These are people whose sole contribution to the proceedings of the board is to move motions of thanks or congratulations. They never ask the tough questions. They need to be loved and that is not a need that contributes to an energetic exchange of ideas. Their contribution to the organisation will remain limited.

CELEBRITIES AND SOCIALITES

Board members must be workers. Famous names and social members will often not be able to put in the time the organisation needs. Whether they are male or female, socialites can open doors to power and money but contrary to popular myth, socialites are not necessarily very good fundraisers. The socialites worth having on the board are those who are there for the organisation rather than merely to be admired.

SLEEPERS

How many board members do you know who attend every meeting and yet contribute nothing substantial to the discussion? Sometimes sleepers are really only timid or overly cautious about expressing an opinion, or they may just feel that they are too new to the board. A good Chair must direct specific questions to sleepers to help them and thus assist the board to have the benefit of those members' talents. If that doesn't work, the Chair should consider discussing their role on the board with them, and encourage them to reconsider the nature of their commitment to the board.

BULLIES

Bullies need to get their own way. Bullies are not good listeners. Bullies are good tellers. If you have a bully on the board you will need a very strong and judicious Chair. The Chair must control the time allowed to bullies yet make them feel that they have been heard. Reflective, summarising techniques are often useful to achieve this. Above all, the Chair must ensure that the other members of the board are not intimidated and have a proper chance to express their own views - even if they are contrary to those of the bully. The Chair must make the other board members safe.

If the bully is the Chair, the board, and thus the organisation, is in real trouble. Many of the board's most talented people will eventually resign and the Chair will attract either friends or martyrs to the board. After a while, nobody of outstanding talent will be bothered to offer themselves for election to the board and the organisation is well on the way to being, at best, a private club.

LIFERS

Lifers are members who have been on the board too long. Every board member has a 'use by' date. Board membership is about determined, devoted, energetic commitment to the organisation and its goals. You maximise the effort by having people commit themselves to a finite term of effort. At the end of their period they should leave with regret; tired but still committed. It is time for new people, with new skills, new ideas and new energies.

Although they can never admit it (because they will never recognise it), lifers are on the board for their own purposes, to satisfy their own needs. The organisation is a mere instrument. The Constitution should always provide for rotation of membership. Because lifers are so apparently selfless in their contribution to the organisation, the least offensive way of dealing with them is to ensure that the constitution provides for a maximum number of consecutive terms of appointment.

Some organisations have rotation of board membership but then allow departing members to immediately stand again for reappointment. This is a sham. You must build a wall, not merely a revolving door. The constitution should provide for a maximum term (five years is often a good guideline), and must provide that the member has a compulsory rest period of one or two years before being again eligible for election.

MARTYRS

Martyrs are professional sufferers. They are a source of discontent within a board because they never feel that they have been heard, that the board doesn't follow their suggestions, that their efforts on behalf of the organisation are unrecognised. They are negative in a passive way. They complain outside the walls of the boardroom and in this way, can be very destructive.

SECRET AGENTS

These are people with a hidden agenda. They can make life difficult for even the most experienced Chair and can be very destructive on any board. You might pick that there is a hidden agenda through their comportment, through the person's choice of language or tone of voice. You might not pick it at all. You deal with secret agents by either ignoring what you perceive to be their hidden agenda or bringing it out into the open.

TWO SECRET AGENTS MAKE A CONSPIRACY. THIS CAN ONLY BE TACKLED BY CONFRONTATION.

A wise Chair will often take the secret agent aside and have an informal chat about things and determine whether there is something of significance for the organisation going on. If the Chair is the secret agent, it is going to take a very forthright board member to raise it - but raise it you must. No hidden agenda is threatening when it is revealed and can be openly discussed by the whole board.

TALKERS

Talkers are infuriating. They often have a very good point to make, but chatter on and on and on and on. Detail, circumstances, exceptions, lead up, let down. They are often intelligent and well meaning but just have no idea when to close their mouth. You don't want to hurt their feelings but after a few meetings you are prepared to kill them. If you feel that way, it is likely that most of the other board members do too. Any good Chair will be able to cope with talkers. They must be given a fair opportunity to express their views, but their time must be firmly limited.

THE DIARY AFFLICTED

There are some board members who simply don't have the time to come to meetings – or if they do, continually have to leave early to fulfil other commitments. Their good will is overcoming their good judgment. They want to help and be supportive but they view their other commitments as more pressing.

It is the Chair's task to have a quiet word with such people. They are doing neither themselves nor the organisation justice. They need to rationalise their priorities so that they can contribute their skills with the profundity that they deserve and the organisation requires. Something is going to have to go. It might be the board member.

THE CONFLICTED

Board members owe their primary responsibility to the company. They must put their duty to the company ahead of their own interests and those of any other organisation (including their employer). Even if they are appointed as staff representatives, once they sit down at the board meeting they must put the benefit of the company ahead of the staff interests. In such a case, they are there to ensure that the board is informed as to the employee's view. It is not to bring discord into the boardroom. (To make this clear, if the staff or some particular interest is to have a specific place on the board it is much better to describe the person as the 'nominee' rather than the 'representative'.)

If a director has a conflict of interest on a particular issue, that conflict must be disclosed. The chair will ensure that the declaration is noted in the minutes and will determine whether it is appropriate that the director be allowed to speak, to vote, or even to remain in the room. It may sometimes be appropriate to allow the conflicted person to express a view but it is rarely appropriate to permit them to vote on an issue upon which they are conflicted. Usually, the safest course is to have them leave the room.

LEGAL RESPONSIBILITIES OF PEOPLE IN AUTHORITY

Every person who has a position of responsibility in the organisation has duties imposed by law. For example, some music organisations are a part of a government department and their employees are departmental employees bound by various laws such as the Public Service Act, Audit Act, Finance Directions and so on.

Other institutions may be statutory bodies, established and funded by government but operating under their own statute. Those established by Local Government will operate under different rules again, including the Local Government Act.

Then there are companies established under the Corporations Act, incorporated associations established under the Incorporated Associations Act and trusts that are governed by the Trustee Act and associated legislation.

These will all impose particular responsibilities. Fortunately, they have a similar theme.

The following can only provide a guide to your rights and responsibilities and does not try to discuss the complexities of the numerous individual circumstances.

STATUTORY BODIES

THE STATUTORY DUTIES

The statute that establishes an organisation (for example the Australia Council), also sets out the basic duties of those responsible for its governance. Necessarily, each such institution is different and all employees and board members should be familiar with the terms of their statute.

THE DUTY TO OBSERVE NATURAL JUSTICE

In addition to the statute that establishes a statutory body, those invested with power have an obligation to observe the rules of natural justice. These include the duty to act fairly, to take into account all relevant matters and to omit all extraneous considerations when decision-making.

Each board member's duty is to the institution. Even if he or she is on the governing body as a representative or nominee of a particular interest group (such as staff representative), or has a particularly burning political, ethical or other position, the overriding duty must be to the institution and its purposes.

DUTIES OF COMMITTEE MEMBERS OF UNINCORPORATED ASSOCIATIONS

Because an unincorporated association cannot hold assets in its own right, any member that looks after property or money belonging to the association does so as a trustee on behalf of the association. A trustee must not place his or her own interests above the purposes of the trust because the trustee has a fiduciary duty to the objects of the trust. The duties of a trustee are the most onerous of all. (Refer to the section "Duties of Trustees" below.)

DUTIES OF MANAGEMENT COMMITTEE MEMBERS OF INCORPORATED ASSOCIATIONS

The responsibilities of the management committee of an incorporated association are set down in the relevant state legislation.

The management committee is responsible for holding regular meetings, as well as an annual general meeting and the public officer of the association will be responsible for filing the association's annual statement with the appropriate government department.

It is also important to remember that while the formation of an incorporated association does provide protection to members of the committee and the association from liability for debts incurred by the association, this is not unlimited. Individual committee members could be held personally liable for debts if they authorise expenditure without having reasonable grounds to expect that the debt can be paid.

The legislation governing incorporated associations also provides for the imposition of fines and other penalties if the committee members' actions amount to fraud. This responsibility will not be imposed on members of the Committee who did not authorise or consent to the expenditure. However, if a Committee member ought to have been aware of the debt, for example if they are responsible for overseeing a particular area of the association's operations and they fail to keep informed about that area, they could be held responsible for a debt, even if they did not know about it.

The duties of members of a management committee of an incorporated association under the common law are the same as those of the members of a board of a company limited by guarantee (considered below). In several States the legislation has clarified the nature of these duties. It is essential that all members of a management committee are aware of their responsibilities under the relevant legislation, acquaint themselves with the rules governing the association and keep themselves informed of the activities of the association and its members.

The checklists at the end of this chapter are applicable to all members of boards or management committees, regardless of the type of organisation.

DUTIES OF DIRECTORS OF COMPANIES LIMITED BY GUARANTEE

The responsibilities of a company director are the same, regardless of whether the company is profit making or a non-profit organisation. This point was made clear by the National Safety Council Case (Commonwealth Bank of

Australia v Friedrich (1991) 5 ACSR 115), a case that struck fear into the heart of every person sitting on the board of an arts organisation. There, the elderly, respected Chairman lost his savings, his reputation and his health as a result of the actions of the chief executive when he was found liable as a director for an extraordinary amount of debts incurred without his knowledge. Since then, the HIH, Vizard and the One-Tel cases have given high-profile demonstration that company directors who breach their legal duties, risk financial ruin, jail, and public ignominy.

THE DUTIES OF A DIRECTOR OF A NON-PROFIT COMPANY

- To act honestly, and in the best interests of the company.
- To not make improper use of information.
- To not make improper use of their position.
- To avoid conflicts of interest.
- To act in good faith, and for a proper purpose.
- To demonstrate reasonable skill in the performance of their duties.
- To exercise reasonable care and diligence when making decisions.
- To ensure that the company does not continue to operate after it has become insolvent.

In recent years the courts have become much stricter in imposing liability on 'passive' directors, directors that through ignorance or inactivity fail to carry out their duties properly. You can no longer say you 'didn't know'. You should have known! If you take on the responsibility of board membership, you must take an active interest and care in the operation of the company. You cannot just let others look after business. If you do, you are inviting trouble.

Directors of companies that fail to carry out their duties may lose the protection of limited liability and become personally liable for debts incurred by the company. A member of a board has a duty to keep informed about the operations of the company and must have adequate skills to cope with the demands of company management. It is no longer sufficient to simply do one's best and hope for the best.

For example, if your company is put on notice by the Australia Council that it may not have funding reviewed next year, you should not enter any agreements for next year unless either you are sure that the company can fund them if the Australia Council does withdraw funding, or make the contracts conditional upon receiving continuing and adequate funding.

You cannot assume that the funding review will be successful and that the company will get the money just because it did last year! All such contracts entered during the review period should be subject to the company receiving continuing and adequate funding. Thus a company 'on review' cannot commit to forward programming unless it is assured that the necessary funds are presently held or uncontingently promised. If it does, and the funding does not eventuate, the directors may be personally liable for consequent losses.

It is generally true that directors and employees enjoy very limited liability for losses incurred by their company. However, the Corporations Act does lay down a number of situations in which the corporate veil may be lifted to expose the individual not only to prosecution and penalty but also to a personal civil liability. In considering the following paragraphs it is important to note that the legislation defines 'officer' to include the directors, secretary or senior management of the corporation and anyone from whom those people customarily take direction.

(i)   **The duty of honesty**: An officer of a corporation must act honestly in the exercise of his or her powers and duties.

(ii)   **The duty to take reasonable care and be diligent**: People are often invited to join a board merely for their famous name. Those people run grave risks if they do not actually read the board's documents, attend its meetings and diligently oversee the operation of the company. It is no answer to say that 'I was too busy to get to meetings', or 'I don't understand figures'. Board membership is not appropriate for those wishing to lend their name to a cause but not intending to be involved personally. Such people make good patrons but their membership of boards does not assist control of the company and exposes them to potentially enormous liability.

(iii)   **The duty not to make improper use of information acquired as a result of your position with the corporation:** A board member or an employee owes primary loyalty to the wellbeing of the organisation. Thus, information learned as a result of one's position in the company must be applied to benefit the company and personal interests must take second place.

(iv)   **The duty not to make improper use of your position:** No director or employee is allowed to make improper use of their position to gain personal advantage, or to advantage anyone else, or to disadvantage the corporation.

(v)   **The duty of a director to disclose conflict in contracts:** It is important to emphasise that it is both common and permissible for directors to have conflicts of interest. However, the Corporations Act demands that a director, who is in any way interested in a contract or proposed contract, must declare that interest. This must be done as soon as is practicable after the relevant facts are known.

A person who has declared a conflict of interest is not prevented from speaking to the subject of the contract or even voting on it. The declaration of interest allows the other directors to give those comments the weight that they deem appropriate in the declared circumstances.

Often, of course, when a potential conflict of interest arises it is most appropriate for that director to offer to leave the room until the issue is decided. The other directors may then accept that suggestion or invite the interested person to remain. That, however, is a matter of etiquette and not law. All that one need do is declare the interest.

'Interest' is interpreted very broadly. It may arise through board membership, employment, consultancies, family connections, investment, and so on. To lessen the repetitious intrusion of such declarations into the business of the board, a director may give a general notice of interest to the effect that he or she is an officer, director or member of a specified corporation or firm and is therefore to be regarded as interested in any contract which may be made with that corporation or firm.

For this reason, it makes good sense for all board members to disclose, at the first board meeting after each Annual General Meeting, all current employment, directorships or memberships. Such declarations should be in writing. This process helps to provide a transparent decision-making process and protects the individual from later accusations of improper conduct. Moreover, it is interesting for the other board members, it saves the tedious interruption of board business by directors making repetitive declarations of interest, and it lessens the risk of receiving a $1,000 fine or three months' imprisonment. If it is discovered that a director has not disclosed a conflict of interest in a contract being entered by the company, that contract may be voidable by the company.

LIABILITY OF DIRECTORS AND EMPLOYEES TO PAY COMPANY DEBTS

As a general rule, incorporation protects the individuals from personal liability. If the company goes to the wall, its directors and employees may walk away with their reputations in tatters but their bank accounts intact.

However, if a person fails to act honestly or act with reasonable care and diligence, or makes improper use of either information or position, the corporation can sue that person and recover any profit that any person made, and any sum that the corporation has lost as a result of the failure.

Moreover, section 592 (1) of the Corporations Act states that if:

(a) *a company incurs a debt, whether within or outside the State; and*

(b) *immediately before the time when the debt is incurred there are reasonable grounds to expect that either –*

> (i)   the company will not be able to pay all its debts as and when they become due; or
>
> (ii) if the company incurs the debt, it will not be able to pay all its debts as and when they become due;
>
> then any person who was a director of the company, or who took part in the management of the company, at the time when the debt was incurred is guilty of an offence and the company and that person or, if there are 2 or more such people, those people are jointly and severally liable for the payment of the debt.

The legislation goes on to provide a defence for defendants who can prove that such debts were incurred without their implied authority or that they could not have had reasonable cause to suspect that the company would not be able to pay its debts when they came due.

The Corporations Act provides both civil and criminal sanctions for the breach of this section. If criminal proceedings are commenced the defendant is liable to large fines, imprisonment, or both. If civil proceedings are started, the directors and senior employees and any other persons involved with the management of the company may be held personally liable for the company's debts.

The duties imposed on directors and other officers can have serious implications for all cultural organisations, for nearly all live according to the hazardous and uncertain principles of government funding. Quite simply, most public cultural organisations in Australia lose money and depend for their continued existence upon subsidy. For their part, most funding bodies refuse to guarantee even core funding to their client groups. One year's funding does not guarantee a grant the next. Nor can the organisation assume that the level of grant will remain as high, let alone increase with inflation or in line with an expansion of program needs.

For years, the directors and management of such organisations have accepted this position and blithely entered ongoing commitments on the assumption that there would always be public money available at (at least) the same level as the previous year. Now, with this imposition of personal liability and the increasingly restricted budgets available to funding bodies, such assumptions are dangerous.

For example, no publicly funded organisation should employ staff for a fixed term of more than a year without ensuring that the contract is conditional upon continued and adequate funding. Otherwise, if funding is cut off, there is a real (if remote) possibility that the board members may find themselves personally liable for paying staff salaries. Leases on premises raise similar problems.

Part of the difficulty lies with policies of funding bodies. They all warn client groups that ongoing funding is not guaranteed and some have warned of the onerous liability under the Corporations Act. Aware of this potential danger, funding bodies will generally put an organisation on notice or review before cutting off funding. Similarly, the introduction of triennial funding has considerably reduced this danger for many organisations.

Cultural organisations, large or small, can only exist because of the generosity of thousands of people who donate their time, expertise and efforts as board members. In order to protect these people from personal liability should that funding be suddenly cut or sharply decreased, funding bodies should set out in their funding guidelines that organisations which receive administrative or core funding may expect that (whilst funding can never be guaranteed) such organisations may expect phasing of reductions in funding over, say, three years. Of course, the funding body would have to retain the right to 'terminate with sudden and extreme prejudice' but such a guideline would protect those thousands of volunteers who now have good cause to worry about their personal liability in the event that funding is suddenly discontinued.

Section 592 of the Corporations Act also has the important effect of making the decision-makers in the group more aware of the need for reasonable, attainable, well-budgeted and tightly administered programs. If an incorporated body takes on a huge project and hocks itself to the hilt in the unreasonable belief that things will work out and things don't, the creditors will be looking for their money. If the company can't meet the debts, one can be sure that the creditors will look to the people who were in control when the company incurred the debt. Culture has become a multi-million dollar industry and as with other industries, programs must be financed, debts must be paid, loan repayments must be met and losses must be recovered. It cannot be reasonably assumed that public money will be available to bail you out. The days are long gone when ailing arts organisations were allowed to suffer a long and quiet death. Now, the end is quick, the noise is often excruciating and the legal consequences for directors and senior management can be dire.

PEOPLE FORBIDDEN TO BE INVOLVED WITH MANAGEMENT OF THE ORGANISATION

These may be summarised (only slightly inaccurately) as the poor, the criminal and the insane.

(i)   **Insolvency.** Persons who are bankrupt or whose affairs are under the control of an administrator, cannot in any way be involved with the management of a corporation without the leave of the court. This includes being a director, promoter or manager of a company.

(ii)   **Prior Conviction.** There are considerable limitations upon people who have been convicted of a serious offence in connection with the promotion, formation or management of a corporation; or any offence involving serious fraud; or any number of specified offences under the Corporations Act or similar legislation.

(iii)   **Insanity**. Persons who have been legally declared insane are not permitted to be company directors. (Just because you think they should have been declared insane is not quite enough.)

These people may not, without leave of the court, be involved in the management of a corporation for five years from the date of conviction or release from prison (whichever is the later). If they wish to take part in management during this period, they must obtain the leave of the court.

DUTIES OF TRUSTEES

The duties of a trustee are perhaps the most onerous of all. They include the following duties:

- **To know and understand the terms of the trust.**
- **To obey the terms of the trust.** One can only depart from the terms of the trust if directed to do so by all beneficiaries, or the court.
- **To adhere to and carry out the terms of the trust.** Only if a statute or the court allows non-adherence, can one avoid this obligation. If it is necessary to not carry out the strict terms of the trust, the trustees should approach the court for a declaration, for otherwise, non-adherence to the terms of the trust will be at the peril of the trustees.
- **To act impartially between the beneficiaries.** One cannot favour one beneficiary over another, unless the trust document provides such a power. Sometimes an act will turn out to benefit one beneficiary more than another. This is not a problem for the law does not expect the trustees to be psychic. Their duty is considered in the circumstances that prevailed at the time when the act was done by the trustee.
- **To act gratuitously.** Trustees are not, as a matter of course, entitled to be paid for their labours. If the trust deed provides for such payments, they are permissible but there are very few exceptions to the general rule and trustees should take legal advice before assuming that they fall within an exception.
- **To not profit by the trust.** The trustee may not use the trust property for their own benefit.
- **To pay the trust property to the right persons.** It is this obligation that strikes fear into many trustees. It is really only an extension on the duty to comply with the terms of the trust. The trustees will be personally liable for such errors unless they can show that they acted honestly and reasonably and that in the circumstances they should be excused.

- **To properly invest trust funds.** Legislation specifies the places in which trust moneys may be invested. These are usually secure investments such as the major banks. Not all building societies qualify, and investment in institutions such as property trusts, shares, in other speculative ways of maintaining the fund are restricted.
- **To keep and render proper accounts.** If the treasurer of the trust is not an accountant (or someone with those skills) the trustees would be well advised to either retain one professionally, or invite one onto the Board. Even if the trust uses an accountant, the trustees are not absolved from all responsibilities. One cannot escape one's responsibilities by simply putting them onto someone else's shoulders.
- **To exercise reasonable care.** Trustees must act with the same care and diligence as would an ordinary prudent business person. It is an objective test. Otherwise a normally careless or lazy person would be excused when a normally careful and skilful person would not. This is a high onus, for the courts have long held that ordinary prudent business persons take a very great care when investing or using other people's money and would not take the same sorts of risks with the money of others as they might with their own.

The court has the power under the Trustee Act to relieve a trustee from liability so long as the trustee has acted in good faith, honestly, reasonably and, in the discretion of the court, it is fair that the trustee be excused.

CHECKLIST FOR BOARDS AND MANAGERS OF NON-PROFIT ARTS ORGANISATIONS IN AUSTRALIA

(Issued by and available from the Australia Council. The checklist is reproduced here with kind permission.)

1. **Setting objectives**
1.1 Do the board and senior management review and set company objectives once a year?
1.2 Are these objectives adequately documented to ensure that staff and other people with an interest in the company can find out what they are?
1.3 Does the board ensure that the company measures its performance against these objectives?
1.4 What steps are taken to ensure that adequate long-term planning is carried out?
1.5 Are the results of all performance reviews adequately documented and included in the company's annual report?

1.6   Are these results communicated to all funding bodies?

1.7   Does the board actively promote excellence in reporting by entering its annual report in yearly competitions – for example, that run by the Australian Institute of Management?

2.   **Corporations Act**

2.1   Have all board members and all managers received a copy of the booklet The Corporations Act and the Arts published by the Australia Council?

2.2   Has the board identified which managers should be classified as 'officers' under the Corporations Act?

2.3   Has the company's chairperson made sure that all board members and all managers participating in the administration of the company's affairs are aware of their responsibilities under the Corporations Act and accept them?

2.4   Have duty statements been issued to individual members and to senior staff?

2.5   Has the board considered the adoption of specific skills criteria for board membership?

2.6   Have all members of the board and all senior managers read the company's Memorandum and Articles of Association?

2.7   Does the board invite relevant managers to attend board meetings for items dealing with their area of responsibility?

2.8   Does the board maintain records of attendance by board members for items dealing with their area of responsibility?

2.9   Does the board actively encourage open membership of the company?

3.   **Organisation and management**

3.1   Has the board reviewed, within the last twelve months, the company's structure, especially the duties and responsibilities of all senior staff?

3.2   Within the last six months, have board members reviewed their duties and responsibilities to ensure sufficient checks and balances exist to guard against misuse of company funds or manipulation of information going to the board or funding authorities?

3.3   Do the board and senior management take an active interest in the company's industrial relations?

3.4   Do both a member of the board and a member of senior management have skills in this area?

3.5   Is the company observing all awards relating to both full-time and part-time employees?

3.6   Do the chairperson and/or a board nominee meet regularly with the staff?

3.7   Do the artistic director and the administrator have regular meetings with the staff?

3.8   Is independent legal advice sought before any significant or controversial decisions are taken?

3.9   Does the board ensure that stocks held by the company are regularly checked?

4.   **Financial management**

4.1   Does the board member with qualifications and experience in finance advise the board on financial matters and, in particular, the monitoring of financial reports?

4.2   Does that person attend all board meetings?

4.3.   Does the person responsible for preparing the financial statements for the board attend that part of a board meeting at which finance is discussed?

4.4   Does the administrator personally check all financial reports before they are distributed to the board?

4.5   Is the person who prepares the financial statements free to discuss with the board any matters relating to the accounts?

4.6   Is a standard format used for all financial reports?

4.7   Does the board receive:
      (a)   monthly financial statements prepared on an accrual basis of accounting?
      (b)   monthly cash flow statements?
      (c)   all reports on a timely basis?

4.8   Does the board receive a standard written report from the administrator highlighting any items of exception in the financial statements?

4.9   Is a regular comparison made of budgeted income and expenditure with actual income and expenditure?

4.10   Does the board take appropriate action if actual results differ significantly from budget?

4.11   Does the board ensure that revised estimates are prepared for the balance of the year (to reflect actual income and expenditure to date) for each board meeting?

4.12   Are detailed budgets prepared for all activities?

4.13   Does the board insist that:
      (a)   feasibility studies are carried out and tabled with the board showing how all capital will be paid before any final decisions are taken?
      (b)   at least three quotes are obtained from potential suppliers before considering any major capital expenditure?

4.14 Does the board ensure that actual capital expenditure is compared with budgeted capital expenditure on a regular basis?

4.15 Are detailed work papers prepared and kept by staff to support figures in all financial statements prepared for the board?

4.16 Are all questions asked at a board meeting properly answered or, if not, carried through to the next meeting?

4.17 Does the board ensure that the investment of company funds at call or otherwise with an institution is in line with company policy?

4.18 Does the board ensure that the company has an adequate system of internal control over all financial transactions and the control of company's assets?

4.19 Does the chairperson meet at least twice a year with the company's external auditor?

4.20 Does the board review all management letters from the external auditor?

4.21 Is the board satisfied with the quality of financial information provided for board meetings?

4.22 Has electronic data processing been considered/introduced by the company?

5. **Liaison with funding bodies**

5.1 Have all members of the board and management read the most recent conditions of grant from funding authorities?

5.2 Are all board members and senior staff aware of what the funding bodies expect from the organisation?

5.3 Do the full board and senior management meet representatives of funding authorities once a year to discuss mutual plans and problems?

5.4 Does the company's chairperson make contact at least twice a year with a nominated person in all funding authorities?

5.5 Is the tenor of those discussions reported to the board?

5.6 Has the board considered periodically inviting representatives from funding bodies to a routine board meeting for discussion?

5.7 Have the company's chairperson and the board member responsible for monitoring the company's financial affairs:

    (a) read the accounting questionnaire presented by the Australia Council?

    (b) taken appropriate action to ensure that its completion will not adversely affect the company's ability to receive further funding?

    (c) ensured that any specific conditions relating to finance in the conditions of grant will be complied with?

6. **Marketing and public relations**

6.1 Does the board ensure that the company maintains a high public profile in order to attract audiences and private support?

6.2 Do individual board members:

(a) attend all first nights, openings and other important functions and take an active interest in the company's operations, especially the less prominent activities such as workshops, theatre-in-education programs, training schools, play readings, etc?

(b) make sure that they are known to senior and middle management?

(c) familiarise themselves with the location and state of repair of all premises used by the company?

6.3 Do the individual board members take an active interest in helping to promote the arts by:

(a) inviting parliamentarians, local council members and potential corporate sponsors to performances, exhibitions, or other events?

(b) personally seeking private support from individuals and others?

(c) taking stock of how much other board members have raised for the company through their personal endeavours?

6.4 Does the board have a member skilled in marketing?

6.5 Does the board monitor marketing growth rates and similar measures?

6.6 Has the board considered using unsold seats to promote the company's interests or social objectives, such as increasing access for the unemployed?

4
AGENTS

AGENTS PROVIDE A CENTRAL FUNCTION FOR PERFORMING ARTISTS. FOR MANY, THE AGENT IS THE PRINCIPAL SOURCE OF INCOME FROM LIVE WORK. THIS CHAPTER DISCUSSES THE FUNCTION AND POWERS OF AN AGENT, EXAMINES HOW THEY ARE REMUNERATED AND ALSO DISCUSSES THE VENUE CONSULTANT'S ROLE. SAMPLE AGENCY AND BOOKING AGREEMENTS ARE PROVIDED.

Agents play a central role in the industry. They are the conduit between the performer and the engagement; they source the work or the artist; negotiate performance terms and administer the fees.

The agency business in Australia is not as developed and sophisticated as it has become in the United States or the United Kingdom. Companies like the William Morris Agency or International Creative Management have hundreds of employees throughout the world and have billion-dollar turnovers. They are so large, they 'package' their own product; that is, they have the resources to put together whole movie or music ventures from beginning to end, using talent from within their own client base.

In Australia, agencies tend to be smaller and more specialised in their general industry focus (music, theatrical, film, publishing, modelling, etc). Even within those groups, there is a high degree of specialisation, so agents working in the music industry tend to specialise in particular categories of performers, such as rock/contemporary, country, classical, cabaret, jazz and so on.

Another feature of Australian agencies is that they have tended to represent both artists and 'employers', as they are called in Australian labour laws. That means that, as well as being the agent for the artist, some also act as '**venue consultants**' to those who engage the artist to perform. There is an inherent conflict of interest in this dual role. Being the agent for both sides of the transaction may have some attractions, but negotiating with yourself is rarely a rigorous process.

In 1989, in the Report Of The Ministerial Committee to Review Theatrical Agents and Employers Legislation in New South Wales, the Association of Theatrical Agents and Employers stated that 78% of its members conducted business in more than one role. The Association argued that this was necessary for their economic viability and that their links with employers benefited performers, by providing employment opportunities for the performers that they would not otherwise have had. The unions answered this by arguing that most of their problems with agencies were a result of agents having conflicts of interest. The unions recognised there can be work opportunity benefits in agents having a dual role, but asked that safeguards be built into the relationship by law.

In 1989 the *Entertainment Industry Act (NSW)* provided that an agent could not be paid by the venue and also take a commission from the performer; for more detail see Chapter 6, **Controlling Managers, Agents and Venue Consultants By Legislation**.

Why agencies demonstrate such a wide range of professional standards is no great puzzle: Agencies reflect the span of the industry. Many are highly skilled, professionally trained and of impeccable reputation, but some are somewhat lower on the evolutionary scale. The latter will always exist while there are more musicians seeking representation than there are agents looking for artists to represent, while aspiring musicians are willing to take any offer of employment on any terms, while artists do not properly look after their own business affairs and while legislation controlling agents (and managers) remains inadequate.

THE FUNCTION OF AGENTS

An agent's primary function is to find, negotiate and conclude contracts for the professional engagement of the artists on their books. (Remember that most management agreements specifically exclude the finding of live performance work from the manager's role.) Secondary functions include receiving fees and security deposits for engagements, arranging publicity, keeping proper records and accounting in relation to the work, forwarding payments to the artist and generally providing career advice.

These functions can be reduced or expanded by agreement between the agent and the artist, e.g. some of the more established acts insist that all final offers for performances must be submitted to them for approval before signing. Some insist that only they (or their manager) have the right to sign agreements relating to their engagements, though this is not always convenient if they are touring or otherwise unavailable to sign documents.

THE POWERS AND AUTHORITIES OF AGENTS

As we have seen above, the word 'agent' is used in two senses in the music industry. It also has another, legal, meaning. Before examining the power of agents in the music industry it is worth briefly explaining the 'legal' meaning of the word because it turns up in so many industry agreements.

At law, an agent may perform any function or exercise any power delegated to it by the principal. This delegation can be in writing, oral or implied by the way the parties behave. By doing so, the principal (the person appointing the agent) is authorising the other party to stand in their shoes and to make commitments on their behalf. What the agent does on the principal's behalf is just as binding as if the principal had done it personally.

The delegation of such trust is sometimes essential in the industry; there are times that record companies, managers and agents all need such delegated powers. In contrast to the Australian practice, in California and New York an agent must be appointed by written contract and there is very strict controlling legislation and labour agreements. The American cases are not of much relevance in Australia because of this difference.

It is unwise to grant any third party, powers of that extend beyond the immediate requirements of that person's function. The essential thing is to limit that power to that which is absolutely necessary or desirable, e.g. with a booking agency, why should your agent have an unrestricted power to negotiate and execute contracts on your behalf? Shouldn't you have the right to be consulted, to approve the terms of the booking and authorise its acceptance? Isn't it wise to require these limitations to be specified in the contract of appointment? Answer 'no' to either question and you are either being naïve or are independently wealthy.

When you appoint an agent, the agreement can be written or oral. That agreement should specify the powers that are being conferred. Those powers should be restricted to those that are needed to perform the appointed function.

THE AUTHORITY TO REPRESENT

The most basic power of the music industry agent is to 'represent'. It is from this basic authority that its other powers are derived or may be inferred.

Major booking agencies require their acts to sign exclusive contracts, meaning that they become the artist's exclusive representative for contracting live work. Other, smaller agents represent less established artists and are prepared to work on a non-exclusive basis.

THE AUTHORITY TO RECEIVE AND NEGOTIATE OFFERS OF EMPLOYMENT

The agent's authority to receive offers of employment is inherent in the agency function. It may be limited to particular areas of the entertainment or music industry, or to particular territories or periods.

The agent is usually authorised to negotiate the terms of employment, including the performance fee, approval for and selection of support acts, order of appearance, performance time, publicity, method of payment, use of other artists' equipment such as public address ("PA"), lights and mixing desk.

As the agent's commission is based on the artist's fee, it is in the agent's interest (unless there is a conflict of interest) to negotiate a fee that reflects the artist's market value. Judging that value is one of the core skills of a good agent. Moreover, it is often the case that, because of the agent's connections and reputation, he or she may be able to secure a better package than the artist would have been able to negotiate.

However, musicians should not leave negotiation of the deal points entirely to the discretion of the agent. The musician will eventually have to perform the contract as it is negotiated and will have to accept all its benefits and drawbacks. Accordingly, performers should liaise with their agent and set the extent of the agent's authority so both parties are clear as to what the agent can and cannot do.

THE AUTHORITY TO SIGN BOOKING AGREEMENTS ON THE MUSICIAN'S BEHALF

Once both the agent and the employer have accepted the terms of a booking agreement, a written agreement between them should be signed as soon as possible.

It is the agent's responsibility to prepare the booking agreement and to submit it to the employer before the performance date. Although some major acts reserve strict control over the agent's right to negotiate or sign contracts on their behalf, in most cases the agent will have the artist's authority to negotiate and sign booking agreements which conform to the usual business practices of the industry.

THE AUTHORITY TO COLLECT DEPOSITS AND PERFORMANCE FEES

The payment of performance fees can be made by several methods, e. g.:

(a) Part-payment of the deposit (in advance) to the agent pending performance, with the balance paid to the agent or musician once the performance is over.

(b) Payment in full to the agent or musician immediately before the performance.

(c) Payment in full to the agent or musician immediately after the performance.

The entertainment industry is notorious for being a cash business and payments for regular bookings are usually made immediately before or after the performance. In the case of new venues or promoters, agents will often ask for a substantial deposit (or even payment in full) to be made at the time the agreement is signed by the employer. Deposits are virtually always paid when booking major artists or booking artists to appear in a large promotion.

Where money is paid to an agent on the artist's behalf, the agent should bank it in a trust account immediately and not mix it with the agency's own funds. This is compulsory in New South Wales, but should be standard practice everywhere. After all, the artist is not a bank, so the artist's money should not be used to fund the agency's operations. Both the agency agreement and the booking agreement should clearly specify that the agent is to maintain a separate account for all deposits or fees paid to the agent and also specify the purposes for which the agent may withdraw money from the account.

AGENTS' FEES AND COMMISSIONS

The standard agency commission for booking live work is 10% of the gross fee paid by employers. Some agents say this is uneconomic and provide (or, if the artist is unlucky, merely purport to provide) management functions as well, to justify charging a larger percentage. In New South Wales the Entertainment Industry Act sets down specific rules which must be complied with if this percentage is to be exceeded: see Chapter 6, **Controlling Managers, Agents And Venue Consultants By Legislation**.

WRITTEN AGENCY AGREEMENTS

Agencies should all have written agreements with the musicians they represent. The agreements are usually brief but some are not paragons of drafting skill. To make them work in practice, it may be necessary to imply further powers and obligations into the agency relationship. It's not hard to imagine the difficulties that can arise if an agency agreement is not written down, or where the terms are vague, contradictory or incomplete.

It benefits both the musician and the agent when a well-drafted agency agreement is used. The contract should include the following:

(a) The agent's authority to represent the artist and whether the relationship is exclusive or non-exclusive.

(b) The fields of activity in which the agent is authorised to represent the artist (e.g. live work, motion pictures, television, composition).

(c) The functions of the agent (e.g. to obtain and negotiate offers).

(d) The agent's powers (e.g. the authority to execute agreements).

(e) The period of the agency agreement.

(f) The amount of commission to be paid to the agent (and also to any sub-agent), including a definition of when the commission is deemed to be earned by the agent.

(g) An obligation to pay all money received on behalf of the musician, into a trust account.

(h) Any restrictions on the agent's powers.

(i) A description of the artist's obligations.

(j) A mechanism specifying what happens if engagements are cancelled.

The following sample may be downloaded from simpsons.com.au/documents/music:

SAMPLE EXCLUSIVE AGENCY–ARTIST AGREEMENT

To: ....

From: ....

Agent Appointment

Further to our discussions we confirm that we agree to represent you. The following sets out the conditions of representation.

1. We will be your exclusive agent for the purpose of booking your live performances in Australia.

2. In representing you, we undertake to:
    (a) Seek, throughout Australia, engagements and other contracts related to your musical activities.
    (b) In consultation with you, obtain offers, negotiate engagements and terms of contracts, and execute agreements.
    (c) Maintain, update and revise as necessary all your publicity material, including brochures, media releases and photographs.
    (d) Keep a record of press notices and interviews.
    (e) Liaise with all relevant organisations to ensure they have up-to-date material about you and pursue media promotion in cases where it is clearly not the prerogative of an entrepreneur or commissioning body to do so.
    (f) Ensure that you receive adequate and appropriate advice from lawyers, accountants or others, if and when this becomes necessary.
    (g) Make travel and accommodation arrangements as necessary and provide detailed schedules and itineraries ('worksheets').

(h) Keep full accounts and financial records (but we will not provide personal, financial, investment, or taxation advice).

(i) Observe the confidentiality of your secrets, private finances and relationships about which we may learn in the course of representing you.

(j) Exercise powers delegated to us, reasonably and honestly.

3. You must refer all inquiries or offers to us and must make full disclosure of all contracts, arrangements and understandings not initiated by us, which affect your musical activities. Although it is essential that we have the exclusive power to negotiate and enter contracts on your behalf we undertake to consult with you and obtain your prior agreement to the terms of such contracts.

4. You agree to perform every contract so entered, fully and to the best of your ability, unless prevented from doing so by reasons that are bona fide beyond your control.

5. In return for our representation you will pay us a commission based upon your gross fees (exclusive of GST). If you accept payment in kind rather than money, commission on the value of that remuneration will be payable, unless otherwise agreed. Commission will be calculated as follows:

    (a) for contracts entered before but performed during the period of this agreement :   %

    (b) for contracts entered during and performed during the period of this agreement :   %

    (c) for contracts entered during but performed after the termination of this agreement :   %

6. Expenses
   We will meet all the cost of:
   You will meet all the cost of:

7. Term
   Our agreement will continue until either party terminates it having served .... months notice in writing.

Yours sincerely,

....
Agent

I agree to the terms and conditions set out in this letter of agreement.

Signed: ....Date: ....

BOOKING AGREEMENTS AND ENGAGEMENT CONFIRMATIONS

Some agencies use written booking agreements with venues but many, presumably because the industry has traditionally been so scared of anything as concrete as a written contract, use a so-called 'confirmation' which they send to the employer, setting out the terms of the deal.

A confirmation is not in itself a booking agreement. However, it is legally correct to refer to it as a 'confirmation' if you argue that the booking contract was really entered orally (e.g. on the phone) and that the written material is just a confirmation and record of the terms of that oral agreement.

All agents use written booking agreements or confirmations. An agent who does not confirm a booking in writing is probably acting negligently in failing to fulfil one of an agent's fundamental functions.

There is no standard form booking agreement. Each agency has different ways of operating and each deal may have different issues of importance, depending on the type of music, the employer, the artist and the event.

Following is a skeleton agreement that provides at least the minimum deal points and the basic information needed if both the employer and the artist are to be sure of each other's basic needs. Established acts are likely have their own, much more developed, agreements and will insist that these are used in place of their agent's basic form.

SAMPLE BOOKING CONTRACT

(short form)

BETWEEN:

Artist:

(a) name..

(b) address ....

AND:

Employer:

(a) name..

(b) address ....

PERFORMANCE DETAILS:

(a) **Venue:** ....

(b) **Date(s):** ....

(c) **Fee** (or basis of calculation): ....

    (i) Deposit: ....

    (ii) Time of payment: ....

    (iii) Payment shall be by cash immediately after each performance.

(d) **Times:**

    (i) Equipment access:..

    (ii) Sound check:...

    (iii) Doors open:..

    (iv) Performance:..

    (v) Equipment removal:...

(e) **Cover charge:** $ ....

(f) **Stage requirements:** ....

    ....

(g) **Power requirements:**...

(h) **Order of billing:**..

(i) **Transport arrangements:** ....

(j) **Accommodation:** ....

(k) **Special provisions:** ....

    ....

    ....

(l) **Cancellation:** Payment will be in full unless cancellation is made at least 14 days from the date of the contracted performance.

(m) **GST:** If you are registered for GST and you supply us with both a Tax Invoice and your ABN, we will pay the Fee plus GST. If you aren't or you don't, we won't - and you will be liable for any GST payable.

READ UNDERSTOOD AND AGREED :

....

Signed for and on behalf of Employer   date

....

Signed for and on behalf of Artist   date

VENUE CONSULTANTS

As mentioned earlier, many booking agents represent performers and also act as consultants to venues, who retain their services to liaise with agencies and to select, contract with and supervise the live entertainment provided by that venue. The degree of responsibility undertaken by these consultants varies considerably. Some just select and contract the talent. Others do that and also supervise all non-financial administration of the engagement. Still others undertake all of the functions already mentioned, as well as payroll administration.

Many venue consultants have written agreements with the venue (more often than not, drawn up by the venue) but many of these agreements do not sufficiently protect either the venue or the agent. They often do not delineate the parties' respective functional obligations nor adequately define their legal liabilities.

A venue consultancy agreement should specify the sort of entertainment the venue wishes to present; the general performance conditions such as sound check and rehearsal time availability, starting times, compulsory finishing times, requirements as to sound levels, performance restrictions (e.g. swearing or fireworks or other pyrotechnics); maximum ticket prices; approved methods and timetables for payment of the acts; promotion responsibilities or restrictions; load in and load out procedures; staging and production limitations; and any other matters that the venue consultant will have to observe when selecting, contracting and administering the venue's artists. Getting down to this sort of detail minimises the opportunity for misunderstanding and conflict between venues and the booking consultant. Misunderstandings are not good for anyone's business.

PAYROLL SERVICES

Venue consultants who provide a payroll service for their venues face particular problems with respect to taxation, unless they are very careful.

To show this, let's assume that you are an agent who is operating as venue consultant for a number of hotels. Put simply, you supply the entertainment needs of your hotel clients, i.e. you act as the agent of the hotel in the selection of the talent, liaise with agencies, attend to administration relating to the employment and attend to payment of the artists. For these services you receive (say) a monthly cheque from the hotel for the entertainment. The amount is all-inclusive ('global') and it is your responsibility to ensure that the financial arrangements relating to the employment are properly concluded.

In brief, you supply a service which provides entertainment for the hotels and which allows them to be free of obligations, except for payment of your regular global cheque.

In this position you are in very real danger of being classified as the employer for the purposes of the income tax laws and thus liable for deduction of PAYG tax from the payments made to your artists.

exposes you to burdensome GST obligations. This means that even though the hotel is the real employer you will be liable as the deemed employer.

If the artist wants you to pay the whole of their fee without you first deducting PAYG tax, the artist has to provide you with the following details:

(a) If the artists say they are a registered company, they must supply you with the company's ABN.

(b) If they say they are a registered company, but have not yet obtained an ABN, you are probably safe if they sign the employment contract as a director of the company. Otherwise, you must insist upon a letter from their accountant or tax agent confirming that a partnership return has been lodged and accepted by the Commissioner.

(c) If they say they are a partnership, they must supply you with the tax file number of their partnership.

(d) If they say they are a partnership, but have not yet filed a tax return and therefore have not yet got a tax file number, only a letter from their accountant or tax agent will do.

If the artist does provide these details, you may pay the whole of the fee and it becomes their responsibility to pay tax. If the musicians are individuals or any groups who do not conform with any of the above, you must deduct the tax from their payments (these deductions are rather engagingly called 'Group Tax' - who said the Commissioner hasn't got a sense of whimsy?) and at the end of the financial year, you must issue Group Certificates to everyone from whom you have deducted tax.

If the artists want the fee to be exclusive of GST they have to provide the venue (or its agent) with their ABN and a Tax Invoice. Without this, the artist (as the provider of the services) may be liable for the tax and if so will have to pay it out of the fee. (See Chapter 35, Keeping the Books.) GST is presently 10% of the cost of the supply. The artist is usually paid the fee plus 10% GST and the venue (or its agent) remits the tax to the ATO. The venue then charges the customer the ticket price plus 10% GST and remits the net tax to the ATO. In this way there is no double tax paid but the government receives tax on the whole transaction.

All this can make the venue consultant unpopular with agents and artists, but there is really no alternative. Venue consultants undertaking payroll services must be very cautious, for they are the ones the Commissioner is going to chase if there is any unpaid tax to be collected.

To avoid these problems, venue consultants providing payroll services should use a very carefully drafted form, which provides all the artists' relevant taxation details. They should also provide standard GST Tax Invoices for use by their artists (because not many are in the habit of carrying them around).

5
THE MANAGER

THE RELATIONSHIP BETWEEN ARTIST AND MANAGER IS HUGELY IMPORTANT. FEW ARTISTS CAN ACHIEVE MORE THAN A MODICUM OF SUCCESS WITHOUT COMPETENT AND ENERGETIC MANAGEMENT. THIS CHAPTER EXAMINES THE SELECTION OF MANAGERS, THEIR FUNCTION AND THE BUSINESS RELATIONSHIP BETWEEN ARTIST AND MANAGER. SAMPLES FROM MANAGEMENT AGREEMENTS (WITH COMMENTARY) ARE PROVIDED.

Although an outsider might view the music industry as simple (indeed primitive) in its structures, like any billion-dollar industry it has many, many subtleties and nuances. Managers must comprehend and manipulate these nuances or risk the act's career becoming stagnant and even going down the plug-hole altogether.

Unfortunately, in the past, management acquired a tarnished reputation. Music management was seen as one of the few ways that someone with enough rat-cunning could drag themselves out of the mire and make a fortune without having to step into a boxing ring, provided he or she got to manage the right act. Nowadays, a top manager has to be as tough as a marine with an accounting degree, be a capable business person and still retain the suave charm of an international diplomat.

The musician's search for the perfect manager is never over. The 'Perfect Manager' would be an amalgam of hard-headed business executive, snake oil seller, economist, Tangier rug trader, kick-boxer, parent, stand-in spouse, friend, confessor, psychologist, fall-guy, punching-bag and stand-over merchant. He or she would also be on first-name terms with all the big-hitters of the business in three continents, enjoy an independent source of income, love your music and have a bullet-proof belief in your future.

QUALIFICATIONS

Too many musicians employ inexperienced and untrained friends, parents or admirers as their managers. This may work for a while but, once your career starts to take off, you will need a manager with real skills!

Once stardom arrives, many artists think that they can now afford to appoint a trusted loved one as their manager rather than an experienced industry professional. They forget how important good management was to their success and give their own talent all the credit. Tread cautiously. Many will be familiar with how Delta Goodrem appointed her mother as manager at the end of her contract with Glenn Wheatley. Many will also be familiar with Delta's rather rapid subsequent search for a new international manager amid public controversy.

One of the most noticeable changes in the last few years has been the increase in younger talented managers and, in particular, the increase in female managers. That said, there are all too few 'exhibition-quality' managers. There are numerous capable ones who may well become top managers but, unfortunately, there are also hundreds of undeniably enthusiastic but nonetheless untrained, unqualified, inexperienced and unduly over-confident people acting as managers. These are the ones who, in all probability, will never make it and may even inadvertently harm the artists who put themselves into these managers' hands.

No degree course can guarantee that anyone can actually 'manage' anything. Nevertheless, it is no longer true that the best university for a manager is the University of Hunger and Hard Knocks. The music business has become sophisticated. Successful managers have to possess much higher levels of skill and knowledge than they did in the past. The traditional route to management was to start out as a musician or road crew and to learn the trade by long exposure in the real world. This apprenticeship was (and remains) valuable, but it does not train individual managers to higher standards of performance in marketing, accounting, law and the other survival skills needed in an increasingly complex business world.

Managers really should have backgrounds in accountancy, marketing or administration. They need to know how to put a proficient marketing campaign together, run efficient offices, prepare and read a balance sheet and understand that accrual accounting is not just the work of 'a cruel accountant'.

The artist looking for the perfect manager is, of course, doomed to disappointment. Even the best have, like all professionals, their strengths and weaknesses. Look for a reasonable match between the artist's needs and the manager's talents.

In selecting a manager, consider the following factors:

- Has the manager had previous experience within the industry as a manager?
- Does the manager have established contacts and business connections that will assist the musician's career?
- Has the manager proven skills to perform all management functions and to comply with all the requirements of the management contract?
- If the manager is currently managing other acts, what is the level of success of those acts? Will the manager be looking after the act's affairs exclusively or delegating the work to a personal manager?
- If the manager has other business experience or interests, are they compatible and is that experience relevant?
- Is the manager genuinely interested in the group and its music and prepared to put the artist's interests ahead of personal interests at all times?
- If the manager offers loans to, or investment in, the group, what are the terms of such loans? Is getting a loan the deciding factor, rather than the manager's business skills?
- Has the manager demonstrated honesty and integrity?
- Is he or she a person you can work with? Can you spend a lot of time with this person?
- Is this the kind of person you want to represent you, both within the music industry and to the public?
- Are the terms that the manager is requiring, fair? Do they indicate that this is going to be a relationship in which the interests are mutually beneficial?

WHEN DO YOU NEED MANAGEMENT?

There is no standard answer to this question. It depends on your individual circumstances. Many new groups acquire a manager almost as a designer accessory; a status symbol. Even though they don't yet need a manager, saying they have one suggests that they are serious and successful - even though the manager may be a friend from school who goes out with the lead singer's sister and enjoys being able to call himself a manager. This sort of posturing doesn't hurt, unless the band actually does get a break. Unfortunately, unless your manager is already competent, he or she is unlikely to be able learn in time the skills that you will need if you are to capitalise on your opportunity.

Don't commit to management too early. Many bands do not really need a manager when they start out. You need to realise that, until you can attract a good manager, you may be better looking after your own affairs and instead retain a good accountant and a good lawyer upon whom you can call as needed.

If you wait until you have developed a reputation and had some success, you will find it easier to attract better quality management. Moreover, you have more bargaining power when negotiating the management contract. If you have interest from a record label, and, even better, the promise of a large advance, good management will be even easier to attract as the manager will have a financial reward immediately in sight. Even then, do not rush to sign with management. Remember that you have done most of the hard work to date. You've established the act, stabilised the line-up, developed the repertoire, obtained agency support, and perhaps record company interest and now you are looking for a manager and will have to sign a percentage (perhaps a large percentage) of your income away!

Bear in mind also that your record company (or future one) may have particular ideas about management. For example, some record companies refuse to deal with some managers after bad experiences and may ask that you give up or change management. Such requests should be considered cautiously, while your manager must have a good working relationship with the record company, he or she is also there to represent your interests (not those of the record company).

There is no right time to have management. Each act's needs are different.

THE LEGAL RELATIONSHIP BETWEEN MANAGER AND ARTIST

Most managers have a written contract with the artists they manage. This is just good business practice (and in NSW it is compulsory). By describing each party's rights and obligations, the contract sets out the terms of the relationship. The function of the contract is to protect both parties' rights, not just those of the manager or the artist.

Even if there is no valid contract between the artist and the manager, this does not mean the artist can avoid paying the manager for his or her services. In a remarkable case, *Brenner & Ors v. First Artists' Management Pty Ltd and Braithwaite* (No. 3606 of 1988, 30 October 1992), Daryl Braithwaite was sued by his ex-managers. The facts of the case are complicated and a brief outline is all but impossible.

Suffice it to say, Braithwaite's career had languished for some time. Having been the lead singer in a hugely successful group, his solo career had slowly slipped to the stage that he was performing in clubs and hotels - something that would have been unthinkable in his heyday. The managers were retained to assist in resurrecting his career. There was no signed management agreement. Eventually, their services were terminated.

It is common in the music business (perhaps more common in times past) for managers to supply their services on the basis of a handshake deal. The only term discussed may be the amount of the commission. Nevertheless, it has been widely assumed that the relationship is a contractual one and that any deficiency in the terms would be overcome by implied terms determined by the 'trade and custom' of the business.

In this case, from the outset, the ex-managers (the plaintiffs) argued that although they had performed services at his request and for his benefit, there was no enforceable management agreement with him. They sought reasonable payment for work and services provided in assisting him to further his career. In other words, unlike most management disputes, this was a claim based on the law of unjust enrichment, rather than upon the existence of any express or implied management agreement.

His Honour, the judge, found that Braithwaite had benefited from the plaintiffs' services and that those services had been provided pursuant to a request which had been accompanied by a discussion about payment. He found that Braithwaite had accepted the benefit of the managers' services, in circumstances where it would be unjust for him to do so without paying them.

The short message of the Braithwaite case is, if you use a manager's services, you must expect to pay for them. But more about payment later.

THE FINANCIAL RELATIONSHIP BETWEEN MANAGER AND ARTIST

Although it is possible to hire a manager on a salary, this is very rarely done. The standard expectation is that the manager will be paid on a contingency basis (i.e. according to success).

There are two main methods used by managers to structure their relationships with the artists they represent:

1. MANAGER AS GROUP MEMBER

The manager may be treated as a non-performing group member and entitled to an equal share of net profits. In this kind of deal, the manager is an equal participant in the business of the group and is therefore entitled to be treated as an equal partner or shareholder in all the group's activities.

As a partner or shareholder, the manager is a part-owner of the business and has an equal vote in the conduct of the business, but is subject to the directions of the majority of group members. Moreover, as a part-owner, the manager may be entitled to rights in the group name, the benefit of recording contracts and to receive a share of the band's profits after payment of all expenses including group costs and management costs.

This form may have initial appeal because it gives everyone a sense of 'All for one and one for all!' However, its disadvantages (these have been proven over the years) mean it is now almost extinct. The disadvantages include:

(a) Conflicts arising from the allocation of income to necessary group or management expenses.

(b) Conflicts of interest and allocation of management expenses if the manager takes on other artists.

(c) Upon termination, conflicts as to the nature and extent of the manager's rights in the group's name, benefit of recording and publishing contracts, ownership of copyrights and goodwill in the continuing business.

It is significant that 20 years ago this was the most common management structure. Now it is hardly used at all. There are still occasions when it is useful, but they are exceptional and need a lot of discussion and careful drafting.

2. MANAGER AS SEPARATE BUSINESS

More commonly these days, the manager is contracted by the artist to supply management services on a non-salaried, contingency basis whereby the manager is entitled to a percentage of the artist's income but owns no part of the artist's business.

This has become the accepted structure because it reflects the fact that the business of the band and the business of the manager are quite distinct. Each is a separate business and each has its own functions, goals and interests. In particular:

(a) The manager and act are each the sole owners of their respective business. The manager does not own a part of the act's business.

(b) The manager and the act are each solely responsible for the allocation and payment of expenses associated with their particular activities.

(c) The manager may undertake management of other acts, without any conflict of interest or dispute about allocation of expenses.

(d) The manager will not have any property interests in the act's name, its contracts, copyrights, goodwill and so on, which makes separation easier and cleaner when that time comes.

SCOPE OF MANAGEMENT

A manager usually becomes responsible for all of the act's entertainment industry activities. The management contract will probably provide that the management function and duties will include the following:

> All of the Artist's entertainment industry activities, in particular:
> (a) the making, distribution, sale and promotion of audio and audiovisual recordings in every medium and by every technology, whether now known or yet to be invented;
> (b) personal live appearances before an audience whether in public or private, paying or not;
> (c) personal recorded appearances for video, film, television or Internet, irrespective of the medium or technology of delivery;
> (d) performance as a program presenter and as an actor in films in any medium;
> (e) the writing of lyrics and the composing of music including (but not limited to) songs for records, commercial jingles, TV or film theme or background music and for any other use;
> (f) the provision of services as an engineer or producer or director of audio or audiovisual recordings of the Artist's own performances or the performances of others;
> (g) the merchandising and other commercial use of the Artist's name, likeness and reputation by way of licence or otherwise in connection with products or services and sponsorship, product endorsement or otherwise; and
> (h) any other activity service or performance by the Artist in connection with any of the above as may be agreed between the parties from time to time.

As you can see, a clause like this covers all of the musician's entertainment industry activities. The scope is wide because the manager is, presumably, at least partly responsible for establishing the profile and success of the musician which (hopefully) will lead to film and television work, the autobiography, advertising opportunities, merchandising deals and so on. Moreover, the manager is usually expected to assist in the negotiation and administration of these associated areas of work. Also, the manager will expect to share in the income from these sources because, while the musician is acting or writing books rather than performing or recording, the term of the manager's contract is ticking away without reward.

At the outset of the relationship, when the management agreement is first negotiated, it is important to question the appropriate scope of the manager's activities and if you wish some of your activities to remain outside the scope of the relationship, these should be specifically written into the agreement. Some musicians already have an acting career (and an agent who already looks after that side of the business). Some have a jingle-writing business, while others work in a music store or teach an instrument or whatever. No matter what this other work may be, you should discuss it with your would-be manager and come to a mutually acceptable arrangement. When this is done up-front, there is rarely a problem. If there is a problem, it is best to find out before you commit yourself.

EXCLUSIVITY

All management agreements provide that the musician will have no other manager without the contracted manager's express agreement. Managers have to demand exclusivity otherwise, as soon as the dollars start flowing, the vultures will start circling in the hope of juicy pickings.

Almost all management agreements provide that the manager may look after more than one act. Few acts earn enough, in the early days at least, to support a manager and the costs of administration. Even established managers tend to look after more than one act. There are at least two good reasons for this: First they are able to recover their overheads and administration costs across a greater income base and secondly, because the shelf-life of many acts is so short, they can develop new acts at the same time as looking after the affairs of the established one, which is good for the continuity of the manager's business.

This obviously can create conflict of interests between the musicians, who want the maximum attention from their manager, and the managers who need to maximise their cost effectiveness and profitability. For this reason, management contracts that allow the manager to look after more than one artist often provide that this is subject to the proviso that:

> ...the Manager shall not devote so much time to other business activities as to jeopardise the Artist's career and interests.

Of course, when you start arguing about these sorts of issues, it is often the beginning of the end of the relationship in any event.

CO-MANAGERS

It is common for artists to have co-managers when they get to the stage of having international careers. Few Australian managers are physically able to take on the major overseas markets, particularly the United States, Japan and Europe, so local co-managers are often appointed for those territories. The appointment of a co-manager must always be subject to prior consultation with, and the approval of, the artist. Moreover, the commission payable where another manager is introduced must be carefully negotiated and agreed in writing. The most common arrangement is for the co-managers either to split the principal manager's commission, or to divide up the territories so that each gets a full commission on their own territory but nothing from the others. Of course, paying of double commissions is not on!

PERSONAL MANAGERS

It is customary to allow managers to appoint a 'personal manager' to perform their duties and tasks. Many of the busier managers who have several artists on their books, will designate a staff member to have particular responsibility for an artist. The salary of a personal manager is a management expense and should not be charged to the artist. Given the personal nature of the management relationship, the artist should always have the power of approval over the appointment of such individuals. Many artists insist on the right to end or replace the personal manager's services.

It is essential that the artist be involved in the selection and appointment of any personal manager or co-manager. After all, the artist-manager relationship is one that demands great faith and confidence. Perhaps the most famous case that demonstrates this involved the Kinks.

In 1964 the Kinks appointed Boscobel Productions Ltd to manage them for 40% commission (a rate that would never stand up today!) In turn, Boscobel retained a co-manager (Denmark Productions Ltd, which was half owned by Larry Page) to actually carry out the management functions. Boscobel agreed to pay Denmark a 10% commission which was paid out of Boscobel's 40%.

In 1965 the group undertook a tour of the United States. Ray Davies (leader of the Kinks) had not wanted to tour but had eventually agreed on the condition that Larry Page acted as personal manager for the tour. Halfway through the tour Page returned to England without warning Davies, and appointed another personal manager to the group. Ray Davies did not approve of the new manager. Unhappiness followed.

In the resulting case, one of the things that was made very clear by the judge was that the relationship of artist and manager is one which demands great trust and confidence and, because of that, the artist should not be locked into such a relationship if the management has breached its obligations in such a way as to destroy that fundamental trust.

TERRITORY

Most managers would prefer to be the manager for the whole world. If a band gets a break overseas, its income (and consequently the manager's income) can grow from nil to millions in a matter of months. Peter Frampton's prodigious success with his live album in the early 1970s and Savage Garden's emergence in the 1990s are classic examples. These artists are reputed to have become multimillionaires within two years from the proceeds of touring, publishing and record royalties.

As the musician, you must ask whether your manager has the skills (or the potential to develop them) to create that international opportunity and then adequately manage your affairs in that tough competitive arena. Less than a dozen Australian managers have a proven record of success overseas although more are starting actively to seek the overseas experience and contacts that are so important. If in doubt, artists should limit the territory as much as possible and include ways of measuring the manager's achievements, perhaps in terms of media coverage, gigs booked or whatever. It is always possible to enlarge a territory if the manager does a good job in the local territory, but it is very difficult to reduce a world territory if it turns out that the manager is not up to the job after all.

The issues raised by co-management are relevant here because, if a manager is given world rights, it may be necessary for the management role to be subcontracted to co-management for particular territories. Indeed it may also be sensible to include a clause that states that the manager must appoint a co-manager in a particular overseas territory if so required by the artist. That said, because of the very personal nature of the management relationship, the management contract should specify that co-management is an issue that requires both consultation and consent.

LENGTH OF THE MANAGEMENT CONTRACT

Most management contracts are for periods of between three and five years. Certainly where the act is not established, three years is usually the minimum a manager will accept. The manager will probably not earn anything in the first year, may balance the books in the second year and will (hopefully) start making a profit in the third. Management of new acts (even when they include musicians who have been successful in other line-ups), is speculative and needs time for the risk to pay off.

Usually, the contract period is split into an initial period, followed by one or two options to extend the period. The options are almost always in favour of the manager. That is to say, it is the manager's decision whether or not to extend the term of the contract. This, of course, depends on the relative bargaining power of artist and manager. There is usually little justification for this when both artist and manager are at an equal level in their careers.

A standard Term clause will look something like this:

> **Initial period**
> *This Agreement commences on the date first written in this Agreement and will continue for an initial period of one (1) year ('the initial period'), unless earlier terminated in accordance with the terms hereof.*
>
> **Option**
> *For the consideration of one dollar ($1) (payment of which is hereby acknowledged) the Artist agrees that this Agreement may be extended (at the sole discretion of the Manager) for two (2) further periods, each of two (2) years (each such period being 'a contract period'). To exercise any such option, the Manager must give the Artist notice, in writing, of the Manager's intention to exercise any option. Such notice must be given at least one month before the expiration of the then current contract period. Each option period shall run from the expiration of the preceding contract period.*
>
> **Continuation upon expiration**
> *Notwithstanding expiration of the initial period, the Term will continue from month to month unless and until either party gives to the other at least thirty days' written notice of termination.*

If the artist has more bargaining power, he or she can insist that options be subject to the parties' mutual consent.

A more common way of building equity into the agreement is to build in some simple performance criteria, e.g. management contracts for non-established artists commonly provide that if the musician does not obtain a recording agreement (and/or a publishing contract) within the initial period, the option can only be exercised by mutual consent. Some deals provide for specific weekly income goals.

Most experienced managers realise that the fundamental characteristic of the management relationship is its personal nature. If the relationship breaks down it is an impossible situation for both parties. (Not even a court will force a musician to continue management with someone if the relationship has broken down. You might have to buy your way out, but you certainly don't have to work together!) Consequently, if you can build objective performance indicators into the agreement, you reduce the chance of friction when the time comes to exercise an option.

THE FUNCTIONS OF THE MANAGER

Every manager has a different view of the job. Nevertheless, they all have fairly similar basic duties. These are: administration and accounting; promotion and advertising; negotiating with, liaising with and harassing record and publishing companies; providing creative career guidance to the artists; organising production, sound, light and crew; liaising with the booking agency; tour organisation; consulting with and scheduling the musicians; co-ordinating television, radio and personal appearances; obtaining and overseeing sponsorships and merchandising; co-ordinating record and video production.

These may perhaps be best summarised by looking at the relevant clause in a management agreement:

MANAGER'S FUNCTIONS AND OBLIGATIONS
Procuring and Administering Engagements
The Manager must use the Manager's reasonable commercial endeavours to promote and further the Artist's career, including without limitation:
  (a) *procuring suitable engagements for the Artist to which the Artist is suited by talent and ability, or by obtaining an agent to do so; and*
  (b) *commercially exploiting the Activities to the Artist's advantage within the entertainment industry by all appropriate media, methods and formats currently existing or developed from time to time.*

Procuring and Administering Contracts
The Manager will on the Artist's behalf, negotiate and confer to the best of the Manager's ability with agencies, employers, record companies, publishers, sponsors, merchandisers and other users and potential users of the Artist's services or properties, insofar as they relate to the Activities.

Promotion and Publicity
The Manager will plan and implement promotion, publicity and advertising relating to the Artist, and will supervise the provision of services relating to the same if performed by anyone other than the Manager.

Consultation and Advice
The Manager shall regularly confer with and advise the Artist concerning the Artist's Activities throughout the Term, including:
  (a) *being reasonably available to consult with the Artist; and*
  (b) *preparing plans for the future direction of the Artist's career in consultation with the Artist.*

Business Management
The Manager will act as the business manager for the Artist in all matters relating to the Activities and will make best endeavours to do everything that is reasonable and proper to ensure that such affairs are conducted in a competent, honest and professional manner.

Exclusions
This Agreement shall not impose upon the Manager any authority liability or duty to the Artist in connection with:
  (a) *Individual taxation matters;*
  (b) *individual investment advice; or*
  (c) *individual financial advice.*

FINDING WORK

It is a fundamental part of the manager's task to find the musician work that is suited to his or her talents and career direction.

Some of the 'standard' management agreements floating around specify that the manager 'has not offered or attempted or promised to obtain employment or engagements for the artist and is not obligated, authorised or expected to do so'. Managers who have this clause in their contract are either trying to contract out of one of the basic tasks of a manager in Australia, or they merely have a lawyer who has copied an American precedent without knowing the custom of the Australian industry. (American management agreements contain this clause because of local legislation requiring people doing such work to be licensed.)

In Australia, if the manager of a young band is not prepared to get out and find the musicians work, both the manager and the musicians are going to have very little to eat.

Some do this themselves but in most cases it is a priority of the manager's job to find an experienced agent to do the job. Even getting onto the books of a powerful booking agent is no easy task. The competition is considerable because there are more acts than there are work opportunities.

BUSINESS MANAGEMENT

You will note that in the above list, there is no obligation to keep the books, bank the money and so forth. If these tasks are going to be the manager's, obviously this should be included. However, both artists and managers should think twice about this. If lawyers are ever instructed to get an artist out of a management contract, the first thing they do is call for the books and have them audited. Very few managers are also accountants so many find it difficult to produce books of account that can withstand more than a cursory examination. This is not to say that they are necessarily dishonest; just that they will probably have made mistakes and the chances are that the mistakes will be assumed to benefit the manager unless proven otherwise.

Although it is customary in Australia for the manager to take care of the business affairs of the artist, this is certainly not so in the United States. There it is recognised that very few managers have the time or expertise to do the accounting and bookkeeping, efficiently monitor and collect all the income from all sources, prepare and supervise the budgets (both the artist's personal expenditure and those of the act), as well as to supervise insurance protection, investments, tax planning, tour accounting and undertake royalty examinations. In the United States this work is generally perceived to be that of the business manager.

For this work, the business manager usually is paid a fee or 5% commission. Most personal managers in the United States charge 15%, because the business managers charge 5%, thus taking the total commission to the magical 20% figure that is so common.

It is increasingly common for musicians in Australia to structure their business affairs in this way. The advantages should be obvious: the skills necessary for each role are so very different that it is hardly surprising that great all-round managers are hard to find.

Perhaps one of the reasons that Australian managers have been reluctant to adopt the American model is that it has been customary for the manager to hold the artist's money and to operate the bank accounts, paying the band expenses and, when there is enough in the account, paying the artists their share. Although most at least set up separate bank accounts in the artists' names, some managers simply pay the artists' money into their own account and mix the funds. It is not necessarily a case of 'What's yours is mine; what's mine is my own', but it is extremely bad business and may well amount to negligent trusteeship. (In New South Wales, such mixing of funds is illegal.)

This practice, perhaps more than any other, has tended to tarnish managers' reputations generally. It is cause for huge resentment when there is only enough money to pay the expenses and the manager's commission but not enough to feed and water the musicians and is cause for very real suspicion when the management treats the artist's income as its own.

These problems are very easily overcome if the band retains an independent qualified person (usually an accountant) to handle the administration of the money. (Where this is done, the artist pays the accountant and the manager drops the commission by 5% to reflect the lesser workload and responsibility.) In this kind of deal:

- All income is paid to the accountant;
- All expenses are paid by the accountant;
- The manager provides the accountant with receipts for all reimbursable expenses;
- The accountant administers the paying of expenses, calculation and payment of commissions payable and the maintenance of the bank accounts and all of the artists' other financial administration matters.

This creates a clear money trail for both parties and removes the potential for the common accusations about managers misusing the artist's money. It is simple, cost-efficient and removes a potential problem area from the artist-manager relationship.

CONFIDENTIALITY, INTEGRITY AND HARD WORK

Although it should not need stating, it cannot be over-emphasised that the role of the manager is one of great trust and responsibility. There have been several decided cases in which the court made it clear that the relationship of the manager to the artist is 'fiduciary'. This means that managers must put the artists' interests above their own.

It is important that the manager observe the confidentiality of the information, secrets, private finances, dealings and relationships relating to the artist. Similarly, the manager has a duty to exercise his or her powers, zealously, responsibly, with integrity and in absolute good faith. All managers should promise this in the management agreement. However, even if they don't, the courts have made it clear that they will demand this high degree of trust and responsibility of the manager.

THE MANAGER'S REMUNERATION

COMMISSION

The standard rate of commission in Australia is between 15% and 20%. If you are paying more than 20%, you could be paying too much. In *Terzian v Gattelari* [1972] AR (NSW) 591, the court determined that the commission rate of 25% of gross income was excessive in comparison with normal entertainment industry rates and reduced the rate to 10% of the gross income. A contributing factor to this reduction was the manager's inexperience in the industry.

In *Layton v. Vaud Vision Promotions* (unreported, Industrial Commission of NSW, 11th October 1983 No 354 of 1983) the Commission indicated that the agreed commission rate of 40% of the gross income was excessive and indicated that a rate of 17% of the gross income was not unreasonable, taking into account the manager's investment of time and money in a new and unknown musical group.

Of course, the percentage figure is meaningless unless you specify what the percentage is based upon. In earlier days, it was standard practice for managers to charge their percentage on 'gross income from all sources'. Although there are some managers who still insist on this, it is now the exception rather than the rule. The manager who is being paid 20% of gross on everything, will make far more money than any of the band members. It isn't going to take long before the musicians start getting resentful about this and the end of the relationship is almost inevitable.

Even remuneration in goods and services is commissionable. If an artist agrees to be paid in airfares or cars the manager should still get paid. After all, the manager has probably put the deal together! The only question is what value should be put on those goods or services. Some managers agree to a wholesale value or corporate rate while others insist on the full retail value. If you accept the saying 'there are no free lunches', then it is not hard to see why a balance needs to be shown between the cost of the manager's services and what the manager can actually provide. Too low a commission can remove the performance incentive. Too high a commission is a gift.

ADVANCES

Commission is payable on income - but what is income? Is an advance commissionable given that it is actually a payment 'in advance' of receiving income?

The industry practice is quite clear. The manager is generally entitled to commission an advance at the time it is paid to the artist. This is the case irrespective of whether the advance is recoupable or non-recoupable.

Where the manager has commissioned an advance, it cannot also commission the money used to recoup that advance. For example, assume that a writer signs a publishing agreement with a recoupable advance of $100,000. There are two ways that a manager can deal with this. Either:

(a) The manager commissions the writer's advance when it is paid to the writer. Because the advance is recoupable, the publisher will allocate the next $100,000 of writer royalties towards the recoupment of the advance. The royalties used to recoup the advance cannot be commissioned. The royalties were paid in advance and the commission has already been taken in advance; or

(b) The manager does not commission the advance when it is paid to the writer. Rather, it commissions the actual income as it is received. Managers understandably resist this because the commission on advances provides important cash flow for the manager as well as the artist. Also, many advances are never fully recouped. On the other hand, if the management is new and unproven (or, conversely, is coming to an end) this option is usually the fairest way to go. If the manager commissions an advance just before the relationship ends, it is an unfair windfall. That advance is going to take a lot of work to recoup: The exiting manager isn't going to participate and, unless the artist is going to pay double commission, the new manager isn't going to get rewarded.

Whichever way the deal is negotiated the principle remains the same: the manager either commissions the advance and not the income used to recoup the advance or it doesn't commission the advance and commissions the income. If it were otherwise, the manager would be double dipping.

EXCLUSIONS

RECORDING COSTS

In the early days of the industry, record deals were differently structured. Production costs were non-recoupable but the royalty rates were much lower. (This is discussed at greater length in Chapter 23, **Record Royalties**.) The effect of this was that the artists (and thus the managers) started earning from the first record sold. In this situation, it was appropriate for the manager to commission all income.

These days the most common record deal characterises the recording costs as an 'advance' to the artists. They don't earn any royalties until those production costs (and any other advances) are recouped. In this situation, if the manager is commissioning all ('gross') income, he or she will be earning while the artists are not. If the artists don't recoup the cost of production it is very likely that they will have incurred a very considerable debt to the manager. They will only start receiving an income after they have both recouped the production costs and repaid the manager! Clearly, this is not on! It is an example of an old management custom not reflecting current practice in the record industry.

If the manager has reason to be scared that the band will spend half a million dollars on an album and never be able to recoup it, the sensible protection is to provide a maximum production budget which will be non-commissionable and provide that expenditure in excess of that figure will be excluded.

A straightforward production costs clause might look like this:

> *Commission shall not be payable on:*
> *(i) direct recording costs of sound recordings (made for the purpose of creating albums and singles but not demos) and promotional videos; musician, performer or producer fees and royalties payable to persons other than the Artist in connection with the sound recordings; and any reasonable expenses incurred with the Manager's prior written consent. Indirect costs such as travel or accommodation are not excluded.*

LIVE PERFORMANCE COSTS

The cost incurred in earning live-performance income is one of the most contentious items when determining what should be deducted from gross income for the purpose of calculating management commissions. The cost of travel and accommodation, renting and transport of gear, hiring the essential support staff, publicity and promotion and so on, all mean that the chance of making a net profit from live work is sometimes slim. In Australia, the ratio of expense to potential earnings is particularly high.

Because of this, you often hear that 'no-one can make money out of touring in Australia'. Of course this is not true. Many Australian artists make very good profits from live work. What is true is that acts have to budget their expenditure in accord with their likely income.

Creating a profile and public following are essential for promoting record sales and thus making more money. Musicians (and record companies) argue that the exposure provided by live performance is essential to establishing a profile for the act and a popular following for their music and that this justifies deduction of expenses and overheads before calculating the manager's commission. Managers agree but argue that, because of the work they have to do to organise and administer the live performance work, a return on the 'net' is simply not economic.

When commission is being paid on gross income, musicians become resentful when they work night after night for little or no cash, if their manager gets 20% of the gross. (This is particularly galling if one of the band's expenses is a tour manager!) Clearly, unless there is some compromise, the resulting resentment will damage the working relationship between artist and manager.

If the parties agree on a net basis of commission calculation, the clause may be along the following lines.

> *In respect of live personal appearances (whether at concerts, on tours or otherwise) the commission will be calculated on the net profit thereof. 'Net profit' means the gross fees received less the total costs incurred reasonably and attributable to staging the event, plus any tour support provided by third parties.*

Note that this example stipulates that any third party tour support money gets taken off the total of the expenses before the calculation of the net. This assumes that the manager has not already commissioned the tour support money! The manager either commissions tour support funds up front or gets the benefit of it in deducting it from the expenses. Either way the manager will benefit from the tour support received, but it must not be commissioned twice.

Managers who are scared that the band will over-spend on production and associated costs should either: specify what costs they are prepared to have subtracted from the gross income received; or commission the whole of the gross, but at a lower rate; say between 5% and 10%.

There is no one right answer. There are a number of factors that have to be taken into account when working out a fair approach to the commissioning of income from live work: the normal costs of delivering the artist's show (from unplugged to major production), genre (from jazz to metal), track record (from development tour to stadium tour), venues (pubs to entertainment centres). No-one commissions the full gross any more; some managers do nett deals, but most managers work on a modified gross deal. A benevolent one might look like this:

> *In respect of live personal appearances (whether at concerts, on tours or otherwise) the commission will be calculated on gross earnings less any booking agent's fees, support band's fees, and any "tour support" monies provided by third parties that have already been commissioned by the Manager.*

TOUR SUPPORT

The commissioning of tour support is always complicated to deal with in a contract because of the various ways in which tour support can be provided. Sometimes the record company may simply provide a recoupable lump sum towards the tour costs or, as is more common, it provides a negative pick-up (where it promises to pay up to a certain amount of any loss that may be incurred). Either way, the contract has to cope.

If the manager commissions the gross receipts, it is taking the commission irrespective of whether the tour makes a profit and commissions the tour support, even though such tour support is provided to mitigate against the losses that would otherwise be incurred by the artist. This is obviously unfair and is an incentive to book high-grossing tours without the incentive to minimise expenses.

Where the manager is on any variant of the net receipts deal, the tour support should not be directly commissioned. Rather, it should be added to the gross receipts from which the expenses are deducted in order to reach the net commissionable figure. This way, all advances (even negative pick-up advances) are commissioned - but in a fair way and only once.

BOOKING AGENTS' COMMISSION

The 10% paid to booking agents is not commissionable by the manager. This custom has arisen in Australia because the agent is fulfilling one of the manager's functions. The agent's commission is taken from the gross before calculating the manager's commission.

Where an agent is also acting as manager, no income should be subject to double commissions. Accordingly, if one person is acting as an agent and as a manager, it is not proper for them to take 10% of the fee as an agency fee plus 20% as a management fee. (In NSW that conduct is illegal.)

MERCHANDISING EXPENSES

Most acts license their merchandising rights to specialist merchandising companies. These companies incur all of the expenses and pay the artist a royalty. That royalty is commissionable. However, if the act is doing its own merchandising, the costs of producing and selling that merchandise should be deducted before calculating the manager's commission.

THE RIGHT TO PAYMENT AFTER TERMINATION

Whether or not a manager has any right to receive commission after the expiration or termination of the management agreement is one of the most vexed parts of any management negotiation. Certainly it is true that the manager's efforts are likely to continue to create income even after the management agreement has ended. On the other hand, the artist needs to be able to get on with his or her career without having to keep paying the old manager for past services. **There is no implied right to receive management commission after termination of the contract**. If the manager believes that such commission is justifiable, it must be in writing.

The variations are almost limitless:

- If the manager is to continue earning a commission after the management period is over, that commission should diminish over no more than three years, e.g. year 1, 10%; year 2, 7.5%; year 3, 5%; year 4, 0%.

- The commission should never be the full commission payable during the term of the contract, because the manager no longer has any expenses or duties in respect of the artist whereas the artist's on-going work, and that of the new manager, will directly and indirectly be promoting the back-catalogue.

- Some managers insist that they receive full commission on any money earned from a contract entered during their time. This is indefensibly unfair. In effect, this means that all recording and publishing income continues to be commissionable by the previous manager. This leaves nothing in it for the new manager who is expected to work the artist's recording and publishing career without reward. The artist will never be able to find a new, competent manager on such terms. Given that, such a term is economically fruitless to both parties: the artist won't have a career and the old manager won't make any money out of the failure that it ensured at the outset of the relationship. No one wins.

At most, the right to commission should be restricted to income derived from product recorded (and live performances actually contracted) during the period. In other words, the commission is directly related to the product on which the manager worked. It should go without saying that no post-termination commission should be payable where the termination has occurred due to breach by the manager.

In *Brenner & Ors v. First Artists' Management Pty Ltd and Braithwaite*, the plaintiffs' claim was for remuneration for the period of their actual work and for the three years after termination of the relationship.

In the period of management, no records were sold. The album 'Edge' had not been released until three months after the termination of management services. The second album 'Rise' was released some two years after termination and was not taken into account at all by the Judge, on the basis that the success or otherwise of this album had not been effected by the ex-managers. He did not accept the managers' argument that the effect of their work would continue to endure for three years after termination.

The judge drew various implications from the evidence before him and found that 'the normal run-off period following termination of a management agreement is six to seven months ... Common sense, however, dictates that this must be dependant upon the management services concerned and the source of the relevant earnings'.

In this case, as the managers had been working to re-establish Braithwaite's career, it was akin to making a debut album. Accordingly, the managers' effect was impliedly of greater effect than for an established artist. The judge went on to decide that the services of the managers would have had a diminishing effect over a period of approximately 12 months. After that date, record sales were considered 'so remote in time as to be considered not to be a benefit of the services provided' by the managers.

Established musicians insist that there will be no post-termination commission payable.

THE MANAGER'S POWERS

Because it is their job to 'look after business', managers usually need to have certain powers delegated to them by their acts. In a legal sense, the manager is the 'agent' and the musician is the 'principal'. The degree of autonomy and control exercised by the manager/agent over the musician/principal varies from time to time and from act to act.

If you look at the old-fashioned contracts that were prevalent up to just a few years ago (and there are quite a few still around), it seemed that the artist was almost the manager's employee. Many of the older contracts stated that 'the artists shall render their services to the manager' and went on to say that the artists could only enter contracts that had the written approval of the manager, that the manager had the power of approval over choice of repertoire and so on.

This is no longer the case. These days the relationship is more balanced and artists expect to have greater control over their own lives and careers. For example, current contracts may include the following provisions:

The Artist authorises the Manager during the Term to:

(a) *collect any monies due to the Artist and to instruct all managements, employers, record companies, publishing companies, sponsors and other persons to make such payment to the Manager or such other person as may be mutually agreed;*

(b) *undertake all promotion, public relations and publicity arrangements for the Artist throughout the World with full authority to use and authorise the use of the Artist's likeness and biographical data PROVIDED THAT the Manager must use the Manager's best efforts to consult with the Artist on such matters;*

(c) *arrange the payment of the Artist's debts and expenses, out of monies, salaries, fees, royalties and other payments received on the Artist's behalf PROVIDED THAT the Manager must not incur any expense over 1,000 dollars or more than 3,000 dollars in any month, in the Artist's name, without first obtaining the Artist's approval;*

(d) *audit and examine books of account, royalty statements and other records of persons with whom the Artist has any contractual or other rights of examination; and*

(e) *enter into and bind the Artist to contracts engagements and arrangements relating to the Artist's entertainment industry activities PROVIDED THAT contracts for tours in excess of two weeks and all publishing and recording contracts must be signed by the Artist.*

You will note that certain sensible safeguards are built into the powers in an attempt to balance the manager's need to 'get on with business' and the artist's need to be informed and retain some basic degree of control.

ENFORCEMENT

A management contract is legally described as 'a contract for the performance of personal services'. For many years the courts have been very reluctant to grant any orders that would have the effect of forcing the parties to such contracts to work together. The courts will order damages to compensate the wronged party but will not, for example, order that an artist must work with a particular manager. The courts recognise the fact that it is very hard to force one person to work with another.

In the Troggs case (*Page One Records Ltd and Dick James Music Ltd v. Britton and Harvey Block Associates Ltd, 1968*), the band alleged that Page One, their manager, had breached their management agreement. They approached Harvey Block to take over their management. Page One commenced legal proceedings. It asked the Court for an injunction forbidding the band signing with Harvey Block. The Court said that although Page One had not breached the management agreement and that the band was in breach of the management agreement, the agreement was one for 'personal services' and refused to grant the injunction. It could award damages for the band's breach but it would not, by forbidding the band from signing with any new manager, force it into working with the old manager.

ENDING THE MANAGEMENT RELATIONSHIP

Sometimes relationships just don't work. The artist-manager relationship is no different. Regardless of everyone's good intentions at the beginning it is highly likely that somewhere along the road, you will need to part ways.

With that in mind, it is important that ground rules are set that allow the relationship to end cleanly. In other words, the contract should provide a mechanism to try and resolve disputes when (rather than if) they arise and if they can't be resolved, how the contract may be terminated (that is, how the obligations under the contract can come to an end).

Many management contracts provide that the contract cannot be terminated unless a series of steps are followed. For example if one party breaches the agreement, the contract may provide that before the other party is allowed to end the contract, it must write to the infringer complaining of the breach and giving them an opportunity to fix the problem. If the problem is not fixed within a certain time, then the contract may provide that the party who is not in breach may write to the other party, terminating the contract.

Whatever the contract says, two things should be remembered:

(a) if the contract provides steps that must be followed to terminate the contract - follow those steps exactly! If it says that you must write to the other side on pink paper clearly marked "DEAR JOHN", then do it;

(b) Every effort should be made to deal with the end of the relationship professionally and courteously. It can be difficult but take a step back, put yourself in the other side's shoes for a second and talk about the issues, the procedure and how to move on together before severing the ties. Much angst, heartache, time (and legal fees) can be saved by doing so.

In *Biscayne Partners Pty Ltd v Valance Corp Pty Ltd & Ors* (2003), Biscayne (through Scott Michaelson) sued Holly Valance (aka Holly Vukadinovic) for breach of their management agreement. Holly and Scott had a detailed management agreement that set out the term of the contract and how it could be ended. The agreement provided for a series of particular steps to be followed. The court found that Holly failed to follow the proper steps on two separate occasions and thus unlawfully tried to terminate the contract. It ended up costing her hundreds of thousands of dollars.

CONCLUSION

Many artists tend to look upon the appointment of a manager as a way of washing their hands of any responsibility for the conduct of the business aspects of their career. A manager is not the parent you buy when you leave home.

If you are an artist, although the appointment of a manager should relieve you of many daily administrative and business functions, it is still very important that you take an active and responsible interest in the work undertaken by the manager on your behalf. You should be aware of and participate in contract negotiation, tour planning, financial planning and other important activities. You may delegate these functions to the manager but remember - Good delegation passes the task but not the responsibility. It is your career. It's your business. It will be your failure or your success.

Popular success may take years to attain and yet may last no longer than one hit album. Proper management must ensure not only that the past efforts of the artist are recouped during the success period but also that proper plans are made to ensure the maximum benefit to the artist as success fades.

MANAGEMENT AGREEMENT CHECKLIST

1. NAME AND ADDRESS OF MANAGER

2. NAME(S) AND ADDRESS(ES) OF ARTIST(S)

3. TERRITORY

4. LENGTH OF INITIAL PERIOD

5. OPTIONS:

   (a) number

   (b) length

   (c) performance triggers

6. REMUNERATION:

   (a) commission

   (b) exclusions:

      (i) sound recording costs?

      (ii) live performance costs?

      (iii) other?

7. SERVICES OF MANAGER

8. POWERS OF MANAGER

9. LIMITATIONS TO MANAGER'S POWERS

10. ARRANGEMENTS FOR BANKING AND ACCOUNTING

11. REMUNERATION UPON TERMINATION (if any)

    (a) recording

    (b) publishing

    (c) live work

    (d) other

12. PERIOD OF POST-TERMINATION REMUNERATION (if any)

    (a) years

    (b) percentages

(Only New South Wales has legislation that specifically affects managers. The Entertainment Industry Act (1991) is discussed fully in the following chapter.)

6
CONTROLLING MANAGERS, AGENTS AND VENUE CONSULTANTS BY LEGISLATION

THE NEW SOUTH WALES MODEL

THE ENTERTAINMENT INDUSTRY ACT 1989 (NSW) IS THE MOST HIGHLY EVOLVED FORM OF REGULATION IN AUSTRALIA OF THE RELATIONSHIP BETWEEN MANAGERS, AGENTS AND PERFORMERS. AMONG OTHER THINGS, IT PROVIDES A SYSTEM OF LICENSING, REGULATES COMMISSION RATES, SETS OUT OBLIGATIONS, AND PROVIDES FOR PENALTIES WHEN THOSE OBLIGATIONS ARE NOT MET.

In 1935, the New South Wales Industrial Arbitration Act 1912 was amended to introduce requirements for the licensing of theatrical agents and employers. In 1952, a Regulation was introduced, limiting agents' fees to 10%.

These laws remained virtually unchanged until in 1987, when a new piece of legislation was passed - the Industrial Arbitration (Theatrical Agents and Employers) Amendment Act (NSW). The uproar from the industry was so great that the government effectively reintroduced the old provisions of the Industrial Arbitration Act in April 1988 and by September of that year, the New South Wales Parliament revoked the 1987 Act altogether. (See the rather grandly titled Industrial Arbitration (Revocation of Proclamation) Act 1988.)

The process of industry consultation that followed was probably unsurpassed in the history of any legislation affecting the Australian entertainment industry. The Minister set up a Committee of Review (headed by the Hon. John Hannaford) which was made up of representatives from various industry organisations, spanning most branches of the industry.

The Committee received 56 submissions from a wide range of groups and individuals.

After this industry consultation the Committee, in an excellent report, recommended establishing a system by which the entertainment industry would 'self-regulate'. (See the Report of the Ministerial Committee To Review

Theatrical Agents and Employers Legislation, February 1989.) At first glance, the concept of a law to help an industry self-regulate looks like a contradiction in terms. In fact, the idea was to impose, on an otherwise unregulated industry, a structure for licences to be issued and policed by representatives of the industry, rather than by bureaucrats. Seen this way, the idea looks much less absurd.

The Entertainment Industry Act (NSW) 1989 came into effect on 18 May 1990. The Act, although not perfect, is the most ambitious and fully articulated system of regulating entertainment industry representatives in Australia. When it was first introduced, other States said that they would treat the experience of New South Wales as a pilot before deciding whether to use it as a model for their own legislation. If they did, it would appear that they either didn't like what they saw or they thought that there were other politically more pressing priorities. No other State has such legislation.

This is an industry that cries out for co-ordinated national treatment. At the moment, the fact that only New South Wales requires licensing, in an industry which by its nature crosses many State borders, continues to cause confusion and uncertainty for performers' representatives based outside New South Wales but who place acts in that State. This is discussed at the end of this chapter.

PURPOSE

The purpose of the Act is to regulate the business relationships between performers and their representatives. The definition of 'performer' for the purposes of the Act includes any actor, singer, dancer, acrobat, model, musician or other performer of any kind.

In this context, 'regulate' means applying certain standards of behaviour and controls to minimise unfair practices or exploitation of inexperienced performers or those with little negotiation power. It is meant to be a life-ring for performers, not a straitjacket on them or their representatives.

THE ENTERTAINMENT INDUSTRY INTERIM COUNCIL

The Act established the Entertainment Industry Interim Council (EIIC) which was given the task of developing a Code of Ethics and the other framework necessary for self-regulation of the industry (such as issuing licences and establishing a tribunal for hearing industry complaints). It was called an Interim Council because it was seen as perhaps being superseded by another body if the Interim Council made recommendations to that effect to the Minister. That was never to be. At the end of the term of its statutorily determined life, the Interim Council dissolved and was not replaced with any other mechanism for industry representation. Now, the former functions of the Industry Council are dealt with as merely administrative issues and are administered entirely by the NSW Department of Industrial Relations.

Before it went, the Interim Council produced a Code of Ethics, though only in draft form. It was far too vague and too general to be of practical assistance to the regulation of the industry. With a few changes of terminology it could have been a model for real estate agents or plumbers. Codes of Ethics are very difficult to draft and if they are to be useful to the industry they seek to regulate, they must be full, detailed and industry specific. This wasn't. It was a waste of time and opportunity.

Any Code of Ethics is largely of cosmetic value unless there is some force or sanction that may be applied to enforce it. The power to grant and remove licences is the single most potent sanction and one that must be exercised with great discretion, since the decision to grant or revoke a licence may have tremendous financial consequences. Refusal to grant a licence, or revocation of an existing licence, would prevent the person from working in the industry. Goodbye Entertainment Industry licence. Hello taxi licence.

ENTERTAINMENT INDUSTRY REPRESENTATIVES

The Act regulates the professional activities of all people acting as entertainment industry representatives. It divides these into the following categories.

'ENTERTAINMENT INDUSTRY AGENT'

This is defined as anyone who:

for financial benefit, carries out any one or more of the following entertainment industry activities on behalf of a performer:

(a) seeking or finding work opportunities for the performer;

(b) negotiating the terms of an agreement for, and the conditions of, a performance;

(c) finalising arrangements concerning the payment of the performer;

(d) negotiating arrangements relating to the attendance of the performer at a performance;

(e) administering the contract of the performer with an entertainment industry employer but does not include a person who carries out those activities solely as an employee of any such agents.

Notice that this applies to anyone who performs these functions for 'financial benefit'. (This expression covers much more than actually being paid money. It covers receiving indirect benefits such as contras and the like.)

The activities covered by the section are very broad. It is hard to think of any activity by performers' representatives that would not come within one or more of the categories of activities. Anyone even remotely involved in the industry should carefully review all their activities to determine whether they are properly licensed under the Act.

The final exemption in this section is included to avoid the absurd situation of all employees having to be licensed as well as their employer.

'MANAGER'

This is defined as being:

> *a person (whether called a personal representative or a personal manager, or otherwise) who, for financial benefit, represents a performer and who agrees, pursuant to a written agreement, to carry out or arrange to be carried out any or all of the activities of an entertainment industry agent and other additional activities or duties specified in the agreement on behalf of the performer but does not include a person who carries out those activities or duties solely as an employee of any such manager.*

Like most legalese, this definition could do with a few full stops to help non-lawyers understand it.

In effect, the definition means that a manager may perform the five functions of an agent but must also perform additional activities or duties for the artist. It is these additional obligations that give rise to the manager's right to charge a greater commission. Given this, it is important that management agreements make it very clear exactly what duties and obligations are being undertaken by the manager in addition to the five functions of an agent.

Also notice that, for a manager to be a 'manager' under the terms of the Act, he or she must have a written agreement with the performer. Unless the manager has a written agreement the 'manager' is restricted to the percentage payable to agents. This is why managers in New South Wales (at least those who know what they are doing) do not do 'hand-shake' deals any more.

'VENUE CONSULTANT'

This is defined as being:

> *a person who acts on behalf of an entertainment industry employer, for a fee or remuneration paid by any such employer and who arranges for a performance by a performer at a particular venue, but does not include a person who arranges for a performance solely as an employee of a venue consultant or an employer.*

This means that venues can arrange for performances without a licence, but anyone arranging performances on a venue's behalf in return for any payment, has to be licensed.

LICENCES

All 'entertainment industry representatives' must have a licence from the Department. The process is cheap. At the time of writing, the application fee is $100 and the licence fees are $200 each.

The expression 'Entertainment Industry Representative' is defined by the Act as meaning an agent, manager or venue consultant. If you work in more than one capacity, you need a licence for each of those activities. For example, being a licensed manager does not authorise you to act as a venue consultant. Venue consultants have their own particular licences. Applicants for any licence must be:

- 'fit and proper';
- over 18 years; and
- with knowledge and experience in the industry.

There are no hard and fast rules as to who is 'fit and proper'. A conviction for an offence involving dishonesty would certainly come within the description but a conviction for driving whilst unlicensed, may not. That said, convictions for drunk driving might well indicate a degree of irresponsibility that would make a person unsuitable for the management role. This is a very subjective criterion.

The last prerequisite is usually met by anyone who can show a reasonable period of activity in the industry or in an area closely related to the activity for which the licence is sought. (Would-be managers who have been performers can usually demonstrate sufficient knowledge simply from having worked in the particular area of the industry for a reasonable time.)

Successful applicants receive 'provisional' licences for the initial 12 months. Licences must be renewed annually. This way, the Department has the opportunity to review licensees who have had complaints lodged against them and can attach conditions to the particular licence.

There are still many managers working in New South Wales who do not know that they have to be licensed. This can be an expensive oversight because unlicensed representatives face penalties of up to $25,000 and may not be able to enforce their management contracts. Of course, merely holding a licence does not instantly make a manager competent, but it does mean there is a mechanism for reviewing their performance, which may benefit the industry in the long run.

One of the other big changes introduced by the Act was that 'theatrical employers' no longer needed to be licensed. This does not mean, however, that those employers are now completely free of regulation. The Department has the power to issue 'directions' to employers and operators of premises concerning any matter relating to the employment of performers and it has the power to enforce these directions.

REGULATION OF FEES

The Act sets maximum fees that industry representatives can charge. These are set out in the Regulations and, in theory, they can be changed at any time if the Minister thinks it appropriate.

AGENTS

Regulation 5 states that the maximum percentage that may be charged is as follows:

> (a) in the case of an engagement involving film, television or electronic media - 10%;
>
> (b) in the case of an engagement involving live theatre or a live musical or variety performance (being an engagement that does not involve film, television or electronic media) - 10% for any period up to 5 weeks and then 5% for any period after 5 weeks;
>
> (c) in all other cases - 10%.

The regulation goes on to state that:

> the following amounts (being amounts payable to performers) are to be excluded when calculating the percentage of fees or other remuneration that an entertainment industry agent or a manager may demand or receive for or in respect of the engagement of a performer:
>
> (a) travelling and meal allowances;
>
> (b) holiday pay;
>
> (c) any long service leave and superannuation payments;
>
> (d) any overtime or penalty payments which are paid on an irregular basis;
>
> (e) any award or minimum payments in respect of rehearsals.

MANAGERS

Section 38 (4) of the Act states that where there is no written agreement between manager and artist 'in respect of an engagement' the manager is limited to charging the agent's commission of 10%. Obviously this is considerably below the usual 15%-20% allowed by most written management agreements. This reference to 'engagements' is ambiguous. This term is not defined in the Act but usually would be given a restricted meaning, namely, 'contracts for live performance'. This would exclude other income such as endorsements and royalties - whether from records or merchandising. If this is so and you are acting as a manager in NSW, unless you have a written agreement with the artist you cannot charge more than 10% for income from live work but may be able to charge the usual rates on everything else.

Although the 10% limit for agents was fairly standard (even if often breached), the 10% limit as to managers' commissions was unheard of before the Act. Now, managers can only charge more than the prescribed 10% in respect of live work if they have a written agreement to that effect with the performer. The whole idea is to force managers to produce written contracts so the performers will be fully aware of what the manager is promising to do, what the manager will charge commission on, and what the manager is permitted to do on the performer's behalf. By requiring the agreement to be put in writing, the chances of 'misunderstandings' and nasty surprises (for both parties) are reduced.

VENUE CONSULTANTS

In the past, people who performed two functions often charged two fees. For example, if the performer's agent also acted as a consultant to the venue, he or she would often charge the act for obtaining the employment and would charge the venue for obtaining the act. This kind of behaviour was always a clear conflict of duty. Under the Entertainment Industry Act, it is also illegal. As a general rule, venue consultants can only receive payment from the venue/employer. The Act also makes it illegal for the venue to deduct any money from the performer's income and pay it to the venue consultant.

In times past, some performers' agents often acted simultaneously as the venue consultant and charged both parties a fee for placing the performer in the venue. Now, if the performer's agent also happens to be a consultant to the venue in respect of the performance, the agent can only charge the venue/employer. If the performer's manager happens to be a consultant to the venue, the manager can collect a commission from the performer but cannot also charge the venue, unless the manager and the performer have a written agreement that permits this.

TRUST ACCOUNTS

It was a long-standing criticism of many managers and agents that they received money for their artists' performances and either banked it in their own account and got it all muddled up with their own money, or failed to keep proper books of account. This prevented even a cursory investigation of where the money might have gone. Fortunately, the Act addresses those problems in a very practical way. It effectively prohibits performers' funds being mixed up with those of the agent or manager.

Now, if entertainment industry agents or managers hold money on behalf of their performer clients, they must establish a separate trust account for each artist. The requirements for the accounts are set out in the Regulations. This is not optional.

The artist's money cannot be held for more than 14 days after the performer becomes entitled to receive it. This overcomes the old problem of managers holding onto their artists' money, using it for their own benefit, and all too often depriving artists of access to their own funds.

RECORDS

Both entertainment industry agents and managers who receive money on behalf of a performer, must maintain proper financial accounts on behalf of that artist. These must be accurate and properly maintained so that they show the true position as regards money received on the performer's behalf. These financial records must be kept at the representative's principal place of business and be made available to the performer upon request.

The Regulations also require that, where an agent or manager receives money on behalf of a performer in relation to an engagement, that person must provide certain (minimum) information to the performer and any other agent or manager who acted for the performer, in respect of that particular performance. These records include:

(a) a statement of the amount received by the agent or the manager on behalf of the performer; and

(b) a statement of the amount paid to the performer for the engagement.

In addition, the manager or agent who receives money on behalf of the performer must provide a statement to the employer (or other person) who paid the performer for the engagement with a statement setting out the amount of money received from that employer.

These statements may vary in form as some managers and agents will have sophisticated computerised systems and smaller operators may use written receipts with carbon copies. Whatever the form, this provides a clear paper trail for the manager, the agent and the performer and emphasises that regular and accurate accounting is a fundamental duty of every manager or agent who receives money on behalf of an artist.

BONDS

If entertainment industry agents and managers hold performers' money, they must lodge a bond with the NSW Department of Industrial Relations. The amount of the bond is $2,000 unless otherwise determined by the Department. This bond can be either be in the form of cash, bank guarantee or other security approved by the Department. If entertainment industry agents are not holding performers' money, they do not need to lodge a bond.

If the agent or manager does anything that causes the performer loss, the Department may assist the performer by releasing all or part of the bond. It can then demand that the agent or manager lodge a further bond. If he or she fails to comply, the licence may be suspended until he or she pays the further bond.

The provision is comparable to the situation with rental bonds. It means that if a problem arises, the expense and delay of obtaining a remedy is minimal because the money is readily available (rather than having to sue for it).

COMPLAINTS COMMITTEE

The Act established a Complaints Committee to investigate complaints regarding:
(a) unfair or dishonest conduct;
(b) unfair entertainment industry contracts; and
(c) any failure to pay amounts owing under an award, industrial agreement or entertainment industry contract.
With the abolition of the EIIC, the Department handles any complaints internally. The complaints procedure is not complex. All that is required is a written complaint to the Department.

If the Department finds that a person is guilty of unfair or dishonest conduct it can order a penalty of up to $500. If it finds that an entertainment industry contract is unfair, harsh or unconscionable, it can redraft the offending clauses. Provided that the parties agree to be bound at the beginning of the inquiry, the Department can make orders up to $20,000 in respect of any failure to pay moneys owed.

The Act contains a very important exception to this power of review. Section 12(4) states that 'An entertainment industry contract or a provision of such a contract which has been fully executed may not be varied under this section'. This is very confusing because 'executed' can mean 'formally signed' or it can mean simply 'performed'. The former meaning doesn't make much sense in this context, because it would mean that any written agreement that had been signed by both parties was outside the scope of the Act. If one party had more bargaining power than the other, it would be easy to insist that the weaker party sign an agreement which contained unfair terms. This would defeat the purpose of the Act, which is to protect both artists and industry agents.

It is more logical to infer that the section uses 'executed' as a synonym for 'performed'. Thus, if both parties have fulfilled their obligations under a contract, neither can go back later and complain that it was unfair.

INTERSTATE REPRESENTATIVES

The application of the Act to interstate managers and agents continues to be uncertain. The generally prevailing view is that any entertainment industry agent, manager or venue consultant carrying on any business within New South Wales must be licensed and, with respect to such activity within New South Wales, must conform to the requirements of the Act. It does not appear to be relevant that the manager, agent, consultant or the performer is usually resident in another State. It is the location of the activity that is relevant.

CONCLUSION

The Act only imposes obligations that even most agents, managers and venue consultants regard as reasonable. Most already had many of the requirements in place before the Act was introduced, but the fact that everyone was not already using these practices made the Act worthwhile.

Having lived with the Act for a few years now, there is a growing realisation that the different branches of the entertainment industry are so varied that different procedures may be needed for different branches. Theatrical agents' operations and needs are quite different from those applicable to musicians' agents. Those of modelling agents differ from those of classical music agents.

This legislation was a bright new industry-backed initiative. Almost two decades later, one has to question whether it was a success. With the demise of the Entertainment Industry Council, the mechanism lost its industry representation and the registration requirement became seen as just another bureaucratic procedure. The industry lost its voice and its feeling of ownership or involvement. The industry didn't fight to retain the Council and there was little evidence of industry commitment to it. The effectiveness of self-regulation always presumes responsibility and perhaps the industry just didn't have it and didn't want it.

In the past, the Department has called for submissions as to the future of the Entertainment Industry Act. Given that its future is uncertain, it is timely to make a few observations.

(a) When the Department took over the operation of the Entertainment Industry Interim Council and the Complaints Committee, it removed the industry's active participation in achieving the goals of the legislation. It became just another bureaucratic procedure.

(b) The Department has never publicly released the necessary data to judge either the effectiveness of the Act or the Department's administrative role. To make such judgments, one needs to know things such as:

- What efforts has the Department made to advertise the existence of the Act and to educate the industry about its responsibilities under it?
- How many complaints have been made under the Act?
- What were the subjects of those complaints?
- Was any type of industry representative more prone to complaint than another?
- What were the findings in respect of the complaints?
- What sanctions have been applied? Has anyone lost their licence?
- Have any agreements been redrafted on the basis of unfairness?
- Has anyone been fined for acting as an industry representative without a licence?
- Has the Department ever exercised its power to issue 'directions' to employers or operators of venues?
- In what circumstances and to what effect?

Without this kind of basic information, it is impossible to respond sensibly to the Department's call for submissions as to the future of the Act. When the Department was asked (twice) to provide answers to these questions for the purposes of this book, the only response was, 'Look at the Department website'. The information was not on the website. This does not indicate great commitment to purposes of the Act on the part of the Department. Indeed, there has been considerable rumour that the government wishes to abolish the Act and by the time you read this, that rumour may have become a reality.

7
PERFORMING LIVE

LIVE PERFORMANCE IS THE BREAD AND BUTTER
OF MOST MUSICIANS. WHETHER YOU ARE A ROCK
STAR, AN OPERA SINGER OR A RESTAURANT PIANO
PLAYER, YOUR INCOME FROM LIVE PERFORMANCE
IS PROBABLY YOUR STAPLE SOURCE OF INCOME.
THIS CHAPTER DISCUSSES THE PROBLEMS INVOLVED
IN PERFORMING AND TOURING, WORKING WITH
AGENTS AND PROMOTERS, OR ORGANISING IT
YOURSELF. IT EXAMINES MANY OF THE BUSINESS
ISSUES THAT MUST BE CONSIDERED WHEN
NEGOTIATING CONTRACTS WITH VENUES AND
PROMOTERS. SAMPLE CONTRACTS ARE INCLUDED.

STARTING OUT ON THE ROAD

Live performance is a fundamental component of the music industry. It's not always pretty, but it's basic. From the 1996 Census it would appear that there are approximately 7,000 professional musicians in Australia and it's a safe bet that 95% of them have played clubs and pubs at some time in their careers.

Many bands play the live circuit in their local area, with little likelihood or expectation of getting further. Every night, there are thousands of musicians playing in pubs and clubs throughout the country. For these people, this is their only work, and for those musicians with families and mortgages and all the usual expenses of adult life, it's a very serious business. Most of these will never be famous nor wealthy (at least from their work as performers). They are professional musicians, providing entertainment to the public. There might be a lot of satisfaction for them, but not much glamour!

For others, particularly in the contemporary/rock scene, playing live is used for honing the skills of the band and attracting a loyal following and attracting the notice that may eventually lead to a record contract. Indeed, delivering a great live show (or a potentially great live show) can be the single critical factor in advancing a band's career. A great live show can attract notice from record companies, publishing companies, and booking agents (who are always looking for a good act to add to their roster).

Once a musician is a successful recording artist, the world changes. Playing live is no longer an end in itself. The clubs and pubs are replaced by specialised music performance venues, concert halls and entertainment centres and the deals get much more complex (in direct proportion to the expectation of profits). Live appearances start to become promotional devices to sell records and T-shirts, rather than the primary income source. Even then, no artist can afford to stop giving value for money at concerts. Meanwhile, the public's expectations of the artist's live work tends to escalate in direct proportion with the number of records the artist sells, as does the cost of performing and the consequences of a below-par performance.

BARGAINING POWER

As in all contractual relationships, the terms governing live performances are directly related to the respective bargaining power of the parties. Musicians at the beginning of their career will do almost anything to get a gig and will accept almost any terms. Those who have a record that is selling well can negotiate reasonable terms, while super-stars can demand terms that can make a promoter's eyes water.

DEALING WITH POTENTIAL EMPLOYERS

If you are starting out, you probably won't have an experienced manager and almost certainly won't have a powerful agent.

You will be personally responsible for scrounging opportunities to perform. This can be lonely and very depressing. Your success in getting work will be almost completely dependent on your own level of energy, persuasion and talents.

You must approach potential venues in an organised and professional way. A disorganised approach will not endear you (unless, perhaps, you are a comedy act) and will only reduce your chances of competing with experienced professionals. Some venues do their own booking but, more commonly, they retain a booking agent or venue consultant to organise the hiring and organising of entertainers. Find out, in advance, how each potential venue does it. The *Australasian Music Industry Directory* is a good place to start. It will provide you with the contact details of the venues and the booking agents. Get on the phone!

How are you going to persuade them to hire you? Not every venue is a potential market for your music, so you might as well do your homework; be selective and be persistent. You will have to sort out which venues are realistic possibilities. Find out what style of music the venue features and what levels of success musicians are expected to have achieved before they are invited to perform there. Often the best way of doing this research is to look at the gig guides and ads in the free street press. If you are not already familiar with your target venues, it is a good idea to go along and familiarise yourself with the way the venue operates, the atmosphere it has and the type of crowd it attracts.

Do you have a top-quality demo CD to show venues, their bookers and agents what you do and how well you do it? Put your best track first. The demo should only have three tracks and must exemplify the style of your music and the quality of your performance. It can be a live performance (because it shows that you can make the transition from the studio to the stage) but there must be no excuses. The demo is your sales instrument. Can you get a friend who is known and trusted by the venue operator to put in a good word for you? Do you have a photo and other publicity and promotional material that can be adapted for the venue to use? Potential employers are not going to put themselves out for you and nor are they likely to take a risk on you. Why should they? It's up to you to convince them!

BASIC TERMS

When you start out, you will find that you are not in a position to demand very favourable terms and you are certainly not going to be getting into heavy negotiations for fear of not being offered the job.

All live performance deals have the same core issues:
- Who is to perform?
- Where is the performance?
- When is it to happen?
- How long must the performance run?
- What will you be performing?
- How much will you be paid, and when?

Then you can add as much detail as you like: transport and accommodation; provision of sound and lighting equipment; arrangements for access for and timing of load in, sound and lighting checks and load out; billing with other artists; promotional responsibilities; food and drink riders, parking and so on.

Venues of any reasonable size will supply you with their 'standard form' booking contract, though some aren't that organised. Some contracts are quite good. Some may be more hindrance than help. You will only find out if you take the trouble to read them before committing yourself to the venue.

If the employer hasn't or won't put the deal in writing, make sure you discuss all the relevant points and then confirm them in writing yourself. Your letter doesn't have to be formal and full of legalese.

Dear Anna,

I enjoyed our discussions on Monday and am pleased that you've booked us to play on March 13th. The following is just a confirmation of my understanding of our deal. If I have misunderstood anything, please contact me at once so that we can sort it out.

Best regards,

You can enclose a **Short Form Booking Confirmation** that will contain the necessary details. The purpose of this document is twofold:

- to ensure that you have the expectations of the venue absolutely clear (and vice versa); and
- to provide some evidence of the terms of the deal in the unfortunate event that things go wrong.

It doesn't have to be signed by both parties: you can be sure that if you have got something wrong, you will get a call from the venue very quickly indeed! Most problems are due to confusion or misinterpretation rather than malice. If you confirm the terms, you can avoid a lot of unnecessary pain.

A short form booking confirmation can look something like this.

SHORT FORM BOOKING CONFIRMATION

ARTIST (a) name ....

(b) address: ....

EMPLOYER (a) name ....

(b) address: ....

PERFORMANCE DETAILS

(a) **Venue**............................... at ....

(b) **Capacity**...

(c) **Date(s)** ....

(d) **Fee** (or basis of calculation) ....

(i) Deposit ....

(ii) Time of deposit payment ....

(iii) Payment shall be by cash immediately after each performance.

(iv) GST: Fee is exclusive of GST. Artist is registered for GST and must provide a GST Tax Invoice.

(e) **Times**

    (i) Equipment access...

    (ii) Sound check..

    (iii) Doors open...

    (iv) Performance

        (a) no. of sets...

        (b) duration of a set...

        (c) duration of breaks..

    (v) Equipment removal ....

(f) **Cover charge** $ ....

(g) **Stage requirements**..

....

(h) **Power requirements** ....

(i) **Order of billing**..

(j) **Transport arrangements**...

(k) **Accommodation** ....

(l) **Promotion arrangements** ....

(m) **Refreshments arrangements** ....

(n) **Special provisions**..

Signed by/for and

on behalf of Artist...

Date ....

Signed by/for and

on behalf of Employer..

Date ....

ENFORCEMENT OF THE DEAL

The best thing you can do is to join the Musicians' Union or the Media Arts and Entertainment Alliance. This way you gain at least some protection and someone to be on your side. These Unions act to make sure employers do not impose less than the minimum conditions of employment. Of course, most musicians at the beginning of their career will accept almost any deal in the hope that they will get a break. Most don't even go to the trouble of finding out what their union believes are minimum conditions. You should.

Sharp operators who abuse young musicians often end the evening with the biggest insult of all: they don't pay up. If you are a member of a Union, you can call on its help. They have full-time officers who chew ankles on behalf of their members. If you're not a member, your choices are limited, generally expensive, and very lonely.

TAX

Don't destroy your relationship with the venue (or its consultants) by complaining because it insists on deducting tax from your fees. It is obliged to do this unless you can prove that you are a registered company or a formal partnership with a tax file number.

Some of the venues won't know their legal obligations, but most do. If you don't want the tax taken out at source, make it easy for the venue and be prepared to provide all of the requirements they need, which are as follows.

(i) If your group is a registered company, you must supply the employer with the ABN of your company.

(ii) If your group is a partnership, you must supply the ABN of the partnership.

(iii) If you haven't formalised a company or partnership structure, at least make sure that you can supply the ABN of everyone in the group. However, most venues just want to deal with one ABN and usually, one of the members of the group gives his or her ABN to the venue, gets paid, and then has to pay the other members of the group. This means that the person who distributes the money has to make sure that he or she has the ABN of each of the band members. It is unsatisfactory, but if the venue demands it, what small band can refuse?

(iv) If you turn over $50,000 (or in the course of the year might do so), make sure that you are registered for GST and always supply a valid tax invoice. If GST is payable and you aren't registered or haven't supplied a proper tax invoice, there is no way that the venue can pay you the GST component of the fee and claim it back. You will have to pay the tax out of your fee. Even if you do not expect to earn $50,000 or more, many musicians are finding that it is worth registering for GST simply because it is reassuring for the venue to know that it has fulfilled its GST obligations and that it can off-set the payment against the GST that it has collected. (For further information on GST, see Chapter 35, **Keeping the Books**.)

THE ROLE OF THE AGENT

In every city there are a few key agencies and every band wants to be on their books. If you need an agent, the first step is to read the Booking Agents' listings in the *Australasian Music Industry Directory*. Consider the alternatives. Some are quite large organisations. Some are very small. Size, as they say, is not necessarily important. You may be better off in a small agency where you may get more individual service than in the larger agencies, where the priority is likely to be given to the most established money earners. On the other hand, being in a larger agency may give you the opportunity to share the bill with established acts and this can provide valuable exposure and experience.

Moreover, it is important to work out which agencies specialise in your sort of music. Agents who book rock usually don't book dance music, children's music, chamber orchestras, jazz or country music. To save time, and your dignity, make sure that the agent you approach is at least interested in your genre of music.

Once you have sorted out some preferences, nothing beats going around asking other artists and venues of their experiences with various booking agents.

An honest, enthusiastic agent can make you a lot of money and get you good, high-profile venues. The alternative doesn't bear thinking about! Assuming you can get a serious agent to take you on, he or she will try to get you work that is suitable to your talent and level of development. If you are in big demand, your agent will sift the offers and act as a first line of defence!

For further information, refer to Chapter 4, **Agents**.

TOURING

There is a myth in the music industry that you can't make money out of touring in Australia. Like all myths, although the statement itself is demonstrably wrong, it hints at some important truths.

As a general rule, 'agents' book Australian acts for performances in Australia, whereas 'promoters' book international acts for performances in Australia. That said, there are situations in which a local promoter conceives of a completely local show and decides to put it all together. The promoter hires the venue, contracts with the act, arranges sound, lights and publicity, contracts with suppliers of food and beverages. It then sets and charges a ticket price reflecting the costs of mounting the show plus the desired profit margin. In this chapter, references to 'promoters' are local promoters who are staging the entire show.

Where the act uses an agent, it is the agent who has to sell the act to the venues and contract those venues. The performer's manager or tour manager will arrange transport and accommodation and liaise with the venue about sound, lighting, publicity, media and so on. As well as taking on most of the administrative nightmares, the agent may guarantee the act minimum fees that will be paid whether or not an audience shows up. If you are organising the tour yourself, you don't have the luxury of having an agent to do most of the basic administration. It's all up to you.

Remember that in the field of live performance, nobody has to stay in concrete roles: depending on the circumstances (and the potential for profit), the hat that one wears in one venture may be quite different in another. For example, sometimes the artist acts as a DIY-agent and does deals directly with the venues. At other times, an artist's agent may be retained by a venue to act as its booker; that venue may be only interested in booking acts for its own venue or may also operate as a quasi-promoter, funding the whole tour and selling-off shows to other venues. In still other situations, the agent of a tour will be dealing with some venues that act only as venue operators and others that are acting both as venue operators and quasi-promoters. Obviously there are important differences between these deals. Theoretically they are completely different but in practice, because so many venue operators also act as quasi-promoters, and so many agents act as quasi-promoters, the line between venue and promoter and between promoter and agent, can often be a thin one.

At the end of the day it comes down to negotiating exactly what each party is going to contribute to the staging of the event. Because of this, labels are often misleading and it is only functions that are important.

DOING IT YOURSELF
PLANNING THE TOUR
Whether the tour is interstate or only intrastate, because of the distances between cities, the pre-tour planning must be meticulous.

Planning the itinerary is an art form in itself. Whether you book the shows yourself or through an agent, make sure that the routing is cost effective. No doubling back, no touring out from a central base (and thus doubling the distance travelled). Travel costs have to be kept to a minimum.

How many people do you really need in your entourage? Keeping the touring party as small as possible is a good start. Every wage, fare and hotel tab comes out of your profit. Could you pick up the people you will need to run the shows while you are on the road, or do you have to take them with you? You might choose to take your own sound person, but you might find that a local operator (who is used to the dynamics of the room and its sound system) would be both cheaper and more effective. If you require accompaniment or additional musicians, does it make sense to take them with you or is it more cost effective to pick up new musicians in each city or region? Do you really need to take a guitar technician as well as a roadie? Will having both make the proposed tour uneconomic? Can you afford not to take technical help? Although precautions against technical and instrument problems can cost money, a performance marred by unnecessary and annoying technical glitches will be remembered long after you leave town.

You must leave yourself enough time between performances to do the necessary travel and to recuperate from the strains of both travel and performance. It's a difficult balancing act. You must maximise your earning potential without exhausting yourself. The longer the tour, the greater the strain. Do too much and, by the end of the tour, you will hate yourself and the whole touring party. Whatever Neil Young may say about it being better to burn out than fade away, if you are too exhausted to bring 100% to the show, a mediocre performance has the potential to do untold damage to your credibility with the audience.

Whether you fly, train bus or drive, is a matter for your individual budget and the requirements of the tour schedule. If the tour is Sydney- Melbourne-Adelaide-Perth in two weeks, planes are the answer. If you are touring from Brisbane to Melbourne, performing at thirty secondary population centres in between, air travel is probably the most expensive and least convenient way of doing it.

Accommodation is always an issue on a tour. Everyone likes to stay in ritzy hotels with gold-plated taps, but hotels like that cost a lot and all those costs come out of your pocket. Choose good-value accommodation, ask for the corporate rate and remember to avoid the usual traps like the mini-bar and using the telephone in your hotel room. You pay a fortune for those little conveniences. Those who have gone before you and established a touring circuit will know about the good-value motels and hotels which can tolerate tired musicians coming back late at night, and might even allow a late check-out to accommodate your need for rest. It pays to ask around.

BUDGET PREPARATION

Budget the tour costs thoroughly and pessimistically. Remember the general rule is - things always cost more than you think and you always make less than you deserve. If you budget accordingly, you won't go far wrong. Where you can get an accurate costing on a budget item, do so. If you have to use an estimate, talk to others who have done similar tours and find out what their actual costs were and add in a factor for cost increases. To these costs, add a 10%-15% contingency. You will need it.

An example of a tour budget is set out at the end of this section. It shows the expenditure items down the left side. Each day's expenditure is set out in columns, to give a total figure. Don't forget to set a reasonable per diem for everyone. Food, drink, accommodation and local travel requirements all have to be taken into account in striking an allowance for each member of the travelling group. These costs, called 'per diems' should be paid - not only because it is fair to the individuals but also because it provides budgeting certainty for the business. If someone wants to order a bottle of Veuve Cliquot after the show, they can, but it goes on their personal bill, not the band's.

A competent manager and tour manager will know the likely costs for each item, how to assemble accurate costings, how to minimise your costs and how to keep the tour on budget. This expertise is essential, but choose carefully. If you haven't worked with a particular tour manager before, don't just put your faith in the big-time names they put on their resumes. Talk to the people who used them.

EXAMPLE TOUR BUDGET			
EXPENSES	**DAY 1**	**DAY 2**	**DAY 3**
Transport			
Air-fares			
Freight			
Insurances			
Sound mixer			
Lighting			
Hired lighting			
Equipment Hire			
Electrician			
Rigger			
Loaders			
Guitars/drum tech			
Door person			
Catering			
Accommodation			
Publicist			
Media Production			
Posters – artwork/printing			
Communication			
APRA (if promoter/venue)			
PPCA (if promoter/venue)			
Per diems			
Postage and couriers			
Contingency			
Sub totals			

FUNDING THE TOUR

A budget is no use unless it can be funded. Once you have a budget that is as accurate as you can achieve, work out how you are going to cover the costs. There are many options. Is it coming from your savings; is the record company advancing the tour costs; are you using advances from your publishing company; do you have a sponsor; are you gambling on making enough from ticket sales to cash flow the tour? If you are relying on ticket sales, you are entering very risky waters indeed. Such grand gestures are usually rewarded with great pain.

Don't forget that you may be able to avoid some of your costs by getting those engagingly named benefits, 'freebies' and 'contras'. For example, you may get free accommodation with a motel chain, poster printing or perhaps reduced van-hire, in return for some quite simple promotion work during the tour or in the show.

CONTRACTING THE PERFORMANCES

Performers who are sufficiently established to mount a tour of any real size will probably have an agency to take care of much of the negotiating and contracting with venues and venue bookers. Whether you have an agent or not, you or your manager should always be involved in the planning for and the negotiations of tour dates and conditions. After all, you are the one that will have to perform on the night. It's your reputation on the line.

DOING IT WITH AN AGENT OR A PROMOTER

Even Dick Smith doesn't sell a gauge that will measure the honesty and professionalism of agents or promoters. You don't need any formal qualifications to call yourself either an agent or a promoter. They are relatively unregulated. There is no real industry supervision of standards. There are those who survive and there are those who don't. They come from many different backgrounds: some were musicians, tour managers, roadies, accountants or lawyers. Some are business men and women who are devotees of particular acts. Most are inspired by the belief that their individual talents will give them the edge needed to make dollars from an act which other promoters either didn't recognise as a money spinner or couldn't sign.

One glance at the 'Agent' and 'Promoter' listings in the *Australasian Music Industry Directory* shows some are large and famous companies. Others aren't and never will be. Some have substantial administrations while others have only a mobile phone and an old station wagon with a stained mattress in the back. Some deal with tours of major entertainment centres and huge open-air venues. Others deal with city clubs and country dance halls.

At every level of the live performance business, life is highly competitive. The agents and promoters who are well established and have national and international reputations vie for the biggest national and international acts. These operators maintain substantial offices and staff; if you ring them this week they will be on the same number next week. There is a frighteningly fast turnover amongst smaller fry, simply because one substantial loss is likely to harpoon the whole operation, unless it has substantial cash reserves or an amazingly understanding bank manager.

The smaller companies attract less famous acts but run smaller operations. This doesn't necessarily mean they make less money. Quite the reverse. They can make more over-all, because they can negotiate favourable deals with artists who do not have the commercial clout of a major act, they spend less on establishing and maintaining the relationships and can have much lower overheads. In other words, they can turn over many small deals at a profit, rather than have to take on the riskier business of taking on a relatively small number of large promotions, each of which may reap large profits but which might just as easily end as an enormous loss. When touring the largest acts, one act that fails to draw the anticipated crowds can wipe out the profit earned from all the other events promoted during the year.

PROMOTER ATTITUDES

If you are a musician and have been offered a deal with a local or overseas promoter, it is important to find out about the individual and the company. Talk to people who know about and have dealt with the promoter. Remember that a promoter is a sales professional so you expect the spiel to be good. They won't volunteer to tell you of their weaknesses. Why should they be different from the rest of humanity? You have to find out about those for yourself. In other words, your decision must be an informed one.

As a musician, you must remember that your interests will not always coincide with the promoter's. You need to have a long-term view of your career, but some promoters (certainly not the majority of them) can be preoccupied with turning a profit out of the immediate opportunity. You may see the tour as a means of promoting your new album, whereas the promoter is hoping to sell enough seats to cover the costs and have enough left over to pay the rent on Monday. Your album only matters to the promoter if publicity for it will help sell tickets.

The promoter's prime concern is to make a profit (or at least to lose as little as possible) on the first tour. After that, the promoter can see if the first tour created a demand that would justify another tour and another and so on. By then, the promoter will be able to make a profit (if all goes according to plan) and the artist will probably get a better deal too. Of course, superstars or artists with established 'draw' cause promoters less worry, but the same considerations apply; a good tour will encourage more touring by that artist, which should benefit both the artist and the promoter.

Because of this different perspective and motivation, the parties to the touring agreement must take particular care over the details of the relationship. What you take to be obvious and 'goes without saying' may not be part of the other party's needs, desires or intentions.

THE LETTER OF INTENT

The first conflict between the promoter's interests and those of the artist, is that the promoter will not wish to enter a binding commitment with the act until it is sure that the necessary tour arrangements are in place. The act, on the other hand, does not want to block out a large section of its bookings-diary, merely on the strength of a 'may-be', nor does the act want a promoter using the act's name or starting rumours about a forthcoming tour, unless the tour will definitely happen.

To avoid this, promoters and artists usually enter a Letter of Intent. This should make it clear that the parties are prepared to negotiate but have not entered a final and binding agreement. Its wording should give the promoter sufficient security to make preliminary inquiries, arrangements and venue reservations but should limit the extent to which the promoter can use the artist's name and reputation. Frequently, they will contain a requirement that the artist not negotiate with any other promoter, at least until the detailed negotiations with the present promoter are concluded.

If the negotiations drag on, the delay can disadvantage either or both parties. If negotiations fall through at the last moment, the promoter may already be financially committed and this could be used by a hard-hearted artist's manager as a bargaining tool to negotiate for better terms. On the other hand, if the deal falls through at the last moment, the artist may not have an opportunity to get other work during the period. Both are at risk of losing money. Both have an incentive to make it work.

REMUNERATION

Although the financial arrangements between artists and venues or artists and promoters vary enormously, there are a number of classic deal types.

THE SET PERFORMANCE FEE

Some acts simply contract for a set fee per performance. They get that fee whether 1,000 people turn up or just the drummer's mum. This type of deal is the most secure arrangement for the artist, but does not provide any opportunity for it to participate in the profits, assuming there are any.

THE PERCENTAGE OF GROSS OR NET

Many of the major popular music acts work on a percentage of the gross revenue earned by the performance before any deductions are made for overheads or costs ('the gross'). Obviously this gives the act the greatest opportunity for 'blue sky' profit. On the other hand, it limits the potential profits for the promoter. In Australia at least, this kind of deal seems to be very much the exception rather than the rule. In the United States, deals based on the gross are more common. Some of the super-groups can demand up to 85% of the gross, where they supply their show as a complete package, leaving the venue/promoter to be, in effect, a glorified administrator. When those stars come to Australia, they demand similar deals from the local promoters.

Promoters are wary of deals based on the gross, because they can leave the promoter in a very precarious position if the promoter has to meet the costs out of its small share before it sees any profits. Any hiccup could mean financial disaster.

In Australia, it is usual for the promoter to pay for lighting, accommodation and freight within Australia for personnel and gear. Deals that provide for the promoter to deduct nominated expenses before calculating the artist's percentage ('net' deals) are preferred here, because they give the promoter some comfort, by allowing it to recover its expenses 'off the top'. If the percentage is to be calculated on net rather than on the gross, the percentages will be between 75% and (absolute tops) 90% of net.

Ironically, what works for the most powerful musicians is also used by some of the weakest. All Australian musicians who have worked in pubs will be familiar with the 'door deal'. As with any payment arrangement, there are numerous variations but, basically, the band doesn't get a fee for performing but instead, gets the venue's cover-charge (or a share of the cover charge) paid by the audience while the pub gets the bar-profits. No risk for the pub, high risk for the artist. It is also in breach of the Musicians' Award.

FEE AGAINST PERCENTAGE OF THE GROSS OR NET

This provides the artist with a minimum fee but also a potential share in the profits, e.g. the deal may be $20,000 against either 50% of the gross or a larger percentage of the net. (What this means is that you get the greater of $20,000 or 50% of the gross.)

As an example: if the gross turned out to be $80,000, the act would get $40,000 (i.e. the $2,000 fee plus another $20,000, to make it up to 50% of the gross). If, however, the event was not so successful and only grossed $30,000, the act would still get its $20,000, but that would be all, because the minimum fee was greater than 50% of the gross. The same principles apply if done on a net basis, but of course the percentages would change accordingly.

For a smaller act doing its own deal with a venue, this is the proper way to do a legal 'door deal'. There has to be a guaranteed minimum fee (which is not less than the minimum Award payment see http://www.musicians.asn.au/union/rates.html) against the artist's share of the door takings. In other words, the artist gets whichever amount is the greater.

FEE AGAINST STAGGERED PERCENTAGE OF THE GROSS

Again this provides a minimum fee, but the artist's entitlement to participate in the gross escalates with the success of the venture, so the artist may receive the minimum fee but no percentage unless the gross reaches certain trigger points. For example:

Gross 0 – $20,000   = zero participation
Gross $20,001 – $40,000   = escalation to 10% of gross
Gross $40,001 – $60,000   = escalation to 15% of gross
Gross $60,001 – $80,000   = escalation to 20% of gross
Gross $80,001 +   = escalation to 25% of gross

This is a frequently used structure, as it provides the artist with a guaranteed fee and still allows for equitable profit participation as the increments are gradual and the promoter still has an incentive to make the gross as big as possible.

NET PARTICIPATION DEALS

The net deals which are favoured in Australia (all the major promoters here do net deals), can be just as fair to both parties, but the fact that certain expenses can be deducted 'off the top' complicates the contracting and the accounting somewhat. As with any deal based on net figures, two problems arise: first, what expenses are permissible deductions from the gross; and, second, what proof is there that the money was actually spent? Only certain types of expenses should be allowed as deductible and the artist should always be supplied with documentary verification of all expenses that are to be deducted from the gross.

THE FOUR WALLS DEAL

These are many variations on this one. Sometimes the venue operator acts as the promoter of an event, so it supplies the venue and the artist supplies the whole package that goes in it. Sometimes the venue will supply the staff and all sound and lighting production, leaving publicity material and so on to be supplied by the act. If the act is bigger, the venue often supplies the staff but the act supplies all sound and lighting production. Because of the flexibility of this deal, it is frequently used by major acts, who don't need guarantees and who can supply a show as a complete package.

Even the means by which the venue makes a profit varies. Some will want just a set hire fee, others take a hire fee against a share of the profits and still others work on a straight profit-split. Sometimes the merchandising will be handled by the venue.

PAYMENT

When working out the basic performance fee, always define the amount of the deposit and the timing of its payment. Similarly, make it clear when the balance will be due and whether it will be paid by bank cheque, cash or (as Chuck Berry made famous) gold bullion.

Getting paid is probably the greatest area of concern - at least for the act. Again, you will get no better information about promoters and venues than what you can learn from artists who have been there before you. What is the proposed venue's or promoter's reputation in the business? How efficient has the administration been? Was there any delay in paying for the transport costs or paying the deposit? Was the promised standard of accommodation provided, or was it approaching the kennel end of the market? Was the promotion of the promised quality? Look for signs of financial trouble and keep several grains of salt handy when listening to any (no doubt very plausible) explanations to justify digressions from the agreed plan.

It is easy to say that you should only work with promoters or venues that have a nice fat bank account but the fact is even the biggest operators have their cash-flow problems from time to time. Promoters who are handling the lower end of the market will often be scratching to make the final payment. All too often it is the artists who end up losing out when another ambitious, convincing, but under-funded promoter goes broke.

Most of the big acts demand 50% of their total fee to be paid as a deposit. This deposit is payable when the contract is signed. To protect each party's interests, the balance is often paid into an 'escrow account' (i.e. a kind of trust account, in which the money is held until it is due to be paid to the artist) well before the performance. Bank guarantees or letters of credit are also used, particularly where the fees are large.

The first time a major act signs with a promoter, each party will be very cautious about payment arrangements. Often, however, after they have worked together a few times and developed a more personal relationship, the rigour of the arrangements as to payment may well relax. This eases the pressure on everyone, but is no reason for either to become complacent. If the fees relate to a tour (rather than just one or two performances) the contract will usually include a schedule showing when payments are due to the artist. The deposit will be paid at the time of contracting and the balance (less an agreed proportion that is held in escrow) will be paid before the first concert. The papers, authorising the release of the sum held in escrow, are often signed just before the final show starts.

International acts present a special problem as the promoter has to withhold a large proportion of the artist's fee until tax returns have been processed. As the returns cannot be submitted until the tour has finished, this means the act will be long-gone from these shores by the time the tax is sorted out. For this reason, a local accountant experienced in touring Australia and New Zealand is appointed to supervise the process. When the figures have been finalised, the withholding tax is deducted from the escrow account before the balance is paid to the artist.

AUDIENCE NUMBERS

Most tour agreements will set a maximum number of people permitted into the venue at any performance. This is important for safety reasons, but it also affects the artist's fee when it is calculated on the number of tickets sold. Knowing the venue's capacity (excluding complimentary seats) means the artist can estimate the maximum fee likely to be earned in that venue.

Setting a maximum number is easy. Setting a minimum is harder, but a minimum figure should also be provided. In this type of deal, the promoter guarantees a minimum number of ticket sales (even if the tickets are not eventually sold) or a minimum percentage of the maximum figure. This way, the musicians know they can meet their budget break-even point, even if the ticket sales are less than 100% of the venue's capacity. This obviously creates a risk for everyone else, which is one of the reasons why, in this kind of deal, usually only a limited number of concerts will be committed to at any one time, though the promoter/venue operator will want options for further concerts, should ticket sales warrant them.

TICKET PRICES

Setting the right ticket price is a mix of accounting and black magic. Experienced promoters, venue operators and artist managers know the limits of their market very well. Artists must remember that the ticket price determines how much the artist and the promoter will each make. Set the price too high and the venue might be empty. Too low and tickets could sell well, but the show still lose money. For those who do attend, their memory of an overcrowded show will certainly include their perception of whether they thought that they got value for money, which will influence whether they will buy a ticket the next time you tour. It might also influence whether they will buy your just-released album.

TICKET SALES

In almost all situations, the box-office will be operated by the venue management. While most play the game honestly, many notorious tricks have been used over the years to short-pay artists. A few years ago, a major Australian entertainment auditorium was hit by scandal when it was discovered that senior individuals in the management were running a scam to get an unauthorised slice of the money paid by or to people hiring the venue. (The laws of defamation prevent the tale being told!) The important point is if the biggest venues can have these problems, you can bet the smaller, less well-supervised venues have their share of problems too.

Most of the scams can be overcome by careful supervision of ticket sales. The contract might include the following safeguards.

> *A designated representative of the Artist will have access to the box office at all times and must view both opening and closing ticket stubs or register roll. Further, the Employer must permit the Artist's nominee to supervise each entrance and all door takings.*

Similarly, even if you are just doing a 'door deal', include a term in the contract that allows you to have a representative on the door to check the count of patrons and the operation of the guest list.

Remember, having this in the contract is fine, but why bother including the clause if you do not actually use it to inspect the tickets and verify sales? Be active in looking after your own interests.

It is standard that the venue be required to sell tickets in numerical order and the agreement often even specifies how the cash register itself will be operated. For example:

> *The Employer must sell tickets to all patrons, in numerical order. If a cash register is used, then every sale must be rung up from a zero point on the register.*

Counterfeit tickets are always a concern for big concerts. Generally, the employer will be responsible for losses incurred through fraud so they have an incentive to put detection procedures in place. The bigger the act, the greater the incentive for counterfeiters and the more elaborate the protections needed.

COMPLIMENTARY TICKETS

This is always a matter for discussion, because the number of tickets given away (by any of the parties involved) will affect the profitability of the show. Everyone in town wants a ticket if it is a freebie. The musicians will want tickets for family and friends, the promoter will want some, the venue will sometimes try to build in some freebies; and not giving a reasonable number of free tickets to the record company is not a great career move. Sometimes the matter of free entry to the performance will be simply handled with a "door list" of guests' names. It is important to liaise with the promoter and venue about the door list policy for each performance.

The artist and the promoter have an incentive to keep down the number of free seats because free tickets affect the profit line. Obviously, allocating some to potentially useful people (e.g. relevant record company and publishing staff) is a good move. Giving free tickets to press reviewers and the winners of competitions or give-aways may be a good use of tickets.

Free tickets for the venue should be resisted unless there is a really good reason for them. Unless kept under control, the venue could simply sell its allocated quota of free seats and pocket the whole ticket price. This amounts to either greater profits for the venue or (if it genuinely doesn't know this is happening) a handsome 'under the table' business for someone working for the venue.

On the other hand, if sales are down, you will probably give a lot of tickets away and giving them away costs you nothing if they were not going to sell anyway. If you wallpaper the room with complimentary guests, at least you can create a decent atmosphere so that the critics (and those who actually paid for their tickets) don't slaughter you. The only thing more miserable than attending a half-empty concert is to play at one.

SUPPORT ACTS

This is the position in which most start-out acts find themselves. Having a support act benefits more or less everyone involved in the tour because:
- (a) the audience probably feels it is getting better value for money - two acts (or more) instead of one;
- (b) it relieves the pressure on the headline act, provided they select a good support act (though headline acts are well aware that a headline act always runs the risk of being blown off the stage by a really hot support act);
- (c) the promoter gets more to promote and support acts don't add all that much to the cost of putting a show on;
- (d) the support act gets experience and may benefit from being associated with a headline act.

Generally, the headlining act will have the right of approval of all support acts, the order of billing and all of the publicity material for the show. This is particularly relevant where an act is selected to support a really major international act. As soon as a major act announces a forthcoming tour there is usually a sustained battle behind the scenes, as a flotilla of managers jostle for position in the hope of getting their act onto the tour as the support.

Sometimes support acts are paid, sometimes they aren't. Commonly, they are paid their usual fee but sometimes the promoter will only make the offer on the basis that the gig will be done for free. (This isn't always the promoter's fault; sometimes where the headline act is responsible for the cost of the support act, it is the act that is responsible. How soon we forget how hard it used to be!) In Europe and the United States there have been examples where the support act (or rather its record company) is charged a large fee for the honour of performing. (See **Buying In**, below.) The question is: How much is the promotional opportunity worth?

When a support band is booked, there has to be negotiation as to the use of production facilities (mixing desks, instruments, backline, mikes etc.) and lights. Some headline acts allow the support act to use their equipment but others don't. Some will charge the support act a fee for use, which may help offset the hire costs or might just be a bit extra on the bottom line. It should go without saying, but being objectionable to the headline act and/or its road crew is both childish and bad business. They can make your touring very easy and enjoyable or very difficult, simply by increasing or decreasing your access to the equipment they control. Most major acts remember what it was like to be a support act, but don't push your luck by antagonising them or their crew.

BUYING IN

In Europe, the really major acts turn this competition into a nice little earner - they often put the support spot out to tender. Best offer gets the gig. This can cost a support act (or its record company) a lot of money if the tour is likely to be really major. It doesn't happen (we are told!) in Australia or North America.

At one level, it can be looked upon as a sad abuse of young talent by those who have made it to the top. Buy-in fees of $50,000-$80,000 are not uncommon in Europe, so you would have to hope that the gamble pays off! If you are looking to your record company to make the payment, you will have to negotiate the basis of the payment. Will it be paid as 'tour support', which is usually either fully or 50% recoupable, or will it come out of the promotion budget and therefore be non-recoupable?

On the other hand, buying-in might be a great career move. The support act (if the publicist is good) stands to get dozens of column-inches of free publicity, plus entry to industry parties and the chance to meet real power brokers in the industry. It can be a major turning point for an act's career if fate is kind although, as always, there are no guarantees! The support act has to hope that the cost of buying onto the tour will be recovered from record sales, or the advance account will start to look like the national debt of some smaller South American nations.

FESTIVALS AND EVENTS

Several regular and large multi-artist music festivals have become a fixture of the Australian touring circuit. These include the Big Days Out, The Falls Festival, Splendour in the Grass and the Byron Bay Blues Festival. Getting a billing on these is a sought-after gig. An appearance at such a festival is likely to expose an artist's music to a large and possibly new crowd. Sometimes the festival features more than one stage area, often loosely organised by genre, which can increase the chance of an artist who performs in such a genre securing a spot. Each act has to look after its interests and fight for a position on the billing. If there are going to be several acts on the one show, the order of performance is always a matter of negotiation. Usually, the show starts with the least established act and works through to the headliners, but this is not always so.

Co-operation in the use of available facilities is very important where numerous acts are using limited stage areas, with little set-up time between performances.

PUBLICITY

INTERVIEWS

Most of the big-name touring musicians have a clause in their contract that forbids the employer from setting up any personal appearances, interviews or any other form of promotion without their consent. This is not to prevent publicity. Promotion is in everyone's interests. Rather, it is to make sure that the artists' time, and the opportunity for promotion, is used as effectively as possible while remaining considerate of personal needs such as rest and recreation. Less established acts will probably be delighted that the employer has bothered and been able to organise some press interest. Any limitations or obligations in regard to media and publicity will be specified in the performance agreement.

PROMOTIONAL MATERIALS

Artists should, whenever possible, supply their own publicity material. This way they can be sure that it will be right. Artists should have a standard media package containing up-to-date photographs, biographical and professional profiles on each artist, perhaps a sampler CD containing some strong tracks, posters and handbills (or at least the artwork for the promotional material) which the local employers can use to promote the concert.

If there are other acts on the bill, there will have to be negotiation as to their order and manner of representation in the publicity material. Generally the order of performance reflects the order in which acts are promoted.

Often, discussions even get down to the comparative size and typeface of the names in publicity material.

PRESS RELEASES

Really organised artists even prepare and deliver their own pre-concert press releases so that they can be sure that the local media know the artists are coming to town and issue post-concert press releases, so those who didn't send a reporter to cover the concert will still hear about it. Many regional and local newspapers will run with these press releases, because they are short of local news. If the press release is well prepared, you often find it being used almost word for word. Remember; half the difficulty of getting newspaper coverage is putting the story into a form that makes it easy for an overworked journalist (or one who intends not to be overworked).

USING THE RECORD COMPANY

If you are signed to a record company, the company's promotions department may want to be involved in all the negotiations affecting publicity. It may want to make sure that there are advertisements in the program, as well as posters advertising your recorded product. No promoter objects to the involvement of the record company. It is in everyone's interests to maximise promotion of the artists and the show. The record company may supply records and other publicity material to be given away in conjunction with the radio promotions for the concert. The record company wants to be involved because successful shows usually result in record sales.

If you are really persuasive, and the record company agrees that it is a good idea, it might even contribute to the advertising campaign for the tour and take the opportunity to cross-promote the record.

OTHER USES OF THE ARTIST'S NAME
AND REPUTATION

Musicians are becoming increasingly aware of how a reputation can be affected by corporate tie-ups and, conversely, how their reputations are valuable to advertisers. Elton John, Ray Charles, Michael Jackson, Kylie Minogue, Pink, Beyonce and Britney Spears have all had very public associations with particular sweet, fizzy drinks. Those relationships are complex and fiercely negotiated and are mutually very rewarding. No sponsored artists can be associated with a rival cola or even seen with a can of 'the other brand' in their hands, for fear of breaching their agreements with their 'own' brand of drink.

All uses of the name and photographs of an artist should be approved by the artist's management and their use limited to advertisements for the show. For example, the name or photograph of the artist should not be used to endorse any commercial product or company, except with the artist's prior written consent.

Conversely, resist signs, banners or advertising material being displayed on or near the stage, unless the artist has approved it. After all, that advertiser is promoting its goods or services by associating them with the talent and reputation of the acts appearing on stage. In a perfect world, artists would always be able to insist on being advised of any advertisers or sponsors at the time they sign their performance contract. Alternatively, they would have the right of approval of corporate tie-ups. It's a pity this is not a perfect world.

MERCHANDISING

The contract will specify who has the merchandising rights to the performance, what can be sold and what will happen to the profits. There is no rule: sometimes the artist controls it completely; others the employer does; sometimes the venue does. (See Chapter 27, **Merchandising**.)

PRACTICAL CONSIDERATIONS

Experienced touring artists know the joys and aggravation of touring. Those new to the business need to be aware of some of the traps and practical matters with which they will have to deal. Following are some of the more important ones.

SET UP

On the day of the engagement, the road crew usually needs full and unrestricted access to the venue, stage, and power supply at least seven hours before the audience is admitted. If a support act is used, then the headlining artist usually has the first right to set up all instruments, equipment and risers to be used in the performance. This equipment should never be moved, or used by anyone other than the headline artist's crew, without approval of either the headliner's production manager or stage manager. All of this can (and should) be set out in the performance contract.

Necessary sound and lighting checks should be arranged before the audience is admitted, at any time set by the tour manager. Most artists seem to need at least an hour to set up and have a sound check. Access to the venue should be limited strictly to authorised personnel during checks. After all, this is the time for making errors and correcting them. You don't want anyone (other than those in the inner sanctum) listening to the preparation process.

The placement of the sound and lighting consoles should be subject to the approval of the tour manager. Where any public address system, amplifier, lights, or any instrument or equipment is to be provided by the venue, it must be to the specifications of the tour manager, of proper quality and in good working condition. The contract should specify this.

Remember too that basic activities, such as parking the musicians' vehicles, can cause problems unless prior arrangements have been made. Always try to arrange for the musicians' vehicles to be parked as close to the venue as possible.

PERFORMANCE DETAILS

Most venues are very specific about the minimum time that the performance should last. After all, an audience that has paid top dollar for a thirty-five minute show is not going to be happy.

If a master of ceremonies is required, this should be discussed at the outset. Many bands include a clause prohibiting the use of an MC. Most crowds are annoyed by the distraction of an MC. They have paid to hear the music, not a speech perhaps littered with bad jokes.

SECURITY ARRANGEMENTS

The venue should provide adequate security to ensure the safety of the musicians and their employees and equipment at all times, as well as proper supervision and orderly conduct of the audience. The stage has to be safe, properly constructed and sheltered.

Backstage, the venue has to provide the musicians with security from their arrival until they leave the venue. All but the smallest concert venues need to supply security at the mixing position, from the time the audience is admitted until the venue is clear.

If it is impossible to reach the stage without passing through the audience, security personnel may be necessary to escort the artists on and off stage.

Of course these requirements vary enormously depending on the type of music and audience. Chamber orchestra musicians rarely need personal guards around the stage but their instruments need special care, as they can be extremely valuable and fragile. Heavy rock musicians who may be valuable but who are only occasionally fragile, will need very different security arrangements. All of these requirements must be discussed at the time of booking and must be contracted accordingly. Ideally, the venue will be able to provide a secure room or lock-up for the temporary storage of equipment. There are lots of horror stories about the post-show disappearance of valuable vintage instruments and long-assembled backlines.

STAGING

Again, each show is going to have different requirements. Although the needs of a solo acoustic act may be minimal, most five piece rock groups will ideally have a stage area at least ten metres wide, seven metres deep and a minimum of a metre high with a further four metres to the ceiling. As a vast majority of artists play on stages which have fixed dimensions and cannot be modified for their individual needs, staging requirements may not in fact be a negotiable term of the performance contract. However the dimensions of the stage should be set out in the contract so that the tour manager can best decide how to use the available space. It should also be specified whether the musicians will be sharing the stage area with the PA, or whether the PA can be set-up above or to either side of the stage.

POWER REQUIREMENTS

It is the employer's responsibility to provide adequate power to the stage.
Any contemporary band will require a minimum of two 3-phase outlets with 45 amps per phase. Should the venue's power supply not be adequate, a licensed electrician must be available to adapt the existing circuits. The isolators should terminate not more than 10 metres from the stage. If normal power supplies are not available the employer must provide a safe, properly supervised generating system operated by qualified persons.

The adequacy and means of power supply is not just a production issue. It is central to the safety of the performers.

In the early 1970s, Led Zeppelin was booked to play at an open-air venue in Auckland. It was the first open-air super-group concert in New Zealand and used a huge amount of production. The press was full of stories about the number of planeloads of equipment that was being flown in for the night. From the hillside seating you had a beautiful view of the night-lights of the urban sprawl. The spots came on as Jimmy Page played the first five notes of 'The Immigrant Song'... Those 10 seconds of the performance sucked so much power that the power grid for the city couldn't cope. Northwest Auckland dropped into darkness and the concert into silence. Somebody hadn't done their homework and hundreds of thousands of people were inconvenienced. It took 20 minutes to redirect more power to the area. Led Zep proceeded to give one of their great performances.

DRESSING ROOMS

All musicians who have spent time on the road have ghastly stories about facilities that are passed off as dressing rooms. It is always worth finding out what is available so that you can either force the venue to improve the facilities or brace yourself for the horror.

Specify that the room be a properly equipped dressing room and that it be for the group's exclusive use and of a size that is sufficient for your needs. The room should be lockable or, alternatively, the employer should provide adequate security personnel to protect your possessions in the dressing room at all times. Theft of instruments, cash and personal belongings from dressing rooms is all too common.

'Real' dressing rooms have hot and cold running water, soap, a full-length mirror, a large lined garbage bin and seating for at least 10 people. There should be at least two 15 amp power outlets. The room should be adequately lit, heated and ventilated and in close proximity to clean and private toilet facilities.

CATERING

Some of the industry's more excessive contract riders, specifying all sorts of fantastic catering requirements, are legendary. Most of this feeds little more than the performer's ego. It's probably a waste of money and, one way or another, it always ends up coming out of the performer's pocket. At the risk of sounding cynical, there are no free meals in the music industry. Order what you need, not all you can get. Artists who are playing in venues that also serve food should negotiate a meal into the deal. A square meal can make all the difference after a long drive along the Hume Highway.

RECORDING THE PERFORMANCE

It is essential that no part of the performance be recorded on film or tape without the artist's permission. These rights must be absolutely reserved by the artist. To facilitate this, the contract should specify that nobody with any audio or visual recording device will be permitted to enter the place where the performance is to take place, except with the artist's permission. If the venue baulks at enforcing this term against audience members who wield multi-media recording mobile phones, it is practicable to allow them an exception, at least until the quality of audio and audiovisual recordings on mobile phones reaches a commercially useful standard that might encourage piracy.

The converse is that artists are usually permitted to record, tape or film their own performance.

PHOTOGRAPHERS

Good photographers create valuable promotional items. Think about how best to use them, and implement a policy. Press photographers and freelance photographers should be considered separately. The former is there to cover you as a news item, while the latter is there to get a 'great picture' that may or may not be of use to you.

Make sure you know what the venue's policy is too, so you don't inadvertently have your invited photographer thrown out by one of the venue's security guards who is faithfully carrying out his employer's instructions to 'keep the front of house area clear'.

Photographers used to have unlimited access to venues - they just bought a ticket and stood at the front of the stage, taking shots without interference from security guards, artists or the artist's management. The photographers owned the photographs outright and could use them as they liked.

That changed in the mid-1980s, when artists began to see the benefit (i.e. profitability) of controlling their images. Since then, photographers have often had to sign special consent forms that restrict their access (each may get as little as 15 minutes with their cameras, at the front of the stage). The consent forms often also restrict the ways in which the resulting photographs can be used and often include an assignment of all copyright in the photographs to the artist.

PERMITS AND CONSENTS

It is the employer's duty to get all permits and consents needed from all authorities for the performance to be given in the particular venue or location.

It must also comply with all conditions imposed in those permits and consents. These may include venue permits from the Australasian Performing Right Association (APRA), the Phonographic Performance Company of Australia (PPCA), the police, the fire department, health and hygiene authorities, local councils, liquor licensing authorities and so on. Obtaining and complying with all the rules and regulations is just part and parcel of doing business as a promoter or venue operator.

In this regard, performance contracts usually impose only one duty on the performers - the duty to keep within certain decibel levels. If the venue is constrained by the local authorities to keep the noise down, that responsibility is usually passed on to the musicians. They control the volume knob. Some venues go even further and connect the power to a sound-level meter, so if it goes into the red, off goes the power. Ask beforehand, to avoid surprises. This can be crucial for inner city venues that have experienced complaints from neighbours in the past. Forewarned is for-armed if musicians know the relevant sound limit and can plan to accommodate that limit, for example by the use of power-soaking devices on amplifiers and by padding drums.

INSURANCE

Musicians should carry their own public liability insurance. The venue and promoter should each carry their own insurance too. Why should both have insurance cover? Because those insurance policies only protect the contracting party.

In one case, a certain Sydney band was known for its use of pyrotechnics in its stage show. During a performance, one of the incendiaries misfired and hit a member of the audience in the face. She could have sued the venue (which had public liability insurance) but she didn't. She could have sued the pyrotechnics company (which also had public liability insurance) but she didn't. She chose to sue the manager of the band for negligent supervision of the special effects. He didn't have public liability insurance.

ACCOMMODATION

Who will provide the accommodation? If this is to be an obligation of the employer, the standard of accommodation must be defined. For example the contract might specify that:

> *The Employer shall provide at its cost the accommodation stipulated above. Such accommodation shall be good quality motel-style accommodation with each room containing its own bathroom and direct-dial telephone. The accommodation is to be booked by the Employer and proof of booking shall be provided to the Artist at least forty-eight hours prior.*

TERMINATION

If the employer wishes to cancel a contracted performance, it should provide reasonable written notice of cancellation. It should be not less than twenty-one days from the date of the performance, as this is the minimum period provided in the Musicians Union Award. In such a case, the employer should forfeit its deposit. If the employer does not give sufficient notice, the musician will be entitled to the whole performance fee.

If the performer cancels a performance, he or she must send written notice to the employer not later than twenty-one days before the scheduled date of the performance and refund the deposit to the employer. The contract should specify that the performer can cancel at any time prior to the performance:

> *...in the event of sickness to any performer, inability to perform due to accident, means of transport, Act of God, riots, strikes, any act of public authority or any cause similar or dissimilar beyond the control of the Artist.*

8

MUSIC COPYRIGHT — THE BASICS

COPYRIGHT IS FUNDAMENTAL TO EARNING INCOME IN THE MUSIC INDUSTRY. THE RIGHTS IN THE MUSIC AND THE LYRICS, THE SOUND RECORDINGS, THE PERFORMANCE AND THE PUBLISHED EDITIONS, TOGETHER WITH THE RIGHTS UNDERLYING THE MERCHANDISING, ARE THE SOURCE OF THE MONEY THAT FLOWS THROUGH THE MUSIC INDUSTRY. UNLESS ARTISTS AND THEIR ADVISERS UNDERSTAND THE BASICS OF COPYRIGHT, THEY CANNOT MAXIMISE THEIR INCOME OR FULLY PROTECT THE INTEGRITY OF THEIR WORK.

TWELVE COMMON MISCONCEPTIONS

- Copyright is for lawyers and it's their job to understand copyright.
- All lawyers understand copyright.
- The copyright is in the notes, not in the way those notes are arranged.
- The band playing on the record owns all copyright in the record.
- If you wrote it no one else can change it.
- You can record any song no matter who wrote it.
- You can't record any song unless you have the composer's permission.
- Mechanical royalties are called that, because they are automatic.
- Mechanical royalties are the same as record royalties.
- You own all the rights at the end of the contract.
- If you sign a record contract you have to sign away your publishing.
- Always go for the biggest advance you can.

WHY IS COPYRIGHT IMPORTANT?

Copyright plays an essential role in any developed sophisticated society. If society is to recognise creativity, innovation and imagination, then copyright is the principal tool by which we accord that recognition. This is economically expressed by the award of a range of exclusive rights that grant the owner the power of control and the right of commercial exploitation.

At the end of the day, the rights of copyright are an award for innovation, creativity and risk taking. It is a recognition that both the culture and the economy of our community is dependent on encouraging and fostering these characteristics.

Copyright underlies most of the ways that people make money out of music. It is fundamental. To make real money in the music industry, talent is optional but copyright is indispensable. When you consider the following points, you will see why. They all involve payment for the use of copyright material.

- Most songs that are recorded are copyright. Even the sound recording itself has a copyright.
- Much of the sheet music published is of works that are in copyright and are only able to be published because the publisher has bought or licensed the necessary rights of copyright to do so.
- There is a copyright in the published edition, distinct from the copyright in the composition itself.
- Most of the popular music played in live performances is in copyright.
- Merchandising involves the use of copyright material.
- Playing music in public places, such as shops and lifts, usually requires payment of licence fees to the copyright owners.
- Communicating music on the Internet usually requires the consent of copyright owners.
- Virtually no film or television drama is now made without the use of music and thus the use of copyright.
- Most radio and television commercials use copyright music.
- Every time you listen to music on the radio you are listening to the result of several contracts involving copyright.

Like the beat, the list goes on.

Whether you are a musician, a manager, a publisher, a record company executive or an entertainment lawyer, your income is based largely on copyright. You should spend some effort on getting to understand the basics so that you maximise your rewards. It is by exploiting your copyright that you make real money from your music.

WHAT IS THE SOURCE OF COPYRIGHT?

Copyright protection in Australia is provided by the Copyright Act 1968. It is Federal legislation. It superseded the 1911 Act that was modelled closely on the English Act. Many people forget that the 1911 Act can still apply in some instances, though this is quite rare now.

In addition, Australia belongs to a number of international treaties, including the treaty known as the Berne Convention, which dovetail into the Australian laws. Australian copyright owners can use these treaties to get reciprocal copyright protection in other treaty countries.

Most countries use the Berne Convention as the basis for their national copyright laws, but there are differences from country to country. Sometimes the duration of protection differs from country to country; sometimes the actual rights that are recognised differ. International copyright law is not for the squeamish. The differences in international treatment are discussed in more detail in the following chapters, where relevant to the particular subject.

WHAT IS COVERED BY COPYRIGHT?

Copyright protection is given to two classes of things:
(a) 'works' (including artistic, musical, literary and dramatic works); and
(b) 'subject matter other than works' (e.g. sound recordings, cinematograph works, broadcasts and published editions).

WHAT RIGHTS DOES COPYRIGHT INCLUDE?

Copyright is a bundle of rights. Copyright in a work includes the right to:
(a) reproduce the work (this includes reproducing it in sheet music or on records or synchronising it in films, television programs and advertisements);
(b) communicate the work to the public (examples include 'live' performances, playing recorded music in public, playing music on the radio, television or the Internet); and
(c) make an adaptation of the work (for example, arrangements, transcriptions, parodies).

COMMUNICATION TO THE PUBLIC

On 4 March 2001, a new right for copyright owners, the right to 'communicate' their work to the public, was introduced into the Copyright Act. This was a major development in Australian copyright law. Contracts spanning over or commencing after this date must effectively manage this new right.

The Copyright Act has made the communication right far-reaching - expanding upon and clarifying the existing bundle of rights. It is broad enough to cover free-to-air television, cable, radio, the Internet and mobile phones. Not only does it provide new on-line rights, it has replaced the existing broadcasting and cable rights and extended the copyright protection afforded to sound recordings over cable.

In relation to the Internet (and its future re-incarnations) the communication right not only includes the right to 'electronically transmit' (such as emailing Missy Higgins' new track) but also to 'make available on-line' which would include simply having your computer on a file-sharing system and allowing others to access that track from your hard drive.

Importantly, the right covers communications not only within Australia but ones originating here and received overseas. Australian copyright owners can thus seek to prevent the unauthorised communication of their works offshore. For example, the right could be used to stop an Australian-based website from making a film or song available not just in Australia but anywhere in the world. Given the global nature of the Internet such recourse is, of course, essential if owners are to protect their works.

Where the old Act did not contemplate the Internet, the communication right provides specifically for 'on-line' distribution. Furthermore, the Government has aimed to keep the right 'technology neutral' so that the right will continue to operate and withstand the semantics and processes of scientific innovation that would outdate a definition based on existing technology.

In a nutshell, the right to 'communicate' works to the public is extremely broad. It clarifies and reinforces the copyright owner's basic and exclusive right to control the use of their work in the digital environment.

USA FREE TRADE AGREEMENT

On 16 August 2004, the Australian Government assented to the US Free Trade Agreement Implementation Act 2004 ("Implementation Act"). The Implementation Act does as its name suggests - implements the amendments necessary to the law in Australia as a result of the signing of the Australia-United States Free Trade Agreement. The Implementation Act introduced significant changes to the Copyright Act 1968 that directly impact on the music industry. New performer's rights were created and the duration of copyright protection was extended for most copyright material.

Performers now have ownership rights in sound recordings of their performances. The term of copyright in musical compositions, lyrics and sound recordings was extended from 50 to 70 years from the end of the year in which the author died (in the case of musical and literary works) or from the end of the year in which the recording was first published (in the case of sound recordings). The Implementation Act also introduced moral rights in both live performances and recordings of performances. Further details of these amendments will be referred to where appropriate below.

REPRODUCTION

Although the term 'Reproduction' is used a lot when talking about copyright, many people misunderstand the term. Reproduction may take many forms. Although it is most usually used as a synonym for copy it actually has a wider meaning in copyright law, for the copy does not have to be exact.

It need not be a copy of the whole work, merely a 'substantial portion' of it. For example, using four notes from a piece of music would not usually be thought of as a 'substantial portion', but in the case of, say, the opening four notes of Beethoven's Fifth, the answer would be different. The test of substantiality is qualitative not quantitative.

It need not be in the same medium. For example, a song may be based on a book. Paul Kelly's 'Everything's Turning To White' on the 'So Much Water...' album is based on a Carver short story. A licence had to be negotiated with the Carver estate. The lyrics are clearly not copied from the story but they do re-tell it.

PUBLICATION

Similarly, the term 'Publication' is given a special meaning by the Copyright Act. It is defined as meaning the supply to the public (whether by sale or otherwise) of reproductions of the work. For a musical composition, this may be by means of sheet music. Surprisingly, supplying records of musical works, whether for sale or not, is not publication of the work, even though this is the most common way works are exploited. Many are never even 'published' in printed form.

WHAT FORMALITIES ARE NECESSARY?

The Australian Copyright Act provides **automatic** protection. No formalities are necessary provided the person claiming copyright meets the criterion of being a 'qualified person' (i.e. an Australian citizen, company or someone normally resident here). As soon as a thing that is capable of protection is given '**material form**', copyright exists in it. To put a musical work (melody) or a literary work (lyric) into a 'material form' it needs to be notated or written down or recorded in some way. If you make a recording of a song, you have reduced it to a material form (s.22). There used to be much debate as to whether the material form had to be visible to the eye but the Act is now clear that it covers any form of storage from which the work can be reproduced. This covers digital storage. (Remember that in the world of copyright, the 'author' is merely the generic term given to the person who put the work into a material form. It is not 'authorship' in the usual sense of the word.)

To get copyright protection in Australia, you don't have to put your name, the copyright symbol © and the year on your songs or demos, but there is still a good reason for doing so. To benefit from copyright protection overseas under the Universal Copyright Convention (UCC), every published copy of the work or recording has to bear a copyright symbol, the year of first publication and the owner, otherwise it doesn't qualify. The UCC is important because, until 1989, the United States was not a member of the older, and arguably more important, Berne Convention. The UCC used to be the basis for copyright recognition in the United States of Australian compositions, records and films, etc. until the United States joined the Berne Convention. Putting the copyright symbol and the other details on the work met the United States' requirements for copyright protection, without you having to register the copyright there. For Australians, putting the copyright symbol, your name and the date is not necessary although it can be useful simply to remind would-be users that the work is subject to copyright and that permission is required to reproduce and exploit it.

Many people are mystified by the ℗ symbol on records. The ℗ symbol stands for "phonograph" and comes from the Rome Convention (yet another treaty!) It came into force in 1964 and this was the first time sound recordings were given copyright recognition in an international treaty. Again, all published copies have to have a ℗ symbol, the year of first publication and the owner or the person who published the record itself (not always the same person).

The degree of protection given to sound recordings varies from country to country. As mentioned earlier, the United States does not recognise public performance or broadcast copyrights in records, so, in general terms, we do not recognise those rights in records made in the United States or owned by United States nationals/companies. The minimum term of copyright protection allowed under the Rome Convention is 14 years from when the recording is 'fixed', but most countries have adopted a longer term. In Australia, as a general rule, sound recordings are protected for 70 years from first publication.

If you are worried that someone is going to steal your song (which, let's face it, is statistically unlikely) the best idea is to keep a regular diary of your work, showing when you worked on a particular song, what it was called, when it was finished, to whom you played it and when.

Copyright is automatic and it is free. All the diary provides is some proof as to what you wrote and when you wrote it. It's just evidence that what you say is true.

So-called 'copyright registration services' do nothing to improve the validity of the copyright itself in Australia and are, at best, a marginal benefit to proving copyright ownership. Take up smoking seaweed instead. It'll do you as much good. Don't bother posting songs to yourself and leaving the envelopes unopened, unless you have some glandular urge to do so. You will soon need a larger apartment to store all the envelopes and the increased rental will outweigh any advantage. You can prove your copyright in easier ways.

WHO OWNS THE COPYRIGHT?
MUSICAL WORKS

It is important to distinguish between the musical work reproduced on a record, and the recording itself. Remember, there is only one owner of the song 'Blue Suede Shoes' but hundreds of recorded versions - each new recording is owned by other people.

The general rule is that the 'author' of the song is the owner of copyright. The author of the music is of course the composer. The author of the lyrics is the lyricist.

The lyrics are protected as a literary work and the music as a musical work. If their authors are different people, then separate permissions will have to be obtained from each one if you want to reproduce the song. This is discussed in more detail under **Co-Writers**.

Even if a composer is commissioned to write the music, he or she still retains the copyright. However, where composers are actually employed to write songs (such as the 'Tin Pan Alley' composers earlier last century in New York), the employer owns the copyright. Avoid contracts that use words deeming the composer to be 'a servant for hire'. Some publishers still use contracts that use this phrase. This must always be struck out. If they refuse, demand superannuation and holiday pay!

SOUND RECORDINGS

The Implementation Act provided performers with an ownership right in a sound recording of their live performance. Importantly, this provides performers with the ability to control the use and exploitation of the recordings on which they perform. Prior to 1 January 2005, the 'maker' of a sound recording was usually the owner of copyright in the sound recording. The maker of the recording was usually the person who made the arrangements and paid for the master recording to be completed.

However, as result of the Implementation Act, as of 1 January 2005, a 'performer' gained part ownership of the copyright in a sound recording of their live performance. The new provisions are retrospective in that they apply to all sound recordings of live performances in which copyright subsists as of 1 January 2005. However, special treatment is given to those recordings made before 1 January 2005.

Under the new provisions, unless there is an agreement to the contrary, the Copyright Act provides that the owner of copyright in a sound recording is the:

- person who owns the record at the time the recording is made; and
- performer(s) who performed in the live performance.

If there is more than one owner of the sound recording, the owners own the copyright as tenants in common in equal shares. Each owner's permission will be required to exercise (or to authorise a third party to exercise) rights in the sound recording. Part-ownership of copyright in the sound recording improves the bargaining position of a performer by giving the performer the right to control the use and exploitation of the recording.

Who is a performer? A performer in a live performance is each person who contributes to the sounds of the performance. If the performance includes the performance of a musical work, the conductor is also deemed to be a performer. So all singers and musicians, including session musicians who perform on a recording will own a part of the copyright in the recording.

Prior to the Implementation Act, the owner of the sound recording was usually an established record company. Accordingly, it was usually reasonably simple to track the owner(s) down, even if the company had ceased trading or been bought by another. The new rules make it somewhat harder to track down the owner(s) of a sound recording, which will now include the performer(s). You will need to ask not only 'Who paid for the making of the recording?' but also 'Who performed on that recording?' They will be the people to go to if you want permission to copy or otherwise use the recording's copyright.

The new rules are likely to have little practical effect as most recording contracts will continue to specify that the record company will own all the copyright in the recordings they make, in spite of the fact that all the costs of producing and manufacturing the record may be recoupable from the artist's royalties. It is understandable that the company should own the copyright until the costs are recouped but there is a good argument that once recoupment is achieved, copyright should be transferred to the artists. After all, it is their performance and their money that, at the end of the day, has paid for it. These copyrights can be seen as the artist's superannuation.

On the other hand, artists can disappear after a few years. Most have no arrangements for anyone else to grant licences in their place. If there is no-one companies can contact for permission to re-release records, the master will probably languish in the vaults, even if there is demand for the recording. It quite often happens with old recordings (i.e. recordings by groups that split up a few years ago, or artists who have gone 'bush' - or somewhere more permanent). In an attempt to counter this problem, the Implementation Act introduced an implicit consent for the owner of a sound recording to use or exploit the recording if a co-owner cannot be located after reasonable enquiries are made. However, the owner that uses or exploits the recording must retain in trust the co-owners share of the profits for a period of four years. It is better for the recording to be administered by a record company, than end up with it not being exploited at all.

SPECIAL RULES APPLYING TO SOUND RECORDINGS MADE PRIOR TO 1 JANUARY 2005

So, how do the new rules work if you made the recording prior to 1 January 2005 and your recording contract provides that the record company owns copyright in the recordings you have made? The new rules apply to those recordings with some limitations (but only if copyright subsisted in those recordings as of 1 January 2005).

The new rules provide that the owner of copyright in the sound recording prior to 1 January 2005 (for example, the record company) retains ownership of half of the copyright in the recording. The remaining half of the copyright is now owned by the performer(s) who performed on the recording (for example, you). No, unfortunately your new rights do not mean that you can now demand a bigger advance or a larger cut of the royalties. Importantly, the acquisition of copyright by performers in pre-January 2005 recordings does not stop the former copyright owner (the owner of the recording prior to 1 January 2005), its licensees and successors in title and any person authorised by such persons, exploiting the recording without having to seek the permission of the new copyright owners, nor does it affect any existing agreement.

Further, the new owners of copyright in sound recordings are severely limited in the remedies they may seek for infringement. Damages and account of profits are not available. A scheme has also been introduced to compensate former owners of copyright if the new owners acquisition would be considered not on 'just terms'.

The table below sets out the different treatment of recordings made before and after 1 January 2005.

RECORDINGS MADE BEFORE 1 JANUARY 2005	RECORDINGS MADE AFTER 1 JANUARY 2005
COPYRIGHT OWNERSHIP	
Whoever owned the copyright in the sound recording before 1 January 2005 will continue to own copyright in the same proportion as they did, but now limited to 50%. Eligible* performers will share the remaining 50% equally. For example, if the record company owned the entire copyright in the master made in 2004, after 1 January 2005 they will own 50%. If there were three artists who performed on that recording, they would then own one third of the remaining 50% each (about 16.5%). *If a performer was employed under a contract for service or apprenticeship then the employer (not the performer) is entitled to own that share of copyright.	The copyright will be shared *equally* and *jointly* between all performers and whoever paid for the recording to be made (usually the record company). For example, if there are three artists performing and a record company has financed the recording, there will be 4 owners of copyright in the sound recording. Each artist and the record company will own 25% of the copyright in the master.
PERMISSIONS	
Performers (or their employers) who acquire copyright are taken to have licensed the former owner of copyright to do any act of copyright (e.g. reproduction of the master) or any act in relation to copyright. This extends to the first owner's licensees and successors. Earlier permissions by performers to use the sound recordings are unaffected.	Permission will be required from all owners (ie all performers and the person who paid for the recording) to do any act of copyright (e.g. reproduction of the master).

RECORDINGS MADE BEFORE 1 JANUARY 2005	RECORDINGS MADE AFTER 1 JANUARY 2005
COMPENSATION	
Performers (or their employers) who acquire copyright may be obliged to compensate the former owner if their acquisition would be considered not on "just terms".	No equivalent provision.
LIMITATIONS ON COPYRIGHT ACTIONS & ENTITLEMENTS	
Performers (or their employers) who acquire copyright in a sound recording after 1 January 2005 (in a recording made before 1 January 2005) have limited remedies available to them if their copyright is infringed (for example, damages or account of profits are generally unavailable).	No equivalent provision.

LIMITS ON RIGHTS GIVEN TO PERFORMERS

The Implementation Act placed some limitations on the new rights given to performers. The first limitation relates to instances in which a person commissions the making of a sound recording by another person. In the absence of any agreement to the contrary, the person who commissioned the recording (for example, the record company) will be the sole owner of the copyright in the sound recording made in pursuance of the agreement.

The second limitation arises in the case of employment. If the live performance was recorded as part of your employment, your employer is taken to be the owner of copyright in the sound recording. Examples of this situation include musicians who are employed by a jingle-house or musicians who are employed to play in a group (side-players).

Thirdly and perhaps most importantly, consent to use a sound recording of a live performance is deemed to have been given if the performer has given consent to record the performance for a particular purpose and the recording is used for that purpose. (For example: session musicians who are hired to play on a record. However, it is still prudent to insist on written consents so that the extent of the consent is clear. You do not want the session musician alleging that he only agreed to record a demo, not a record that was going to be commercially released.)

PUBLISHED EDITIONS

The copyright owner for a published edition of a musical work (the sheet music) is the publisher of the edition. This does not affect the author's copyright in the music itself.

HOW LONG DOES COPYRIGHT LAST?

MUSICAL WORKS AND LITERARY WORKS

Prior to 1 January 2005, the general rule was that copyright in the musical composition and in the lyric, lasted for 50 years from the end of the year in which the author died. However, as of 1 January 2005, the term of protection was extended to 70 years from the end of the year in which the author died. The extended term applies only to those works in which copyright existed as of 1 January 2005. If the copyright in a musical or literary work expired prior to January 2005, it did not revive.

If the work has not during the composer's lifetime been 'published' (say as sheet music), publicly performed, broadcast, or sold in the form of records, the copyright period does not start running until the end of the calendar year in which the first of those events occurs (if ever!)

SOUND RECORDINGS MADE BEFORE 1 MAY 1969

If recorded before 1 May 1969, copyright in these recordings lasts for 50 years from the end of the year in which the recording was made.

RECORDINGS MADE AFTER 1 MAY 1969

The copyright term was extended from 50 to 70 years by the Implementation Act. The copyright period of 70 years starts to run from the end of the year in which the recording is first published. Basically this means the year of its release to the public, so if a master recording is made but, for whatever reason, a decision is made not to release the record, copyright will remain indefinitely because the 70-year period will never start to run.

(The distinction between pre-1969 recordings and post-1969 recordings was caused by the introduction of the new Copyright Act 1968, which came into effect on 1 May 1969.)

PUBLISHED EDITIONS

There was no copyright in published editions before 1 May 1969. Editions published after that date enjoy copyright protection for 25 years from the date of their first publication.

ANONYMOUS OR PSEUDONYMOUS WORKS

From 1 January 2005, the copyright in these works was extended from 50 to 70 years after the end of the calendar year in which the work was first published. However, if the composer's identity is generally known, or could be ascertained by reasonable inquiry, the general rule applies. If the copyright in an anonymous or pseudonymous work expired prior to 1 January 2005, those rights were not revived by the extension of the copyright term. Once they're dead, they're dead.

WORKS OF JOINT AUTHORSHIP

Again, whether or not the work has been published is significant. Where it has been, the 70-year period runs from the end of the calendar year in which the last remaining author dies. However, where the work is first published after the author's death, the period runs for 70 years from the end of the calendar year in which the work was first published.

Where one or some (but not all) of the joint authors uses a pseudonym, the 70-year period runs from the end of the year in which the last author, whose identity has been revealed, dies.

Similarly, where all of them use pseudonyms, if at any time within 70 years of publication the identity of one of the authors is or could be discovered, the period runs from the end of the year in which the author, whose identity has been revealed, dies.

FILMS

Films made before 1 May 1969 are not protected, though the individual frames can be protected as photographs. There are also provisions protecting films made before that date that were 'dramatic works'. Films made after that date are protected for 70 years from first publication. The expression 'film' includes video.

Who said copyright was simple?

COPYRIGHT TRANSACTIONS

The statutory provisions as to the ownership of copyright are all subject to variation by contract. The most common methods are set out in the following section.

THE ASSIGNMENT OF COPYRIGHT

Assignment is essentially a transfer of ownership and rights. It is just like a sale of the rights. Thus, you should always beware of assigning your rights as it means losing ownership of them (and usually control as well). Assignments are only effective if in writing, signed by or on behalf of the owner of copyright.

It used to be common for record companies, and publishers dealing with copyright to adopt a rather heavy hand in this regard. They used their considerable power not only to acquire assignments of copyright but also to get a free hand in the way in which they exploited those copyrights. Fortunately, the general approach has improved greatly. Most companies now will negotiate their deals so that the composer/artist retains at least a degree of control over how their works and recordings may be exploited. If nothing else, this helps maintain relations between publisher and composer or record company and artist, as the case may be.

Remember that when you assign your copyrights, you are exposing yourself to Capital Gains Tax. You must do your tax planning before you have that big hit - not after! If you leave it until after you have the hit, your copyrights, once worth only a nominal amount, suddenly have a new taxable value.

LICENSING THE RIGHTS

When a copyright owner grants a licence, he or she permits another to use the right but still retains ownership and thus a certain control over that right.

Licences allow the usage to be limited to the real needs of the licensee. It also means that you don't lose total control of your rights. Where possible, copyright owners should license, not assign! Exclusive licences must be in writing, signed by the 'licensor' (the one granting the licence) or their agent.

BASIC TERMS

A copyright is a very flexible piece of property. Some elements which must be considered and included in licensing and assignment contracts are:

1. PARTIES INVOLVED

Who is the contract between? Who is the grantor and who is the grantee? Although it may seem obvious, in an era of complex legal structures, it is sometimes not as easy as it seems.

2. WORKS INVOLVED

What work(s) are included in the transaction? Include an attachment or schedule showing what works are part of the deal.

3. RIGHTS

What rights are being granted? What parts of the 'bundle of rights' are included in the agreement? Is it to include all of the rights of copyright or only some of them?

4. DURATION

For how long are the rights to be granted? You can assign or license copyright for a set number of years.

5. USES
What uses are you going to permit? You may be happy for your song to be used for a Holden commercial but not for a toilet cleanser commercial.

6. EXCLUSIVITY
The grant of rights may be exclusive or non-exclusive. Even where they are 'exclusive', the extent of that exclusivity can be limited. You can grant exclusive rights to different people for different uses in the same territory. For example you may grant an exclusive license to use a song for car commercials yet still grant a film producer the right to include that song in a film.

7. TERRITORY
You can license or assign someone the right to use your rights in a particular territory, but retain the rights in other territories.

8. CREATIVE CONTROL
What changes to your work are you going to permit? What degree of control are you going to retain? Will these affect your royalties? Who may approve changes?

9. PAYMENT
How will the copyright owner be paid: With an up-front fee or by royalties or a mixture of both? This will be largely determined by the type of deal and the relative bargaining power of the parties.

10. OBLIGATIONS AND GUARANTEES
What obligations and guarantees are the parties offering each other?

11. ACCOUNTING AND INSPECTION
How can the copyright owner check that they are being paid the right amount?

12. FURTHER GRANT OF RIGHTS
Can the grantee license the rights to anyone else?

13. ENFORCEMENT
Who will protect the rights against infringements? Who will pay the legal costs? Who may 'settle' a dispute if it goes to court? How will damages and costs be split?

14. TERMINATION
Are there circumstances in which the contract can be terminated?

15. DISPUTES

How will you settle disputes? Is there a mechanism in the contract that makes the parties undergo mediation or arbitration of a dispute that cannot be resolved by negotiation?

IS ALL USE OF COPYRIGHT MATERIAL FORBIDDEN UNLESS YOU HAVE A LICENCE?

The Copyright Act provides for a number of situations in which reproducing a work will not amount to an infringement of copyright.

FAIR DEALING

This specifically covers the use of artistic, literary and musical works (not recordings or films), for the purposes of:

(a) Research or study.

(b) Criticism or review (although sufficient acknowledgement must be made).

(c) Reporting news in a newspaper, magazine, film or television broadcast (although in the case of the print media, sufficient acknowledgement must be made).

To determine whether or not a dealing is 'fair', regard is given to several factors:

(a) The purpose and the character of the dealing.

(b) The nature of the work.

(c) The possibility of obtaining the work within a reasonable time at an ordinary price.

(d) The effect of the dealing on the value of or market for the work.

(e) Where only a part of the work is copied, the amount and substantiality of the portion copied, taken in relation to the whole.

At the time of writing, 'parody' is not one of the fair dealing exceptions. However the Attorney General has announced an intention to amend the fair dealing povision to permit parody - thus bringing it into line with the U.S. position.

USE OF AN INSUBSTANTIAL PORTION

To be an infringement, the use must be a reproduction of a 'substantial' portion of the work. Of course, what is substantial is a question of fact and degree in every case.

There are no simple rules of thumb you can use, although you may hear glib and reassuring little phrases such as 'You can use up to 14 bars of music', or 'It's OK if you change a note here or there'. None of these are true. It will vary in each case. George Harrison of 'The Beatles' had to pay millions to the composer of 'He's So Fine' because a court found that he had (unconsciously) used that melody in writing his big hit, 'My Sweet Lord'. In a major computer case, a defendant was found to have breached copyright because its computer-widget used the same series of numbers in its calculations as did another company's computer-widget.

Anyone who suggests there is some magic rule that lets you use grabs of copyright material for free, is woefully misinformed or no friend of yours.

HOME COPYING

Virtually all Australian households contain privately made reproductions of musical recordings and radio broadcasts. How many times have you gone into a restaurant and seen a pile of homemade recordings being played as background music? Over the years, making such cassettes and RW-CDs has become one of the most publicly recognised examples of community-sanctioned unlawful behaviour. It seems that virtually everybody does it, and no one (except copyright lawyers!) feels particularly guilty about it and nobody can do anything about it.

Any law is only as powerful as the determination of the community to observe it. In the case of home taping, the intrusion of a court official into the lounge room of every home in Australia would be practically, politically, financially, commercially and morally unthinkable, even though home taping is illegal and cheats writers, performers and the industry generally.

After discussion (for nearly a decade) about reform, the legislature decided to make home audio taping legal, in return for a copyright royalty on blank tapes.

The cynical might say that it was a tax to ease our consciences. To some extent that was true, but it was intended to do much more: it was intended to introduce a mechanism by which the copyright owners (who are presently being cheated of their rightful income) could receive some, if not their due, compensation. Several European countries have enacted similar legislation.

The legislation was passed, but immediately challenged by the blank tape manufacturers, who feared that the imposition of a levy would reduce sales. The High Court heard the matter in late 1992, and ruled the legislation was unconstitutional. No replacement legislation was attempted, probably because the evolution of technology has made the issue less significant: the CD has won the battle over the cassette tape. In May 2006 the government announced that it intended to amend the Copyright Act to allow for time-shifting and also to allow a person who has purchased a legitimate piece of copyright material, to store it on a personal MP3 player or computer. (It will remain illegal to upload that material onto the Internet.)

PROTECTION OF NON-COPYRIGHT RIGHTS OF PERFORMERS AND THEIR PERFORMANCE

Throughout the history of copyright in Australia, the performance itself - that primary focus of the music, theatre, dance and film industries - has had little or no protection, except for that provided by the law of contract and (occasionally) defamation and passing off. The problem was the Copyright Act's fixation with 'fixation' (to turn a phrase). It is well known that copyright provides no protection for ideas. It protects the material form in which those ideas are expressed. This simple proposition has been an enormous stumbling block to the introduction of performers' protection because the performance is, by definition, live, temporary and ephemeral. To fix it in a material form, one must destroy those inherent features that make it a 'performance'.

Copyright has been largely based upon traditional notions of property and property ownership. Prior to the Implementation Act, it was an unpleasant irony that the maker of a bootleg recording of a performance enjoyed copyright ownership of (and protection for) that sound recording, yet the poor performer had no right to determine whether or not the performance was recorded at all, what would be recorded, how, when and by whom the recording would be made, let alone receive remuneration from sales of the recording.

In 1989 the Copyright Act was amended to remedy this state of affairs. This amendment did not create a new kind of copyright. An Australian performer has a right to take action (including getting injunctions) against any 'unauthorised use' of their performance. In effect, the new law created a 'neighbouring right' (that is, one that is derived from, or is dependent upon, the copyright in the work that is performed, recorded or broadcast, but is not itself a copyright. It's not really as hard as it first sounds).

No one may make an 'unauthorised' use of a performance during the 20 year protection period without the permission of the performer. 'Unauthorised use' is exhaustively defined and was extended by the Implementation Act to include 'the communication of the performance to the public without the authority of the performer'.

Prior to the Implementation Act, the recording of a performance from a broadcast (or a re-broadcast) or via a diffusion service for the private and domestic use of the person who made it, was exempt from these provisions. The Implementation Act however removed this exemption.

The Implementation Act has introduced provisions to prevent performers doubling up on their damages by receiving compensation for both infringement of copyright in a sound recording and infringement of the performer's neighbouring 'non-copyright' rights (arising from the one event). If a performer has already been granted damages in an action for infringement of copyright, those damages will be taken into account by the court in assessing damages for infringement of the performer's neighbouring rights.

It is essential that everyone who performs on a record, signs a properly drafted '**Performer's Consent**' form. This should be an absolutely standard, no exception, practice. All of the artists, the session musicians and the producer, must sign off.

PERFORMER'S CONSENT

All performers, without exception, must sign this form before recording of their performance commences

RECORDING: (give actual working title of track or Album as the case may be)

FEATURED ARTIST:

RECORD COMPANY:

PRODUCER:
I confirm that I have been retained to perform on this Recording so that records (in any format) embodying my performance may be released to the public and that my fee (if any) is the sole remuneration due to me. Once any fee payable is paid, I will have no further claim in relation to the Recording or for my services.

I also confirm that the Recording may be included with visual images and any copies of the Recording may be retained indefinitely.

Name: ....Signature: ....Date: ....

PERFORMERS' COPYRIGHT?

As mentioned above, there is no copyright in a performance itself. The copyright only subsists in the embodiment of the performance - the recording, the video, the film.

In 1992, the Labor government established an industry advisory group called the Music Industry Advisory Council (MIAC). One of its functions was to advise government on the introduction of legislation to protect performers. In 1994 it published a useful report (*Performers' Copyright*) that set out the pros and cons of performers' copyright. The interest groups were clearly divided along the lines of self-interest: unions for; record companies and broadcasters against.

In 1995, the Liberal government commissioned an independent report. (Sherman and Bently, *Performers Rights: Options for Reform,* see www.dca.gov.au). Although the Implementation Act significantly strengthened and extended the rights of performers in Australia - there is still no copyright in the performance itself.

MORAL RIGHTS

While Australia's obligations to implement a Moral Rights framework have existed under the Berne Convention since 1935, it was not until 21 December 2000 that Moral Rights became Law in Australia. They relate only to musical, literary, artistic and dramatic works.

The introduction of these new rights was the result of over twenty years of often heated lobbying and negotiation with governments of both persuasions. Changing the status quo of a copyright regime was no easy task. Many copyright users resisted the introduction of Moral Rights. The film industry, for example, argued that the rights would interfere with the smooth production, sale and distribution of films. They successfully lobbied the government to provide their industry with certain indulgences in the way Moral Rights would operate. The differential treatment obtained by the film industry is an important reminder about the strengths of collective political lobbying.

The Implementation Act introduced moral rights for performers in both live performances and recordings of performances. The new performer's moral rights will take effect when the WIPO Performances and Phonograms Treaty (1996) comes into force in Australia. The rights will apply only to performances that take place after the commencement of the Treaty.

The Copyright Act provides authors and performers with three Moral Rights:
- the right of attribution;
- the right not to be falsely attributed; and
- the right of integrity.

These rights are owned by the authors of musical, literary, artistic, dramatic works as well as films (that is, directors, producers and screenwriters) and performers in live or recorded performances. The precise application of the rights varies depending on what kind of work has been created. They cannot be assigned; they are personal. However, when an author or performer dies, his or her beneficiary can exercise the rights.

THE RIGHT OF ATTRIBUTION
(a) Musical and Literary Works

This gives the author of a work the right to be credited as author. This means that the author (i.e. the composer or the lyricist) has the right to be identified clearly and reasonably prominently with the work when it is reproduced, published, publicly performed or communicated to the public. If the work is musical or literary (i.e. the lyrics), the right also applies to adaptations of the work. If the author makes it known what form he or she wants the identification to take, that should be done if it is 'reasonable in the circumstances'. Yes, it's vague, but the concept of 'reasonableness' is always contextual.

(b) Live Performances and Recordings of Performances

This gives a performer in a live or recorded performance the right to be credited as a performer in their performance. Identification of the performer is required when:

- communicating a live performance to the public;
- staging (making arrangements necessary for) a live performance in public;
- a recording of a performance, or a substantial part of a performance, is copied (from the master or otherwise) or communicated to the public.

Performers should be credited in a clear and reasonably prominent or audible way. Notably, if you are a member of a band, using the band's name is sufficient identification. Performers and bands should now be credited on the recording (and any recording that includes a substantial part of the recording) in a manner that enables someone buying the recording to notice the credit. As with literary and musical works, if the performer makes it known what form the identification should take, this should be done if it is reasonable in the circumstances.

THE RIGHT NOT TO BE FALSELY ATTRIBUTED
(a) Musical and Literary Works

This right is not likely to be as important in the music industry as in the visual arts. However, it may be relevant to successful recording artists that insist on getting a share of the copyright in works composed by others in return for putting the track on their album. This is a common practice really designed to procure a share of the actual composer's mechanical income. The artist gets attributed as a co-writer when he or she had nothing to do with creation of the work - merely its exploitation.

(b) Live Performances and Recordings of Performances

If the performance is in public or communicated to the public it is an act of false attribution if the stager of the performance states or falsely implies to an audience, immediately before, during or immediately after a performance, that:

- a particular person is, was or will be performing; or
- a particular group is, was or will be presenting the performance.

Acts of false attribution in respect of a recorded performance are:

- inserting or affixing a person's (or group's) name (or authorising others to do so), falsely implying that person (or group) performs on the recording;
- dealing with a recording knowing that a person (or group) named in or on the recording is not the performer on the recording or communicating the recording to the public; or
- dealing with a recording of a performance as if it were an unaltered copy knowing that the recording has been altered by a person other than the performer in the recording.

THE RIGHT OF INTEGRITY

This is the right not to have a work subjected to 'derogatory treatment'. 'Derogatory treatment' is the doing of anything that results in the distortion, mutilation or alteration to the work or performance (or anything else to it that is prejudicial to honour or reputation).

In the music industry, we already have this concept to a limited extent in that artists who do covers can not avail themselves of the statutory mechanical licence if their version is a 'debasement' of the original. (See the discussion of the *Carmina Burana* case, below.) This right certainly gives another weapon to an artist objecting to a sample of his or her work. It is particularly important because authors and performers retain their Moral Rights whether or not they are still the owners of the copyright.

It may affect the rearranging, remixing, and sampling of work. It could also be used to prevent the use of a work or recording in association with 'premiums', advertisements and other licensed uses. In other words, the right of integrity protects against those who would debase the work or recording by changes they make to it and also, against those who would seek to use the work or recording in a context that would be debasing.

DURATION

(a) Musical and Literary Works

Moral Rights in music, lyrics and artistic works last for the full period of copyright: 70 years from the author's death. Composers will have to take particular care to appoint an executor in their will who will take appropriate care of their work after they die. This may mean appointing one executor to take care of the ordinary duties of divvying out the ordinary assets and another who will take care of the musical/copyright assets.

(b) Recordings of Performances

A performer's right of attribution of performership in a recorded performance and right not to have performership falsely attributed, continues for the full period of copyright in the recording: 70 years from the end of the year in which the recording is first published. Whereas, a performer's right of integrity of performership in respect of a recorded performance continues until the performer dies.

REMEDIES FOR INFRINGEMENTS

If your Moral Rights have been infringed, you may seek a wide variety of remedies from the courts. These include an injunction to stop further infringements, an order to pay damages for financial loss suffered as a result of the infringement, a declaration that your Moral Rights have been infringed and an order that the defendant make a public apology. When the court considers what remedies are appropriate it takes into account all the circumstances. These include whether the defendant was aware of your Moral Rights, the likely effect of any damage to the work or recording or your honour or reputation and how many other people have seen the infringement.

Such remedies can be far reaching. For example, if a lyricist's Moral Rights have been infringed by someone putting out a record with the author's lyrics reworked in a derogatory way, the worldwide distribution of that record could be stopped. Before charging down to see your lawyer with a handful of Moral Rights abuses, bear in mind the availability of such remedies are tempered by various defences.

DEFENCES TO INFRINGEMENTS

Firstly, if you **consent** to the event that would otherwise be an infringement of Moral Rights, there is no infringement. The consent must be in writing. Most consents for artistic, literary and musical works must be for specific events or types of events. For example, one might consent to 'using a 30-second excerpt of the music for advertising'. Consents for 'all uses of the music in any way' would be too broad to be valid.

A performer's consent can relate to all or any acts or omissions occurring before or after the consent is given. The consent may also be given in relation to a specified performance or performances of a particular description.

While recognised in other countries, **waiving** Moral Rights is not permitted under the Australian Copyright Act. (A waiver indicates that the consent given is too non-specific.) However, if a work is a film or is to be included in a film a slightly different set of rules apply. In such cases the consent does not have to be in relation to specific events or types of events. In film deals, the consents can be very broad and 'waiver' language is often used.

If any consent is obtained by misleading statements (such as 'just sign it, it doesn't mean anything') or duress (such as 'if you don't sign we'll take your house'), the consent will be ineffective.

Secondly, it is not an infringement of Moral Rights if the act (or the failure to act) was **reasonable** in all the circumstances. The Copyright Act provides a shopping list of things for judges to consider when ascertaining whether something was reasonable. These are very broad and include:

- whether there are any industry standards or agreements;
- the context and manner in which the work or performance was used;
- if the work had more than one author, what the other authors thought about the infringement; and
- if the performance involved more than one performer, what the other performers thought about the infringement.

NO CAUSE FOR ALARM

Even before the introduction of Moral Rights, we were seeing many of the Majors including terms in their recording and publishing contracts by which artists and composers had to waive their Moral Rights. This was absurd. After all, companies should be striving to protect the reputation of their writers and artists and not be acting contrary to them. The rationale is that they don't want to be exposed to such a claim by mistake. Well-run companies do not commit acts of debasement or fail to give due credits. If they do, by accident, then fixing the error and making an apology should be the automatic response.

There are many protections built into the legislation to ensure that the rights are not used capriciously. The remedies are all discretionary and take into account the circumstances of the breach, the extent of the damage caused and the action taken to remedy the problem.

No one should be threatened by this legislation provided that they act in a manner that respects the role of the author or the performer in the creative process. This should already happen. Moral rights confer little more than an obligation to treat the creative person with a reasonable degree of respect. It may be hard to believe that this does not always happen in the music business.

SAMPLING

One of the most contentious and yet widespread practices that technology has endowed upon the music industry is 'sampling'. It is now common in rock, jazz, rap and dance music. Many of the most popular contemporary artists, such as Janet Jackson (Joni Mitchell's 'Big Yellow Taxi'); the Beastie

Boys, Oasis ('Hello', thanks to Gary Glitter and/Mike Leander); Puff Daddy; Verve ('Bittersweet Symphony' using strings provided by the Rolling Stones); Vanilla Ice ('Ice Ice Baby' using a melody from the Bowie/Queen 'Under Pressure'); MC Hammer (using Rick James' 'U Can't Touch This'). On and on it goes.

Unfortunately, the term is inconsistently used. Sometimes people use it to mean creation of a sound envelope for emulation in some form of synthesiser. Sometimes, people use the expression 'sampling' when referring to the copying of whole phrases from other recordings. This particular activity undoubtedly amounts to 'substantial reproduction' - a phrase well known to copyright lawyers!

The usual case of sampling is when a musician or the producer takes a sound or series of sounds from its original context and makes a new use of it. For example, the producer of a dance record may take a riff from a BB King guitar solo recorded in the 1960s and the drum track from a James Brown album recorded in the early 1970s and use computer technology to combine these with the performance of the present-day recording artist.

Sampling often involves the breach of three different sets of rights: the copyright in the composition, the copyright in the sound recording and the breach of the performer's right to control the use of his or her performance. Under the Moral Rights legislation, sampling is also a potential breach of the Moral Rights of the composers whose works are sampled.

The use of pre-existing material in an entirely new social, political and intellectual context is a feature of many forms of modern (or so-called 'post-modern') art practice. The arts world usually refers to this practice as 'deconstruction' or 're-contextualisation'. In the visual arts, it is described as 'appropriation' (what a quaint euphemism for 'copied'!). In the music business it is called 'sampling'. A copyright lawyer, however, will most likely describe the same conduct when applied to recordings as any or all of the following:

- a breach of copyright in the sound recording from which the sound bite is taken;
- a breach of the copyright of the underlying musical work;
- an unauthorised use of the artist's performance; or
- a possible breach of Moral Rights.

Bringing a legal action on the basis of breach of copyright in the sound recording used to be difficult, because it was not always easy to identify the sampled performance and prove that it was indeed a reproduction of the earlier recorded performance, rather than a 'sound-alike performance' (in which a later artist is imitating the original). Nowadays there is no such problem. A simple electronic matching process allows easy identification of most sampled material. Once that is done, it is 'game, set and match' to the owner.

The real reason that few owners have been prepared to undertake the expense of copyright litigation against unlawful sampling and re-use of an earlier recording, is simply that it is rarely cost-effective. However, try sampling The Beatles, AC/DC or The Eagles and see how fast the record company moves! The weight of the artist will be sufficient to force the company into action, merely to keep the artist happy. When a producer of dance music took a Susan Vega track and added a backing music-bed, her record company, A & M, quickly jumped on them and the matter was settled by A & M licensing the original recording to the producer in return for most of the income earned by the record's sales.

Similarly when Negativland sampled U2's 'I Still Haven't Found What I'm looking For', U2 sued. Although the case settled, Negativland agreed to recall the record and hand all copies over to U2's record company for destruction. (See www.negativland.com/edge.html). Also, in *Grand Upright Music Ltd v. Warner Bros Records*, Gilbert O'Sullivan successfully sued rap artist Biz Markie for sampling 'Alone Again Naturally'.

As to the breach of the copyright in the musical work, there must be a very real doubt as to whether sampling is covered by the statutory mechanical licence or indeed any formal industry agreement. So long as the sample is of a 'substantial' portion of the work, there is a breach of copyright. 'Substantial portion' is really just another way of saying the 'essence', so it is clear that many samples do fit within this description. After all, capturing the essence of the earlier work and re-contextualising it is part of the very purpose of sampling. It makes no difference whether the material sampled is extensive or small: the issue is whether the sample captures the essence of the earlier work.

Again, however, the expense of legal action is great and the return quite small. Most publishers would agree to grant a licence for a sample, particularly if they were asked during production of the sample rather than after release of the record! Usually, they charge a modest one-time flat fee rather than a percentage of mechanicals, but this depends upon the song in question. Some composers are very much against the practice and will force their publishers to refuse to license the use of their songs in others' works.

In most cases, it is the artists who are most angered by the re-use of their talents without permission or reward and it is they who will press the recording or publishing companies to bring proceedings. Since the introduction of Performers' Protection powers in the Copyright Act, artists have been given the ability to bring their own proceedings against samplers. Now, if the plaintiff artist can prove that the defendant has made an unauthorised use of his or her performance, the artist will be able to seek an injunction and damages.

Throughout the world, the process of sampling has become so commonplace that record companies are now no longer discussing the legality or otherwise of the process but rather, discussing:

- to whom should the licence fee be paid?
- how much should the licence fee be? and
- should that fee be recoupable from the earnings of the artist or be met by the record company?

WHO PAYS AND GETS PAID FOR THE SAMPLE?

If you are sampling a record and a song that are in copyright, you have to get permission of both the owner of the rights in the sound recording (usually the record company and the performers) and the owner of the rights in the composition (usually the publishing company). If you ask, you might get permission for free but, usually, there will be a fee.

The fee is usually calculated in cents rather than percentages of the selling price. The latter generates such complicated royalty accounting statements that most sampled artists prefer to use the simpler, set-fee method. Small bites may be licensed for $100 to $10,000 per bite or 1c to 4c per record manufactured. The actual figure depends on the fame of the sampled performer, whether or not the original recording was a hit, how long ago it was released and all the other commercial factors that usually determine the value of a licence. The fee is calculated on the number of units to be pressed and is often payable up-front.

Sometimes, where the sampling artist is also the principal composer of the track into which the sample is going to be inserted, the record company giving permission for the use of the sample, demands all or part of the composer's mechanical royalties from the track. It is rumoured that Fatboy Slim's sampling bill on one record was 250% of mechanical royalties. The price of spurning originality certainly comes high.

The fee to the publisher is generally calculated either as a percentage of the standard mechanical royalty payable under the statutory licence scheme or as a flat fee. Common figures seem to be in the region of 25% to 50% of the mechanical royalty, again depending on the commercial circumstances of the licence.

It is all well and good to talk merrily of paying cents here and percentages there, but who is actually paying this money? The record companies argue that these payments are in the nature of recording costs and therefore (assuming that the recording costs are recoupable under the recording contract) should be recouped from the artist's share of income.

The artists argue that this allows companies faced with the bother of clearing sampled performances to take the risk of not obtaining clearances and merely relying on the artist's warranty (and indemnity) in the recording contract that he or she has the necessary rights. Then, in the event that a claim is made, the company simply settles the matter using the artist's royalties.

Musicians and record producers who use sampling techniques should ensure that, before they start to record, they work out who will be responsible for the clearance costs and provide the record company with a listing of all samples to be used, detailing where they have been taken from and the use to be made of each sample (both as to nature and length of use).

Record companies are very concerned by the risks that their artists run when they use unauthorised samples. Sampled artists are almost always financially powerful and their record company will not hesitate to sue. Accordingly, most record contracts now contain a clause requiring the artist to inform the company of any samples used, to obtain all necessary consents and to pay any associated costs.

One other aspect of the sampling controversy highlights the industrial nature of the problems underlying their use and re-contextualisation of performances. A few years ago, a very successful Australian rock band incurred the wrath of the Musicians' Union by lifting from its own record, the performance of the backing vocalists who had been hired to perform on the record. By doing so, whenever that band played live, they could achieve the sound of the backing vocalists with the flick of a computer switch. Backing vocalists argued that it was wrong for bands to use and re-use their voices, without further payment. Nowadays the answer is easy. The band would have to have a release or contract with the backing vocalist to use and reuse their performances in that way.

PARALLEL IMPORTING

The international trading system for copyright material (such as records, films, books, compositions, artwork and so on) has traditionally been divided into geographic territories. The company that owns the world rights may choose which company should represent its product in each particular country. In Australia, the local rights holder has been protected by giving it exclusivity within the territory.

Parallel imports are not pirated goods. They are genuine goods sold in the country of export with the permission of the rights holder, but imported by a reseller without the authority of the rights holder in the country of importation. For example, if Simpson Music USA owns the world rights in a work and grants an exclusive licence to Simpson Music (Australia) to manufacture and distribute its sheet in Australia, no competitor could buy the sheet music in the USA, import it, and go into competition against Simpson Music in the local market.

So, when we talk of abolishing 'Parallel Importation', we really mean to say exactly the opposite - we really mean permitting parallel imports by the abolition of parallel import restrictions. Clear?

This general position no longer applies to sound recordings.

IMPORTING SOUND RECORDINGS

The fight waged against the abolition of protection against parallel importation of sound recordings was probably the most public and bitter political fight ever waged between the Federal Government and the Australian music industry.

To understand what the fight was about, it is essential to remember that the copyright business is based on the territoriality of the exclusive rights of copyright. If you have the rights for the territory, you can stop your competition from importing and selling the same goods on your home turf. The whole economy of world record industry is based on the granting of exclusive territories. The local industry could not perceive a future in which retailers could buy their stock from the cheapest legitimate source anywhere in the world. That said, the government could smell voter approval in forcing the lowering of the price of CDs. The Prices Surveillance Authority argued that allowing copyright owners to control importation reduced competition and thus resulted in higher CD prices. The government agreed.

In 1998, notwithstanding the public controversy, the Federal Government amended the Copyright Act and opened the gates to allow 'parallel' importing of records. This made it possible for retailers to import their stock direct from overseas and bypass the local distributors.

One of the record companies' main concerns was that if parallel imports were allowed, it would be impossible to stop the import of pirate CDs. In response, a number of procedural changes have been implemented to provide anti-piracy measures. For example, only goods that are manufactured in certain countries with adequate copyright protection may be imported. Mechanical royalties must have been paid in the country of manufacture. Further, the maximum penalties for unauthorised commercial dealings in or possession of infringing copies have been increased to $60,500 and/or five years' imprisonment for individuals and $302,500 for companies. In civil actions related to the infringement of copyright by importation of pirated sound recordings, the onus of proof is on the importer to establish any defence that the sound recordings are legitimate and not pirated. All you have to do is catch them!

HOW PARALLEL IMPORT OF SOUND RECORDINGS WORKS

Copyright in a sound recording will not be infringed by importing into Australia a 'non-infringing' copy of a sound recording. Section 10AA of the Copyright Act states that a sound recording will be a 'non-infringing copy' only if:

> 1. *the copy is made by, or with the consent of:*
>   (i) *the owner of the copyright in the sound recording in the country in which the copy was made ('the copy country');*
>   (ii) *the owner of the copyright in the country in which the original sound recording was made, if the copy country does not provide copyright protection for sound recordings; or*
>   (iii) *the maker of the sound recording, if there is no copyright protection provided for sound recordings in either the copy country or the country in which the sound recording was originally made;*
> 2. *the making of a copy does not infringe copyright in the copy country; and*
> 3. *the copy country is a party to the Berne Convention, a member of the WTO, and complies with TRIPS with respect to copyright in literary, dramatic and musical works.*

All three components must be proved.

It didn't take the lawyers long to find a way around the legislation. The amendments only related to the copyright in the music and lyrics and the sound recording in which they were embodied. It didn't cover the copyright in the packaging. Nor did it cover film material. So record companies started putting music video clips on CDs (calling them 'enhanced CDs'). For a while, this strategy worked (albeit in a way that was as cumbersome and expensive as any loophole fashioned by lawyers through which their clients have to fit). Most loopholes are easily plugged if the government has the willpower and on this issue, it had plenty. It took the government 18 months to get legislation through the Senate, but the new millennium also saw a new era: Full parallel importing of records was permitted.

COMPETITION POLICY

All of these changes are part of the Federal Government's attempt to subject copyright to the principles of competition policy. There have been two very significant developments in this regard: the Ergas Report; and the legal action taken by the Australian Competition and Consumer Commission (ACCC).

ERGAS REPORT - COPYRIGHT AND COMPETITION

One of the most important reports of recent times in Australia is the Ergas Report. An independent Intellectual Property and Competition Review Committee was set up in 1999 by the Federal Government, chaired by Professor Henry Ergas to investigate areas of conflict between intellectual property legislation and competition law as it is embodied in the Trade Practices Act. The Ergas Report is likely to be a trigger for a great revolution in copyright. It is the opening shot in a war that has been threatened for years but, until now, has never really got above the status of a skirmish: the cult of the anti-monopolists versus the religion of exclusive rights.

The copyright regime's system of exclusive rights has long aroused allegations of monopolistic and anti-competitive behaviour of copyright owners. Let's face it, monopoly is the very essence of exclusive rights.

The Trade Practices Act 1974 was the first major intervention in intellectual property by non-IP legislation. Basically, the legislation specifically provided that the exclusive rights of copyright could not be used in a manner that amounted to a misuse of market power or retail price maintenance but provided a number of exceptions which benefited copyright owners. The Ergas Report acknowledged that the IP system promotes innovation and that this is a key form of competition, but nevertheless concluded that there are a number of areas of conflict between IP laws and competition policy.

Some of the submissions to the Committee supporting the removal of parallel import restrictions included the argument that the Copyright Act is not an appropriate mechanism for addressing issues such as piracy, censorship or product safety, in answer to fears of cheap, low quality copyright goods flooding the markets in the absence of import restrictions. E-commerce businesses argued that parallel import restrictions are hampering the development of the e-commerce industry in Australia, as businesses are forced to buy products through the exclusive Australian distributor rather than sourcing more cheaply off shore. Many argued that 'the globalisation of trade and the development of the Internet are making the restrictions redundant'.

In its submissions to the Committee, unsurprisingly, the ACCC argued that copyright should be treated like all other forms of property and should not receive special treatment under the Trade Practices Act. It further argued that the parallel import restrictions are unjustified because they extend copyright protection into the sphere of distribution, as opposed to just that of production, which was the original legislative intention.

The ACCC also emphasised that restrictions on parallel imports 'do nothing to protect domestic industry, they simply provide the domestic rights holder with an exclusive right to import. Whether they choose to invest and manufacture domestically are separate decisions which will be influenced by factors such as the likely international returns from investing in local R&D and the costs of local versus offshore manufacturing.'

In contrast, the Ergas Committee recognised that copyright has important features to differentiate it from other property or assets. Notably, these include the fact that 'contractual arrangements are likely to be especially important in the efficient development and exploitation of intellectual property, as these arrangements allow for gains to be realised by specialisation in the various functions and stages involved in the innovation process'.

Notwithstanding their approval of special treatment for copyright, the Committee found that some of the exclusions granted to copyright under the Trade Practices Act confer protections that can reach too far.

In particular, most committee members were of the view that removing all parallel import restrictions would 'not undermine the efficacy of copyright as a stimulus to creativity' and that it would give the small economy of Australia the opportunity 'to benefit from the intense competition, low prices and wide product availability associated with large, integrated markets' such as the European Union and the USA. It recommended the removal of parallel import protection (with a 12-month transitional window for books.) Mr John Stonier's dissenting opinion is very powerful. He attacks the arguments of the majority and scores powerful blows. To take just two examples:

The majority pointed out that the European Union has done away with parallel importing and suggested that this has not deleteriously affected the intellectual capital of those countries. Stonier pointed out that while the European Union has done away with parallel import restrictions between its members - it still maintains them against outsiders. Another point worth drawing from Stonier's dissent is that parallel importing restricts only intra-brand competition - not inter-brand competition. Thus the only advantage that may be gained from removal of the laws is one of cost reduction - a consequence that he seriously questioned.

The Government accepted the recommendation of the majority and in 2003 amended the Copyright Act to allow parallel importation of books, periodicals, printed music and software products, including computer-based games. (As a result, provided that they have been lawfully purchased in the country of origin, digital downloads no longer breach the parallel import rules.)

GETTING USED TO PARALLEL IMPORTING

The industry is still in a state of considerable flux as a result of the parallel import changes – but the early fears have now become less hysterical. The fall in the Australian dollar has meant that the advantage of importing records was instantly reduced. Also, it must be said that many of the retailers do not appear to be passing on all of the savings to their customers. Further, the retailers who import from overseas are concentrating on Top 20 records rather than specialist lines and back catalogue. Accordingly, while the prices of the former have dropped a little, the rest of the repertoire hasn't become any cheaper. Try buying any current jazz or classical CD and see how much cheaper it has become since parallel imports were permitted!

The record companies have negotiated new deals with major retailers to dissuade them from importing. After all, a cheap wholesale price is only one of the considerations for a record shop: defective records or unsold stock cannot be returned and that some of the imported records have poor quality, mistake-riddled artwork.

Australian music publishers feel just as endangered by parallel imports as their record company colleagues. They are understandably determined to prevent imports on which mechanical royalties have not been paid and will remain at the forefront of the war against those who threaten the Australian music industry by the import of pirate records.

Because this area is so complex, the Federal Government has an on-line advice site for music retailers. It provides 'information about sourcing CDs, ensuring their supplies are legitimate, importing and dealing with Customs, freight and delivery issues, using the Internet and e-commerce, understanding the law, and useful contacts'. (See www.dcita.gov.au/ip). For discussion of the impact of parallel importing on the industry, see *Australian Competition and Consumer Commission v Universal Music Australia & Ors* (N925 of 2000, Federal Court, Hill J., 14.12.01).

CONCLUSION

The rights of copyright are very valuable. They are what feed, house and clothe both composers and recording musicians and they provide the profit incentive for record and publishing companies to promote those musicians and their work. The rights are valuable and they are complex.

FURTHER INFORMATION

If you need comprehensive information about copyright law, policy and practice, see www.dcita.gov.au/ip. It is designed for IP professionals but is useful for non-professionals too.

You can also contact the Australian Copyright Council for free copyright advice on (02) 9318 1788, or write to it at 245 Chalmers Street, Redfern NSW 2016. Its website is at www.copyright.org.au.

You can access the Copyright Act 1968 online at:
http://www.austlii.edu.au

9
MUSIC PUBLISHING

THIS CHAPTER IS AN INTRODUCTION TO THE
FUNCTIONS OF THE MUSIC PUBLISHER. IT DISCUSSES
THE VARIOUS SOURCES OF PUBLISHING INCOME,
HOW THAT INCOME IS COLLECTED AND HOW
ROYALTIES ARE CALCULATED AND DISTRIBUTED.

Music publishing is one of the oldest branches of the music industry and is central to it. Composers, lyricists, librettists, translators and arrangers (for convenience, we will generally use the term 'writer') all create works that need to be administered if they are to generate money. Most writers are too busy, or have no inclination, or do not have the administrative infrastructure, to get involved in the day-to-day business of keeping track of all the ways their works are used by others, so they do deals with music publishers to do it for them in return for the publisher retaining a percentage of what it collects. This is good for the writer because the publisher has a strong commercial incentive to do the best job possible. Like any relationship, both parties have to play their part; the publisher has to be as efficient and active as possible in exploiting and protecting the works, while the writer has to deliver works as and when promised and generally be an active partner in exploiting his or her own works.

You will hear the word 'exploit' a lot in this business. Despite conjuring up images of grimy-faced waifs in Dickensian sweatshops, it is actually just a grab-bag word to cover the multitude of ways music and lyrics can generate income for those who own and control the copyrights. Just because publishers exploit music does not mean they exploit composers (though, as in any business, there are good and bad examples of the species, which is why writers need good legal and business advisers). Music publishing is a business. Any writer who forgets this is likely to regret the memory lapse.

WHAT A PUBLISHER DOES

The principal functions of a music publisher may be summarised as follows.
* Publishing sheet music or licensing others to publish it.
* Persuading artists and record companies to record the copyright material that it owns or controls.
* Persuading other users of music, such as film and television producers and advertisers, either to commission new works from its writers or use its existing works.
* Collecting fees and royalties earned by the commissioning and exploitation of music.
* Promoting the reputation of its composers so that the market for their work is enhanced.
* Protecting the work from demeaning or unauthorised uses.
* Doing all the administration involved in registering, maintaining and protecting the copyrights.
* Pitching songs to record companies, film and television production companies and advertising agencies.
* Helping writers get record deals and funding demos.
* Helping writer/artists get good management.
* Giving general career advice.
* Participating in industry associations such as APRA, AMCOS and AMPAL through which they negotiate rates for the use of their works with users, e.g. ARIA, Free TV Australia, CRA and websites.

Although it is not something they see as their function, publishers have an important secondary role in that their royalty advances are also an important source of non-bank finance in the industry.

PUBLISHING INCOME AND COPYRIGHT

There is no purer form of copyright business than Music Publishing. All music publishing income is earned through the administration, collection and enforcement of copyright. The rights of copyright are like veins through which the money flows. If you don't own or control the vein, you don't get the sustenance.

'Publishing income' is the income flowing from the composition. It includes: mechanical royalties; sale of sheet music; commissions for new works; licensing compositions for subsidiary uses such as film, television and advertisements; licence fees for the playing and broadcasting of works in public.

RIGHTS, USES AND MONEY

You will remember from the previous chapter that the Copyright Act gives the owner of the copyright in a musical work (the composition) and a literary work (the lyrics) a number of exclusive rights. When you read the dry legislative provision (s.31) it may be hard to see how they underlie every moneymaking mechanism in the music publishing industry. But as you will see, they do.

THE RIGHT TO PUBLISH

The most common way of exercising this right is printing sheet music. (The Copyright Act specifically says that the right to publish does not include making records or live performance.) Many musical works are never 'published'.

Money from this source is called **print income**.

THE RIGHT TO REPRODUCE

This is the right to capture or embody a composition in a medium that allows it to be heard later. Common reproduction media include CD, vinyl, audio-tape, video, DVD, film, hard disk, memory card.

When the reproduction is audio-only, we usually refer to the tariff for making the reproduction as **mechanical income**.

When the reproduction is audiovisual (such as film, television or other forms of combining recorded music with moving images, such income is referred to as **synchronisation (or 'synch') income**.

Both mechanical and synch income, flow from the exercise of the copyright owner's exclusive right to reproduce the work.

THE RIGHT TO COMMUNICATE TO THE PUBLIC

This right covers all the situations in which music is communicated publicly - rather than privately. It includes live performance, radio and television broadcast, and streaming, broadband or telephone line etc. This income stream is generally called **public performance income**.

THE RIGHT TO MAKE AN ADAPTATION

This is the right to change the work. The most common example of this is the making of arrangements or transcriptions.

If you do your own arrangement of someone else's work (unless the work is out of copyright or unless you have a contract with the rights owner) you will not earn any part of the original work's publishing income. By reworking or rearranging, you don't get any ownership of the original or its income stream.

For example, if Eric Dolphy rearranges a Mingus composition, he can record it and perform it live. Dolphy would get the box office and the record royalties - but it would be the Mingus estate that gets the publishing income.

COMBINATIONS OF RIGHTS

Some uses necessarily involve the exercise of more than one of the exclusive rights, at the same time.

An example of this is the digital download: The process requires an exercise of the reproduction right and the public communication right. Accordingly when a song or ring tone is legally downloaded, the composer receives mechanical and public performance income.

SOURCES OF PUBLISHING INCOME

According to the National Music Publishers Association (U.S.), the latest reported world publishing revenues during 2001 amounted to US$6.63 billion. This is not chickenfeed. The United States generated $1.940 billion followed by Germany with $808 million, Japan $702 million, U.K. $670 million, France $549 million and Italy $353 million. Australia/NZ was 11th in the lists with $99 million.

Predictably, by far the most important sources were performance income (US$3 billion) and mechanical income (US$2.7 billion), but synchronisation income (US$619.2 million and print music (US$767.2 million) were also significant contributors.

Some countries showed huge leaps (such as Croatia where, in 2001, music publishing revenue increased a massive 674% as improvements were made in the collection mechanisms, albeit off a small base.) Generally however, the total world publishing income is barely keeping pace with inflation.

1999	$6,429.4	(+2%)
2000	$6,877.3	(+6.7%)
2001	$6,626.8	(-4%)

Since then, although the figures are not available at the time of writing, it is likely that with the worldwide contraction in record sales, the related publishing income has also reduced.

It is sometimes said (inaccurately) that publishers are the banks of the music industry, but during the same period, the banks did a lot better than that.

SHEET MUSIC

Although the publishing of sheet music used to be a publisher's primary activity and source of revenue, this is no longer so. The advances of technology over the last 50 years have superseded the publication of sheet music as the primary means of distributing music to the public. However, although the sale of sheet music has been swamped by records, tapes, downloads and CDs, it remains a multi-million dollar business. US$767.2 million ain't bad!

A large percentage of print music is sold to schools and other educational institutions. Further, sheet music is still hugely important to classical music publishers in that hundred of thousands of students and professionals learn and play this genre of music. A Messiaen quartet is not something you can learn just by listening to a record.

MECHANICAL RIGHTS INCOME

These days the single most important source of income for publishers (and therefore for composers) from the reproduction of their works, is 'mechanical royalties'. Basically, the payment of mechanical royalties is the way that composers share in the income that recording artists and record companies make from the use of their material.

WHAT ARE MECHANICAL ROYALTIES?

The mechanical royalty is the royalty paid to the owner of the copyright in music (or the lyric) in return for the licence to include that work on a record.

It is called a mechanical royalty because, in the days before records, the main method of reproducing songs was music boxes and later on player pianos using piano-rolls. (They truly were mechanical devices.) In the early Copyright Acts these were referred to as 'mechanical devices'. A royalty was paid to the composer for the right to put his or her music on a player piano roll. Thus the term 'mechanical royalty' was introduced and stuck. It was introduced to break the monopoly that certain piano-roll makers were getting over popular songs by securing an exclusive right to reproduce the song on piano rolls.

Although mechanical royalties were a modest source of income in the early part of last century, it was not until modern means of technological reproduction permitted truly mass distribution and sales that the mechanical income became the flow of gold that it is today. (It is ironic that mechanical income became important because the means of reproduction was in fact electronic rather than truly mechanical.)

'Mechanicals' (used in this context) is an industry term rather than a legal term and is not technology specific. After all, the CD process is a digital one, not mechanical but we still use the term to describe the right to use a composition on a CD. But what about digital downloads? Thanks to the Digital Agenda Amendments to the Copyright Act, it is now clear that mechanical royalties are also payable in respect of digital downloads.

Now that digital downloads are an increasingly important form of distribution, it is important to note that the process of downloading involves the use of two distinct rights: the communication right (through transmission on the internet) and mechanical reproduction right. Consequently, both mechanical and performing royalties are payable.

It is not too cynical to suggest that the potential for income from mechanical royalties has been the greatest single reason for the development of the singer-songwriter in the last thirty years. The Gershwins, Rogers and Hammerstein, Cole Porter and most of the great names in popular composing between the 1920s and 1930s, made their fortunes by writing primarily for others. Virtually all of them had their songs popularised by someone else's performances. The Tin Pan Alley-style songwriter, who sat at a desk and turned out songs for others to perform and record, suffered for a while, but songwriters such as Leiber and Stoller, Goffin and King, Burt Bacharach/Hal David and others like them who all specialised in writing songs for major artists, had a revival in the 1970s and early 1980s. They made a more than comfortable living by writing songs for major artists such as Elvis Presley, Frank Sinatra, Whitney Houston, Celine Dion, Cher and John Farnham, who are not themselves composers.

COVERS

Although only the owner of the copyright in the composition can authorise the first release of a record, when that has been released on a record provided that the mechanicals are paid, anyone can record a 'cover'. This is a right granted by the Copyright Act and it is known as the **statutory licence**.

You often hear people say that a certain musician performs 'all originals'. To the outsider, this is not particularly helpful as they might quite properly assume that all material is original to somebody. In this context, however, it simply means that the material was written by the performer. On the other hand, in the publishing business, the term 'cover' means a musician's performance of material written by somebody else. Carl Perkins (who wrote 'Blue Suede Shoes' while he was a young session musician with aspirations to fame) had a car accident on the way to the studio to record 'his' song. In hospital, he had the disconcerting experience of hearing Elvis' version hit the air before he could record his own. It was another example of the 'cover' finding the success. By the time Carl Perkins recorded the song, everyone assumed he was covering the Elvis hit. Still, in the world of music publishing, no one had cause to cry. Perkins might not have sold a lot of records but he certainly made a lot of money from the mechanicals earned from Elvis' success. (The Perkins incident is not likely to happen in Australia because the composer has the right to make or authorise the first release of the recording. This right is given to the publisher under the publishing agreement and the publisher would move to stop the ambush release.)

A publishing agreement for a singer-songwriter must contain different terms to those for a songwriter who is not a performer. For the former, it makes sense to distinguish between songs they release and popularise and versions of those songs recorded by others, but for the latter the distinction is meaningless. If a composer does not record and release his or her own songs then, in a sense, every release is a 'cover'. To get over this, the publishing contract should not have a wide (or perhaps, any) royalty differential between 'originals' and 'covers'. (In such a case, the only important distinction in the royalty clause should be whether the cover is secured by the writer or the publisher.) However, in these cases, because the writer has no natural outlet for his or her material, the general royalty rate will usually be less generous.

Given that mechanical income is paid regardless of who is recording the work, it is clearly to the composer's advantage to have as many people as possible record that work. The more versions recorded, the more potential sales and the greater opportunity to earn mechanical royalties. If it is true that 'River Deep Mountain High' has been recorded by about 250 different artists, you can imagine that the mechanical income from that one song is a fortune.

Dolly Parton's song 'I Will Always Love You', which was a huge hit for Whitney Houston in 1993, almost certainly made Dolly more money as a 'cover' than Dolly's own version. According to industry legend, at one stage the Whitney Houston version was outselling the combined sales of the other ninety-nine records in the US Top 100 Singles Chart.

Publishers would always like to be more successful at getting recording artists to record the work of third party writers but, in Australia, the opportunity for placing a cover is restricted because the cult of the singer-songwriter is so very strong here. It is not uncommon to hear musicians speak unkindly of performers who do covers. It is (quite wrongly) perceived as some kind of indication of inferior talent even though, in recent times, the best selling Australian recording artists have been artists such as John Farnham, Jimmy Barnes, Anthony Warlow, Guy Sebastian and Kylie Minogue, to name only a few, who have mainly recorded other people's songs. Ask Joe Cocker about the value of covers - he even made a Beatles' song his own! All of these performers have attained huge sales of albums featuring material written by others, proving that a good song will always justify being recorded, no matter who writes it.

It is no wonder that when one of these artists prepares for a new album, the publishers get flushed with excitement. If they can place just one of their songs on a platinum-selling album in Australia, it is likely to be worth about

$10,000 in mechanicals alone, not to mention the likely public performance income if it gets airplay too. If they can get a cover on the record of a best-selling international artist, the royalties from just one album track can be many times more. Even the 'B' tracks on a single are valuable, because, although they earn no performance royalties (assuming they don't get airplay), the amount of mechanical income they earn is identical to that of the feature track.

If a cover of your song is included on a 'Various Artists' compilation album you will be paid your mechanical rate, pro rata to the number of tracks on the album.

Of course, sometimes the owner of the copyright in a work does not like the cover version. There are many dire covers of fabulous works. However, provided that the cover artist pays the mechanical royalty to AMCOS, there is not much that the owner can do. The only angle is to argue that the cover is a 'debasement' of the original work and therefore not allowed under the statutory licence. In 1996 we saw Australia's most important case in this field: *Schott Music International GmbH v. Colossal Records*.

In that case, a Spanish group had done a techno version of 'O Fortuna' from the classical work 'Carmina Burana' by Carl Orff. The publishers of Carmina Burana sued on the basis that the new work was a debasement of the original and was therefore outside the terms of the statutory licence. Justice Tamberlin's judgment in the Federal Court, which was upheld on appeal, will be the benchmark for similar cases in the future. He extensively discussed the meaning of 'debasement'. Essentially, he decided that the term 'debase' calls for a value judgment based on a significant lowering in integrity, value, esteem or quality of the work. This, he decided, had to take into account the broad spectrum of taste and values of the community (not just those of the composer or a limited section of the musical industry). At the end of the day, the court had to decide whether the adaptation of the original was so extensive, detrimental or inferior, as a whole, which it amounted to a debasement. (See (1996) 36 IPR 267 at 274). He decided that the techno version was not a 'debasement' and was therefore covered by the statutory licence. The permission of the widow Orff was not required. So long as the record company paid the mechanical royalty, the record was legal.

(Although the judge was at pains to say that the case was not about Moral Rights, now that Moral Rights legislation has been introduced in Australia, we will see Justice Tamberlin's arguments once again put to the blowtorch. Given that there are no other cases on the meaning of 'debasement' in Australia, it will be of considerable importance.)

SYNCHRONISATION IN FILM OR TELEVISION

All films and television programs use music on their soundtracks. To allow them to do this, the film producer must obtain what is known as the 'synchronisation rights' to the music. (This is the case whether the film is intended for theatrical or non-theatrical exhibition, transmission by cable or closed circuit, for television or whatever.) It is called the synchronisation right because the producer is synchronising the music with the moving images.

Producers have a choice; they can either use so-called 'production music' (also called 'library music' or 'mood library music'), commission a composer to write new music for the film, or license particular tracks of material which has already been released on record. Sometimes a producer may use a combination of all three.

USING PRODUCTION MUSIC

Production music is basically an archive of generic material composed and recorded especially for use in film. If you want 'love music', 'earthquake music', 'battle music' or whatever, all you have to do is use the library's index. It is owned by the publisher and, because it is not available for exclusive licences, it is generally quite cheap to license. Production music, unlike other sources of music, is licensed at fixed rates for particular uses.

You select the material you want and pay for the amount you actually use. The licensing is done through AMCOS. Between 2002 and 2005, the amount of production music licensed by AMCOS increased by 75%.

COMMISSIONING OF ORIGINAL SOUND-TRACK MATERIAL

The commissioning of new works for use on soundtracks is very important to the financial health of many composers. Composers are sometimes commissioned to write just one featured song, or to write the whole soundtrack, or to write the sound-track plus supply the fully leadered and cued sound recording of the commissioned music.

If you have signed a standard term agreement with your publisher, you will probably have assigned to the publisher all rights in the works you compose during the term of the agreement. Accordingly, if a producer approaches you directly, you cannot legally commit to the deal before discussing it with your publisher and getting the publisher's approval. Not only is this legally correct (because you may not have the necessary rights to do the deal yourself), it is commercially sensible. Your publisher may be more knowledgeable about the going rates and terms for such deals and may well have greater bargaining power. For example, the publisher might be able to offer assistance from its affiliates in other territories to help publicise the film or, in some other way, convince the producer to improve your deal. Negotiations and final agreement for film commissions must be between the publisher and the film producer, rather than with you, though you can obviously assist in the negotiations.

LICENSING PRE-RECORDED AND RELEASED MATERIAL

The third choice, licensing the use of material that has already been released on records, has been used for decades, particularly for use over opening and closing credits. During the last 20 years, however, there have been many hugely successful movies that have moved the music up from the background and made it the centrepiece of the film. Examples like 'Saturday Night Fever' (the biggest selling soundtrack of all time), 'Titanic', 'Romeo + Juliet', 'Reservoir Dogs', 'The Bodyguard' and '8 Mile', show the commercial attractiveness of combining popular and familiar music with the story-telling capabilities of movies. Apart from anything else, it creates a wonderful opportunity to sell the soundtrack album, which can turn a break-even film into a commercial success.

For further discussion, see the Chapter 30, **Music in Advertising** and Chapter 31, **Music in Film**.

THE PROMOTION OF THIRD PARTY GOODS AND SERVICES

Those in the marketing and promotion business have for many years realised that an association with music can enhance the image of the service or product that they wish to promote. Many composers make their entire living (and a very good living too) writing jingles for radio and television advertisements and other corporate promotions.

More recently there has been a great increase in the amount of licensing of standards or hit songs from the not very distant past for this purpose. 'I Still Call Australia Home' has obvious appeal for a Qantas commercial and 'Who Wants To Be A Millionaire' was a natural for Lotto.

Classical music has become rather more popular with advertisers since the 'Three Tenors' video and CD was so successful. Advertising agencies love using classical works to enhance the 'class' of products. The fact that most classical works (though not the recording itself) are out of copyright and so can be used free is, of course, entirely incidental. A word of warning though: particular arrangements of very old classical pieces may still be in copyright, so never assume a work is out of copyright. Always check carefully first, to avoid a nasty surprise.

Until recent years, most publishers in Australia had a reactive approach to this income source. They would wait for an advertiser to approach them for permission to use a song, rather than chase the advertiser. In the last decade though, this has changed. Now, all of the major publishers have hired Licensing Managers to promote actively the use of their catalogue by advertisers. (In the US there was a species of song salesmen called 'pluggers' because they went from studio to studio, plugging a publisher's songs to name artists, to get them to record the publisher's song. That doesn't happen any more. The business has become more sophisticated.)

Whether or not composers are prepared to allow their material to be used this way, is a matter for negotiation when entering the publishing contract. Most, quite rightly, want to maintain some control (see Chapter 13, **Common Clauses In Publishing Deals**, where it deals with artistic control).

COMMUNICATION TO THE PUBLIC

Every time copyright music is performed in public or broadcast, a royalty is payable to the copyright owner for that use. Because it would be impractical and too expensive for individual composers to collect the fees, composers and publishers formed companies to administer the public performance and broadcast rights on their behalf.

In Australasia, the Australasian Performing Right Association (APRA) performs that role. APRA is a non-profit company, established by copyright owners (both publishers and writers) to administer public performance of music. APRA's role is dealt with in detail in Chapter 26, **Collecting Societies** but, in brief, it operates by having its members assign to it the right to perform the composition in public and to communicate it to the public (including by way of broadcasting). That way, it can grant licences and collect fees from a wide range of public users of music such as radio and television stations, shopping arcades and venues. The money collected is then placed in revenue pools (e.g. commercial radio income, ABC concert, etc) and distributed according to each work's share of the total performances.

Every composer should be an APRA member. To do so, you must either have had your songs performed or otherwise exploited, or have a contract with a publisher which is a member of APRA or one of the equivalent bodies overseas which are affiliated to APRA.

The rules of APRA provide that no less than 50% of the income collected is to be paid directly to the writer. Accordingly, the writer gets a minimum of 50% of the APRA income. In practice, there are very few 50/50 deals. Most publishing agreements grant the writer a greater split of the APRA income. How this is described in the agreement will vary from contract to contract but it is common for a publishing agreement to say something like the following:

> *The Writer will receive 70% of the gross fees paid by the collecting society in relation to performing rights in the Compositions (it being understood that you will receive 50% of the gross directly from the collecting society and 50% will be paid to us, of which we will pay you 40%.)*

It is simpler than it looks: The gross income is 100%. The collecting society directly pays the writer the minimum 50%. It pays the publisher the other 50%. However, if we assume the contract specifies that the writer is to receive 70% of gross public performance income, the writer is still 20% short. This comes out of the 50% paid to the publisher. Given that the publisher has been paid 50% of the gross it must pay or credit the writer with 40% of that amount (40% of 50% equals 20% of the gross amount) to bring the writer's receipts up to 70%.

The 50% share paid by APRA directly to the writer is a 'minimum'. It is perfectly possible to negotiate a deal with the publisher whereby the writer is paid its full percentage directly by APRA. However, this is uncommon for two reasons:

- *First*, publishers need to recoup their advances: although they can't touch the 50% minimum paid direct to the writer, they can use the balance to recoup any outstanding advances. Using the same example as above, if the writer was unrecouped $50,000, the publisher would not actually pay the additional 20% of gross in royalties. Instead, it would credit that amount to the recoupment of the advance.

- *Secondly*, even if there is no advance to be recouped, it means that the publisher will have the use of the money (and thus the interest on it), for several months, until the next accounting is due to the writer. (Even in this era of low interest rates, six monthly accounting means that considerable sums are earned by publishers from the interest on the writers' share of revenue.)

This means that even if you are heavily unrecouped with both your record and publishing company, if you are doing a lot of live work and you make sure you submit your APRA Returns at the end of each live performance, your APRA cheque can be quite substantial. (How this is collected, calculated and distributed is discussed in some detail in the next section.)

SUNDRY INCOME

All publishing agreements have (or should have) a clause relating to sundry income - all the bits and pieces that don't fall in the major categories already discussed. This is the catch-all category.

Sundry income is derived from (say) the hiring of the orchestral parts of a full score or licensing a newspaper to publish the words of a lyric or a clothing manufacturer to print lyrics on a T-shirt. If and when a 'recordable CD royalty' is introduced in Australia, the publishing share of that income will be classified as sundry.

COLLECTION, CALCULATION AND DISTRIBUTION OF PUBLISHING INCOME
SHEET MUSIC

In the popular music field, most publishers in Australia do not even publish sheet music. Most issue a print licence to other publishers such as Music Sales, Allans or Hal Leonard that have specialist skills, to manufacture and distribute it on their behalf. This is simply because of the high cost of specialist printing, administering the publication, warehousing and distribution. It makes commercial sense to minimise the overheads and license a specialist to do the task, underwrite the costs and to run the commercial risks. (Before 2001 and the intervention of the Australian Competition and Consumer Commission, two competitors in the field, Music Sales and Warner/Chappell, wished to share warehousing and distribution (the non-competitive aspect of their businesses), and compete on the input and sales area. The ACCC said no: to do so would be anti-competitive. So Warner/Chappell withdrew from all print distribution in Australia, saying that anyone could import their material from now on - provided that they bought it from Warner/Chappell Florida! So much for the effectiveness of the ACCC approach. Thank god for we consumers that purity of competition ideology has been maintained.)

Print licences can be restricted to the publication of single works, special 'mixed folios' or may encompass the whole catalogue of the publisher.

For example:
- Company A and Company B enter a print licence.
- Company A (the licensee publisher) prints, distributes and administers the sheet music and as well, collects, accounts for and pays through the royalties due to Company B (the licensor publisher).
- Company B merely supplies the compositions (and the necessary rights) and receives its share of income from Company A.
- Depending on the deal, Company B will either pay through to the writer a share of that income or may have Company A perform that function as well.

The writer's share of sheet music income is usually based on a royalty between 10% and 14% of the recommended retail price of copies sold. Where the music is included in a folio (i.e. a collection of works), the royalty is reduced in proportion to the number of 'your' works in the edition. The publisher meets the cost of printing, distributing and promoting the material.

Although publishers usually process their sheet music sales invoices on a monthly basis they will not account separately for sheet music sales. This is not negotiable. Accounting for sheet music sales will be included in the usual six monthly royalty accounting statement.

MECHANICAL INCOME FROM RECORDS

The Copyright Act 1968 (ss 54-64) provides that the mechanical royalty rate will be:

(i) *the royalty agreed between the manufacturer of the record and the owner of the copyright in the musical work; or if no agreement can be reached,*

(ii) *an amount determined by the Copyright Tribunal; or*

(iii) *if no such agreement or determination is in force, 'an amount equal to 6.25% of the retail selling price of the record'.*

This is referred to as 'the statutory rate'.

In New Zealand the rate is 5.6% of the recommended selling price of the recording (excluding GST).

Although the Act sets the basic rate, the rate can be varied by contract. For many years there was in place an agreement between the Australian Mechanical Copyright Owners Society (AMCOS) and the Australian Record Industry Association (ARIA) to vary the statutory rate that applies to ARIA members. It was a complex agreement, one that was negotiated hard. Perhaps because it was so hard to come to terms, as from January 2006 the old approach was abandoned, and AMCOS has introduced its own Physical Product Licence Scheme.

The most obvious changes to the statutory scheme are that the rate is lower and more flexible and that the percentage is based not on the retail selling price (RRP) but on the PPD (the published price to dealer - the maker's listed wholesale price to dealers.) These days it is easier for both parties if the rate is calculated on the PPD because the retail price can vary so much. The current mechanical rate, calculated on PPD, is 8.25%. Where there are a number of tracks on the recording, the mechanical royalty is divided equally between each musical work. (This is referred to as 'pro rata per track' in contrast to 'pro rata by time' where the longer tracks attract larger fees than shorter ones.) If one of the tracks on the recording is a medley, each song in the medley receives a pro-rata share of that track. Therefore an album with 12 tracks where one of the tracks is a medley of three songs, the medley track receives $1/12$ and each song in the medley gets $1/3$ of that $1/12$.

MECHANICAL INCOME PAYABLE IN OTHER SITUATIONS

Although the manufacture and sale of recordings is the most important, there are a huge number of different situations in which a mechanical licence is required from AMCOS. Some of these include:

(i) **Demo/Audition**: Audio-only recordings specifically designed for submission to music publishers, record companies, artists, orchestras, bands, etc. to promote the artist and/or composer's work appearing on the recording.

(ii) **Background Music**: Audio-only recordings made specifically for your own use as background to a performance or other event. These recordings cannot be used for advertisement purposes or for the purposes of promotion of an event or product. Background music licences are also obtained by pubs and shops and other businesses that recognise the importance of music (and in particular, the right music) to their customers and thus to their profitability

(iii) **Educational**: Audio-only recordings made by an educational institution where the recordings are made available free of charge to the students. Where the institution intends to sell the recordings to students, such recordings come within the 'for retail sale' category. Where a person is making recordings for an educational purpose and supplying them to educational institutions or their students, again such recordings come within the 'for retail sale' category.

(iv) **Premiums**: Where the record is going to be given away to promote a product (such as a magazine) the specific approval of the publisher will be required. AMCOS cannot grant a licence or nominate a fee. You must get the publisher's approval (see below).

(v) **Ringtones and Downloads**: When musical works are sold as downloads or used as mobile phone ringtones, reproduction and communication rights are both being exercised. To facilitate the process, APRA and AMCOS operate joint licence schemes. The current mechanical rate is 6.25% of retail price (ie what the consumer pays for the download.) An additional 1.75% of retail price is payable for the transmission of the work to consumers. So the total publishing royalty applicable to downloads is 8% of retail price.

THE MECHANICAL LICENCE PROCESS

Since 2001, mechanical licensing has been done electronically, replacing the old paper-based system that was so complex, inaccurate and time consuming. It uses the copyright information stored in APRA/AMCOS' extensive works database, Copyright Management System. It works for large and small record companies alike.

REPORTING THE USE

For each new release clients must submit the same information - including details of the production as a whole (title, artist, catalogue number, etc) and of each track featured on the production (track title, writers, etc). A matching algorithm processes the information submitted and either links the tracks to existing works in the database or creates new records. The results of this are checked manually and then made available to publishers to view and to make claims online.

CLAIMING THE WORK AND THE ROYALTY

Any publisher who claims ownership or control of any part of the mechanical right of the work must make its claim within 10 working days and, if its permission is required, must state whether or not the intended reproduction is permitted. The publisher's permission is only relevant if recordings of the particular work have not previously been released. This is the so-called "first use" right and it applies equally to songs and instrumental works.

To explain, let's assume a publisher controls the song. (The right belongs to the composer if the work has not been assigned to a publisher.) If this recording will be the "first recording" of the song, then the publisher may withhold permission to make the recording. However, once the first recording of a particular song has been released, the Copyright Act provides a 'statutory licence' allowing anyone to make and release records of that song provided they pay the proper mechanical copyright royalty.

If two publishers claim the same piece of music (and this does happen), the publishers have to work the "Disputed Claim" out between them - the record company just has to keep accruing the proper amount of royalty for each record it sells in the meantime.

ISSUING THE PRESCRIBED NOTICE

At the end of the 10 day notice period, an initial Prescribed Notice is created. The whole process takes some 12 working days, a fraction of the time taken under the paper-based inquiry system. The Prescribed Notice shows the current mechanical ownership details. As and when ownership changes to works attached to the production occur, new Prescribed Notices are generated to reflect the new position. In this way ownership information is always kept up to date, allowing accurate allocation of the mechanical royalties.

PAYMENT

The major record companies - which pay mechanical royalties directly to the publishers - can upload the latest Prescribed Notices to their copyright systems to ensure each quarter's payments are made accurately. Non-major labels - which pay via AMCOS - are informed if the "AMCOS royalty" has changed and the transparent nature of the process allows labels to check information easily.

Then, when the label supplies the sales reports, AMCOS' distribution system splits the amount under invoice and distributes to each sharer of each work according to the details on the Prescribed Notice. It even takes into account any retention allowances and maintains an historical record of sales and returns.

One of the important terms of the AMCOS licence is that the manufacturer must supply manufacturing information to AMCOS. This also applies to manufacturers of third party product. This allows AMCOS to effectively supervise the mechanical right by comparing the figures provided by the label and the manufacturer, thus making it difficult for record companies (big and small) to under-report.

ACCOUNTING

The accounting will detail the title, catalogue number, royalty rate, number of units sold and amount of royalty.

Record companies have to account to the publisher on a quarterly basis, or to be precise, within 60 days from the end of each quarter. This does not mean, however, that you will be able to persuade your publisher to account to you for your mechanicals on a quarterly basis. This is not negotiable.

RETURNS AND RETENTIONS

Although the Copyright Act refers to royalties being payable on records manufactured, one of the important concessions that was negotiated into the AMCOS-ARIA Agreement is that mechanicals are in fact only paid on records that are sold. ('Records sold' is the number of records delivered or invoiced to a retailer, less the number returned.)

In order to protect the record company from excess payments of mechanical royalties, the AMCOS-ARIA Agreement allowed the record companies to retain a proportion of mechanical income that would otherwise be payable, to take into account the returns. In the United States, the retentions are frequently between 50% and 75%! This crazy situation is largely due to the fact that virtually all records are sold there on 'sale or return' (meaning the retailer can return any unsold records for a full credit), but apart from that, the American record companies tend to over-ship stock to the shops, especially if the act is touring. This means (in the dreaded record industry expression) records can 'ship platinum and return gold'!

In Australia sale or return is becoming more widespread although over-shipping tends to be due to market miscalculation rather than a marketing technique.

There are two kinds of retentions provided in the current AMCOS licence:

RETENTIONS ON STANDARD WHOLESALE SALES

On these, a record company is allowed to keep a retention of 10% calculated on the net number of units of the record delivered during that accounting period. This is permitted for each of the first four accounting periods after a record's release. Thereafter, no retention is allowed.

RETENTIONS ON SALE-OR-RETURN PRODUCT

For records that have been distributed on a sale-or-return basis (the most usual of these being records sold in conjunction with large-scale television advertising campaigns) greater retentions are permitted.

THE FINANCIAL RESULTS

The mechanical royalty can mean large amounts of money for the publisher and composer, if a record is commercially successful.

On a CD with a standard PPD of $18.60, the current statutory mechanical copyright royalty in Australia is approximately $1.35 per unit. If the record sells 50,000 units, the gross mechanical royalties generated are about $67,860 in Australia alone. That amount would then be split between the publisher and the writer in the proportion set down in the writer's publishing agreement. If it were a 75/25 deal, the writer would earn about $50,000, provided all the songs were that writer's. If there were 10 tracks on the album, and a different publisher and composer controlled each track, each publisher would receive $6,786, of which the relevant composer would get $5,090.

UNITED KINGDOM PRACTICE

In the UK, there is no statutory rate. The mechanical royalty is set by agreement between representative organisations of the record industry and the composers.

For all European Union member states except Ireland and the UK, the mechanical royalty rate is set by a contract between the *International Federation of the Phonographic Industry* (IFPI) and the *Bureau International des Sociétés Gerant les Droits d'Enregistrement et de Reproduction Mècanique* (BIEM). The current rate is 9.306% of the wholesale price of the CD or cassette. The rates in Ireland and the UK are 7.5% and 8.5% respectively. These rates are subject to national variations and certain discounts.

UNITED STATES PRACTICE

The USA uses what is called a 'penny rate'. It is based on a fixed number of cents not a percentage figure. The mechanical royalty rate in the USA was fixed at a low 2.75 cents per track for many years. When an escalating rate came into effect, the US record companies promptly amended their standard controlled composition clause to neutralise the increase by capping the rate at 75% of the full rate, with special provisions to cover discounted records and records which are distributed but not sold for money. The royalty will continue to increase automatically: In 2002, it was 8.0 cents; in 2004, it was 8.5 cents; and in 2006 it became 9.1 cents. It is to be reviewed in 2007.

CONTROLLED COMPOSITION CLAUSES

For a discussion of controlled composition clauses and other caps on mechanical income imposed by record contracts, see the section on Controlled Compositions in Chapter 23, **Record Royalties**.

SYNCHRONISATION WITH FILM OR TELEVISION

As was described earlier in this chapter, when a film or TV producer needs music, there are standard sources: Production music; original, commissioned music; and sound recordings that have already been recorded and commercially released.

PRODUCTION MUSIC

Licences for the use of production music (which used to be called library music or mood music) are issued by AMCOS on behalf of the music publishers. Most other synchronisation licences are issued directly from the publisher. This is because most publishers have to consult their writers (or the licensor, where the songs are licensed from a third party) whenever their works are to be synchronised. Good publishers will consult this way, even if the contract does not actually require it.

The cost of licensing production music is considerably less than of the cost of licensing a musical work that has already been published (excluding the cost of licensing the sound recording that embodies that work). For producers, it is the most inexpensive way of obtaining music for synchronisation.

COMMISSIONED MATERIAL

Even though the Australian fees are much lower than in the United States, a small documentary can still attract a commission fee of $15,000 and a film or a television series can be worth between $40,000 for low-budget and $150,000 for high-end productions. Of course the fees vary enormously, depending on the budget of the production and the experience and reputation of the composer.

PRE-RECORDED AND RELEASED MATERIAL

The cost of licensing such music depends on the success the song has enjoyed on record, the place of intended exhibition - theatrical or non-theatrical - and the territory of the licence sought, how often the song has been used in synch before, and the type of rights sought (i.e. the producer may also want to secure cable television, free television and home video rights but not, usually, rights for the use in games). Each kind of use attracts an additional fee.

Expect the synchronisation rights for million-sellers to cost more than those for songs that stiffed, assuming comparable use in the sound-track (i.e. featured or as background). Theatrical costs more than non-theatrical and 'world' rights cost more than Australian rights. This said, as only the roughest of guides, the licence fee for world theatrical rights can be between $1,400 and $2,500 per 30-second grab, but the rights to 'contemporary standards' can cost a lot more than that.

Producers should ask for a quote from the publisher for each of the rights. Then, the producer can secure and pay for the rights 'as needed' at the agreed quoted rate, rather than buy them all up front. This is common when securing rights in sound recordings, but seems less common when licensing from publishers. (Note however that it is usually more expensive to buy the rights piecemeal.)

THE PROMOTION OF THIRD PARTY GOODS AND SERVICES

Licences for use of songs in commercials and the like are granted by the music's publisher. Before granting such a licence, it is standard practice for the publisher to consult with the writer and obtain his or her consent to the use. Some writers object to their songs being used to promote certain types of goods. It was only a dozen years ago that any of the Lennon-McCartney songs were licensed for advertising uses.

The fee is negotiated directly with the music publisher. The rates charged will vary according to the success enjoyed by the song, the reputation of the writer, the nature of the product that wishes to associate itself with the song, the territory, the duration of the promotional usage, the intended audience, and how determined the intended user is to secure the rights. Even in Australia, national advertising campaigns have been known to attract fees well in excess of $500,000 for a 12-month licence. In larger markets, the fees can be much greater.

COMMUNICATION TO THE PUBLIC

Every time copyright music is performed in public or broadcast, a royalty is payable. Most 'public performance' of music is licensed by APRA (discussed briefly earlier in this chapter).

As soon as a publisher enters the contract with a writer, it will notify APRA that it controls the works of that writer and notifies it of income splits.

LICENSING OF USERS

APRA has established a network of 'blanket' licences with the users of publicly performed music: radio stations; television stations; ring tone providers; digital service providers; webcasters; live music venues; halls; function centres; aerobic and fitness classes; film screenings; churches; schools; sports stadia; jukebox and video jukebox operators; public transport operators; cinemas; dancing schools; electrical appliance shops; dance clubs (including mobile discos); skating rinks; background music users and so on. This can amount to big money: Although the organisers tried to negotiate a voluntary licence for the inclusion of music in the Olympic Games, after difficult negotiations, the APRA fee was rumoured to be in the vicinity of $100,000.

The manner of calculating how much will be payable to APRA for the right to publicly perform music depends on the type of use. Each type has a different formula. There is no point in detailing all of these formulae here, but generally they are based on a percentage of gross income. Some examples follow.

- **Cinemas**: A licensee will pay a fee of 0.55% of net box office receipts revenue (this rate is currently being reviewed by the Copyright Tribunal).
- **Dance Parties**: Dance Parties with a box office, i.e. ticket sales, are generally licensed on APRA's Dance Party Licence. Fees are calculated at 1.859% of gross box office receipts (1.69%+GST) or 10.791 cents per person admitted (10.89 cents +GST) whichever is greater. Licence fees are generally paid after the event, but in some cases an advance payment is required. APRA may also request a lists of the works played by each DJ on the night. The play lists are important because they allow APRA to identify the composers who should receive royalty payments. If your dance party is free to the public, you still need to take out an APRA licence to play copyright music. The licence fee is calculated at 10.791 cents per person admitted to the party with a minimum fee of $38.50.
- **Jukeboxes**: $119.19 per annum plus $1.07 per additional speaker.
- **Live Musical Performances**: Either 2% of gross annual expenditure upon all performing artists or where admission fees are charged and

collected by performers or their agents, 1.5% of the gross annual sums paid for admission.

- **One-off Concerts**: 1.5% of the gross admission receipts.
- **Jingles**: Public performance royalties are paid for music used in radio and television advertisements. How they are calculated depends on whether the advertising campaign is local, state or national, frequency of play and so on.
- **Commercial TV Services** (including local stations): A negotiated, industry-wide, lump sum.
- **Commercial Radio**: a new scheme started on 1 January 2000. Monthly fees are based on a percentage of the station's gross advertising revenue which varies between 0.4% and 3.5% depending on the proportion of APRA works broadcast as a percentage of total airtime. Stations provide quarterly reports detailing songs played and number of times per quarter.
- **Subscription TV Services**: These pay a fixed rate of 28.5c per subscriber per month irrespective of number of channels per service. Commercial premises (businesses, pubs and hotels) pay a higher monthly rate. This scheme is under review too.
- **Community Radio and TV**: For these licences, fees are assessed on licensees' music usage, grant revenue and the split of their income between exempt and non-exempt sources. Stations pay a flat rate of $150/year or 1.5% revenue if it's greater than $25,000/year.
- **Narrowcast TV**: 0.9% of total revenue.
- **Narrowcast Radio**: the rate varies depending on amount of APRA works broadcast, from 3.5% - 0.5% of applicable revenue.

Of course these figures are varied from time to time, so they should only be treated as guidelines. The current figures can be obtained readily from APRA.

EXCEPTION FOR GRAND RIGHTS

APRA does not collect income earned from 'Grand Rights'. These relate to works performed in:

- A 'dramatic context' (i.e. with costume, scenery or other dramatic effects).
- Oratorios and large choral works (i.e. those over 20 minutes).
- In association with ballet. In other words, performance of ballet music by itself (e.g. in a concert) does not involve Grand Rights, while a staged ballet does.

If Grand Rights are involved, you must negotiate directly with the publisher who controls the rights (although with smaller shows APRA often acts as the publishers' agent and streamlines the process). Ask early. Do not assume that you will be given the rights. In many cases permission will be refused: an exclusive licence may already have been granted to somebody else; the publisher may not be convinced of your ability to mount the show; or the copyright owner may simply choose not to grant the licence.

TRACING PERFORMANCES

The validity of any system of royalty allocation demands that the right people are getting paid. This is achieved by a combination of means which are of varying precision. Some of the performance calculations are achieved by making statistical inferences from surveys, some of it is based on mere cost effectiveness, some are precisely calculated:

- **Radio**: APRA conducts 'census' logging - meaning that all broadcast featured music is logged.
- **Television**: The survey system is exemplified by the treatment of television. The music that is broadcast on television is calculated using reports supplied by the stations as to the music used over particular survey periods.

  An example of pooling of income (to save unjustified administrative expenses) is the adding of money obtained from juke box licences to radio income, on the basis that what's popular on radio is probably popular on jukeboxes. (This is referred to as the 'follow the dollar' approach.)
- **Concert performances** are analysed individually, and performance royalties are allocated to the specific copyright owners involved.

DISTRIBUTION

After deducting its expenses (generally around 13-14%), APRA allocates its income to members. The method of income calculation necessarily mirrors the method of usage calculation.

For example, station X pays its APRA licence fee and supplies census electronic logs of all music put to air. The music reported on those logs is paid out of station X's licence fees. If there are 260 commercial radio stations in Australia, there are effectively 260 commercial radio 'pools'. (In contrast, the calculation of royalties payable as a result of concert performances is done on the basis of actual works performed and reported.)

SELF-REPORTING

APRA Returns are the method for reporting to APRA each use of your songs - even your own performances of them! A Return should be completed and sent to APRA each time you perform your own (or anyone else's) songs. By doing this whenever you perform your original material, you can earn APRA income. Similarly, if you hear your material being broadcast you should self-report in case that particular broadcast was not part of the station's survey period.

TIMING OF PAYMENTS

The APRA royalty payments are based on six-monthly accounting periods. For the period from June to 31 December, a distribution is generally made the following May or June. For the following six months, the distribution is generally made in December (just in time for writers to have some money over Christmas).

OVERSEAS INCOME

Most Australian publishers insist on acquiring world rights when signing writers. (This is of course negotiable but is certainly the natural desire of the publisher.) In order to administer their catalogue and represent their interests in a foreign territory, all major publishers have established an international network of publishers. In the case of multinational publishing companies the sub-publisher will usually be the local office of the parent company. Independent publishers will usually do a sub-publishing deal on a territory-by-territory basis with one of the Majors or come to some arrangement with another independent company.

Similarly, the collecting societies (APRA and AMCOS) have an international network of like societies. In the United States there is no equivalent of AMCOS (except for the privately owned Harry Fox Agency) and there are three rival organisations (BMI, ASCAP and SESAC) that fulfil the APRA role.

10
ANATOMY OF A MUSIC PUBLISHER

IF YOU ARE DEALING WITH MUSIC PUBLISHERS IT IS
IMPORTANT TO UNDERSTAND WHO DOES WHAT IN
THE COMPANY. THIS CHAPTER INTRODUCES YOU TO
THE DRAMATIS PERSONAE: WHO THEY ARE AND WHAT
THEY DO.

Music publishing does its business differently from the record business. Each
deals in different rights and activities. At its core, publishing is about three
things - controlling and protecting copyrights, exploiting (i.e. licensing
commercial and other uses) those copyrights and administering the flow of
income to the copyright owners. Without these basic activities the whole
industry would grind to a halt, paralysed by lack of repertoire (i.e. the works
controlled by a particular publisher or written by a particular composer) and
inability to distribute royalties.

Most music publishing deals tend to be a bit like courtship - lots of action
in the early days until the formalities are done, then things quieten down to a
routine. This is unlike in the record industry where the real business only
starts after the deal is signed and planning the recording starts. However,
publishing is not just about music and songs, it is also about relationships, so
good publishers and sensible writers actively work on developing that
professional relationship.

Following is a brief guided tour through the main positions in any
music publishing company. In smaller operations, one person will usually
perform several (perhaps all) functions, but the functions themselves are
fairly standard.

THE MANAGING DIRECTOR

Publishers are very much influenced by the character of their managing directors (MDs). Different MDs have different strengths. Some are great at picking songs and writers and happily become the company's main talent scout. Others claim no musical sense but are terrific administrators and are happy to leave the talent scouting to their professional manager. Some exhibit both qualities.

MDs of the multi-national publishers all report to regional managers based overseas. This means that their actions must be within corporate policies, but most still enjoy considerable freedom. MDs of independent publishers can be more maverick if they wish but, in the long run, they face the same financial pressures and industry structures as the multinationals.

When looking at any publishing company, make sure you can get along with its MD. Get to know his or her management style. You will have no trouble finding out those who support their writers and those who seem to be otherwise engaged whenever their writers need advice or a royalty advance. A supportive and patient MD can help a writer get through tough times. Remember though - a lot depends upon personalities. Some writers get on fine with MDs who others think of as fiends. MDs, like most people, respond badly to gratuitous unpleasantness. Who can blame them? If you don't like the MD before you sign a deal, don't expect to like him or her afterwards (when it's too late to change).

THE CREATIVE SERVICES MANAGER

Creative Services Managers (also known as Professional Managers) are the publishers' equivalent of the record companies' A&R managers. They generally answer directly to the MD and work closely with whoever looks after Business Affairs and Accounting.

Their primary role is to look for songs, writers and catalogues for the company to acquire. They have to be able to recognise songs and writers with potential and to evaluate what is a commercially realistic price when acquiring established catalogues and works.

Professional managers also liaise with record companies and artists. They are responsible for finding ways to exploit the musical works the company controls. This means keeping in touch with A&R departments, to stay aware of who is recording and who might need songs. If John Farnham, Jimmy Barnes or an Australian Idol is recording, the publishers are aware that their records will be largely made up of songs written by other writers. They audition literally hundreds of songs, before deciding on a track listing. (The story goes that 'You're the Voice' was only auditioned and included on

'Whispering Jack' at the last minute, after someone checked to make sure the demo had arrived safely. Such is life, and luck, in this business.)

LICENSING MANAGER

Licensing managers put the songs to work. They deal with the multitude of ways music can be commercially exploited. (In some companies, the Business Affairs manager's job includes Licensing but this is now unusual given the importance placed on licensing.)

Licensing managers usually receive the initial requests from third parties for permission to use particular works. In the past, they tended to be reactive rather than pro-active, but there are now some notable licensing managers who are active out in the marketplace and seeking opportunities, rather than waiting for potential customers (e.g. advertising agencies and film producers) to approach them.

They have to:

- Determine whether the work is actually controlled by the publisher. This is not always an easy thing to determine, especially when dealing with old works. Computerised databases help, but a work's ownership may be riddled with uncertainties.
- Ensure all the contractual obligations are met. This can range from getting written permission (from whoever owns or controls the copyrights) for a particular use, through to establishing any obligations regarding the kind of credits the writer and publisher require.
- Ensure there are no conflicting licences already granted or pending. This is especially important when considering advertising campaigns. A careless licence could be hugely embarrassing and costly if it fouls a pre-existing licence for a competing product or campaign.

Assuming everything is clear, the licensing manager will negotiate the licence.

TRANSCRIBERS

The largest publishers often employ or hire specialists to transcribe music (and to decipher lyrics) from recorded versions. This is often needed, as few modern pop songs are written before being recorded. So, to create a printed edition, someone (usually whoever owns the publishing rights) has to transcribe the song. Sometimes this is quite simple. Sometimes songs do not lend themselves to easy transcription. Pity the transcriber who had to convert songs by The Vines or You Am I, into a beginner-grade score for solo piano.

Transcribers have to be skilled musicians, able to convert a recording of a work into printed notation. Often the same work will be issued in numerous grades - from ham-fisted to finger-knotting.

Computer programs now make it simple to digitise a recording, analyse it and produce printed scores for any nominated instrument. The end result may need only cosmetic surgery to make it suitable for release as parts or sheet music. The same program can produce a computer disc suitable for direct transfer to the printing works (or laser printer) to produce hard copies with hardly any intermediate steps.

Publishers who do not have their own transcribers generally license transcriptions from the owner. Many writer agreements specify that each song must be delivered to the publisher in written notation as well as on CD, so the good old writer may end up doing it (or paying for it to be done) anyway. The alternative is for the publisher to commission a transcription.

PRINT MUSIC

Until mechanical copyright royalties took over as the main source of income for publishers, sheet music used to be the backbone of the industry. Most publishers now find it uneconomic to operate their own print divisions, though the advances in desktop publishing and computer-assisted transcription mentioned earlier might see that trend reversed to some extent.

Most publishers used to have whole departments devoted to transcribing music into printed notation and having them typeset and printed. Only a few do it now. Most still produce sheet music, but the work is often subcontracted.

Printed music does not only mean sheet music. It includes lyric sheets, magazines that reproduce lyrics and notation as a part of their usual content and special publications having particular themes or featuring a particular artist. These are increasingly valuable as income earners, though producing them can be more complicated than simply printing sheet music, e.g. there may be other rights to be cleared before photographs or biographical information can be reproduced, or there may be several publishers each controlling a portion of the copyright. Where things get complicated, the Business Affairs department will certainly be involved.

PRINT MUSIC SALES

Publishers, like record companies, have to promote and sell their product to retailers. This involves producing catalogues, advertising the current and back catalogues, and (if the publisher does its own distribution) sending sales representatives out to retail outlets to take orders and generally sell the product.

Retail outlets for printed music are quite diverse but specialist music shops who sell musical instruments, local record/music shops and some large bookshops are the main areas. Educational use is a major area too, and publishers are well aware of the needs of educational institutions for variously graded sheet music.

PLUGGERS

The unfortunate name given to this role may have something to do with its demise. From the earliest days of the business, right up to the 1950s, pluggers were very active, going from record company to record company with the sole purpose of getting the plugger's songs recorded, if possible by 'name' artists.

Getting a performer of the stature of an Al Jolson or Frank Sinatra to record one of your works was almost a solid gold money-maker for the writer and the publisher. Remember - if someone like this records even one of your songs you will make a mint, because the song has a chance of being an industry 'standard' - the most desirable song a publisher can control. Irving Berlin wrote a lot of standards. So did Leiber and Stoller ('You Ain't Nothin' But A Houndog' for starters). All got rich from others performing songs they wrote.

This was before the singer-songwriter became the dominant species in the music jungle. It's a pity, but pluggers don't seem to exist as a distinct species any more, though several of the major publishers are consciously promoting their catalogues to advertisers and other companies for use in commercials and the like. Once you call someone a licensing manager you lose that mental picture of a pushy, hustler salesman with a bag of songs and a smile that is just a bit too wide.

BUSINESS AFFAIRS

This is the department in charge of deal-making and contract administration. The business affairs manager is one of the most influential people in most publishing companies, because he or she is the custodian of the copyrights upon which the publisher's business depends.

Often the commercial shape of the deal is negotiated with the Managing Director or General Manager and given to Business Affairs to do the paperwork. In other companies the negotiation is with Business Affairs. They draft and issue contracts, check licensing policy and liaise with the accounts department to make sure they comply with royalty obligations both to and from owners and writers. If disputes arise, they are usually the first people to be called. Do not put business affairs managers off-side. They will usually be very helpful if you have a contract problem or a dispute with a third party. After all, the company's writers are its primary source of income, so its writers' problems are likely to be the company's problems too. They can often give helpful commercial advice, or put the company's weight behind you in third party negotiations.

COPYRIGHT AND ACCOUNTS

Although often two separate departments, it is convenient to consider them together because they have a symbiotic relationship - each depends upon the other to be able to operate.

The Copyright Department or Manager is responsible for maintaining the company's most valuable resource - its copyright files. These list all the works the company controls or in which it has an interest, the writers, the owners, the rights controlled by the company, the term, the territory and so on. Without this data, the publisher cannot identify the works it controls nor collect or distribute the appropriate licence and royalty income. Publishers have had a long time to perfect bureaucracies for processing royalties.

The Copyright Departments in the international publishing companies (and all but the smallest Independents now) have sophisticated computer databases, linked to the Accounts Department. These assist them to identify their works in APRA Returns and in the hundreds of inquiry notices submitted by record companies who intend to make records of musical works.

The Copyright Department has to update its files constantly. Rights ebb into and flow out of the company's control all the time: at the end of a contract term the writer might sign with another publisher; catalogues are won and lost and eventually, the copyright period expires and the works go into the public domain. Similarly, each time a new work is delivered by writers, the files have to be updated and the relevant performing rights society advised. All these steps are routine and comparatively simple but if they are not done, the works cannot generate royalties for either the publisher or the writer.

The Accounts Department is the immediate user of the Copyright Department's labours. The data is the basis for all royalty accounting. The Accounts Department has to match income with the relevant works, check that it is correct, apportion the income according to the contract, deduct the publisher's share and remit the balance (or credit it to the writer's account, depending on whether the writer has any unrecouped advances), within the time allowed under the contract.

It is worth noting that in some companies, Accounts is split into two different departments: the Financial Department (which handles all the general accounting for the organisation) and the Royalty Department.

WAREHOUSE

Only a few publishers have warehouses now, since so few distribute their own sheet music. Most contract with other publishers for warehouse and distribution services.

The warehouse fulfils orders placed with the publisher from the retail outlets, and deals with any returned stock. To that extent, its functions are much the same as in any other industry, though the task of keeping track of the literally hundreds of different titles is by no means simple.

Publishers with warehouse facilities usually also offer distribution services to other parties as this helps them keep the facilities fully used and the income earned from distributing other publishers' sheet music can help offset the warehouse costs which would otherwise be entirely paid by the warehouse operator.

11

COMPOSING AND WRITING WITH OTHERS

CO-WRITING CAN BE BOTH A SOURCE OF INSPIRATION AND A LEGAL NIGHTMARE. FOR IT TO WORK, THE WRITERS HAVE TO RESOLVE THE BUSINESS ELEMENTS OF THEIR RELATIONSHIP. THIS INCLUDES THE LEGAL FORM OF THE RELATIONSHIP, HOW COPYRIGHT WILL BE OWNED AND CONTROLLED, THE DIVISION OF ADVANCES AND ROYALTIES AND HOW TO DEAL WITH OTHER PARTIES SUCH AS ARRANGERS, PRODUCERS, TRANSLATORS AND ADDITIONAL WRITERS.

When musicians want to work with other people, they form a band and get involved in all of those issues discussed in earlier chapters such as Structures and Group Contracts. Composers have a less complicated existence. When they want to work with others, they get co-writers.

This chapter explores the amorphous world of co-writing. We will use the expression 'co-writers' to cover anyone who is involved in creating a musical work and acquires a copyright interest in it. (Arrangers and translators are treated separately, because their involvement comes after the original work has come into being.)

Complications are always implicit when writers work collaboratively. In a way, the legal and financial interests of each co-writer competes with the interests of the other, so it is vital that everyone involved understands their position. The principles apply regardless of the number of co-writers involved.

The separateness of the writers' interests becomes particularly evident if the relationship between the co-writers breaks down, or there is a legal problem with the work (for instance, a competing copyright claim by a third party). Because of this, co-writers should always document their intentions at the beginning of their relationship while they can still talk reasonably together about difficult issues. If problems erupt later, it is often too late for calm and reasonable discussions.

DOCUMENTING THE RELATIONSHIP

We will use a hypothetical pair of writers - you and an acquaintance we will call Oscar. You write lyrics. He composes music. Over a meeting lasting several large drinks, you and Oscar decide to co-write a few songs, so you discuss who will write what, when you will meet, how you and he will exchange ideas and how any royalties will be split. You might even get round to discussing questions of artistic control before the bar closes.

Even if not put into writing, this is likely to be an enforceable contract, particularly if either of you perform a part of your side of the bargain. Unfortunately, there is a strong chance that you each have a slightly different recollection of the terms of your agreement. This is why making a written record is so important. Putting it in writing makes your respective lives a whole lot easier. If a dispute should arise, if you can't negotiate a solution, a court would have to decide what the terms of the agreement were, having regard to your respective versions of what was discussed over a few drinks. This isn't good for either party because if the song has been recorded, no royalties will be paid to either party until the dispute between the writers is resolved.

A court may even have to 'imply' additional terms if there is a gap in your agreement. Courts have the power to make assumptions about what you and Oscar would have agreed, had you actually got around to considering the particular issue. These assumptions are then taken as a term of your agreement. This process of telepathy usually ends up pleasing neither party.

In most cases, a brief letter confirming the agreement, even in point form, will be sufficient. However, if the project is a major one (e.g. a commissioned musical show or a major performance work) then a proper agreement would be well worthwhile. If you are already bound by a publishing agreement at the time, you should, and may be contractually obliged to, consult with your publisher in relation to the effect of the co-writing agreement on the publisher's rights in your songs. Many writers' agreements include a clause requiring the writer to try to secure (for the publisher) the publishing rights for any co-writer who is not already subject to a contract. (As you can imagine, this is rarely successful.) In any event, agreements covering major co-writing projects should be drafted by a lawyer. The resulting document can, suitably amended, then form the basis of any subsequent projects where you work with other co-writers.

You should always keep a work diary. Faithfully note your meetings and any agreements reached. Also note any significant dates or events such as the date you actually delivered your part of a song. If your diary is kept as a matter of routine, it is likely to be admissible to a court as a business record and could provide vital evidence to help you in a copyright claim, whether the claim is by you or by another person against you claiming breach of their copyright.

Sometimes, it is useful to confirm decisions by sending an informal letter or note of some kind to the co-writer. This is particularly important if there is more than one co-writer. This way there will be a record of your mutual understandings should things become unpleasant or merely complicated.

Also, don't forget to give your publisher demos of all of your songs, together with a note stating the agreed writer shares. This is a very simple, basic part of having a professional approach towards the protection of your material and keeps your publisher fully informed about and interested in your work. (You only have one publisher; they have hundreds, even thousands of writers. Being practical, if you want your publisher's involvement in your career, which one of you is going to have to take the initiative in the relationship?)

PARTNERSHIPS

If the co-writing venture is entered with the intention of making a profit then, depending upon your agreement, you and Oscar are likely to have formed a legally recognised 'partnership'. (Partnerships are discussed in some detail in Chapter 2, **Business Structures**.) A partnership is not a separate legal entity. It is a legal relationship, governed by legislation and common-law.

The good thing about partnerships is that there is a lot of law covering them so, even if you do not document it properly, the courts are usually able to unravel any problems and reach what everyone hopes will be a reasonable solution.

The downside of partnerships is that partners are individually and collectively responsible for the liabilities of the partnership. As a result, if a song has a credit 'Words and music by X (i.e. you) and Oscar', then both of you may be liable if the music infringes someone else's copyright, or the lyrics are defamatory. Claimants will always sue the partner with money, leaving the partners to sort out the contribution questions. The 'innocent' partner may have a right to recover damages from the other partner, though this is cold comfort if the other partner has no assets or money.

COPYRIGHT OWNERSHIP – JOINT AND COLLECTIVE WORKS

Co-written works can be either 'joint' works or they can be (as they are sometimes called) 'collective' works (though that expression is not strictly a technical term). The distinction between joint and collective works can have important ramifications upon who controls exploitation of the song.

COLLECTIVE WORK

When each co-writer's contribution is a literary or musical work in its own right, and is identifiable as separate from the other's contribution, the parts are owned separately. Therefore, if you write the lyrics and Oscar quite separately writes the music, then each of you has a distinct part of the song. Unless you and Oscar agree otherwise, you separately own the copyright in the lyrics and Oscar owns the copyright in the music. The song is a collective work when the two parts are combined, but each part can exist by itself too. If the credits say 'Lyrics by X. Music by Oscar' this implies it is a collective work. Bernie Taupin and Elton John work this way - Taupin writes poetry. He sends it to John, who puts it to music. They do not actually 'collaborate' in the creative process.

In a collective work, unless you both agree to the contrary, you can sell, assign or license your lyrics separately from Oscar's music and Oscar has no copyright claim to any income you might receive from that activity and vice versa. To put it simply, you own 100% of the lyrics and Oscar owns 100% of the music.

JOINT WORKS

Remember that a song is made up of two 'works': the literary work (the lyric) and the musical work (the melody). Assume that you and Oscar write the melody together and you write the lyric alone. If you collaborate in a way that makes it impossible to separate each other's contribution to the music, then you are creating a work of joint authorship (a term defined in the Copyright Act) and together, you will own the copyright in that work in equal shares (unless you agree otherwise).

You will own 100% of the lyric and you and Oscar would each own 50% of the copyright in the music. Although you are free to licence the lyrics, you would not be entitled to exploit the copyright in the music without Oscar's permission. To do so would constitute copyright infringement even though you are a part owner of the copyright in the work.

In *Prior v Sheldon and Others* [2000] FCA 438, Zelda Sheldon was ordered to pay around $77,000 to John Prior following her failure to acknowledge his part ownership in musical works associated with the television series "The Great Outdoors". Sheldon had attended Prior's studio with a view to composing a theme for the series based on her preliminary ideas. She drummed semi-quavers on her lap and sung 3 notes to give him an idea of what she was thinking. He recorded variations of the notes, selected the tempo, selected samples, selected sounds including bass, piano and synthesiser sounds, added notes, added structural elements including accompanying chords, bass line and counter-melody (all of which she approved). The court regarded the theme as a work of joint authorship. The court's view was that Ms Sheldon took only a few ideas to Mr Prior's studio and that Mr Prior made a major creative contribution to the theme, "possibly the major creative contribution".

Examples of joint works are common: e.g. if the credits for the work say, 'Words and music by X and Oscar', this implies joint authorship and ownership of both the lyrics and the music.

You have to make a significant and original contribution to be considered a joint owner of a work. For example, where a group works-up a melody in the studio, it may be nothing more than an arrangement. In 1999, three members of the English group Spandau Ballet sued the fourth member, Garry Kemp, alleging that they were joint authors of the works performed by the band. It was common ground that Kemp developed the melody, the chords and the structure of the songs - in his head. He would play a song in its rough state to the others; they would develop it, arrange it, rehearse it and eventually record it. The judge held that the songs thus recorded, were not the result of a collective creation. The band members had not made a 'significant and original contribution to the creation of the work'. Their contributions were to the interpretation and performance of the work, not the creation of it. If the band members wished to receive a portion of the publishing income, they should have had a formal contract in place. (See *Hadley v. Kemp*, unreported, 30 April 1999).

CONTROL

Right at the outset, to remove any ambiguity and avoid complications later on, you and Oscar should sort out your individual interests in the works that you are about to write together. The most important reason to do this is ensure that you have a mechanism to ensure the orderly control of the work: Do both of you have the right to record the work? Can either of you license it? Are there any limitations? What will be the splits? What will the credit be?

Each contributor is a copyright owner and therefore can have his or her own publisher to handle their share of the song. This means that two (or even more) different publishers may control the one song simultaneously. This is a common situation, but you can imagine the problems if the co-writers have not agreed upon the policy to apply when granting licences for commercial licensing. Commonly, stalemates occur and neither publisher can fully exploit the value of the song.

THE ROYALTY SPLITS

Co-writers commonly agree to share the rights in the lyrics and the music equally, but you can make whatever arrangement you like. You can change the agreed split at any time but, if you do, remember to tell your publisher so the change can be registered in its copyright files and it can notify any sub-publishers. Similarly, where the splits are changed, APRA will continue to divide the royalty pay out on the old basis unless you or your publisher advise them to do it another way.

There are no definitive rules as to the splits. The law will generally assume equal shares between co-writers unless there is compelling evidence to the contrary. This presumption is included in many publishers' writer-agreements too. If you have a fetish about counting lines or words, and everyone is happy to go with it, then fine. Most people prefer to go for the 'all for one and one for all' principle and give equal shares, even if one person does more 'work' on a particular song than the other writers. Lennon and McCartney worked this way. Even where one wrote the whole of a particular song, the other got a credit as co-writer. It keeps things simple and, where the writing load is similar, the royalties generally average out in the long term.

APRA REGISTRATION

Co-writers need to be careful when registering their interests with APRA because frequently this will be the only formal indication of the ownership split. Remember to advise APRA of any changes (or get the publisher to do it).

CONTRACTUAL OBLIGATIONS

If you are bound by an 'exclusive writer' music publishing contract, remember that co-writing can have important ramifications on your royalties and advances. Most contracts stipulate that royalties and advances will be reduced pro rata in the case of songs not 100% written and owned by the relevant writer. It may also affect any minimum delivery clause in the contract. Too many co-written songs may result in an extension of the term of the contract until the minimum number of songs are delivered.

On the other hand, some writers are signed by publishers precisely because they are so good at writing with other people. They seem to do their best work with others. Agreements based on this premise need to be structured accordingly or they can disadvantage the writer. Standard writer agreements usually contain provisions that are inappropriate if the writer will be writing primarily with others. For example, most 'term' publishing agreements require that the composer will deliver 10 works a year. If you do co-writes the drafting of the minimum commitment clause should make it clear that what is required is the 'equivalent' of 10 songs: e.g. it would be fulfilled by 5 wholly written songs and ten co-writes.

ARRANGERS AND TRANSLATORS

The right to adapt a musical work is one of the exclusive rights given under the Copyright Act to the owner of a musical work. The right to adapt is defined as being the right to arrange and transcribe the work. Under the right circumstances, a separate copyright can arise in relation to the adaptation and writers need to be cautious when engaging someone to adapt a work.

ARRANGEMENTS

The Copyright Act doesn't mention 'arrangements'; it talks about 'adaptations'. The Act provides that the writer of the musical work has the exclusive right to make adaptations of that work.

An adaptation must have a certain quality of creativity and an input of talent and labour by the arranger that distinguishes it from the original work. So, for example, a cover will not be an adaptation if it merely involves change of key or instrumentation. The distinction becomes blurred, however, when an arrangement is so comprehensive that it becomes a new musical work in its own right.

The test the courts apply is an objective one. Just because the arranger thinks he or she has created a new work does not really matter. What matters, is whether the court thinks a new work has been created. The law is unclear in this area but, needless to say, an arranger who needs to establish that his or her work is a new 'work', faces the prospect of a long and expensive argument.

Even if a particular arrangement meets the test and is recognised as having an independent copyright, the arranger has only limited rights. The copyright only relates to that particular arrangement, so anyone else can go to the original work and make another arrangement, which might be uncannily like the earlier, but will not infringe its copyright provided it was independently created. The arranger does not have the legal right to authorise new adaptations of the original work. If this were otherwise, the original's owner would have his or her copyrights eroded over time.

The original owner can stop various uses even of the adaptation, because the adaptation can never be completely separated from the original work. To use an analogy, if the arrangement is thought of as the paintwork on a car, the paintwork does not really have an independent existence. It cannot be driven by itself. The car's owner has final say over where the car, with its paintwork, will go.

Where an arrangement is legally recognised as a true adaptation and there is no contrary agreement, the arranger will be entitled to receive a share of income produced by that particular arrangement, but not otherwise. That share is usually worked out by negotiation between publishers. In Europe, most public performance societies will distribute part of the public performance fee to the arranger at the same time as it distributes to the composer and the publisher. The usual share is two-twelfths of the total.

If you decide to get a third party to arrange your songs, you may face a demand from the arranger (or a producer) for a share of the copyright as a condition for arranging the song. Owners should avoid giving copyright in the song to an arranger, if at all possible. At most, the arranger should get a share in his or her particular arrangement of the work rather than a share of the copyright in the original work.

A once-only fee for services is the usual basis for arranging, and is better for the composer because it saves fragmenting the copyright. Even if you agree to pay a royalty, this can be done without assigning any copyright over to the arranger. (There is a difference between granting a share of the income stream and a share of the copyright. Both result in a split of the income but only one results in a split of the copyright.) Ultimately, it depends whether the arranger can turn a dud song into a killer song. It's a decision that has to be made at the time.

TRANSLATORS

Translators are essentially in the same position as arrangers. The right to authorise translations is held by the copyright owner, who can impose whatever conditions it considers appropriate. In most cases, the translation will have its own copyright, provided its creation involved the necessary degree of skill and labour.

If it has a separate copyright then, in the absence of a particular agreement, the translator will be entitled to receive a share of income from that translation. Again, publishers usually negotiate this for their writers. Your publishing agreement will determine who pays for the translator's services, and what impact this will have on your royalty income. In Europe, public performance societies will often distribute two-twelfths of the performance income to translators.

Although translation is comparatively rare in Australia, it is of course common in Europe and becoming more so in North America, where the growth in Spanish and other languages has created a market for non-English language versions of pop songs. Sting put out a Spanish and Portuguese language album of several tracks from his album '...Nothing Like the Sun'. Similarly, Bachelor Girl generated a lot of interest with their Japanese versions of their songs and it's likely this helped them to get into a notoriously difficult market for non-Japanese artists. There are plenty of other examples of the industry recognising the value of translated lyrics, so translations will undoubtedly become more common.

The usual process for getting a lyric translated is for a literal translation to be prepared. Sometimes a translation changes the original (say for purposes of rhythm or rhyme, which is an adaptation. Good publishers will consult with their writers, to make sure they are happy with the translation before approving it. A translator will usually get a nominated percentage of all income derived from the translation (in the region of 10%). Public performance splits are determined by the local collection society's rules.

RECORD PRODUCERS

Beware of record producers who insist on claiming a writer's credit on the songs they produce. These producers are very expensive.

Production of a sound recording does not automatically give any basis for a claim for copyright in the musical work or the sound recording. The claim is based purely upon the commercial clout of the producer. It may be that the cost of getting a given producer (particularly an internationally renowned name) is an enormous fee and a copyright share. You have to decide whether the cost is justified. You also have to consider the impact on your publishing agreement.

Producers who want a share of the copyright are intending to share in your on-going publishing income generated by the song. This can even include covers on which they have not worked, for the life of copyright. Consider carefully whether you can afford this person. It may be better to pay higher points under the producer agreement than to give away a share of the publishing rights forever.

Some producers are considered to be so valuable to a recording's success that they may be worth the expense. Only you and your co-writers can decide. If you do decide to part with some of the publishing, don't go mad with generosity. Make sure you get your lawyer to negotiate and document the agreement. Any producer participation in the copyright should be restricted to his or her particular arrangement of the song, but not in the original work itself.

ADDITIONAL WRITERS

A slightly different situation arises where the original writers all agree to give a co-written song to (say) a third writer to finish or improve it. There is an argument that there is a creative input into the song itself which might justify the original writers each relinquishing a part of their respective shares to give the third party a share.

If the re-written song is more likely to be a hit than the original, it may be better to take 30% of a hit, than 50% of a song that no-one wants to know about. Remember that a re-written song is likely to become a new song, though the original version obviously continues to exist and remains subject to copyright. The distinction between a re-write of an incomplete song and adapting a completed one can be quite blurred at times. Re-writing involves substantially reproducing part of the original song, so re-writing without the owners' consent is a breach of copyright.

Co-writing can be artistically satisfying and financially worthwhile, but if things start going wrong, there is a lot of comfort to be gained from having an agreement which anticipates the more likely areas of dispute and then provides a mechanism for resolving them.

ACCIDENTAL CO-WRITERS

This is not as silly as it sounds. Many songs are composed in the recording studio and are not 'written' in advance. The band gets together, a chord becomes a sequence, the sequence becomes a melody, the melody gets words which are only slightly more complicated than ga-ga, then the drummer has a great idea for a lyric line and, before the week is out, a terrific song is born - but with perhaps five proud parents. Who claims what? Unless the contributions are clearly separable, it is likely to be a joint work, and in the absence of any other agreement, copyright and proceeds will be shared equally. Those members with publishers will not be affected, provided they notify their publisher of their share. Those without a publisher should consider doing a single song assignment to the main publisher, if only to keep copyright administration simple. (More about these agreements in the next chapter.)

This process becomes harder when songs are created on computer synthesisers by the producer, particularly in electronica and hip hop, where the 'melody' is often largely replaced by a highly distinctive drum-machine pattern or sound loop. Then, sounds and samples are 'pasted' over this pattern as various people suggest new sounds and effects to add. Deciding who wrote what part is a real problem here. In fact, it raises quite nice legal points about the nature of the work and whether it has the necessary qualities to make it subject to copyright as a musical work, but that's lawyer talk. As far as you are concerned, you should make every effort to simplify your life, by thinking about the possibilities, anticipating complications and documenting your work.

If the creation process has involved the use of samples, remember that they are likely to be copyright works and you can't use them without a licence. (Samples are dealt with in more detail in Chapter 8.)

12
TYPES OF PUBLISHING CONTRACTS

THERE ARE MANY TYPES OF PUBLISHING AGREEMENT. THIS CHAPTER LOOKS AT THE CLASSIC TYPES: WRITER FOR HIRE AGREEMENTS, SINGLE-SONG ASSIGNMENTS, TERM PUBLISHING CONTRACTS, ADMINISTRATION DEALS AND THE ALTERNATIVE OF BEING YOUR OWN PUBLISHER. SAMPLE AGREEMENTS ARE PROVIDED. THE AGREEMENTS ARE LOOKED AT FROM THE WRITER'S PERSPECTIVE, BUT ALWAYS REMEMBER THAT PUBLISHERS NEED (AND DESERVE) REASONABLE PROTECTION OF THEIR INTERESTS AND A REASONABLE RETURN FOR THEIR INVOLVEMENT AND INVESTMENT.

WRITER-FOR-HIRE AGREEMENTS

The days of Tin Pan Alley are gone. Publishing houses in Australia do not keep staff writers on salary any more. Of course there are companies that do employ composers, but the contracts are not publishing deals in the ordinary meaning of those words; e.g. advertising houses may hire jingle writers, but it is very rare for those companies to insist on owning all of their writers' work - they only want the jingles they write for the company's clients.

For modern publishers, the cost of having a writer on staff and having to supply office space, pay superannuation, holiday pay, sick leave and all the other things that are the duties of modern employers, is prohibitive. They can achieve a similar result to Tin Pan Alley-style writers, without having to take on the responsibilities of being an employer. The modern way is to sign the writer to a term deal (say three or five years) and pay periodic advances, perhaps monthly. Depending on the writer's ability to generate income, this could be in the vicinity of $48,000 per year in 12 monthly payments of $4,000. In return the publisher will require delivery of a minimum number of works - often 10 or 12 per year. Indeed, these days, the publisher often gives the writer various projects to work on because it is rarely productive to have writers sitting in studios writing songs that they hope someone will like someday.

In this way, the publisher gets a catalogue of works from the writer without having to meet the additional overheads which employment entails, while the writer gets a regular source of income without losing independence. The best part of the deal for the publisher is that, instead of paying salary, the money paid to the writer is all treated as a recoupable advance.

SINGLE-SONG ASSIGNMENT

Perhaps the simplest publishing deal of all is the assignment of a single song, where the songwriter transfers the copyright in a song to a publisher for an agreed period, at an agreed royalty.

Single-song assignments are usually offered by a publisher so it can acquire a particular song (or songs), though sometimes they are offered to new writers who have not yet established their reputations as songwriters but who have produced a couple of good, strong compositions. These deals can be a stepping-stone towards a long-term, more comprehensive relationship. They provide you with an opportunity to have your works 'published' and for the publisher to administer them, without either party having to make a long-term commitment to the other. These days, publishers rarely bother with a single-song deal unless the work is about to be recorded and likely to generate income.

Single-song assignments are also sometimes used for people such as band members, producers, arrangers, managers and anyone else who is not a writer, but who somehow or other ends up owning a share in the copyright of a song which is going to be exploited commercially. In such a case, there is an obvious advantage for the publisher to rake up all of the pieces of the copyright in the work in order to better control it.

There is an obvious benefit to the writer too, in having a publisher administer the paperwork and clearances involved when having a song recorded. The paperwork is usually fairly simple (a few pages). Given that the advances will be small, having your lawyer negotiate it is often not justified, though your lawyer can advise in general terms whether the deal is a reasonable one.

This said, if you are in the early stages of your career, be wary of the small, fringe publishers, who call themselves music publishers but who are often little more than copyright-acquisition schemes. There are many working in the country, Christian and ethnic-music genres. They usually have a contract misleadingly headed 'Standard Music Publishing Agreement' or something similar, so the naive will think that it's a non-negotiable (but nonetheless fair) deal. They don't offer advances and the royalty splits are usually 50/50. The deal usually requires the writer to spend money on material or services that the 'publisher' promises to provide. Despite the individuals being charming and having a great spiel, if you sign one of these deals, you will undoubtedly learn a comprehensive lesson.

THE RIGHTS PERIOD

The total period for which the publisher owns or controls your copyrights under a single-song assignment agreement is called the rights period.

If the deal is merely for an assignment or licence of specific works, you don't have a separate 'term' and retention period, merely a rights period. However, if there is an advance of any seriousness, the publisher may not use the rights period approach and may opt for a term plus a retention period. This gives the publisher more assurance that it will have the opportunity to recoup the advance.

THE ADVANCE

For the novice songwriter, the advance is often not as important as the opportunity to forge a relationship with the publisher. The fact is, few publishers will take even a single song, unless they see some commercial benefit in it (which usually translates as 'The publisher likes it').

The advance for a single song assignment is usually quite modest, unless the writer is established and the publisher really loves the song. It all depends upon the work's estimated capacity to generate income. It might be $500 or $15,000. Whatever it is, some advance, no matter how modest, is desirable, both as a sign of faith by the publisher and as a little extra incentive for the publisher to actively 'work' the song. At the very least, it will help pay the cost of any legal or other professional work needed.

If the songwriter is established or the song is going to be recorded (and is therefore likely to generate mechanical income) you can expect a greater advance, based upon the song's earning capacity.

ROYALTIES

The royalty split on single-song assignments varies from 60/40 to 80/20 in the writer's favour. It depends on the writer, the song and the publisher. Only exceptional deals are 50/50 any more. There would have to be many other benefits for the writer for a 50/50 deal to be at all attractive.

OTHER SPECIFIC-WORKS AGREEMENTS

While the single-song assignment is usually for beginners, established writers - particularly those who are also recording artists - sometimes do a publishing deal for a larger number of specific works. These are sometimes referred to as 'single-song' assignments, but such deals may actually deal with more than one song at a time. They are more accurately described as 'specific-song' agreements - to distinguish them from deals based on a set period of time or a yet to be recorded number of albums.

A writer often sees this as a way of getting an advance without the commitment and exclusivity of a term agreement. It is little more than a funding device for the writer, so the publisher will not agree to it unless the figures show a high likelihood of financial return. After all, in this sort of deal, the publisher's commitment to the writer can hardly be expected to be greater than the writer's commitment to the publisher!

In this sort of deal, the paperwork is likely to be about as long and complex as a term agreement. Because the dollars are significant and the writer is likely to be established, this kind of specific works assignment is likely to spell out the deal points in greater detail than a simple single-song assignment. These are certainly deals you will need a lawyer to negotiate, particularly if you don't want to be thin-lipped about the industry in your old age.

SAMPLE SPECIFIC-SONG ASSIGNMENT AGREEMENT

THIS AGREEMENT is made the   day of   2006

BETWEEN *publisher*   ('we/us');

AND   *composer*   ('you');

TERMS:

DEFINITIONS

1. In this agreement, the following words in bold type will have the following meanings:

   (a) **Composition** means the music and lyrics of the song entitled: 'OVER THE HIGHWAY'.
   (b) **Territory** means the world.
   (c) **Net Royalties Received** means the total royalties arising directly and identifiably from the exploitation of the Composition which are received by or credited to us in Australia less only:
       (i) taxes required to be and actually deducted;
       (ii) third party collection society and APRA charges;
       (iii) sums payable by way of remuneration to arrangers, adaptors and translators of the Composition; and

(iv) sums permitted to be retained by our sub-publishers or licensees which may not exceed .... per cent (%), except in the case of covers and synchronisations for which the retention may be .... per cent (%), of the sums arising at source and directly and identifiably from the exploitation of the Composition less only the deductions mentioned in (i) and (iii) above.

(d) **Covers** means any commercially released recording of the Composition which does not embody a performance by the Writer.

(e) **Copyright** means copyright as defined by the *Copyright Act 1968 (Cth)*.

(f) **GST Law** is defined in the *A New Tax System (Goods and Services Tax) Act 1999 (Cth)*. **GST** means a tax, levy, duty, charge or deduction, together with any related additional tax, interest, penalty, fine or other damage, imposed by or under a GST Law. The meaning of **Tax Invoice** is as defined in the GST Law.

ASSIGNMENT

2. In consideration of the advance and royalties payable to you under this agreement, you assign to us all the Copyright throughout the Territory in the Composition for a rights period of .... years.

3. Without prejudice to the generality of the foregoing, the rights assigned to us which will be ours, solely and exclusively, for the Territory include the following:

(a) The right to grant licences to communicate the Composition to the public by any and all means, subject to the rights of the Australian Performing Rights Association (APRA).

(b) The right, subject to our obtaining your prior written consent, to make adaptations, additions, alterations, arrangements and translations of the Composition in whole or in part.

(c) The right to grant mechanical licences.

(d) The right, subject to our obtaining your prior written consent, to grant non-exclusive synchronisation licences.

(e) The right to use the title of the Composition for all purposes in connection with the Composition.

(f) The right to publish, print and reproduce the Composition.

(g) The right to authorise others to exercise any of the above rights.

All other rights in the Composition are reserved by you.

PROMISES AND WARRANTIES

4. You agree that you will (if so requested by us) promptly:

(a) Execute or sign any other documents and do all other acts and things which may be reasonably required of you to vest in us the rights granted under this agreement.

(b) Deliver a lead sheet or a recording of the Composition.

(c) Allow or obtain for us to use your name, professional name, approved photograph, likeness and approved biography and allow us to exploit the Composition.

5. You warrant and declare that:
   (a) The composition is an original work and does not and will not infringe the copyright in any other work and shall not be obscene or defamatory of any person.
   (b) You have good right and full power to grant to us the rights set forth above.
   (c) You indemnify us (and our successors and assigns) against all costs damages losses and expenses (including legal expenses) that we suffer because of any breach of your contractual promises provided that this breach is found proved by final order or award of a court or settled with your consent. This clause will continue to be effective after termination or expiration of this agreement.
   (d) You will (if so requested by us) permit your name to be used as a plaintiff or party in any actions or proceedings that may be necessary for us to secure, establish or enforce the rights in the Composition. The expense of any such action or proceeding will be borne by us except that all such expenses will be recoupable from any sums obtained or derived from such action or proceeding and any residue therefrom will be dealt with pursuant to clause 7 (b) (vi).

PUBLISHER PROMISES AND WARRANTIES

6. (a) We promise to use reasonable endeavours to exploit the Composition and exploitation by our licensees will be deemed to be exploitation for the purposes of this clause.
   (b) Without prejudice to the generality of the above we will use all reasonable endeavours to:
      (i) obtain Covers of the Composition;
      (ii) collect all income arising from the exploitation of the Composition; and
      (iii) protect the copyright and all like rights in and to the Composition.

ROYALTIES

7. Provided that you fully perform all of your obligations hereunder we agree to pay to you:
   (a) On execution of this agreement, an advance of *$1,000* dollars, which will be recoupable only from all royalties or other income otherwise due to you under this contract; and
   (b) The following royalties:
      (i) mechanical income (other than from Covers): seventy per cent (70%) the Net Royalties Received;

    (ii) mechanical income arising from Covers: sixty percent (60%) of the Net Royalties Received where such licences are procured by us and seventy per cent (70%) where such licences are procured by you;

    (iii) synchronisation licences: sixty per cent (60%) of the Net Royalties Received where such licences are procured by us and seventy per cent (70%) where such licences are procured by you;

    (iv) print: twelve per cent (12%) of the suggested retail selling price of each such copy of sheet music sold for which we receive payment or credit or sixty-five per cent (65%) of sub-licence fees received from third parties. In either case in respect of folios or other compilations, such percentage will be pro-rated according to the total number of songs contained therein;

    (v) performing rights: we acknowledge that you are entitled to be paid the so-called 'writer's share' direct by APRA. We will also pay you (or credit your unrecouped Advance account with) forty per cent (40%) of the so-called 'publisher's share' of performance income collected by APRA; and

    (vi) sundry income: seventy per cent (70%) of the Net Royalties Received.

ACCOUNTING

8. (a) Twice a year we will prepare and submit to you a statement of account showing the amount due to you under this agreement and will pay to you the amount (if any) shown to be due. Such accounting will be made within sixty days of the close of the relevant accounting period. The accounting periods will close on 30th June and 31st December in each year.

  (b) All statements of account rendered to you will be binding upon you and not subject to any objection unless you give us a written notice which states the basis of objection within three (3) years from the date of the statement.

  (c) You will have the right at your expense to appoint a chartered accountant to inspect our books of accounts at our usual place of business insofar as they relate to the exploitation of the Compositions. If the inspection reveals a discrepancy in excess of 5%, we will pay your reasonable costs of the inspection. Such right may be exercised not more than once in each calendar year nor more than once in respect of any statement, by giving reasonable notice in writing to us before any proposed inspection.

  (d) All payments will be subject to the deduction or withholding of all taxes required to be deducted or withheld under the laws of any country or territory and to the exchange control regulations of any country or territory from which those payments emanate.

  (e) All copies of the Composition in whatever form which are distributed to the trade and profession or otherwise for the purpose of exploiting or popularising the Composition and also all reproductions of the Composition or parts thereof published in any newspapers and other periodicals, will be free of all royalty or payment to you where we receive no payment or payment below cost.

(f) We shall make all reasonable efforts to ensure that your share of money earned overseas is remitted to Australia as promptly as is practicable.

ASSIGNMENT

9. You may not assign transfer or license any of the benefits or rights of this agreement.

TERMINATION

10. (a) If you have a receiving order in bankruptcy made against you or if we enter into liquidation (other than a voluntary liquidation for the purposes of reconstruction or amalgamation) or if either party makes any composition with that party's creditors, the other party may terminate this agreement forthwith upon giving written notice thereof.

(b) In the event that either party breaches or is in default of its obligations hereunder, the party not in breach or default ('the innocent party') must serve notice on the other, specifying the breach or default. If the breach or default is not remedied within 21 days the innocent party may terminate the agreement forthwith by notice in writing.

(c) Any such termination will be without prejudice to our rights in respect of the Composition to which we are entitled at the date of such termination.

ENFORCEMENT OF RIGHTS

11. You irrevocably grant us the sole right to enforce and protect all rights in and to the Composition in the Territory. We may join you or such others as we may deem advisable in any suits and proceedings and we may proceed with and dispose of proceedings or suits at our sole discretion. If any third party suit or proceeding is due to your default or the breach of any promise by you hereunder, any legal costs or disbursements incurred by us will be borne (on an indemnity basis) by you. If the suit or proceeding is not due to your breach or default the costs or disbursements incurred by us will be borne equally (on an indemnity basis) and any sums recovered by you and/or us by way of damages or otherwise (but after the payment of all legal costs or disbursements) shall be shared according to clause 7(b)(vi). We warrant we will not settle any action involving your interests without first consulting with you

PUBLISHER WARRANTIES

12. We warrant that we will at all times act in good faith and deal at arms length on a proper and customary commercial basis and without limiting the generality of the foregoing, this warranty shall apply to our dealings with our affiliates, subsidiaries, licensees and sub-licensees and any collection agencies that we may retain.

GST

13. The royalties that we pay you are calculated exclusive of GST. We will pay you the royalty plus the GST payable in respect of that amount provided that you provide us with a GST Tax Invoice for the amount of GST paid.

ENTIRE AGREEMENT

14. This agreement constitutes the entire agreement between the parties with respect to the subject matter hereof and cannot be altered, amended or modified except by an instrument in writing signed by the parties.

INDEPENDENT ADVICE

15. You warrant that you have obtained independent legal advice in respect of this agreement.

JURISDICTION

16. The laws of .... govern this contract and the Courts of that State have exclusive jurisdiction.

READ UNDERSTOOD AND AGREED

Signed (etc).

SCHEDULE OF COMPOSITIONS

1.
2.
3.

TERM PUBLISHING AGREEMENTS

DURATION

The 'term' of a publishing agreement is the period during which you, the composer, provide your exclusive services to the publisher. The contract will usually deliver ownership or control of all of your copyrights that either come into existence or become available during the term. This will include works written by you:

(a) During the term;
(b) Prior to the date of agreement and not previously licensed or assigned to another publishing company;
(c) Prior to the date of agreement and which were previously licensed or assigned to another publishing company, where the rights revert to you during the term.

So, if your deal is for a three-year term, the publishing company will own or control all of your copyrights that come into existence or become available during that time and you cannot deal on your own behalf in respect of those works. That is the exclusive right and power of your publisher.

For obvious reasons, this sort of deal is usually referred to as a 'Term Contract'.

THE RETENTION PERIOD

A Retention Period is usually included in all term publishing agreements. It is the period immediately following the end of the term, during which the publisher will retain ownership and/or control of all the copyrights it acquired from you during the term.

To illustrate how this works, assume that the term is three years and that the Retention Period is ten years. If you write a song at the beginning of the first year of the contract, the publisher will control that song for thirteen years. If you write the song at the beginning of the third year, the publisher will control it for eleven years.

Your exclusive commitment to the publisher lasts only for as long as the term and, therefore, is over when the term expires. This means you are free to sign up with a different publisher in respect of any works you might write during the Retention Period.

GENERAL

Until the 1980s, it was commonplace for Retention Periods and rights periods in publishing deals to be for the life of copyright (i.e. for as long as the work is protected by copyright). This is no longer the market unless there are unusual circumstances that would justify such a long Retention Period. Publishers these days do not expect to control a work forever, though such deals are occasionally done if the circumstances are such that it is fair to both parties.

One school of thought amongst lawyers who represent writers is that the Retention Period should be as short as possible. Others say it doesn't matter, provided the original deal is 'fair', because continuity of control tends to minimise administrative errors that inevitably creep in whenever a catalogue or song changes hands. Administrative errors mean lost income. Sometimes the retention period will be for a much longer period than usual but with a higher royalty paid to the writer (if the publisher is recouped). There is no 'right' view. Like all important deal points, the duration of the various periods reflects the market power of the writer. As a general rule, try to keep the various periods as short as possible unless there are good reasons to do otherwise.

For a term deal, the Term will usually be between three and five years, unless there are unusual circumstances. The Retention Period will vary from two years to 20 years.

For an assignment of specific works, the period for which the publisher will control the work is rarely less than three years. Control periods can range up to 10 years or even longer, depending on the deal (though this would be unusual).

As you can see there is a certain symmetry to these figures. From the publisher's point of view, the period that it will have control of the work determines the likelihood of it making a profit from the work in particular and from the deal in general.

In cases where the song is going to be used in a film soundtrack, the assignment or licence might well be for life of copyright. The reason is simple enough - most film producers need to have the right to use the film music for as long as the film might be shown, so they can legitimately (and probably will) insist on obtaining that right for the maximum period. This is dealt with in detail in Chapter 31, **Music in Film**.

THE ADVANCE

There is no rule for determining the proper amount of an advance, except what the market will bear. Many writers have unrealistic expectations of what they can get.

One basis for setting the amount is to make a realistic estimate of the royalties that your publishing is likely to earn over a reasonable period. Obviously this is as much a guess as anything else (no-one can predict whether a song will be successful at all, let alone whether it will become a standard), but it looks nice on paper and is a starting point for negotiations. This is probably the maximum amount that you could realistically expect as an advance.

If you were paid this, you would be receiving all of the income that would be payable to you during the term, in one up-front payment. This sort of deal is described as 'front-end loaded' for obvious reasons. No publishers like this sort of deal because it leaves them very exposed. They know from unhappy experience that too many very talented writers never achieve the success they probably deserve, so only established writers with a proven track record can get deals of this kind.

If a writer cannot demonstrate a history of successful songs, the advance will be a matter of sheer guesswork. If you are a rookie with nothing more than some new songs in your bag, but your would-be publisher likes your work and sees real prospects of getting it commercially exploited, you might get an advance of $50. Or $500. Or $50,000.

If you have a recording contract and are going to record an album of self-written material, you are well on the way to getting a good publishing deal because you have more bargaining power. The publisher can see the likelihood of recouping some of its risk money and will be more willing to give ground on major deal points - such as advances. The amount of the advance is governed by factors such as whether the record company is a Major or an Independent, the amount of promotion that the record company is committing to the project and generally what the 'vibe' is for the material. In fact, there may be several publishers interested, in which case you could select not just the publisher you like best, but the most generous (though this is definitely not the best way of selecting a publisher!).

Hugely successful writers have been paid hundreds of thousands of dollars in publishing advances. Very exceptionally, even new writers who have a recording contract and the 'vibe', can receive very significant advances if the bidding war gets out of hand ($80,000 and more) but these are very exceptional.

If you are offered a publishing contract with no advance, there has to be a reason for doing the deal, but what is it? Ask yourself, 'Why am I willing to sign this?' Remember that it is very unusual for a publishing deal to attract no advance at all. After all, the advance is the most obvious symbol (though of course, not the only one) of the publisher's expectations of your success.

On the other hand, getting a huge advance is not everything. All too often, writers insist on squeezing the last dollar out of the advance and overlook the other more important terms of the deal. An advance is only the prepayment of money that you expect to earn anyway. It can also have disadvantageous tax implications for you. It is more important to negotiate other matters, such as the royalty splits and the degree of control that you wish to retain, than using the publisher as a credit card.

It is often said that if you get a large advance the publisher can't afford to let you fail. If only it were true. Like all aphorisms, whilst it contains an element of truth, practice has proven that you can't rely on it. A publisher that has paid too much for a writer will rarely blame itself for the miscalculation. It is more likely the writer will be blamed! If the royalty account remains hugely unrecouped for too long, the managing director of the company will get the blowtorch treatment from his superiors and you will soon feel the heat of the reflected glare.

SPLIT PUBLISHING DEALS

As we have already indicated, the old 50/50 split of income is not usually a reasonable royalty division in the Australian industry and ought to be accepted only in unusual situations.

Nevertheless, you may hear the expression 'split publishing'. This is an American term, which isn't used in Australia. If you assume (as the Americans do) that the basic split is 50/50, if the writer receives, say, 60%, he or she is in fact getting 20% of the 'publisher's share'. The publisher is 'splitting' its share with the writer. Almost all term deals done in Australia are, according to the American definition, split publishing deals.

In Australia, the expression split publishing is usually used to indicate that more than one publisher has an interest in a work (e.g. two writers - each with their own publisher), rather than telling you anything about royalty splits.

RECOUPMENT

All advances paid by the publisher will be recoupable from the writer's publishing earnings. An advance, as that term is usually understood, is a pre-payment of royalties that would otherwise by payable under the contract.

Look at your contract to see what else is going to be recoupable. Many contracts state that any money paid by the publisher on behalf of the writer is deemed an advance and is therefore recoupable. The problem is in determining exactly what expenses are paid "on behalf of the writer"! Are demo costs? Contributions made by the publisher to the record company towards the promotion of your record? Demo duplication costs? The cost of preparing lead sheets or arrangements? Administrative costs? Travel? Beware!

Now you see the danger of a phrase that states that 'any money paid by the publisher on behalf of the writer is deemed an advance and is therefore recoupable'! It looks very reasonable at first blush but, if applied unscrupulously, it could work most harshly. It is quite unreasonable for a publisher to use this kind of clause to get you to contribute to basic costs of running the company. After all, the company gets its own percentage of the income earned by your works. You need to ensure that recoupable expenditure is not being incurred without your knowledge.

The only sums that should be recoupable without prior mutual agreement are advances and any amounts you have specifically asked the publisher to spend on your behalf and agreed (in writing) may be charged to your royalty account. Remember though, publishers are not in the business of spending for the sake of spending. Sometimes, they can only justify certain expenditure if it is recoupable (i.e. treated as an advance). If you do not agree to any particular expenditure being recoupable, it may not get spent at all, which could be to your detriment. The only way you can make an informed decision is by knowing what is planned and being part of the decision-making process.

Demo costs are always a subject of contract negotiation. Publishers' policies as to the recoupability of demo costs vary widely. Many will advance money for demo costs provided the advance is recoupable. Non-recoupable or partly recoupable payments are harder to get unless you have some negotiating clout.

Remember that advances are pre-payments of royalties, so they almost certainly constitute income for tax purposes and should be declared in the year you receive them. The tax laws give writers a concession by allowing income averaging, to allow for good and bad years (farmers and sports stars have the same concession). The formula is too complex to go into here and (like most tax laws) might be changed while we are all asleep one night. See your accountant, and make sure you set up your financial affairs properly.

PRODUCTIVITY COMMITMENT

It is common for publishers to insist on the delivery of a minimum number of compositions a year. In some cases 'product commitment' calls for 'recorded and released' compositions. The publisher's financial commitment is based on the assumption that it will get a flow of songs capable of earning income. Assuming that the writer is talented, the more songs the publisher has to exploit, the greater the chance of one being a hit.

Because of this, publishers encourage writers to create new songs. This is one reason that advances are frequently tied to the number of new songs to be delivered in any given period. Some writers can't help themselves - they have to write. Others need a bit of encouragement.

Product Commitments are often requested where the advance is significant and the publisher has a term of (say) only three years. It wants to make sure that it is getting something for its money and something with which to work. After all, most publishers have had the unhappy experience of signing a writer to a three-year deal, paying a sizeable advance, and then getting very few works in return while the writer has either an extended holiday or a sudden and unexpected health breakdown.

Because of this, many agreements specify that unless the writer delivers a minimum number of works in a contract year, that year will be deemed to extend until the minimum commitment is delivered. This way, the publisher has a way of keeping tabs on the writer's output. Also, a publisher can look at a three-year deal and at least calculate that it will have, say, 30 works to exploit during the Retention Period (assuming the writer performs as per the agreement).

SAMPLE TERM PUBLISHING AGREEMENT
(AND COMMENTARY)

THIS AGREEMENT is made the   day of   2006

BETWEEN   THE PUBLISHER PTY LIMITED, of
             (hereinafter called 'we/us');

AND   THE COMPOSER, of
             (hereinafter called 'you');

WHEREBY IT IS AGREED AS FOLLOWS:

DEFINITIONS
1. (a) **Compositions** means: those compositions –
    (i) (including those listed in the Schedule hereto) written in whole or in part by you (whether alone or with third parties) prior to the commencement hereof and which are not presently licensed or assigned to a genuine 'third party publishing Company' (which expression does not include any company owned or controlled directly or indirectly by you);
    (ii) written in whole or in part by you (whether alone or with third parties) during the Term;
    (iii) the rights in and to which revert to you (or any of you) during the Term.

This clause defines which 'works' will be the subject of the agreement. The clause is intended to include all material that is already in existence and is not assigned to another publisher plus material that is assigned to another publisher at the time of signing but reverts to you during the course of the contract, and all works that you write during the term.

  (b) **Territory** means the world.

The other common territory is 'Australia and New Zealand and any of the Australasian Performing Right Association territories'. The extent of the territory depends on your commercial needs, the size of the advance required and, above all, your negotiating strength.

  (c) **Net Royalties Received** means the total royalties arising directly and identifiably from the exploitation of the Compositions and which are received by or credited to us in Australia less only:

(i) Withholding Tax and any other taxes required to be and actually deducted;

(ii) any third party non-affiliated collection society charges (if applicable);

(iii) any sums payable by way of remuneration to arrangers adapters and translators of the Compositions; and

(iv) any sums permitted to be retained by our sub-publishers or licensees which shall not exceed .... per cent (...........%), except in the case of covers for which the retention may be per cent (...........%), of the sums arising at source and directly and identifiably from the exploitation of the Compositions less only the like deductions mentioned in (i) and (iii) above.

This is a 'pro-writer' provision, in that it limits the amount of commission that can be deducted from the gross income before overseas royalties are remitted to Australia. It allows you to control the amount of the administration commission but still provides the overseas sub-publisher with an incentive to obtain covers.

(d) **Covers** means any exploitation of a Composition which embodies the performance of a party other than you (or any group of which you may be a featured member) and obtained as a result of our efforts *whether or not such efforts are exclusive or non-exclusive*. In this agreement, synchronisations will be deemed to be Covers for the purpose of calculating royalties.

Notice the phrase in italics. This is to help avoid disputes between the publisher and the writer as to who got the cover. The actual extent of the parties' respective involvement in securing any particular cover is often impossible to determine.

(e) **Copyright** means copyright (as defined by the Copyright Act 1968) throughout the territory to which that Act may now or may at any time hereafter extend together with all rights now and hereafter thereunder existing and together with all other rights of a like nature as are now conferred by the laws in force in all other territories throughout the world, including: the right to renew and extend the copyright and the ownership of such renewed and extended copyrights; and such other rights as may hereafter be conferred or created by law of international arrangement or convention in any part of the world whether by way of new or additional rights not now comprised in copyright or by way of extension of the period of then or now existing rights.

(f) **Retention Period** means the Term (including any extension thereof) and ....(.......) years from the end of the Term PROVIDED that if the Retention Period does not expire on 30 June or 31 December, the Retention Period will automatically be extended to the end of the 30 June or 31 December whichever first occurs.

The retention period clause is one of the most important negotiable clauses of any publishing agreement. In earlier times, the retention period was life of copyright. Even 15 years ago, it was only top writers who could demand a retention period of 15 or 20 years. These days, a retention period of between 3 and 10 years is the market.

In this clause, the extension to 30th June or 31st December is for the publisher's ease of accounting. The extension merely moves the end of the term to the end of the publisher's normal accounting period.

(g) **Term** means ....years calculated from 1 January .... but if we are unrecouped at the expiration of the said ..... year period, the Term will automatically extend (for a period which will not exceed ..... years) until the end of the accounting period in which you recoup.

The term is obviously important as it defines the period of direct relationship between publisher and writer. Three years is very common. Anything less is not worth the trouble.

Note that the term automatically extends until any outstanding advances are recouped. This lessens the likelihood of the publisher being burnt by a writer who gets a large advance but doesn't prove to be as productive or successful as expected. Commonly, the writer will negotiate the right to repay advances that are outstanding at the end of the term rather than just wait for the publisher to recoup, so if you wish to change publishers you might persuade your new publisher to provide the money for the buy-out. Be warned, however, it is common for the publisher to require a repayment of more than 100% of unrecouped advances if they are going to let you go. After all, if they only get back their advance, they will have not even recovered their costs, let alone made a profit.

ASSIGNMENT

2. In consideration of the sum of one dollar ($1.00) paid by us to you, you assign to us all the Copyright throughout the Territory in the Compositions for the Term.

The one dollar business is legal paranoia. It ensures that 'consideration' (or 'value') is present. This is one of the requirements of a valid contract. More importantly, by this clause, all of the rights in all your compositions are transferred to the publisher. You no longer own your works.

Writers with some clout may convince the publisher to accept an exclusive licence of the copyright rather than an assignment.

3. Without limiting the generality of the foregoing, the rights assigned to us (which will be sole and exclusive for the Territory) include:
    (a) the right to grant licences to communicate the Compositions to the public by any and all means, subject to the rights of the Australasian Performing Right Association ('APRA');
    (b) the right, subject to our obtaining your prior written consent, to make adaptations additions alterations arrangements and translations of the Compositions in whole or in part;
    (c) the right to grant mechanical licences;
    (d) the right, subject to our obtaining your prior written consent, to grant non-exclusive synchronisation licences;
    (e) the right to use the titles of the Compositions for all purposes in connection with the Compositions;
    (f) the right to publish print and reproduce the Compositions;
    (g) the right to authorise others to exercise any of the above rights; and
    (h) collect any other income relating to the Compositions.

This clause is in fairly standard form. It specifies the rights that the publisher will be able to exercise. If you want to withhold any rights from the deal, or put limitations on the publisher's power to exercise certain rights, this is the place to do it. For example, you may wish to limit the right of the publisher to grant licences for the promotion of third party goods and services. (Seeing your favourite composition used to sell toilet paper may not bring joy; on the other hand, the licence fee paid by the company might ease the pain.)

COMPOSER PROMISES AND WARRANTIES

4. You agree that you will (if so requested by us):
    (a) execute or sign any other document and do all other acts and things which may be reasonably required of you to vest in us the rights granted hereunder;
    (b) deliver a lead sheet(s) and a recording of all Compositions;

If you don't give the publisher a copy of the composition in an easily accessible form, it is going to be very difficult for the publisher to do anything with it. These days many composers do not (cannot) actually write out lead sheets, so writers generally deliver demonstration recordings of their material.

(c) sign a separate agreement or assignment in respect of each or any of the Compositions; and

(d) allow us to use your name, professional name, approved photograph likeness and approved biography to exploit the Compositions PROVIDED THAT we will at all times obtain your prior written consent before making such use in relation to any merchandising or the promotion of the goods or services of any third party.

Note the approval protections built into the paragraph.

5. You hereby warrant and declare that:
   (a) the Compositions are original works and do not and will not infringe the Copyright in any other work and will not be obscene nor defamatory of any person;
   (b) you have good right and full power to grant to us the rights set forth above and every one of them in the manner aforesaid;

Paragraphs (a) and (b) are central to any publishing deal. It is fundamental to the relationship that the works are original and that you have the rights you say you have. These provisions should never be treated lightly. The next paragraph shows why

(c) you indemnify us our successors and assigns against all costs damages losses and expenses (including legal expenses) suffered by us as a result of any breach by you of the warranties and declarations on your part contained herein as are provided by final order or award of a court or settled with your consent; and

It is only fair that you 'indemnify' (i.e. reimburse) the publisher if you do not comply with the fundamental promises of the above warranties. This clause is fair when compared with some which require the writer to indemnify the publisher in respect of all third party claims made in relation to the warranties. The companies argue that, if somebody makes such a claim, it costs them considerable amounts of money to defend themselves even if they win the dispute at the end of the day. The writers argue that they should only have to indemnify the publisher for proven breaches of their (the writers) warranties. After all, you can't stop anyone from making a claim, no matter how ill-founded that claim may be. This is a point which doesn't get called upon in more than a tiny percentage of publishing relationships - but if it is, you may find that even though you win, you have to pay the difference between the amount the publisher recovers as legal costs and its actual legal costs (which are likely to be between $30,000 and $150,000). The difference *can be quite substantial, even if the publisher wins the case.*

As a result, the risk of the writer should be limited to actual breaches of the warranties. If claims are made, and those claims are unfounded, it seems unfair for the publisher to demand that the writer pay the publisher's costs. These should be treated by both writer and publisher as a cost of being in business.

(d) you will (if so requested by us) permit your name to be used as a Plaintiff or party in any actions or proceedings that may be necessary for us to secure establish or enforce the rights in each of the Compositions hereby assigned. The expense of any such action or proceeding will be borne by us except that all such expenses may be recouped from any sums obtained or derived from such action or proceeding.

PUBLISHER PROMISES AND WARRANTIES

6. (a) We agree to use reasonable endeavours to exploit the Compositions and exploitation by our licensees shall be deemed exploitation for the purposes of this clause.

This doesn't sound like much but it's about all most publishers promise to do. Of course, given that the industry is so speculative, it is difficult for the publisher to actually guarantee to achieve anything. The following paragraph at least attempts to put some specifics into the publisher's obligations. Good publishers will do all of these things, and more, as a matter of course, so it does no harm to include them!

(b) Without prejudice to the generality of the above we will use all reasonable endeavours to:
   (i) (where you do not have a recording agreement) assist you in obtaining a recording agreement;
   (ii) obtain Covers of the Compositions;
   (iii) collect all income arising from the exploitation of the Compositions during the Retention Period; and
   (iv) protect the copyright and all like rights in and to the Compositions.

If you have particular needs, this is the time to raise them. For example, if the publisher is expected to provide money for producing demo recordings or for living in Nashville for a spot of co-writing, these should be specified.

ROYALTIES

7. In consideration of your execution of this agreement and provided that you fully perform all of your obligations hereunder we agree to pay to you:

(a) on execution of this agreement, an advance of .... dollars ($............), which shall be recoupable only from all royalties or other income otherwise due to you hereunder; and

Note that the advance is recoupable. There is no 'cross-collateralisation' (meaning that recoupment is only allowed from income earned pursuant to this agreement and not from any other agreement or source).

Some publishers have a reputation as having large chequebooks. Others can be tightwads. Advances vary from zero to $500,000 or more. It all depends on the earning capacity of the copyrights and the other terms of the deal, such as royalty rates and control periods. In other words the advance is necessarily linked to the publisher's estimation of its ability to recoup (though other factors can obviously be relevant).

(b) the following royalties:
  (i) in respect of mechanical income (other than from Covers) from exploitation of Compositions delivered hereunder .... per cent (........%) of the Net Royalties Received;
  (ii) in respect of income arising from and directly attributable to Covers and synchronisation licences we procure, ... per cent (........%) of the Net Royalties Received, or .... per cent (........%) where such licences are procured by you;

This clause recognises the fact that writers often find their own film and television work. Where they do, there is no justification in the publisher enjoying a bigger share of the income. After all, the greater publisher's share is designed to be an incentive for the publisher to obtain such exploitations.

  (iii) .... per cent (........%) of the suggested retail selling price excluding GST of each such copy of sheet music sold for which we receive payment or credit (such percentage to be pro-rated in respect of folios or other compilations by the number of Compositions contained therein as compared to the total number of songs contained therein);
  (iv) .... per cent (........%) of the gross fees paid by APRA in relation to performing rights in the Compositions (it being understood that you will receive 50% of the gross directly from APRA, and one half will be paid to us, of which we will pay you .... per cent (........%) of same;
  (v) In respect of income earned overseas, ... per cent (........%) of Net Royalties Received; and

This deal is based on income actually received by the publisher in Australia. It is not an 'at source' deal.

> (vi) in respect of all other income from the creation and exploitation of the Compositions delivered hereunder .... per cent (........%) of the Net Royalties Received by us.

ACCOUNTING

8. (a) We will, by 30 September for the period ending the preceding 30 June and by the 31 March for the period ending the preceding 31 December in each year, prepare and submit to you a statement of account showing the amount due to you hereunder and will pay to you the amount (if any) shown to be due.

You will never improve on half-yearly accounting. This is not negotiable. The whole collection system is based on it. The accounting periods end on 30 June and 31 December. After that, there is a period required in which the publisher prepares its accounts relating to the immediately past accounting period. This is usually 60 or 90 days.

> (b) All Statements of account rendered to you hereunder will be binding upon you and not subject to any objection unless you give written notice of objection stating the basis thereof to us within two (2) years from the date rendered.

Publishing agreements limit the period within which you may query the accounting. Your lawyer will try to extend this period because, if the limitation period is two years, you are almost obliged to go to the expense and trouble of auditing the company every two years just to protect your interests. It would make sense if companies, at least during the term of the agreement, agreed to extend it to, say, six months after the expiration of the term or Retention Period. Then, one audit would be enough and both parties would be saved a lot of trouble. On the other hand, publishers want to have a definite time at which they can 'close off' their accounts and not worry about audits, which are very intrusive and interrupt normal work.

Remember that many errors, once made, are simply repeated year after year and it may be necessary to go back many years to get a true accounting of the amount actually owed.

> (c) You will have the right at your expense to appoint a chartered accountant to inspect our books of accounts at our usual place of business insofar as the same relate to the exploitation of the Compositions. If the inspection

reveals a discrepancy in excess of ....% of the amount properly due for the audited period but in any event greater than $1,000, we shall pay the reasonable cost of the inspection. Such right may be exercised not more than once in each calendar year nor more than once in respect of any statement, by you giving reasonable notice in writing to us before any proposed inspection.

(d) All payments will be subject to the deduction or withholding of all taxes required to be deducted or withheld under the laws of any country or territory and to the exchange control regulations of any country or territory from which those payments emanate.

(e) All copies of the Compositions in whatever form which may be distributed to the trade and profession or otherwise for the purpose of exploiting or popularising the Compositions and also all reproductions of Compositions or parts thereof published in any newspapers and other periodicals will be free of all royalty or payment to you where we receive no payment or payment below cost.

(f) We may only account for monies received by us in Australia although we do warrant that we will make all reasonable efforts to ensure that your share of money earned overseas is remitted to Australia as promptly as is practicable.

This is a 'receipts' deal, not an 'at source' deal.

LIMITATIONS ON POWER TO DEAL

9. (a) You may not assign transfer or license or agree to assign transfer or license any of the benefits or rights of this Agreement.

(b) We will not assign any of the benefits or rights of this Agreement except with your prior written consent PROVIDED THAT we will at all times have the right to assign this Agreement to a related company or as an inclusion in the assignment of the whole of our catalogue.

Note that the company's right to deal with the rights is greater than yours. This is only common sense. The company must be able to license the rights because that is one of the functions of a publisher, but writers always argue that, because of the personal relationship needed with their publisher, the publisher should not be allowed to assign rights except as a part of an internal corporate rearrangement or the sale of the catalogue as a whole (and even then, many writers want prior approval rights).

TERMINATION

10. (a) If you have a receiving order in bankruptcy made against you or if we enter into liquidation (other than a voluntary liquidation for the purposes of reconstruction or amalgamation) or if either party makes any

composition with that party's creditors the other party will have the option to terminate this Agreement forthwith upon giving written notice thereof.

(b) Any such termination will be without prejudice to our rights hereunder in respect of each and all of the Compositions to which we are entitled to at the date of such termination.

ENFORCEMENT OF RIGHTS

11. You irrevocably vest in us the sole right to enforce and protect all rights in and to the Compositions and the copyright therein in the Territory. We may join you or such others as we may deem advisable in any suits and proceedings and we may proceed with and dispose of proceedings or suits at our sole discretion. If any third party suit or proceeding is due to your default or the breach of any promise by you hereunder, any legal costs or disbursements incurred by us shall be borne (on an indemnity basis) by you. If the suit or proceeding is not due to your breach or default the costs or disbursements incurred by us shall be borne equally (on an indemnity basis) and any sums recovered by you and/or us by way of damages or otherwise (but after the payment of all legal costs or disbursements) shall be shared according to clause 7(b)(vi) hereof. We warrant that we shall not settle any action involving your interests without first consulting with you.

Part of the publisher's job is to protect your copyrights. It must have the right to commence proceedings and to involve you in those proceedings. It is reasonable that you grant the publisher an indemnity in the event that it is found that you have breached the terms or warranties in the agreement. The drafting of this clause is very important and complex. Just a very small change in wording can cost a lot of money if you get involved in a legal action. Beware!

PUBLISHER WARRANTIES

12. We warrant that we will at all times act in good faith and deal at arms length on a proper and customary commercial basis and without limiting the generality of the foregoing this warranty will apply to our dealings with our affiliates, subsidiaries, licensees and sub-licensees and any collection agencies that we may retain.

These may not seem much, but it is more than many publishing agreements contain! These warranties show the publisher has the right spirit.

ENTIRE AGREEMENT

13. This Agreement constitutes the entire agreement between the parties with respect to the subject matter hereof and cannot be altered amended or modified except by an instrument in writing signed by the parties hereto.

Once you have signed this agreement, nothing that was discussed before has much worth. If the publisher has made a promise that is an important reason for you agreeing to enter the deal, make sure that it is spelt out in the contract. Similarly, if the parties agree to change the terms of the deal, those changes must be put in writing and signed by both parties. If it isn't written, it may not be binding.

NOTICES

14. Any notice required to be given pursuant to this Agreement will be deemed to have been sufficiently given if sent by recorded delivery or registered post to the party to whom it is addressed at the address hereinbefore mentioned or any address of that party subsequently notified in accordance with this clause and will be deemed served on the day of posting.

Keep your publisher up to date with your various house shifts. If you don't, this clause can hurt you.

15. In the event of a material default on our part you must serve written notice to us stating the nature thereof and requiring the same to be remedied within 45 days from receipt of such notice and you will not be entitled to take any action against us unless such notice has been served on us.

It is always sensible to include a provision that requires the other side to notify you of any actual or suspected breach of the agreement and gives you an opportunity to remedy that breach. Nobody likes to be bushwhacked.

INDEPENDENT ADVICE

16. This Agreement contains important provisions relating to your career as a songwriter and you are strongly urged to seek independent legal advice from a solicitor specialising in this area of law.

There is now much case law, both here and in England, which makes it clear that one of the factors a court will take into account, when determining whether or not contracting artists and writers have been treated harshly or unfairly, is to see if they had the benefit of independent legal advice before entering the agreement. All wise companies now demand that their writers get independent legal advice.

JURISDICTION

17. This Agreement will be governed by and construed according to Australian Law and the federal courts and the courts of (New South Wales) will have exclusive jurisdiction.

This rather dull seeming clause is very important in a country that is subject to a federal system. It is also very important when you are dealing with a foreign company (or one that is multi-national). The difficulty and expense involved in fighting a case hundreds or thousands of miles from your home is hard to appreciate, unless you have been put through the nightmare.

GST

18. The royalties that we pay you are calculated exclusive of GST. We will pay you the royalty plus the GST payable in respect of that amount provided that you are registered for GST and you provide us with your ABN and a GST Tax Invoice for the amount of GST paid.

   (a) **GST Law** is defined in the *A New Tax System (Goods and Services Tax) Act 1999 (Cth)*. **GST** means a tax, levy, duty, charge or deduction, together with any related additional tax, interest, penalty, fine or other damage, imposed by or under a GST Law. The meaning of **Tax Invoice** is as defined in the GST Law.

Royalties are always calculated exclusive of GST. Provided you are registered for GST, provide your ABN and give the publisher a tax invoice (which the publisher will provide for you) it will pay the royalties plus the GST on those royalties. It is then your responsibility to forward the GST to the Australian Tax Office. If the contract doesn't specify that the publisher pays the GST, you will be liable to pay it anyway. In effect this would mean that you would be getting 10% less royalty. Not good.

SELF-PUBLISHING

Many established writers who wish to maintain control of their own catalogue, establish their own publishing company. They don't need the funding a publisher can provide and they can get their material recorded through their own contacts or simply record it themselves. To administer it, they either use a lawyer or the administrative staff of their management company. In this way they receive a greater proportion of publishing income because they earn both the writer's and the publisher's share.

If you are prepared to handle the administration yourself, fund yourself and promote your catalogue yourself, that's fine. Many prefer to take a halfway-house approach and maintain overall control but pass the day-to-day work over to a publisher, via an administration deal.

ADMINISTRATION DEALS

These deals are usually only available to writers who are established and have an attractive catalogue or to people who are in a position to acquire copyrights from other writers, such as record producers.

In an administration deal the publisher will provide the administration necessary to register the songs, grant licences, collect, account for and distribute the income and provide some finance but both parties are expected to find opportunities for exploitation of the catalogue.

LENGTH OF CONTRACT

Administration deals are usually for either three or five years. Unlike term contracts, there are no retention periods, although there is often some extension provided for in the event that the writer's advance is unrecouped at the end of the agreement.

COPYRIGHT OWNERSHIP

In an administration deal, the publisher does not acquire ownership of the copyrights. It is granted an exclusive licence for the territory, authorising it to be the only party to administer, exploit and collect on the writer's behalf.

ADVANCES

Advances paid for administration deals are generally lower than for 'term' deals. The publisher will control the rights for a quite limited period (and therefore will have a shorter earning period), so it will be disinclined to pay a huge advance - if any. (For example, as the writer is the owner of the copyrights, he or she would be expected to pay for all demo costs.) Of course there are exceptions but they only prove the rule, don't they?

INCOME SPLITS

An administration deal usually provides the writer with a greater share of income than that generally provided by a 'term' deal. A common split would be 80/20 or 85/15. Only the really top writers can demand more. After all, the publisher has to cover its costs and make a reasonable profit from their work!

You hear some of the 'great rumours of modern publishing' when some deals are whispered about. One writer is supposed to have been on a 100/0 deal by a major publisher, and Supertramp supposedly did a 105/-5 deal with its publisher. Yes, for every $100 earned, the publisher would pay through $105! How does this make sense? It may not! Nevertheless you can point to two factors that might have made it possible: first, the publisher was looking to sign a big name. Second, the writer/artist was selling so many records and was generating such huge volumes of income that the interest earned on that income (while it was being held by the publisher - in between six-monthly accountings), meant that the company could anticipate making a profit out of the interest alone! Don't expect to do such a deal. They are more rare (and much more fun) than appearances of Halley's Comet.

COVERS

Because the margins are so small in an administration deal, it is usually assumed that the publisher will not be expected to actively promote the catalogue. Rather, its function will be restricted largely to simple administration. If the writer wants the publisher to be more active, it is usual for the agreement to give the publisher an incentive to look for synchronisations and covers. The incentives can include:

INCREASED ROYALTY SPLIT

The publisher will expect to retain 25%-35% instead of 15%-20% of the royalty receipts. It makes sense to give the publisher a reasonable incentive to work the material and to procure additional exploitations.

The difficulty here is whether the different rate applies to all uses of that song once it has been covered, or whether it just applies to the cover version. The publisher will pitch for the former and the writer for the latter. The publisher will quite rightly say that it is difficult (if not impossible) to clearly differentiate the public performance income earned from various versions of the same song. (Indeed in respect of public performance income, APRA cannot distinguish between different recordings of the same song.) The writer will argue for a proportion reduction of the income so the performance income is in direct proportion to the more easily calculable mechanical income. There are problems to both approaches, but there are also various solutions - though they may be imperfect.

EXTENSION OF RIGHTS PERIOD

If the rights period of the agreement is, say three years, the contract may provide that if the publisher obtains a cover, the publisher will continue to control the rights to that work for an extended period. An extra three to seven years is not uncommon.

COPYRIGHT OWNERSHIP

Some smaller publishers try to insist that they will become the owners of the copyright in the work if they get a cover of it. Sometimes this may be worth the cost but usually it is not. A publisher who wants that much flesh is probably too greedy to be safe. If you have to do this deal, make sure that there are guarantees that it will only be triggered if the cover record sells a poultice. If you have to lose control of a work make sure that you are going to get money for it.

If the publisher is going to get extra benefits for obtaining covers, you will have to examine very carefully the definition of what constitutes a 'cover' for the purposes of the agreement. Very tight definitions are essential.

13
COMMON CLAUSES IN PUBLISHING DEALS

MANY OF THE MOST IMPORTANT CLAUSES IN PUBLISHING CONTRACTS WERE DISCUSSED IN THE PREVIOUS CHAPTER. HOWEVER, THERE ARE A FEW OTHER MATTERS THAT YOU MUST TAKE INTO ACCOUNT.

ASSIGNMENTS AND LICENCES

All publishing contracts involve the writer handing ownership (or at least control) of the song over to a publisher. Whether the deal is based on assignment of copyright or merely a licence, the underlying principle remains the same. The publisher must have the rights necessary to permit and encourage it to exploit and protect the work.

The publisher will always prefer to have an assignment of the copyright because this is the most absolute transfer of rights. When you assign rights you are transferring them. The assignment will usually be for a limited period but, during the period of the assignment, the rights that you have assigned are no longer yours.

In contrast, when you license rights, they remain your property; you are merely formally permitting another party to use some of those rights. That permission can either be on an exclusive or a non-exclusive basis.

Both assignments and licences can be limited in all sorts of ways. Both can be limited as to duration, territory, the rights granted and so on. Importantly, both can be terminated in similar ways and the effect of termination can be identical. In other words, both assignment and licence deals can provide similar levels of protection for each party. The answer lies in the detail of the drafting.

At the bottom of the assignment/licence debate:

1. *The publisher wants an assignment* because, if it has to sue someone for infringement, it has to establish a chain of copyright to the owner. If it is itself the owner, that chain is rather short! The assignment gives the publisher the ability to protect the work in its own name, whereas if the publisher is an exclusive licensee, it must join the writer (who would normally be the owner, unless the writer has interposed a company which owns the works) as a party to the proceedings in order to establish that chain of title.

2. *The writer wants a licence* because of the security of knowing that the writer still owns the work, even if he or she does not absolutely control it. It means that in the event of a breach of the terms of the agreement by the publisher, it is easier to argue that a mere licence has been revoked, as it does not involve transferring ownership of the rights. It is merely a matter of withdrawing a privilege.

More important than the question 'Is it a licence or an assignment?' are the following questions.

- As a songwriter, how long will you be tied to this publisher?
- How long will your work be tied to this publisher?
- What do you expect your publisher to achieve?
- What would your publisher expect of you?
- What controls will you maintain over your work and reputation?
- What income will you earn from your work?
- If the publisher should breach its obligations to you, how will you get back full control of your works?

PUBLISHER'S OBLIGATION TO EXPLOIT

No matter how the publisher acquires its rights, the writer has to be assured that the publisher will be active and not just be in the business of building up a catalogue as a business asset.

There is an obvious commercial incentive for a publisher to be active when an advance has been paid, but that is no guarantee. Better to have some objective yardsticks by which to measure the publisher's performance.

Most publishing agreements now contain clauses giving the writer the right to retrieve the copyright in any works the publisher does not exploit. For example, if a particular work has not appeared on a record, been broadcast or synchronised into a film soundtrack, within (say) two years, then the writer can get the work re-assigned. Note that it is not sufficient that such a clause says that the work can be retrieved if it is not 'published' within a certain period. That is too low a performance criterion. It could mean merely releasing a cheap print version of the work. Instead, such a clause should specify types of exploitation that will **earn income** such as obtaining a synchronisation or a cover.

(For more on re-assignment, see the end of this chapter.)

ROYALTY SPLITS

GENERAL

These days, no matter how inexperienced you are, you should never sign a single-song assignment for less than 60/40 of mechanical, public performance and sundry income. Publishers who ask for the old style 50/50 are not meeting the general market rate. There are always a few of these operators working the market, promising the world and delivering very little. Avoid them and their 50/50 deals.

The most normal rates are 70/30 to 75/25. The absolute maximum rate is 80/20, unless you are in superstar-writer class. Above 80/20, you cannot expect the publisher to do much for you because the margin just isn't there (unless, of course, your works are generating huge amounts of money). All the publisher will do is administer the catalogue, collect income and account.

SYNCHRONISATIONS AND COVERS

The royalty rate for income from covers may, in some deals, be lower than the basic royalty rate for mechanical, public performance and sundry income. The cover rate paid to the writer for these forms of exploitation is commonly 10% to 20% less than the basic royalty rate (e.g. the basic rate may be 70/30, but on covers, 60/40). Some publishers also reduce the rate on synchronisation licences (e.g. licensing the work for use in a film sound track or a television commercial.

There are several theories (or, as some would put it, justifications) for this difference between the two rates. One theory is that the reduction is an additional reward to publishers who go to the trouble and expense of looking for covers and opportunities for synchronisation licences.

The cynical theory is that publishers will be more inclined to work a song from which they are going to get a bigger percentage of the gross. The theory goes that, if a publisher has a choice between pitching a song from which it will earn 10% and a song from which it will earn 40%, it will pitch the one with the better margin. Right? Well, maybe. Publishing is rarely that simple or predictable. Publishers would prefer all their hits were on 60/40, but the fact is, a hit is a hit and any publisher will be grateful for a hit, even at 90/10. In most cases, the people in the publishing company who are pitching the song may not even know the comparative royalty rates and probably wouldn't care, even if they did know.

To avoid this problem your lawyer will usually negotiate a different split depending on whether it is the publisher or the writer that secures the cover or synchronisation.

All this is perhaps somewhat theoretical if you only have a single song assignment (unless it is a real zinger of a song, with hit written all over it) because the publisher is not very likely to go out looking for synchronisations and covers for an orphan song. It is more likely to try and get these exploitations for its longer-term writers.

SHEET MUSIC INCOME

The writer's share of sheet music income is usually based on a royalty between 10% and 15% (commonly 12.5%) of the retail selling price of sold copies. (In the United States this royalty is calculated in cents rather than percentages: five cents to seven cents per copy is common unless the writer has negotiating clout.)

In Australia, the rates paid for sheet music and for folios is the same. (In the United States, sheet royalties are calculated on retail and folio income is often calculated on wholesale.)

Where a composition is included in a folio, the royalty is reduced in proportion to the total number of works in the folio (this calculation is usually referred to a being pro rated). So, if you are on a royalty of 10% of the retail selling price and there are 20 works in the book of which one work is yours, for every $100 of net sales you will get $10 ÷ 20 = 50 cents.

It is important that the contract specifies that the pro-rating takes into account only works that are still in copyright (which can include new arrangements of traditional works), otherwise your earnings will be reduced by the inclusion of those works on which the publisher is not paying any royalties anyway. The larger the denominator in the fraction, the smaller each share will be, so it makes sense for the writer to exclude all non-copyright works.

PUBLIC PERFORMANCE AND COMMUNICATION INCOME

All writers should join the Australian Performing Right Association (APRA). APRA pays a minimum of 50% (the writer's share) of the income it collects, direct to its member writers and the balance to the relevant publisher. If there is more than one writer (i.e. the copyright is split between several writers), APRA will divide it in the proportions as notified by the writers or their publishers.

If the writer should by chance not be an APRA member, APRA will still only pay 50% to the publisher. The writer can then claim the writer's share from APRA in the usual way by joining it, or one of its affiliates. If no publisher is involved with a particular work, 100% will be paid directly to the writer.

Most publishing agreements provide for the publisher to pay through a proportion of the publisher's share to the writer. This is usually the difference between the standard writer's share (50%) of APRA fees, and the percentage payable to the writer (under the contract) of the publisher's income from other sources. For example, if the usual split is 75/25 under the contract, then on public performance income, the writer should receive 50% of the publisher's share (i.e. 25% of the total paid out by APRA for the particular song) in addition to the 50% paid directly as the writer's share.

There is an alternative method sometimes used: APRA is advised that the writer's share is (say) 75%, so APRA pays 75% of performance fees directly to the writer. This method disadvantages the publisher because, if the writer is unrecouped, recoupment will be even slower since the publisher cannot treat 50% of the publisher's share as part of the writer's royalty and apply it towards recoupment.

Let's apply this to a simple example: Assume that APRA collects $100. Unless the publishing agreement specifies that the full $75 be paid to the writer, APRA will pay $50 to the writer and $50 to the publisher. Out of its share, the publisher will pay or credit the writer, $25. The writer gets $75 and the publisher ends up with $25.

OVERSEAS INCOME
THE SUB-PUBLISHER'S COMMISSION
The division of overseas income is always detailed in the publishing agreement and you must take particular care to make sure that you are getting your fair share.

Sub-publishers are third-party publishers who are licensed by your publisher to administer and exploit your works in that sub-publisher's 'territory'. As the sub-publisher is working in its own backyard, the theory is that it will better know its local industry and will therefore more effectively exploit your works. The territory may be one country or several. The licence may also allow the sub-publisher to appoint sub-publishers (sub-sub-publishers) or it may administer the whole territory itself. Sub-sub-publishers are not desirable, as they are just another party taking a percentage of the fees before you get them.

All sub-publishers charge a commission for administering your copyrights. That is, after all, how they make their money. The commission is usually between 10% and 15% of the total royalty income collected by that sub-publisher (the gross), depending on the terms of the sub-licence. If the sub-publisher makes a special effort to procure a cover of your song, it will usually expect a greater commission in return for its additional work.

The commission on covers usually increases to about 20% of the gross, but can be as much as 50% in really exceptional circumstances. This greater commission is a reward for or an incentive to the sub-publisher to obtain a cover of your song.

NET RECEIPTS V. AT SOURCE

Great care must be taken in working out the basis upon which overseas income will be divided between the writer and the writer's publisher. There are two basic methods: "net receipts" and "at source".

NET RECEIPTS

In essence, net receipts deals work on the basis that your royalty is calculated as a percentage of the money actually received by your publisher in Australia. The term 'receipts' should, of course, include any royalty **credits** that the publisher might earn. The net receipts figure, at least in the case of royalties earned outside Australia, is reached after deduction of the sub-publisher's commission from the total amount of income earned in its territory.

For example, say your song earns mechanical royalties of US$100 in the United States. Your publisher has a sub-publisher in the United States and given it the right to collect royalties on your songs and retain commission of 10% of the gross in its territory.

The sub-publisher will retain US$10, deduct any withholding tax required under United States' law (say, another 10% of the original US$100) and remit the balance to your publisher.

	US$
Gross earned in United States	100
less withholding tax @10%	10
less sub-publisher's commission	10
Net receipts in Australia	80

To calculate your royalty your publisher will multiply the net receipts by the percentage in the publishing agreement, after converting the net receipts to Australian currency. Conversion will increase or decrease the total, depending on the exchange rate. Let's assume US$80 equals $A160. On a 75/25 deal, your royalty account will be credited with $A120.

Most publishers prefer to work on a net receipts basis. They are usually unwilling to work on an at source basis though, in the final analysis, a comparable result can be achieved for both parties provided the writer's royalty is calculated at a rate which gives the publisher sufficient margin to allow for the sub-publisher's commission on the gross earnings. In effect, the royalty rate has to be set at a low enough rate to leave the publisher with sufficient margin for both it, and its sub-publisher, to make a reasonable commission. As an alternative, the sub-publisher's commission can be capped to a set percentage. This way, no matter what the sub-publisher actually retains under its deal with your publisher (as they could always agree between themselves to vary the sub-publisher's commission), your net receipts will be worked out using the capped rate.

Net receipts deals are simple enough, but the system fell into disrepute some time ago when some publishers abused it. The scam went like this (slightly exaggerated, to highlight the trick): The (say) United States publisher obtained world rights; it sub-licensed its Canadian affiliate which in turn sub-licensed its English affiliate, which sub-licensed its French affiliate; which sub-licensed its German affiliate; which sub-licensed the Swedish affiliate... All of them worked on a net receipts basis and each of them could retain (say) 15% of those receipts as its commission. You don't have to be very bright to work out that, by the time the royalties from Sweden have gone through the chain, they will have been whittled away to almost nothing.

To avoid this, make sure that the contract specifies that only one bite can be taken out of the overseas income before it is remitted to Australia, irrespective of the number of hands that it passes through. Fortunately, most publishers need to make a profit in their own home territories, and it is not in their interests to do the old 'sub-publisher run around' (quite apart from the horrible publicity this kind of sharp practice would generate, if done today). That said, it certainly pays to ask how things are done by each particular publisher. If your publisher is accounted to at source by its sub-publishers, then the receipts in Australia will be the gross royalties generated in the sub-publisher's territory, less only the sub-publisher's administration charges and any taxes. After that, it is only a matter of limiting the permitted sub-publisher's commission so that you can be assured that the royalty return will be fair to you.

The alternative method is to calculate income at source.

AT SOURCE

If your overseas income is calculated at source, it means that your percentage is based on the gross receipts in the overseas territory, only allowing specifically nominated deductions (e.g. withholding or other taxes the foreign government might apply).

True at source accounting provides for your royalty to be calculated on virtually 100% of the gross generated in the sub-publisher's territory and disregards the sub-publisher's percentage. To maintain the dollar value of the royalty your publisher will have to pay you, the royalty rate in your publishing contract has to be adjusted, e.g. assuming the sub-publisher is retaining 10% of the gross in its territory, a 75/25 net receipts deal is about the same as a 67/33 at source deal.

Using the same assumptions as were used above and assuming the definition of at source allows deduction of local taxes:

	US$
Gross earned in United States	100
less withholding tax @10%	10
at source	90

To calculate your royalty, your publisher will multiply the at source amount by the percentage in the publishing agreement, after converting the amount to Australian currency. Let's assume US$90 equals $A180. Then the calculation would be $A180 x 75 % = $135. As you can immediately see, it is better than a receipts deal.

The advantage of at source accounting is that you know what deductions your publisher may apply before the division of income is made. With a net receipts deal (unless the clauses are properly negotiated), you may have less knowledge of, or control over, any amounts which will be deducted before the money gets back to Australia.

Not many writers have the negotiating strength to demand a pure at source deal. All publishers resist it and most simply refuse it.

But beware! There is a surprising number of publishing agreements around which use the phrase "at source" but actually mean no such thing. These agreements use a definition of at source that changes the usual meaning of the phrase so that it actually means net receipts! It is just a ruse to catch the poorly advised writer who, seeing the magic phrase, assumes that he or she has the optimum protection. It is a feel-good-now, feel-awful-later definition.

MECHANICAL ROYALTY REDUCTIONS IN THE UNITED STATES AND CANADA

Controlled compositions and reduced mechanical copyright royalty rates are dealt with in detail in Chapter 23, **Record Royalties**, so we will deal with them only briefly here. They are relevant to performer-songwriters because they reduce the mechanical royalties that can be earned in the territories where the clauses apply. If you are a performer-songwriter with publishing and recording contracts, these clauses will affect both you and your publisher. In some publishing agreements, the publishers try to get themselves a more favourable commission rate on mechanical royalties earned in countries where controlled composition clauses apply.

The custom in the United States and Canada is that record companies demand special conditions on the way mechanical royalties will be paid on records which contain works written or otherwise controlled by that artist (controlled compositions). These are generally defined as being works owned or controlled by the recording artist. Some record companies try to expand the definition to include songs the recording artist does not own or control.

Works already assigned to a publisher (including those not yet written, but which must be assigned as they are created) should never be treated as controlled compositions. Your lawyer should try to knock these expansions out.

Why do artists agree to these terms? Because they have a choice: do the deal that way, or not do a deal at all. Mega stars might (emphasise might) get to negotiate minimum concessions, but for everyone else, the terms are non-negotiable in the sense that you will never get rid of them completely.

Essentially, they affect the otherwise applicable mechanical copyright rate by:
- limiting the royalty to only three-quarters of the otherwise applicable statutory rate;
- paying on no more than 10 tracks (even if the album has, say, 12 tracks). A similar cap is often applied to singles, etc.
- paying no royalties on 'free goods' (the term is usually widely defined).

As far as anyone can tell, all Australian artists who have had releases in the United States have had to suffer this diminished rate and there is nothing to make anyone think that situation will change (but that's no reason not to negotiate hard, to get the best deal you can!).

There is a rationale for the provisions (as you will see in the detailed study), but they have too often been abused and blatantly used as a way of reducing the record companies' royalty expenses. They argue that they shouldn't have to be paying their own recording artists to record their own material, though they (conveniently) overlook the fact that recording music and writing it are different skills AND DIFFERENT RIGHTS and are properly the subject of separate remuneration. If a corporate analogy may be drawn, if a company makes both compact discs and CD players, no-one suggests that if you buy the company's hardware, you get a 50% reduction on their discs. (Perhaps it should be suggested!)

No matter how good your lawyer is, on sales of your record in the United States and Canada you will suffer a reduction in mechanical royalties payable in respect of controlled compositions. Your lawyer's knowledge and ability will be important, however, in limiting the scope of the definition in your particular record contract.

(For further discussion of controlled composition clauses and mechanical royalty caps, see the last section of Chapter 23, **Record Royalties**.)

GST

Publishing income is subject to the Goods and Services Tax. As this tax is designed to be an 'end-user' tax, publishing contracts must make it clear that any GST payable in respect of the writer's royalty, will be actually paid by the publisher. Various publishers adopt different procedures but essentially they should all be variants on the following process.

- The royalty payable is calculated in the normal way.
- Then the GST payable on that amount is calculated.
- If the composer is registered for GST purposes, he or she will be advised by the publisher of the royalty payable and the amount of any associated GST.
- The composer then invoices the publisher for the royalty plus the GST payable.
- On receipt, the composer pays the GST with the publisher's money (or has the publisher pay it on his or her behalf).
- The publisher then claims the GST payment as an input credit and off-sets the amount against any other tax that it would otherwise have to pay.

If the composer is not registered for GST purposes, he or she will not have a tax liability in respect of the royalty. The composer doesn't invoice the publisher for the GST payable. None is payable. That's the theory but you only have a choice of registering or not if your income is under the $50000 threshold. Given that everyone wants to earn more than that (and the publisher funds the GST payment), why wouldn't you register for GST and set yourself up on the basis that you are going to be successful?

ACCOUNTING

Publishers account to their writers on a six-monthly basis. The accounting periods traditionally run from 1 January to 30 June and 1 July to 31 December. This does not mean that you will get your cheque on 30 June and 31 December. These are the close-off dates for the accounts. You will actually receive the royalty statement between 60 and 90 days after the close-off date. This gives the publisher's accounts department a chance to make all the necessary calculations and prepare all of the individual statements for its writers.

The publisher has an absolute obligation to account to the writer. Many a writer has terminated a publishing agreement for a breach of this fundamental duty. Failing to account can be grounds for immediate termination of the contract, depending on the terms of the contract. The reality is, though, that termination is not usually the most appropriate response unless the writer already wants to be out of the contract for other reasons. Often, the writer is quite happy with the publisher in all other respects: the writer just wants the royalties. Immediately.

The accounting clause can limit your right to challenge the accounting statement and your right to commence action in respect of that statement. Most contracts state that, if you wish to make any objection to a statement, you must do so within (say) two years of receiving it and must commence any legal proceedings within three years. The justification given by publishers is that they have to be able to rule their books off at some stage, send them out to storage and eventually destroy them. They argue that it is reasonable to force a writer to verify the accounts promptly and make any complaints without undue delay.

There is truth in this, but two points should be borne in mind:

1. The limitation forces successful writers to audit their publisher more often than would otherwise be necessary. This is inconvenient and expensive for both parties and therefore it should be in the interests of both to extend the limitation period to three or even five years.

2. The limitation can operate very unfairly. For example, mistakes, defaults or frauds may have gone on for years (and across many accountings) without being detected. It would be a brave (or foolhardy) publisher who, in such circumstances, refused the writer's auditors access to the earlier figures on the ground of this contractual limitation. The publisher always has a duty to account honestly and accurately for money that does not rightfully belong to it and it is unlikely that Australian courts will let such a limitation clause operate unjustly.

CREATIVE CONTROL

All writer agreements have clauses giving the publisher some right to alter the works, add new lyrics, translate them into other languages, license them for others to use and so on. The publishers quite correctly say that these are rights they need, to maximise the financial potential of the work. The writers also correctly state that their professional reputation is inherently intertwined with their work and that some alterations and uses can detrimentally affect their professional reputation.

Almost all publishers in Australia will agree to include clauses protecting the works' integrity, but you have to ask for them. As usual, how readily (and to what extent) these requests will be met will be influenced by your bargaining power. Most publishers, as a matter of course, consult their writers before varying a work or authorising new words or music to be written.

Perhaps the most contentious of these creative controls is the right to license the work for synchronisation, both with film and television programs and into commercials. Most publishers resist giving the writer absolute control over the licensing of their works. They argue that this is really the publisher's role in the relationship and it is in the publisher's interest, as much as the writer's, to ensure that the licensing is done in such a way as to protect the integrity (and therefore the value) of the work.

On the other hand, the writers ask, 'where did all those terrible films and television programs get their music from if publishers were looking after the greater interests of their writers?'

In practice, it is very rare that a writer refuses permission for a synchronisation licence. Why would you? Synchronisation income is an important part of a writer's income flow. The common exceptions are commercials and X-rated movies. This all becomes very idiosyncratic, because no two writers will have the same attitudes to, and standards in, these matters. For some, the use of their song in a beer commercial is acceptable but a cigarette advertisement is not. For others it's sex, violence, politics and who knows what. One publisher was approached for permission to use a song in a commercial for sliced bread. When the composer was asked if he consented, after much turmoil, he eventually refused. He could not stand the thought of waking up every morning and hearing his favourite composition being used to sell sliced bread. No logic, and it cost him the average Australian wage, but it was important to him. What is more, his publisher understood and accepted his decision. That is one terrific publisher.

All reasonable publishers are prepared to give the writer certain power of control over these uses. The degree of control depends very much on the trust that the writer has for the publisher and the respect that the publisher has for the writer.

WRITER'S WARRANTIES

All publishing contracts have a section in which the writer has to promise the publisher that a whole array of things are true. They may seem to have little in common, but the thread running through them all is that they are all fundamental to the publisher's authority and ability to exploit and protect the work.

Most warranty clauses make the writer promise that:

- each of the compositions will be original and not infringe the copyright in any other work and is not to be obscene nor defamatory;
- the writer has the right and power to enter the agreement and to grant the publisher the rights granted in the agreement;
- the writer will indemnify the publisher against all losses it may suffer as a result of any breach of the agreement or the warranties; and
- the writer will assist the publisher in various ways in any actions or proceedings which may be necessary for it to secure, establish or enforce the rights in the work.

As you can see, in principle they are commercially necessary. Your lawyer will make sure that the clauses do not expose you to unreasonable risk.

PUBLISHER WARRANTIES

Contracts drafted by publishers rarely put much of a burden on them. This is understandable because the publisher's lawyers drafted the contract.

It is reasonable to expect the publisher to promise to try to exploit your compositions, collect all income arising from the exploitation of the compositions and to protect them.

They can't promise to get covers and synchronisations but they can promise to try. On the other hand, the collection of income and the protection of the copyrights is a fundamental obligation.

REVERSION OF COPYRIGHT

Reversion of copyright is relevant to the Term and Retention Period of the contract. As already noted, contracts that transfer the copyright in a work to a publisher for the duration of copyright, have (largely) been relegated to the scrapbooks as an unfortunate historical anomaly. Mind you, sell enough songs and you'll get rich even in a 50/50 deal. It will take a lot longer though. As a general rule, don't do them.

Lovers of fables will recall that, when the clock struck midnight, Cinderella's fairy godmother took back her magic. Writers should always have the option to take back the copyright in their works at the end of a publishing deal. A writer may decide to leave them there (after all, continuity of administration is a valuable thing) or decide there is more to be made by shifting control to another publisher. This is one of the great incentives for a publisher to keep doing the right thing.

Fortunately, most publishers do not expect life of copyright deals now. It's swings and roundabouts for them - they might lose one writer's catalogue at the end of the retention period, but pick up another writer's catalogue that had been controlled by a competitor until the retention period had similarly expired.

Most publishing deals give the writer the explicit right to require the works (which were assigned to the publisher during the deal) to be reassigned to the writer at the end of a specified time. The usual way of doing this is to have an appropriate clause in the section setting out the period during which the publisher may control the works. This may involve executing specific documents, though this can be avoided by careful drafting.

There is some debate over the Capital Gains Tax (CGT) implications of re-assignments and these need to be considered on a case-by-case basis. A recent amendment to the law probably catches such reassignments. The real problem is how to value the works. This is an area of law that is still developing. Keep it in mind though that CGT is one of the fairer taxes, because it deducts the effects of inflation before the 'capital gain' in value is calculated.

14
TECHNOLOGY AND MUSIC: EVOLUTION TO REVOLUTION

WITH DEVELOPMENTS IN TECHNOLOGY WE ARE SEEING NEW FORMS OF COMMERCIAL EXPLOITATION, NEW RIGHTS BEING CREATED AND NEW CONTRACTUAL PROVISIONS AND STRATEGIES BEING INTRODUCED TO DEAL WITH THOSE NEW SITUATIONS. IN UNDERSTANDING LEGAL AND COMMERCIAL DEVELOPMENTS, IT IS IMPORTANT TO HAVE AN UNDERSTANDING OF THE TECHNOLOGICAL BACKGROUND.

Performers now can have international reputations without having to leave their shores. What is more, audiences can enjoy those performances without even leaving their bedrooms. Technology has changed the nature of the music experience from one of personal presence and public participation to one of imagined presence and personal fantasy.

During the past two centuries there has been a great change in the way music is made available. This in turn has affected how, where and when music is used or enjoyed. It also affects what music is available and to whom.

Even though this book is about the music industry as it is today, there is a lot to be learned by taking a look at the past. If you were to wander back through history, you would see that the industry has already resisted, weathered and adopted many technological advances. Each has demonstrated the awkward tension that exists between the proponents of new technologies and the copyright owners that have grown attached to (and financially reliant on) existing technologies. Each has shown that new technologies open new markets and commercial opportunities, but also challenge the existing market structures and distribution networks. Innovations challenge the status quo of the day and then become part of it themselves.

Educated guesses about the future can help too. It can help you anticipate and prepare for change. All survivors in this business must realise that the industry is in the early stages of a revolution: we have moved out of the mechanical and electric ages that have stolidly shaped our last two centuries and into a globally networked digital age, the ultimate effect of which we can only surmise. Whether you like it or not, the music business is part of this revolution. It will affect both your personal lives and your professional lives. The only choice you have is whether you will be leading the tumbrel or be a passenger on it.

THE MECHANICAL AGE

Delivering music to the public has always been dependent upon the technology available at the time. Before sounds could be recorded and stored, written notation was the only way of keeping music for later use. Music had to be 'live', played by skilled musicians. But once sounds could be recorded and stored (and played later, over and over) it was only a matter of time before the performance of music became independent of the musicians. What an extraordinary concept! What a recent one!

EARLY RECORDINGS

The first means by which the sound of music could be mechanically mass-produced was the music box. Much of the philosophy regarding copyright and the international protection of music, and many of the conventions and practices still applicable to the industry, were developed when music boxes were hi-tech. We now think of music boxes as quaint historical oddities: hardly the stuff of which marketing managers' dreams are made. But in their day they were important; they were very fashionable; they were at the cutting edge.

The fact that many of these practices and theories have survived to the present day (though adapted to suit changing conditions and new technologies) seems to confirm the basic soundness of these early approaches.

Then in the mid-19th century, the piano roll became the most popular form of mechanical reproduction of music for home entertainment. In a way, it was an early form of karaoke. Even people who couldn't actually play the piano could still pedal out the accompaniment to a sing-along around the Pianola. Piano rolls sold in their millions and were a useful source of mechanical copyright income to many of the great popular composers of the 1930s such as Cole Porter and Irving Berlin. Piano rolls had quite a long life in terms of popularity, although by the 1950s they were reduced to being a curiosity, having been superseded by new media and interests.

What was the significance of the piano roll? For the first time, technology permitted the public to experience superior performances by performers whom they had never met (and who would certainly never want to meet them!) in the cosiness of their own home. Music was still essentially a personal medium but, for the first time, live performance had become a creature of mass-reproduction technology.

In 1877, that archetypal inventor, Thomas Edison, recorded and played 'Mary Had A Little Lamb' on a fragile tinfoil cylinder. It was a monumental moment, albeit a bizarre choice of music, but the physical problems of reproducing large numbers of cylinders or rolls could not be overcome. In most cases, each cylinder was an original recording, a 'direct-to-disc' recording which was a unique performance. Indeed, it would be another eleven years before the sound recording moved from a scientific curiosity to a robust commercial reality.

The first mass-produced music cylinders emerged on the United States market in 1888. This attempt to mass-produce rolls was not especially successful either but in 1889 The Columbia Phonograph Co, the world's first record company, published a one-page list of music cylinder titles. It was the first record catalogue.

The following years saw a format war between manufacturers of different types of cylinders and discs. Consumers were caught in the crossfire, uncertain as to which format to support. One thing was certain; as the technology developed, durable sound recordings allowed consumers to listen to their favourite musicians perform in the comfort of their own homes. It was a luxury that people were prepared to pay for.

FLAT RECORDS

On 16 May 1888, Emil Berliner gave the first public demonstration of the flat phonograph record (which was based on the work of a French painter, Leon Scott de Martinville who, in 1857, had invented a way of recording sound on paper). Berliner's invention was critical for the development of the modern record industry.

Unlike the cylinder and the piano roll, the flat disc could be produced in automated presses, so it became possible to manufacture many cheap copies of any recording. Mass production began around 1892. In 1894, the United States Gramophone Company sold 1,000 gramophones that played flat hard rubber discs. It sold 25,000 discs that year, effectively competing with Edison and Columbia's cylinders.

In 1900, Thomas Lambert developed a method for the mass duplication of 'indestructible' cylinders of celluloid. His method would substantially lower the cost of the cylinders and threatened to drive Edison out of business. Lambert sought legal protection for his invention and applied for a patent.

Edison challenged the application. Although, Lambert's patent was eventually upheld by the courts, Edison effectively used costly lawsuits to drive Lambert's company and his cylinders out of business. This was not the last time lawsuits were used to drive out competitors.

Edison's victory was, however, short lived. Developments in new material technologies saw Edison admit defeat in 1913 and give up on cylinder technology in favour of the flat shellac and then plastic records that reigned supreme for over 75 years. Think of its significance: it was the invention that gave birth to the record industry. It made superior performers available for mass domestic performances that were not limited by number, social class or political boundary.

THE ELECTRONIC AGE

The electric microphone was the breakthrough which allowed sound to be recorded electronically. The electric microphone was developed in 1925 by Bell Laboratories in the United States, by a team headed by Joe Maxfield. Physical recordings could finally be superseded by electrical recordings. The sound quality improved enormously.

In 1933, the first stereo master recordings were made by Electric & Music Industries – which later became known as EMI – in England. EMI pioneered the shellac record, which became the basis for the industry for many years.

The long-playing record meant that popular songs did not have to finish within 3 minutes, or be played at breakneck speed so as to finish before the side ran out. (Most jazz recordings of the 1930s were played at a fast tempo because of this technical problem.) Long-play records and compact discs freed artists and composers from the tyranny of the three-minute song, though it has still not disappeared. Just listen to commercial radio for proof!

ELECTRICITY

The first known radio broadcast to the public occurred on Christmas Eve, 1906 in Massachusetts. It is not known how large the audience was that night but it's unlikely anyone who happened to hear it could have anticipated the industry that would eventually develop from that half-hour session.

No longer was mass influence dependent upon getting pieces of paper to a target market. The means of production and delivery were cheap and the new science called 'programming' permitted the message to be designed for maximum pleasure and thus influence. From the beginning of the radio age, music has been a fundamental component of this medium.

Just as the disc had revolutionised individual access to and choice of music, radio made music available as a community experience. It also changed the way that music and its performers could be promoted. It was the basis of the use of music as mass culture and thus mass communication. Indeed, perhaps it changed music itself.

In 1937, Alan Reeves patented his ideas for digital recording, but found that vacuum tube technology was an insurmountable obstacle to the idea being put into practice. The sheer computing power needed to manipulate digital data was beyond the room-filling computers of the day. Besides, they were so primitive that they would have taken a month to decipher a few seconds of music, even if they could have been programmed to do it. They could calculate the ballistics of cannon shells (their main task during the Second World War), but not a lot more.

In 1948, the early 78 rpm shellac discs were superseded by plastic long-play (33 rpm microgroove) records. Using technology developed during the Second World War, the new materials meant that faster record presses could be used, which helped the industry meet demand. As a result, records became cheaper, in real terms, when compared with the cost of other basic consumer items. It also resulted in another leap of huge cultural influence: It was largely responsible for a rebirth in the popularity of opera and many of the major symphonic works. At last, home listeners could dispense with the huge piles of records (being changed every 3 minutes!), previously needed to play a complete opera or symphony. Now, virtually anyone could own a complete opera – and play it in their own home.

HI-FI

Simultaneously, advances in reproduction technology, inspired at least in part by the anticipation of increased demand for records, created hi-fi (this name was an abbreviation of 'high fidelity' – so named because of its true-to-life character). In 1948, RCA issued the first microgroove record, followed closely by the more successful CBS version, invented by Peter Goldmark.

Stereo records were released in 1958, when Pye and Decca and Audio Fidelity first released records which used theories largely developed in 1933 by an EMI employee, Alan Blumlein, who had patented the idea for stereo recordings back in 1931. EMI extended the patent to 1952, but the patent expired just before the first stereo recording was released. That's show biz.

In 1958, with the first commercial release of stereo records we were no longer fascinated by mere availability, we started the search for realism. How close could we get to the concert experience without leaving our lounge room? It didn't change music but it certainly changed the way that we appreciated it. It meant that musicians who dared to perform live, could and would, unfairly but inevitably, be compared to the recordings of the greatest performers in the world.

THE TRANSISTOR – MUSIC ON THE MOVE

The development of the transistor had a more fundamental role in re-shaping the music and record industry than is generally recognised. Invented in 1947 by John Bardeen and Walter Brattain and others in the team at Bell Laboratories, transistors were the successor to delicate vacuum tubes and were a classic case of a solution looking for problems to solve. Two Japanese electrical engineers purchased the patent rights for a pittance (virtually no one else saw the potential) and went home to make a portable tape recorder. Their enterprise grew into the giant electrical company, Sony.

The first integrated circuit was made in about 1958. The following year, Professor Okamura patented his ideas for putting large amounts of data on magnetic tape. Unfortunately, the patent expired in 1973, too soon for him to benefit from the developments in home video and digital formats.

Before transistors were generally available, radios and amplifiers relied upon valves. They were expensive to manufacture and limited to mains power supplies, so they could never be truly portable. Transistorised amplifiers and radios could follow their owners out of the house. Car radios and cassette players became standard items after transistorised units became cheap and robust. By 1957, there were 30 million transistors being produced annually. Youth, music and transistor radios seemed almost synonymous terms! Music became a part of everyday life. Life acquired a soundtrack of background music, just like a Hollywood movie.

AUDIO AND VIDEO TAPE

Magnetic tape was developed in Germany in the 1930s. Its development was critical for technological and artistic developments in the recording process. It affected the artistic direction by finally allowing time-shifting of performances and permitting editing of performances that until then, had to be re-recorded if flawed performances were to be corrected.

The significance of all this was enormous: Recording technology allowed the public to listen to music without the presence of the musician. It also changed what the public listened to in private, where they could listen to music and how often they could listen to it. It made the music of the privileged, available to almost everyone.

In 1956, AMPEX developed videotape, to help television stations in the United States overcome the problems of broadcasting over four time zones. Videotape technology created a whole new industry and revolutionised television programming.

The 'compact cassette' format was released by Philips in the 1960s. It was a development from the first magnetic tape system that had been developed by AEG Telefunken and I.G. Farben in 1935. The cassette was intended to be a dictation system for offices. There was no thought of it becoming a format for recorded music because magnetic tape formulations were simply not capable of the required performance. They were too noisy and could not record the high frequencies needed for realistic music reproduction. Yet, in only a few years, the quality of cassettes was improved and noise reduction systems developed to the point that they were regarded as true hi-fi items.

Of the noise reduction systems, one invented by Ray Dolby was particularly successful. He was very astute in the way he sold his Dolby Noise Reduction System to the tape-machine manufacturers and thereby made it the industry standard.

Now the public could record their favourite pieces from their records and take them with them to the beach and in the car. Gone was the restraint of having to keep the playing surface flat and stable. Youth wanted to move and cassette music allowed them to move with their personal choice of music – without the physical restrictions of record players or the content restrictions of radio.

PORTABLE RECORDING

Portable recording methods meant that recording in remote areas and capturing the ancient music and sounds of Africa, Asia, South America and, yes, Australia, became a technically simple activity. Technology not only provided the means by which western music would encroach upon and overwhelm less technologically sophisticated cultures, it would provide the means by which the indigenous music of those endangered cultures might be captured, retained and perhaps fight back (remember 'Deep Forest'? No?).

DIGITAL TECHNOLOGY

Digital recording of sound (and of course, vision) has opened up amazing possibilities for new media. Digital recording is the basis for virtually all the new 'record' formats. Now, sound recordings can be manipulated and stored in the same way as any other computer data. The traditional lines have become blurred as data and music are combined in the same medium. Digital encoding enables even old (analogue) recordings to be modified and the vocals removed. Abracadabra – Karaoke!

The compact disc was cutting-edge technology when it was conceived in the 1970s. The science was formidable. New materials (such as polycarbonate – the same stuff used in many crash helmets), lasers (which are a direct result of the Theory of Relativity and were another example of a solution looking for a problem) and digital recording, all combined to record sounds and images. What was science fiction, is now in your lounge room.

Making the science work in the real world was hard work. Philips and Sony spent many millions of dollars developing the medium. Then they had to spend millions more selling the medium to the general public to make sure that it sold lots and lots of discs and players.

It was 1982 and, in many ways, compact disc was the right technology at the right time. The world's economy was booming. Conspicuous consumption was not a dirty concept. The public had spare money and was feeling optimistic. The product looked fabulous. The public took to it immediately and switched to the new format, buying the new hardware and replacing their records with compact discs.

The vinyl record rapidly ceased to be an economically viable format. There is no doubt that vinyl records had been developed to a quite astounding degree, and hi-fi enthusiasts mourned (and still mourn) its passing, but people wanted something they could handle easily. Few were prepared to buy a $2,000 turntable when a compact disc gave pretty impressive performance for a lot less and the discs didn't wear out. Old recordings were re-released and repackaged, the music industry boomed and the vinyl format finally crept off into the woods, to die alone.

Although the vinyl record re-emerged as an integral part of the hip hop and dance music culture it never came back to life as a mass consumer product. Perhaps it metamorphosed: In the hands of the skilled DJ, vinyl has become an instrument rather than a medium.

It was digital technology that enabled the CD to deliver its superior audio quality. Sounds were translated into a computer code, a complex combination of 1s and 0s where a certain string of 1s and 0s would represent a certain sound. The code was compressed and finely etched into a disc that could then be read by a laser, decoded and played by a hi-fi system as a virtually exact replica of the music it represented. Each CD of a particular performance was exactly the same as the master digital recording (and here lies one of the foundations of the digital revolution). Unlike its analogue predecessors, digital copies suffer no degradation in quality. When, the millionth copy is indistinguishable from the first, a pirate copy sounds just as good as the legitimate.

THE BIRTH OF THE © BLUES

We all too often forget that technology has no value in itself. Its value as well as its dangers, are the results of human imposition. Accordingly, it is precisely in times of boom that we often make the mistakes that will later cost us dearly.

The 80s and 90s was a period of marketing and retail heaven. No one spent time thinking about the consequences of what they were doing. To do so was negative; just get out and sell; make budget; make bonus! Record companies sold millions of sound recordings to consumers around the world in high-quality digital file format. The files were not encrypted or encoded with markings to identify their source or deliver other rights management information. In so doing, it was the record companies themselves who eagerly and unwittingly handed over the same digital files that would later be used by music pirates – both corporate and domestic.

OTHER DIGITAL FORMATS

The last ten years has been a time of expensive trial and error in the attempt to develop and market a digital recording technology to replace the dying analogue cassette. Although the DAT cassette format was more successful than some earlier attempts to improve the cassette format (remember eight track cartridges and Elcassettes? No?) it never cracked the domestic market. When it was first introduced, though, DAT was thought to present a huge threat to the record industry because its reproduction quality was so high. The industry was so worried that it embarked on an international campaign to have spoiler circuits installed in all domestic machines to stop second generation copies sounding as good as the first. Professional machines didn't have these circuits but were a lot more expensive than domestic machines. The campaign was successful and the format never took off in the way that its creators had no doubt hoped. It lasted for a while in studios but never became a feature of suburban lounge rooms. Perhaps consumers were already wary of anything tape based.

Philips' Digital Compact Cassette (DCC) format, was a digital recording system using a stationary record/play-back head so it could also read ordinary analogue cassettes. It had little success and never really had a chance to make its mark when everyone was throwing out their cassettes and replacing them with CDs. Right product, wrong time.

Sony's three-inch (75 mm) diameter MiniDisc looks like a small version of the usual five-inch (125 mm) compact disc, but uses a very different method of encoding and replaying the signal. Most importantly, users were able to record their own MiniDiscs. This format looked fabulous but took a long time to get any market acceptance. The problem was that compression technology does not allow the MiniDisc to match the reproduction quality of the normal CD. Fine for Aerosmith but inadequate for Wagner. It is still used for semi-pro recording (which the MP3 market is yet to address) but never achieved significant market penetration.

CD ROMs too, had their moment in the sun during the 1990s. For a moment, everyone thought that they would be the next wonder product. People not only wanted to migrate from audio entertainment to audiovisual; they wanted to inter-act with the material and the artist. The assumption that audiences wished to move from linear to non-linear entertainments and from passive to active involvement, was never proved by the sales figures. While useful for educational purposes, software delivery, games and maybe porn, CD ROM never became a significant technology in the music business.

Laser Discs? Another loser. They were bigger and more expensive than DVD and suffered lower horizontal resolution but as VHS proved over Beta, the absence of quality is not fatal. The killer of laser disc was the PC: No-one ever made a PC with a Laserdisc burner.

DVD was the killer technology that all the hardware companies had been looking for. It allows the recording and encoding of massive amounts of data and enables albums to provide visual as well as audio content. DVD has taken off because it is the natural replacement for videotape and most Australian homes are replacing their video machine with a DVD player – or keeping the latter to time-shift. The figures have been extraordinary. There were just 45,000 DVD players sold in 1999 (average price $1,005) for a total value of $45.1 million. 1.4 million were sold in 2003 (average price $223), for a total value of $312 million (see http://www.afc.gov.au/gtp/wvanalysis.html). The proportion of metropolitan households with DVD players has risen from 43 per cent in 2003 to 62 per cent in 2004. They are eloquent figures.

Re-writeable DVD is one of those winner technologies that is simple to use, cheap when mass-produced and takes on a familiar technology (tape) and does it better. Already there are a large number of DVDs in the music catalogue. These are, so far, mostly recordings of 'live' performances or a compilation of music videos put onto disc format. That won't last. Given the massive capacity of DVDs, it will not take long before musicians start to find more creative applications for the technology.

Recordable CD (CD-R) has had a big effect in recent years. Its effect continues to grow. The threat that this technology poses is analogous to that posed by cassettes when they were first introduced. CD-R can record from other CDs but it can also record on-line downloads. Providing 700 megabyte capacity, they can contain 74 minutes of music – although this is nothing in comparison to the even newer re-writeable DVDs which hold up to 8.4 gigabytes! The total number of DVD-R/RW machines sold in 2002 was 205 million. In 2004 it increased to 1,935 million, worldwide (see http://www.recordingmedia.org/news/stat-recordable-worldwide.html). Storage capacity has increased from 40GB to hundreds of gigabytes.

Whilst perhaps the majority of these were bought for data storage, the technology is just as relevant for music applications (see http://mmislueck.com/WhatsNews.htm). All of this ignores the fact that many PCs now have internal DVD burners and most entertainment users don't need a separate piece of hardware to achieve their purposes.

True audiophile recordings, in the form of SACD and DVD-Audio pressings, have failed, at least to date, to arouse much enthusiasm from anyone anywhere. Despite their potential, according to the latest data, (as of August 20 2004), there were only 324 titles available in the DVD-Audio format and 1,314 titles in SACD (see http://www.mmislueck.com/Archives/090104.htm). One would think that the audiophile segment of the music-buying public would have welcomed these improved digital formats with open arms, but they have not. Although the music industry insists it is spending more time and money on promoting these two beleaguered formats, there is growing feeling in the industry that they will never gain general acceptance and will probably disappear altogether from the market place over the next three or four years. However, all of this may change now that the five Majors have all agreed to introduce "DualDiscs", in which a specific album is reproduced in standard CD on one side of the disc, and in DVD-Audio on the other.

A large percentage of all CD-listening today is done using portable players and earphones, and the quality of sound reproduction is anything but "high fidelity". Moreover, in America alone, there are now more than 20 online services, similar to Apple's "iTunes", that offer recorded music for purchase and downloading, and millions of tunes are still being downloaded illegally each day over peer-to-peer Internet connections. Most of this music will be heard either on a PC or a portable device (with earphones), and again, the quality of the music reproduced could never be called "high fidelity". As of April 2005, Apple had sold 3 million iPods and by February 2006, one billion legitimate downloads: Digital music on the move; convenience over fidelity.

One of the other successful technological developments of the past decade has been the development of smart card technology. (Smart cards resemble ordinary credit cards, but store data). Smart cards have already taken over the personal finance industry and as our personal technology becomes increasingly smaller, more mobile and more intelligent, smart cards that interface with other technologies such as mobile phones, personal computers, internet-banking systems and sound delivery systems will just become part of the wallpaper. Combine smart cards with mobile telephone and you have a very serious new music product.

If iPod caused a stir, the iPod phone is the next evolution. The idea is beautifully simple: Put two popular technologies into one. Already it is not uncommon for phones to have hard drives, to play MP3s (and these also take SD memory cards, so you can have up to 2GB – 24 hours – of music), to play videos, show television, and which connect to the Internet. There are very few parts of the business model to be coloured in before we simply expect the mobile phone to be our integrated communications and entertainment mobile device. We may still call it a phone but it is already much more.

PERSONAL COMPUTERS

Through the 1990s, personal computers spread like honey across the world. No longer the lonely domain of tech heads, they became an integral part of daily school and office life and overflowed into the home. Spurred by new techniques for the mass production of silicon chips and plummeting production costs, PCs became cheaper and more powerful. The average laptop now has more computing power than the supercomputers that were revered a decade ago.

Coupled with increasingly complex software packages, the PC fast became capable of processing large amounts of data, be it text, images or sound. With the advent of the CD-ROM drive that enabled PCs to access data on compact discs, it was not long before they were adapted to play music CDs. Software soon became available that empowered the user to easily access the music tracks on CD, copy it to the computer's hard drive and modify the track in just about any way imaginable. It was easy and the sound quality remained virtually indistinguishable from the CD.

Beyond accessing and manipulating existing audio files, computers and audio software packages forever changed the way in which music was created. 'Desktop studios' emerged, powerful computers linked to racks of synthesisers and other instruments and MIDI (Musical Instrument Digital Interface) conveying the musical notation between them all. The music created was already in digital form; there was no need for it to be converted from analogue.

It is interesting to note that personal computers could have been manufactured so as to hinder the copying of music from CDs. Other devices were. Take, for example, the digital audiotape. Like the CD, DAT carried digital music, but, unlike the CD player, the DAT player could also record digital music – each copy a perfect reproduction of the master. While DAT never caught on in the consumer market due to the high cost of DAT players, the record industry saw the proliferation of an unlimited number of perfect copies as a major threat. In the United States, consumer electronics manufacturers and the record industry lobbied for legislation to limit digital recording of copyright music. The legislation required manufacturers to design digital recording devices that would recognise and obey copy protection information embedded into a CD. For example, a CD could be coded with a "copy once" direction whereby the device could make one copy but that copy would then contain a "copy no more" direction so that no further copies could be made.

Due to the heavy lobbying of the computer industry, however, the legislation did not apply to computers or computer peripheral devices. If the music industry had been more conscious of the inevitable direction of delivery technologies, it is hard to imagine that it could not have marshalled a counter-balancing lobby force. But no, it was too busy selling CDs to put executive time into thinking about the long term. Had it been otherwise, we may never have seen the download phenomenon that now threatens the traditional record business.

THE INTERNET

Driven by the increasing use of computers in military communities, the United States developed a network of machines each capable of communicating with (or surviving the demise of) the others. The Advanced Research Projects Agency network (ARPAnet) began with only four computers. The computers were inter-connected but self-sufficient. The network concept spread from the military to the scientific and university communities and was the birth of the Internet, as we now know it. From isolated communities the network grew and continues to grow, joining communities and individuals together on a local, regional and global level. At the end of September 2004, total Internet subscribers in Australia numbered over 5.7 million (see http://www.abs.gov.au/Ausstats/). By any standards, this is a successful technology.

Without clear national boundaries and a uniform application of law, the Internet has fostered unique cultures. It has melded previously disparate social and geographical groups into new communities with common interests, etiquette and values. Ironically, given its military history, the most prolific beliefs have been based on the utopian notion of freedom: freedom of speech and freedom of access to information (or more sourly, anarchy and stealing). This has been particularly so within many of the early 'cyber' communities. However, as the Internet slowly has become more commercialised, regulated and governed by national interests, such cultures have become less dominant. Nevertheless, early Internet culture has shaped its development and many people's expectations about what should be freely available.

Clearly, a culture based on freedom of access to information does not sit well with any industry based on notions of individual ownership and economic rights. For better or for worse, this has been one of the challenges to the commercialisation of the Internet.

Most countries recognise the value of proprietary information and have entrenched its protection in their intellectual property laws. Copyright, confidential information, trademarks, designs and patents all provide for limited protection for the owners and creators of information. Such laws confer on the owners an exclusive or monopolistic right to stop others from using their material. While such laws are well established and widely accepted in most countries, the Internet challenged their application to what was seen as a borderless, ephemeral on-line world.

For many, the Internet was a refuge from an over-commercialised society governed by multinational corporations, where money not only talks but also introduces itself with a smirk at dinner parties. Cries of 'copyright is dead, long live the Internet' echoed around chat-rooms as intellectual property laws were flaunted and copyright works were copied and distributed around the world with a lone finger raised in the general direction of the owners. A subversive culture of an elite and technically savvy minority grew, fostering hacking and piracy in this mild, mild west.

ON-LINE DELIVERY

Without the development of digital technology, we could not have had the personal computer or the Internet. Without the personal computer becoming a pervasive business and domestic technology, the Internet could never have become so significant. Without the confluence of each of these, on-line distribution could not have been born.

The phenomenal success (from a technological point of view) of downloaded music illustrates that the on-line delivery of music is no longer news. Whether it is legal or illegal, good or bad, the fact is irrebuttable: On-line delivery of music has already become one of the principal sources by which consumers access music. There are now many companies (not just Telstra) that are providing legal, licensed, music to the on-line market. With the development of digital radio, the legitimate download market will be enhanced because one of the services that will eventually be provided by the digital radio service will be the ability to buy, down-load and own the music that the listener has just heard and enjoyed.

Australia already has one of the most extensive and developed optical fibre networks in the world. A single optical fibre can carry 117 television channels and many times more radio channels, but a single strand of the new 'dark fibre' can in theory carry 2.5 thousand million radio channels! These will revolutionise on-line services that, until recently, were reliant on ordinary copper wires that can only carry a few channels at a time. When compared to the cost of setting up a radio station, the cost of becoming a program provider to a diffusion network is comparatively low, because there is no need for an expensive transmitter. The program provider just connects into the network.

Such services have the potential to make 'records' largely redundant, at least for the mainstream of popular music. Instead of buying a record, through a simple-to-operate home computer, the public simply order it to be delivered by the program provider. It is instantly delivered in glorious digital signal, ideal for recording onto compact disc, DCC, CDV, DVD or whatever

– for those who feel the need to keep a copy at home.

On-line services are unlikely to completely supersede other sound carriers, but records are likely to be a smaller part of the total music market. Records (in whatever format) will probably remain, but are likely to be more important to the non-mainstream areas of music.

For further discussion see Chapter 15, "**Download Delivery – Evolution in Technology: Revolution in Business**".

MP3

One of the initial hurdles to on-line music distribution was the physical difficulty of sending large music files through the old telephone lines that make up a large proportion of the Internet. When digital audio is created the resultant sound files are generally large and not easily transferred.

Technically speaking, such files are typically created by taking 16-bit (digital) binary samples of an analogue sound signal. Since this signal is typically spread out over a spectrum from twenty to twenty thousand cycles per second (kHz), and each cycle needs to be sampled a minimum of twice for accurate reproduction, samples must be taken at a rate of at least 40 kHz. In fact, CD quality audio is sampled at 44.1 kHz. This means that one second of CD quality sound requires 1.4 million bits of data (or 175 kilobytes whereas the typical text e-mail is about 2 kilobytes).

Rather than convince the telephone companies to change the phone lines to push through larger bits of information, software developers worked on a system that would compress those files into more manageable sizes. This was done by encoding the file using mathematical algorithms.

At the time of writing, MP3 (gratefully short for Motion Picture Experts Group-1 Audio Layer-3) was the most powerful of these algorithms. It was developed in association with the Motion Picture Experts Group (MPEG) and formalised by the International Organisation for Standardisation. The MP3 compression algorithm cleverly deletes data (a lot of the bass) from the sound files. In doing so, it compresses sound sequences into a much smaller file (about one-twelfth the size of the original file) while preserving a reasonable level of sound quality when it is played.

MP3 files have become a household name. It was postulated in 2000, that MP3 had become the most searched-for 'word' on the Internet, surpassing the other adolescent boys looking for 'sex'.

MP3 files are widely available and require software capable of recognising and playing the file. Most computers are sold with built-in MP3 compatibility. Alternatively, players can be downloaded from any number of MP3 sites.

To create an MP3 file, a software program called a 'ripper' is used to move a track from a CD onto the hard disk and another program called an 'encoder' to convert the selection to an MP3 file. Most people, however, simply download MP3s from someone's web site and play them, which takes us to Napster, P2P networks, Limewire, Kazaa, Grokster, Morpheus, Gnutella, BitTorrent. Unsurprisingly these have given rise to an enormous range of MP3 blogs and forums (for example see http://tofuhut.blogspot.com/; http://www.livejournal.com/community/audiography/; http://jefitoblog.com/blog/index.php?cat=2). This is viral marketing at its most basic. Because they are so idiosyncratic and personal, blogs are difficult to harness yet they are a new phenomenon in music marketing.

MP3 is a technology that is now more than ten years old. Its compression technology has meant that sound quality has never been of a similar standard as that of the pre-compressed recording. With MPEG4, that is changing. MPEG4 is the new multimedia standard that uses Advanced Audio Coding (AAC) and provides more efficient compression and thus better sound. It is an open system which means that it is inter-operable between rival companies' systems.

Already further developments are underway. MPEG-21 is going to include object-based coding and metadata that will facilitate the licensing and administration of content. It may well be that the technology that enabled the download revolution evolves into the product that delivers the music industry the solution that it so desperately seeks.

WEBCASTING

Webcasting is really just coming of age but its early manifestations proved illusory. Compression technology now permits live performances to be webcast and distributed to the screen of your PC or mobile phone. Various companies have based at least part of their business plan on the preparedness of their public to pay to see performances that they cannot attend, or similarly, pay to access the archive of performances that such companies are building. The digital distribution companies seem to be from one of two camps: those aligned with concert promoters and those aligned with clubs. For example, MCY.com is the exclusive digital music distributor of SFX Entertainment, the largest concert promoter in the United States.

One of the earliest club-based webcasters in the United States was The House of Blues (HOB); it is a webcaster and has a pay-per-view concert archive. But it is also much more than that. HOB also controls a large network of venues. Seven of these are HOB-branded clubs and restaurants; It has a record company (specialising in unsigned acts) which releases CDs and DVDs of the live performances that it records; a music publishing company; a merchandising operation and a TV syndication section. In brief, HOB is not a company that sees webcasting itself as a business model. It is just part of a much larger model in which all forms of digital distribution of music are included.

Knitting Factory has gone for a different market: avant-garde jazz. It too has a record company (including the fabulously named JAM label (which stands for Jewish Alternative Music); has jazz clubs in New York and Los Angeles; a jazz festival division; video distribution; TV syndication; and webstreaming. In other words, Knitting Factory is not basing its success on one element of the digital music industry. It is merely one arrow in their strategic quiver.

In Australia, there were many brave companies that started webcasting. All of them struggled to find a sustaining business model. Advertisers were unwilling to spend the same sums advertising to the tiny audience attracted to webcasts and despite attempting a cocktail of advertisers, sponsors and investors, they all withered and died. The longest to survive was the Basement.com.au. This was an interesting venture because it combined a complete audiovisual delivery with live webcasts from the stage of The Basement (one of Australia's best known venues), and sold a range of CDs and DVDs of musicians who had performed on their webcasts. It also sold commercials but its main source of revenue was Telstra, which used it as a test bed and means of showcasing the possibilities of it's broadband services. Eventually Telstra bought out the shareholders and turned it into an on-line production studio. It closed public access to its services in 2003 and with it, the last independent webcaster died.

One of the reasons that independent webcasters had a short life was that the existing media players all recognised the ability of the Internet to enrich their existing services. Now, every radio and television station offers its listeners a sophisticated menu of on-line fare and given that they are able to pay for it through their existing advertiser base, and are able to rely on their already existing administrative and program overheads, their on-line services are both content rich and financially viable.

RINGTONES

The downloadable ringtone market started in Finland in 1998, initiated by Vesa-Matti Paananen, the same gentleman who had written the first ringtone composer software for the new Nokia phones that allowed user programmable, monophonic ringtones. Shortly after the launch of the service in Finland, pirated ringtones, 15 seconds of carefully sequenced beeping, were available for $10 in Hong Kong.

In 1999 in the UK, which would become the West's ground breaking market for ringtones and associated businesses, James Winsoar started the "My Nokia" website (later renamed "Phat Tonez", years before a mobile phone could produce anything resembling bass) to sell bespoke ringtones to customers, later automating delivery, hiring composers and arrangers and creating a business model that would be heavily copied.

Instead of grinding to a halt at the turn of the millennium, 2000 saw mobile phones appearing with polyphonic sound ability. A few years later this was augmented by phone manufacturers adding more voices, adopting the MIDI standard to describe ringtones and embedding industry standard sample banks, allowing ringtone purveyors and composers to improve the quality, and thus the appeal, of ringtones.

2004 saw the introduction of phones capable of playing short samples and 2005 brought the "iPod" phones that would incorporate MP3 players and provide access to music download services. In 2005, all the technology is available: All that is necessary is for the hardware owners to conclude their deals with the content owners. If they leave it too long the urge will pass and the business model will not survive the universal availability of unlicensed music.

In tandem with ringtone technology improving, the ringtone business matured and gained respect, mostly due to the surprising size of the market – in 2003 ringtones accounted for approximately 10% of the $32.2 billion in global music sales. Music publishers were taking their cut of every download, and with the introduction of sampled ringtones, the record labels got their hands in the honey jar as well. Even if revenue were not the gauge of success, you know you have arrived when Billboard devotes a chart to you: In October 2004 Billboard introduced the "Hot Ringtones" chart.

In 2005, the UK saw the peak of the "Crazy Frog" phenomenon, a sampled ringtone from Jamster that set the record for sales and marketing spend. If you are not aware of it, words are inadequate for capturing the high-pitched, frantic vocal rendition of a Formula 1 engine, or the accompanying mascot – a bug-eyed frog with vestigial genitals and an old-fashioned, leather driving helmet (perhaps conjuring up Toad of Toad Hall in the collective unconscious of the UK population). Despite this, or perhaps because of this, it was downloaded 11 million times at the behest of 36,382 TV spots across the UK (for perspective, McDonalds had 9,780 spots during the same period). Mixed together with "Axel F", the 80s synth pop theme of "Beverley Hills Cop", "Crazy Frog" had the honour of beating Cold Play to the number one spot on the UK singles chart and had ringtone purveyors staking out their claim in the commercial mainstream. With all these triumphs perhaps we could ignore Jamster's troubles with regulators over not clearly informing downloaders they were signing up for a monthly subscription and not just a single ringtone.

Ringtones, and other phone downloads such as wallpapers and games, are being integrated into the income streams for artists. Robbie Williams is an early adopter of this strategy. His "Greatest Hits" CD released in the UK in October 2004 had the WAP (Wireless Application Protocol, or, the internet from your phone) codes for 57 ringtones and 100 wallpapers printed on the inside cover of the CD. Some 300,000 registered fans also received an email from Robbie, encouraging them to buy these items.

In Australia the current ringtone market is valued at approximately $50 million per year. Very little of the product available is locally sourced and we have not escaped the "Crazy Frog". There is currently debate over whether or not the market has peaked, with some analysts saying that consumers are already moving onto phones that can play MP3s, while others suggest that since only 30% of people have phones that could play polyphonic ringtones there was plenty of room for growth as people upgraded.

Although ringtones seem too faddish and ephemeral to be an enduring source of music income, they have already been a phenomenon that few predicted. They might fade away or they might just become one of the standard sounds of life that people are prepared to pay for.

DIGITAL BROADCAST

Since the last edition, extensive trials of digital radio have been undertaken. It will provide higher quality of reproduction than either AM or FM and reception will be much more stable. It will also allow broadcasters to include more than audio-only material. After all, once the data is digitised, the potential for delivery of complex media, is enhanced. This comes at a price because consumers have to replace their existing analogue tuners with digital tuners but the UK experience certainly indicates that Australian consumer resistance will be low and uptake of the new technology will be rapid.

When digital radio is introduced we are perhaps unlikely to hear the same plaintive sounds that were heard from record companies when FM was introduced. They learned from that experience that good reception does not necessarily mean more piracy: It means more appreciation of the production and performance values in the recording and a greater likelihood that the listener will be interested in buying the recording. Indeed digital radio's capacity to deliver text and other audiovisual content means that the owners of the music will be able to use the new technological capabilities to enhance their marketing of the broadcast recording. Digital radio is the best thing that has happened for a long time to the marketing directors in record companies. Those who think creatively and strategically will realise that this new platform means the radio stations have to rethink the way they relate to their audiences. They will need lots of additional material to make use of the data-rich format and the record companies, publishers and artists are going to be the best (and cheapest) source of this material.

Digital broadcasting means 'pay radio' is feasible. It would permit subscribers to select particular tracks and be charged per track: a kind of 'broadcast juke box'. On the bright side, digital encoding means it is perfectly possible to encode every digitised recording with the equivalent of a bar-code. Every recording can be identified. Every use can be logged. This will have an obvious impact on performance and licensing revenues.

MOBILE PHONE

Mobile phones have been one of the most successful mass-market technologies of the last decade. For those old enough to remember the impact of the portable transistor radio and the thrill of, at last, being able to listen to your music on the move, it is easy to see that the mobile phone would be just as influential. If music of choice can be played through your mobile, all your music needs can just slip into your pocket.

In September 2000, Vivendi Universal, owner of the world's largest record company UMG, launched Universal Music Mobile in France. It allowed WAP mobile phone subscribers to hear tracks from UMG artists and get news updates, buy CDs and concert tickets. The phone users could also download MP3 files (if the handset is MP3 enabled). When it went on trial in France, the monthly subscription fee was between US$16.60 and $41.78 and the 20-30 minute download time didn't help either! All that changed quickly. By July 2005, Virgin Mobile was publicly musing whether they would have to introduce unlimited music access to mobile phone users. They estimated that consumers had spent $1.5 billion in the last three years on buying songs for their phones with digital music players (see www.mobilemag.com/content/100/104/C4261/). This is also interesting because it provides an eloquent example of the inherent clash of interests between the record companies (that want to sell downloads) and phone companies that want to sell hardware and time. Still, in Australia, that delicious spat is some way off. Until 3G technology gets a grip and mobile broadband becomes widely adopted, most music consumers are going to have to put up with transferring MP3s from their PC to their mobile. Tedious.

The great news is that by the time you finish reading this Chapter, most of it will be out of date.

15

DOWNLOAD DELIVERY: EVOLUTION IN BUSINESS – REVOLUTION IN THINKING

THE BIRTH OF DIGITAL DOWNLOADS DEMANDED THAT THE RECORD COMPANIES TAKE NOTICE. ONE OF THE MOST IMPORTANT ISSUES IS HOW BEST TO MANAGE COPYRIGHT MATERIAL IN THE DIGITAL ENVIRONMENT. THIS CHAPTER LOOKS AT SOME OF THE DEVELOPING MECHANISMS OF DISTRIBUTION AND COLLECTION IN THIS CONTEXT.

To become dominant, a new technology must provide consumers with a clear advantage over existing technologies. This will provide the motivation for consumers to invest, financially and culturally, in the new product. Manufacturers will compete heavily to enter the market early to establish their brand names. They will do all they can do to win, including using lawsuits to drive their competitors out of the market and to drive the demand. Most of the old players will survive and prosper but new businesses and alliances will emerge.

History has shown that both the law and the business of music have adapted to and grown because of these new technologies. On-line music delivery is the latest of these technological challenges and the music industry is still feeling its way.

Let's face it, the pioneers of on-line music distribution were not the record companies – they were the fans. Lovers of music have always distributed their recommendations to friends whether as sheet music, vinyl, cassette or CD. With powerful computers easily able to copy the digital music files from CDs and the Internet, it was no great conceptual leap to foresee that popular on-line music distribution was waiting to happen.

The adoring public created a new market based on a new delivery mechanism that demanded that the record companies take notice. But how did it all come about?

THE BIRTH OF DOWNLOAD DELIVERY

Compact discs, increasingly capable domestic computers and the Internet gave the music-loving public the tools they needed to start the revolution. CDs provided the music in unencrypted digital form. The personal computer had become sufficiently powerful to read, translate, copy and manipulate the digital files. Audio formats such as MP3 enabled such files to be compressed so that they were more easily stored and transferred. The Internet linked all those people together and enabled them to swap music files. People now had the power to copy, store, play, manipulate and transfer music.

The Internet was seen by many as the saviour of the indignant artist and consumer who had suffered too long under the tyranny of the record companies, inequitable contracts and overpriced CDs. For nascent rock stars and indeed all creators of music, it provided an independent means to contact and deliver news, music and video to their fans. Thousands of official and unofficial fan sites sprouted like spring flowers across the Internet.

Through the 1990s, when it was already evident that the Internet would become an important medium for music delivery, the record companies and the music publishers gave it insufficient attention. The Majors in the Australian industry were predictably reliant on their head office in the United States or England for their direction and answers, and head office just didn't focus early enough. As a result, the music industry has had to play catch-up. It is now in the position of being reactive to a reality, the shaping of which it played no part. The download war that they are now fighting as a rear-guard action is one that the industry lost, through inaction and a failure of strategic planning by those in control of the Majors in the mid-1990s. Quite simply, at that early stage in the campaign, when it mattered, they failed to allocate financial and intellectual resources to deep study of the changing role of copyright; the effect of the new technologies on the economy of music; how the new technologies would change the way we perform, conserve, distribute, market, promote, sell, study or enjoy, music.

When the Major record companies, who control the distribution of about 83% of sound recordings, initially refused to license emerging on-line music sites to distribute their catalogues, a market vacuum emerged. Internet start-up companies like Emusic.com, Napster, MP3.com and Scour, emerged everywhere, determined to take power away from the multinationals and deliver it into the hands of the individuals (whilst trying to make a small fortune in the process). The culture of the Internet, coupled with uncertainty over the particular application of law to these transactions and the complete absence of legitimate alternatives, motivated the users to disregard intellectual property laws and copy and distribute music all over the world.

In 2000 and the following years, the record companies took legal action to stop the on-line music pirates. The most infamous case was the one against Napster, the on-line distributor of music whose members peaked at sixty-two million people across the world. While Napster's infamy is eroding as other pirate systems jostle for supremacy and legitimate systems emerge, the Napster story is an important part of on-line music history.

NAPSTER

Napster was an ingenious system. By accessing the Napster website, users could download a software package that would enable them to search for and download music files. At its peak, it was actually a challenge trying to find songs that weren't available through Napster. But rather than go to the expense of copying and storing music files on to its own computer servers, Napster relied on a database of songs that were stored on their members' personal computers. When a user found a title, the Napster software enabled the user to directly access the other user's computer and retrieve a copy of the music file. It was the users who paid for the storage and connection costs. It was the users who made and downloaded copies of the sound recordings. Napster simply facilitated the transaction. It provided free music.

Napster became a household name and challenged the record companies' control of the distribution of their music repertoire. While there is some debate as to what extent, if any, illegal downloads compete with traditional music sales, the record companies decided that Napster must be closed down.

In December 1999, the record labels began legal proceedings against Napster (*A&M Records, Inc v. Napster, Inc.* 114 F. Supp 2d 896 (N.D. Cal. 2000)). It alleged, among other things, that Napster was infringing copyright by permitting the duplication and distribution of copyright works on the Internet.

The District Court of Northern California granted the record labels an injunction stopping Napster from engaging in (or helping others engage in) copying, downloading, uploading or distributing the record labels' copyright works. The decision was appealed.

On appeal, one of Napster's defences was that what it was doing constituted 'fair use' under U.S. copyright law. Lawyers argued that people used Napster to sample tracks before they bought them and transfer music they already owned (on say CD) onto their computers (so called 'space-shifting'). It was also argued that Napster had a role as a distributor of legitimate music as users also used it to distribute sound recordings of artists who had permitted such distribution.

The court on appeal, dismissed Napster's arguments and its other more technical defences, concluding that sampling and space-shifting in these circumstances were a commercial rather than fair use and competed with the record companies' legitimate commercial interests.

The court then went on to find that although Napster itself was not infringing copyright by copying and distributing protected music (its users were), Napster was likely to have had knowledge of such infringing conduct. The court said that Napster 'induces, causes or materially contributes' to that infringement and fails to take any action to prevent it. Napster was found to have turned a 'blind eye' to the illegal actions of its users whilst profiting from those actions and was found to be vicariously liable.

In March 2001, following the delivery of these findings by the appeal court, Judge Patel of the Federal District Court of Northern California issued a preliminary injunction against Napster. The record labels were required to identify their copyright music and Napster was required to block access to it through their system within three days. As the vast majority of music available through Napster was copyright controlled by the record labels, Napster was effectively sunk.

POST NAPSTER

Even before the final judgments had been handed down in the Napster case, BMG moved in and bought what was left of the company. It was a clever move because they acquired the rights to the Napster name and brand without having to invest huge amounts into promoting a completely new on-line identity. Of course the new manifestation of Napster no longer promotes illegal downloads. It has been completely redesigned as an on-line source of legal downloads.

However, even though the old Napster had been brought down by the court decision, many other companies filled the void. One of the larger distributors was Grokster. It, too, was sued and the court asked to decide the tricky question: "When should the distributor of a multi-purpose tool be held liable for the infringements that may be committed by end-users of the tool?" (see http://www.eff.org/IP/P2P/MGM_v_Grokster/). It was particularly significant because it revisited the 1984 decision in *Sony Corporation of America v. Universal City Studios Inc* (known as the Sony Betamax case. This earlier case had held that if you supplied a machine that could be used for legal purposes as well as illegal purposes (in that case a dual recording tape machine) you were not liable for the illegal uses to which it was put. Perhaps it wasn't a great surprise given that the same approach that has been taken for many years with regard to guns.)

In 2005, the courts finally handed down their judgement in favour of the record companies and against Grokster.

In the same year, the Australian Federal court was given the opportunity to consider the legitimacy of the Kazaa website in the case of *Universal Music Australia Pty Ltd v Sharman License Holdings Ltd* [2005] FCA 1242. At the beginning of 2004, Kazaa was the most used website for peer-to-peer file sharing activities and over 317 million people had downloaded Kazaa onto their computers.

Kazaa enabled users to share sound recordings by placing the material in a file called 'My Shared Folder'. Other users could then search and download for free any material from another user's 'My Shared Folder'. These files were referred to as 'blue files'. Kazaa also enabled users to access licensed works (works made available to users pursuant to arrangements made with the owners of copyright in those works). These files were referred to as 'gold files'.

The 30 applicants in the case, including the major record companies, claimed that the sharing of blue files constituted an infringement of their copyright in certain sound recordings.

While the court was not prepared to find Sharman Networks guilty of direct copyright infringement, the court had no difficulty in finding Sharman Networks guilty of authorising copyright infringement. It was held that once Sharman Networks knew Kazaa was being used to infringe copyright in various sound recordings, they should have taken preventative measures. Displaying warnings on the website and making users agree not to infringe copyright under an end user licence agreement, was not enough to excuse Sharman Networks from liability for authorising copyright infringement because it was obvious to Sharman Networks that these measures were ineffective. The court expected Sharman Networks to take further measures to curtail infringement by implementing technical measures involving keyword filtering and gold file flood filtering. These measures would have prevented copyright protected files being searched and limited search results to licensed files. It was clear to the court that because Sharman Networks made its revenue mostly from advertising, it was in Sharman Network's financial interests to maximise music file sharing. Sharman Networks' desire to maximise file sharing was also apparent through the website encouraging users to 'Join the Revolution' and expressly criticising record companies for opposing peer-to-peer file sharing.

With these factors in mind, the court ordered that the Kazaa system be modified through a system of keyword and gold file filtering so as to protect copyright interests whilst allowing sharing of permitted files. Sharman Networks appealed the court's decision and the appeal is expected to be handed down soon.

THE BATTLE WON, THE WAR RAGES ON

That is not to say we have seen the death of on-line music piracy. Far from it; it has just been marginalised. In the wake of Napster and Kazaa, and while similar systems operate, personal computers have been and are still being stocked with an enormous catalogue of unencrypted music. Each of these computers is connected by the Internet: All that remains is for file sharing software to act as an intermediary. Inevitably, when one dies another grows.

One such peer-to-peer file sharing software that has grown in popularity recently is BitTorrent. Much like Napster in its infant days, BitTorrent has provided users of the Internet a more efficient way of file transfer. However, unlike Napster, BitTorrent does not store files on a central server. Instead, files are stored locally on the user's computer and distributed from one computer to the next. This makes it difficult for record companies to fight: Because the files are not stored on a central server, it is harder to shut down all the users of BitTorrent (who number in the millions), than one central server (like Napster or Kazaa).

Of course, the practicalities of commencing complex and expensive litigation against every new Napster, Grokster, BitTorrent or Kazaa (or their users) is an entirely different issue altogether.

THE WAY FORWARD

The real alternative for the record companies is to go with the flow and provide a viable alternative for consumers: one that is cheap, easy and legal and of course, one that maintains their control over their copyright works.

The model for the way forward has been illustrated by iTunes. In February 2006, iTunes announced that it has sold one billion legitimate downloads. That same month EMI, which has been perhaps the most innovative of the Majors in its approach to marketing and commercialising music downloads, announced that almost 6% of its gross income worldwide, came from digital downloads. The International Federation of the Phonographic Industry (IFPI) says that global sales of digital music zoomed to $1.1 billion in 2005, up from $380 million in 2004.

It is perhaps not surprising that the light was provided not by record companies that had been moulded on an old paradigm but by a computer manufacturer that prided itself on providing new and elegant solutions to old market problems. Apple didn't have to worry about protecting its (non-existent) investment in music copyrights. It figured that if music consumers were given an opportunity to buy legitimate product for a reasonable price and deliver it through well designed, simple to use hardware, a lot of them would. And they did.

The report from Entertainment Media Research shows around 35% of online music buyers are paying for legal downloads versus the 40% who have pirated music. (The online research company used data collected from 4,000 music consumers to compile the *2006 Digital Music Survey* in association with UK media law firm Olswang.) This is a turn-around in consumer attitudes that would have be inconceivable just four years earlier.

CHANGE IN THE WAY COMPANIES DO BUSINESS

Irrespective of technological or legal developments, the ways in which we do business will change.

The early efforts of the Majors seemed almost ludicrous. First, they ignored the public-lead download revolution. Then they acknowledged it but forbade their repertoire to be downloaded. Then they allowed certain material to be downloaded but only for the payment of a fee that no net-customer would possibly be interested in paying. Why would they do such an apparently self-defeating thing, as to charge for a download, a price that is similar to that paid by its customers for a compact disc? Could it really have been as stupid as it seemed? Obviously, the young people that make up the potential cyber customers were not going to pay that much. We have to assume that the companies knew this.

Continuing this benign analysis, we must assume that this was a deliberate attempt to limit the usage of their systems so that they could trial them and perfect them before they were tested by large volume usage. If on the other hand, the companies were simply trying to maintain their old profit structures, by such a seemingly primitive price maintenance scheme, they were clearly going to fail; customers ignored them and, it became very apparent that - like all businesses that abuse their customers – if they continued, they would wither and die.

Until record companies have chief executives who were born too late to own vinyl records and never did play pinball, we are unlikely to see management that is completely comfortable with the Internet and plan the corporate future accordingly. At the moment, there is a generation gap in record company and music publishing management. Did any of the horse breeders of the late 18th century contribute to the development of the motorcar? Both were means of transport but they required very different skills, experience and comfort zones. When it comes to executives in the rapidly evolving music business, like soldiers, 'age does not weary them'. It kills them.

Of course that is exaggeration. Alain Levy, the former head of PolyGram and the current CEO of EMI, is an obvious example of a successful record man who realised that the industry had to find a way of making money out of music downloads. Record companies need to hire flexible and creative minds because they have to completely rethink and redefine the way that they do business.

Does anyone want to run a book?

- They will become principally production and promotion houses. For many companies, pressing and distribution functions will virtually disappear. These will be outsourced in the same way as most music publishers outsource their print music publishing.
- Their promotion staff are going to be focusing, not on how to sell records, but on how to persuade the public to select their artists' product from the extensive menu of choice and to visit their own cyber-download shops.
- One of the major determinants of a record company's commercial success will be its ability to attract Net surfers to pay-for-play services. These services will have to be a mix of company, cross-company and company-independent. It is the artist's brand, not the company's, which sells the download.

Present trends already indicate that we will see a number of strategic alliances formed (both formal and informal). We are seeing that through conventional advertising, on-line service providers are using existing broadcasters and print media as tools for attracting the public to their on-line services and products. But this is just the start: record companies or on-line service providers will enter joint-ventures with existing radio networks so that each cross-promotes the delivery of services of the other; record companies will form alliances with telcos for the delivery of their content; large record retailers will establish alliances with those with dominant web presences to distribute and promote product. One thing that we have learned from the two massive crashes of the dot com share market is that e-commerce requires alliances. No matter how big the cash box, the financial demands of establishment, promotion, financial administration and product fulfilment in e-commerce, are punishing if you try to do it alone.

Mainstream publishers, record companies, record retailers, newspapers, film studios etc are only now, committed to the Internet. They know that it is not going away and that unless they embrace it, get comfortable with it, learn how to make it work for them, learn how to dominate it, they will lose market share.

This creates an internal conflict for the companies: they know that if they continue to delay their involvement, they endanger their potential for market predominance and indeed give even more encouragement to free file swapping; if they do embrace the Internet, they know that they are ordaining the death of the market-place that is their own present comfort zone and the foundation of their current prosperity. It is a hard choice.

That said, after their early bumbling efforts, the record companies have clawed back considerable control of on-line music distribution. By combining business acumen, lawsuits and market power, they have bankrupted, acquired or effectively marginalised many of their pirate competitors. At the same time, by licensing product either directly or to legitimate on-line distributors, they are creating a legal alternative for consumers.

There have been many casualties. Of the victims of the two dot com crashes of 1998 and 2000, many were music-based companies. Virgin Megastores ceased on-line distribution and went back to its bricks and mortar business. Momentarily high-profile Atomic Pop.com, died in 2000. Early 2001 saw the collapse of Musicmaker.com which was a well funded public company backed by AOL and BMG. Discjockey.com couldn't make a business of it. Napster never did have a business model and eventually sold out to Bertelsmann under the weight of lawsuits. CDNow, which in the late 1990s seemed to be a coming heavyweight, nearly went broke and had to negotiate acquisition by Bertelsmann. (The German company was early to recognise the significance of on-line delivery and while every one was busy suing Napster, it realised the value of the brand and acquired the name very cheaply - so that it could later resurrect it.)

All of this was perhaps predictable when the share price in all the dot coms listed on the NASDAQ, fell by no less than 92% during the 1999-2000 period. This was an astonishing fall out. Very few businesses can survive this kind of haemorrhage. Even those that survived, shed both staff and rhetoric.

Part of the problem was that, for a long time, the record companies were not prepared to accept that consumers were not prepared to pay high prices for on-line music. It was not until iTunes became successful as a retailer that the message was made clear: The old pricing structures based on hard-fought-for record prices (despite the pressure from the record retailers) could not be maintained. iTunes demonstrated that the subscription service was not the only financial model; if the price was right, customers would buy individual tracks. Indeed, that was what they wanted!

Just as it was a computer company that cracked the legal download market, it seems to be the on-line companies and the telcos that are beginning to dominate the nascent business of on-line music stores: iTunes, BigPond Music, Yahoo Music, eMusic are dominant although there are many smaller players, including labels and, of course, artists. In the on-line world it would appear that the Majors might be losing their dominance as distributors of music. The present trend indicates that record companies will be predominately makers and marketers of music product. The old industries of manufacture and distribution will be relegated to minor parts of their business.

And what about the record store? It is impossible to discuss the impact of the download without thinking of the effect that the download has already had on this traditional form of retailing. In February 2006, the director of Brazin (the company that runs HMV, Sanity and Virgin record stores in Australia) announced the introduction of Fast Tracks Kiosks to allow customers to buy single tracks for download on either CDs or MP3 players. Record stores are not taking the download lightly. They realise that they have to learn ways of retaining relevance in a different distribution environment.

THE SLOGANS THAT COME AND GO

In the mid-1990s, every article about success on the Net seemed to stress brand recognition. Certainly, one of the ways that the public can gain reassurance and comfort in a new environment, is through brand recognition. Quite simply, people will be more likely to use an unfamiliar medium for commerce if they are dealing with people or things that they trust. That is what brand recognition is all about. Nowadays, so few years later, we realise that brand recognition is valuable but not determinative. No one buys a record because Sony is distributing it. They buy it for the content. (Perhaps the exception to this is the product of smaller, quality labels such as ECM were someone might buy on the basis that they don't release anything that is not, at least, interesting.)

These days, we don't hear so much about the role of brand recognition. Experience is proving that content and price is more determinative on the Internet.

Similarly, at the end of the 1990s, the catch-cry became 'on-line communities': the presence of like-minded fellow travellers provided the comfort zone necessary for on-line business to flourish. The NASDAQ crash of 2000 killed off many of those warm and fuzzy thinkers.

In the on-line music world there are only three words that should be accorded icon status: 'content', 'access' and 'price'.

NEW TECHNOLOGY AND ARTISTS' ROYALTIES

Fortunately, instead of being the beginning of the end for musicians, each advance in recording technology seems to have increased demand for music and for musicians. Each new technology always has a definite impact on recording contracts. Unfortunately, unless recording contracts have provision for the new media, the artists risk not being remunerated properly for their efforts and the artistic integrity of their recordings may be at risk.

When the compact disc was being introduced, the record companies immediately made sure the artists contributed to offsetting the enormous re-tooling costs by taking a royalty cut on records sold in the new medium. First the 'black-disc equivalent' clause was used. This capped compact disc royalties at the same dollar values as was paid for the equivalent vinyl records. When that fiction became too embarrassing to defend any longer, it was superseded by a royalty reduction for new technology and/or with so-called packaging deductions.

They were (and largely remain) 'non-negotiable'. There is an argument that the new medium boosted sales and that it was 'only fair that the artist share in the establishment costs'. On the other hand, if this is so, it is one of the few examples in the history of commerce where the cost of product development was recouped from a part of the creative team rather than from the consumer of the end product!

The same thing happened with the introduction of DCC and the MiniDisc format. Now the audiovisual and digital download technologies are the focus of the debate. There is always a new technology.

It is unclear at this time, how much users will be expected (or are prepared) to pay for legitimate music from on-line retailers. That said, it would seem that the success of iTunes has set the first reasonable price indictor. Nevertheless, until the content owners experiment with different pricing regimes there is much uncertainty. It remains very difficult for record companies and artists to evaluate the commercial worth of their copyright in the on-line environment. Certainly, most record companies are being cautious in dividing on-line revenue with their artists. From their perspective, considerable sums are invested in developing new technologies and they argue that in order to recoup this research and development cost, the artists should be paid less (up to 35% less) for sales in such developing markets. Let's face it, CDs had become the dominant sound carrier for years before record companies ceased treating CDs as a new technology and subject to such royalty reductions.

That said, on-line delivery is a very different system to traditional physical delivery and bears potentially enormous cost savings for record companies in the manufacture, packaging, storage and distribution processes. There are, of course, costs involved in on-line delivery. There are the costs involved in encoding and watermarking music files including the licence costs for using such proprietary software, web development costs and there are the digital storage costs in running large computer servers. But this is nothing compared to the costs of making, pressing, packaging, warehousing and physically distributing CDs. Once an encrypted, watermarked music file is created and is sitting happily on a hard drive, all that is left is to procure a licence for the track, send the sound file to an on-line distributor, retailer, or customer and then collect and distribute the sales income. This is largely an IT function. No warehouses to buy, secure, insure, maintain and staff; no delivery trucks and drivers; no defective returns to administer. The list goes on.

Now, in a perfect market, if the record companies are making more money per unit through on-line delivery then, competition principles suggest that they should pass these savings on to consumers and impart higher royalty rates to artists. In most cases this has not yet happened.

Many record companies are still treating on-line sales as though they were physical sales. In other words, artists receive a percentage of the sale price using the same royalty formulation that it applies to the sale of CDs. If, based on wholesale price, the royalty for a single might be 17% less of course 'new format' deductions (say 25%) and 'packaging deductions' (say 25%). The deductions erode the end royalty to about 9.5% of the wholesale price. So if a track is sold on-line for $1.00 (excluding GST) the artist gets 8 cents. The record company pockets 92 cents. There is something wrong in that model!

Other companies, more appropriately, treat the download not as a sale but as a licence – which strictly speaking it is. (Either the company is licensing the customer to reproduce the recording by means of download or it is licensing an on-line retailer to grant sub-licences to its customers.) When analysed this way it is apparent that the artist should receive a much higher royalty. After all, record agreements provide generally that where the record company licenses a third party to use a recording (such as in a film) the artist receives 50%-75% of the net amounts received by the record company.

The record companies' concern is that, if on-line music becomes the predominant form of music sales and if the record companies are locked into a high artist royalty rate, they may be unable to recoup their large financial investment in the recording and promotion of the artist. Almost any analysis of this argument shows that it is flawed. What it fails to recognise is that the economics of the record business are not going to remain as they are. On-line distribution changes the economic model. Nothing remains constant - not even the traditional paradigm for calculating record company overheads or artist royalties.

For the moment, however, the record companies are being cautious. Until the commercial profit models are abundantly clear, the record companies are hesitant to commit to higher artist royalties or to lower consumer pricing. The cynical would say that the companies have no incentive to allow such benefits to flow through to either the artist or the consumer when the savings produced by on-line distribution can be better applied to company profits and executive bonuses. Damn the cynics!

If companies continue to adopt this passive-resistant approach, we must take comfort in the application of competition principles: A company that wishes to attract top artists will have to offer a competitive royalty calculation model; if it wishes to sell large volumes of product on-line, its pricing is going to have to reflect the consumers' price sensitivities.

In any event, the move from free to fee will not be an easy one for the record companies. Firstly, as we have seen above, those people who are familiar with and see value in downloading music onto their computers have become accustomed to getting what they want for free. Secondly, there are many people who do not see (or do not understand) the additional value of downloaded or streaming music. Thirdly, particularly in Australia and despite encryption technologies, there is still a reluctance to divulge credit card details on-line.

What is certain, however, is that the music available through legitimate systems must be in a relatively secure format that allows record companies to maintain control of their music. Software developers are creating complex rights management systems that enable copyright owners to control how digital works are used. By embedding information into a music file, instructions can be given to the file player, such as a computer or MP3 player, to limit the way in which the music is used. (For example, instructions can be given such that the file can be downloaded for free but only be played for 30 seconds after which the user is obliged to purchase the song.) Hackers will always enjoy the sport of cracking such systems. That said, so long as there is a hurdle to deter the amateurs and a clear benefit to consumers, the legitimate market will continue to emerge. Indeed it is likely that technological methods controlling the use of intellectual property will deter pirate use much more effectively than threats of lawsuits.

ARTISTIC CONTROL IN THE DIGITAL AGE

Digital manipulation already enables artists' voices to be added or erased, instrumentation changed, stereo synthesised and so on. The technical ability to alter recordings, even without access to the original multi-track tapes, means that recordings are vulnerable to radical alteration by third parties. Artists are likely to hear very different versions of their recordings, as others manipulate the originals.

Apart from the obvious problems this creates for copyright owners, it means artists, who often pay thousands of dollars to producers to get the sound 'just so', risk having their recordings changed - not always for the better. Copyright and moral rights go some way to preventing travesties from being produced but these only protect the composers and lyricists. In contract, artists who want to control manipulation of their recordings have to rely on contractual provisions that are inherently inadequate for the purpose.

COPYRIGHT ISSUES ARISING FROM RECENT AND FUTURE TECHNOLOGICAL DEVELOPMENTS

DOES COPYRIGHT HAVE A FUTURE?

There is a modern myth that the Internet is some sort of law-free zone. In spite of the popular writings of commentators such as John Perry Barlow, this is not so. The laws of the country apply to Internet just as any other form of communication such as mail or radio.

It is argued that because the Internet is based on a digital system, it is impossible to regulate bits in any meaningful way using the existing legal framework. It is certainly difficult at the moment (for the law always reacts to technological development and is therefore always a little behind), but many of the copyright problems thrown up by the Internet are not so very different from those posed in relation to other areas of social regulation: Defamation and obscenity are obvious examples.

It is also argued that the Internet is unique in that it is a medium that ignores national boundaries and thus national government control. Not so. Radio and TV broadcasts are everyday examples of media that have footprints that extend far beyond national boundaries and far beyond the possibility of local regulation.

Whenever a new reproduction or transmission technology comes along, one has to ask, 'Can the existing formulations of the law cope with the effects of the new technology?' The Internet is no greater challenge to the copyright system than the photocopier, which when it was introduced was supposed to presage the end of the text publishing industry. The Internet is just the latest in a long line of challenges to copyright provided by technology.

The continued existence of copyright is hardly worth arguing. It is an economic and cultural given. There are at least three indicators that this is so:

- First, copyright has long been entrenched in Western Europe and the United States and in countries such as ours which have been legally, socially and economically sculpted by those influences. This predominantly Western intellectual construct has developed into a powerful international network of treaties and organisations and through the internationalisation of communications and commerce, it has influenced the world.

- Secondly, the copyright-based industries are among the largest in our society. Intellectual property contributes billions of dollars to our corporate balance sheets every year and it is improbable that these corporations are going to simply allow these billions to be wiped off their asset registers on the strength of a few articles in Wired

Magazine or the IT pages of the local newspaper. In other words, commerce will demand an evolution, not a revolution.

What developed as a mode of cultural remuneration for individual creators is now established as integral to the balance sheets of many of the most powerful companies on earth and, as such, has become a fundamental part of the world economy.

- Thirdly, is history: The phonograph didn't kill the live performance industry as it was prophesied (although thankfully it probably did kill off the music box)! The tape recorder didn't kill the record business! Television didn't kill the cinema! The photocopier didn't kill text publishing! All developments in the law of copyright are technology-driven and all significant changes in the copyright industries are similarly technology-driven.

It is not the future existence of copyright but rather the future design of copyright that should be the concern of the industry. Given that:

- copyright is now inextricably a part of the cultural expression in which it is embodied; and
- copyright has now become an important factor in the national and world economy.

Simultaneous with the revolutionary effects of the Internet, or perhaps it is merely a part of it, we also have the impact of fibre optics, broadband, convergence and interactivity. Each of these technologies is influencing and enabling the others. Together, they have created a turmoil that is going to influence, if not completely change, the way we study, perform, record, market, distribute and enjoy music.

It is always useful to remember that most of these technologies were not invented as part of some considered social or cultural strategy. They are largely an accidental by-product of the scientific method that demands that the researcher reject all questions of cultural value and influence. The companies develop and market the technologies. We adopt and we adapt. The impact of these technologies on copyright is but one example of the way that we are forced to adapt.

Technology and culture are not enemies, they are inextricable; but we have a duty to consider the impact of technological developments on culture in general and, in particular, its effect on the rights owners who are, and will always be, vital to the provision of content and thus vital to the cultural richness of our community.

The challenge, just one of many, is to ensure that the laws of copyright adapt to the new technological environment in a way that feeds and encourages creative activity rather than in a way that inhibits or overwhelms it.

As we have seen in previous chapters, Australia has implemented a range of legislative amendments such as the Copyright (Digital Agenda) Amendment Act and the Broadcast Services Act to clarify parliament's intention that, in essence, what is protected in the off-line world is protected in the on-line world.

Given that technological advances continue to modify the way in which intellectual property is created and used, the laws will need to be continuously revised by parliament and interpreted by the courts to cover the ongoing process of technological change. What is clear beyond doubt, however, is that the Internet is no longer a lawless wonderland or an anarchic state. It is governed by the rule of law.

With a clearer legal framework, the commercial risks associated with investment in the Internet have been reduced. This has soothed the investors who have begun to pour millions into the development of legitimate on-line music ventures.

There are many matters that will influence what music copyright will look like and how it is exploited in the music industry.

COPYRIGHT MANAGEMENT

One of the most important issues is how best to manage copyright material in the digital environment. It is now extraordinarily cheap and easy to store, re-purpose, manipulate and distort, and distribute.

These are characteristics that can greatly enhance the commercial value of the copyrights and this is reflected in the macroscopic view of corporations which are acquiring content through takeovers or strategic alliances and in the microscopic view which sees the release of a record and video featuring a long-dead Nat King Cole singing with his very much alive daughter thanks to the miracles of digital technology (and our ability to suspend belief). It sees Forrest Gump talking with President Kennedy.

On the other side of the coin, distortion and manipulation is an important moral rights issue for the authors of content. It is also important for every company whose business is the administration, exploitation and control of that content. The use of copyright without remuneration obviously affects the rights owner's ability to make income from their work, but the distortion and manipulation of one's work can not only deprive the rights owner of income in respect of that reuse, but also derogate the value of the original. Copyright control and supervision is not just an issue for the creators, it is an issue for the boardrooms.

PROMOTING CONTROLLED COPYRIGHT ACCESS

The cost of getting lawful access to copyright material is considerable. The traditional forms of licensing take time, skill and money. Interactive technologies require us to look for new ways of granting access.

The granting of statutory compulsory licences (such as the mechanical licence administered by AMCOS) is one way that the community ensures access but generally, compulsory licences are an unwarranted interference with the right to control one's own valuable property. There are other approaches that should be investigated and encouraged. They are all based on a balancing of competing interests. On the one hand, easy access by the user and on the other, protection of the commercial and cultural interests of the owner.

The development of an international, reliable mechanism for the authoritative identification of works, uses, permissions, income collection and distribution, is essential. There are two ways that this might go.

(I) ROLE OF COLLECTING SOCIETIES

The role of the copyright collecting societies will become even more important than they are today. To achieve this, these societies themselves are going to have to be at the forefront of IT research, development and implementation. They are going to be responsible for the design, administration and supervision of the process by which uses are identified, royalties are collected and by which rights owners are identified and remunerated. Few individual rights owners will have the resources effectively to administer their own rights.

The proof of this has been the facilitative approach of APRA, AMCOS and the PPCA in negotiating a regime for downloads and web-casting.

(II) DIGITAL OBJECT IDENTIFIERS

As part of this strategy, many of the major international societies together with a number of the major content owners combined in a major research initiative called the INDECS project. This was based on the need to develop digital object identifiers (DOIs) by which users and uses could be identified and administered. It was an ambitious project and resulted in a cataloguing system that may yet provide the basis for a reliable international DOI structure and standard. Quite simply, until there is such a standard in place, the effective and reliable administration of copyright on the Internet is going to be cumbersome and expensive and the prophesies above, concerning the online access to the world repertoire of legitimate content, will be impossible.

The digital age may be one in which everyone has the ability to be a content provider but only those who administer their rights collectively will be able to maximise their commercial benefit. This is one of the great ironies of the digital revolution: The mechanisms of freedom of expression will be anarchic, but the income mechanisms will be largely collectivised. Or is this so?

The emergence of a DOI standard, while essential for collecting societies to administer web-based transactions, is also the seed that may grow to make the role of societies virtually redundant.

There are now several companies investing very large amounts of money in developing software that will permit the trading of intellectual property material online. There are various models, each too complicated for this discussion but each seeks to provide a simple way of distributing digital content for a fee that is determined by the content, the user and the use. The largest and best funded of these initiatives, Intertrust, is a United States-based strategic alliance of massive companies rich in copyright and content. It was due to launch in mid-2001 but it got enmeshed in a legal battle with Microsoft - a fight that was only settled in mid-2005. There is nothing like the payment of a $440 million settlement and the inking of a nice long-term licence agreement for Intertrust's digital rights management tools, to bring joy to a boardroom. (See www.intertrust.com).

These systems could largely do away with the need for collective administration and thus the role of collecting societies. Each content owner will theoretically be able to mark, distribute, trace, set terms, trade and collect payment for, his or her own material. That said, this is likely to assist only large-scale owners, as the small distributors such as individual artists are unlikely to have the resources to administer the various component functions. There will still need to be a degree of collective administration to support such owners. (This is a bit like the current functioning of AMCOS; large record companies don't need to use AMCOS to license the mechanical rights from publishers - they can do this themselves, direct with the relevant publishers. AMCOS is essential for the smaller operators that do not have the administrative resources to do it themselves.)

POLICING COPYRIGHT

Copyright tagging, watermarking and unique identifiers permit the owners of digital material to be able to identify their property wherever it is and however it has been modified or distorted. This technology already exists and, as it develops, will overcome many of the present problems of identification.

Of course it is only useful in respect of material that has been tagged or watermarked. This takes resources. Then it takes even more resources effectively to use, supervise the tagged or marked material, administer the granting of access to it and operate some system of stopping non-authorised use.

This is going to give rise to the 'killer app'. It doesn't exist at the moment but every copyright owner looking to trade content on the Internet wants it and needs it. Bad.

Let's call it the 'Exocet bot': a very directional and efficient destructor. We already have 'intelligent agents' or 'bots' that are capable of trolling cyberspace identifying these tags and tracking the copyright material across the Internet wherever they may be. What does not exist is a bot that can identify an unauthorised use of a digital object and simply disable that object while it is sitting in the user's hard disk. In a sense it would be a 'white virus' - affecting only material that was illegitimate. Of course, the legal issues arising out of such technology are considerable (but that's not all bad!).

COLLECTION OF COPYRIGHT INCOME FOR INTERNET USE

None of the payment collection mechanisms currently used on the Internet is ideal. Each has its disadvantages. Most of the problems are related to security issues and the cost of financial administration. This is where the telcos have the great advantage over most other service providers: they have highly automated and reasonably reliable billing systems already in place. What is more, they are internationally available and already familiar to millions of phone users. As such they are readily accessible and have a major comfort and confidence factor. The provision of billing services for intellectual property trades is potentially a very large business for the telcos. Accordingly, it is predictable that most content providers will seek to form strategic alliances with Telstra or its competitors, to provide the billing backbone of their business.

The other likely enabling technology will be the new generation of smart cards. Although this technology was probably over-hyped in its early days, it is now coming of age. For example, imagine a card, loaded with the necessary financial information which, when inserted in your computer or mobile phone, simply conducts the payment part of the transaction automatically. This technology presently exists. It allows the payment and collection of revenue with minimal administration and expense.

With intellectual property transactions on the Internet, the multi-layered nature of the licensing means that the transaction is much more complex than most e-commerce. One digital object (or song) may embody rights owned or controlled by several entities. Each requires a small piece of the payment for use. This can certainly be done most cost-effectively in a computerised transaction but it is still to be seen whether that is most effectively achieved by distributing the necessary software to each user's computer (say bundled with the operating system) or through the operation of ASPs that would permit greater security and would make software upgrades comparatively simple to implement.

THE FUTURE OF ON-LINE MUSIC – 'THE TIMES THEY ARE A CHANGIN'

When Bob Dylan sang of the radical social changes of the 1960s, his song was a plaintive cry to the conservatives of the day to accept that the world will never be the same. While forty years old, the song is still used as a revolutionary anthem. The message is one that needs to be heard by the record industry today: 'you better start swimmin', or you'll sink like a stone'.

At the time this chapter was written, the music industry was in the early stages of its latest metamorphosis, the online delivery revolution. As this and the previous chapter have tried to show, the music industry has been continuously subjected to technological developments and with each such development, the industry has embraced the change and turned it to a profit.

With the development of digital technology and ever cheaper and more powerful computers, technology has changed the way music is created, used, copied and enjoyed. The Internet has provided new ways for it to be delivered. Where consumers have been faster than the big record companies to adapt to these changes, opportunities have appeared for new players. These more agile new businesses have challenged the record companies' traditional business models and income streams, leaving them with Dylan's ultimatum - learn to swim, or sink.

Although they have been slow off the mark, the major record companies have finally made clear their intention to lead the industry through its next big change - on-line music delivery. With their financial and market muscle, not to mention their enormous catalogues, the Majors have the power to transform access to music - and thus the business of music.

This will be no easy task. The music industry is heavily entrenched, physically and conceptually, in a business model that has been fine-tuned over the last 100 years. No wonder the record companies have been such reluctant supporters of the revolution.

The key to overcoming consumer resistance is 'access'. On-line music's real drawcard is that it potentially offers access to the world's entire record repertoire, past and present, directly from the record company. That access should be cheaper and easier than going down to the local record store.

On-line music is a great idea. There is no shortage of prophets foretelling the time when every mobile phone can access any song ever recorded and stream it to your stereo or headphones, you'll pay 5c per song to go on your phone bill to be split between the various rights owners and the telco. Sounds great. We're waiting.

A POSSIBLE FUTURE

Having covered so much ground focused on the past and the present, we should have a think about what the future might look like. This is true risk taking!

A STORY

The following scenario is based on current and emerging technologies: It assumes the ongoing development of interactive media, of community access to broadband and ever-increasing computing speed. (This piece of future - gazing was written in 1994 and still remains relevant!)

Let's imagine a person wants to see an opera at the Sydney Opera House. She is in her lounge room in Singapore. She turns on the media centre. The media centre delivers the household's complete entertainment and telephony requirements. Through it, on a pay-for-play basis, she can access the world's music repertoire, an enormous library of films and other audiovisual programming and she has the option of both aural and audiovisual telephony. It is, of course, also a computer and has the usual email and fax facilities. What is not self-adjusting is voice activated and voice controlled. By voice instruction given to the remote control, she requests access to the Music Channel; Opera; Sydney Opera House.... (and so on).

The media centre immediately accesses the desired channel and program. She is able to watch live or recorded events. If she wants to see a performance or an incident from a different camera angle, she has only to ask. If she wants to know the performance history of a particular singer, she has only to ask. The data is immediately thrown up on the screen in the right-hand corner so that she doesn't miss the live action. If she wonders how the singer trained to achieve such a level of performance or what the singer's home town looks like, she has only to ask. She can buy some genuine Opera Australia merchandising by requesting to see the range, making her selection and paying without leaving her chair. If she wants to listen to a recording before purchase, she can do so. The whole transaction is voice controlled. The media centre automatically does the form filling on the basis of her pre-programmed personal details. She approves the transactions before they are completed. Then she leaves a message on the viewer response line. Seeing the world's best has excited her and she immediately calls up the on-line music reservation service and books her seats for the Singapore Opera next January.

At the end of the month she will get a statement of account that will include all her purchases, her bookings and her on-line access fees.

She may never have been to an auditorium. Yet she is an active participant in music. She doesn't know it, but she is a very valuable asset to all participants in the music business.

FEATURES OF THE POSSIBLE FUTURE

This is a possible future. Most of it is already technologically possible. It is neither science fiction nor mere speculation. In an age when media rights are negotiated for several years at a time, it is important to spend expert time trying to work out what the most likely future will be. If you don't, the future becomes the present and you are unprepared for the change.

In the world of music media, if you miss the technological change, you can miss the opportunity. This can cost you dearly. Rather, you must develop and implement strategies to maximise the opportunities that this inevitable future presents. It is a future with many unknowns but some things are certain: multi-format media and interactivity will be basic elements in the way that you communicate and present your music and music services to the world.

What are some of the features of the futuristic tale?

- The technology was a basic home facility.
- The technology was simple to use. It didn't require knowledge of systems or software. The cleverness of the technology was invisible.
- The response time of the technology was almost immediate.
- The viewer had no resistance to using the service for shopping.
- The machine could respond to various programmed languages.
- The machine had a fuzzy logic capacity; it could make inferences as to what the viewer wanted or meant.
- The machine was truly multimedia.
- The available programming was diverse in interest although thematically consistent. Everything related to the music but it had action, lifestyle programming, travel, etc.
- The viewer was more actively participating than a television viewer, radio listener, newspaper reader or record listener.
- Although the activity was in another country it could be used to stimulate audience attendance and other benefits in the viewer's local country (International presentation; local stimulation).
- The activity represents an integration of music, commerce, domestic life and technology in a seamless and effortless continuum.

TIMING

When will it happen? The arrival date of a technology is determined by what might be called confluence. Basically, the future tale cannot be realised until there are a number of ducks in a row. Let's just take 12 of them:

- Watermarking and tagging of copyright material to allow effective tracing and identification of rights usage;
- Development and invisible availability of effective encryption technology to protect financial transactions and reduce user resistance;
- Increased speed of information transfer: not just top-end but rather, the public average;
- Increased storage capacity: hard discs and other technologies that permit enormous quantities of data to be stored and accessed by vast numbers of users simultaneously;
- Domestic media hardware that has the technical capacity to be truly multi-format and truly interactive - at a price that allows it to be pervasive and with an ease of function that disarms the average person's resistance to complicated technology;
- Reliable and trusted information technology solutions to the charging, collection and distribution of micro-payments;
- Easy-to-use online copyright licensing software that permits flexible, 'granular' licensing;
- Multi-industry acceptance and implementation of a universal system of identifying digital objects;
- Content that makes the public want to adopt and pay for the new technology;
- Content makers (including musicians and record companies) who are prepared to make material that is suitable for the new delivery formats and who are prepared to rethink their traditional business models;
- New marketing paradigms that are based on the digital, online environment rather than the old, atom-based world;
- Confluence: these developments have to come together before we can have a real, online, interactive, entertainment economy;
- And when will we have confluence? The most unreliable thing about trying to guess the future is to judge the timing. Still, by the time you see the next edition of this book, this chapter will look quaint and old fashioned. Confluence will have occurred and today's future will have arrived.

CONCLUSION

Technology and culture are not enemies, they are agents of mutual influence and change. All participants in this process have a duty to consider the impact of technological developments on culture in general and, in particular, its effect on the rights owners who are and will always be, vital to the provision of content and thus vital to the cultural richness of our community.

New technologies can kill older technologies. Their introduction is rarely fatal to any art form. The invention of the camera did not mean the death of painting; film did not kill the theatre; the photocopier did not ruin the book, and so on. Rather, technological innovations act as catalysts and modifiers of the arts. Each changes the way we practice, conserve, distribute, market, promote, sell, study, criticise and enjoy, the arts.

The power of technology undoubtedly influences the music industry but in doing so it creates new forms and new opportunities for enhancing its aesthetic, social and economic impact.

Technological invention is rarely part of some considered social or cultural strategy. It is largely a by-product of the scientific method that demands that the researcher reject all questions of cultural value and influence. Corporations develop and market the technologies. We adopt and we adapt. The impact of these technologies on copyright is but one example of the way that we are forced to adapt. In spite of the 'copyright is dead' cant that it has been generating, the Internet poses no greater challenge to the copyright system than the photocopier. It is just the latest in a long line of challenges provided by technology.

Given that copyright is now inextricably a part of the cultural expression in which it is embodied and has now become an important factor in the national and world economy, it is not the future existence of copyright but rather the future design of copyright that should be the concern of the music community: how we manage copyright material in the digital environment; how we protect it from theft, manipulation and distortion; how we do that while still promoting access to it?

Copyright must continue to play an essential role in any modern, developed, sophisticated society. At the end of the day, the rights of copyright are an award for innovation, creativity and risk taking. This recognises that both the culture and the economy of our community is dependant on encouraging and fostering these characteristics.

Whatever happens, there is no reason to think that the demand for music will decrease in any way. If anything, it is likely to increase. It will certainly become even easier to access. Online delivery of music is going to mean great changes in the way that publishers and record companies operate; it will change the way that performers and composers work and the sort of material they produce; it will change the legal relationships between the talent and the companies; it will change the exploitation media available to the companies; it will change the way you use music to communicate with your market.

As you can see from the brief history provided by this chapter, we can look back and see how fast the future arrives, is overtaken and dismissed. For record and publishing companies to survive and flourish in the digital age, they will have to overcome the disadvantage of being creatures of an earlier age. The old media tools and existing marketing recipes will no longer necessarily be relevant. That is why it's a revolution. All of the old paradigms must be challenged. We cannot know what the future will be, but we must acknowledge that if we are to be part of the new commercial, social and cultural order, we must be part of the revolutionary force, not its subject.

16
THE GROWTH OF THE AUSTRALIAN RECORD BUSINESS

THIS CHAPTER STARTS WITH A BRIEF HISTORICAL SKETCH OF THE DEVELOPMENT OF THE AUSTRALIAN RECORD BUSINESS. WHILE THE BUSINESS HAS ITS OWN CHARACTERISTICS THAT MAKE IT DIFFERENT FROM ITS OVERSEAS COUNTERPARTS, THERE ARE MANY FEATURES THAT MAKE COMPARISONS BETWEEN THE AUSTRALIAN AND THE UNITED STATES RECORD INDUSTRIES INEVITABLE. THE CHAPTER THEN GIVES BRIEF PROFILES OF SOME OF THE MAJORS, INDEPENDENTS AND OTHER PLAYERS SUCH AS RECORD CLUBS AND DISTRIBUTORS.

The record industry has evolved from fairly uncomplicated beginnings, into a complex group of interrelated companies. These generate billions of dollars each year and have made the music industry one of the biggest businesses in the world. To put that into perspective, even in the early 1980s, global record sales generated an annual turnover in the order of US$4,000 million dollars (give or take a bit). Compare this with the figures for 2004: According to London-based International Federation of the Phonographic Industry (IFPI), IFPI reports that in 2004, sales of physical formats (ie excluding downloads) generated US$33.6 billion:

> "Even excluding digital sales, 2004 was the best year-on-year trend in global music sales for five years. Sales of top-selling albums reversed several years of decline. Top 10 albums sales globally rose by 14%, while the top 50 albums were up 8% in value. Eight albums sold more than five million in 2004, up from five in 2003.
>
> Digital sales rose exponentially, with the total number of tracks downloaded in 2004 (including album tracks) up more than tenfold on 2003, to over 200 million in the four major digital music markets (US, UK, France, Germany). The trend has continued in 2005, with digital sales in the US in the first two months more than double that of the same period in 2004; Eight albums sold more than 5 million in

2004, up from five in 2003; Music DVD sales rose 23% and have doubled their share of the world music market from 4% in 2002 to 8% in 2004 - with a value of US$2.6 billion dollars."

http://www.ifpi.org/site-content/publications/rin_order.html

We are talking about very large piles of money here.

The Australian Record Industry Association (ARIA) reports that for the year ending December 2004, Australian record companies shipped over 57.9 million audio and music video units. The following ARIA charts provide a snapshot of the local industry.

SALES BY VALUE FOR THE YEARS ENDED 31 DECEMBER (000'S)

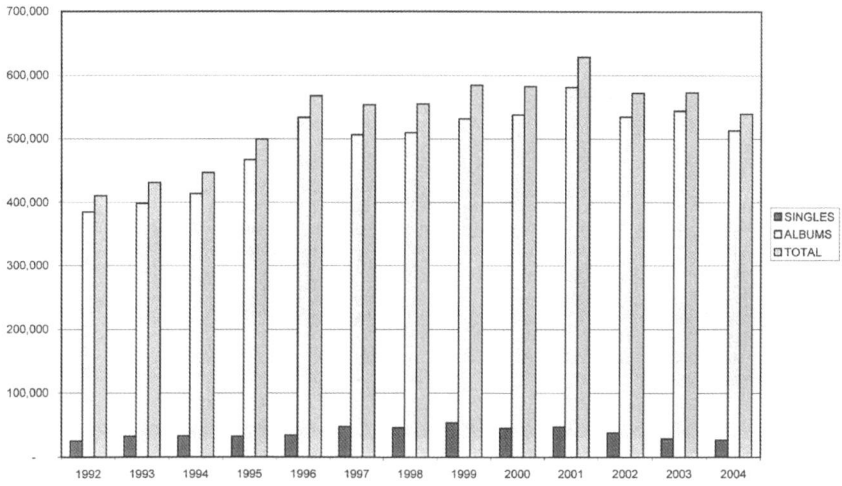

SALES BY UNIT FOR THE YEARS ENDED 31 DECEMBER (000'S)

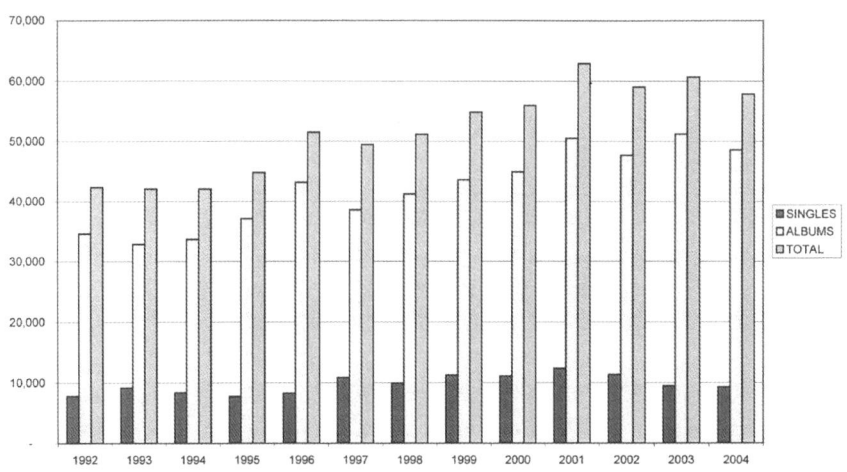

AUSTRALIAN SALES AT WHOLESALE VALUE FOR THE YEARS ENDED 31 DECEMBER

$000's	1994	1995	1996	1997	1998	1999	2000	2001	2002	2003	2004
SINGLES											
7&12" Vinyl	81	68	66	132	86	118	93	70	67	98	61
CDs	24,700	27,273	31,090	46,194	45,631	53,373	44,571	46,659	37,460	28,509	26,670
Cassettes	8,371	5,090	3,295	1,279	86	(4)	-	1	-	-	1
DVD/Other								52	(4)	(1)	13
TOTAL	33,152	32,431	34,451	47,605	45,803	53,487	44,664	46,782	37,523	28,606	26,745
ALBUMS											
12" Vinyl	457	213	346	316	225	342	336	394	426	525	385
CDs	351,368	421,519	499,507	486,041	498,324	524,994	531,972	576,484	528,401	539,609	509,807
Cassettes	62,078	45,578	33,823	20,237	11,207	6,283	6,063	4,739	4,317	1,681	942
DVD/Other							89	226	1,938	2,788	2,179
TOTAL	413,903	467,310	533,676	506,594	509,756	531,619	538,460	581,843	535,082	544,603	513,313
TOTAL	447,055	499,741	568,127	554,199	555,559	585,106	583,124	628,625	572,605	573,209	540,058

AUSTRALIAN SALES BY UNIT FOR THE YEARS ENDED 31 DECEMBER

000's	1994	1995	1996	1997	1998	1999	2000	2001	2002	2003	2004
SINGLES											
7&12" Vinyl	14	10	10	19	12	15	18	9	8	12	7
CDs	5,638	6,002	7,196	10,427	9,900	11,290	11,099	12,367	11,343	9,464	9,286
Cassettes	2,751	1,678	1,109	437	37	(2)	9	-	-	-	-
DVD/Other								4	-	-	3
TOTAL	8,403	7,690	8,315	10,883	9,949	11,303	11,126	12,380	11,351	9,476	9,296
ALBUMS											
12" Vinyl	28	19	31	24	18	30	37	31	32	43	30
CDs	25,948	31,136	38,330	36,218	39,631	42,672	43,917	49,670	46,954	50,640	48,234
Cassettes	7,705	5,978	4,833	2,367	1,604	909	949	811	598	360	194
DVD/Other							5	10	107	180	143
TOTAL	33,681	37,133	43,194	38,609	41,253	43,611	44,908	50,522	47,691	51,223	48,601
TOTAL	42,084	44,823	51,509	49,492	51,202	54,914	56,034	62,902	59,042	60,699	57,897

SEASONALITY (PERCENTAGES)

The seasonality weighting of sales as follows:

Total sound recordings

Units %	1992	1993	1994	1995	1996	1997	1998	1999	2000	2001	2002	2003	2004
January - March	17.3	19.8	17.3	17.7	17.5	18.7	17.1	17.6	17.1	18.6	19.7	19.4	19.6
April - June	21.9	20.1	20.7	21.0	22.7	20.0	20.7	20.6	18.6	21.7	21.7	20.6	19.7
July - September	22.5	24.2	24.8	23.0	21.6	22.3	22.9	22.2	25.2	22.9	22.5	23.8	22.8
October - December	38.3	35.9	37.2	38.3	38.2	39.1	39.3	39.6	39.0	36.8	36.1	36.2	37.9
TOTAL	100.0	100.0	100.0	100.0	100.0	100.0	100.0	100.0	100.0	100.0	100.0	100.0	100.0

Wholesale Value %	1992	1993	1994	1995	1996	1997	1998	1999	2000	2001	2002	2003	2004
January - March	18.2	18.7	17.1	17.4	17.5	18.2	17.9	18.1	17.5	18.7	19.4	19.9	19.6
April - June	21.3	19.6	20.9	21.6	22.2	19.9	20.9	20.6	18.3	21.3	21.7	21.2	19.5
July - September	22.2	22.4	24.0	22.0	22.1	22.1	21.9	21.9	24.4	22.6	22.2	22.6	21.5
October - December	38.3	39.3	38.0	39.0	38.2	39.8	39.3	39.3	39.8	37.4	36.7	36.3	39.4
TOTAL	100.0	100.0	100.0	100.0	100.0	100.0	100.0	100.0	100.0	100.0	100.0	100.0	100.0

Source: www.aria.com.au

Although sales were down in 2004 in comparison to the previous three years, they are still vastly higher than they were 10 years ago. Despite the cries that the end of the world was coming, CD sales still reached 48.2 million. The seesaw is the continued demise of cassettes and the continued buoyancy of the DVD. The Australian Music Retailers Association in 2005 predicted that by the end of 2006, DVD sales would be 20% of the number of CD sales: DVD would no longer be an emerging technology – it would be a dominant technology.

Today, the Australian industry is made up of a central core of Majors and Independents, surrounded by dozens of spin-off industries which provide services and specialist facilities to the record companies. They provide the services and equipment needed to turn a performance into what is, when stripped of the glamour and art, essentially a piece of injection-moulded plastic in fancy wrapping.

The interrelationship between the various interests makes the industry a complex one and maddeningly difficult to analyse. Generalisations tend to be misleading unless heavily qualified, but generalisations are often all we have to go on. The Australian industry does not collect and publish statistics as readily as its American and European counterparts and without such data it is difficult for outsiders to quantify the nature and economic direction of the industry. Rather, outsiders have a 'keyhole' view, often based on rumour rather than hard data. This has tended to encourage observers to see dark motives in most of the industry's activities, or to be over-awed by the promotional hype (which rarely fools anyone on the inside). The industry is often criticised for being crass and heartless. It can be, but they are hardly characteristics unique to this business.

The fact is, the degree of competition between the record companies is difficult to quantify, but compete they certainly do. In spite of this, there are business practices and methods that are standard throughout the industry. These similarities are not, in themselves, evidence of collusion between the companies. The record companies all sell records and they all face essentially the same problems and pressures. It is hardly surprising that the solutions adopted by the companies are frequently similar.

Record companies all have to formulate internal and external policies. Internal policies are usually treated as confidential. External policies (which relate to matters of common concern such as copyright charges, GST, technological developments and the like) obviously have to be seen as applicable to the majority of companies. Accordingly, the development of industry policies should not automatically be thought of as sinister. Any 'co-operation' between record companies has to be seen in the context that, on a day-to-day level, they are competing fiercely amongst themselves (and with other industries) for consumers' attention and money.

PROFIT – SKILL OR LUCK

Because the primary commodity of the record business (i.e. music) is regarded as something 'cultural' and different from selling egg beaters or socks, it is frequently criticised as being venal and 'just worried about money'. But it should never be forgotten that this industry is just as driven by the need for profit as any other. Criticism of the profit motive ultimately misses the point. If they are to survive, the record companies, whether Majors or Independents, have to generate sufficient cashflow from their activities to meet running costs and have enough left over to re-invest in artists and recordings - and make a profit. Any company that makes records that do not sell, faces a short future, regardless of the artistic merit of its recordings. Perhaps the recordings will be appreciated by a later generation... as back catalogue, but then, the company will be long gone.

Considerations of artistic merit are just one of a number of factors which must be considered whenever a record company contemplates signing an artist or making a recording. At the end of the day, the judgment that the company has to make is, 'Will this record earn more than it costs to sell?'

Sometimes, though, a record will be released despite any realistic expectation that it will recover its cost. This is the kind of thinking that leaves the record companies' accountants distraught. It would be naive in the extreme to think there is a great tradition of philanthropic record releases, although they do happen. Often, such releases are founded on the belief of one executive in an artist; a 'gut-feel' that it is worth the risk. One of the great fascinations of this industry is to work out why this happens even occasionally, but we should be grateful that it does. Without the occasional reliance on ears and belief over surveys and commercial radio formats, we would end up with a very monochromatic musical world.

The mining industry faces similar problems to the music industry. Mining is a high-risk, capital-intensive industry, where most of the costs are incurred before anyone can say whether the mine will pay off. Geological reports come in, the company's experts say 'dig' so a hole is gouged out. If they are right, everyone will say, 'I told you so'. If they are wrong, everyone will run for cover and deny involvement. As they say, 'Many mining fortunes have been lost by actually digging a hole'.

So, too, the record industry. Each year, it spends millions of dollars on making new recordings, of which only a small percentage will recover their costs. There are no sure-fire hits. Fortunately, records can have long lives. Similarly, the possibility that a recording or artist can make a comeback is another reason record companies put money into long-shots. Remember that John Paul Young's 'Love Is In The Air' made much more money on its second and even its third time around (in 2005, it was still one of the most performed Australian works, internationally). A record company gets to be successful if it guesses correctly more often than it guesses incorrectly, or if its correct guesses are sufficiently successful that they more than compensate for all the bad ones.

Someone in each record company has the job of deciding which records are likely to earn more than they cost. The people responsible for making that judgment are the artist and repertoire (A&R) managers. Their role is considered in detail in Chapter 17, **Anatomy of a Record Company**, but for the moment, it is enough to note that these people have the professional life expectancy of a human cannon ball, but while they are in the job, they have enormous influence in a record company. They can shape the company's artistic direction and, ultimately, its commercial fate for years to come.

A SHORT HISTORY

When looking at the Australian record industry it is worth considering a little history. This is by no means a deep history, but will help put the industry into perspective.

LANGUAGE AND GEOGRAPHY

The record industry in Australia evolved to suit its particular circumstances. It had to come to terms with the country's comparatively small population, physical isolation and primary language.

Artists in Australia had to deal with a problem not faced by artists in non-English speaking countries. Sharing the same language as the United States and England, which together dominated the industry from its early days, has always created problems for the local industry. The volume of records coming out of the United States and England made the job of establishing Australian artists and music even more difficult than it would have been if Australia had a different national language.

The record industry in France, for example, could rely on the domestic demand for French language records on which to base its industry. Meeting that demand provided the financial basis for the whole French industry and English-language records were just a sub-category of the overall market, rather than being the entire market.

COVERS

Until the early 1960s, it took a long time to get a master tape from overseas, so simultaneous Australian release of the original version was impossible. The Australian record companies usually had to make local versions of songs that were the hits in the United States and English charts.

Many of the hits here were covers of overseas versions, locally recorded by Australian artists. They almost always beat the overseas originals onto the market. To the Australian record-buying public, the locally recorded versions were the originals at least until the overseas recordings were released here (usually too late to capture the market for that song).

Those early days may not have been exactly glorious in terms of creativity, but they were vital to the local industry's development. They provided training for artists, studios and the local companies that made and distributed the records. The profits provided the finance for companies to create an industry that was to become a disproportionately strong source of recordings of Australian artists.

THE 1960s

By the mid-1960s, local artists were recording and having hits with original songs. The glorious days of 'Bandstand' and similar programs, were a sign of the increasing influence and demand for local artists. 'Hoadley's Battle of the Sounds' provided an opportunity for Australian bands to compete nationally, get radio exposure and free publicity and to win trips to England (though the value of those trips to the winners' careers was probably questionable).

This was the period in which Australia gave the world Rolf Harris, the Seekers and the Easybeats. Now that's cultural diversity! The Easybeats was perhaps Australia's first international success (if we don't count Dame Nellie Melba). It was reputedly one of David Bowie's favourite bands and one that influenced his early days as a recording artist.

Surfing became a national obsession, while folk music could be heard in coffee lounges across the country. Meanwhile, popular culture became increasingly focused on music and recording artists. The Mersey Sound inspired a phenomenal number of artists in Great Britain and the United States, which accelerated the process while increasing the dollars being generated by the industry. Then came Beatlemania. Anyone seriously interested in this era should read *The Sound of the City* by Charlie Gillett (Souvenir Press) and any of the many excellent biographies of major artists of the era.

THE 1970s

Local artists had begun to secure a significant portion of the recorded music market by the early 1970s. Australian companies had notable success with local artists and the whole industry grew. In large part, it was funded by the phenomenal sales of records such as 'Hot August Night', 'Grease', 'Saturday Night Fever', 'Dark Side of the Moon' and the thousands of other releases by the international acts who had become heroes and icons of popular culture - and managed to sell a lot of records while they were at it. More and more local artists were being accepted as stars and the industry began to develop an identity. This was when most of the Majors began establishing Australian subsidiaries, recognising the market as being both a consumer and a supplier of new talent.

In many ways these were the golden years of the record industry around the world, despite the slump in about 1979, which saw all the record companies suffer a large fall in turnover and profits. The demographics of the post-war baby boom and the prolonged period of economic growth from the 1950s vastly increased the market for recorded music. The demand was unprecedented and sales during this period injected a remarkable amount of money into the industry and propelled it from being a peripheral commercial activity to being a major business sector.

The 1970s were probably unique in the way recorded music dominated popular culture. It would take, at the very least, a major book to do justice to this era. The point is that the music industry achieved its extraordinary power and wealth during this era. The book *Hit Men* (Times Books) provides a very depressing but instructive insight into the record industry and the main players (at least in the United States) at the time. During this period, Australian music was mainly a local product but there were some important exceptions such as Little River Band, Air Supply and AC/DC.

THE 1980S

The 1980s, by comparison, were something of a period of consolidation. Most of the industry's main companies (i.e. the Major record companies, with their international affiliates in most major markets) had settled in for the long haul and the business closely resembled the one you see now. The Beatles were not quite the colossus astride the industry that they had been and acts like The Police, Sex Pistols, Michael Jackson, Dire Straits and many others, representing many diverse musical styles, took their place. What is more, Australian acts such as Midnight Oil and INXS became international stars with hit records in the United States, United Kingdom and Europe.

Musical styles started to diversify. Independent labels became more and more important as a source of new talent and the Majors recognised this by buying or forming strategic alliances with Independents.

This was the time compact discs took hold. This is also the time music videos came of age. Virtually every significant single release included a video. Frequently, the video cost several times more to make than the single. Television started to see the potential and the record companies themselves desperately sought ways of generating income from the clips.

It was also a time that the artists, who had dominated the industry for a decade, were slowly displaced by newer musical styles and fashion trends. Electronic percussion became cheap and widely used.

THE 1990s

In the early 1990s, Midnight Oil and INXS continued their success and Kylie Minogue became the darling of the United Kingdom. In fact, the impact of Australian TV soaps in the United Kingdom was such that, for a while, it seemed that if you were a star on 'Neighbours' or 'Home and Away', it was only a matter of time before you got a recording contract and 15 seconds of music industry fame.

For a while it seemed that the musical styles had fragmented to the extent that no one company or act could dominate the market. Dance, rap, hip-hop, heavy and thrash metal, indie rock, rockabilly, thrash-country (!), acid house... were all representative of separate subcultures and each produced its own stars and hits, although comparatively few 'crossed over' to have gigantic international success in the way Silverchair did in 1995-96 and Savage Garden did in 1997. Tina Arena moved to France and became their no.1 female recording star. John Farnham and Jimmy Barnes proved that you could sell millions of records at home and yet not get a meal overseas.

Naturally, this diversifying of musical styles has had an effect on the structure of the record industry generally. It has diversified the sources of new artists, but in a curious way, has (arguably) made Independents rather more reliant upon the Majors for funds, physical resources and marketing muscle because, as the costs and risks increased, the average wholesale price contracted. The prize-money contracted, but the cost of competing, if anything, increased.

As for the corporate trend of the 1990s, the big word was takeover. This was a decade in which the number of players shrank and many of the old guard of managing directors found themselves in retirement or looking for new work. Suddenly, the industry was no longer controlled by men who remembered the days of vinyl.

THE 2000s

The Australian record companies entered the new decade with a certain trepidation. The companies remained concerned by the potential consequences of the removal of parallel import protection. While the immediate reaction was to threaten to cut back on the local rosters, this was a temporary, knee-jerk reaction. The parallel import debacle did not have the promised consequence of reducing record retail prices by a significant amount. Certainly the top twenty records dropped a few dollars but the bulk of the repertoire remained largely unaffected. The record companies dropped the wholesale prices because the large retail chains threatened to import the product if they didn't. However, many of the retailers simply absorbed that cost saving and did not pass it on to the public.

The buzz of the early days of this decade is 'new technology'. The emergence of DVD has already become significant in Australia. It is creating new opportunities to repackage existing product (always a great money-maker) and to present performances to the market. The record business, which has always been audio, has started to become audiovisual. It needed to because the MP3 generation, the children of the MTV generation, already expect it.

For many, CD and even DVD is a temporary technology. The Internet's download phenomenon is the greatest challenge ever faced by the record companies and their early efforts at meeting this challenge have not covered them in glory. Perhaps unsurprisingly, it was a computer company rather than a music company that revolutionised the legitimate download market: Apple's software iTunes provided the first commercially successful, legitimate model and its iPod hardware did for the youth of its generation, what the invention of the transistor had done for the youth of the 60's. Now, however, it was not just 'music on the move' it was 'music of individual choice, anywhere, anytime'.

The licensing of digital content is still pre-pubescent but just as this is the decade in which the CD single and the cassette tape died, it is the era in which the digital, downloadable, programmable, transferable, mobile and accessible musical content became ascendant.

VERTICAL INTEGRATION

The music business in general is growing, thanks in part to the interconnectedness of entertainment media. The Majors have deliberately widened their activities, to enable them to maximise the revenue from their resources.

By the early 1960s, the money generated by the United States record industry made it immensely attractive to other areas of business. These other businesses could see the remarkable sums being made as rock'n'roll took hold of the United States teen market. They saw it as a logical extension for their own activities. As Paul Petersen (who starred in the hugely successful 1960s television series 'The Donna Reed Show') once observed: 'When you're on television and 30 million people watch you every week, you can sell a lot of records. Of course, that doesn't mean that they're good records'. Enough said.

Vertical integration (in this context) is the technique whereby groups of companies owned by the same parent company combine their resources to control several stages in the production and distribution of a product or service. This is done in order to rationalize costs, maximize the value of the assets of each participating company, and to increase the power of the whole, in the marketplace. Vertical integration enabled popular music, in the broadest sense, to become an international cultural phenomenon unlike anything before it. Depending on the makeup of the corporate group, member companies could:

- publish a song;
- sign the artist to an 'all media' contract;
- record and release the song on record;
- sell the hardware on which the record would be played;
- put the song into a film soundtrack and promote the artist in films produced in associated studios or in programs broadcast on associated television networks;
- publish books about the artist;
- promote the music product through their magazines; and
- sell T-shirts through a wholly owned merchandising company;
- broadcast performances or promote artists on their TV or radio network;
- present performances in their stadiums or concert halls.

Warner Brothers was one of the first and certainly one of the most successful at vertical integration. In the late 1950s, it began contracting young talent, grooming them and putting them into its televised variety show, 'Warner Brothers Presents'. If the public reacted positively, a special show would be created to capitalise on the personality cult. As early as 1959, Ed Byrnes, for example, was lifted out of the Warner Brothers television series '77 Sunset Strip' and transformed into a record star (albeit briefly). His records generated a lot of dollars and kept promoting the show for little or no cost to the studio. Then they started the same routine on his co-star, Connie Stevens. Meanwhile, Walt Disney discovered that the Mousketeers could sell records too and Annette Funicello became a recording artist. Even Lurch, from the Addams Family, had a record released.

Given the power of vertical integration it was perhaps not a great surprise when Universal Music was bought by a major United States alcohol company. However, when AOL bought Time Warner, everyone was surprised. An Internet cash box company purchasing one of the giants of the business! In 2000, when Vivendi bought Universal (for US$34 billion), we were almost complacent. After the AOL-Warner shock, it already seemed natural that a communications company would take over a content company.

During the next five years, the concept of vertical integration (along with shareholders' funds) took a battering. Vivendi nearly went to the wall and ended up selling-off Universal and returning to what was left of its once core business. Eventually the rocket scientists worked out that AOL was populated by people with a gene pool that was quite distinct from that of the Time-

Warner staff: Another merger, another disaster, another corporate fire-sale. Hubris is expensive.

Sony Music is part of a company that has both a powerful hardware arm and a motion picture business. In 2005, the record division of Sony merged with the record division of BMG. BMG has been vertically integrated since it started in Australia. It is part of the Bertelsmann Group that, among many other interests, is already the largest book publisher in the world.

Universal, which has large international film and television interests (as well as being part of the massive Philips hardware conglomerate) has started trying to acquire film and television rights from its recording artists.

Probably the most powerful example of local vertical integration was Michael Gudinski's group of companies. Even after selling Mushroom Records to Festival (itself now eaten by Warner Music), his companies still include recording, music publishing, management, touring, agency, merchandising, film and television. In a microcosm, it has demonstrated the best and the worst features of industry integration.

There are many other examples. The point of this section is not to provide a comprehensive list of vertically integrated companies; it is to indicate that vertical integration is a reality of the Australian music industry. If you are a pessimist, it means that the terms of the deal can be influenced by the record company's other tentacles. If you are an optimist, it can mean that you will have additional opportunities for cross-promotion.

THE RECORD COMPANIES

The record industry is generally spoken about as though it was neatly divided into two classes of record company - the Majors and the Independents. Of course, the real world is not that neat and trim. These names are no more than convenient labels; a shorthand way of saying, 'This company is a subsidiary of one of the Big Four multinationals. If it's not one of theirs, it's some variety of Independent'.

Having said that, we will still use the terms but, as you will see, they are at best indicators. They are not reliable descriptions.

The Majors are the multinational corporations, with subsidiaries in most major markets. They draw their repertoire from many countries and all musical styles. They are big. They have structures and rules. They are also the bankers for the industry. The Majors are all affiliates of international corporations, whose businesses are based on selling records, music and films. In Australia they are Warner, Sony/BMG, Universal (which has now subsumed PolyGram and MCA) and EMI.

There is a subcategory to the Majors that could be thought of as 'local Majors' that do not comfortably fit in either category since they are not part of the Majors, but are large enough to be very important players in the Australian industry. These are Shock and the ABC (because of its activities in so many different media, of which recorded music is only a part). Until late-2005 Festival/Mushroom also came within this category - but it was bought by Warner.

Independents, on the other hand, are free spirits, or so they would have you believe. They both benefit and lose from their independence. They benefit by being less constrained in the kind of deals they can do but, at the same time, they find it harder to compete with the sheer marketing muscle and financial resources of the Majors. This is one reason Independents try to establish close rapport with similarly minded Independents in other major territories. This way they can more or less emulate the Majors' networks, without sacrificing their status as an Independent.

There are so many Independents operating at any one time (some for years, others for brief bursts of activity before disappearing apparently without trace), that I will not even try to profile them.

MAJORS' STRUCTURES

Each local company is still expected to be a source of repertoire in its own right. The intention is, of course, that product will have success outside its originating territory. This improves the odds of getting a commercial return on the investment. Bookmakers know that the more bets you place, the wider you spread your risk and the better your chances of winning. So it is in the record industry. The more records and the greater the catalogue diversity, the better the odds of finding commercially successful recordings. At least that's one theory! The scattergun approach can also send you broke.

Each local subsidiary of the Majors is regarded by its parent company as a potential profit centre. This means they each have to work to annual budgets, long-term marketing plans and follow corporate policies. Corporate policies can be thought of as the skeleton in a body. They give the corporate body a particular shape and simplify inter-company dealings by harmonising contract policies and the like. Each company group has its distinctive corporate manner and methods. The subsidiaries frequently disagree with their head offices and with other subsidiaries, so they are not mere clones of their parent companies.

Despite being answerable to an overseas head office, the Majors' Australian subsidiaries have considerable autonomy. The distance from their head offices may have something to do with this. They still have to comply with group policies and directives but, within that framework, they can largely determine their own methods for achieving acceptable results.

To get an idea of the 'shape' of each of the Majors, visualise a wheel, with the group's head office at the hub. There are other models, but this is the most usual because it is relatively simple to create and administer.

HEAD OFFICE

The head office provides the policy and administration for the group, as well as co-ordinating the various local companies, which are around the rim of the wheel. Joining the hub to the rim are pairs of spokes. One has an arrow pointing to the hub (OUT). The other of the pair has an arrow pointing out from the hub to the subsidiary on the rim (IN). These represent the inter-company rules and the licensing agreements, needed to enable each local company to license its recordings to others within the group. The IN-spoke is the local company's source or repertoire from the hub. The OUT-spoke is the licence by which the hub gets repertoire from the local company. To license their repertoire to another subsidiary, the rights go via its OUT-spoke to the hub and from there to the other local company via that company's IN-spoke. The royalties flow in the opposite direction. Simple.

The head office is also responsible for setting long-term goals and group objectives. It issues policy directives to the local companies, setting the rules by which they may conduct their business. These rules cover most matters relating to all the usual corporate issues such as accounting procedures, staffing policies, contract parameters and the myriad of policy matters which crop up in the operation of any record company. They determine what terms can be accepted in record contracts and which terms are non-negotiable as a matter of company policy. This way the companies will not make contracts inconsistent with their affiliates, but still gives them room to negotiate the most appropriate deals for the local circumstances.

If a proposed deal is inconsistent with these rules, the local company will have to clear it with the head office. Generally, this would only be done for a very important signing because it is both time-consuming and aggravating for the local company's Business Affairs Manager and for the head office.

MULTINATIONAL MAJORS

It can be useful to know something of the history of any record company with which you are dealing. This can give an insight into the way the particular company works, its A&R philosophy, and where the real lines of command lie in its organisation. These are only snapshots, meant to give an indication of where the major players in the Australian industry originate. They are in no particular order.

EMI

The company was originally called Electric & Musical Industries and was founded on the principle that the best way to maximise profits from music was to make both the records and the machines upon which to play them. Vertical Integration was recognised as the way to go, even then.

The company was a pioneer of the 78 rpm shellac record, on which its early fortunes were based.

EMI was one of the main forces in Great Britain from the earliest days of popular music and made a fortune over the years from Cliff Richard and The Shadows. But that looked like small beans in comparison with the money it made from its Beatles catalogue that is still a major part of EMI's justly admired back-catalogue. This catalogue provides the company with a comfortable turnover even in otherwise lean years. It has always had a significant classical repertoire that has also provided a buffer against the bad times.

It had a growth spurt when it bought Virgin Records and Chrysalis Music. Both were very significant catalogue acquisitions. Although it is the only UK-based Major, it has been on the takeover block for several years. In 1999 it seemed that AOL-Time Warner was going to take it over, forming the largest music company in the world, but the deal was eventually sunk by United States and European pro-competition authorities. Indeed, given the anti-competition difficulties, it is unlikely that any of the international Majors could buy it. Certainly, it is most likely to be acquired by a non-music company interested in vertical integration rather than one of the more obvious suspects.

In 2006, EMI announced that it had returned to profit for the first time since 2000 (revenues of US$1.64 billion). It had a very creative approach to commercialising music downloads and reports that 5% of revenue is from downloads (up from zero two years ago.)

EMI has had a strong local roster for many years: Slim Dusty, Air Supply, Little River Band, The Angels, Australian Crawl, the Seekers, Paul Kelly, Missy Higgins, Jet and Kasey Chambers.

EMI has also long been important in Australia and New Zealand as a record manufacturer. It used to make vinyl and now its compact disc plant (a joint venture with Warner Music) continues to be a major supplier to the other Majors, as well as Independents and individuals.

SONY-BMG

Where do you start a story like this? There are beginnings, several disjointed middles and no apparent end. The history of this new company embraces much of the history of recorded music but this is something that is valueless to those concerned with branding and marketing the next teen moment.

One is tempted to observe that this is not the first time that the Germans and the Japanese have joined forces to dominate the world and this time they may succeed. However what is more interesting is the story of how this giant came to be. The historical roots of these companies are neither German nor Japanese: They are American. The confusion arises because companies are a bit like dogs. The name of the dog only tells you about its current owner and nothing about the dog or its breeding. In this case, both Sony and BMG were the result of intense corporate inter-breeding and each of them had hardware invention and manufacturing and media interests in their bloodline.

SONY

Go back to 2004, before Sony Music 'merged' (was bought by) BMG Music. Sony was probably the most successful record company in Australia.

Sony Music was formerly known as CBS Records and was a subsidiary of Columbia Broadcasting System until it was bought by the Japanese electronics company Sony.

Alexander Graham Bell (reputed to be the inventor of the telephone, though some claim it was invented by an Italian inventor from whom Bell appropriated the idea while he was a clerk in the United States Patent Office) started the Columbia Phonograph Company in about 1887.

In 1938, William Paley bought the company and immediately made a small fortune from it. This became a very large fortune in the late 1940s when CBS released its version of the long-play phonograph record and became one of the most aggressive marketers of new acts.

Mitch Miller (once a household name for his television show and 'sing-along' albums, which sold over 20 million copies) was an amazingly successful A&R manager. His work arguably gave CBS its financial basis. Another A&R manager, John Hammond, had been at Columbia since about 1937. He spotted and groomed dozens of artists, including Billie Holiday, Count Basie, Bob Dylan, Aretha Franklin and many, many more.

In Australia, the company started out in 1936 as Featuradio Sound Productions making and distributing 16-inch (40 cm) vinyl disks recording radio serials. In 1938 Featuradio merged with The Australian Record Company and in 1939 started recording and distributing commercial 78 rpm gramophone records (mostly on the Macquarie label and then on Rodeo and Pacific Records). For those interested in trivia, in 1956 when ARC started distributing Columbia records, it did so under the Coronet label (because EMI had registered the Columbia trademark). It used an octagonal record label - the only time such a shape has ever been used on a record! Its early releases tell something of the sociology of the time: the first 78 rpm release on Coronet was 'The Bible Tells Me So' by Mahalia Jackson and the first 12-inch (30 cm) LP was 'Presenting Father MacEwan'.

ARC was acquired by Columbia in the 1960s and was renamed CBS Records in 1977. In 1988, Sony bought CBS Records. For Sony, it meant that it at last had a repertoire source to complement its electrical and consumer products division. Philips was already in that position, and had succeeded with its launch of the new compact disc format. Sony wanted the same advantage for its own new record and video formats. After the purchase, CBS Records was re-named Sony Music Entertainment Australia.

In 2004, the record division of Sony merged with the record division of BMG. This has resulted in the most powerful record company in Australia: John Farnham meets Delta Goodrem.

BMG

BMG Arista/Ariola started as the Victor Talking Machine Company. The company was started in 1901 by Emil Berliner (who invented the flat phonograph record) and Eldridge Johnson. It had early success with recordings by Caruso and Al Jolson and by 1920 it had released 6 million-selling records.

The company was bought by the Radio Corporation of America in 1929. RCA was a major maker and distributor of radio and heavy electronic equipment, so the record operation was a logical extension of its domestic appliance operations. RCA made and installed much of the television station equipment when television was introduced into Australia.

It has always tended to be stronger in the United States than the rest of the world. It has been a major force in Nashville and has had many successes with country music. Its phenomenal success with Elvis Presley has tended to overshadow its earlier successes with artists such as Perry Como, Eartha Kitt and Harry Belafonte, the Isley Brothers, and its more recent A&R activities which have seen the company grow internationally. The Presley deal was the deal of a lifetime. The catalogue was reputed to have cost RCA only $100,000.

In the mid-1980s the company was bought by the remarkable German-based Bertelsmann family conglomerate, which has major interests in printing, transport and manufacturing. After the sale, the company was re-named the Bertelsmann Music Group. Before the merger with Sony, Bertelsmann AG had annual revenues of $17.6 billion and BMG Entertainment accounted for $4.7 billion of that! BMG owned more than 200 labels world-wide, including Arista, RCA and Ariola.

Both internationally and locally, BMG was one of the first of the Majors to invest heavily in on-line technology and was also one of the first to set up a retail download website, GetMusic (although it subsequently sold its interest in GetMusic to UMG.) It continued this commitment when it formed a strategic alliance with Napster, lending the beleaguered company US$60 million when it was in the middle of the infamous Napster litigation. BMG's digital rights management company Digital World Services then started driving the new-look, legal form of Napster. It is continuing its investment in on-line delivery and in 2000 purchased the subscription-based service MyPlay and was a partner in the development of MusicNet with RealNetworks, EMI and AOL Time Warner.

It has a major investment in state-of-the-art printing, artwork, CD and DVD mastering at a complex in western Sydney as well as a one-third share in EDC, a major distribution joint venture with Warners and EMI.

UNIVERSAL

Universal has an important local roster, but for the most part, it gained its strength through company buy-outs, notably MCA and the PolyGram group.

In 1962 the Dutch electrical goods conglomerate, Philips (which had had its own record company since about 1950) started a joint venture with a German company, Siemens AG. Siemens owned the record company Deutsche Grammophon Gesellschaft, which had been in operation since about 1898. They combined their record operations to create PolyGram and Polydor. Its headquarters were in London.

Like the other Majors, PolyGram accelerated its growth in the 1970s by buying various Independents and labels (such as Mercury and the jazz specialist Verve) and entering ventures, such as that with the Robert Stigwood Organisation. In the mid-1970s, it bought the Chappell Music Publishing Group, which it sold to Warners in the mid-1980s.

Around 1989, PolyGram bought two of the largest Independent record companies - A&M Records and Island Records (both previously distributed in Australia by Festival for about 20 years).

PolyGram was traditionally seen as being strongest in Europe, where it dominated for years. Its companies were all active in recording local-language repertoire and its classical labels (DGG, Philips and Decca) were among the most active producers of classical and operatic recordings. In the 1980s there were plans to merge with Warners, which was seen as being strong in North America but not in Europe. A legal challenge in the United States, by other Majors, put a stop to those plans.

The Australian operation began in the early 1960s. In the mid-1970s it bought the Melbourne-based company Astor Records, which had had a strong local roster.

Now PolyGram does not exist. In 1998, Seagram Co. (a large Montreal-based alcohol manufacturer) and owner of Universal Studios, bought PolyGram. This was a very expensive bid (US$10.6 billion) to become one of the biggest entertainment conglomerations. It meant a merger not only of the two companies' record businesses, but also their music publishing, movie and TV businesses. Universal was never considered a Major in the music industry; it certainly is now. It's amazing what you can do with US$10.6 billion!

And then in 2000, the French communications giant Vivendi bought Universal. It paid US$34 billion. Media meets content. It's a rich mix. Actually, it's a dangerous mix. The company lost 23.3 billion euros in 2002. Those who are interested should look at the history of this company through this stage of its history. It shows that chief executives, boardrooms and investors are readily susceptible to testosterone poisoning. Over the next few years, Vivendi shares went through the floor as the scandals and ineptitudes of its top management were publicly exposed. Nevertheless, the Universal Music Group (with international revenue of $7 billion a year) remains the biggest of the Majors. The Universal Music Group had a 24.7% estimated share of global sales in 2004.

WARNER MUSIC

The famous siblings of the film industry, the Warner Brothers, started their own record label in 1958. In 1963, they bought Reprise Records (Frank Sinatra's own label) and combined the two. The record and film operations of the old film studio were sold to Seven Arts in 1966. In 1967, Seven Arts sold the music and record operations to Kinney Corporation (headed by Stephen J. Ross). Warners started operations in Australia in 1970.

The company grew very quickly because it adopted a 'buy and combine' policy and used it to great effect to secure Atlantic Records, Elektra Records, Asylum Records, and several others. In the mid-1980s, it acquired Chappell Music Publishing from Philips, which was a tremendous boost to its music publishing enterprises. Chappell alone controlled over 700,000 titles and many of the great writers of this century.

Warners had early successes from artists such as Trini Lopez, Bill Cosby and Peter, Paul and Mary. It had phenomenal A&R hits in the 1970s, which gave it one of the strongest pop catalogues in the business. It was not afraid to spend big money on artist signings and the policy certainly proved to be correct. Its back-catalogue enabled it to capitalise on the mid-price compact disc boom of the late 1980s.

It has become a hugely successful (and profitable) company, with interlocking interests in electronic entertainment media, computer games, films and film-distribution companies. These gave it a remarkable degree of control over its creative and distribution systems.

Its back catalogue of records generates millions of dollars annually and has enabled it to run an aggressive A&R policy.

In the mid-1980s, Warner and PolyGram were on the brink of merging their operations. Warner's strength in North America would have complemented PolyGram's strength in the rest of the world. It is difficult to imagine the impact such a combination would have had. The rest of the industry, particularly CBS, had no intention of waiting to find out. An anti-trust suit (the United States equivalent of the Trade Practices Act here) was started in the United States Supreme Court and sank the idea. Instead, Warner merged with Time-Life a few years later. Suddenly, one of the world's most powerful music companies had joined forces with one of the great print media organisations. It seemed that this vertical integration would make the company into an unstoppable behemoth. But that was not the end of the story.

On 10 January 2000, Time Warner was itself bought - by an Internet company. Flush with dot com investors' money, AOL bought out one of the largest media companies on earth. At the time, it rocked the industry but AOL Time Warner was the company that everyone was looking to for leadership as to how the old record economy might migrate to the on-line world. In the meantime, before it could solve such a complex problem, it had to first withstand the pressures inevitably caused by the merger of two such different business models and management cultures. It could not. The music arm of the company, the Warner Music Group, was sold off in February 2004 to help pay the debts of the parent company but not even that could stop the eventual split of AOL and Time Warner. In less than five years, the dream of a content-rich online giant had proved unmanageable.

This experiment should be a poignant lesson for others who believe that the integration of content and on-line distribution in the one company is either necessary or even desirable. Theoretically, the merger should have been fabulously successful but perhaps it shows that the human qualities that drive a content business are different from those that drive the on-line distributors. Perhaps it indicates that on-line companies should create partnerships and co-ventures with content providers but should not try to own them: that 'vertical integration' in the on-line environment is not as productive as 'vertical relationships'.

Warner Music Group was bought by a group of investors headed by Edgar Bronfman Jr in February 2004. That year it had revenues of $1.769 billion (down 47.6%). Interestingly, in its third quarter results for 2005, its financial reports showed that digital music sales had increased to 6% of revenues.

In late-2005, Warner bought Festival/Mushroom Records. This company was an amalgamation of two important Australian companies - Festival, founded in 1954 and responsible for the recording careers of many of the great early names of Australia rock 'n roll, and Mushroom which has been the tearaway success of the 80's and 90's. The merger was never a thing of joy and now both companies are no more - another illustration of the continuing concentration of market power.

In Australia, Warner and EMI have a joint venture for pressing records and Warner has large plants in North America and Europe. Initially distributed by CBS, it began its own distribution in 1972, which it handled until it started EDC (a joint venture with Sony and EMI). This is a very interesting example of how major corporations can compete aggressively at both ends of the supply chain (from A&R and recording at the beginning of the chain, through to retail sales at the other end), yet co-operate in the middle sections of the chain (in the manufacture and distribution sections). In a sense, this is a good illustration of the 'core business' of record companies: they are in the A&R business, the record production business and the marketing business. This is where the competition lies. Record companies may, as a matter of convenience, history or philosophy, also own manufacturing, distribution and even record retail businesses - but for most companies, those are just ancillary to the commercial heart of the record company.

LOCAL MAJORS

ABC

The ABC operated symphony orchestras (as part of its Charter) for many years, but only got into popular records in the early 1980s. The ABC has been under increasing pressure to become self-funding for some time, and the record division was a logical step towards that goal. Its distribution has always been undertaken by other Majors.

It has built up a significant catalogue of popular, jazz and classical recordings, and was almost entirely responsible for the development of the country music market in Australia. The success of artists like Lee Kernaghan had every other record company scrambling to sign country artists when for years most of them had ignored (and quietly derided) the genre.

It has complementary print and video divisions that are being included in cross-media marketing campaigns. ABC Music may be the offspring of a bureaucracy, but its people have learned fast and it is an important supporter of local artists and songwriters. It is also one of the major producers of 'spoken word' and children's recordings: Both The Wiggles and Bananas In Pyjamas are huge international businesses but their earlier success was largely due the cross-promotional power of ABC television, ABC Radio, ABC Records, ABC Video and the ABC Shops network. In this respect, the ABC has an unusual capacity to sell its product.

THE INDEPENDENTS

It is very difficult to define exactly what makes an Independent record company. It is a term that encompasses such a diverse range of record companies that it almost defies meaningful definition. It doesn't even mean that it is not part of a Major because many of them are at least funded and distributed by a Major. Indeed, the 1990s is significant for the demise of independence amongst the Independents. Most of the major independents were funded by their Major distributors; they were closer to the street, heard the whispers of talent more quickly, and best of all, saved the Major's A&R Manager from having to go to a lot of late-night gigs. The Majors do not really see most Independents as big threats; they are usually just another A&R source of product.

Nevertheless, Independents go to great lengths to differentiate themselves from the Majors and would be most put-out if mistaken for one. They are generally smaller than the Majors, both in terms of number of personnel and financial size. This is meant to make them lean and agile. That can often be translated as under-funded, under-staffed and, because they so often depend for their survival on the fire in the founder's belly, idiosyncratic.

However, it is true that they are often quicker to recognise and release new musical trends. They can release music before it is sufficiently 'commercial' for the Majors to do so, because the Independents generally have lower overheads. This means they can recover their money on fewer sales - or so the theory goes.

Size is not necessarily conclusive evidence of a record company being an Independent. One successful local Independent worked out of a converted chicken coop at the bottom of the garden. By contrast, Mushroom Records, before it was bought by Festival, was a hybrid Independent because it had many of the characteristics of a Major, yet was so obviously identified with and directed by its founder, Michael Gudinski.

Independents generally have access to artists who would not otherwise be willing to be involved with a Major. Independents certainly tend to appeal to artists who are looking for control over the creative process of making recordings or who feel uncomfortable being seen as part of the mainstream of the industry.

Independents also frequently claim the ability to be able to record artists more cheaply than the Majors can. This very much depends upon the expertise of the Independent's staff. Some Independents go the other way, shunning the 'cheap and cheerful' image, instead trying to create an elite, almost 'boutique', image. Most Majors can confirm from bitter experience that getting an Independent to make a recording is not always cheaper than the Major doing the job itself.

Independents that are not tied to a Major's affiliates can license product to any company outside Australia. Majors' affiliates do not pay advances to others in the group when they license product from them, whereas an independent licensor can generally expect to get an advance as a pre-condition for granting the licence.

Independents have an ambivalent attitude to the Majors. Most would prefer not to have to deal with the Majors, but they recognise that they need the Majors because only the Majors have the financial resources to invest in expensive capital items and infrastructure such as warehouses, pressing plants and distribution networks. In other words, the Majors can get records to retailers. Most companies simply cannot afford these infrastructure costs.

The exception to much of the above discussion is Shock Records. This has quickly become a real force in the Australian industry. It does not get its funding or its distribution from a relationship with a Major. Founded in 1988, primarily as a distributor, it has quickly grown and by 2001 had an annual turnover of approximately $80 million. It is very committed to local music, energetic and ambitious. That's the strength of independents. The fire in the belly.

RECORD DISTRIBUTORS

As already explained, the Majors are responsible for most record distribution in Australia. Nearly all the Independents use the Majors for their distribution. Even the Majors usually have joint ventures to create cost efficiencies. Basically, because of the enormous distances between the main market centres in Australia, distribution is not a highly profitable business. Everybody needs it done but nobody wants to do it.

There are a few independent distributors. They tend to be specialists in a particular niche of the market (such as classical, country, jazz, ambient). Some of the most important distributors, at the moment, are Shock Records Distribution, Shock Dance Distribution, Phantom/MGM Distribution, Rajon, Inertia, Oracle Distribution and, with a fabulous classics and jazz catalogue, Sonart.

TELE-MARKETERS

These are Independents that specialise in selling records in conjunction with television advertising campaigns. Most do not record their own material. They license it from the Majors, Independents and from an international network of repertoire suppliers who specialise in recordings for this segment of the market. The vast majority of the repertoire sold by tele-marketers is from back catalogue and recent-but-not-current hits. All specialise in creating special television advertisements that are placed on national television to coincide with a particular release. Many of the releases are theme compilations using tracks from many sources.

This area of the industry is valuable because it can extend the life of product not otherwise considered suitable for continued top-line release. It is another way of marketing back-catalogue and it has an important place in the Australian industry, not least because it generates such a significant number of sales.

The major tele-marketers have mostly disappeared. Rajon is still in this market but it is an exception. Time Life, too, is active, promoting its music packages through long-form late night television infomercials. However, over the last decade, most of the Majors started to question why they were licensing their back catalogue to other companies when they could do it themselves. They brought the business in-house and most of the tele-marketers died.

BUDGET RECORD COMPANIES

'Budget records' usually get a special mention in recording contracts, so you need to know about them. They are usually defined in terms of their selling price being 50% or 60% of the price of so-called top-line records. For details on how this works, refer to the section on Budget Records in Chapter 23, **Record Royalties**.

All specialise in high-volume, low-margin product (most do both records and videos) sold in the major retailers and non-traditional record outlets such as supermarkets and petrol stations. Most do not create their own repertoire.

Budget companies work in an area of the market that the Majors are reasonably happy to leave alone, because it is so specialised (and often a bit tacky). Some find it easier to license their product to the Budget companies than trying to do it themselves. The Majors prefer to operate in the 'mid-price' area (dearer than budget but rather less than full price) and do so as a way of extending the life of their repertoire.

RECORD CLUBS

These are companies that sell records to subscribers or members. By their nature, they do not carry anything other than mainstream pop and classical repertoire, or (in the case of Readers Digest) their own special compilation packages which are offered to members only. If your record is not already a hit, it probably won't interest any of the record clubs.

They operate by distributing regular catalogues to their members, who place orders and receive their records by mail. The record clubs attract customers from traditional retailers by a combination of convenience (not everyone has a record store close at hand - especially in rural areas) and discounting. The discount is given either by a reduction in the price (although they must compete with the major discount retailers) or by giving 'bonus' records ('Buy five, get one free'). The joining incentive is usually a special deal such as 10 records for $10 or some such. Most use a form of inertia selling. Unless the member advises to the contrary, they will be sent a record and billed in the usual way.

Independent record clubs get their supplies either by manufacturing their own stocks under licence or by buying stocks directly from the record companies. However, given that most of the independent clubs have died, the most clubs these days are operated by record companies as an on-line method of distribution of their own records.

This is an area that is likely to be deeply affected by the Internet. If you are a monthly subscriber to one of the Internet music services, why would you join a 'record' club? Rather than killing the club business, the Internet will reshape and re-energise this part of the business.

17
ANATOMY OF A RECORD COMPANY

IF YOU ARE DEALING WITH RECORD COMPANIES, IT IS IMPORTANT TO UNDERSTAND WHO DOES WHAT IN THE COMPANY. THIS CHAPTER INTRODUCES YOU TO THE CAST, WHO THEY ARE AND WHAT THEY DO.

Every artist needs to understand the way record companies work. Obviously each company has its peculiarities, but a short tour of a hypothetical record company should give you an idea how each part of the company interrelates with the others and how the decision-making process works.

ARTIST AND REPERTOIRE (A&R)

Your first contact with any record company, whether a Major or an Independent, is likely to be the A&R department. This is the department (or, more usually, the person) responsible for finding new talent and administering the recording process. It can be one person or a whole department with specialists for different areas of music.

The A&R manager should be your best friend in the company. This is the person who has to have sufficient faith in you and your work to put his or her name on a memo to the highest people in the company, requesting the funds and the approval to sign you.

A&R managers have frantic but, all too often, short professional lives. They are hired to find 'successful' artists for the company. If success eludes them for too long, people both in and outside the company will start to make loud comments about them having 'cloth ears'. This is the beginning of the end for any A&R manager, unless there is intervening success.

The A&R manager's other qualities are largely irrelevant. Astonishing efficiency and powers of organisation are wonderful, and he or she may never have had a project go over budget, but these abilities are only valued if combined with an ability to pick successful acts and recordings. At the end of the day, if a record proves successful, no one will be particularly bothered whether it was over or under budget. Success tends to cause a kind of collective amnesia about any problems there might have been during the recording process. Of course, unsuccessful recordings are not especially popular in any record company and an A&R manager who is responsible for too many of these is likely to be replaced even if they have been recorded within budget.

Some A&R managers are given great freedom to pursue their particular ideas and preferences. Others may have to work with the knowledge that job reviews happen once a year and that many companies (especially the Majors) lack compassion for those who do not have chart success within 'a reasonable time'. In the early days of the industry, A&R managers could hold the position for years. John Hammond, for example, started his time with A&R for CBS in the United States in about 1937, signed Bob Dylan in 1961 and was still there to sign Bruce Springsteen!

The pressure to deliver hits can mute any A&R manager's sense of adventure when it comes to deciding what music to record. It is hardly surprising that until they have a few 'hits' to their name, most simply cannot take a fiercely independent A&R line.

The turnover of A&R managers led to the development of '**key man**' clauses being put into some artists' contracts. Artists often feel that a particular A&R manager has their interests at heart and will support them and their music against criticism, particularly any from within the company. However, most companies will not, as a matter of corporate policy, allow a 'key man' clause because it gives that individual executive too much power within the company if the artist has success.

Still, although A&R managers can change like the seasons, whoever has the job at the time has to be your best ally in the record company, and must believe in you and your music. The A&R manager has to be your advocate and mentor between the time you sign to the company and when your first record is released. After all, if you are a success, he or she will share in that success. Similarly, the A&R manager will be associated with you if you are not a success. This makes your career a matter of great personal interest to the A&R manager.

BUSINESS AFFAIRS

This is one of the 'backroom' departments of a record company. It is the department that ensures that the company's business policies are maintained, sets the deal terms (with input from the CEO, A&R and Finance) to see that the deal adds up financially, and produces the contracts. The business affairs department is there to protect the company's interests - not yours - and usually has to approve any deal before it can go ahead. Don't underestimate the influence that the business affairs managers have on the deal. They are crucial in the 'behind closed doors' discussions about the deal.

Smaller record companies may not engage a specialist business affairs manager. Companies in this position usually have an accountant to do the necessary financial analysis and then the deal outline will be forwarded to the company's lawyers for drafting and negotiation. Either way, your manager and your lawyer will spend a lot of time communicating with this department.

The communication does not stop when the deal is signed. Inevitably there will be matters needing clarification or disagreements needing business affairs' advice. Some of these issues will be contractual, but many of them will not have been specifically covered in the contract. Many are just day-to-day business dealings that arise in the process of developing and marketing the act.

This department is also usually responsible for administration of the recording contract (e.g. exercising options where applicable) and the associated contracts for video production and the like. An important part of this function is to administer the copyrights, ensure that they are registered where necessary and that they are protected. After all, copyright is a key corporate asset.

ART DEPARTMENT

Whether you have your record cover artwork created yourself or you have the record company do it for you, you will deal with the art department. This department designs record and promotional packaging.

When the designs are done outside the company, the art department will usually oversee it being put into production. Record packaging is a specialised area of the graphic arts and you ignore the art department's advice at your peril. The people there may not always be right, but they know what can and cannot be put into production at a reasonable cost and what designs are likely to be successful.

Obviously visual impact is important in the overall marketing of your records. This is why artistic control of packaging is so often an area of heated negotiation when contracts are being worked out. Whether you retain final say regarding the design of your record packaging or have agreed to let the record company do the design work for you:

(i) check your contract to make sure that you are familiar with what amounts to non-standard packaging, as this may have an impact on your royalties; and

(ii) consult with the art department before the designing starts, to give them a definite idea of your wishes. They may not always agree with you, but you can find out what is possible and what is expensive (e.g. gold lettering, embossing, extra fold-out pages in booklets and cassette sleeves). It will also help them co-ordinate the other materials that they will no doubt have to create and produce to promote your records.

If you are having the work done yourself, by an independent artist, make sure you acquire the copyright in the artwork so that you can use the artwork for additional purposes such as merchandising. You should also insist that the artist discusses the technical aspects of the work with the record company's art department. This can help avoid costly printing specifications, such as unusual colours, which can cause production costs to escalate. These problems can be the genesis of disagreements with the record company, but are easily avoided.

PRODUCTION DEPARTMENT AND STOCK CONTROL

These are separate departments within the Majors but their roles are related. The production department (the name varies from company to company) is responsible for getting records made and put into stock. It is involved in:

- receiving the record master tapes and sending them to the record manufacturer;
- ordering initial quantities, usually as requested by the Marketing manager or (in the case of recordings obtained from third parties or affiliated labels) the label manager;
- co-ordinating manufacture of record packaging, in consultation with the art department;
- co-ordinating manufacture of advertising materials such as posters, special record bins and other promotional materials to be put into record shops as 'point of sale' advertising;
- ensuring the finished records (in all formats) are manufactured and in the record company's warehouse by the release date; and
- ordering duplicates of promotional clips, to be sent to television stations and as otherwise needed by the promotions department.

Stock control involves monitoring the outward and inward (i.e. new stock and returns from retailers) flow of records so that there are just enough records in stock at any one time to meet demand. This involves a lot of educated guesswork and daily sales analysis. At one time or another, many artists will hear the words 'out of stock' in relation to their records.

While a record is out of stock, there are no copies in the warehouse to meet orders placed by retailers. This may be due to unforeseen demand or perhaps because of delays by the manufacturer in delivering replacement stocks. Sometimes it is just oversight (human error). Whatever the reason, it has to be remedied without delay, especially if the release coincides with a major promotional campaign or a tour by the artist.

MARKETING AND PROMOTIONS DEPARTMENT

The marketing and promotions department often is the department with the highest profile inside and outside the record company. In many ways, it is the glamour area of the business and the one most people first think of when the record industry is mentioned.

This is the department responsible for advertising you and your records. Its staff is there to convince the public that owning your records is the most important thing in the world. Promotions departments have to develop and implement advertising plans for your records and do it within a budget. Simultaneously, they are promoting all the other records being released by the company. Decisions as to which records are given priority are usually made after the A&R and the marketing and promotions departments have consulted, though it can be as a result of a directive from the highest levels in the company. If a major international artist has a new release, or is touring, there is no question which recordings will get top priority.

If your records are made a company priority, then your chances of success are increased. Human nature being as it is, despite directives, if the people in the promotions department like your records, they may unofficially become a priority, simply because of enthusiasm for the product. If, however, you make yourself unpopular (being rude, demanding, or unreliable are all sure-fire ways), you may find that your records stop being priorities. They may slip to the bottom of the pile of work the promotions department has to do.

This is not to suggest you should become a fawning sycophant. Just remember the two-way nature of the interrelationship between you and the record company.

SALES REPRESENTATIVES

The Majors all employ sales representatives who liase with major customers. Usually, each has a designated area and visits retailers in that area, showing new releases and taking orders, installing in-store promotional materials, checking the stores' stock to see if any titles are low or unfavourably displayed (or are in the wrong area of the store) and dealing with requests for returns of faulty or excess stock to the warehouse. Representatives do not usually visit retailers who order less than a certain amount of stock each month.

The sales representatives are the personal connection between retailers and the companies. They try to induce retailers to stock more product, while the retailers try to keep stocks to the minimum they need to satisfy demand. Record industry lore says that representatives from companies with hits are more welcome than those from companies going through a lean time. This may be the origin of the industry adage that when a company is 'on a roll', with unusually strong chart success, the success will help sell the rest of its catalogue.

As has happened in so many other areas of business, many companies are consolidating and rationalising their sales representatives and are using call centres to undertake some of these functions.

ORDERS AND WAREHOUSE

The Majors have their own departments where telephone operators take orders and transmit them to the warehouse. The representatives also place their orders here. Independents who are distributed by the Majors use their distributor's order system too.

As far as the retailer is concerned, all they need to know is from whom they can order the particular recording. The Majors, until a few years ago, each put out new release sheets and catalogues but this was superseded by the Australian Record Industry Catalogue in which all the ARIA members now list new releases and back catalogue. Most retailers subscribe to this, and use it when ordering both new releases and back catalogue.

The orders are transmitted to the warehouse, which then assembles the order, packs it and dispatches it to the retailer. The warehouse also usually receives and processes returns of stocks from retailers.

The greatest change that we have seen in the last few years has been the computerisation of catalogue and ordering services. The last five years has seen an explosion of B2B (business to business) uses of the Internet and the ordering process is one that is ideally suited to this technology. Already we have seen huge savings in time and administrative expense through on-line ordering and reporting, and this trend will increase.

ACCOUNTS AND ROYALTY ACCOUNTS

The accounts department bills the retailers and collects payment for sales. Its data comes from the warehouse's records which should, after deducting returns from the total number of units shipped from the warehouse, give the net sales figure for each record in the catalogue.

The accounts department's figures for sales are used by the royalty accounts department when calculating the royalties due to artists and licensors, and also the appropriate mechanical copyright royalties.

ON-LINE

The only new department to have been added to record companies for years is the team that has responsibility for devising and implementing the company's on-line strategy. Some companies don't separate this function into a separate management centre; others do. Moving the company from traditional distribution methods to a digital platform, is something that all companies are having to face. Some leave primary responsibility for planning to their overseas head office, but the wise ones know that there are no right answers at the moment and that what may seem sensible in New York or London is not necessarily an appropriate solution in Sydney or Wellington. Like it or not, it is in the hands of this department that the future shape and indeed the very existence of the record company rests.

18
CHOOSING A RECORD COMPANY

WHICH RECORD COMPANY SHOULD YOU CHOOSE?
NOT MANY MUSICIANS HAVE THE LUXURY OF CHOICE.
STILL, THERE IS NO POINT SIGNING WITH A COMPANY
MERELY BECAUSE THEY ARE THE ONLY ONE THAT
HAS OFFERED YOU A DEAL SO FAR. GIVEN THAT
RECORD CONTRACTS ARE VERY LONG-TERM
RELATIONSHIPS, YOU NEED TO BE VERY CAREFUL
ABOUT YOUR CHOICE. IF YOU MAKE A DECISION IN
HASTE, YOU WILL HAVE YEARS TO REGRET IT.

THE ARTIST ROSTER

Record companies all tend to have particular strengths in their catalogues and artist rosters. It is worthwhile having a good look at the ARIA Catalogue (most record shops have them), the company website and the *Australasia Music Industry Directory*, to see in which areas they seem to be strongest. If you are a Country act, there's not much point putting your efforts into getting a deal with a company that clearly is happiest working with jazz or dance.

WHO'S HOT

It seems each of the Majors has a period (sometimes of years) when it dominates the charts around the world. Success comes in cycles in the record industry. The old adage 'success makes success' seems to apply. A strong record company seems to have a run of hits.

This may be because the company has plenty of cash to spend, the staff may be buoyant and work that little bit harder, or maybe retailers just relax a bit when the sales representative of the company with the current hits comes in to take re-orders for existing releases and sell other titles.

Whatever it is, a 'hot' record company is the place everyone wants to be. Unfortunately, this may mean you will find it harder than ever to get to the

A&R manager. On the other hand, a record company that is experiencing a run of success tends to be more acquisitive, so it can be a good time for new artists, especially if they are in the same genre as the company's hottest artist.

WHO'S THE BEST AT PROMOTING RECORDS?

This is hard to answer, unless you know someone who can give you an educated appraisal. Many people have an opinion on the subject and will share it with you if you ask. You should be able to make a preliminary judgment by looking at the music press and looking (and asking) in record shops, to see which artists have the most in-store advertisements and support from their companies. Television advertising is not, of itself, especially indicative unless it is apparent the record company does it more often, or better, than the opposition.

Every record company claims to be the best marketer, but the fact is they can't all be the best at all times or even for all types of music or artists. This is where you need to do some asking around. Talk to artists' managers, other artists and even record company representatives.

Some companies have particular strengths, or preferences for particular types of promotion. Some will use large-scale television campaigns more readily than others. Some have strong contacts with the electronic media. Some have unusually creative or adventurous promotions managers, who will try new or innovative campaigns. Most promotions managers got their skills by doing the job. They all have particular favourites and prejudices that influence their decisions.

When you are talking seriously to a company about a record deal, there is no substitute for questioning the executives closely about their promotion methods, budgets and policies. This way, you have a chance of getting an idea of their usual methods and of their intentions in relation to your records. It is very difficult to get any commitments to promotional expenditure, but ask the right questions early on.

CAN I WORK WITH THEM?

Signing a record contract is only the start of your relationship with a record company.

Record contracts usually require the company to commit to spending a lot of cash in the recording process, before they even see the outcome. Until the final recording has been made and auditioned, no one can have any basis for estimating (a euphemism for guessing) potential sales. Even when the artist has a history of record releases, the guesses are just that - guesses.

This is when tempers fray. Having a solid relationship with the people with whom you have to deal every day can make the difference between a disaster and a successful relationship. If, after early meetings with a record company, you find you have an urge to throttle the executive who is sitting across the table from you, think carefully about whether you should do the deal. If you think you can barely keep your hands off their neck at this stage, think how much worse that urge will be when things get tough!

WHAT DO I WANT MY RECORD COMPANY TO DO?

Ask yourself: 'What exactly do I want my record company to do for me?'. Formulate your expectations in advance, so you can discuss them with your lawyer and your management. They will need this information for the contract negotiations.

If you can't answer this question, that's fine - it just means you need to improve your knowledge of what record companies can and should do. That's one of the objectives of this book.

WHO'S GIVING THE BEST DEALS?

This is hard to determine. Record companies jealously guard the details of their deals. They would all love to know what royalties and funding have been agreed by their competitors for their major acts. Rumours always spread after a major deal is done but deal points will never be revealed except in the witness box. Besides, the best deal for one artist may be totally inappropriate for another.

Basically, the people best placed to know this, are those who regularly negotiate deals with the record companies - the top managers and music lawyers. They may not be at liberty (or willing) to tell you details of specific deals, but they can usually tell you who is offering the best royalty rates, advances and general conditions.

Talk to other artists too. Usually someone will know someone who did a deal with this or that record company. Bad deals tend to be talked about. The true figures of a good deal are rarely revealed. Smart artists know that the Taxation Office routinely scans the papers, to see who is getting deals and what they are getting paid.

Sometimes, people will talk in awed tones of a million dollar deal. Don't get too excited. They may have got their figure by adding up all the recording budgets if all the options were exercised. This is a very different thing from the artist actually getting a million dollars in the hand. Recording budgets are just expense items. True artist advances are another story altogether.

19
GETTING A RECORD CONTRACT

**THERE IS NO EASY WAY TO GET A RECORD DEAL.
THERE ARE RIGHT WAYS TO DO THINGS AND WRONG
WAYS. EVEN THE WRONG WAYS CAN TURN OUT RIGHT
– IF YOU ARE LUCKY. THIS CHAPTER IS ABOUT HOW
TO IMPROVE YOUR CHANCES OF GETTING LUCKY.**

DREAMS OF INSTANT SUCCESS

Most performers dream of being plucked from obscurity to become an overnight success. For the majority of artists, a record contract is the pay-off for years of focus and effort.

Don't feel depressed because you have been trying hard for so long, but have not been signed. There are precious few overnight successes. Behind every successful artist are years of often disappointing work, but it's the thought that 'It Just Might Happen' that keeps people going. Elton John started as a tea-boy at Dick James Music. INXS spent many, many years on the road, playing hundreds of minor venues, before they signed a record contract. Be patient. The Police were rejected by just about every record company in England ('Roxanne' was reputed to be the demo) before finally getting a deal with A&M. One of the Beatles' earliest recordings was as backing band to a solo act who the record company thought was the real talent. The history of the industry is full of such stories. That's what makes it so fascinating. It is also what makes it addictive: intermittent reinforcement is a powerful agent in moulding behaviour. It's what gets otherwise sensible people to spend thousands of dollars on poker machines, horse races and lottery tickets; it helps them look for another partner after a break-up; it sends laboratory mice in the Skinner Box mad; it keeps musicians believing that they can achieve stardom.

CREATING AWARENESS OF YOUR MUSIC

You have to create awareness of and interest in you and your music. A&R managers are flooded with offers from artists of all kinds - from mainstream pop to buskers with ambitions. They all want recording deals and they all believe they deserve a break ahead of everyone else. This tends to make A&R managers pretty cynical - they have to be to survive the onslaught.

More importantly, A&R managers never forget that they have budgets to meet and that they have finite resources. They have to be selective in choosing the artists upon whom they will spend the company's time and money.

You have to win the A&R people over, or you have to create so much interest in your music and your personality that you cannot be ignored. That said, it helps to know someone, who knows someone, who knows ...

KNOWING SOMEONE

There is no doubt that knowing well-connected people can help you get a record deal, but that's no different from any other line of business.

A record deal needs trust on both sides. Record companies like to know with whom they are dealing. Negotiations are likely to be quicker (though not necessarily any more favourable in terms of the actual deal points) if you are introduced by someone known to, and trusted by, people in the record company.

This is when an active publisher can be invaluable. A publisher's support can sometimes convince a record company to do a deal that it might not otherwise do, because it can see there is someone (the publisher) who might be able to help contribute to certain costs (e.g. touring or publicity) and who is likely to help secure overseas releases.

Experienced managers and music lawyers can also be valuable in this area. They know most of the people and the companies and are aware of each company's strengths, weaknesses, interests and priorities.

Artists without the help of an 'insider' have to work that much harder to be recognised and remembered by the record company's people. This is not to say that talented acts with strong demos will not get a break unless they are introduced by someone who knows someone in the record company. However, it is only human nature that people will naturally listen to people they already know and whose judgment they trust. Never forget - all the talk about 'the record company' obscures the fact that all the decisions made by the record company are made by people.

Most new acts, however, do not have top management, nor do they have the funds needed to mount publicity campaigns or hire top entertainment lawyers. They have to use other, admittedly rather less romantic, methods that may seem somewhat mundane. But they still work.

LIVE WORK

The Australian record industry seems to place unusually high emphasis on 'live' work. It is generally accepted by executives as a self-evident truth that all artists have to do live work to succeed. Lots of it. The more the better. The theory has much to commend it. Anyone who is constantly in front of the public has a better chance of winning over new fans, consolidating support from existing ones, and honing essential performing skills. Record companies tend to avoid acts that won't tour.

Of course, some acts are signed even if they won't or can't tour. Stars of television soaps can always be signed on the strength of their television appearances, which give them a ready-made vehicle for promotion. They do not need to tour to get essential publicity. The same goes for any well-known personality who gets media attention.

Although no musician enjoys the endless grind, live performances do give you the opportunity to you're your performance skills. Not only does the music have to be sensational, so too does your stagecraft. (One of the humbling tests of your stagecraft is to hire a room with a full-wall mirror, play a set, and see for yourself what you look like to your audience. If it looks ordinary to you, it is going to look extremely ordinary to any A&R guy who has four more bands to see that week and who would rather be at home with his family.)

Live work also gives you the opportunity to create a loyal group of followers. They also give the A&R scouts a chance to see if the crowds react well to your act and your music. A&R managers want to see a host of ecstatic fans - it makes their decision relatively easy and they can report it when they apply for approval to offer you a record deal.

A&R managers take a chance whenever they offer a recording deal - they are putting their reputation and their jobs right on the line. Being only human, they prefer safe(ish) bets to long shots.

The ideal situation is for more than one A&R manager to be hot on your trail. A&R managers tend to react a little oddly when other A&R managers are in the vicinity. Imagine fish in a feeding-frenzy and you will get the general idea of what can happen if several record companies are competing to sign the same act. If the word gets out that you are hot ('They must be hot. Why else would so many A&R managers be at their gigs?') there is a chance of a bidding war erupting. This can be an exhilarating but risky time for artists. Egos can become dangerously inflated and unrealistic expectations can make it difficult to evaluate offers properly. Keeping a sense of proportion can be very difficult with all that attention.

For most artists, though, the usual path to a recording contract involves a combination of talent, hard work and cunning.

PUBLICITY STUNTS

You can try donning a chicken-suit and standing on the A&R manager's desk while singing to a ghetto blaster, but you are likely to be thrown out by a security guard. On the other hand, good promotions people (and managers) can dream up ideas that, if done properly, will make it impossible to ignore your work. (Mind you, given some of the stunts that record companies get up to for record promotions, unless the stunt is a real stinker with no style, you will almost always get grudging admiration for having a go - though you may be dismissed as a flake, which can be a disadvantage.) Making yourself stand out from the crowd is not all that easy, if you also want to retain your dignity.

Anyone can wear funny hats (remember Devo?) but that isn't everyone's idea of a good career move. Besides, if it really worked, everyone would do it.

Several years ago, an artist blitzed the Sydney metropolitan area's power poles with posters 'X is coming'. It was one of the great teaser campaigns. It seemed everyone in the record industry saw the posters and their curiosity was aroused because no-one knew the artist or where he came from. His management was able to use the campaign to get appointments with the A&R managers and to get the A&R people to listen to the demos. Regrettably, there was no happy ending. The campaign was the artist's career high point - no contract resulted, but the campaign was remembered long after everyone had forgotten who was supposed to be coming.

Any stunt has to match your music and image. There is no point having an inappropriate campaign that could make the A&R managers categorise you and your music before they have even heard it. Initial impressions are hard to shift from peoples' minds. It can be counter-productive to have a huge fanfare, if it creates great expectations that cannot be met in real life.

IMAGE

You need to create and develop a professional image. Quality photographs and biographies are invaluable when making a pitch to record companies. If you don't have any contacts in the promotions business, speak to a few managers and other acts. Most will have a favourite photographer and names of people who specialise in creating 'images' or distinctive styles for artists. Some video clip makers are terrific at this, too.

Your primary aim is to get people's attention. Tiny Tim became an international star after he appeared on 'Laugh In'. Cher starred in a highly successful variety program on United States television and went on to attract media attention with a combination of unusual clothes and unlikely boyfriends. For Kylie Minogue, it was 'Neighbours'. Major stars all have an 'image' of some kind. Acquiring an image is not necessarily a compromise of your artistic abilities. It's giving the public what they want - someone to relate to in some way.

People don't just buy a record because they like the sound. The record can be a way of getting a piece of a hero to take home.

DEMOS

Demonstration CDs (demos) are the usual way of introducing your music to A&R managers.

Demos can be rough, lap-top recordings or elaborate productions (approaching release quality) recorded and mixed in a studio. The purpose is always the same - to enable your music to be heard and evaluated.

The better the demo, the less there is to distract from the performance and the songs. A&R managers often hear the excuse: 'Of course the song would sound different (read 'better') if it was mixed/properly recorded/the lead singer didn't have a cold', etc. A&R managers will always say they can hear a good act and song, no matter how bad the demo, but why risk it? If you have to apologise for the quality, stay at home.

Spend as much as you dare on recording demos that are truly representative of your abilities. Shop for deals and rates. Recording studios are a lot cheaper in the unpopular 'midnight to dawn' hours and this can significantly reduce your costs and help you afford better quality recordings. Watch out for the 'add-on' costs of outboard gear, which can quickly inflate a budget. Wherever possible, try to get experienced help in mixing and production. An experienced friend is fine. Most studios have a resident engineer you can hire. You need someone who can help get the best sound recorded in the shortest possible time.

If you have a publisher, you can try to get funds to help produce high-quality demos. Your publisher will be just as keen as you are for you to get a record contract and will generally see this kind of expense as an investment, rather like pump-priming.

The A&R manager's assessment of an artist's ability and potential is made on a range of considerations. The demo may well be the most important. Fortunately, if the material is strong enough, a merely 'adequate' demo is unlikely to be fatal to your chances. On the other hand, a fabulous demo might just save an otherwise ordinary performance or song.

If your demo is not the very best you can do, it doesn't fairly reflect your talent. Don't present a demo unless it's your best shot. There can be no excuses! None. Understand? None.

Once the recording is as good as you can make it, remember that how you present your demo can be almost as important as what it sounds like. If it never gets played, it's a wasted effort. Make sure it is presented in a way that invites a listen. You are selling something. Advertising agencies know how important it is to present any product properly. Record companies spend thousands of dollars creating visually attractive packaging for their records. You should do the same, within the limits of your budget.

Imagine yourself in the A&R manager's shoes. The morning's mail contains a dozen demos. You've had a rough time the night before and you are in no mood to listen to anything. Ask yourself: why should a jaded A&R manager listen to your demo rather than one of the others on his or her desk? Think about what you can include in the package.

- What will attract attention to it? What is there about it that encourages someone to open it?
- Does it have a visual appeal?
- Is there a useful biography included? (Do not send pages of gushing prose. That will almost certainly guarantee that your tape will land in the bin before any of the others.)
- Is there a photo of the artist included in the package?
- Is there a clip?

Make sure the demo disc and the crystal box are both clearly marked with a contact name, phone number and copyright line. It's amazing how many demos arrive without basic information, get separated from their boxes and remain anonymous forever. All because no-one thought to put a name and phone number on it.

The post office provides a terrific service but it is the least desirable means of delivering your demo to a record company. Material delivered by mail is the last to get listened to.

Some A&R managers say they are just too busy to listen to demos! What are they there for? You might well ask. The fact is, they are busy and any tapes that arrived in the morning post will probably go on the pile of demos received the day before, unless there is something to attract the A&R manager's attention.

There is probably no better way to get heard than to have the demo supplied by someone, preferably someone the A&R manager knows already. Common conduits include well-connected managers or one of the top music lawyers. The manager is unlikely to do it for you unless he or she is going to get a percentage. The lawyer will want a fee for 'deal shopping' because it takes more time than you might expect - especially to do a good job. The A&R managers know that top managers and lawyers will only put their reputations on the line in this way if they have listened to the demo and believe it has credibility. It's like sending your demo with a good reference.

Selecting which songs to use in the demo needs careful thought. Some people believe that every demo should include at least one cover of a well-known song. There is something to be said for this - it removes one variable in that there is one less thing to distract the A&R manager. A familiar song will leave the listener free to concentrate on the performance itself. It also provides a kind of mental yardstick against which to compare your version with the earlier, more familiar, version.

Don't try to prove that your interests and talents span all musical styles. Make the demo concise. Don't fill a CD! Two or three songs, well recorded and performed, will have more impact than fifteen songs indifferently presented. If the A&R manager is interested, you'll get plenty of chances to audition your other material. And put your best track first: first impressions are important.

Some acts are fortunate enough to be able to pay for fully produced records to be pressed from their masters. This is usually only possible with relatively expensive recordings. There are exceptions though. For example, Michelle Shocked made a 'live' recording for around $10 - recorded outdoors, on a portable tape machine beside a campfire. An Independent record company released the recording 'as it was' and a Major later released it and it sold well in most major markets.

TALENT SHOWS

In television shows, others control the performance. There is always the risk that a bad performance will be seen (and remembered!) by thousands.

You have to decide whether the show is a genuine showcase for talent or a thinly disguised freak show. If it is a legitimate showcase, it might be worth a shot. Avoid freak shows if you want to be taken seriously. A&R managers are unlikely to be impressed by a competition win unless the show has credibility in the industry. There are talent shows, sponsored by non-record businesses (e.g. brewers and the like), that are held in significant venues. They can attract a good deal of attention and crowds. Ask around, to see if past winners have benefited or suffered from their win.

Finally, when you're looking for a record contract, remember that there are no rules. The competition is tough. You have to be dedicated, talented and lucky (but not necessarily in that order).

STARTING NEGOTIATIONS

Assuming you have an A&R manager's interest, you or your manager will need to have a few meetings to get to know each other better. These tend to be informal ('let's do lunch'), but are no less important for that.

For the relationship to work properly, the A&R manager has to (in rough order of priority):
- Believe in your ability to succeed;
- Trust you and your management;
- Believe that he or she can work well with you;

- Be able to give proof to others in the company of your commitment to the project; and
- Believe you can deliver the recordings on time and within budget.

The A&R manager is going to be looking hard at you, and your management, for signs of the attributes listed above. This may take quite a long time, or it may be almost immediate. There is no way of anticipating whether the mixture of artist and A&R manager will work or not.

If the A&R manager sees the right signs, the next stage is to talk about deals. It is a critical time, as you and the A&R manager ascertain exactly what each of you are looking for from the relationship and what each has to offer to the other to make it successful. You must use this time to find out as much as you can about the company and how its policies are likely to affect you and your records. For example:

- A&R policies and directions in the long and short term;
- Long-term plans in terms of its direction and expansion;
- Personnel and the frequency of changes;
- Budgets and the company's willingness to support developing artists;
- Promotions policies (i.e. does it readily use television advertising, press or whatever);
- The company's internal structure (i.e. who answers to whom);
- The company's policies for exploitation of repertoire overseas (i.e. timing of servicing its associates with samples, how soon releases can be procured, what efforts are made to secure overseas release);
- The company's attitude to tour support;
- How exactly it gets its records distributed here and overseas;
- Accounting procedures;
- The company's policies in relation to old repertoire (e.g. back catalogue sales and artist's consents for non-usual use of recordings).

If the initial meetings go well, the A&R manager is likely to put a proposal to you. At this stage of play, you are likely to be introduced to the company's lawyer, or (in the case of the larger record companies) their business affairs department. This is the gateway to the next stage of your career.

20
RECORD CONTRACTS

**THIS CHAPTER LOOKS AT THE FORM OF RECORD
CONTRACTS AND THEIR KEY ISSUES AND TERMS.
THESE INCLUDE DURATION, OPTIONS, TERRITORY,
DELIVERY AND RELEASE COMMITMENTS, FUNDING,
OWNERSHIP, ARTISTIC CONTROL, TERMINATION AND
SO ON. THE GENERAL ISSUES DISCUSSED ARE
COMMON TO MOST RECORD DEALS.**

The formal start of your relationship with your record company is the signing of the record contract. The contract is always long. It is always expensive to negotiate. Then, oddly, once it is signed, neither party refers to it – until there is a problem.

To most people, a contract means a thick bundle of closely typed documents with fine print and no pictures. This is an accurate description of most recording contracts but they vary greatly in size, style and content, from company to company.

There is really no such thing as a standard-form recording contract. Each company's corporate policies determine the form and content of that company's recording contracts. That said, even though the form and content changes from company to company and from contract to contract within any given company, there are certain basics that have to appear in all recording contracts. Remember that many clauses affect others in the contract and it would be misleading to think that any one part can be properly understood in isolation from the others.

An observation about contracts generally: when negotiations start getting technical, or there are real sticking points on issues, you may hear someone say, "Don't worry about that clause. The company takes no notice of that clause anyway". If that were really true, the clause wouldn't be in the draft. It is there for a reason. The person with whom you are negotiating may be a lovely, reasonable person. Their successor may be the complete opposite. Don't ever assume that any particular term of the contract will not be applied should the circumstances make it relevant. There may be a lot of money at stake. The contract is the basic mechanism regulating your relationship with the company. Either side is entitled to, and usually will, use everything available to it under the contract when the going gets tough.

Always assume that the terms of the contract you eventually sign, are the exact terms by which you must operate.

WHY HAVE A RECORD CONTRACT?

All record companies work on the assumption that their prospective artists will be successful. If they thought otherwise, they would not do deals. Similarly, artists need to feel confident that they will have a productive relationship with the record company and its personnel over an extended period. If either has serious doubt, they should not agree to the long-term commitments usually required as a part of most record contracts. The parties create the recording contract with the expectation that it will form the basis of a long-term relationship. Getting it right the first time is usually better than the trials of re-negotiation.

The contract is the framework of the relationship. The participants create it in advance, trying to ascertain each other's expectations and anticipate what each other's actions and reactions will be in particular circumstances. The old game of 'What if ...?' has to be played so they can establish acceptable responses to anticipated situations. Without a contract, neither the company nor the artist could feel secure when making the kind of commitments needed to create and market recordings.

THE FORM OF THE RECORD CONTRACT
ORAL AGREEMENTS

Remember that a contract does not actually have to be in writing to be binding. The law recognises that people sometimes create a contract without ever putting it on paper. As long as there is an intention to create a set of mutually binding obligations, and there is the necessary transfer of value in return for a promise, a court may infer a contract by looking at the parties' actions, their conversations and any correspondence between them.

In the absence of anything else to go on, the courts have to rely on the respective parties' testimony as to what was agreed (these versions rarely coincide) and then imply other terms, on the assumption that the parties would have agreed certain things, had they actually turned their minds to the problem. It is not surprising that sometimes the end result of this process does not resemble the parties' actual intentions.

It should be obvious that this situation is unsatisfactory to all concerned and is to be avoided if at all possible. Be aware of the risks, and be suitably cautious. Do not be afraid of documents. Do not be afraid of the word 'contract'. Contracts are facts of life and are there to be used, but you must understand the rules.

WRITTEN CONTRACTS
INFORMAL DEAL MEMOS
Once preliminary negotiations are over (and assuming you and the record company agree on the basic points of the proposed deal) the record company usually will send you either a letter setting out its offer, or a draft contract.

Usually, these deal offers are headed 'Subject to Contract' or words to that effect. This is an important phrase. It means that, even though the document may be called an 'offer', it is not intended to be binding on either party. This allows the parties to get on with negotiations about the details of the deal, without actually committing either party to it. This also means you would be unwise, in the extreme, if you were to make commitments or incur any liabilities in anticipation of concluding the deal. At this stage, all you have are pieces of paper and a warm inner glow. There is no binding contract – yet.

HEADS OF AGREEMENT
In exceptional circumstances – for example, to speed up a contract when time is short – record companies may be willing to conclude a deal based upon a 'Heads of Agreement'. This is a short-form contract, containing the basic terms of agreement but omitting most of the precise drafting and technical clauses that make up so much of long-form contracts. Heads of Agreement have their place, but are no substitute for a full-length contract. Just because they are shorter than a full-length contract does not make them any less binding – just less certain. If a dispute did arise, a court may have to infer terms not actually written in the document, which can lead to unintended and unsatisfactory results for both parties.

INDUCEMENT LETTERS
Many artists use a company structure through which they run all their music business activities. Such companies are often referred to as 'loan out' or 'service' companies because when they enter contracts they provide (or loan) the services of the relevant individual.

The use of service companies is considered in Chapter 2, **Business Structures**. If you are using a service company, then it will be the party contracting with the record company. You will be contracting with your service company to provide the services it needs to carry out its agreement with the record or publishing company. It is the service company which promises to deliver your services as specified in the contract.

Generally, record and publishing companies will prefer to contract directly with you. However, the Majors are more familiar with the use of service companies than most Independents.

Most Majors will be reasonably willing to co-operate, although they will need to be satisfied that your service company can actually deliver what it promises (i.e. your exclusive services). Also, unless they take certain precautions, they could be left in a situation where you could hide behind the service company to get out of your obligations under the agreement. To deal with this, whenever a service company is involved, record companies will insist on you signing an inducement letter.

Inducement letters are usually drafted in the form of a brief agreement (or a letter), cross-referenced to the recording contract and are signed by each member of the band. They contain various terms that provide that, even though the record company is contracting with a service company, if it doesn't fulfil its obligations, you will personally deliver the record company everything the service company had promised to deliver. If you don't, you will be personally liable and may be sued.

KEY ISSUES IN RECORDING CONTRACTS

The following sections look at the basic concepts and clauses common to all recording contracts. There are many variables and special terms in each contract, and it is not possible to deal with all of them here. (The particular problems or clauses relating to group deals, master lease deals and label deals, all have specific chapters. Publishing and distribution deals are different again and they have a specific chapter too.)

The expression 'the record company' will be used here to refer to the party securing your services under the recording contract, even though that person might not technically be a company.

Just remember that there is a reason behind each clause. Record contracts are like a coded history of the record business – they reflect bitter experience. Take for example the seemingly strange and tortuous clauses that provide that the artist cannot deliver more than a particular number of masters within a nominated period. They seem to be lawyer over-kill but they came about when Frank Zappa signed a seven album deal and the next day delivered seven albums to his record company. It didn't take long for the story to get around and ever since, all record companies include a clause that ensures that they won't be taken for a similar ride.

CONTRACT FOR SERVICES

Recording contracts are contracts for personal services. They are about a person or several people providing special skills at agreed times and places to make master recordings and videos, participate in promotional photo sessions, attend press conferences and generally do what is needed to make and sell records.

Recording contracts are not employment contracts. The artist is not an employee. In fact, most record companies are so keen to avoid that situation that they include a specific clause in their contracts to the effect that the artist is an 'independent contractor' and not an employee. Oddly enough, those same contracts sometimes then go on to say that the recordings are 'works for hire' which is an American legal term to indicate that the artist is an employee. That term does not apply in Australian copyright law, but it does show the internal contradictions that some contracts contain. The lawyer's job (or at least one of them) is to remove those that are harmful to the client's interests.

No matter what is written in the recording contract, some industrial laws may still apply to your contract, even though those laws are meant to apply to employees.

Most States have legislation such as the Contracts Review Act (NSW) which provide remedies for harsh and unfair contracts. The branch of law known as Equity (which is a very old concept, all about fairness rather than technicalities) has provided some protection in the past, but putting it into the statute books increased awareness of the remedy and predictability of the law.

Remember, record contracts are all about artists providing their services to someone else, perhaps for a long time, in a complex industry. That is why the contracts are so detailed.

EXCLUSIVITY

Virtually all recording contracts will require you, as the artist, to deliver your services exclusively to the record company for the duration of the contract.

This means that the record company may apply to the courts to prevent anyone else making recordings of 'its' artist (i.e. you) for as long as the contract is in force. Your record company could also apply for court orders, preventing anyone else from recording your performances or otherwise using your services when these have already been granted exclusively to your record company. If infringing records are made with your co-operation, your record company may also seek damages from you as well as from whoever made the recording.

THE ARTIST'S 'SERVICES'

The contract sets out exactly which of your services as an artist will be exclusive to the record company. Some companies are quite modest in their demands. They restrict their claims to just making sound recordings and video clips. Others go for the works. The wording varies from contract to contract, depending upon what the contract is meant to achieve.

'ALL MEDIA' CONTRACTS

Some companies (and not just the Majors!) regard the recording contract as an 'all-media' deal. They will try to tie up all possible activities in which the artist's musical performances are recorded (including session work, studio work, walk-on performances and even work in movies). This aspect of cross-media contracting is dealt with in more detail in the section Working in Other Media later in this chapter.

Keeping your record company informed of what you are doing is an effective way of avoiding problems, even if you are stuck with a very restrictive contract. Few record companies can resist the lure of free publicity for their artists. Basically, if the activity legitimately furthers your career and the record company gets a benefit, it is likely to agree to you recording with or for someone else. Telling them early on means there are no nasty surprises. If you tell them and they do not object at the time, it would be quite difficult for your record company to stop it later.

If in doubt, speak first to the A&R manager. Explain what you want to do. The A&R manager is there to handle this kind of issue. Then make sure that Business Affairs finalises the 'release': sometimes A&R will agree to something just to avoid confrontation with the artist. If documents have to be prepared, the record company will provide them. It makes sense to have your lawyer have a careful look at them, to make sure everything is in order.

GUEST APPEARANCES AND STUDIO WORK

A quick glance at any record store will prove that a lot of artists record with other artists on other labels. The credits will usually say 'X appears courtesy of Major Co'. In reality, the gig was probably arranged by the artists and the record companies gave it their seal of approval after the event.

Just consider recordings as varied as 'Woodstock' or Santana's 'Supernatural' and the countless guest appearances by major artists on other stars' records. Few things aggravate a record company more than unexpectedly finding one of its artists listed as appearing on their arch-competitor's record. Tell your record company before going into the studio. This way, you will not upset your record company, and it may welcome the opportunity to co-operate with the release.

These projects are recognised to be of mutual benefit to the careers of all artists involved. In many cases, the record company will agree to the idea and simply put it down as publicity, unless the artist is a major act. For major acts, they may insist on participating in any income generated by the record. The record companies then have to come to some arrangement as to how they will share the income generated by the recordings which come out of the session or project. Fortunately, because these situations arise quite often, the deal terms should not be difficult to close.

OVERRIDE ROYALTIES

The usual deal is that your company will exchange your services for a royalty from the company putting out the record. This is called an "override" royalty. It is paid directly to the company that has the artist under contract and is quite distinct from any royalty or payment the artists might receive either from their own record company or from the third party.

Alternatively, the record companies might agree to share the income on an agreed formula which will give each enough to cover their royalty obligations to you and still leave some over as profit. If there are a lot of guest artists, the record company which will be selling the record might even do a joint venture with the others, splitting the cost and the profits on a predetermined basis.

WORKING IN OTHER MEDIA

Compared with their modern equivalents, recording contracts from the early days look primitive. The early agreements only had to worry about live performances and performances in the recording studio. It was simply not necessary for them to deal with any other activities. Films, videos, DVD, CD extra and the Internet were not anticipated. This meant that when these new media and technologies came along, there was often a hole in these old contracts. For example, some record companies had problems proving that they had the right to issue some of their back catalogue in new record formats.

These days, the activities included within the 'exclusivity' are usually very wide. The rationale is that 'recording artists' have become multi-format artists. The companies argue that, by spending money on promoting the artist and the artist's recordings, they are making the artist famous. They say they ought to share in income generated by the artist from the sale of all media in which the artist's work or image is exploited, because the sales are at least in part the result of the record company's work.

In some cases, the record company actually invests in these other media and will be able to provide the artist with tangible benefits. If that is contemplated as part of the contract, then fine; strike a deal with proper provisions to cover these other areas, but there has to be something for the artist in return for the rights which are outside the usual scope of a recording contract. There must be appropriate artistic controls, remuneration clauses and the like. A fair investment deserves a fair return for all parties.

FILM AND TELEVISION

Capturing live performances, which can be readily duplicated and sold to the public on new media such as CD extra, DVD and the Internet, are having a real impact on the content of record contracts. So has television. Record companies are always alert to the possibility that an artist might make a television appearance that might later be repackaged on disc.

Record companies have the capacity to use their recordings and their artists in many different ways and media, provided their contracts with their artists are sufficiently comprehensive.

You must make sure you understand the scope of the services covered by the agreement and make sure your legal adviser explains it to you, in detail, early in the negotiating process.

NON-MUSICAL ROLES

Some of the Majors (such as Universal) now try to include the artist's appearances in films and videos. This is usually, but not always, limited to situations where the artist actually performs or mimes music. Some recording contracts even include 'dramatic' performances by artists (e.g. in non-singing roles in films and in television shows, etc.) as an activity that can only be performed for the record company or with its consent. These are legitimate if used only to prevent clashes between recording and film obligations. On the other hand, a widely drafted clause might be a way of securing further control over the artist's activities in the entertainment business. Ask your lawyer.

Most artists feel uncomfortable (with good reason) about giving the record company the exclusive right to decide whether to make, or not make, films of the artist where the artist's roles have little to do with the artist's musical career. This power could interfere with what could be quite a distinct career path for the artist. Film work can also be an important promotional vehicle for some artists and can give them access to a completely new audience from the one that usually buys their records. Film work can also be a separate source of income for artists. On the other hand, for a record company that is part of a larger corporate structure that also contains a film production company, why wouldn't you try and vertically integrate your talent?

Recording contracts must include mechanisms to enable you and the record company to discuss and decide these matters quickly. You may not be able to afford to wait (and possibly miss an opportunity) while the record company makes a decision. It could take weeks, especially if it hasn't happened before or the decision is likely to have ramifications for the company's A&R policies.

The best way of avoiding the problem is to ensure that the scope of the 'services' definition in your record contract accurately reflects the services you will be providing – nothing more and nothing less. If you do decide to give the record company exclusive rights to your services for audiovisual devices (such as 'sell-through video' and DVD), make sure the contract includes comprehensive provisions dealing with the type of performances covered and the methods of payment. The audiovisual industry has huge potential for further growth and technological breakthroughs. Failing to deal with it properly could leave you in the same position that many artists found themselves in when their video clips began to be sold to the public, but there was no provision in the contract for them to get any payments or royalties on the sales. So they didn't get any.

INTERNET AND WEB SITE CONTROL

As the commercial importance of the Internet becomes more and more obvious, some of the Majors are attempting to control the on-line presence of their artists. For example, some recording agreements demand that the artist assigns all rights to the company to control the artist's official web-site – even after the contract is terminated. Their rationale is that they will still want to promote their back catalogue featuring the artist even though the contract has finished. Clearly, these sorts of efforts to control the artist's ability to control his or her own name and reputation, must be resisted. The most benevolent interpretation of this kind of clause is that the commercial structure of the Internet is still evolving and the company is simply being heavy-handed out of an excess of caution and anxiety. Be that as it may, it is hardly an inspired attitude to artist relations. Sometimes you wonder whether record companies would be better off hiring more psychologists and fewer lawyers.

That said, it makes sense for the record company to be intimately involved in the artist's web presence during the term of the recording agreement. The Internet is the distribution system of the future and both the company and the artist must recognise that the artist's official website is increasingly going to be an important portal for download distribution.

CONTRACT DEFINITIONS

One of the hardest things about reading recording contracts is the fact that many words used in them do not mean what you might first assume they mean. They acquire special meanings by being redefined in the contract. Some contracts are famous for going one better. They try to hide the definitions as well, just in case you or your lawyer might actually want to read them. Sometimes the same word will have more than one definition. Sometimes the definitions look similar, but with subtle differences. You should assume the differences are intentional, unless convinced to the contrary. If the differences are not deliberate, it indicates poor drafting, which can be an even bigger problem for your lawyer to have to deal with.

Never assume a word has its common meaning. If it is not defined, make certain there is no uncertainty about its meaning. The courts tend to assume that terms commonly used in a particular industry will have that meaning if used in an agreement originating in or involving that industry. Sometimes, the courts decide on a meaning that neither party intended or wanted.

The Definitions section often contains important operational parts of the contract. It is common for the 'Packaging Deductions' to be set out here, as well as vital terms such as 'net sales' and the 'Royalty Base Price', which determine how generous that royalty rate really is.

THE 'TERM' OF THE CONTRACT

You must understand the 'Term' and the various ways it can be increased or decreased. The Term of the recording contract determines how long you and the record company will be bound together. Even if you stop liking each other. The Term can be shortened by mutual agreement although, as George Michael found out, this is not necessarily easy.

The Term is commonly defined in terms of an initial period (usually a 'year' but watch what happens to that word!), followed by a number of optional years. These 'years' may not, in fact, have much at all to do with a calendar year.

CONTRACT YEARS

A year in a contract can be defined to be as long, or as short, as the parties agree. Usually, a year will be defined as being the longer of either:
- 12 months from the date of signing (but there are creative alternatives); or
- a nominated period (usually between 90 and 180 days) after either completion of the relevant master recording, or first release of records from that master.

In each case, the actual 'Contract Year' is likely to extend for much longer than just 12 months.

OPTIONS

In most recording contracts, the initial year is followed by a number of 'optional' contract years. The options belong to the record company, not you. Record companies will rarely commit to recording more than one album at a time, unless they are dealing with a major artist. Options mean they can make a particular recording, release it, and then evaluate the response before having to decide whether to make another one.

As an artist, you may feel this kind of approach does not exactly demonstrate unqualified faith, or a commitment to your career. Take heart: it isn't personal! Record companies are realistic about their ability to predict the response to a new record or artist. If they had perfect powers of prediction, there would be no unsuccessful records. Their mistakes appear in their financial accounts at the end of the year, so they have to do all they can to tilt the odds in their favour, by maximising the number of option years, and minimising the amount of recording they are obliged to do, as opposed to the amount they may choose to do.

This is only smart risk management on their part. The record company will make decisions based upon past performance, potential for growth, success of already-released product, public reaction to the act's live performances and prevailing market conditions. It will also have to adjust for changes in musical fashions. Decisions about exercising options are rarely taken lightly. Of course, sometimes no decision is made (i.e. if someone forgets the option date) but that is another story.

Take special note of the time each option must be exercised, and how it is to be exercised. If an option is not exercised in time, the Term will end. If that happens, the only way the record company could continue to make new recordings would be if you make a new contract with them. If they want you back, it's because they think you have potential. If you have potential, the price you set for making a new contract is likely to be higher than it was when you did the original deal as a new, unknown recording artist with limited bargaining power. That's one aspect of 'contract renegotiation'.

'WAKE-UP' CLAUSES

Record companies know that they sometimes miss option dates, so most now include 'wake-up' clauses in their contracts. These take different forms but, basically, they require the artist to remind the company that the option date is coming up, and give the record company time to reconsider its position. The clauses are intended to protect the company's option rights. They do the artist no favours.

Artists generally resist this kind of clause. The options are for the record company's benefit. The company should be capable of monitoring its own contracts. More than one act has had reason to thank a lapsed option, which enabled it to make a new, more favourable, deal with another record company or to renegotiate with their old company – something they could not have done if there had been a 'wake-up' clause in the contract. Mind you, if they had been happy with the other party, they probably would not have taken advantage of the technicality after all. Leaving a record company because of a failure to exercise an option probably reflects a deeper problem in the relationship.

DELAYS AND INTERRUPTIONS

EFFECT ON THE TERM

Delays in completing or delivering any particular master or video can have a major impact on the current Contract Year. Usually it will continue to run until you deliver the master recording that is due under the contract.

This could be many months after recording started. Extension of a Contract Year will also effectively extend the Term of the contract, so there should always be a cap on the extension period in such cases (particularly if the delays are not caused by the artist). Although it will depend upon individual circumstances, six months should be ample.

WHO IS LIABLE?

You might be liable to compensate the record company if the delays are your fault. The contract should always draw a distinction between delays caused by the artist and delays caused by circumstances beyond the artist's control. Artists should not be liable to compensate the company for delays they did not cause. Similarly, the record company should not be liable to the artist for any delays not reasonably within the company's control; a change of personnel would not usually fall into this class of events.

SUSPENSION CLAUSES

Record companies include suspension clauses so that they can put the contract into a kind of 'limbo' if the artist cannot record for some reason. The most usual reason is illness, but sometimes tours get in the way, or there is no new material ready to record. Either way, the record company will not want the Term ticking by. Suspension clauses were devised to enable the contract to be put on 'hold'.

The widely reported court case between Sharon O'Neill and CBS in the 1980s was the leading Australian case on suspension clauses. The court did not award CBS the injunction it was looking for but, on appeal, the court did not dismiss the possibility that a record company could suspend an artist indefinitely and without notice – a worrying prospect for many reasons, not least because while in suspension, the Term does not run.

THE 'TERRITORY'

The Territory is a basic concept of any contract. It defines the places in which the record company has the rights to your services and where it may exploit the recordings you make.

The 'exclusive rights' granted elsewhere in the contract are exclusive only within the contract's Territory. Record companies will generally try to get the maximum Territory. World-wide rights if possible. Some contracts even define the Territory as 'The Universe including the World'. This accounts for the use of satellites to transmit music and to avoid any suggestion that once the radio waves leave the Earth's atmosphere, they belong to no one!

The 'Territory' determines:

1. the countries in which the record company has your exclusive services as a recording artist; and
2. the countries in which the record company has rights in any recordings resulting from the contract, including the countries in which the record company may sub-license others to commercially exploit those master recordings.

For example, you might agree that the record company can have world-wide exclusivity to your services, but you might agree that you reserve the right to license the recordings in certain countries. In that case, example 1 would be for the World, but example 2 would be for a lesser territory.

OVERSEAS RELEASES – RELEASE OPTIONS

Artists must always ask, 'What will happen if the record company cannot get a release overseas?'. The Majors are usually obliged to offer their recordings to their overseas affiliates before offering them to anyone else, but they usually can't guarantee that they will achieve a release. This is not the local company's 'fault'. It is a fact of life. Each overseas company has to assess its local conditions and decide whether to release the record. Super-stars can get overseas release guarantees (and they would probably have been released anyway, so it's no great concession). Everyone else has to take their chances.

Independents do not have that 'problem' – theirs is usually that they have to look for potential licensees, which takes time and money. Some are better than others. Some take longer than others. They also have to co-ordinate the promotional work and release schedules, which can be a disadvantage over Majors, but a well organised Independent is likely to be the equal of a well organised Major in that regard.

In any event, artists are always justifiably anxious to see efforts being made to get a release in other territories. The record company deserves and needs a 'reasonable' time to secure sub-licences but, at some stage, the artist should be able to seek release commitments too. Given the many people and tasks needed to get a record actually released, it is not unreasonable to give the record company between 180 and 270 days after release in the 'home' territory, to secure release commitments overseas.

The contract will have royalty rates predicated upon the record company securing the release, but if the artist secures the release, the artist should get some additional benefit, by way of a larger share of the overseas royalties.

ARTIST'S MINIMUM DELIVERY COMMITMENTS

The Minimum Delivery Commitment can have a major impact on the duration of the Term. It specifies the minimum number of new recordings that you have to finish in any given year of the contract. It is not a maximum. It can be changed by mutual agreement, but some contracts try to give the record company the power to unilaterally increase any year's commitment. This has to be resisted, for obvious reasons!

EFFECT ON THE TERM

There is often a degree of fantasy in these clauses in any event. All too often, impossible timetables are set. Many contracts call for an album of entirely new tracks every 12 months, which is usually unrealistic. The previous recording may still be being promoted; you may still be touring to support an earlier release (so there will be no time to write or rehearse new material anyway, let alone record it); the next option may not be due to be exercised yet; or the record company may not want to spend funds at that time. A blow-out in the recording schedule can also cause everyone to overlook option dates, which is another reason record companies like wake-up clauses!

Unmet minimum recording commitments will extend the Term. If you do not deliver the minimum commitment in any year, the then-current contract year will usually keep running until you deliver the required number of tracks. This can easily extend the Term by many months (or even by years) and there may be nothing you can do to prevent it. That said, provided there is good communication between artist and company, it is unusual for the company to exact penalties when the artist fails to meet the technical requirements of the delivery commitment. Most artists are in breach of this provision at some time or another!

The moral is: only agree to realistic targets, consistent with your own ability to write, rehearse and record new material.

THE RECORD COMPANY'S RECORDING COMMITMENT

Record companies will naturally try to limit the number of tracks they must record in any year. Many will only agree to record one or perhaps two singles in the first year, with an album for each subsequent year. More established artists, or artists who have convinced the A&R manager that they have a dozen good songs ready to record, will get an album commitment from the first year.

SINGLES VERSUS ALBUMS

New acts frequently regard the singles-only approach as an insult, but it's not necessarily a bad thing. From the record company's point of view, consider the analogy with roulette. The record company has a specific amount of cash to spend on each artist. It can either put all its funds into making an album (i.e. putting all its gambling money into one very expensive chip) or it can spread the same amount to make several singles (i.e. spread its funds over several cheaper chips). Obviously, it can gamble for longer with a pocket full of chips.

From the artist's point of view, a singles deal can also be advantageous. A suck-it-and-see deal like this may provide an opening that the artist wouldn't otherwise get: the company may be prepared to risk an investment in a singles deal but not in an album deal. If the single works, the album will surely follow. Secondly, if the single doesn't work and the record company loses faith in your potential, you will be out of the agreement quickly and will have the opportunity of seeking another record company who believes in you.

There can, however, be definite disadvantages to a singles-only deal. If the first single takes off, will it be possible to finish a second single and then the album in time to capitalise on the first single's success? Can an overseas release be secured with only a single immediately available? Generally, the answer will be no – particularly in the case of the Majors, who have to have an album ready in the vaults before their affiliates will even listen to the artist's work, let alone think about releasing it. There are no definitive answers to these questions: being able to answer them successfully is the mark of a great A&R manager.

ARTISTIC CONTROL

Artistic control is always a vexed area of negotiation. It is often the area that causes the most heated discussions, unless the artist and the A&R manager have come to an understanding before the lawyers get involved. Unfortunately, it is rarely dealt with fully in contracts – yet it permeates them all and decides who has the final say as to what your recordings will sound like.

All artists want to have control of their artistic direction and output. After all, if the record company wants to sign someone, they should be reasonably impressed by that artist's work to date. On the other hand, as far as the record company is concerned, if they are writing the cheques, they want final say as to how their money will be spent and what recordings will be released.

Artists with strong bargaining power can demand complete freedom to select the material they record, their producer, their video concepts and their image. These are artists whose ability has been proven by an established history of success. Everyone else has to argue and bargain for control of the recording process and how their image will be presented.

The norm is to provide mutual control so that neither the artist nor the record company is stuck with material that they do not believe in.

WORKING WITH A&R

Unfortunately, there are limits to what can be achieved in a written document. Creative control is an issue that is often an important part of the pre-contract discussions between the artist and the A&R manager. The trick is to take the essence of those discussions and embody them into the agreement. The contract sets out the respective parties' rights and remedies. It does not instantly make the parties reasonable. It does not mean they agree on everything. 'Agreement' requires communication and an understanding of the other party's aims and constraints. The alternative is 'force' but it is generally not a productive technique in this business.

PLANNING THE RECORDING BUDGET

The contract should establish the process to be followed before recording takes place, to ensure the artist and the company agree on the basic issues relating to creative control, including:

- the amount available to be spent;
- the songs to be recorded;
- record packaging and design;
- the producer;
- the studio; and
- the video budget and the 'concept' (if there is one) to be promoted.

All these things can then be included in the recording budget. It is in everyone's interests for the recording budget to be written down and made available to all concerned, so there can be no confusion later. The secret is to work closely with A&R and constantly communicate ideas and preferences so that there are no surprises and so that A&R becomes your supporter for the budget sought.

DISPUTES

Artistic control can be a major source of disputes if:

- the A&R manager no longer trusts your judgment;
- someone high up in the hierarchy of the record company has heard the demos and hates them; or
- the only people who bought your last record were close friends and relatives.

Beware of clauses which require masters to be 'artistically acceptable' (or, even worse, 'commercially acceptable') to the record company. These expressions could leave you open to capricious A&R directives that could force you back into the studio again and again, while the Contract Year rolls on and on until you deliver acceptable masters. It is vital that there be some mechanism for settling deadlocks and disagreements quickly. The record companies will usually offer to resolve the problem by giving themselves final say in artistic matters – not exactly the approach most artists have in mind. Of course, the record company has a vested interest in the record being the best it can get, and if the record company is unhappy about having to release, the artist cannot expect much enthusiasm for expensive promotional efforts. A balance is needed.

The easiest thing is for artists to keep the record company fully aware of what is being recorded, so any differences of opinion will be spotted early in the process, instead of after the multi-track is finished.

CREATIVE DEVELOPMENT

Record companies are always worried that artists will be unpredictable in their artistic direction. Some can get away with it: Frank Black is a great musical chameleon, but even he must have had his record company gasping when he delivered his 'Honeycomb' album (an country album recorded with Nashville session players, totally unlike anything he had done in the past). This happens in all genres: who would have guessed that Keith Jarrett, the master of jazz extemporisation, would start recording wonderful, formal, classical records?

Record companies, no matter whether they are Majors or Independents, recoil at the thought of getting a 'maverick' recording. They rarely want their artists to remain in a musical time-warp but, at the same time, they know that the record-buying public frequently wants more of the same from their artists. How many artists, who had major success years ago, find that a change of musical direction is greeted by cries of 'play your hits' when they perform now? Delivery of a recording in a style related to the proven formula is more likely to please your record company (at least initially) than a stunning (but uncharacteristic) recording. Of course, if your break-through album goes Platinum, all will be forgiven!

'A SATISFACTORY RECORD'

Some Majors are remarkably up-front about what is satisfactory. They include a clause to the effect that each recording must be technically and artistically similar to your previous recordings! Others try to be more flexible by being less precise which, in the end, may not be much better.

The interaction between the artist and the A&R manager may end up with this result (i.e. a similar sounding recording) more often than not anyway, but this kind of clause seems guaranteed to create more problems than it is meant to solve because:
 • it seems inevitable that this will tend to stifle creativity;
 • it gives the record company power to veto release of recordings, yet the rationale for rejection of any recording may be entirely subjective and (at least for the artist) unpredictable; and

- it means the artist, for his or her own protection, should try to get written confirmation from the A&R manager early on in the recording process, acknowledging that the artistic direction being taken is acceptable to the record company. Without this, the artist risks having the recording rejected once completed if, for example, the A&R manager leaves or is overruled by someone higher in the company.

RELEASE COMMITMENT

The corollary of the artist's commitment to record a minimum number of tracks in any year, is the record company's obligation to release records of the masters it records.

WHEN THE RECORD COMPANY HESITATES

Now, you might think that a record company, after spending perhaps hundreds of thousands of dollars making an album, would be only too keen to release it no matter what but, fortunately, that is not the way the industry works. Record companies (especially the Majors) are only too aware that their costs are only just beginning once the master is delivered. The records have to be manufactured, artwork produced, packaging printed, advertising campaigns planned and paid for. This is often several times the recording cost and takes up a lot of company staff's time, which it would rather spend on records that it feels have commercial potential.

If the record company feels the master is not commercially viable, it certainly does not want to be compelled to release it. That is why record companies almost always resist inclusion of a release commitment. The artist's opinion that the record is a masterpiece will no doubt be taken into consideration, but then the artist will not actually be paying for the release, so may (quite understandably) be less than completely objective at this point. This is, of course, a part of the larger issue of artistic control.

WHEN THE ARTIST HESITATES

If the artist wants to see the record released, but the record company does not want to do it, there is a battle looming. If the record company wants to release but the artist does not, there is a battle looming again. Sometimes, an artist will decide the recording is a failure and try to bury it. This will displease the record company, even if it agrees that it is not really a hot product. There is cold comfort in knowing that everyone agrees the record company wasted its recording costs.

Sometimes, the record company (i.e. the A&R department) and the artist genuinely disagree about a recording's merits. Eric Clapton didn't want to release the album he recorded live on MTV. It won a Grammy and sold millions of copies. Unfortunately, not every artist is so happily wrong.

BREAKING THE DEADLOCK

Resolving this dilemma requires a great deal of trust and patience on both sides. Calling in a mediator might be worth considering, as a way of helping resolve the issue. Ultimately, someone (usually the record company, as it is paying for the whole process) has to decide whether to try to salvage the recording, start again, or, if things are really bad, try to walk away from the whole project. In any event, the artist's relations with the company will certainly be strained to, or beyond, breaking point by this time. This jeopardises the parties' ability to continue working together in the short term or on future projects.

CONTROL OF RELEASES

Being pragmatic, you have to give the record company a recording it likes, because their publicity department has to promote it and their sales staff has to sell it. That can be hard work if the general feeling back in head office is that the recording is a turkey and only released because it was a contractual obligation album. Conversely, artists are unlikely to be overjoyed at having to make another recording for a record company because of contractual obligations. (This may explain the 'Contractual Obligation' album by Monty Python's Flying Circus.)

Most record companies try to retain unrestricted control over:
- whether to release your records at all;
- if it does decide to release them, when to release them;
- when and whether to do any of the things noted above or license others to use the recordings in those ways; and
- whether and when to delete the records from its catalogue.

The record company does not want to have to manufacture and stock records that sell fewer than commercially viable numbers, but the artist cannot earn royalties if the record is not available. The reality is that the record company will happily reissue a recording if it believes that it will sell sufficient numbers. Unfortunately, the delay in re-releasing records can be significant and it is notoriously difficult to create interest in a record once it has been deleted.

There is no 'correct' solution to this dilemma. It is one of the matters that seem to defy resolution by mere words in a contract. For the artist's protection, agreements should always contain:
- a commitment from the company to release the record(s) within a certain number of months after delivery of the finished masters;
- limitations on the right of the company to license the masters, particularly for uses associated with advertising third party products and services; and
- protection against deletions within a certain period of initial release in a territory.

PUBLICITY AND IMAGE

The issue of artistic control is also important to the packaging of your records and their accompanying promotional material. Artists' incomes are increasingly affected by selling their image, so their image has to be protected and kept within their control. For this reason, photographs, biographies and the like really should to be specified as being subject to your prior approval.

CHANGING THE IMAGE

The publicity photographs and other images have to be consistent with your then-current image. Maintaining control over biographical materials will help reduce the possibility of incorrect or inappropriate material being given to the media.

When Kiss changed its image and dropped the make-up and theatricals, the whole basis of the band's publicity had to change. It had to re-educate the public and redefine the band's image. The change must have worried the record company, which probably anticipated dire consequences. The old adage 'If it ain't broken – don't fix it' is popular amongst promotional staff and in record companies generally. As it happened, the public wanted the old Kiss image and gave the record company hell over the new one.

FUNDING RECORDINGS – ADVANCES AND RECORDING COSTS

Royalties are usually thought of as the main reason for doing a record deal. They are certainly important – that is why there is a chapter devoted just to that topic. But there are many other aspects to recording contracts. They need to be considered together when assessing whether a particular offer is good or not. Good royalty rates but low-level promotion is usually equal to lousy royalty rates. It may even be worth trading points for other benefits from the record company, such as guaranteed promotional efforts or higher video budgets or whatever. That is all part of the art of deal-making.

FUNDING

Unless you are independently wealthy or have a private investor, you will be looking to the record company to provide the funding to make recordings and videos and to promote you and your records. Banks are simply not interested, and finding investors is time-consuming and expensive.

For many years, record companies absorbed recording costs by treating them as a business expense. They set the budgets and paid the studios directly. The artists did not have to know how much the recording cost because the cost had no direct impact on them, other than perhaps influencing the technical quality of the eventual recording. Since the recording costs were generally low anyway (given the relatively unsophisticated recording technology), record companies could afford to take a pragmatic attitude. Deals of this kind are called 'non-recoupable' deals, because the artist is paid a royalty from the first record sold.

The distinction between recoupable and non-recoupable deals is dealt with in more detail in the Chapter 23, **Record Royalties**. Briefly, 'recoupable' means that an artist's royalties are retained by the record company and applied to off-set all of the record company's costs that are identified in the recording contract as being recoupable.

'Non-recoupable' means the record company has to treat those costs as an expense, and the artist gets a royalty from the first record sold. There is much to be said for receiving royalties from the first record sold, rather than having to wait until royalty receipts exceed recording costs; but there is a catch. The artist's royalty rates in non-recoupable deals have to be much lower than in a recoupable deal. They are costs paid by the artist out of his or her sales. It is not a debt (because it is not repayable from other sources). Hence the common phrase "recoupable but not repayable".

Artists' royalty rates started off at only two or three percent of the retail selling price. The record companies argued (usually successfully) that the low royalty rate was necessary by saying they needed a greater profit margin on each record they sold, because they had to recover the recording costs paid out. As the industry grew and artists acquired greater bargaining power, the royalty rates gradually crept up. By the late 1970s, in Australia, non-recoupable royalties to artists on sales in Australia were between 6% and 10% of the retail selling price, subject to the usual deductions for packaging and the like (see Chapter 23, **Record Royalties**).

In the late 1960s and early 1970s, the super groups decided that they would make a lot more money if they paid for the recording process and, in return, received a higher royalty on sales. They could afford to invest in their own product and were reasonably assured of large volume sales. After a while, the record companies realised that it was to their advantage to extend the 'super group' approach to all artists. They could advance the artist the money to make the recording and then recoup it from the artist's share of sales. This strengthened their hold over the artist.

Recoupable deals largely replaced non-recoupable deals as the record companies' favoured type of deal. As a trade-off, the artists' royalty rates virtually doubled. In effect, the artists had to take a gamble: if they were successful, a recoupable deal would give them a significantly greater royalty per record, whereas if they were only moderately successful, they would be better off under a non-recoupable deal.

WHY MOST DEALS ARE RECOUPABLE NOW

For the record companies, recoupable deals have two main advantages.

- Recording costs were rapidly escalating and artists' demands were becoming more expensive to fulfil. Recoupable deals made the artist aware of the costs of making recordings.
- With a recoupable deal, the company can off-set the recording costs and other expenses against the artist's royalty. This means that until the costs are recouped, the artist's royalty is merely a book entry in the record company's accounts.

Very few recording contracts are non-recoupable now. It is not unknown in contracts to record classical music, but rare otherwise.

SECONDARY EXPLOITATION OF RECORDS

RELEASES AT SPECIAL PRICES

Unusual marketing methods (television, club) are dealt with in detail in Chapter 23, **Record Royalties.** These sales methods are obviously important if they affect the artist's royalties, but there is another aspect to be considered. These sales methods are very public. They can send a message to the public that may disadvantage the artist's image.

Selling records at mid-price or budget price is a perfectly normal part of the record business, but selling at a 'special price' (the uncharitable would just call it 'discounted') is usually reserved for records that have stopped being top-line catalogue. It is exploitation after the initial release demand has been met. If a record appears with a 'mid-price' sticker, or appears in a budget line catalogue, the assumption is that it has had its day as top-line product. This can affect the public's perception of the artist. This may not be a problem for artists currently with a high public profile, which will dispel any doubts, but most artists do not have that luxury.

If your contract does not give you a right to prevent releases in special price points at least during the early stages after first release, you will have to hope that your friend, the A&R manager, will be able to convince the marketing manager not to include your records in the special price roster against your wishes.

ADVERTISING AND SOUNDTRACKS

Recordings have multiple uses. Granting licences to third parties to allow your recordings to be put into the soundtrack of a film or a commercial can be lucrative but, as always, needs to be considered in the greater context of your career. A carelessly placed synchronisation licence could have your recording appearing in the soundtrack of a real dog of a movie, which could take years to live down.

Worse, your recording might get put into the soundtrack for a commercial just after you signed a mega deal with a competitor, or an exclusive endorsement deal. Would your face be red? Yes. Would you be happy? No. Could you have avoided the problem? Yes, if your contract included a veto or prior approval right over the record company's otherwise virtually unlimited power to grant licences of this kind.

Record companies prefer not to have their powers limited in this way but, assuming you care about artistic control, you have a legitimate right to be able to control how your reputation and works are used. Like so many aspects of the contractual relationship, it is a two-way affair. If the record company refuses to concede this, you really have to consider whether you can afford to deal with them in the long term.

This whole question of control over the uses to which the recordings can be put, is tied in with copyright ownership and physical ownership and control of the master tapes. If you do not own the recordings themselves, you must rely on contractual restrictions.

WHO OWNS THE RECORDINGS?

As a matter of law, copyright ownership is shared between the persons who performed on the recording and the person who actually pays the recording costs of the resulting master, unless otherwise agreed in writing.

Negotiations over record contracts usually include heated argument as to who will ultimately own the masters and videos. Record companies are very reluctant to relinquish copyright ownership because the masters are the only tangible asset which survive the end of a recording contract. Artists are equally keen to retain ownership for the same reason. In the final analysis, ownership of the masters will be decided by your relative bargaining strengths.

If you cannot retain your share of ownership of copyright in the master, you can try to have ownership revert to you after recoupment, but if this is rejected, take heart. You will never win that one! The industry practice is that the artist pays for the cost of the recording and when the company has recouped those recording expenses from the artist's royalties, the company keeps ownership of the masters and all rights in them. Good work if you can get it! The upside is that if the record company owns the master:

- it has the job of storing it; and
- it will be easier for potential licensees to locate a record company than it will be to locate an individual. (The job of finding the owners and getting clearance to exploit the recording is even more difficult when the master is jointly owned by several people.)

The master is only valuable because of its potential to generate royalties. Ownership of the master(s) is less important than the need to ensure that the master(s) will always be readily available for commercial exploitation and that licences will be granted unless there is a really good reason not to. The master will not be used if there is no one to grant a valid licence.

COVER ART

In the case of record cover artwork the general rule is: if you paid for it, you own the copyright in it. If the record company pays for it, it will own the art and will have a legitimate claim to having final say as to the design.

If your band has a registered trademark, the record company will require a written licence to reproduce the trademark on records, promotional materials and packaging.

Ownership gives you the opportunity to use the artwork for merchandising. It also gives you greater artistic control. If the record company pays for it, the company will own it and you will have no automatic right to use it for your merchandising. This can be very important, as the record cover art helps define your public profile.

Most artists are best served by supplying and paying for their own cover art. It is very galling if you have to pay the company a royalty for the right to use 'your' cover art on your own merchandising – particularly if the cost of producing it in the first place was a fully recoupable cost!

If you are providing the cover art, the record company will usually insist it be licensed for as long as the records are being sold. The licence may be limited to reproduction on record covers, or it may include merchandising rights. This is a matter for negotiation.

RE-RECORDING RESTRICTIONS

Most recording contracts contain a clause which states that upon the expiration of the current agreement, for a set a period of time, the artist can not re-record material which was recorded during the term of the agreement. This prevents artists from getting out of contract, immediately re-recording and selling records in competition with the first company's version. Reasonable restrictions are a legitimate means of protecting the record company's investment.

Usually, the time period is measured either from the end of the contract or the date of first release of any particular recording. Typically, the restriction will apply for either three years from release or two years from the end of the Term, whichever is the later.

You should always try to keep the restriction periods as short as possible. It should only apply to recordings actually released by the record company.

Some companies try to include recordings made but not released (which would include demos). This could obviously be highly prejudicial to your career. When a recording has been put into the vaults, you have to be careful about when (and if) you are willing for it to be released sometime in the future – particularly if it was initially rejected and stored as 'not being, in the company's opinion, artistically or commercially acceptable'!

It is important to recognise both the interests of the company that funded the tracks and those of the artist, who has legitimate artistic concerns about release of dated material.

MORAL RIGHTS AND REMIXING

Mixing is an important aspect of artistic control. So too is remixing. You may not be thrilled by unauthorised re-mixes of your recordings being released some time in the future. After all, you will have spent a lot of time and money getting them to sound just right. Remixes could be disasters or could ruin your reputation as an artist. Always try to retain prior-approval rights on remixing. The company's response will give you an idea of its attitude to artistic integrity generally.

In Australia, we now have Moral Rights legislation under which an artist's consent is required for changes to his or her work. This right (known as the 'right of integrity') recognises that an artist's professional reputation and public image, is inextricably intertwined with the music they perform and the records they release. Even so, it is still a sensible idea to ensure the right to stop unauthorised changes by having appropriate clauses in your contract.

AMERICAN FEDERATION OF MUSICIANS

This body (commonly called the AF of M) is the professional musicians' union in the United States. The important thing for non-United States artists to know about it, is that the AF of M levies a fee on records recorded in the United States.

Following a long musicians' strike, the AF of M established a trust fund, into which the levies are paid. The AF of M has an agreement with the record companies that covers union members and instrumentalists who make recordings. They do not cover artists who are getting a royalty over a minimum threshold. The agreement is similar in effect to the relevant industrial awards in Australia that set minimum session rates and conditions.

The AF of M's rules affect non-American artists if they record in the United States and use AF of M union members as session musicians. If this happens, the record company is obliged to make certain deductions and pay them to the trustee of the Music Performance Trust Agreement (MPTF) and a separate one to the Administrator of the Special Payments Fund (SPF).

Naturally, the record companies do not pay this themselves – they deduct it from the artist; either by treating payments as an advance, or actually invoicing the artist.

The rates vary, depending on the selling price of the record. There is an allowance for 'free goods' that varies by format. The combined MPTF and SPF royalty comes to between about three cents and just over four cents per unit, depending on format and selling price. These MPTF payments relate to sales made for five years after release, while the SPF payments are on sales for 10 years.

THE RIGHT TO ASSIGN THE CONTRACT

Most contracts include some provision specifying whether either the record company, the artist, or both of them, can assign their rights under the contract.

The fact is, if you are the artist, you cannot assign the obligation to provide the personal artistic services required under the contract, but there may come a time when you want to assign either your copyright or the income that flows from your copyrights (e.g. to a company or trust structure established for tax reasons). This is rarely a problem for the record company.

Giving the record company an unrestricted power to assign its rights, however, is a very different thing. Assignment usually arises from one of three scenarios.

1. The record company wants to restructure its organisation and needs to transfer contracts from one company to another within the group. This rarely causes any problems, provided the artist is not disadvantaged, or suddenly comes under the control of someone they cannot work with.

2. The record company sells all or part of its catalogue of recordings to a third party and wants to prevent any veto by its artists. It will also be anxious not to have to argue with artists about them sharing any of the purchase price with the company, which is, after all, selling only its own right to receive income from the catalogue – the artist's rights to royalties are not being sold, though they obviously have many other interests in this kind of transaction.

3. The record company sells its exclusive right to the artist's services, by assigning the contract to a third party. From the artist's perspective there are two major problems with this. First, the artist signed with the record company for its particular attributes, which the new company may not demonstrate. The new company may even be a company the artist specifically decided not to sign with in the first instance; and second, the company gets 100% of the purchase price, but the artist does not get any of it. Again, the company will argue that it is selling its own right to income – not the artist's. The artist will argue that the artist's services are the thing of value being sold, and so the artist ought to share in the proceeds.

In the real world, record companies know that an angry artist is not an especially productive one, so they will usually try to avoid antagonising them, but if the offer is too good to refuse...

Try not to give the record company an unfettered right to assign the contract, if at all possible.

WARRANTIES AND INDEMNITIES

WARRANTIES

These are the statements each party gives to the other, confirming that each has an unrestricted right to enter and perform the agreement. Often they will be quite long clauses that also cover promises that the recordings will not be defamatory, obscene or infringe any third party's copyright.

Problems arise if the warranties by the artist are absolute. The artist can usually say that they will not deliberately or negligently record obscene or defamatory songs, but an absolute warranty that the recordings will not infringe a third party's copyright could be risky. The only way the artist can be sure that there is no risk is by keeping strict control over any sampling or inclusion of other recordings into the final mix by (for example) the producer.

The record company's best defence is to make sure the A&R manager keeps a close watch on what is being recorded. The artist's best defence is to make sure the A&R manager is kept informed, even if the A&R manager shows no interest in the problem.

INDEMNITIES

Indemnities apply if one of the parties to the contract has been 'economical with the truth' (as it was so delicately put in the Spycatcher Trial), or forgot to mention a critical fact, such as that they are still under contract to another record company. Don't laugh, it happens!

The indemnities are a kind of insurance policy for the other side. They are a promise, which the courts are happy to enforce, that the party at fault will reimburse the 'innocent' party for any losses or expenses they incur because of the fib, failure to disclose or outright foul-up. They are very serious things. Having an indemnity enforced against an artist can effectively end their career and leave them in debt forever. If the amount is sufficiently great, it could force an Independent record company into bankruptcy.

Indemnities are a two-edged sword. If you are on the receiving end, having been the innocent victim of the other party's errors, you will give thanks for the skill of your lawyer for drawing a cunning clause which allows you to reclaim every cent that the mistake or breach of contract cost you. If you are on the paying end, you will be appalled when the clause seems to open up an unending vista of liability and expense.

Although the saying about blood from stones applies to indemnity clauses, they are very serious matters. Be warned.

GIVING NOTICE

If either party fails to carry out its side of the bargain, and negotiation has failed to resolve the problem, the other party is quite entitled to give the other side formal notice that it must fix the problem or suffer the consequences. This process of telling the other side to get its act together is usually referred to as 'giving notice of breach'. Notice clauses tell you how this must be done.

Notice clauses set out:

- the actual methods by which notices can to be sent by one party to another;
- how long after dispatch the notice will be assumed to have been received;
- to what address they must be sent; and
- the minimum information that any notice must contain (particularly if it is a notice of a breach of the contract's terms).

You have to be aware of these because if the worst happens, and you have to give notice, you must abide strictly by the contract. If the contract says it must be a letter, by registered post, to a particular address, send it that way. For example, in such a case, a facsimile will not amount to giving proper notice.

Sometimes these clauses have absurdly short delivery times allowed, particularly if the notice has to be posted. Always allow a reasonable time for the post to do its job.

Beware of clauses that 'deem' the notice to have been received from the date it is sent. It might not actually reach you, but a clause like this puts you in a terrible position because the other side can terminate without you being aware of the problem or the termination.

Assuming the other side has ignored the notice to rectify the problem it has caused, the innocent party has to decide whether to:

- continue with the contract and, perhaps, get a court order to force the other side to abide by the contract's terms; or
- terminate the contract (and if it does that, whether to sue for damages).

Termination clauses are usually among the last clauses to be considered in negotiations and do not always get the attention they deserve. This is most unfortunate because, although they are technical and are pretty dry reading, the artist must understand what the provisions mean, and what happens if they are activated. The clauses are not mere decoration. They are there for a reason.

The parties have to agree what events will be regarded as so serious and fundamental that, if they happen, the contract can be terminated by one or other of the parties. Some events can be 'cured' and there is usually a specified period ('days to cure') allowed to the party that is in breach. This involves the innocent party sending the other a notice specifying the problem and demanding that it cure the breach within a nominated time; usually between 14 and 30 days. If it is not fixed by that time, the innocent party may terminate the contract.

Some events cannot be rectified, or are so serious that they justify immediate termination. Refusal or serious failure to pay royalties on time usually qualifies, as would bankruptcy or the like. If a record company is declared bankrupt, giving it another 14 days 'to cure' will make absolutely no difference. Events of this scale are generally regarded as the end of the line and the contract may be terminated immediately. It is debatable whether an artist's bankruptcy would really justify terminating the contract, though most contracts provide for this to happen.

Sometimes one or other of the parties has sufficient bargaining skill/power to have special conditions included. These include 'key man clauses', which would allow the contract to be terminated if nominated people leave the record company or the band (depending on which side had the clause inserted). Few record companies will agree to a 'key-man clause' because if they lose that important employee, they may also lose the artist or, if the artist becomes successful, it gives the employee too much power!

21
RECORD DISTRIBUTION DEALS

THERE ARE THREE CLASSIC TYPES OF RECORD DISTRIBUTION DEAL. THESE ARE LABEL DEALS, PRESSING AND DISTRIBUTION DEALS, AND MASTER LICENCE (OR TAPE-LEASE) DEALS. THEY ALL INVOLVE THE DISTRIBUTION OF THE RECORD BUT INVOLVE VARIOUS PERFORMANCE OBLIGATIONS. IT MUST BE EMPHASISED THAT THERE ARE MANY VARIATIONS TO THE CLASSIC TYPES DISCUSSED.

LABEL DEALS

You will often come across the expression 'label deal' in the record industry. It is a generic description for a whole range of structures and schemes which are meant to give Independents and individuals access to the Majors' facilities, while allowing the Independents to sell records in their own name.

Most label deals resemble complicated master licence deals. They set out how the Independent will make its master recordings, who will provide the funding and how, and the terms of the licence to the Major. The Major's role is to manufacture records from the masters delivered by the Independent, promote them and sell them. The Independent gets a royalty from the Major for each of its records the Major sells. That's the theory anyway.

In most label deals, the Independent is responsible for:
- contracting with the artists;
- administering the recording process;
- delivering the audio and video master recordings to the Major;
- creating artwork for record covers; and
- making sure the artist is available to support the Major's promotional activities.

Before considering the mechanics of label deals, it is worthwhile considering just what 'labels' are, and what label deals are supposed to achieve.

WHAT ARE LABELS?

Record companies sell their records under a variety of so-called labels. The label itself is a distinctive name or logo which can be a trademark, an image, or just a name or words. The Majors each use many different labels at any one time. The labels are used to help record buyers tell where the particular record came from and (perhaps) what kind of music it is, before they have even heard it. Record companies go to great lengths to protect labels. There is no point in having a label and promoting it if it can be confused with someone else's, or if someone else uses it without consent.

Labels can get a reputation for quality or a particular musical style, which helps marketing. The ECM jazz label is a perfect example of one which managed to define its musical style so powerfully that the record buying public can more or less tell what they will get as soon as they see an ECM label on the record. The label identification is so strong that when the company decided to release classical recordings, it had to devise another label for those new recordings.

Labels in other genres of music have been successful in defining themselves by their labels too. No one would expect Harmonia Mundi to release rock and roll any more than Def American would release chamber music. Any potential buyer looking at a record on the Verve label would know the recording's musical genre.

A successful label helps to sell records. Often, they are one of the most valuable assets an Independent can acquire, besides its master tapes. We will look at the ways to protect labels later in this chapter.

LABEL OWNERSHIP

You can see the diversity of labels, just by browsing through any record shop. If you are unsure who owns a particular label, or who is licensed to use it, ARIA keeps a register of the owners and licensees of many of the labels used in Australia. It is updated annually, to keep track of label movements between record companies and to note any new labels as they are introduced. Sometimes old labels are dropped and replaced by new ones. Sometimes old ones are revived after years of disuse.

If a label has been registered as a trademark, it is easy to search the trademark registry to find who owns (or owned) it. Many, though, are just used for a while, then fade away. Some are sold off to new owners, or change hands as companies are sold or merged over the years. This can make them hard to track down, but may have little adverse effect on the label's worth as a marketing tool.

WHY DO A LABEL DEAL?

Label deals are usually structured so an Independent can sell records under its own label. This way, if the recording or artist is successful, the artist is associated with the label rather than the Major which distributes the records, so the label can acquire a public profile, which attracts other artists who want to be associated with its success.

Often, the idea behind a label deal (at least in the minds of the people starting the Independent) is that the label will sign new artists (using a Major's funds as its bank), have a few successes and eventually sell the company off. This process has actually been one of the features of the growth of the music industry over the years. In fact, most of the Majors achieved their accelerated growth by buying and absorbing third party labels. A few examples: the Atlantic label started as an Independent, distributed by Warner, who eventually bought it (along with another Independent, Elektra) and combined their operations to form the WEA company. Herb Alpert learned (and earned) enough from his days heading the Tijuana Brass, to form A&M Records with Jerry Moss. A&M was remarkably successful and was bought eventually by PolyGram. Robert Stigwood's RSO label made a fortune during the disco-fever phase and its catalogue was too attractive for PolyGram to ignore. In turn, PolyGram was snapped up by Universal, one of the world's biggest Majors.

The Independents are usually the result of the fire in the belly of one person. For example, David Geffen was manager to many of the big names of the 1960s, such as Joni Mitchell, Neil Young and Crosby, Stills and Nash. In 1970 he founded Asylum records. Asylum's roster included the major names of the 1970s and was eventually sold to Elektra, which was sold to Warner, creating WEA. Not content with that, in 1980 (presumably when the non-compete clause in his contract expired), he founded Geffen Records which carried Guns N' Roses, Elton John, Don Henley, Whitesnake and Aerosmith. MCA bought Geffen Records in 1989. Geffen then went off to be a founder of Dreamworks. Who said that 'rust never sleeps'?

The great Australian example of fire in the belly was Michael Gudinski who founded Mushroom Records (and an octopus of vertically integrated entertainment businesses.) Mushroom had a label deal with Festival. Over two decades it amassed a large and important catalogue and was eventually taken over by Festival (which in turn was bought by Warner Music).

The list of successful labels goes on and on. Unfortunately, the list of unsuccessful labels is many times longer!

Label deals have been rather unkindly criticised as being a "Clayton's A&R policy" for Majors, because the Major is relying on the Independent to make the A&R decisions. Despite the apparent inherent contradiction of a Major paying someone else to make A&R decisions, most Majors recognise the value of this kind of deal and continue to do them. By doing a label deal with an Independent, the Major gets a fully recoupable A&R department. In the Major's books, the advances that fund the label are advances against the label's royalties. As the Major will not actually have to pay any royalties until the advances have been recouped in its books, the deal can be quite advantageous for it, if the label sells a good quantity of records.

In addition, the Major can get the wholesale margin (the profit on the sale to the retailers) when it also distributes the records. Of course, it is still only profitable if enough records are sold.

NEGOTIATING LABEL DEALS

A label deal has to work at two levels. Before it even gets to the mechanics of record distribution (royalties, rights, etc.), it has to define the relationship between the Independent and the Major that will distribute its records. This is rarely easy, because of the basic conflict between the Independent wanting to have as little interference as possible from the Major, and the Major wanting to influence how the Independent spends the funds that the Major will be providing.

The parties have to spend a lot of time making sure they agree on the basics of the relationship. This can be strongly influenced by the personalities of the people involved and this is the great intangible that can make or break a label deal. If either side has unrealistic expectations, negotiations can be very difficult. Making promises that cannot be met will almost certainly result in a fundamentally flawed deal. Experienced advisers, involved from the start, can do much to minimise these problems.

LABEL IDENTITY

The agreement has to set out the extent of the label's freedom to make A & R decisions. This will largely depend on how financially independent the label is and the relationship between the people involved in the label and those in the Major.

The label should always insist on having the final say as to what records will be released. 'Cherry picking' by the Major is the alternative – a very unsatisfactory situation for a label, where the Major can decide whether or not to release any particular recording. If this is the case, the label cannot give its artists any guarantee that their records will be released. Without a release guarantee, if the Major says 'no thanks', the artists and the label will be in a difficult position. They will have significant recording costs but may never see the recording released, so cannot earn royalties to recoup them. The Independent will have to find another way of releasing the record which, at the very least, will delay any release and may antagonise the artist and put extreme financial pressure on the Independent.

FUNDING

The label needs sufficient funds to run its infrastructure and make recordings. There is no future for the deal if the Major keeps the purse strings so tightly drawn that the label slowly starves. Good budgets are essential, so the Independent can make a realistic estimate of its needs.

In most deals, all the funds advanced by the Major will be recoupable from all royalties payable to the label. This is usually called a 'cross-recoupable' deal because all royalties, regardless of which of the label's artists earned them, are retained by the Major until all the advances are recouped. This can lead to problems if, say, one of the artists has a huge success and starts earning royalties, but the Major is still retaining all royalties because there are other advances (for other artists) still to be recouped. This possibility has to be considered and a mutually acceptable solution worked out before it happens. (One solution is for the agreement to state that the Major will pay-though the artist royalty to any artist who actually is recouped.)

Sometimes the Major will agree to treat each artist separately. Each artist has a separate account in the Major's royalty account system and as advances are paid to the label, they are recorded in the relevant artist's account. That way, the successful artists do not, in effect, subsidise the unsuccessful ones. This structure only works if a label has a small roster of artists. Once it gets the size of (say) Interscope or the like, the label can generate enough cash flow to easily meet its royalty commitments, so it does not need to worry about cross-recoupment.

As in all record deals, it is vital that the contract spells out exactly when advances are payable. The Independent needs the money in advance, to pay recording costs, but the Major will usually want to have the funds payable on delivery of master tapes, video clips or whatever the funds were spent on. The usual compromise is half in advance and half on delivery, or progress payments. Whatever is agreed, the contract must be unambiguous as to when the payments are due and how they are to be paid.

GRANT OF RIGHTS

The rights granted in the master recordings are much the same as in any master licence, so it is not necessary to repeat them here. Obviously, the label has to make sure that the rights it gives to the Major do not exceed the rights it has under its recording contract with the artist. If they do, things can become extremely tense (for example, if the artist asks the label why their records were released as a budget record without the artist's permission, in breach of the artist's contract with the label). It is important to remember that the label really should retain the right to approve any unusual sales methods or activities that might adversely affect the royalty it receives.

DURING THE TERM
During the term, the label will deliver more than one master tape and will certainly deliver quite a few different batches of expensive artwork and video clips. Assuming the Major has to release everything delivered to it, then there will be quite a few different releases by different artists. It is in the label's own interests to keep accurate files recording:
- when each recording was completed;
- when it was delivered to the Major (remembering that 'delivered' may be defined to mean very much more than just sending a master recording to the Major's office);
- what artwork was sent (and keeping a copy of the signed assignment letter from whoever designed the art, otherwise the label may not actually have the right to deal with the artwork);
- to whom each master recording was sent and how;
- any video clips or other promotional material supplied, to whom and how sent;
- any costs which the Major is meant to repay (this will depend on the terms of the agreement);
- when records are scheduled to be released;
- the date they are actually released;
- any special arrangements made with the Major for promotional efforts and expenditure;
- whether copies have been sent to the Major's affiliates overseas, in an effort to secure an overseas release; and
- how much every item cost! (If the label does not know this, it cannot hope to keep any useful books of account, nor can it tell how much it is to recoup from each of its artists before it has to start writing royalty cheques.)

It is amazing how many label deals are done without any thought being given to who will keep accounting records. It is absolutely essential to have a competent accountant if the label is to have any hope of surviving. Anyone setting up a label deal owes it to themselves, their artists and to the Major which is probably providing the funds to run the operation, to keep track of funds moving in and out of the label. Specialist accounting and legal advice will pay for itself many times over by minimising foul-ups and avoidable errors which could leave the label, and the people running it, liable for thousands of dollars in damages. Besides, if you don't have proper accounts, you are wide open when the Taxation Department decides to audit you and the label. Without proper accounts and files, all those deductions you claimed won't be allowed. Penalty tax will be charged. End of story.

REVERSION OF RIGHTS

There are particular things to consider when a label deal comes to the end of its term. The label naturally wants to be in the position to take its catalogue and its artists and deal with it without interference from the Major. On the other hand, the Major will want to ensure that it has a chance to recover its investment because, from past experience, it expects to be unrecouped at the end of the term. This is one of the main areas for negotiation when the deal is being put together. The lawyers' job is to find a balance between the parties' wishes.

Most Majors will insist that they keep the exclusive licence of any recordings for some period after the end of the deal.

For example, say Label A does a three-year deal with Majorco. At the end of the three-year term, Label A will be free to do a deal with another Major, but the recordings delivered to Majorco during that time will remain with Majorco for some additional period. Sometimes it is expressed as a number of years (often referred to as the retention period). Sometimes, it is 'until recouped'.

Unfortunately, this approach creates several problems because:
- Majorco will want to keep selling the records in their original packaging, and will not want to have to remove the label from the remaining or future stocks of records;
- the label may not want to have its catalogue split up over two or more Majors, especially as this may mean some artists will have records released by two different Majors (which can confuse retailers when they come to order stocks); and
- the new Major may want an exclusive right to use the 'labels', but Majorco may want to have the right to keep using it.

In spite of the fact that there are lots of examples of labels that have product split between two distributors (particularly while the first company's retention period is running out), it is to the label's advantage to find a way to consolidate its catalogue. This usually means paying back any unrecouped advances, or paying some percentage of future sales to Majorco. Leave the negotiating and structuring of this to the lawyers!

TERRITORY

Like any other licence deal, label deals can give Majorco rights for the world, one country, or anything between. This will be the subject of much negotiation when the deal is being worked out.

From the label's point of view, the important thing is to achieve releases in as many countries as possible. If Majorco cannot secure overseas releases in a reasonable time, the label has to have the right to seek offers elsewhere. These releases should be under the label's own label, but sometimes overseas licensees will resist this. If this happens, the label has to decide whether this is a deal-breaking point, or whether to agree and be satisfied with a big production credit on the record and its packaging and any promotional material.

ROYALTIES

More importantly though, a label's primary source of income is the royalty from each record sold. Labels do not have the benefit of getting the margin between the wholesale price and the actual cost of the record, as the Major/distributor keeps that. This means the only opportunity for the label to make a profit is to keep the difference between the royalty it receives and the royalty it pays the artist. Accordingly, labels have to offer lower royalty rates to their artists than those a Major can afford to offer (assuming, of course, it was ever willing to pay the maximum).

Also, royalties from overseas sources have to come through yet another party, which will, of course, take a share for its trouble. With a Major, the royalties usually go from the local company to the central company, and from the central company to the Australian company, which distributes it to the artist. This can delay the royalty accounting for perhaps 18 months or more, especially if the Major works on half-yearly accounting.

Quarterly accounting will significantly reduce the telescoping of royalty accounting. Fortunately, most of the Majors use monthly accounting within their respective inter-company accountings.

AUDIT RIGHTS

Though something likely to affect only a few artists, it ought to be remembered that if you are an artist who is contracted to a Independent, you do not have audit rights which extend to the Major's books of account. You could certainly audit the label's books, but that is as far as you could go. If you did an audit and happened to discover a problem, the label (not you) would have to take the matter up with the Major, which might be a bit unnerving for the label, seeing the Major is its main source of funds.

ARTISTS AND LABEL DEALS
ADVANTAGES FOR ARTISTS

As an artist signed to an Independent with a label deal, you stand to get personal attention and (if you are lucky) greater artistic freedom. You can also benefit from being associated with a successful label, which can boost your profile. If a label is perceived as being 'hot' then, by association, everyone signed to them is seen as having the potential to be 'hot' too.

Label deals particularly suit developing artists but the fact is, most artists who are successful under a label deal will eventually move from the Independent label to a Major. After all, Majors generally have bigger chequebooks, come record contract renegotiation time.

POINTS FOR ARTISTS TO WATCH

If you are an artist signed to an Independent that has a label deal with a Major, you are affected in several vital ways because the label relies upon the Major for:

- **Funding**. If the label deal should end, your label could be left without funds to make your recordings or, in a worst-case scenario, may not be able to pay your royalties.
- **Manufacture and distribution of the label's recordings**. If there is no deal with a Major, the label may have no facilities for getting records made or distributed.
- **Funds for promotion and/or use of the Major's promotions staff**. If the label deal should be terminated, there may be no funds to promote the label's catalogue or artists.
- **Many policies relating to** accounting, retention of royalties to allow for returned records, and sales policies (all of which have an impact on your royalties) may not be in the control of the Independent label. The label's records will be sold under the Major's usual trading terms, so these terms have to be reflected in the terms of your recording agreement, which can reduce the label's flexibility in negotiations with its own artists.

If you are negotiating a record deal with an Independent which relies upon a label deal with a Major for its funding/distribution, try to find out everything you can about the Major's policies, its relationship with the label, the depth of that relationship, the term of the deal and whether the Major has to release everything recorded by the label or can cherry pick. Try to meet with the people in the Major who will be working your product – don't just rely on the say-so of the Independent.

PRESSING AND DISTRIBUTING DEALS

Pressing and Distribution deals are usually abbreviated to P&D deals. You need to be careful with the terminology though. The term is a bit rubbery. Some people use it when they actually mean a master licence deal. This can cause confusion because there are quite fundamental differences between P&D deals and master licences. This will become clear as we get into this chapter. For the moment, just remember: P&D deals do not involve the licensing of copyright but rather, just the physical distribution of the product.

We will use the expression 'distributor' here, rather than 'record company' because the distributor need not be a record company. Anyone who can deliver records to retailers and collect payment could do the job, although record companies are the logical choice because they are already set up to do it.

There are two basic kinds of P&D deal: one is selling and distribution (where you use the Major's sale's force); and the other is distribution-only, and the Independent does the sell-in to the retailers.

WHY DO P&D DEALS?

Let's assume you own a master recording but need the records made and distributed. P&D deals give you maximum control over the way the records are presented and advertised. Once the records are in the warehouse, all the distributor need do is take orders and ship goods. The distributor has no financial stake in the goods, no money at risk, and need not have any involvement in how the goods are promoted, unless it chooses to. As far as the distributor is concerned, you could be selling carpet slippers for all it mattered. If you do a P&D deal with a Major, you can get access to the Major's national distribution network, while remaining essentially independent of any A&R intrusion.

P&D VERSUS MASTER LICENCE

Under a P&D deal, you own the master recording from which the records are made and also the records themselves, at least until they are sold to retailers. In a master licence deal, however, the record company pays for the records and owns them. This makes the record company worry about the number pressed, the number sold and any returns. In a P&D deal, the distributor just keeps the records in the warehouse and ships them out to meet demand whipped up, no doubt, by your brilliant promotional campaign (which, by the way, you have to pay for).

Owning the records not only gives you great control over how the records will be presented and promoted, it also means you can get a greater share of the total dollars generated from the sale of your records. In a master licence deal, the record company pays you a royalty of (assuming it was being generous) around 20% of the retail price, less the usual deductions. By comparison in a P&D deal the distributor keeps around 20% to 25% (it can vary a bit, especially if you are a big label, but this is a ball-park figure) of the proceeds of each sale, and you get the rest.

A word of caution though: P&D deals can be very hungry for capital funds. (This is dealt with in detail later in this chapter in the section headed Funding.) In a P&D deal, if your records start to sell really well, you still have to pay for additional stocks to be manufactured. This may be fine once the cheques start coming in. Meanwhile, unless the distributor is prepared to make an advance against future sales, you have to find the funds. Fortunately, if your records start selling really well there is a good chance of flipping the deal over to a licence deal. Then, the distributor will be paying for the stock to be made and will carry the risk of not selling all of them.

SELECTING A DISTRIBUTOR

You can go via the independent distributors or you can go for one of the Majors that still offer P&D deals. Some will only do master licence deals. Others will also give you the option to flip a P&D deal over to a licence deal, should sales really take off.

You have to shop around. Find out who their main customers are. The Majors deal with traditional record outlets but tend not to deal with independent outlets. Independent distributors sometimes do not supply major retail outlets. You can only find out by asking. Check the *Australasian Music Industry Directory*. It lists distributors and the labels they distribute. There is no substitute for doing your homework.

Once you have decided which distributors seem the most suitable, see whether they can or will take the job. This usually involves you convincing them that you will sell a reasonable number of records. Unless you can sell more than a minimum number, it is not worth any distributor's time to take on the work. Be realistic, most single artist or single album P&D deals don't make much money for anyone.

Ask for details of their distribution terms. If you can get it, a copy of their standard agreement is the best place to start. You can compare terms and conditions, to see who offers what services and at what cost. Then ask around retailers, to see if the distributors you have short-listed have a good reputation for service.

EXPENSES

In P&D deals, the owner gets most of the proceeds from each sale. Up to 70% – 75%, depending upon the distribution fee. Before you get excited though, remember that out of that 80%, you still have to pay:
- all risk funding of the entire recording process;
- the manufacturing cost of the record and its packaging;
- artwork origination;
- artist's royalties;
- mechanical copyright royalties;
- marketing and promotional costs;
- GST;
- business overhead, including warehousing of stock (distributors may only be willing to hold the number of records they feel they need, not the number pressed); and

- returns and obsolescence of stock. The administrative processing is done by the distributor, but the cost of it (i.e. the loss of value of records returned or which become obsolete, damaged etc), is all borne by you. Both parties suffer when there are returns or obsolete stock.

The residue (if any) after all these deductions is your profit. Welcome to the world of being a record company!

FUNDING

The down-side of P&D deals is that you have to fund them. You have to fund not only the recording process itself but also any promotional materials (e.g. videos, record packaging, art) as well as the costs of manufacturing and promoting your records. You need plenty of capital to be able to do this properly. Most people in the music business do not have private wealth or a tame bank manager. They usually have to do a deal with a Major record company, just to get an advance to pay for the recording costs. Paying for manufacturing and promotion is out of the question for most people.

Subject to complying with the horribly complex tax and corporation laws, it may be possible to arrange for a group of investors to finance you. This is lawyer territory and requires planning and a great deal of expert advice. This is particularly true if you intend to raise funds in a way that legally requires a prospectus to be produced. A prospectus is a very formal (and expensive) document, setting out the whole scheme in detail. This kind of thing is only justified if the returns will be truly spectacular, or some of your friends need a tax loss.

There are ways that the capital drain can be at least slowed down a bit. With the distributor's agreement, you may be able to defer manufacturing costs and mechanicals until you actually start to receive income from record sales. This has to be dealt with when you first do your deal with the distributor and is usually only possible if the distributor is a Major record company.

WHO DOES WHAT?

You should take a look at the list at the beginning of Master Licences, to check the licensee's responsibilities in a master licence agreement. This will highlight the differences between master licence deals and P&D deals.

In typical P&D deals, the owner of the master recording is responsible for:

- paying for the records and their packaging to be manufactured and delivered to the distributor's warehouse;
- advertising the records;
- keeping adequate stocks of records in the warehouse;
- ensuring mechanical copyright royalties are paid;

- taking back any surplus stocks of records left in the warehouse at the end of the deal and disposing of them (hopefully, in a way which will help give a return on them, rather than just having them dumped at the local tip);
- ensuring that the proper GST is paid.

The distributor is responsible for:

- including the records in release sheets and putting the titles and catalogue numbers into the distributor's catalogue;
- fulfilling orders and shipping the records to the retailers;
- collecting payment; and
- remitting the owner's proceeds, after deducting the various costs and fees.

If the distributor is a Major, it will often arrange for the records to be made for the owner (unless the owner has already done this, by making arrangements directly with another manufacturer), although the cost is charged to the owner.

MANUFACTURING

You pay for the records manufactured. If your distributor is a record company that has its own manufacturing plant, there are obvious benefits in doing a deal for their plant to make your records. The record company will bill you. You will have to pay the whole lot within (usually) 30 days, or (if they are generous) the record company might agree to treat it as an advance against your proceeds from the sale of those records and deduct it when the accounting is done.

Record companies have usually negotiated very cheap rates with record manufacturers. As an individual, you are very unlikely to get a comparable price. If you are using a record company as a distributor, try to get the records ordered from their usual manufacturer on your behalf. This is likely to reduce your manufacturing costs considerably.

If you make your own arrangements to have the records manufactured, you will probably have to pay for the records on delivery. This will drain your capital rapidly. Remember, a compact disc can cost you around $3 to $3.50 per unit once you include the costs of creating and printing artwork, getting the discs made, having the packaging inserted and the whole lot delivered to your door. You can negotiate better prices if you are ordering larger quantities but it is always important to judge carefully whether the savings are real or illusory: if you can sell the stock readily the savings will be real. If not, the cost of storage, insurance, handling, interest, and the general inconvenience, make the ordering process one of keen judgment rather than mere optimism.

It is always worth seeing if the distributor will agree to you deferring payment of the manufacturing costs until they can be deducted by the distributor from the proceeds of the sales. This can be done in the course of their accounting to you.

WHO OWNS THE RECORDS?

You pay for the records, so you own them. You should always have final say as to how they are to be sold, though this has to be consistent with the distributor's methods and trading terms.

Make absolutely sure that the distributor knows that you, not it, own the records. Otherwise, your records may be gathered up inadvertently in the course of a warehouse clear-up (which distributors regularly do to remove surplus stock). Stocks of your records may be scrapped along with the distributor's own stock unless precautions are taken. Worse still, they might be sold as 'deletions' to retailers. The distributor would ordinarily have to reimburse you for any records it mishandled (and probably for any loss of profits you might sustain) but it could take quite a while to convince the record company to find its chequebook (even if it acknowledged its mistake). In the meantime, your records are out of stock as far as the company's computer is concerned.

Any records returned by retailers have to be put back into your stock or a full credit given by the Major that is doing the distribution.

STOCK CONTROL

Most distributors will try to put the responsibility for stock control back onto you. This means the distributor will not order new stocks unless you say to. You have to watch the stock levels and sales trends constantly. If, for example, you have a big promotional campaign planned, don't forget to top-up the stock levels or to prepare your manufacturer so it can respond promptly to orders for additional stock if needed. An out of stock television-advertised album is an embarrassing thing to behold and makes you no money either.

PROMOTION

Since this is likely to be your concern, there will be no one else to blame if things go wrong. Plan this properly. Do not overestimate your abilities, or underestimate the cost. If in doubt, engage an experienced freelance promotions person.

Distributors may agree to take promotion over from you and to pay for it but, in return, they will take a bigger percentage of the takings. Only you can decide if this is a worthwhile trade-off. Sometimes you can do it cheaper and better than the distributor. Sometimes the campaign will simply demand more money and resources than you can muster.

PROMOTIONAL COPIES

It is in your interest to keep tight reign on the number of promotional copies, including limiting copies that can be ordered by your distributor's staff. There is certainly promotional value in having the record available to the staff, even if they do not pay for it, but the numbers have to be reasonable. Any records given away free by the distributor should be exempt from its distribution fee (or subject to a reduced fee).

You should try to retain sufficient copies to meet promotional needs, rather than take copies out of the distributor's warehouse. This will save you time and money. Make sure the distributor knows what your promotional plans are and agree in advance to whom, if anyone, the distributor may provide promotional copies. Usually, if you are dealing with a Major, they will agree to simply drop copies off to their main media connections (radio programmers, DJs and the like) as part of their usual promotions work, provided it does not require any additional time or effort.

DISTRIBUTION

Most P&D deals give the distributor 'the exclusive right to distribute' in the nominated territory. This is not a copyright licence, but is still enforceable as a condition of the contract. If you think you will want to distribute any records yourself, then reserve that right in the contract. This right can be particularly useful if you do a lot of live work and can sell records after the show. (Now quickly read the chapter on Merchandising!) You might even be able to arrange some to be sold through mail order or via your website. To do these things, you need to reserve the rights up-front, or risk annoying your distributor when your records turn up in unexpected places. Basically, record companies are good at selling to record retailers. Other non-traditional outlets are outside their area, so you will have to tackle those yourself. A bit of creative thinking can generate a surprising number of sales.

Assuming you made your own arrangements for the records and packaging to be manufactured, the distributor's work only starts once the records are delivered to its warehouse. Then, it will load the record's catalogue number into its sales system and put the title into its catalogue. From then on, the records are available for dealers to order in the same way they would order any other record. As far as the retailers are concerned, for most purposes (except returns) there is no difference between records sold by the distributor under its own labels, and those it is distributing on your behalf.

TRADING TERMS

The retailer buys the records in accordance with the distributor's 'trading terms'. These are the rules that regulate the distributor's interaction with its customers (the retailers). The terms of trade determine:

- how records are ordered by the retailers;
- how and when they will be delivered;
- if and how records may be returned by the retailer; and
- when and how the retailer pays for them.

You have to accept that the distributor's trading terms will apply to all its transactions. You cannot expect them to be changed just for your product. You have to find out what those terms are, before you do the deal, so you can make appropriate plans to deal with any parts you might not like.

For example, you should reserve the right to set the selling price of your records. If you do not reserve control over price, you could get a very nasty surprise should your records come out at a reduced (or increased) price. You should also determine whether sales must be 'firm'; or whether they can be 'sale or return'. You should insist on being advised, in advance, of any changes to the relevant trading terms. You will get an unpleasant surprise if the distributor's firm sales policy is changed so that retailers are permitted to take the stock 'on spec' and then return it at any time if the stock doesn't sell.

DISTRIBUTION FEES

Like most things in the record industry, the fee the distributor wants in return for its services is negotiable. It will vary according to your bargaining strength and the amount of work the distributor will have to do to get its fee. The more it does, the more it will charge. You have to decide what work is genuinely extra and what work is routine and effectively not costing the distributor anything it would not ordinarily spend anyway. Hanging out for a bottom-line fee will be false economy if this encourages the distributor to put your record even lower down its list of priorities than it already is.

Most record companies will calculate and pay mechanical copyright royalties for you at no extra cost. Their computer will be processing your record sales anyway, so it's very little extra work to have it calculate the mechanicals at the end of the quarter and send off a cheque on your behalf. Naturally, the payment will be deducted from any payments due to you from sales of those records.

Be very wary of distribution fees exceeding 30% of the wholesale price less GST. This is the top rate for physical distribution, unless the distributor is handling and paying for advertising. Distribution fees above this may leave you with too little from the proceeds of each sale to cover all your costs, let alone to make a profit.

Also, be wary of additional handling fees charged as administration fees. (What do they think you are paying them the distribution fee for? Out of pity?) Shun delivery fees and the like. The distribution fee is meant to cover the distributor's costs and leave it with a profit. Any added-on fees have to be questioned. Some may be legitimate but most are just another way of making a 20% distribution fee add up to a 30% one.

Because the handling and administration of returns is expensive, some companies will also charge an additional fee for returns. As you will have no control over returns policy (it is determined by the distributor's terms of trade – remember?) you must try to cap this. Others allow a percentage as returns, but will charge an additional fee per returned record once a certain number has been reached, usually calculated as a percentage of the number of records shipped to retailers in that period. Either way, these additional fees can bump up your distribution costs, so watch out for them and whenever they are proposed, get them explained to you in full before signing on the dotted line.

DEDUCTIONS AND ACCOUNTING

You must make sure what the actual basis of the payment calculations of net proceeds will be. The usual basis will be either the retail price after deduction of GST, or the wholesale price after deduction of GST. Either way, you need to be sure that there are no other deductions (such as delivery charges or processing fees) applied before division of the proceeds.

Typically, an accounting from a distributor will show:

Net proceeds from sales
minus   mechanical copyright fees (1)
minus   distribution fee (2)
minus   cost of record (3)

leaves   your share (4)

1. This assumes that this will be calculated and paid in accordance with the Copyright Act and the ARIA/AMCOS Agreement.
2. This will be calculated as a percentage of the net proceeds figure before deduction of mechanicals or other fees.
3. This will only apply if you have arranged for the record distributor to do this on your behalf and it has agreed to defer such payment. Otherwise, you will already have paid for it.
4. Out of this, you will have to meet your artists' royalty obligations, promotional costs and set-up costs. Anything left over is your profit.

Accounting statements and remittances are usually timed to coincide with the record distributor's usual royalty statement run. Quarterly accounting is common but monthly is better because cashflow is essential for paying all the other costs.

GOODS AND SERVICES TAX

This is a really knotty area of P&D deals and, frankly, is completely misunderstood by most people. GST law is too complex to be dealt with in this book. However, it is vital that you be aware of its importance and that you consult professional help in advance (preferably from an accountant who deals with trading enterprises, rather than doing tax returns for pensioners) to make sure you do not inadvertently pay too little (or too much) GST on records sold through a P&D deal.

Essentially, the manufacturer will charge you the manufacturing cost plus the GST. Assuming you are then selling to the record shop (through the distributor as agent) you will charge the dealer the published price to dealer (PPD) plus GST. Of course you will then be charged GST in respect of the distribution commission and fees that you are charged by the distributor. You then remit the GST to the ATO less the GST you have already paid. Simple, right? NOT!

The moral is: get professional advice on GST and stick to it. The GST issues in P&D deals are very complicated and the companies have had to spend a lot of money getting advice on how to make their systems comply with these laws.

DURING THE DEAL

It pays to check with retailers, to see if the record company is actually making your records available to retailers and delivering them. The best thing to do is to order a few at randomly selected retail outlets and see how they go.

Keep close contact with the departments looking after stock control at your distributor. The people there are best placed to know how well or badly your record is selling and when you should order more stock (or make arrangements with your creditors!).

Call at least every 10 days for a stock report and, if possible, get a copy of the stock report dealing with your record(s) so you can see sales trends, numbers given away, etc... If your distributor's information system allows, get daily reports.

AT THE END OF THE DEAL

When the deal ends, you will usually be required to take your stock out of the warehouse within a specified time otherwise the record company will probably sell or dump it. The removal costs are usually yours. You are, of course, free to do whatever you like with the records after that.

MASTER LICENCE DEALS

For simplicity, the expressions 'master recordings' or 'masters' will be used here to refer to audio-only master recordings, whatever format they are in. In practice of course, masters can take many forms: 2-inch (5-cm) studio tape of the multi-track and the final mix, DAT, U-Matic, quarter inch (6.25 mm), custom compact disc, direct cut mother, or even just a hard drive disc containing the relevant sound files in digital form. Even commercial compact discs are occasionally used when the original tapes cannot be located.

Master licences deal with the end result of the recording contract, not with the recording process itself. They are one of the basic transactions in the record industry. They are the means by which the owner of a master recording can formally permit or license others to use that master and to commercially exploit the copyright in it, without the owner relinquishing copyright ownership.

Master licences can deal with all of the copyright in a master recording, or just a part of it. They can deal with one master recording or many. It all depends upon the agreement. This flexibility is the major attribute of master licensing. The parties can tailor their deals precisely to suit their needs.

EXCLUSIVITY

Like other copyright licensing, master licences can be exclusive or non-exclusive. Exclusive licences are the most common kind, although, as will be seen later, non-exclusive licences have their place. Because of the Copyright Act, exclusive licences must be written down and signed by the party granting the licence (the licensor). If they are not, they risk being unenforceable by the recipient of the licence (generally referred to as the licensee) against infringers. (The terms licensee and licensor will be used in this chapter, though occasionally other names are used in practice so as to reduce the chance of confusion in documents, since the words are not that dissimilar. The name itself is not especially important. It is the nature and extent of the rights granted which count.)

The Copyright Act allows non-exclusive licences to be either verbal or in writing. The basic difference between exclusive and non-exclusive licences is that in an exclusive licence, the licensor gives the rights to the licensee 'to the exclusion of all others' (as the Copyright Act so succinctly puts it), whereas in a non-exclusive licence, there can be any number of non-exclusive licensees, all having identical rights in the masters in question. The commercial ramifications of exclusivity as opposed to non-exclusivity, will be explored in detail in here.

BASIC ELEMENTS OF MASTER LICENCES

The following aspects are essential elements of all master licences, both exclusive and non-exclusive:

THE PARTIES

Master licences are done at all levels of the record industry. For example, a recording made in the United States by an Independent (let's call it Indy Co) might be:

- licensed in the United States by Indy Co to a Major in the same country (let's call it Major Co), giving Major Co exclusive rights for the world;
- Major Co might license the recording to an affiliate in Australia, giving the affiliate exclusive rights in Australia;
- the Australian affiliate might license a television-marketer in Australia, giving it non-exclusive rights to include certain tracks in one of the television-marketer's theme album '20 Great Hunting Songs'; and
- the Australian affiliate might also grant a film producer a non-exclusive licence to reproduce the recording in a film soundtrack and exploit that film throughout the world.

PROOF OF COPYRIGHT

At each step of the chain, the party granting the rights will be a licensor and the recipient of the rights will be a licensee. Each licensor depends upon the person before them for its rights to be valid. If someone in the chain makes a mistake or enters into an agreement that exceeds their authority, this will invalidate the rights of everyone below them in the chain. This is sometimes called the 'withered root' theory of copyright and is based on the obvious analogy of a tree with problems of a fundamental kind. In other words, know who you are dealing with. Get warranties of ownership. If you have any doubts at all, get objective proof of ownership before you conclude a deal with a licensor who you know is not the person who actually made the recording. Remember; a warranty gives nothing more than a right to sue. It cannot cure the defect in the copyright chain.

THE LICENSED RIGHTS

Master licences must give the licensee record company the right to make copies of the master and to sell copies to the public in the nominated territory for a nominated period of time. After that, the rights will be as wide or as narrow as the parties agree.

The rights granted and the degree of scope the licensee will have in dealing with the master, depends upon the relative bargaining strength of the parties and whether the would-be licensor really trusts the would-be licensee. When in doubt, keep the rights under tight control.

The agreement may even specify technical standards which the licensee must meet, limit which formats of records may be released, and specify the ways the records may be marketed.

In most cases, the licensee has no rights in the master other than the licence to make and sell copies. Thus, the licensee may not alter the master in any way, nor attempt to exercise any rights that were not granted by the licensor. Basically, the licensee may only do those things specified in the agreement. Any deviation will usually require the licensor's prior consent. Most licensors even require licensees to get permission before allowing their records to be sold as mid-price or budget records, or in conjunction with a television campaign.

THE MASTERS

Master recordings are usually defined as 'recordings of sound technically suitable for the commercial manufacture of records' or similar. Most licence agreements also specify the format in which the master must be delivered to the licensee. No point getting U-Matic if all you have is DAT or CDR.

Where the masters already exist, it is easy to identify them in the agreement by artist and track. If the masters are yet to be recorded, it becomes more complicated. The contract has to identify the master unambiguously. Unless this is done properly, an unscrupulous licensor could deliver any old rubbish that approximated the description of the master to be delivered and claim to have met its obligations under the contract.

The masters have to contain the correct recordings and be in first class technical condition. If not, they will be commercially useless. Masters should be checked as soon as they are delivered and any faults reported without delay, so a replacement can be supplied (at no charge of course!).

Most licensees will also require delivery of a "PQ sheet" containing data about the location and timing of tracks on the master, as well as details of the International Standard Recording Code (ISRC) setting out the country of origin of the master, as well as the copyright ownership and the designated identification number for each track.

ADDITIONAL MATERIALS

Records are more than flat pieces of plastic, a series of noughts and ones on a hard drive, or spools of magnetic tape. The packaging is an integral part of the goods being offered to the public. A master licence has to specify:

• in what packaging the records are to be sold;
• who will pay for original artwork and production parts (such as negatives or digital files) to be made;

- in what form production parts are to be supplied, assuming the licensor is to supply them (e.g. whether as artwork or as photographic negatives or digital files); and
- when the parts must be delivered. (Remember that it usually takes longer to print packaging than to make the records.)

If you are a licensee and you have to create your own artwork, remember that you should own both the art itself and the copyright in it. A licensee in this position can sometimes do a trade with a licensor that may need artwork itself. In such a case, the licensor may find it cheaper to buy the licensee's artwork than to create its own. This all needs to be documented properly.

Most master licences also require the licensor to deliver an accurate list of musical works reproduced on the Master as this simplifies the licensee's task of complying with mechanical copyright requirements. The licensee can use this list when notifying the publishers of the works being reproduced in the records made from that master.

TERRITORY

This can be as widely or narrowly defined as the parties agree. If you are a licensor, ensure the definition of the territory is neither ambiguous nor extends beyond the territory you actually control. If you are a licensee, you will want the widest possible territory, but your licensor will probably want the narrowest definition it can negotiate.

Where an Independent (Indie Co) is licensing a master to a Major (Major Co), and they know Major Co's affiliates are going to release the records in several territories, it may suit both sides for Major Co to get rights for a territory greater than its own domestic territory, so it can do the licensing. Indie Co could choose to negotiate the licence to the affiliate or it could ask Major Co to act as the licensor because Major Co will probably already have an inter-company licence agreement in place with its affiliates. In most cases though, Major Co will only agree to act as licensor if it gets a percentage of the licence royalty flowing to Indie Co from those external territories.

Conversely, Indie Co might choose to do the additional work of negotiating the licensing directly, if there are significant financial advantages (e.g. additional advances) sufficient to outweigh the extra work.

Major Co might only be prepared to sign the licence deal if it is for 'all available territories' – meaning all countries where Indie Co. has not yet already secured releases itself. This is a matter for negotiation. Indie Co needs to make sure though that if Major Co cannot secure a release in a reasonable time (usually between 90 and 180 days, depending upon the kind of recording), then Indie Co must get back the right to seek alternative licensees overseas. If that happens, Major Co ought not to share in royalty income generated from licences it did not secure, although this will be more difficult to secure if Indie Co is also looking to Major Co for a large royalty advance.

TERM

Most licences are for three years, though there's no magic in the number. It may be that three years is long enough for most licensees to make a profit, but not such a long time that the licensor feels they have lost control of the recording. There is no standard term, but as a general rule, pop recordings are licensed for a fairly short time. Classical and jazz recordings need to be licensed for a longer time because they tend to sell at a slower rate.

Licensors usually want to keep the term as short as possible. As a licensee, you will usually want the term to be as long as possible. Sometimes, licensees are given the opportunity to extend the term, if they achieve specified sales targets or other goals.

Defining the term can become complicated where a licensee has options to acquire additional masters that do not yet exist. For example, Indie Co may have signed an artist and recorded one album. It has the right to record several more. Indie Co and Major Co may agree that Major Co will have first opportunity to obtain a licence of each album as it is finished. This kind of deal will need some fancy drafting by lawyers for the agreement to be workable. The parties need to consider whether all the rights in the repertoire will revert to the licensor at the same time, or whether each recording will be licensed for a number of years as it becomes available. The former is neater but the latter gives the licensee more chance to recoup any advances paid for the master last delivered.

In addition to the term (during which time the licensee can exercise all the rights granted under the licence) there is usually a 'sell-off' period of between 6 and 12 months, during which time the licensee is permitted to sell-off stocks of records that were in existence at the time the term ended. Some agreements include elaborate provisions to prevent the licensee from filling its warehouse with records in anticipation of the term finishing, or selling the records off at discount prices. This is because the sell-off period is usually non-exclusive in that the licensor may grant to another party altogether, a licence for the same recordings and this licence will usually start at the end of the term of the previous licence. This is something that can become very important if the licensed recordings are still selling well as the licence enters its last few months.

RIGHTS LICENSED

Most licences give the licensee the exclusive right in the Territory during the term, to:

- reproduce the master recordings;
- communicate the recordings to the public; and
- reproduce the other materials and video clips supplied as part of the package, subject to whatever particular limitations the licensor requires.

Most licensors go to great lengths to limit the ways its licensee may sell records. The licensee will always be able to sell full-price records through so-called 'traditional or normal retail outlets' (i.e. record shops), but other methods will usually require the licensor's prior approval. The licensor has to protect itself from unscrupulous licensees. It also has to ensure that any special obligations, owed to the artist under the recording contract, are passed along to all licensees via the licence agreements. If a licensee wants to sell records through (say) record clubs or digital download services or as something other than an ordinary full-price record, then the licensor will have to approve first.

In general, licensors tend to restrict the rights granted, so that they retain maximum control over the many ways a master may be exploited. For example, most licensors will specifically reserve the right to authorise synchronisation of their masters into film soundtracks, advertising and the like. This helps stop licensees from getting out of control and also helps the licensor co-ordinate the way the record is marketed in several territories.

Film soundtracks can be a valuable licensing right for licensees. Soundtrack rights usually attract a significant lump-sum payment, which some licensors will try to claim as their own, no matter where the film originates. Other licensors take a more pragmatic attitude and share synchronisation fees with the licensee, which can be a significant incentive for a licensee to propose one recording in favour of another when the time comes! Soundtracks are also useful because they can promote interest in a recording and can even form the basis for a promotional tour by the artist, if the film has sufficient profile. A soundtrack album can revitalise an artist's career and sell a lot of copies in its own right.

Generally, licensors will also forbid a licensee (other than a Major) from itself granting exclusive sub-licences, unless it first gets the licensor's express consent in each instance. Licensors like to know who is dealing with their recordings. Besides, it is that much harder to keep track of, and collect, royalties from sub-licensees.

DELIVERY OF MASTERS AND OTHER
MANUFACTURING PARTS

Most licence agreements are done in haste. There are always time constraints imposed by promotional activities, touring and availability of personnel, as well as the licensor's need for money ('Pay the advance now and trust me!'). Combine that with a licensee who wants to get the records out as soon as possible and soon the licensor starts handing over the master recordings and manufacturing parts even before the deal is actually struck.

Now, this point may seem obvious when you read this at your leisure, but when you are in the middle of frantic last-minute negotiations, do not part with your masters or your manufacturing parts until the deal is actually done and signed. It is quite astonishing how many deals are signed after the records are actually in the shops. This lemming-like behaviour invites disaster because it instantly escalates any last-minute misunderstanding or disagreement into a huge drama with commercial implications and the threat of nasty litigation, rather than it just being another point to negotiate before the final draft of the agreement is printed before signing.

Licensees should always check each master for technical quality (and that it is in fact the correct master) as soon as it arrives. The same applies to manufacturing parts such as negatives or digital artwork files for record packaging, and to promotional videos.

MANUFACTURING RECORDS AND PACKAGING

The licensee is responsible for having the records and the packaging manufactured and getting them in the warehouse by the scheduled release date.

The licensee has to pay for all stocks from the proceeds of each sale. As no sale equals no proceeds, most licensees try to keep initial orders for records to a minimum. Initial quantities should be discussed with the licensee, but the licensor ought to respect the licensee's knowledge of its own market and conditions. It takes less time to top-up stock than to first manufacture it, but the delay can still be inconvenient and, at worst, could lead to the records being out of stock, which means lost sales.

It can take quite a long time from placement of initial orders until records are manufactured and delivered, especially as Christmas approaches. This is when the Majors are gearing up to fill their warehouses in readiness for the most active sales period of the year and manufacturing capacity is usually booked and over-booked in the last quarter of every year.

No matter what the time of year, the licensor should always deliver the parts to the licensee in ample time to allow for mishaps, errors and plain old stupidity. The release date can certainly be adjusted if the records are obviously not going to be ready in time, but this is not desirable as it may force the promotions department to spread their time over more records than they can properly deal with at any one time.

PROMOTION

Licensors will usually want guarantees from licensees that the licensee will make reasonable (and sometimes, even unreasonable) efforts to promote the records. Commercial common sense would suggest that a licensee would do that anyway but just to make sure, some licensors insist on a minimum amount being spent by the licensee on promotional activities. These provisions are usually difficult to enforce and cannot guarantee a record's success anyway.

Most licences oblige the licensee to supply a minimum number of sample records to the licensor. The proper purpose of these is to verify quality of manufacture but sometimes the number to be provided can be very significant. Whatever the number, these copies should be exempt from royalties.

The expression 'promotional activities' can range from a sullen office junior dropping a copy of the video and a sample record onto a radio programmer's desk, through to the promotions department mounting a co-ordinated campaign with a street team, posters, place mats, a media party and a hot air balloon from which the artist dangles, wearing only bicycle shorts and a smile. The point is, if you have a particular promotional campaign in mind, and both the licensor and the licensee agree to it, make that a part of the agreement. This gives the licensor some certainty and protects the licensee from the allegation (should sales not meet expectations) that it did not promote the records properly.

Wherever possible, the licensee should be required to keep the licensor advised of promotional activities as they may be relevant to the licensor's own plans in some way.

Most promotional activities are the licensee's responsibility, but some kinds of promotional work can be so expensive that the licensee has to get assistance from the licensor. Some promotional activities have an impact on the royalty rates. For example, television advertising is so expensive that it is only commercially viable if the retailer pays a premium on the wholesale price of television advertised records (as they do in the United Kingdom) and/or the licensor takes a reduction in royalty rate (which is the usual approach in Australia). The usual reduction is 50%. The tricky part (for your lawyer) is defining the term 'television advertised records'.

MECHANICAL COPYRIGHT FEES

These are the fees payable by the licensee to whichever publisher or person controls the copyright in the music reproduced in the master recording. The licensee has to comply with the requirements of the Copyright Act, though the practice is varied somewhat by the ARIA/AMCOS Agreement (see Chapter 9, **Publishing**, for a description of how this agreement works).

The Majors are all set up to comply with these requirements as a matter of course. If the record company distributing your records is not an ARIA member, contact AMCOS.

ROYALTIES

If you have not already read it, this is a good time to turn to Chapter 23, **Record Royalties**. The principles discussed in that chapter apply here too.

If you are a licensor (like our example, Indie Co) you will want to maximise your royalty but at the same time, you will not want to remove the licensee's incentive to maximise sales. All licensors have to set the royalty rate high enough to cover all their costs (e.g. recording the master and making the video and the cover art), their royalty obligations, and still leave enough to make a profit.

Conversely, a licensee will always be trying to keep the royalty as low as possible, because it is an expense that reduces the licensee's profitability. If you are a licensee, you should to do a proper budget before concluding any deal. Use realistic sales estimates and current costs figures. This is the only way you will be able to see how many records you have to sell before you break even (i.e. make neither a profit nor a loss). Better still, do several calculations. One using worst-case figures, another using the number of units you genuinely feel you will sell and another using wildly optimistic figures (you will need to do this one to restore your confidence after you see the results of the other two calculations!) This is the only way you can sensibly decide whether the deal has any hope of making a profit or whether the advance the licensor is demanding is realistic.

As a licensee, your chief concern is to make sure the royalty rate you have to pay to the licensor is not so high that the exercise becomes uneconomic. Deciding what is a reasonable rate under the circumstances will be influenced by a number of factors.

- The nature of the rights you are getting, the territory of the licence, and the term. You need to determine whether anyone else has competing rights in the territory. Has any previous licensee or importer spoiled the market so that your sales will be affected? Do your rights give you enough scope to exploit the copyrights properly?
- Your financial calculations will vary depending upon whether you are manufacturing and distributing the records yourself or doing it through a third party. Virtually everyone except the Majors rely upon someone else to manufacture and distribute their records. Every licensee in that position has to set its in-coming royalty rate sufficiently high to enable it to cover its royalty obligations and other expenses, and still leave it with a profit. If your outgoing royalty is

more than 60% of your royalty income, you may not have sufficient margin to make it worthwhile, unless the record is a phenomenal success.

- Your set-up costs (e.g. manufacturing records and packaging) will need to be taken into account, as you have to pay these from your income.
- You need to allow for the amount of any advance you have to pay.
- Don't forget your overhead costs. Running a business always involves rents, salaries, stationery, insurances and so on.

The royalty rates for master licences tend to be higher than those paid to recording artists under direct signings. This is because the licensee can judge the finished product for itself, so the risk is lower. Also, whoever actually made the recording will want to make a reasonable return on their investment and effort. The licensor will have royalty obligations, either to the artist or to another licensor. The royalty the licensor gets must comfortably exceed its royalty obligations, or it cannot make a profit, no matter how successful the record might be.

Basic master licence royalty rates in Australia range from a paltry 12% of dealer price (with the usual deductions) up to 30% of dealer price (with the deductions) for a really spectacular catalogue. Master licences for catalogues rarely differentiate between recordings in that catalogue. Major catalogues may attract a premium if they are especially prestigious or can guarantee to provide a significant cashflow to the licensee.

It is standard practice for licensees to request reductions in royalties (a royalty break) for records sold other than at full price. These provisions are dealt with in the Chapter 23, **Record Royalties**. The licensor may agree to adjust the royalty rate, provided it feels the potential benefits outweigh the reduction in royalty per unit – i.e. whether the increase in the number of sales will be great enough to offset the reduction in the royalty per unit otherwise paid on a full price record. Most licensors insist that non-standard methods of selling be subject to their prior approval, especially if it has an effect on the royalty rate.

When masters are licensed from overseas, it is usual for the licensee also to get the right to control public performance and broadcast copyrights. The licensor will allow the licensee to retain a percentage (up to 50%) of fees received from the Phonographic Performance Company of Australia Ltd (PPCA) to whoever is the copyright owner/exclusive licensee in Australia.

Most licensors reserve the right to approve requests to synchronise their recordings into film and television soundtracks. Some will let their licensees negotiate such licensing provided they consult with the licensor. Others insist on doing it themselves and keeping any fees due.

ADVANCES

An advance is supposed to be a pre-payment of royalties. If a licensor wants an advance that is more than that, the would-be licensee has to evaluate whether the extra money (and risk) is justified under the circumstances. Sometimes the excess is just part of the price of securing the deal, especially if there are several parties interested in it.

Overseas licensors keep forgetting that the potential market in Australia is only slightly larger than New York or Greater London, so their initial suggestions for advances tend to be excessive.

Something every potential licensee must remember is that the anti-parallel importation provisions of the Copyright Act no longer apply to recordings. Imports invariably account for a number of sales of both moderately popular and niche market records that originate from overseas. This means that the number of sales the licensee can make may not bear any relationship with the total market for that recording. It is extremely difficult to calculate a reasonable advance in such circumstances. In spite of this, most licensees still have to pay advances because this is the best way a licensor has to guarantee at least a minimum payment for the licence. In the unlikely event that the total royalties due to the licensor exceed the advance, the licensor will no doubt be pleased, if perhaps surprised, to start getting royalty cheques.

If you are a licensee and you have to pay an advance, try to get a concession from the licensor, allowing you to extend the term if you are under-recouped at the date that the term would otherwise end. This way, you can even agree to a slightly higher advance than would otherwise be prudent, because you have the opportunity to continue exploiting the masters and generating royalties.

ACCOUNTING

This is usually quarterly, but can be every half year, depending on the terms of the deal. Licensees should always comply strictly with all accounting dates and requirements and so must be careful not to agree to any accounting requirements they cannot actually fulfil.

The agreement will set out the details to be included in royalty statements. Licensees must make sure they do not promise to supply accounting information they do not have or cannot get. Any deviation or late payment could give an aggressive licensor the opportunity to terminate the licence for breach of the contract. This could be catastrophic, especially if the licensee paid a big advance and it is still unrecouped.

Most licence agreements include detailed clauses that give the licensor the right to conduct detailed financial examinations of the licensee's books of account. If you are a licensee, it is in your interest to keep the terms of any examination as narrow as possible and to ensure that it occurs no later than two or three years after the end of the Term, in order to give you some finality. Royalty audits are terribly disruptive affairs and tend to be expensive, which is why there have been so few between licensors and licensees in Australia. In the United States, because the market is so big and therefore the amounts of money in the system are so large, there is a great tradition of licensors auditing licensees. Perhaps it will catch on here too, given a little time.

Conversely, if you are a licensor, you will of course be deeply suspicious of the licensee and will try to insist on the right, as part of an audit, to use an endoscope on the licensee's managing director. You will want to insist on unrestricted access to all the licensee's books and records relating to licensing, promotions and manufacturing but, in practice, a licensee that is administering a large number of licences will demand some practical limitations on audit levels so that its own business is not unduly disrupted.

TERMINATION

Licence agreements usually end because the term expires, but sometimes they end because one of the parties does something to give the other cause to terminate the agreement for breach of contract. This is when all the lawyers start turning to the back of the contract to the 'miscellaneous' clauses no-one wanted to look at when the licence agreement was being negotiated.

Well-drafted licence agreements have comprehensive provisions setting out what events will amount to a breach of the contract and what happens if a breach occurs.

Most licences give the licensee some 'days to cure' should they make a mistake, but some events, such as the licensee's bankruptcy or any failure to deliver accounting statements on time, will usually give the licensor the right to terminate the licence immediately. Usually, termination for breach will also annul any sell-off period.

At the end of any licence deal, the licensee should always be obliged to destroy manufacturing parts and provide a sworn statement (a certificate of destruction) verifying that it was done. If there is a sell-off period, then the licensee may continue to sell remaining stocks at full price. Once the sell-off period ends, the licensee should have to destroy any remaining stocks and provide a certificate of destruction. Usually, video masters will be erased, or sent to the new licensee.

MISCELLANEOUS

This is the title usually given to the part of the licence agreement that deals with such things as which country's laws should apply when things go wrong. These clauses can actually be quite important if there is a breach of the agreement. Most overseas licensors try to make sure their own laws and courts have sole jurisdiction over the licence agreement and any disputes. Imagine the problems this could cause for an Australian licensee, if it has to sue in (say) California, under Californian law! Try at least to give Australian courts jurisdiction, even if they have to apply the law of the licensor's nominated country.

WITHHOLDING TAX

This is a subject that deserves a book of its own, so it is not possible to give a comprehensive treatment of its working. However, licensees who deal with overseas licensors need to be aware of it and how it can affect their remittances of advances and royalties to overseas licensors.

Withholding tax is a tax levied on remittances of advances and royalties to licensors outside Australia. There is a specific department of the Australian Taxation Office (ATO) that deals with withholding tax. The people there are helpful and will answer telephone queries and supply the necessary forms on request.

The practical effect of withholding tax laws is that all licensees have to deduct a specific percentage of all royalty and advance payments and pay it to the ATO accompanied by the appropriate form. The percentage varies, depending upon the country to which the royalties are being paid. It can range from 5% to 10% (for countries with tax treaties with Australia) up to over 40% (for non-treaty countries), which is why you have to contact the ATO before you make the remittance.

The licence agreement should always allow the licensee to deduct withholding tax before calculating the remittance, otherwise the licensor could insist that you pay the tax out of your own pocket. For example: if an advance of $10,000 is agreed, and the withholding tax rate is 10%, then you will send $9,000 to your licensor and $1,000 to the ATO. If, however, there is no clause in the contract allowing withholding tax to be deducted from the advance, then the licensor could insist you pay $10,000 to it, and you will still have to pay the $1,000 withholding tax. In that event, your total expenditure has gone up to $11,000 and the extra $1,000 will not be recoupable as part of the advance. The same applies to royalty remittances.

The licensee must obtain a receipt from the ATO, which can take several months. This receipt is then sent to the licensor. As far as the licensor is concerned, withholding tax is usually treated as a pre-payment of tax in its own country. This means the licensor pays $1,000 less tax for that year in its own country. Of course, this only helps a licensor that is actually liable to pay tax in its own country. If the licensor is making a loss, then the tax paid in Australia cannot be reclaimed in its own country.

RECORD RENTAL

One of the little-considered avenues for record distribution is Record Rental. It's just that the distribution isn't controlled by either the artist or the record company.

Of course it was never favoured by either record companies or artists because it might affect sales. In fact record rental was not a great problem while records were vulnerable to damage and wear – new ones had to be bought regularly. Compact discs changed that. The much advertised 'perfect reproduction for ever' virtue, turned out to be a very mixed-blessing for the record industry.

Rental outlets buy the compact discs for the same price as the public, then rent them out for a few dollars a time. Nothing is paid to the songwriters, the artists or the record company for this commercial use of their work. It has taken a long time for governments around the world to accept that renting compact discs is really a commercial use of peoples' artistic efforts, for which the owners of the copyright ought to be paid.

In Australia, that recognition came in 1994 when legislation was introduced as a consequence of the *Trade-Related Aspects of Intellectual Property Rights (TRIPPS) Agreement*. Now, the Copyright Act requires that the owner of the copyright in the musical work, the lyrics and the sound recording, all have to grant a licence to permit the rental of recordings before rental will be legal. The only exception to this is very limited: You can rent someone a CD if:

- you bought the record before the commencement of Part 2 of the Copyright (World Trade Organisation Amendments) Act 1994; and
- the commercial rental of CDs is part of your ordinary course of business; and
- you were already conducting the same (or similar) business when the CD was purchased.

In other words, unless you get a licence from the copyright owners, you can't set up a new rental business and even if you have been running one for years, can only rent out pre-1994 material. It is not a very attractive business model.

22
GROUP RECORDING CONTRACTS

WHEN GROUPS ENTER RECORD CONTRACTS THEY CAN HAVE PARTICULAR PROBLEMS THAT ARE NOT FACED BY SOLO ARTISTS. WHAT IS THE INFLUENCE OF THE GROUP'S STRUCTURE? WHO CAN MAKE DECISIONS FOR THE GROUP? HOW DOES INCOME GET SPLIT? WHAT HAPPENS IF A MEMBER IS SICK OR WISHES TO LEAVE THE GROUP? WHO IS LIABLE FOR UNRECOUPED ADVANCES?

This chapter looks at recording contracts that apply to more than one artist - so-called 'group contracts'. For simplicity, we will use the expression 'group' but this should not be taken as limiting this chapter only to groups as used in popular music. Most of these principles apply to any multi-artist contract, irrespective of the genre of music.

Membership of groups changes over time. This is just as applicable to rock groups as it is to chamber music ensembles. Record contracts which deal with more than one artist have to contain provisions to deal with this possibility, and with the problems which can arise when groups change line-up or disintegrate to the point that it changes so much that the group loses the characteristics which induced the record company to sign it in the first place.

Personnel changes also affect the group's internal structures. Provision has to be made to remunerate leaving members and to introduce new members into the income stream. All this takes time and thought. The details are dealt with in Chapter 2, **Business Structures**. The present chapter concentrates on recording contracts, though the same principles apply to publishing contracts that have more than one writer.

GROUP CONTRACTS

Most of the provisions in a group's contract are the same as those for a solo artist, so their basic structures are similar. The main difference is that, in addition to all the usual matters, a group's contract has to:

- identify exactly who will be the contracting party or parties;
- identify the group's professional name, and how it can be used, and by whom;
- specify a particular place to which notices and royalties should be sent for all members of the group;
- specify who can speak for the group on any matters arising in the course of the contract, and give approvals where needed;
- deal with any in-coming members;
- deal with any out-going members; and
- set out whether the record company can secure the services of a leaving member(s) and, if so, how this will be done.

Each of these areas will be dealt with in detail later in this chapter. If you have not already done so, you should read the Chapter 20, **Record Contracts** and Chapter 23, **Record Royalties**, because the principles dealt with there are just as relevant to group contracts.

THE DYNAMICS OF GROUPS

Being a solo act can be uncomplicated, but solo artists often wish they were not quite so alone. It can be comforting to know someone else will share the good (and not-so-good) parts of the business - but there is a price to pay. For each additional person, you can more or less double the complications that will arise in getting decisions made and implemented. This is why business structures and planning are so vital.

GROUP STRUCTURES

A group can use any of a variety of structures. These are dealt with in detail in Chapter 2, **Business Structures**.

Partnerships or companies are the most common structures. Whatever structure you adopt, make sure it is properly integrated into the group's recording contract, or you could end up with the wrong people contracting with the record company, which would cause many sleepless nights for all concerned. If you set up a company to provide your services to the record company, your company will be the party that enters into the recording contract, no matter how many members there are in the group. Nevertheless, the contract still has to deal with the usual contingencies, such as the possibility that members may leave, or be unavailable to record/tour/make promotional appearances.

Most groups end up with a partnership structure, simply because they never get around to setting up anything else! If you join one or more people in a business venture you have a partnership going, even without signing any documents. Remember: a partnership is not an entity - it is a relationship. Partnerships are easy to create but can be complicated to take apart. Get good professional advice early.

The contractual provisions relating to groups are sometimes not given the consideration they deserve. When the contract is being negotiated, the band's membership is all too often treated as though it will never change. It is easy to become impatient when negotiations focus on what seem to be mere technicalities. But imagine the situation where, two years after the band signs the recording deal, your two lead singers decide to go out on their own, leaving the rest of the group to carry on as best they can. Chaos. The group has a big unrecouped balance with the record company (the usual recording costs and tour-support) and an unrecouped publishing advance (which was spent on instruments and living costs). Now, the record company wants to record another album because there was encouraging public response to the first one.

Somehow, the group has to unravel itself from the mess and (hopefully) retain something valuable for the remaining members, while letting the lead singers get on with their career. Good leaving member clauses in the recording contract and in the group's own structure will help smooth the process, but never expect it to be any fun!

THE CONTRACT PROVISIONS

THE PARTIES

The first thing to be decided, when group artists are to be signed, is whether the contract is to be between the record company and all the members of the group, with just some of the members, or with a company representing them. This is where integration of the group's structure with the contract is so important.

INDIVIDUAL AND GROUP LIABILITY

Group contracts are usually expressed as being 'joint and several' or 'individual and collective' (same thing). This means each member is contractually bound both in his or her capacity as a member of the group, and also in his or her capacity as a solo performer, for as long as the contract is in force.

It is rare for a group contract to give individual members the freedom to make solo records for another record company. As far as the record company is concerned, it is going to spend time and money on making the group famous and wants to share in any benefits flowing from that effort and expenditure. The individuals in it may even enjoy success as solo performers. The solo careers of the individual members of Cream, The Police, Wham, Cold Chisel, Take That and the like are very much in record companies' thoughts when they do group deals.

As far as the record company is concerned, the group it signed is the particular combination of individuals performing together to create a performance of a particular quality or nature. Nevertheless, each member is contracted (exclusively) to the record company, even though each performs and records as a member of the group. The record company pays just one royalty per record, which is split amongst the group members on whatever basis they decide. It sends just the one royalty accounting statement each accounting period.

THE GROUP'S PROFESSIONAL NAME
The record company needs the right to keep using the group's name for promoting and selling records throughout the term of the contract and for as long as it sells the group's records, even if there is a line-up change or the group disbands. This usually takes the form of an exclusive licence during the term of the contract and a non-exclusive one after the term ends. It has to be non-exclusive after the term ends, or the group would have to change its name if it wanted to keep recording. Beware of clauses that do not make this distinction.

The group's name is probably the most valuable asset the group can create. It is the basis for merchandising, promotions, live work and is the label by which the world knows the group. Its ownership and integrity must be protected at all times. Even if the group's membership changes, the name can go on and on and records can be sold using the group's name many years after the group itself ceases to exist.

One of the most contentious issues when a band breaks up, is 'Who owns the name?' Sometimes a change of line-up is so fundamental that the group effectively ceases to exist. Usually, the departure of one member is an interruption but the group's identity remains more or less intact. Accordingly, the recording contract has to specify what will happen to the group name should any members leave. If this clashes with the group's internal agreements, watch the writs fly.

Whatever is decided must be reflected in the agreement governing the group's own structure. Sometimes, one member will claim ownership of the group's name and will want to keep it if he or she leaves the group. Other times, the group will agree that there is more to be gained from the name going on, despite even fundamental line-up changes. Few groups could hope to stay with the same line-up for as long as Status Quo (more than 30 years). That name still sells records. It would, even if none of the original members were still in the group.

There are usually a number of competing but equally valid claims to on-going rights to use the name. There are no right answers to this dilemma. Sometimes, the name goes with the majority. Sometimes one person will take it with them, leaving the others to find another name and create a new identity. How often have you seen an album with a sticker 'Ex-lead singer of X'. This is usually the nearest the ex-lead singer can get to using the name of the group he left. If that ex-lead singer had also signed a 'no use/no association' clause in the partnership agreement, prohibiting any reference to the group's name, that ex-lead singer might not even be able to sticker his or her own albums to let the public know of the former association. It can be a tough world if you don't read the fine print. This might also influence any other record company thinking about signing that ex-lead singer as a solo artist, if that person's main claim to fame cannot be mentioned except in press releases.

LIAISING WITH THE RECORD COMPANY
WHO SPEAKS FOR THE GROUP?

Co-ordinating the group can be a major logistical problem. This is another reason record companies will rarely sign a recording agreement with a group unless the group first secures reliable management. The record company is not interested in trying to organise the group. As far as it is concerned, that is the manager's job.

The manager has to provide the main link between the group and the record company and facilitate putting the contract into effect. This means making sure that any decisions that have to be made actually are made and the record company notified. For example, the group's permission might be needed to synchronise a track into a film soundtrack. With a solo artist, this can be relatively easy to arrange but with a group everyone will want to be consulted. This might mean having to locate them first, which may not necessarily be easy.

Group contracts commonly contain a clause nominating one person to whom the record company can direct all clearance requests. It is up to that person to contact all the others in the group, and advise the company of the decision. The group's internal agreements have to complement this, by giving that person the necessary authority.

WHO MAKES DECISIONS?

It is worthwhile dealing briefly with the decision-making process for groups, because this can influence the structure the group finally adopts, which in turn affects the way the recording contract will be structured.

The group has to be able to make decisions quickly and be sure the decisions will be accepted by all members. There is no point trying to use an inappropriate decision-making process. It has to suit the individuals in the group. This is important for the members' sense of self-worth, the manager's sanity, and the group's ability to work with the record company.

Group artists have to accept that allowances have to be made if differences of opinion within the group are to be resolved. Even the most successful groups do not agree on everything all the time. They survive these disagreements by ensuring (as far as possible) that everyone involved understands the ground rules and by establishing a system by which decisions can be made. Some use consensus. Some resemble benign dictatorships. Most groups work best under some system between those extremes. There are no infallible ways. Try any system on the wrong group and there will be a blood-bath and the group will fragment. Good management can help you work this out. So can a few sessions of 'but say this happens', which are an opportunity for hypothetical possibilities to be thrashed out before they actually happen.

LINE-UP CHANGES

JOINING MEMBERS

New members usually contract to the group's record company on the same terms as the rest of the group. There is no reason in theory why every member of the group has to be under a long-term deal to the record company. It's just that, in practice, the alternatives make life too complicated for the company. It is possible to do a one-off recording deal with the artist, but that is hardly satisfactory in terms of on-going availability and commitment to the group.

There can be exceptions, though. For example, if a singer who is already successful and a major attraction in her or his own right, joins a group that will benefit from being associated with that singer, the singer may demand different terms. The group has to decide whether this is commercially justified. This situation is generally not recommended because it can create tensions that could threaten the group's long-term stability. Why deliberately create sources of tension in an already tense industry?

Suppose your group needs a new percussionist. You find a great one, but unfortunately, she is already signed to another record company. As long as her contract is in force, she may perform with the band, but cannot make any recordings unless the other record company agrees. If the other record company is willing to release her from the contract, then she can immediately sign a contract with your record company. If that cannot be done, arrangements have to be made for her to perform as a session musician.

LEAVING MEMBERS

Most line-up changes are more or less voluntary although, sometimes, members are ejected against their will. Some leave for very permanent reasons, to join the choir celestial. Whatever the reason, while alive, they remain under exclusive contract to the record company until the contract term expires, or they are released from it by the record company.

Option rights are problematic here. The record company may have several option rights and they will usually claim that the term must be calculated by assuming that all the options have been exercised (although this argument would be hard to uphold if it had already indicated that the next option may not be exercised).

Record companies are pragmatic. They recognise the practical and legal difficulties involved in trying to hold an unwilling artist to a contract. It is much easier for all concerned if a mutually acceptable settlement can be negotiated between the leaving members and the record company. Unfortunately, this is not always possible. The very public split between George Michael and his record company at the time, Sony, is a case in point. Few record companies will relinquish their grip on a successful artist without a fight. Record companies in Australia are limited in what they can do to stop an artist pursuing their chosen career. The courts are extremely reluctant to try to stop artists working. The most likely outcome of this kind of dispute is an award of damages, or settlement on the basis of a royalty to the old record company for the remainder of the old contract.

FIRST OPTION RIGHTS OVER LEAVING MEMBERS

Most groups' contracts give the record company the first opportunity to conclude a contract with any leaving member as a solo artist. In practice, this option is usually only exercised to hold those members the record company perceives to be key performers, who have the potential to capitalise on the success of the group and have solo success.

If a leaving member clause is exercised, the terms of the contract will determine if the recoupment account starts afresh, with a zero balance, or whether the solo artist carries-over a portion of any unrecouped advance under the group's contract. The latter can lead to some strange results and ought to be resisted. The group and the record company continues to have the benefit of the group's name and reputation, so it is difficult to see the justification for saddling the leaving member with a negative balance in the recoupment account even before a cent is spent on recording costs for that artist's solo career.

FINANCIAL CONSEQUENCES OF LINE-UP CHANGES

ROYALTIES AND ACCOUNTING

Record companies are not interested in sending multiple copies of royalty statements or splitting up the royalties into individual shares. The group has to nominate a single accounting point - perhaps the manager or, better still, the group's accountant or solicitor. This accounting address is likely to outlive the group, and it should be easy for others to locate. Any changes should always be notified promptly to all concerned, in writing.

RECOUPMENT

The remaining members of any group have to come to grips with the financial consequences of members leaving or others joining mid-way through a recording contract. Line-up changes are irrelevant to recoupment as far as the record company is concerned. All recording costs are lumped together in the one account, irrespective of when the recordings were made. Any advances that have already been debited to the group's royalty account will still have to be recouped from royalties earned from sales of the group's records, even though members come and go.

Suppose a group records two albums under a deal, then the lead singers leave. The record company exercises its option for another album, which is recorded. There may come a time when the recording costs and other advances of the first two albums are recouped, but the third album is still unrecouped. As far as the record company is concerned, the present group members are not due to receive royalty cheques. Of course, the group's account will still be credited with royalties against the unrecouped balance, but there will be no actual money flow at that point. Meanwhile, the ex-members are probably due to get a share of royalties from sales of the two albums in which they performed (unless their agreement with the group specified that they would not receive any payment until the group actually received royalties).

The group partnership agreement should always provide that ex-members will not have to subsidise recoupment of recording costs and advances which arise after they leave the group. From the group's point of view, the situation is not likely to be too bad even though it looks bad at first glance. Most groups that are into their third album have alternative sources of income by then. Live work is likely to be reasonable, as well as merchandising and the like, so it is usually possible to fund the obligations to the ex-members out of current earnings other than record royalties. If there aren't sufficient earnings, the old adage about extracting blood from stones should be borne in mind by all concerned.

ILL AND ABSENTEE MEMBERS

Group artists also need to consider the possibility that one or more members might be unable to participate in a recording. Record companies in Australia rarely have insurance against artists becoming ill during recording sessions. If someone becomes incapacitated, recording either stops or a stand-in has to be found to play that person's part in the sessions. Either way, there will be additional cost that the record company will treat as recoupable.

The group might technically be in breach of its recording agreement if it cannot record as and when required. The recording contract should make it clear exactly what amounts to a breach of the contract if a member of the group cannot perform because of circumstances beyond that member's control. While most record companies are reasonable if the default is beyond the artists' control, they will rarely forgive absences caused by wilful or careless acts.

23
RECORD ROYALTIES

BECAUSE RECORD ROYALTIES ARE THE MAIN SOURCE OF INCOME FOR BOTH RECORD COMPANIES AND RECORDING ARTISTS, THEIR CALCULATION HAS BECOME HUGELY (AND PERHAPS UNNECESSARILY) COMPLEX. THE CONCEPT OF RECOUPABILITY OR NON-RECOUPABILITY, ROYALTY BASE RATES, DEDUCTIONS, SUNDRY INCOME, CONTROLLED COMPOSITION CLAUSES AND SO ON, ARE ALL TREATED DIFFERENTLY FROM COMPANY TO COMPANY AND DEAL TO DEAL. ACCORDINGLY, ALL ARTISTS AND THEIR MANAGERS MUST UNDERSTAND HOW THEIR PARTICULAR ROYALTY MECHANISMS WORK. IT IS THIS UNDERSTANDING THAT WILL KEEP BREAD ON THE TABLE.

Royalties in record deals are usually calculated as a percentage of either the retail or the wholesale price per unit sold. The record company determines which method is used. As you will see though, this apparently simple formula is subject to many subtle (and some not-so-subtle) qualifications and deductions.

By far the majority of deals involve a royalty being credited to the artist for records sold by the record company or its licensees. 'Credited' is a critical word here.

NON-RECOUPABLE DEALS

Originally, record deals were non-recoupable. This means the record company paid the recording costs. The artist got paid a relatively low royalty, but the royalty was paid from the first record sold.

If the artist was pre-paid an advance of royalties, the record company retained the artist's royalties until the amount earned equalled the advance (i.e. the advance was 'recouped'). Once that happened, royalties were paid to the artist.

Each time an advance was paid, the royalty account went into debit and the company retained royalties again until the advance was recouped. But even though the record company was retaining the royalties, the royalties were still technically earned by the artist and had to be shown as credit in the royalty account.

As recording costs began to reach six and even seven figures, record companies wanted to make artists aware of recording costs. They struck on the idea of making the recording costs a recoupable item in the same way that artist advances had always been under the old style of contract. In effect, the recording costs were treated as if they had been paid to the artist as a pre-payment of royalties. As a trade-off, the actual royalty rate was approximately doubled.

This meant that even though the artist got a larger royalty per unit, it made little practical difference to the record company until the artist actually recouped. By that time, the record company had made a profit anyway and could afford the higher royalty per unit sold. The trouble with this system is, of course, that although the advance recoups twice as fast (because the royalty has been doubled) the artist only actually sees the benefit of the increased royalty rate once the advances have been recouped and royalties start to be paid.

As an aside, it is worth noting at this point that royalty rates vary considerably from country to country. Australia actually has quite favourable rates when compared with the United Kingdom and the United States. Whereas a new artist can get a recoupable deal in Australia with a royalty rate of about 12% of the 'retail price' (more on that rubbery term later), in the United States, a comparable artist is likely to get 7% or 8%.

As you will see from the section Royalty Rates later in this chapter, it is usually misleading simply to compare royalty rate percentages, but these figures illustrate the point. You need to evaluate the royalty rate in the context of the prevailing record industry economy. When sales are down, royalty rates will decline. When sales are up, companies can afford to compete for artists and so the rates also tend to go up.

There are many factors influencing the royalty rates other than the status of the artist; competition between companies, the margins companies achieve on their sales, the state of the general economy, corporate policy and so on.

The Australian rate needs to be higher than in the United States. Given the small market size in Australia, a low royalty rate would doom most artists to being unrecouped for ever. The cost of making an album here is not significantly less than in the United States but, because of the size of the market, a top-twenty hit in Australia means that the artist is still unlikely to achieve recoupment, whereas even a minor hit in the American market can still generate enough royalties for the artist to recoup from United States sales alone.

RECOUPABLE DEALS

In deals where the record company can recoup the recording costs, you will get royalty statements, but no royalty cheques, until all recording costs and any other payments that are treated as advances under the contract have been recouped.

Recoupable deals have become the standard deal now and the items which are treated as recoupable now often include video clips, tour support, certain promotional activities (such as hiring independent publicists) and basically anything else the record company can get included during the contract negotiations. Some are legitimate items, but some are not. There are no hard and fast rules.

As with so much in the industry, the parties' relative bargaining strength will ultimately decide which items are recoupable and which are not. Some items are non-negotiable because company policies dictate that certain categories of expenditure must be treated as an advance unless cleared by head office, but artists must question every item. After all, every item treated as recoupable only increases the debit in your advance account and defers the day that your account goes into credit.

The single most contentious recoupable item is the cost of video clips. Many companies insist on them being 100% recoupable. Others will accept 50%. Whatever deal you get, consider exactly what royalty income will be applied towards recoupment. Some companies will agree to apply only income from commercial exploitation of the video. Most will not separate video income from record royalties. They simply lump video costs in with the other expenses and treat it as a single amount. Again, there is no right way to handle this. You just have to decide which will be more advantageous to you and try to negotiate it into the deal.

'NET SALES'

When is a sale not a sale? The contract will usually provide for a variety of situations where, although a particular record may be thought to have been sold, no royalty will accrue to you. This is because of the way the term 'net sales' is usually defined.

You need to be aware of which sales do not attract a royalty. If the record company receives money or credit for any record, you would expect that you would also get a percentage of the selling price. Unfortunately, record contracts are rarely so simple!

Net sales will often be defined to exclude a number of transactions where records are disposed of by the company and for which it gets some benefit but which are not 'sold'. For example:

- **Records given away by the record company as promotional records to publicise you or your records**. This includes copies given to media representatives, copies ordered by record company staff (this is an important way for your record to be heard by the people who will be dealing with it day to day), and copies given away in advertising campaigns.
- **Records returned to the record company as defective or wrongly shipped to dealers**. Defective records have to be replaced or a credit given to the retailer. The record company does not make anything on the sale (in fact, replacing defective records is an expensive exercise for record companies, because of the labour and time it involves) so it is reasonable for these to be non-royalty-bearing records.
- **Records given away by the record company as 'bonus records' to dealers** (commonly called 'free goods'). This is meant to cover such sales incentive schemes as the 'buy 12 and get an extra 1 free, in place of a discount' scheme. These schemes are popular in North America and parts of Europe, but have been slow to catch on in Australia. They are becoming more common here as the record companies fight for market share and shelf space in retail outlets.

  The catch with these schemes is that, unless precluded by your recording contract, your records can be given away as bonus records to assist the sales of any other artists' records! In other words, your records can be used to boost sales of records from any part of the record company's catalogue. This might help you, or it might not. Either way, in effect you are enabling the company to give a discount to its customers but you get no discernible benefit - certainly no royalty. The solution is to insist that free-goods be limited to assisting sales of your own records unless you agree otherwise in any particular case. Sometimes you will win, sometimes you won't. Even if you get the restriction included, it can be very hard to monitor but can be verified should a royalty audit ever be conducted.
- **Records sold at or below cost or in the course of deleting a record from the company's catalogue**. 'Deletions' should not be confused with 'overstocks'. Deletions are records that are being sold off 'at cost' or less because the particular recording is being cut from the company's catalogue. (Deletions are very common with singles; many companies will delete a single when it has reached No.1 to promote sales of the album that contains the track.) It will not be offered for sale again (unless reinstated at some later time) because its commercial life has ended. Overstocks, however, are warehouse-clearing exercises, where surplus records (i.e. usually records ordered

by mistake) are sold off cheaply to retailers, but the record remains in the catalogue. From the artist's point of view, these records are still sold and arguably should generate some income, even if only 10% to 15% of the actual selling price net of tax.

- **Format exceptions**. In the case of records in 'new' formats (i.e. formats not in common use when the contract is signed), some companies try to make the first several thousand sales royalty-free.

    It is hard to justify this practice, given that most of these formats tend to attract a high packaging deduction (see the section heading Packaging Deductions below for an explanation of this term) in any event.

- **First sales**. Some companies (and not just the Majors) even try to exclude the first few thousand sales of certain traditional formats where the record company's profit margins would otherwise be less than those set in the company's A&R policies. In effect, the artist will be contributing towards the promotion costs.

As a general rule, the cost of promoting records is borne by the record company rather than the artist, although this does not preclude the parties from making specific agreements in particular cases.

THE ROYALTY RATE

Do not be impressed by a high royalty percentage figure. By itself, it is meaningless. You have to know the royalty base price (i.e. the amount per record to which that percentage will be applied) before you can evaluate whether the royalty is good or bad. As will become plain from what follows, the royalty base price will bear almost no relationship to the price appearing on the record's price sticker in the store.

THE ROYALTY BASE

Until recently, the royalty base price was calculated using the recommended retail price (RRP) as the starting point. This arose because record companies used to have retail price lists. The Trade Practices Act (and its equivalent in many other countries) meant that record companies could not set the retail price any more. They sometimes set a maximum price but could not set a minimum retail price. Retailer discounting also meant that the recommended retail price often bore little similarity to the actual store price for many records. Retailers who discount heavily usually put great pressure on record companies to discount their wholesale price. If the wholesale price drops, the record company's margins drop too.

Eventually, record companies decided to stop pretending that the retail price had much meaning and began using their wholesale price, which they can still set and which they still publish. Some call it 'published price to dealers' (PPD), or 'dealer price', or 'wholesale price' or some similar name to distinguish it from the retail price. They all mean the same thing – the price that the retailer (or for digital product, the aggregator) purchases from the record company. For convenience, we will use the term "dealer price".

The dealer price is of course considerably lower than the RRP (between three quarters and one half of the RRP, depending upon the prevailing retailer margins in the country of sale). To preserve the royalty's monetary value, the royalty rate (as a percentage of the dealer price) has to be increased by the same margin to compensate for the lower royalty base price. For example, if the margin between the dealer price and the RRP were 25%, then a royalty rate based on RRP would need to be increased by that margin (25%) if it were to maintain the same value when converted into a PPD-based royalty: In that example a royalty of 10% based on RRP would need to be 12.5% if it were based on PPD. Let's look at an example that is more fully worked out.

RRP ROYALTY CALCULATION

Assume you have a contract with a royalty rate of 15% of RRP less GST and packaging deductions. To keep the calculation simple, assume that there are no producer royalties to take into account and that the retail price of a compact disc is $30. Assume for the sake of the exercise that GST is $2.73 and that a packaging deduction of 25% applies. We will disregard shipping charges for the purposes of the exercise, though many companies charge around $0.30 per unit, which is included in the price to the dealer.

RRP	$30.00 (incl. GST)
less GST (11 %)	$ 2.73
	$27.27
less packaging deduction of 25% of $27.27 ($6.82)	$20.45
Apply the royalty @ 15%	
Royalty per unit is	$ 3.07

DEALER PRICE CALCULATION

You may have become a musician to avoid becoming an accountant. If so, just bear with the calculations, because you will learn something that may save you a lot of anguish.

Assume the royalty is calculated on dealer price, being the cost of the record to the dealer less GST and packaging. Assume the dealer price is $18.18

including the shipping charge but excluding GST. If the royalty rate of 15% is retained for the moment, you will see the effect of going from RRP to dealer price accounting.

Dealer Price	$20.00	(incl. GST)
less GST (11 %)	$ 1.82	
	$18.18	
less packaging deduction of 25% of $18.18 ($4.55)	$13.63	
Apply the royalty @ 15%		
Royalty per unit is	$ 2.04	

Hey presto - using dealer price as the basis for the royalty base price, the royalty has dropped to $2.04 instead of $3.07 if calculated on RRP!

To restore the dollar value of the dealer price royalty, the rate has to be increased to 22.5% of the royalty base price, otherwise you are going to lose out. The same logic applies no matter what royalty rate is used.

This is why you should always ask to see fully worked royalty calculations, or you might get a few nasty surprises.

The record companies which use dealer price accounting are gradually converting RRP rates to dealer price rates, but this usually requires the artist's prior approval. You should always see a few worked-out examples of the converted rates.

DEDUCTIONS – CALCULATING THE ROYALTY BASE PRICE

Regardless whether RRP or dealer price is used in the contract, the figure from which the royalty itself will be calculated (the royalty base price) will be further reduced because of the effect of various deductions applied before it is multiplied by the royalty rate.

The most usual deductions are:
- GST;
- delivery charges;
- packaging deductions;
- new technology deductions; and
- arbitrary deductions.

The effect of these deductions can be enormous. What appears to be a generous royalty rate can very quickly be made very modest by substantial deductions. For this reason, people in the record industry do not refer to percentages, but rather to 'points'. Points simply mean the percentage royalty taking into account all deductions. Points are real; percentages are illusory.

GOODS AND SERVICES TAX

GST is excluded from the royalty base because, even though it forms part of the RRP or the dealer price, it is not actually revenue for the record company.

The tax is collected on the government's behalf by the record company, as part of the wholesale price to record dealers. This is why record price lists always show the price of the goods and the GST as separate items. In the United Kingdom it's called VAT, in France TVA. Whatever the name, the effect is the same. France removed sales tax on records about eight years ago on the basis that records, like books, are a cultural item. The move seemed to boost the industry there.

GST is assessed at 10% of the cost of the supply. The record shop pays the record company the PPD plus 10% GST and the record company remits the tax to the Australian Taxation Office (ATO). The shop then charges the customer the retail price plus 10% GST and remits the net tax (the difference between the GST it collects from the customer and the GST it paid to the record company) to the ATO. In this way there is no double tax paid but the government receives tax on the whole retail price.

When you look at the examples given above, many readers say, "GST is 10% - you are using 11%." It is not a mistake. To find out how much of GST inclusive price is actually the GST, you divide by 11 – not 10. In contrast, if you have a GST exclusive price and want to know how much tax will be payable, you use 10%.

DELIVERY CHARGES

These are usually shown as a separate item on the price list. If they are not then, arguably, they ought to be included in the dealer price.

Originally, delivery charges were exempt from the old sales tax (which was an incentive to have them). These days, delivery charges, if applicable, are meant to be cost-recovery items that do not make a profit. It would be almost impossible to prove this either way unless you had unrestricted access to the record company's accounts.

PACKAGING DEDUCTIONS

Packaging deductions are allowances supposed to off-set the cost (to the record company) of artwork for record packaging and for having the packaging manufactured. Shellac records used to be sold in large book-like packages which the industry argued were not records, so ought not be a part of the record price for royalty purposes. The books have gone but not the deduction.

In theory, there is no reason why the same deduction could not be achieved by simply setting a lower royalty rate, but too many artists are impressed by a royalty rate which looks great but which is subject to packaging deductions (even though the actual dollar value is no higher than a lower rate without deductions). It makes for good party talk to boast about a 20% royalty. It sounds great, even if it is meaningless!

Deductions are generally specified as a percentage of the applicable royalty base (RRP or dealer price, net of GST). The actual amount to be deducted will vary, depending on the record format and whether the packaging is standard or non-standard.

You need to be careful that the definition of standard packaging is wide enough to include basic packaging. Some definitions are so narrow that only a brown paper bag qualifies as standard. You have to talk to the A&R department to find out exactly what the company's policies are regarding packaging. This is particularly important if you anticipate that many of your records will have unusual packaging. 'Unusual' includes any item which increases the print or production costs. Embossing, gilt, cut-outs, extra pages, digipack, difficult colours or print techniques. All these are likely to be non-standard.

The amounts deducted for packaging differ from record company to record company and vary from 15% to 25% for CDs. As non-standard packaging reduces your royalties (though it may well have a positive impact on sales), the artist's prior approval should be required before non-standard packaging is adopted.

SPECIFIC PACKAGING DEDUCTIONS
VINYL RECORDS
Packaging deductions for phonograph records (vinyl) range between 6% and 12% of the retail price less sales tax. The shift away from vinyl means that this has become almost irrelevant, but there remains a small demand for this format, at least from dance music artists, so vinyl has not disappeared entirely. According to the Australian Record Industry Association's (ARIA) figures, in 1991, vinyl albums accounted for just 2% of total units sold. In 1992, the percentage was down to 0.1%. To put it another way, sales of vinyl albums suffered a 92% drop from 1991 to 1992. The CD had truly arrived and like any dominant new technology, was ruthless. (By 2004, the ARIA figures showed that out of total unit sales of 57.897 million, only 37,000 of them were vinyl.)

Coloured vinyl and shaped records always attracted a special deduction. Sometimes they were sold at a premium price, which offset the deduction a bit, but most were made for promotional purposes. The artist had to decide whether a funny-shaped record would boost sales enough to offset the lost royalty income.

CASSETTES
Cassettes usually bear a slightly higher deduction than vinyl. The usual rate for cassettes is 12% to 15%.

Like vinyl, cassettes are now a minor format - one that is suffering a lingering death. According to ARIA's figures, in 1991 cassettes accounted for 72% of the number of 'singles' sold in Australia. By 2000, that that figure was less than 0.1%. Of total album sales in 1991, cassettes were 43% of sales. In 2000, they were down to less than 20%. In 2004 it was 0.4%. How long can this keep going on?

COMPACT DISCS

Compact discs are audio-only records. You need to be careful about packaging deductions for compact discs because it is now the main format. When compact discs were first introduced, the record companies were able to get many artists to accept the infamous 'black-vinyl equivalent' clause. This meant that the dollar value of the royalty on compact discs was capped at the same dollar value as the royalty on the corresponding black-vinyl record. Any company trying to impose that clause these days would be laughed at (because no-one would be able to remember what black-vinyl looks like) and risks having the clause (if not the whole contract) struck out as unconscionable. The justification given for the black-vinyl clause was that the cost of developing the new format of compact disc had to be recovered by the record companies. It may have been arguable once. It isn't now.

ARIA's figures show that in 2004 there were 43.234 million sales of CD albums. Add the 9.286 million CD singles and compare the figure to the total unit sales of 57.8 million and it is clear that compact disc is the primary sound carrier in Australia now and is likely to remain so for some time.

The deductions for compact discs tend to be considerably higher than for the equivalent cassettes. Usually the deduction is between 15% and 25% of the royalty base price less GST.

It is a well worth asking the record company to provide worked-out examples of the royalty calculation (per format) so you can see the actual dollar-value of the royalty for each format. In most record contracts, a compact disc single attracts the same packaging deduction as an album in that format, even though the royalty rate is reduced for singles in any format.

NEW TECHNOLOGY DEDUCTIONS

This is a relatively new deduction category, largely triggered by the enormous development costs associated with creating new record formats. The deduction is intended to help the record company recover its cost of developing and introducing these new technologies by increasing its profit margin on sales of records in the new formats. The deductions vary from company to company, but 30% to 35% of the Royalty Base Price is not uncommon. This means a similar reduction in the value of the royalty to the artist, so it is no small thing.

Again, the definition of 'new technology' needs to be thought about. If the deduction cannot be negotiated out of the contract, make sure it applies only to genuinely 'new' formats and that it cuts out once they become commonplace in the market. This will usually require some objective test or you may get bogged down in disputes come the time you challenge the newness of a five-year old 'new technology'. Remember: compact discs were new technology in the mid-1980s. Now they're not. DCC and MiniDisc formats have not been new technologies now for a long time. The new spectre is on-line downloads. The irony is that with this medium, there is no packaging at all. Beware those contracts that have both a new technologies deduction and a packaging deduction for downloads. It is this sort of cute accounting practice that brings record companies into disrepute.

Let's face it, packaging deductions are just another way of reducing the value of the royalty to the artist and thus the expense to the company. As the then worldwide head of PolyGram once proudly told me over cocktails, "PolyGram paid for the retooling for CD, worldwide, out of our artists' packaging deductions". They were good cocktails!

In most industries the companies pass the cost of research and development on to their customers. In the music industry, it is subsidised by the artists. There is no satisfactory explanation for this. Moreover, the deduction is even charged by companies that have not spent a cent on developing and implementing the new technology!

ARBITRARY DEDUCTIONS

This may seem a rather bold title, but it is hard to think of a more apt name for some of the more inventive deductions that are sometimes applied.

One of the most common used to be to calculate royalties on 90% of net sales. Few reputable companies still use this formula. No explanation is usually given. It's just there in the contract definitions.

It originally arose because shellac records broke if they were dropped. Shopkeepers dropped them occasionally or they were broken in transit, so the record companies replaced the broken ones. Have you ever dropped a vinyl record or a CD? It didn't break did it? You probably couldn't even bend it. Once again, the rationale for the deduction has long gone but, for some, the deduction lives on. Reject it with contempt.

There are some companies that try to include 'free goods' as an arbitrary deduction. These are records given away in place of a discount and are discussed under Net Sales in this chapter.

DOUBLE DEDUCTIONS

You must always be careful to ensure that only one deduction applies at a time. For example, a substantial new technology allowance, on top of a hefty packaging deduction, can more than halve the effective royalty rate. For example, an already low royalty rate for downloads will be really hammered if it is reduced by both a 25% packaging deduction and a 30% new technology deduction! The classic example is the digital download: Several companies will try and claim a new technology (or digital delivery deduction) as well as a packaging deduction. Given that there is no packaging on a download ...

ROYALTIES FROM RECORDS SOLD BY UNUSUAL MARKETING METHODS

Although recording contracts are essentially contracts for services, the record company's precise exploitation rights in the recordings must be set out in detail because the royalty that you receive will vary, depending upon the way the records are sold.

Record companies, large or small, all try to get the maximum freedom as to how their records may be sold. They will resist most artists' requests for any 'unusual' marketing methods or sales to be subject to the artist's prior approval. The artist, of course, has a direct interest in the way the records are sold because this will affect (usually by reducing) the royalty and may also be relevant to the artist's performing schedule and promotional activities.

Apart from selling records to retail stores, there are quite a few other ways of commercially selling recordings. These non-traditional outlets are all important in the overall scheme of things and can generate significant additional sales.

RECORD CLUBS

Record club operations are described in Chapter 16, **Growth Of Australian Record Business**. Most offer bonus records to their members in place of discounts and all have a special offer for new members that generally involves a number of records for the price of one, or a variation on that theme.

Record clubs work on the theory that many sales with a low margin equals a few sales with a high one. They are essentially an outlet for current hits and strong-selling back catalogue.

They will either manufacture their own records or buy finished product from the record companies. If they manufacture them, they will usually pay a royalty per unit to the copyright owner and be responsible for paying mechanical copyright fees. If they buy finished product, the price may be inclusive or exclusive of a royalty to the record company.

The record company will usually have to get prior approval for the records to be sold through a club. If the record company owns the recording, it will set the royalty having regard to its own royalty obligations. It will set the royalty at a high enough level to cover the artist's royalty and a margin for itself. This is additional to any profit it may make if it also manufactures the records for the record club.

If a record club buys its stocks exclusive of licensor's royalties, it must provide royalty accounts for all sales. These accounts in turn have to be incorporated into the record company's accounting to its artists. To do this, the record company has to re-calculate the artist's royalties for those sales, using the royalty rate and base price as set out in its contract with the artist. The same applies where the record company has licensed the recording from another record company or another licensor (for example, an overseas label distributed by the record company here).

Most record companies require the artist's royalty on these sales to be half the rate applicable to sales through usual retail outlets. Sometimes it will be specified as being one half of the record company's royalty receipts. Practices vary.

If you can, retain the right of prior approval for club release. That way you can insist on a royalty projection before giving approval.

TV ADVERTISED RECORDS

These are records sold in conjunction with large-scale television advertising campaigns. They may be sold by the record company itself or by a tele-marketer to whom the recording is licensed.

Large-scale television advertising campaigns have proven to be an excellent way of increasing sales, but they are expensive. The record company has to create a specific advertisement and buy time on television over a period of weeks. This can cost over $150,000 for a national campaign, depending upon the cost of the advertisement and the amount of television time bought. Most companies will run a test campaign to see if the advertisement works. If it does, the records will be shipped in bulk to record retailers to coincide with the advertisements being run. Any unsold records can be returned to the record company for a full credit ("sale or return"). Unless this safety net were available, few retailers would risk ordering more than a minimum number of records. They would rather be out of stock for a few days than be caught with a huge number of unsold records in their racks.

To offset the costs of making the advertisement and buying the television time, the record companies usually insist that the artist's royalty be reduced by half on these sales. If you have sufficient clout (i.e. you are a major international star) you might get a slightly better deal but it will not be very much better because the numbers just have to add up or the campaign won't be run. Few record companies will run a campaign if they know in advance that it will not recover its costs. If it does run despite poor financial projections, it is because there is a hidden agenda (e.g. if an international artist is in town to perform, or a record is not performing as hoped after its initial release).

When negotiating your deal, make sure the contract specifies exactly which records will be subject to the reduced rate. Usually, a period is specified (say, from the beginning of the campaign until between one and three months after it has ended) and sales made during that time, in the region where the advertisements have actually been run, will attract the reduced rate.

The record company will also often require the right to withhold a percentage of the royalties in the initial accounting periods, to allow for any surplus records returned by retailers when the campaign ends.

Sometimes the reduced royalty will only apply until the cost of the campaign has been recouped by the record company, but this is less usual. It should probably be standard practice.

PREMIUM RECORDS

These are records sold or given away with goods other than records. Cigarette, magazine, clothing and soft-drink companies are perhaps the most common users of this form of marketing. The artist royalties on this kind of sale are usually very low.

Watch out for unjustified deductions by the record company when the royalty base is specified. It may be acceptable for the company to deduct certain expenses, but it's a bit rich trying to get the manufacturing costs deducted off the top too. Always get fully worked-out examples of royalty calculations, so you will be able to see exactly what costs are going to come off the top before your royalty is calculated.

Most artists do not like being associated with premium records, because they feel these sales demean the recording. In Europe and North America, they are a useful way of exploiting back-catalogue and can generate reasonable royalties if the campaign works particularly well in those large markets. Premium sales should always be subject to your prior approval so you can control the kind of goods your records will accompany and properly evaluate the deal overall.

BUDGET AND MID-PRICE RECORDS

This involves selling records at reduced prices - usually between half (budget-price records) and three-quarters (mid-price records) of the normal full price.

Budget records are at the lowest end of the retail price point for records. Mid-priced records are, as their name suggests, less than full price, but more than budget. It would be a rare budget-priced compact disc which sold for more than $12 at the moment. Most sell for under $10 and there is a large market for compact discs in the $6 to $10 range. Cassettes sell for even less. A mid-price compact disc album would have to sell for less than about $18 to qualify as a mid-price album under the definition used in most recording contracts.

Obviously the margins on these records are very tight indeed. They cost the same as a top-line record to press and package and the mechanical copyright is the same percentage of the selling price, but the records sell for no more than three-quarters (and often less than half) of the price of a top-line record. There has to be a saving somewhere and that saving includes reducing the artist's royalty rate, but then you'd probably guessed that already. There are other economies such as cutting advertising and simplifying the packaging.

When a 'half-rate' is applied to a record with a selling price of half a full price record, the artist's royalty drops, effectively, to 25% of what the artist would get on a full price record. The same logic applies to mid-priced records which attract a 'three-quarter rate'. Either way, the record company has to sell a lot of records if the artist is to overcome this royalty reduction. On the other hand, it may be that the record won't sell as a full price record any more, in which case 25% of something is better than 100% of nothing.

In the United States, new artists are often first released at mid-price to encourage sales. This is not the practice in Australia. Here, records are rarely released at less than full price until sales at full price have stagnated. In fact, the mid-price market has been one of the strongest areas of the Australian industry for some years.

Most mid-price records are sold by the record company responsible for the first release of the record, using generic advertising campaigns and special display bins. In contrast, most budget-price records in Australia are sold by companies which specialise in this area and which license their product from the 'first release' companies.

From an artist's point of view, whilst any sale is welcome, always try to avoid having these sales occur while the record is still current - say within the first year after initial release in each country. The only way to ensure this is to have a suitable limitation in your recording contract.

OTHER INCOME
BROADCAST AND PUBLIC PERFORMANCE ROYALTIES

Broadcasting records on radio and performing them in public places are increasingly becoming important as sources of revenue. They are likely to assume even greater importance in the future, as 'pay streaming' and other media come into existence.

Australia, the United Kingdom and most European countries recognise broadcast copyright and have collection bodies that receive royalties from radio, television and other media outlets. The 'pay for play' disputes in Australia were all about the fees radio and television stations ought to pay for using records (and videos) as the basis for their programs from which they generate their income. Unfortunately, not every country recognises a copyright in broadcasting sound recordings. As far as Australian law is concerned, recordings made or owned by North American companies do not attract broadcast and public performance copyright protection in Australia. This means anyone can broadcast them in North America (or Australia) and there is no right to collect a copyright fee for that particular use. Similarly, Australian artists cannot collect broadcast or performance fees in North America. This whole area is a mystery to most American lawyers because it is irrelevant to most of their artists, which is why it is not mentioned in American books on the record business.

Public performance income generated by the broadcast, transmission and performance of records in Australia, is collected by the Phonographic Performance Company of Australia Ltd (PPCA). It collects the funds and, after having the total divided by an independent accountant, each member company receives a proportional pay-out.

Depending on the terms of your contract, you may have a right to share in that income. Sometimes it will be caught up in a 'sundry income' clause. (This clause would also have covered the ill-fated blank tape levy, which the High Court disallowed in March 1993 after a year's deliberation over the legislation that had already been enacted.) As the fee is a 'blanket licence' fee, not specifically identified with any particular recording, it has to be divided by the record company on some basis. Each record company has its own way of dividing the income and will not make exceptions for any particular artist or licensor. Usually, it will be based on the proportion your records represent of the total sales by the company in that year. So long as you are treated no less favourably than other artists/licensors, you should be reasonably protected.

You should negotiate for at least half of royalty income from this source, and more if possible. It will become an even more important source of revenue as sales of records are superseded by other ways of delivering music to the public.

Remember, public performance income is another part of the income which, if you are under-recouped, the record company can apply towards recoupment in the same way that it recoups against record royalties.

SYNCHRONISATION FEES

Synchronising a recording into a film soundtrack or licensing it for use in advertisements is also becoming a lucrative area for fees. You should get a royalty of at least half of the record company's income from this source. Wherever possible, try to get the right to approve this kind of use in advance.

You don't want to get any nasty surprises finding your recording synchronised into the soundtrack of an ideologically unsound movie...do you?

Movies and advertisements use a lot of music. Most is original, but much is licensed from record companies, especially for movies and videos. There is no set fee scale. The fee will be as much as the market will bear. A relatively unknown track might get a worldwide synchronisation fee of $2,500. A Beach Boys track might justify $80,000. It all depends upon the movie's music budget, the importance of the song in the overall context of the film, the recording in question and the nature of the rights being bought. It costs more for worldwide rights than Australia only. It costs more for an all-media licence than only a home video/DVD licence.

In any event, it is a legitimate use of the recording and the artist should get a share of the revenue. Again, the artist's share is income available to be applied towards recoupment (or against which you could request an advance).

ROYALTY ACCOUNTING

Most contracts require the record company to keep account of each record it sells. It should also keep track of the number it gives away or disposes of in any other way.

The contract will stipulate what the accounting statements must show, how often they have to be provided and to whom. There is usually also a clause setting out the artist's right to audit the record company.

Your accounting statements should show:
- the sales of records in each country, by format;
- the royalty base price for each record;
- the royalty accruing on each record;
- whether you have recouped all recording costs and/or advances; and
- sundry income to which you may be entitled under the contract.

The statements should be delivered to you as soon as possible after the end of each accounting period. Accounting periods vary from company to company, but are usually calculated for each calendar quarter or half year. To allow time for the calculations to be done, there is usually a delay of between 45 and 90 days from the end of the relevant accounting period. Until you have recouped, the royalty statements are usually of academic interest but, nonetheless, you should try to obtain quarterly accounting and keep the statement preparation time to a minimum.

The right to audit is important. Very few artists use the right. Some do not realise it is there, some are deterred by the thought of the cost and some are afraid it will upset the record company (which it will, but that's life).

Most audit clauses are quite detailed as to what the artists can and cannot see or copy, how often audits can be conducted, by whom, and how far they can go back. Most also provide that the record company must reimburse the artist for audit costs if serious errors are discovered. The definition of 'serious' can be the subject of heated debate between business affairs managers and artists' lawyers.

PRODUCERS' ROYALTIES

Producers' contracts are dealt with in detail in Chapter 24, **Record Producers**, but you have to understand how your producer's royalties will affect the royalties you get from your record company.

Most recording contracts specify that the artist's royalty includes any producer's royalties. In other words, artists are responsible for paying the royalty from their own pockets. This creates real complications unless care is taken to co-ordinate the royalty and accounting provisions of the producer's agreement with those in the recording agreement. If possible, agree with your producer that you won't be due to pay royalties until you actually start receiving record royalties.

Sometimes a record company will pay the producer royalties directly. If this happens, your royalty rate under the record contract will be reduced so that the record company's total royalty obligations are not actually increased. Most producers prefer this kind of arrangement. The down-side for you is that, as the royalty is lower for you, it takes longer for you to recoup any advances and recording costs as the royalty per record is less than would be the case if you were being credited with a royalty inclusive of the producer's royalty points.

ALTERNATIVES TO ROYALTY PAYMENTS

Royalties are the usual basis for payment under recording contracts, but there are other methods of payment and these will be covered briefly so you can see their advantages and disadvantages.

LUMP-SUM PAYMENTS

You might be offered a recording deal where the payment is by a lump sum instead of a royalty. Lump sum payments are all-inclusive and intended as 'once and for all' payments. Session musicians are usually paid in this way.

Lump-sum payments can be attractive where a project is high risk and there is little likelihood of getting a royalty in any event. Because no royalties are paid, the fee has to be large enough to make up for that lost opportunity.

Lump-sum deals are quite common where a large number of artists are involved (e.g. recordings of stage-shows or film soundtracks) and when library music is being recorded (see Chapter 31, **Music In Film**). This can work out to everyone's advantage. With a lump-sum, the artists get the fee in their hands with no risk. Besides, if the whole cast of a stage show were to share the usual record royalty, each member would be lucky to get more than a fraction of a cent per record. A $2.50 royalty can only be split so many ways before each share becomes practically worthless. For its part, the record company benefits because it does not have to negotiate perhaps dozens of recording contracts and then produce multiple royalty statements each quarter.

SHARES (EQUITY IN THE RECORD COMPANY)

There has been more than one instance where a major artist has signed a recording agreement in return for shares in the record company. In effect, they were prepared to accept a dividend on each share instead of a royalty. This has the benefit of enabling them to share in the overall success of the company, even if this is not directly related to sales their own records. It has also given the artist the opportunity to share in any profit from sale of the company itself.

Don't expect this kind of deal unless you are already a hugely successful act. In any event, the Majors cannot usually offer that kind of deal because of the way their shares are held. Of course, there's nothing to stop an artist buying shares in record companies and the like on the open market.

BEING CREATIVE

The basis of payment is only limited by the parties' imaginations and by the limitations imposed by the record company's accounting system. But remember - an unusual deal structure means that the record company's routine has to be varied and, bureaucracies being what they are, this increases the risk of something going wrong.

Unusual deal structures usually also cost more to implement and administer than commonly used ones. They are more suited to artists who have already established themselves and/or have a particular need (e.g. a tax problem). They are best avoided, unless you are prepared to accept the additional costs and complications.

MECHANICAL ROYALTY CAPS AND REDUCTIONS

As discussed earlier, mechanical copyright royalties ('mechanicals') are the royalties a record company has to pay to the owner of the composition in return for reproducing that work on a record. Record companies in the USA and Canada insist on getting reductions in the amount of mechanicals that they have to pay. This section explains how those reductions operate.

Mechanical royalty caps and reductions apply only to sales of records in the United States and/or Canada. It is never applied to sales in Australia and New Zealand. The USA and Canada have comparable systems and practices in this regard, so for these purposes we will treat these as one territory and call them 'North America'. To be fair to Canada though, remember that the Harry Fox Agency (the organisation which collects mechanical copyright royalties in the United States) does not operate in Canada, so a separate deal is often worked out for Canada, though the same principles apply in both countries.

Few musicians bother to understand the effect of the mechanical royalty caps and 'controlled composition' clauses in their recording contracts – yet these clauses can gut the financial viability of every artist that tries to break into the North American music market. They are now standard terms in recording contracts in North America. Even superstars cannot get them omitted entirely. No one outside North America likes them, but they are something every artist wanting to get a release in that territory has to accept.

It comes as a very rude shock to artists who find on their royalty statement that the record company has deducted large chunks of their earnings as 'excess mechanical payments'. To avoid this shock it is important to understand how such clauses work. Only then can you work out strategies for minimising their effect.

To have any chance of understanding these clauses, you must know something of their history.

BACKGROUND

Mechanicals are a matter of deep interest to record company accountants and lawyers because they (mechanicals, that is) represent a significant chunk of what would otherwise be company profit. Mechanicals are a cost to the record companies' business, so they rather resent them and will do what they can to minimise them. The companies do all they can to cap their costs by using controlled composition clauses in their recording contracts wherever possible under local law and custom.

Most international contracts now include a clause by which the artist promises to license controlled compositions at no more than the industry rate or the generally prevailing rate.

There is an increasing trend in some local recording contracts to extend the operation of the clauses to territories other than the United States and Canada. Resist. In other countries, the local statutory rate should be sacrosanct.

NORTH AMERICAN PRACTICE

Unlike virtually everywhere else, in the United States and Canada mechanical copyrights are a set number of cents per track. This means that the royalty remains the same, regardless of the selling price of the record. Apart from the fact that the mechanical copyright royalty remains unchanged regardless of the record's price, the total mechanical royalty per record increases as the number of tracks increases.

The move from vinyl to CD saw the average number of tracks increase from 10 to 15. This meant that the mechanical royalties payable per unit sold, increased about 50% and that was something that the record companies were never going to tolerate.

In response to these problems, the record companies in North America took to putting clauses in their recording contracts to cap their exposure to mechanical royalty payments and recoup any mechanicals the company has to pay in excess of the minimums set by the recording contract. These clauses have become a standard and virtually non-negotiable part of any North American record deal.

There are four ways that North American record companies limit the amount that they have to pay for mechanical royalties:
- Mechanicals are only paid on records sold;
- The three-quarter rate;
- The capping of the number of controlled compositions that will be paid mechanical royalties; and
- The capping of the total number of tracks that will be paid mechanical royalties.

All of that may be acceptable if you own the composition and accept the lower rate. However if you record songs written by others, because those other writers have not agreed to accept a lower mechanical royalty rate, they are not affected by the deal you have with your record company. They will get full mechanical royalties and the difference between the 'cap' and the full rate will be taken from your record royalties. This can be very expensive for the recording artist.

PAYMENT OF MECHANICALS ON RECORDS SOLD

The royalty is supposed to be paid on all records '**made and distributed**'. If they are made and distributed but not sold (e.g. promotional records), mechanicals should still be paid. This is particularly relevant in the United States, a market where free goods are regularly distributed in lieu of discounts to dealers and where many hundreds of promotional copies can be given away as a matter of course.

This first way of limiting mechanicals is that record contracts often say that the company will pay mechanicals on records '**sold**'. This is narrower than their legal obligation that is to pay mechanicals on records '**made**'. If the owner of the composition insists on being paid on a 'made and distributed' basis but the record contract limits the record company's obligation to paying for records sold, the publisher still gets paid and the balance is recouped by the record company from the artist's share of royalties.

THREE QUARTER RATE

The clause will stipulate a cap on the royalty per track of 75% of the statutory rate on sales in North America.

Conversely, it will also limit the total mechanical copyright royalty the record company will have to pay on the record, to 10 times 75% of the minimum statutory royalty. This means that the company does not want to pay mechanicals on the eleventh or subsequent tracks.

Don't try and negotiate this unless you are married to the president of the record company: even then it is likely to be just another disappointment in your life.

CAPPING CONTROLLED COMPOSITIONS

The expression '**controlled compositions**' refers to musical works and lyrics owned or controlled by the recording artist. It is standard practice in the United States for record companies to cap the mechanical royalties payable in respect of controlled compositions. Such clauses are referred to as '**Controlled composition clauses**'.

Record contracts will usually limit the number of controlled compositions upon which the record company will pay mechanical royalties. This is usually 10, irrespective of the number of controlled compositions on the album. For example assume the album has 16 tracks. The artist has written 12 tracks and four are covers. The record company will pay on only 14 tracks: (ie the four covers and only 10 of the other tracks.)

CAPPING ALL MECHANICAL ROYALTY BEARING TRACKS

Really nasty mechanical-capping clauses try to limit the **total** number of tracks that will attract mechanicals – whether they are controlled compositions or not. This is a Bad Thing. In effect, you will be underwriting any payments the record company makes in excess of the contractually agreed limit.

The maximum number of tracks varies with the format: on an album, the usual limit is 10 (historically derived from the usual number of tracks on a vinyl album).

Although the record contract purports to reduce the amount of mechanicals payable by the record company, no one can legally give away rights that they do not own. Neither an artist nor a record company can unilaterally reduce any writer's mechanical copyright royalties. You can only agree to accept reduced royalties for songs you actually own and control (i.e. controlled compositions). As a result, the third party owner of the cover will still get paid in full and the artist will have to pay from its artist royalties the difference between the track cap and the actual number of tracks.

For example assume that the CD has 16 tracks. All of them are covers. The artist's recording contract limits the record company's mechanical obligation to 10 tracks. All 16 writers will be paid but the record company will recoup the cost of 6 of those tracks from the artist's royalties.

YOUR PUBLISHER

Even if you already have a publishing contract and have assigned all your copyrights to the publisher, these clauses will be relevant. Most record companies in North America will refuse to release your records unless they get the 'customary' reductions on mechanical copyright rates.

Your publisher has greater bargaining power than you do, so there may be a chance of the full rate being paid, but don't bank on it. You will have to decide whether it is worth holding out for full mechanicals. The fact is, record companies in the United States will simply not negotiate controlled composition clauses unless you have the negotiating clout of a Michael Jackson (and it seems likely that even his contract will not oblige the record company to pay mechanicals on promotional copies, or full rate on mid and budget priced records). The record companies can (and do) say - 'If you don't like it, go somewhere else, and see if you can get a better deal'. As they all apply similar reductions, any difference will be one of degree.

In the last few years, some of the Majors have realised that they have a trump card to play when negotiating deals. Where the record company has an affiliated publishing company, it can regard mechanical copyrights as a payment within the same corporate group. Looked at this way, it costs the company very little to pay 100% mechanicals on controlled compositions where those works are published by an affiliated company. This is also a strong incentive to go against the old record industry adage of not giving your publishing to the same company as your record rights.

Always ask about the policy when you are negotiating the record contract. It could represent up to 25% more for your mechanical copyright income in the biggest record market in the world.

'FIRST USE' RIGHT

There will usually be a clause expressly granting a first use licence to the record company in relation to each controlled composition. This is only relevant if the songs have not been recorded before. Once the songs have been released anyone can record them, provided they pay the mechanical copyright fee.

Some clauses will also include a free synchronisation licence for use in video clips. This should be restricted to promotional video uses and not be in lieu of mechanical copyright fees on videos that are sold.

EXEMPT 'FREE GOODS'

Most record contracts will try to exempt 'free goods' from mechanical copyright royalties. This does you no favours. This should only extend to records given away free for promotional purposes, but often it will be extended subtly to include goods given to retailers and wholesalers in lieu of discounts. It should also be limited to controlled compositions. Again, expect videos to be treated the same way.

ROYALTY RETENTION AND OFFSET

As mentioned above, your artist royalties generated from record sales can be diverted by the record company to reimburse it for any mechanical copyright payments in excess of the maximum mechanical copyright royalties specified in your recording contract. This is the basic security the record company will want. There is no guarantee that there will actually be enough royalties there to be worth retaining, but if there is, the record company does not want to be in a position of having to pay you the record royalty cheque with one hand and then snatch it back with the other. Some clauses will include a right to sue the artist for the excess if there are not enough royalties.

PRO RATA ROYALTY RATES

There is often a mechanicals minimisation clause that seeks to reduce the mechanicals paid on records sold at less than full price or sold through television advertising campaigns. This is not too onerous, provided it does not extend to non-controlled compositions as well.

VIDEO

The clause will usually apply comparable caps on any videos the record company might sell that contain your controlled compositions.

Sell-through videos and DVDs are the main concern. In most countries, videos sold to the public are treated like records. Mechanicals are calculated on the selling price (usually the dealer price) and the mechanicals are paid in much the same way (although at a different rate). However, unlike records, some films are made with an 'all-rights buy-out' licence, which may include the right to reproduce the video and sell copies to the public. If this kind of licence is in place, it supersedes any other mechanical copyright payments.

PRACTICAL EXAMPLES

The following examples start at the optimum and work down to the standard agreement offered by most Majors to a new act. Negotiating skill and leverage will determine how close to optimum you can get.

EXAMPLE 1

Imagine you release an album in the United States with 12 tracks. Assume you wrote six of the tracks and that they are controlled compositions. You sell 200,000 albums. Assume the United States mechanical rate is the 2006 rate of 9.1 cents per track.

(A) FULL MECHANICAL RATE

Applying a full mechanical rate the total mechanicals would be $218,400. Therefore you get half (for your six songs) and the third party writers would share the other half.

200,000 units x 9.1c mechanical royalty x 12 tracks = $218,400
$218,400 ÷ 12 tracks = $18,200 per track
Thus:

> Third party receipts = $18,200 per track x 6 tracks = $109,200
> Your receipts = $18,200 per track x 6 tracks = $109,200
> Total mechanicals paid = $218,400

(B) 75% RATE ON CONTROLLED COMPOSITIONS

Now assume that your record contract states that mechanicals on all controlled compositions will be paid at 75% of the full statutory rate. The third party writers will still share $109,200, but you will get only $81,900 (75% of the full rate). Already the company's mechanical royalty bill is reduced to $191,100.

(C) 75% RATE ON CONTROLLED COMPOSITIONS AND 10 TRACK CAP

In fact, most contracts not only have a reduced rate but also state that the company will not pay mechanicals on more than 10 tracks, no matter how many are actually on the album.

On the same assumptions, the third party writers share $109,200. However, the company only has to pay on 10 tracks, and after the payment of third party writers, there are only four tracks left on which mechanicals are payable. Thus you get paid $34,200. The company has limited its total mechanicals bill to $102,600.

> Payment to third party writers = $18,200 per track x 6 tracks
> = $109,200
> Payment to you = 4 (10 - 6) tracks x $18,200 x 75% = $54,600
> Total mechanicals paid = $109,200 + $54,600 = $163,800

(D) 75% RATE ON ALL COMPOSITIONS AND 10 TRACK CAP

Many agreements are deliberately drafted very widely, to apply the reduced rate to all compositions on your record, whether you control them or not. This may appear harmless, but in this example you only wrote six of the songs on the album. It is very likely that the publishers who do own them will want to be paid their full share of mechanical income. Unless some deal is made with the publisher before the song is recorded, you can expect the publisher to take a hard line. If negotiated early enough, the publisher may agree to take a reduction if it means getting the song covered.

Assuming that there has been no such deal worked out, the third party writers will get all of their $109,200. You will get $27,300 and the company will have further reduced its total mechanical pay-out to $136,500. You just lost $81,900.

Total mechanicals = (200,000 units x 9.1c royalty x 12 tracks)
= $218,400

$21,400 ÷ 12 tracks = $18,200 per track

Thus:

Third party receipts = $18,200 per track x 6 tracks = $109,200
Your receipts = $18,200 per track x 6 tracks = $109,200
Total mechanicals paid = $218,400

Maximum amount payable under your contract to the third party writers = (75% x $109,200) = $81,900

Overpayment of third party writers = ($109,200 - $81,900) = $27,300

Payment to you = 4 tracks x ($18,200 x 75% - $27,300) = $27,300.

So, as you can see, depending on the drafting of the record contract, your mechanical income could vary from $109,200 to $27,300!

EXAMPLE 2

Assume you released a sixteen-track record in the United States. Again assume that you sold 200,000 units. This time, assume that all of the songs are covers, so none are controlled compositions in the sense that you wrote or control them in any way.

(A) FULL MECHANICAL RATE PAYABLE

In the unlikely event that your record contract provides for no reductions in the mechanical royalties payable, the writers' publishers will receive $136,800.

200,000 units x 9.1c royalty x 16 tracks = $291,200

(B) 75% RATE ALL COMPOSITIONS

Things are not looking good for you. The third party publishers will still get $291,200 but your contract says the maximum the record company is supposed to pay is 75% of that - $218,400. Therefore your record royalties will be reduced by $72,800 - assuming your royalty account is in credit. If it's not, it goes into the red even further, or the record company may send you a polite letter, 'asking' for a cheque.

(C) 75% RATE ON ALL COMPOSITIONS AND 10-TRACK CAP

The full mechanical royalty payable by the record company would be $291,200, but you have agreed to cap the mechanicals to 10 tracks, each with a 75% rate, even though you don't actually own them.

You will be horrified to find, when your record royalty statement arrives, that the excess payments to third party writers will have been deducted from your record royalties. That is, $81,900 will have been deducted because you had promised to give the record company a break in respect of material over which you didn't have the rights to be generous.

Mechanical royalties actually paid at full rate = $291,200
Royalties payable at reduced rate = ($291,200 x 75%)= $218,400
Per track rate = ($218,400 ÷ 16) = $13,650
Maximum royalty payable with 10 track cap = ($13,650 x 10)
= $136,500
'Over-payment' of royalties = ($291,200 - $136,500) = $154,700
(You just lost $154,700 without even feeling a thing! Now go back to the section on calculating record royalties and work out the number of extra records you have to sell to recoup $150k!)

24
RECORD PRODUCERS

THE ROLE OF THE PRODUCER IS CENTRAL TO
RECORD PRODUCTION. THE REWARDS CAN BE
CONSIDERABLE, BUT ONLY IN THE LAST DECADE
HAVE PRODUCER'S CONTRACTS STARTED TO
REFLECT THE VALUE OF THE PRODUCER'S ROLE. THIS
CHAPTER DISCUSSES WHO SELECTS, HIRES AND
PAYS THE PRODUCER, EXAMINES THE MOST
IMPORTANT FEATURES OF PRODUCER CONTRACTS
AND DISCUSSES THE RIGHTS OF THE PRODUCER IN
MATTERS SUCH AS BUDGET OVERAGES, COPYRIGHT
AND REMIXING.

In the early days of the industry, record companies had staff record producers who literally controlled the recording session. A&R managers usually got the job and often did it very well. Many of the great recordings of the 1950s and 1960s were produced by A&R managers.

Record production was not nearly as technical as it is now, though. After all, even after stereo was introduced, most recordings went directly onto 2-track tape. The idea of a 32 multi-track tape was literally unthinkable. Microphone placement was simple; most sessions just used two, and they were on the same stick. If the recording was faulty, they did it again. Have a listen to the last seconds of Gene Pitney's 'Twenty-four Hours From Tulsa'. You may catch the guitar twanging away, completely at odds with the rest of the band. He was actually telling the engineer/producer that he (the guitarist) had goofed. The take was used anyway. It would never happen now. The guitarist could come back a month later (or record in a different country) and the track could be grafted into the multi-track. It might only cost $10,000 (fully recoupable of course) to make it perfect.

In 1959, Ella Fitzgerald, with the legendary Nelson Riddle as producer, recorded 'The George & Ira Gershwin Song Book' (a five-album project) - all fully orchestrated, and fewer than a dozen days are listed as recording days! By contrast, the Beach Boys took over six months to record the track 'Good Vibrations'.

In the 1960s, artists became more knowledgeable about the recording process and, more importantly, their success enabled them to begin to be able to dictate terms. They began producing their own sessions. The Beach Boys were a prime example of how successful this could be but it only worked if the band knew what it was doing. Mr Wilson got 'Good Vibrations' right, even if it took a while.

As the recording process became more technically demanding and musical arrangements became more complex, the artists started bringing in expertise from outside. Technology made producers necessary. They started as technicians who knew the studio equipment and could read music. They have developed into a distinct form of creative artist. Their importance is reflected by the fact that, in many cases, the producer earns more royalties than any of the individual artists who played on the record.

WHO PAYS?

The record companies argued that they should not have to pay more royalties just because the artist couldn't produce their own recording sessions. That is why, even now, producer royalties usually come out of the artist's royalties rather than being paid by the record company. The other reason is that the record company wants to put a cap on its royalty obligations. If a high producer's royalty were to be added to a high artist's royalty, the company might find its margin cut to an unacceptably low level. For example, a 15% artist royalty plus an additional 3% producer royalty might be too high, whereas the 15% in total might be acceptable.

THIRD PARTY PRODUCERS

Producer's agreements should be negotiated very carefully. After all, producers can make an enormous difference to whether a recording session is successful and efficient, or an expensive indulgence. Check prospective producers carefully. Some (especially young hopefuls from overseas) will tell you they have 'produced' various name artists, but you will often find that this is an exaggeration. Assistant engineer is more likely the case. Choose carefully. You deserve the best talent you can afford.

The subject of overseas producers raises another area to watch for. A hypothetical example will illustrate the potential pitfall. Remember: this could happen in any country, so even though local in this context means Australia, the same principle applies wherever records are produced.

Let's imagine a young band, about to make its first record. It has a very limited budget, so an international producer is out of the question. A talented young local is brought in and produces the first track. It's released as a single and it's a success. Now it's time for the album. Who's to produce it? The young local, who produced the hit? Not likely! Now it's a big budget item and to show how important it is, in comes the overseas producer (naturally paid a lot more than the local) to record the album that, of course, has to recapture the spirit and feel of the single. To some extent, the new producer's job is easier, because the artistic direction has already been decided. Let's assume another nine tracks are recorded, to make a 10-track album. The local producer's track broke the band, but he or she will only get points on one track; the imported producer will get points on the remaining nine, and will probably get the benefit of being credited as the producer of a successful album.

The questions to be asked (and answered) in the course of contract negotiation are: if a producer is contracted to do one track, should he or she have a 'first option' for the album? If not, should the producer get an override on the album (even if that producer does not produce the rest of the tracks) if it is pretty clear the album relies heavily on the first producer's work? The answers to these questions have to be included in the contract.

WRITTEN CONTRACTS

All established producers use written agreements now. The old days, when a handshake sufficed, are long gone. As with most contracts in the music business, there is no 'standard' deal, although the elements are pretty much the same in all of them. Each is influenced by the terms of the artist's contract with the record company, so the two contracts have to be dovetailed carefully, to avoid inconsistencies.

THE JOB DESCRIPTION

Usually, a producer is needed mainly to provide musical insight or to give new musical direction to a performer's studio work. In some cases, though (this is more prevalent in the United States), the producer might be contracted to provide a complete package of studio, engineer and producer services and, occasionally, even accommodation for the artist while the recording is being made. The principles of such deals are actually not so different, though the cost and documentation most certainly will be.

Personal rapport with a producer is important. There is no point hiring a hot-shot if you can't stand being in the same room. Some producers take control of the studio and really direct things. Others take a rather passive role, making suggestions and responding to the artist's wishes. The producer's working style is one of the main factors that will determine your choice of producer for any particular track. Some are multi-instrumentalists too, which can reduce lost time in the studio and help reduce recording costs.

WHO HIRES THE PRODUCERS?

One matter to be sorted out at the very beginning is whether you or the record company will hire the producer. If you will be paying the producer's royalties, the usual scenario would be for you to be the contracting party. If the record company will be paying the royalties, then it is better if it contracts with the producer. Either way, it is important to keep the terms of the producer's contract in step with the record contract, particularly when defining the 'royalty base' for the producer's royalties. This will save you a lot of work re-calculating royalties (dealt with in more detail later in this chapter under Advances and Recoupment).

SERVICES

A skilled producer can be crucial to the commercial success of a record. The producer's decisions affect the whole 'feel' and 'sound' of the recorded work. For example, any history of the Beatles will inevitably refer to the influence George Martin had on the records and musical development of the group over many years.

The job description in most production contracts is usually pretty prosaic: 'To deliver to [insert name here] a fully edited and leadered stereophonic master recording technically and commercially satisfactory to [insert name] for the manufacture and sale of records'. Translated, this means a 2-track master recording with end-bits, on time and within budget. If it also happens to be an artistic masterpiece, that's a bonus.

If any of those tasks are not fulfilled, you will have a problem with your record company. Naturally, if you have a problem, you will insist your producer share it with you and that he or she contribute to any over-budget expenses caused by them not performing as contracted.

ADMINISTRATIVE AND FINANCIAL SERVICES

In the record producer's relationship with both the company and the artist, there are two primary issues: creative control and financial control.

On an executive level, the producer is usually responsible for supervising the recording process, to ensure that a quality record is delivered within budget.

Sometimes this will involve only supervising the actual sound recording process. Sometimes it will include preparing and administering the budget (after agreeing to work within the one set in your contract); hiring the studio and any additional equipment necessary (for example for mix-down); hiring all personnel such as the engineer, arrangers and session musicians; maintaining job sheets (and their prompt submission to the record company); obtaining and delivering all necessary approvals, consents and permissions under the performers' protection legislation; and delivering all invoices and receipts relating to recording expenses, as proof of the recording costs. If the producer does not do these things, someone has to and that someone is going to be you.

CREATIVE SERVICES

On a creative level, the craft of the producer is more difficult to define. In the end, it comes down to producing a record that pleases the artist, the record company and, most of all, the record-buying public. This is a combination of talent, training, experience, black magic and serendipity.

Until the company (and/or you if you have managed to retain creative control under your recording contract) are satisfied with the result, the producer may have to rerecord, remix, re-edit or remaster. Because of this, the contract should be carefully drafted to make sure there is no uncertainty about who has to do what and who pays if things go wrong.

Some producers also become involved in selecting the songs to be recorded. Some can arrange the songs themselves. Some will rewrite parts of the material so that it fits their artistic plan better. There are many degrees of creative involvement - some more intrusive than others. Some may try to claim co-writing credits in your songs that they arrange. Beware a cuckoo in the nest!

SELECTING A PRODUCER

Both the artist and the record company must be involved in selecting the producer. With new artists, the record company may insist on having final say over this important creative element of the recording process, although few record companies will insist you use a particular producer against your wishes. The A&R manager may, however, think your choice is too expensive, and resist it when the recording budget is being set.

PRODUCER'S REMUNERATION

THE FEE

Producers worked out long ago that most records do not recoup, so most insist on an up-front fee. However, they also have an each-way bet by also taking a royalty. The size of the fee is largely determined by the availability of funds in the recording budget and whether that particular producer is in demand or not. The fee is usually recoupable against royalties (if any) earned by the producer.

Producers may get further fees if they are playing as session musicians on the recording and still further fees if they are also acting as the engineer. Payment is according to function and negotiation.

If they have to travel, they will usually have their travel costs, accommodation and daily costs of living (per diems) paid as well, but these may not be recoupable.

THE TOTAL RECORDING PACKAGE

Because so many producers now have their own recording facilities, record companies have found it advantageous to offer such producers an all-up fee, covering all of the recording costs. In effect, the producer is contracted to make the recording on behalf of whoever is the final copyright owner. If the producer can bring the record in under budget, the savings (the 'underage') are often kept by the producer as an incentive to keep costs down. If the project goes over the agreed budget, the producer pays the additional costs (the 'overage').

The advantage of this system is that everyone can forecast the actual recording costs and limit their risk exposure.

A lot of music is being made using inexpensive computer equipment now, so actual recording costs can be kept down, but the budget tends to be boosted by relatively high mixing costs. Specialist mixing experts are taking over the role previously held by producers. Most charge a fee per track, with no royalties (except in R&B, dance and urban genres where the mix is everything).

FEE PER MASTER

The most common basis for paying producers is a fee for each track produced. The record company usually controls the budget. Novice producers may get less than $500 a track but the fees for established producers range generally between $1,200 and $3,000. A really hot international producer can get very much more, depending on the artist and the recording budget.

If the producer is also acting as the engineer there may be additional fees for this extra work. This is usually no more than half the producer fee. In the United States it is not uncommon for top engineers to get a 1% (of retail, less packaging) royalty as well. This is not usual practice in most other countries.

TIMING OF FEE PAYMENT

Producers are usually paid half the fee on commencement of recording and the balance on completion or delivery and 'acceptance' (which can have a technical meaning, depending upon the contract with the producer) of the master.

ROYALTIES

In recent years, producers have been increasingly treated as a vital part of the creative team and therefore deserving of reward on a similar basis to the artist. This means not just the payment of a one-time fee but also a share in the 'blue sky' royalties.

ROYALTY RATES

The most common range of rates in Australia is between 1% and 2.5% of the retail price less GST and packaging (which roughly translates to between 1.5% and 3.5% of the dealer price, less GST and packaging). Overseas rates are generally a bit higher, although there is always the option of reducing the rate for overseas sales or nominating a rate per territory, to tie in with any reductions to the artist's royalty from the relevant country.

When negotiating their record contracts, artists should try to cap their liability for producer's royalties. Some record companies will agree to cap the artist's share at 2% based on the retail price less GST and packaging, and pay (or split) the cost of producer royalties in excess of that rate. This gives both the artist and the company an incentive to be reasonable in the selection of the producer and negotiation of the producer's contract.

ADVANCES AND RECOUPMENT

If the producer is going to receive a royalty in addition to a fee, the fee should always be treated as a fully recoupable advance of the producer's royalties. Insist that the royalty base for the producer's points be the same as yours under the recording contract. This will simplify royalty accounting for you, especially if you are the one paying the producer's points.

Producers should get royalties when you get them, on the same records, and subject to the same reductions. After all, if the rationale for the producer getting a royalty at all is that he or she is a part of the creative unit, the producer should be paid on the same basis as that other important component of the unit - the artist.

WHEN DOES THE PRODUCER EARN ROYALTIES?

There are two absolutely basic questions to be resolved when looking at a producer's contract:

- **At what time will the producer start to accrue royalties?**
  'Accrue' here does not actually mean receive - it means the royalty may be earned but is not actually due to be paid until some later specified time. Failure to look after these aspects can have diabolic consequences for all concerned. If badly handled, you could be left in the position that you cannot afford to have a hit record, because the producer royalties will be more than you can afford to pay.
- **Who will pay the producer?**
  Producers usually ask to have their royalties payable directly to them by the record company, rather than administered by the artist. Most record companies in Australia are obliging in this respect. After all, the companies have control of the receipts and have the

administrative facilities to provide the accounting. If the company looks after it, the producer is protected, the artists are relieved of a responsibility that they are not set up for and the company knows that all the loose ends are properly tied up.

TIMING OF ROYALTY PAYMENTS

Every producer wants to be paid royalties as soon as possible. Artists generally want to defer the evil day as long as possible, especially as they may not see any royalties from the particular record for a long time.

Only a tiny number of international producers could negotiate a deal where they get royalties regardless of whether the recording costs have been recouped. For example, if the producer's royalty was equal to 10 cents per album, and the record sold 50,000 albums in the first accounting period, the producer would be due to get (subject to any advances paid previously) $5,000. This would have to be paid, no matter whether the album had recouped its recording costs or not. Unless the artist has the money readily available, the producer is likely to be waiting a long, long time to see the royalties, which is why the record company will usually pay the royalties directly. If it does make payments to the producer, it will add the payments to the artist's advance account, to be recouped from record royalties.

Fortunately, most producers will agree to defer getting royalties to a later stage. Those with enough clout may agree to defer receiving royalties until after the record's recording costs have been recouped. This will usually be calculated using the combined artist and producer royalty rates to speed up the process. Really major producers (especially in the United States) can get deals where, once recoupment occurs, the producer's royalties are calculated by going back to the first record sold. More often, though, the royalties just start once recoupment happens.

Of course, just because the recording costs for that record are recouped does not mean the artist is getting royalties. Life isn't that simple in this business. You, the artist, may have already recorded a subsequent album, so your advance account has been charged with the new record's recording costs and there will no doubt be many video clips and advances to be recouped too. As far as the record company is concerned, you are unrecouped, even if your royalties for the first album have exceeded its recording costs.

You have to allow for this and make provisions to meet your obligations. Your producer is an important part of the team that creates your recordings. If he or she is a friend, the relationship will not last if you stiff them for their royalties. If not a friend, the producer will not have second thoughts about suing you for the royalties, if the stakes are sufficiently high. A run-away international hit record could just about do it.

There is some comfort in knowing that if the record really becomes a huge hit, your career will probably experience a timely surge and your income will increase greatly, so money should be coming in from several sources by the time the producer's royalties fall due. But don't assume this will be the case. Plan early.

SHARE OF LICENCE FEES

Whenever a master is licensed, say for synchronisation on film or video, a fee is paid to the company for the licence. Your record contract should always provide for the company's net receipts from these licences to be split in some proportion between the record company and you. Producer agreements are also beginning to include such provisions. The producer will often receive a share of the licence fee in the same proportion as the producer's record royalty bears to the artist record royalty. For example, if the artist is on 12% and the producer is on 2%, the producer would get one-sixth of any licence fee received by the artist.

VIDEO ROYALTIES

Producers with enough negotiating power may demand a share of video income in addition to record income. If agreed, the producer's royalty is usually arrived at by using the same formula as the licence fee above - but with a twist.

Again, if the artist is on (say) 12% and the producer is on (say) 2%, the producer will get one-sixth of the artist's video royalty rate - divided by two. The reduction is based on the rather obvious fact that the sound track is only half of a video - the other half being the visual part to which the producer made no contribution.

ROYALTY REDUCTIONS

As has been stated over and over in this book, what is important is not the percentage but the 'points'; that is, what is left of the royalty after all of the deductions have been taken out.

The producer's royalty should be subject to exactly the same reductions and deductions as those suffered by the artist. If there is any variation in this rule, it is usually when the record company is paying and contracting the producer and not recouping the money from the artist, in which case the record company may be able to negotiate a more advantageous royalty base.

If the artist is being paid on 90% of sales, suffers deductions for taxes, packaging, mid and low price discounts, club sales, premiums and free goods, television-advertised product and so on, so too should the producer. If the artist is paid less for overseas territories, so too should the producer.

PRO-RATA CALCULATIONS

Where the record is a compilation of tracks by various artists, the producer royalties are pro-rated according to the proportion that the number of the producer's tracks bears to the total number of tracks on the compilation. For example, if the producer produced two out of 12 tracks, the producer royalty would be one-sixth of the royalty that would have been received if he or she had produced all 12 tracks.

Similarly, if the album is the work of one artist but the producer has not produced all of the tracks on the album, the royalty is pro-rated according to the proportion that the number of the producer's tracks bears to the total number of tracks on the album. Sometimes this is calculated by the time (rather than the number) of tracks, but this is less usual. There is one common and important exception to this. It is called 'A-Side Protection'.

A-SIDE PROTECTION

In the days of vinyl records, established producers often insisted that if a track they produced was released as the A-side of a single, they would be paid full royalties on the single, regardless of whether they had produced the B-side or not. If there was no A-Side protection and the single contained two tracks, one by the producer and one produced by someone else, the producer of the A-side would receive 50% royalties because of the effect of pro-rating.

If the producer of the A-side had A-side protection, there was no pro-rata reduction in the royalty payable. It was deemed, for the purpose of royalty calculation, that the producer had done both tracks.

The reason for this was two-fold. First, it was argued that no one bought a single for its B-side. Radio played the A-side and the B-side was hardly relevant to singles sales. Second, it was very common for artists (or record company executives) to insist that one of the tracks they produced themselves go on the B-side, either to cut down on the royalties payable or simply make a bit of money on the side.

Now, in the days of the CD single, there is of course no B-side. However, the principles remain the same because additional tracks and remixes are often included on the CD. No big-name producer wants to see his or her royalty diminished just because the artist or the company has filled up the rest of the disc with someone else's productions. Accordingly, we still talk of A-side protection and apply the same principles, even though technology has made the terminology redundant.

RESPONSIBILITY FOR BUDGET OVERAGES

Many record companies insist on a provision that, if the project goes over-budget, the producer will be responsible for the overage. Of course, producers object to this and try to negotiate this out of the contract, or at least restrict it to situations in which the overage was due to circumstances within the producer's control.

If the budget blow-out is due to technical failure, the artist's failure to attend recording sessions, illness or a record company executive's demands for unanticipated changes, or some other such cause, there is no reason why the producer should have to foot the bill. At the very least, producers should insist on there being a contingency factor of, say, 10% provided before they become liable for overages.

COPYRIGHT OWNERSHIP

THE MASTERS

The producer does not own any rights in the masters produced. The contract will specify that all rights are owned exclusively by the artist or the record company, as the case may be.

If the producer is Australian and performed on the master, always get a written Performers' Protection clearance from the producer as well as from the other session musicians and backing singers.

WORKS COMPOSED WITH THE ARTIST

Some producers involve themselves in the re-writing and comprehensive re-arranging of the songs recorded. Some also insist on being given a share of the copyright in the work. This means they are credited as a writer and share in any publishing income generated by the song.

This may be acceptable if the artist is a novice, or the material really needs a lot of shaping before it is commercially acceptable, but otherwise this practice should be resisted. The producer's contribution is already being recognised and paid for by the fee and royalty.

To make the issue of who owns copyright in the work absolutely clear, most producers' contracts have a clause specifically stating that they 'have not contributed to the authorship of any musical composition recorded' and include a warranty that they 'will not assert any right, title or interest therein'.

WORKS COMPOSED BY THIRD PARTIES

As the producer is intimately involved in the selection of material to be recorded, some producers do deals with publishers by which they get a part of the publisher's share of income in return for getting one of the publisher's tracks onto the record. This can be a serious conflict of interest, for although it is in the publisher's interest to procure a cover for its composer, it is not necessarily in the best interests of the recording artist. Certainly if the producer is doing such side deals, the artist should be informed. The taking of secret commissions is, after all, illegal.

REMIXING

Most producer agreements give the company the right to remix the masters using a different producer. Sometimes this is necessary to salvage a record with which either the artist or the company is dissatisfied. It is also particularly important when recordings are licensed into the United States. There, the need to remix Australian product is almost glandular. The American A&R managers have a concept of what the American record-buying public wants and they often spend huge amounts of money remixing product that has already been commercially successful in Australia.

In Australia, most producers who are hired to do a remix do it for a flat fee but in the United States it is common practice for the remix producer to be paid a royalty as well. Established producers protect themselves from the effect of such additional royalties by insisting that, while the company has the right to remix using another producer, the costs of such remix will not deleteriously affect their royalty.

TERMINATION

All producer contracts have explicit clauses describing the circumstances in which the producer's services may be terminated and the consequences of that termination.

They are usually one-sided. That is, the record company has the power to sack the producer even if there has been no breach of contract, but the producer does not have the power to quit for no particular reason.

Both the artists and the record companies argue that they have to retain the power to terminate if they believe the producer is not getting the quality they are looking for. The artists also want to be able to sack the producer if they are simply unable to work together for personal reasons. No breach of contract need be proved.

Obviously there needs to be some negotiation here to ensure that such a clause is not overly harsh.

Sometimes the right of termination is restricted to trigger events that are within the producer's control; sometimes the right remains unfettered, but the company agrees to pay the producer's full fee in the event that they terminate early ('play or pay'). Sometimes the company will agree to pay the full fee and the royalty, although this is rare.

Terrible problems can arise when the producer is sacked after completing some but not all of the tracks, or after doing a considerable amount of work on them but not actually completing them. What proportion of the final instalment of the fee should be payable? If a royalty is due, what proportion should be payable? What credit should be accorded the producer on the record when it is released?

Because the circumstances of every early termination are so different it can be very useful to include in the agreement an arbitration or mediation clause. This allows an independent third party to determine what is fair in that particular situation.

25
MUSIC CLIPS

THE AUDIOVISUAL CLIP HAS BECOME ONE OF THE
MOST IMPORTANT TOOLS IN MARKETING
CONTEMPORARY POPULAR MUSIC. IT HAS ALSO
BECOME A PRODUCT FOR SALE IN ITS OWN RIGHT.
THIS CHAPTER LOOKS BRIEFLY AT THE
DEVELOPMENT OF THIS TOOL, COMMISSIONING
PRODUCERS (AND THE TERMS OF SUCH CONTRACTS),
CREATIVE CONTROL AND INCOME.

Not so long ago, we spoke of 'film clips'. We still use the term 'video clips' and 'music videos' but as the technology continues to evolve and the videocassette quietly dies as a medium, we will probably soon find a more appropriate name. Perhaps they will become technology non-specific and just referred to as 'music clips'. Anyway, clips are short audiovisual productions that have a song as the main element of their soundtrack. Everything is digital. Usually, the images on the film are more or less synchronised with the song, depending upon the director's imagination. Whichever expression is used, it will be used to refer to 'short-form' videos rather than to so-called 'long-form' videos, though of course they have some aspects in common.

Long-form videos/DVDs tend to be special projects in their own right, needing specific contracts and involving most of the problems normally associated with feature-length movies. This puts them outside the scope of this book and the average recording contract. DVD may change this. At last we have a medium that realistically permits artists to communicate to their fans visually, whilst delivering the audio content with sound quality that is not compromised by the tape medium. DVD heralds the birth of a new attitude to making records.

HISTORY

Long ago, when the world was uncomplicated, artists did not need to make music clips. Go back far enough and there was no way to make them (silent movies made lousy music clips) and nowhere to show them. Besides, there were plenty of other, cheaper, ways for artists to be promoted. The development of television and videotape really made clips viable.

Hollywood produced films with music, and even made a few about musicians (e.g. 'The Jazz Singer' and 'The Glenn Miller Story'). In the 1950s, jazz musicians were occasionally filmed in concert but these were still qualitatively different from what we now recognise as music clips. Those productions were generally intended to make money in their own right, whereas clips were primarily promotional tools, so it was irrelevant to the record company whether they made money or not. It was only in the 1980s, when clips got to be so expensive and such a large part of popular culture on television, that pay-for-play became an issue. More on pay-for-play later.

By the early 1960s, it was already beginning to look as if clips were important to augment exposure on radio, but only a few far-sighted souls predicted that they would eventually become the primary medium for showcasing artists and breaking records. The various ways of exploiting videos, such as the development of the various home entertainment formats and of pay television, were not contemplated.

CLIPS AS A PROMOTIONAL TOOL

In the early days of music clips, record companies started to make 8 mm and even 16 mm films of their major acts and sent copies to their affiliates in the major territories for free distribution to television stations. Most were pretty primitive affairs (as anyone who has watched a 'Rage' retrospective will confirm). Nonetheless, they were important promotional tools. Besides, it was much cheaper, and a lot less trouble, to post a film clip to a foreign territory rather than fly a group there, keep them in a hotel room and pay for the repairs to the room afterwards.

Unfortunately, many of the old clips have vanished; heaved out by record companies with bulging storerooms full of dust-covered film canisters. In many cases, the only remaining footage of these early clips is held by television stations. Sometimes this is footage taken in the studio before a gyrating audience. Sometimes it is all or part of the actual clip, inserted into a program. The ABC has a treasure trove of this kind of footage. Strangely, Australian television stations have been an accidental archive for quite a lot of international material generated in the 1960s, since we kept telecasting the programs long after they had become a distant memory in the United States and had been thrown out there.

CONCERT FILMS

By the middle 1970s, feature-length films (e.g. 'Concert for Bangladesh', 'Woodstock', Emerson, Lake & Palmer's 'Pictures at an Exhibition' and The Band's film of their farewell concert, 'The Last Waltz', etc.) were able to make their producers a healthy return from their cinema seasons, quite apart from the cross-media promotional opportunities they offered. All these had spin-off albums. In a way, they were the forerunners of the long-form video format.

TELEVISION

As television gradually increased the opportunities for clips to be screened, demand for the number and quality of clips increased. So did their cost. High production values were seen as important and story lines became more adventurous, while technology and advanced post-production techniques were improving all the time. By the early 1980s, clips were as ubiquitous as Stratocaster look-alikes. Every act, no matter how lowly, made clips to support each single's release. In fact, many acts absolutely demanded that there be a clip for every single. This put considerable pressure on A&R managers and their budgets. A&R managers had to increase their project budgets to allow for several clips and then they had to organise the production in addition to the recording itself.

A&R managers are not film producers and the record companies did not have the in-house expertise. They had to hire film producers to do the work for them. Independent film production houses proliferated, specialising in four-minute epics funded by record companies. Record companies were reluctantly dragged into a video war and spent more and more money on bigger and more elaborate productions, all vying for the attention of television programmers and viewers. The willingness of record companies to agree to substantial budgets for clips in their record contracts was interpreted by many artists as proof of true love. More and more complex productions were made in an effort to attract the attention of an increasingly demanding public. The theory was that a hot clip sold records.

CLIPS AND RECORDING BUDGETS

Meanwhile, the recoupable recording deal ensured that the artists' advance accounts went further and further into the red. Even in Australia, where clip budgets have always been much lower than in the United States or the United Kingdom, it was (and still is) commonplace for an new act's first single to cost $10,000 and the clip to cost $25,000. All of a sudden, the single had a recoupable recording budget of $35,000 before a cent had been spent on other promotional activities. In many cases, the clip was the entire promotional activity, because the record company had no money left after it was made.

Putting this into perspective: if the average single generated 25 cents in artist's royalties, they had to sell the equivalent of 140,000 singles to recoup their advance account. Of course, the real intention was (and still is) to sell albums rather than singles. (It is not uncommon for record companies to delete a single when it has reached No.1. This supposedly forces the fan to buy the album to get the track but these days it merely prompts the frustrated fan to download the track illegally from the Internet.) The extraordinary success of Michael Jackson's 'Thriller' album was a perfect example. Almost every track was successfully released as a single in its own right, each supported by a highly inventive and expensive clip. The album was a landmark in the music business.

MTV

Music clip costs reached an all time high when MTV began going to air in the United States. Suddenly, there was a program that people watched to see how good the clips were. The music often took a subsidiary role to the visual element. Of course, there were other clip shows too, which only compounded the madness. Clip shows favoured artists who had a strong visual element to their performances, whether they were mainstream acts or signed to independent labels. A good clip got viewers and, if the theory worked, sold a lot of records. A dud clip didn't get shown, so the promotions staff at the record company would have to find alternative ways of promoting the record.

Clip producers began to be chosen because they had had a clip on MTV rather than because they had great creative ideas for a particular clip. Video costs began to consume more and more of the total budget for a particular album project. Many times, the cost of the clips approached the cost of the album they were meant to promote. From the record companies' view, the positive side of all this was that a screening on MTV achieved national exposure for the clip, rather than having to get it placed individually with dozens of television stations across the United States, so it was still regarded as reasonably cost-effective.

In Australia, it is hard to say that clips can ever be cost-effective: production costs versus market size is always a problem. Local viewers demand that local clips have the same production values as those from the United States, a country where the production costs are similar but the potential market is almost fifteen times larger.

OTHER USES OF CLIPS

The plethora of clips had an interesting side effect; it created a number of spin-off industries that were based on commercial exploitation of clips.

VIDEO JUKEBOXES
Television broadcast of clips created a demand for video jukeboxes and the widespread use of video projection units in nightclubs. After initial indifference, the record companies found it economic to license third parties to supply the clips to clubs and video juke boxes, rather than have to go to the trouble and expense of setting up a special department themselves.

This was one of the earliest uses of clips that regularly generated income (although minuscule) from the commercial use of the clips. These uses gave the record company a small return (by way of a royalty or fee from the distributing company) and generated additional public performance income for the composers, as well as helping promote the records that were reproduced in the clip's soundtracks.

SELL-THROUGH VIDEO AND DVD
Meanwhile, and quite coincidentally, clips were turning into an art form with a commercial value in their own right. Advances in technology enabled the producers to give them the kind of production values that had previously been the preserve of expensive television commercials for more mundane products. The advent of domestic video players meant that it was finally possible for the public to rent or buy a feature-length movie and take it home. It was only to be expected that demand for music videos would grow in the same way, especially when hi-fi video came along. The public started to want clips they could play at home.

For the record companies, this was great news. Provided they had the necessary contractual rights, they could stick a dozen clips end to end, put a fancy cover on the box, and sell maybe a few thousand copies. At last - a way to make money from these hideously expensive promo films! The more adventurous companies even let their artists make long-form videos to support an album release, with the video tracks corresponding to the album tracks. Retrospective video compilations of old clips were especially good - usually the artist didn't get a royalty and most artists had no contractual right to stop the video being compiled and sold.

Fortunately, most recording contracts now provide for the artist to get a royalty from commercial exploitation of clips and often include a right to approve video compilations. This will be dealt with in more detail later in this chapter.

One of the most significant changes in the last five years has been the unlamented death of the music video and the birth of the music DVD. At last the technology can do justice to the music, the performance and the production. It was yet another bonus for the record companies for they were able to re-release their video stock on the new medium. Reuse of existing material can return a high profit. Then after the excitement of the new technology waned, the prices for that kind of material reflected the CD market: There are now thousands of music DVDs for $9.99 while new release products still commands premium pricing.

TELECAST

'Pay for play', mentioned earlier, is essentially a royalty or fee from telecasters for the right to use clips as program material.

Telecasters have always paid for their other program material, but somehow the logic of paying for clips was slow to catch hold. It still hasn't. The telecasters still object to paying royalties for clips, even when programs consist of a score of clips strung end to end, interrupted by commercials. Programs of this kind are cheap to make, appeal to an attractive demographic, rate well in what would otherwise be a very lack-lustre time of the day and, as a bonus, they count as local content.

The telecasters argue that all air-play is promotion. Some even argue that they ought to be paid to screen them! The record companies say the context is important: put a single pearl in your hand and you really notice the pearl. Put a string of pearls there and you lose sight of the individual pearls. They argue that this applies to clips, too. One clip by itself, with commentary, can have promotional value. Playing clips of records that are already hits is not exactly promotion. As usual, the truth is probably somewhere in between those extremes.

The fact is, of course, telecasters do not actually need clips for their programming. They could get by quite well without them, but (even with pay for play) they are still about the cheapest way of filling screen time, other than running a test pattern.

FUTURE FORMATS

The demand for clips in high quality domestic formats was the incentive for the new hybrid audiovisual formats. The laser disc, which is the usual name given to the 30 cm disc, had a moment of fame but it is the DVD that has now established itself as the industry standard. CD Extra and Dual Disc try to deliver the best of both worlds by delivering both audio and audiovisual and it may withstand the assault from DVD. It really is just a clever way of delivering the music with the clip. It's the Old World graced with new technology.

In contrast, DVD provides for a more creative future, for if musicians and record companies are going to harness the capabilities of the medium, they will have to reconceive the recording process and purpose. It can be used to deliver the usual compilations and to capture whole live performances but it also provides a new medium for integrating music, visual art, drama and cinematography in the delivery of the performance to the home audience. Not convinced? Well, in 2001 Australians bought 4.3 million DVD movies. In 2004-2005 it was 40 million. That indicates that the home entertainment market has adopted the technology and is spending hundreds of millions on it. The musician or record company that ignores this shift is going to get left on the wharf.

CLIP PRODUCERS

Clips are virtually never produced in-house by record companies. Independent producers are commissioned to make the clips. Most producers have production companies that provide the director, the production crew and all the equipment. Often the director will also be responsible for the clip's artistic content, writing the storyboard, selecting the location and arranging for props and extras as needed, arranging transport, shooting the footage, post-production and editing. The elements of production agreements are considered in detail later in this chapter. Clip production agreements have to cover a lot of areas and can be as complex as a contract for a major record producer.

In fairness to music video makers in Australia, most produce phenomenal results on minuscule budgets. This comes from a combination of technical skill, competition between producers and the rather undesirable but common practice of using unpaid 'mates' and film students in the production crew. This is understandable, but it does tend to undervalue the true cost of making a clip. Another area where savings are often made is by not paying insurance premiums.

Most video productions start life as a story or concept explained by the producer or director to the artist and the A&R manager. If it gets the go-ahead, the producer will put a written budget together, itemising the costs for crew, technical equipment, location costs, travel and the other essential items. The budget will usually also show the producer's fee as a separate item. Alternatively, the producer might agree to deliver a finished film for a specified sum. This sounds fine in theory, but you have to have an unusual degree of trust in your producer to agree to a deal like that.

If the budget is approved, the record company will usually produce a standard form production agreement. The agreement defines what the clip will be like, how it will be produced, when it will be delivered (it is critical that the clip be ready for the release date of the relevant record), in what format it will be filmed and the budgets. In all cases, the record company insists that the copyright be assigned to it without restriction.

COMMISSIONING YOUR OWN CLIPS

In some cases, the artist commissions and funds the clip directly. In that case the artist will be the party that contracts with the video producer. Provided the money is available, this is the best option as it gives the artist complete artistic control and also the opportunity to own the copyright outright.

The matter of copyright ownership in clips is being questioned in some quarters now. Some producers feel they should own some (or even all) of the copyright and claim a residual right and/or a royalty if the clip is used in certain ways (e.g. sold for home video/DVD). Whilst this is understandable to an extent, the fact is that most producers get paid a production fee irrespective of the clip's success. It is not the producer's money on the line. If the producer were willing to waive the production fee and take a risk on taking a share of profits instead, then the argument might have more weight. Most producers are (quite understandably) loath to accept a deal like that. Consequently, it is almost unknown for the party who commissions the video to share the copyright with the producer.

MUSIC COPYRIGHT IN CLIPS

You may have noticed the absence of any reference to 'musical copyright fees' in the discussion of budgets. That is because it is customary in the industry for composers and publishers to waive their fee for synchronising their song into a promotional clip (provided that is actually what it is). If the clip is really a film project in its own right, the publisher is quite entitled to demand a synchronisation fee. This is a fee based upon the copyright owner's right to authorise reproduction of a musical work in a film's soundtrack. This fee can range from a few hundred to many thousands of dollars, depending on the project and the work. There is no rule of thumb here. You have to ask well in advance.

If copies of the video or DVD are sold to the public, the publisher is also entitled to claim mechanical copyright royalties on each video and DVD sold. After all, these are not promotional products. They are market products in their own right. (For an explanation as to what the rates are and how they are applied, see Chapter 9, **Music Publishing**.)

CLIPS AND RECORDING CONTRACTS

Your recording contract will determine whether you or your record company contracts the clip producer. Usually, it is the record company that is responsible for:
*   commissioning the producer and establishing the budget;
*   making the necessary contractual arrangements;

- providing the funds; and
- exercising control over the clip's artistic content (though you should have no less input/control than you have in relation to your sound recordings).

Your record contract should specify exactly how many clips actually have to be made and set guidelines as to their budgets. You and the record company can always agree to do more - or fewer - clips but you have to have a bottom line figure. In the old days (up to a couple of years ago) you would negotiate for a clip to accompany the release of each single, but these days, with the decline of the CD single other marketing parameters are perhaps more appropriate. (For example, it may be based on which tracks are promoted to radio.) Even more importantly, you should ask yourself whether you really need any clips at all. If your music is not likely to get played in the major clip shows on television, maybe you would be better off spending the money on other kinds of promotion.

BUDGETARY AND CREATIVE CONTROL

Budgets are a vexed area. In fully recoupable deals, if an album has two or three singles, each with a clip, the total clip budget can equal the album's recording cost. Fortunately for artists, the industry is gradually getting used to 50% recoupable deals (i.e. only half of the cost of the clip to be put against your advance account, with the balance paid by the record company from its promotional account). That said, 100% recoupable deals are still frequently made. It depends upon your bargaining power in negotiations.

The extent to which you have artistic control should be set out in your contract. The contract has to state who may decide which tracks will have clips made for them, what the clips will look like and how you will be presented. It is sensible, at least in the early stage of a career, that these controls be mutual. Both the company and the artist have a valid interest in ensuring that the clip meets the promotional and marketing requirements of a carefully considered strategy.

Control of the uses to which the clip(s) may be put is always important. If you have high bargaining power, you might be able to restrict the uses to which your clips can be put by the record company and define which uses would need your prior consent. Promotional use is obviously alright but use for promoting other people's records or goods should be avoided, except with your prior approval.

ROYALTIES

If the clips are used in any way which generates income for the record company (commercial exploitation), as opposed merely to them being provided free to third parties to advertise your records, then you should get a slice of the income. This royalty should apply to all forms of exploitation including broadcast (pay-for-play) income and the like. There is much to recommend the artist and the record company sharing the receipts 50/50. Watch out for any deductions such as mechanical copyright fees or unspecified 'expenses of collection'.

Sometimes there will be a nominated royalty rate for sales of conventional videotapes and other formats such as DVD. For video, this was usually between 10% and 14% of the wholesale price, after subtracting GST and a huge packaging deduction. Video rates are almost irrelevant these days. The focus is DVD and the royalty for these is usually the CD album rate. How else could it be if the one disc contains audio-only and audiovisual material?

PACKAGING DEDUCTIONS ON SELL-THROUGH VIDEOS AND DVD

Expect heavy packaging deductions off the Royalty Base Price. This can be up to 30% to 35%. Even videocassettes will have packaging deductions of between 20% and 30%. DVD and other new media will often have an even higher deduction.

Unfortunately, the high cost of making videotapes meant that they had a low profit margin for the record companies, so royalty rates reflected the tight margins. It is not clear why this logic should be applied to other formats that do not necessarily share that particular problem, but it usually is! Do not be surprised to hear the words 'new technology' or 'development costs' if you query the deductions for DVD.

THE VIDEO PRODUCER'S CONTRACT

Following is a brief review of the terms typically found in a clip producer's contract.

THE PARTIES

The contract will be with the producer or (more usually) the producer's service company. If with the latter, that company will undertake to provide all facilities, including the director's services, for the duration of the production schedule.

CHOICE OF DIRECTOR

Unless agreed otherwise, the director should be providing his or her services on a 'first priority' basis for your project, until the finished clip has been delivered and accepted. You do not really need the director to head off to Guatemala just when post-production is about to start.

Selecting a director can be difficult. You have to know the director's work and trust him or her to make a clip that will complement your music, not swamp it or be incongruous with either your music or your image.

Often the director is the deciding factor when determining who will produce the clip. It may be because you have seen a particular director's work, or one comes well recommended, or someone offers to do the job because they like the idea (or need the money). Some directors use clips as a stepping-stone to 'real' films. Russell Mulcahy is a case in point. He made many clips before getting a director's chair in a major film production. Students from Film and Television schools are similarly attracted to clip making, although few ever get a chance to make clips for 'name' artists, so they have to establish their credentials by making clips for independent acts and labels.

If your record company is feeling impetuous, it might agree to use a 'name' director from overseas. All else being equal, a top name director can improve a clip's chances of getting added to the television play-lists here and in the United States and Europe. American clip makers are usually accustomed to having huge budgets and high profiles. Consider the impact on your advance account before rushing into this quagmire. The end result has to justify the cost. At least a hugely expensive director will give the music-press journalists something to write about, even if they hate the clip.

STORYBOARD

This is the basic idea of the clip, around which the visual elements will be anchored. Someone has to decide, at the beginning, what kind of clip is going to be made: whether to do a performance clip, which is useful for demonstrating your ability to deliver the goods on stage and which increases the clip's use to the record company if it wants to use it to convince its affiliates or other potential licensees to release the record; or whether it will be a concept or story-telling clip, which is more generally attractive to television clip-show programmers.

Some artists insist on writing their own storyboard, others are happy for the director to do it. Either way, the storyboard will probably be subject to copyright. Assuming that is so, the contract has to include an assignment of the storyboard to whoever commissions the clip. This will usually be dealt with as part of the general assignment of copyright in the film to the appropriate party - usually whoever pays for it.

BUDGETS

The storyboard will influence the overall budget (and vice versa). Setting the budget can be like deciding whether the egg comes before the chicken. The video producer usually regards the budget initially proposed as completely inadequate and the producer's budget will probably be more than the cost of your whole album's recording budget. Somehow, you have to work together to make a clip within the constraints set by your record contract, if not by common sense. If you can't agree, then you can try going back to the record company to get a revised budget agreed, or get a new producer.

Clips made in Australia can cost anything between $10,000 and $250,000 per clip. The average for a television-quality clip seems to be about $25,000 to $40,000. The budgets have held pretty steady for a while now, despite increases in production costs from inflation and use of more sophisticated technology. Indeed, for once, the developments in recording and computing technology have helped keep the costs down.

FACTORS AFFECTING THE BUDGET
These include:
- the status of the director;
- the number of extras;
- the need for special sets or props;
- locations other than local, or which introduce particular logistical difficulties;
- special effects;
- format (16 mm, Super 8, digital video or whatever);
- number of days needed to shoot the footage needed; and
- post-production suites and time needed to edit.

WHO OWNS THE RIGHTS?
Under the Copyright Act a 'cinematograph film' means 'the aggregate of the visual images embodied in an article or thing so as to be capable by the use of that article or thing (a) of being shown as a moving picture; or (b) of being embodied in another article or thing by the use of which it can be shown' (s.10 Copyright Act). That's straightforward enough!

When you have deciphered that clause, you will notice that for copyright purposes, a film is not just a film. Indeed there doesn't have to be any film in the process. It can be completely digital and captured to disc.

The owner of the film is the person who makes it, unless it is made for another person for 'valuable consideration' (s.98 (3) Copyright Act) in which case the latter person is the owner. If a clip were made for no charge, the producer would be the owner, unless the agreement specified otherwise.

In addition to the film, there is the storyboard to be considered. This is an artistic work, which would usually be owned by whoever actually creates it unless the agreement provides otherwise.

To resolve any uncertainty, there is always a general assignment to the commissioning party of all copyright in the film, including unused footage and underlying copyrights in storyboards and the like. Usually, producers and directors will be allowed to keep an excerpt for their 'show reels' that they may show to prospective clients, as examples of their work.

CLEARANCES

Copyright material belonging to third parties is frequently included in clips. The producer is responsible for:

- getting all clearances from performers;
- getting all clearances to reproduce any literary works included in the script or storyboard;
- compliance with union and health and safety rules;
- obtaining insurance policies;
- obtaining consents to use locations;
- obtaining props and contracting extras; and
- completing the clip on time and within budget.

DELIVERY DATES

Delivery dates are critical. They are even more critical than bringing the clip in on budget. Delivery dates are set by reference to the release date for the record. The record company's whole publicity machine is geared to that date. If the clip is not ready on time, either the date has to be set back (never a good idea) or the clip may well become an expensive and useless relic. The contract must specify when the finished clip must be delivered, and to whom. It should also specify who pays if things go wrong.

WHEN THINGS GO WRONG

Contracts come into their own when things go wrong or the director comes down with plague mid-way through the production. When things go seriously wrong, everything stops, except the record company's release schedule for the record!

Producers should have appropriate insurance policies. Wherever possible, key people can be replaced but, where that cannot happen, it may be necessary to give the job to another producer. This is lawyer territory, unless rational decisions are made quickly.

THE FUTURE

Clips will be the raw material for a whole new generation of entertainment industries. The advent of pay television, the Internet and DVD has already become a significant area for exploitation of clips of all kinds. You need to bear this in mind when negotiating your recording agreement for they will be increasingly important avenues of exploitation and recoupment.

26

COLLECTING SOCIETIES

THE COLLECTION AND DISTRIBUTION OF INCOME
FROM THE EXPLOITATION OF THE WIDE RANGE OF
RIGHTS THAT UNDERLIE THE INDUSTRY HAS
NECESSITATED THE CREATION OF SOCIETIES TO
REPRESENT THE INTERESTS OF THE RIGHTS OWNERS.
UNLESS THEY BANDED TOGETHER IN THIS WAY, THE
SUMS THAT EACH INDIVIDUAL COULD COLLECT
WOULD BE FAR LESS THAN THE COSTS OF
COLLECTING THAT MONEY. THIS CHAPTER PROVIDES
AN OVERVIEW OF THE DEVELOPMENT OF COLLECTION
SOCIETIES AND HOW THEY WORK.

Collection societies first arose in France. They were started by composers and authors as a form of self-help. The earliest known collection society was founded in 1791 (for composers) and in about 1837, Alexandre Dumas (who wrote 'The Three Musketeers' and many, many other books) co-founded the Societé des Gens de Lettres, to administer literary rights. The societies were the first practical application of the principle that creative artists had a right to receive remuneration for performance and reproduction of their works and their development roughly coincided with the growing recognition of moral rights.

The first known case of a composer suing for a fee for a public performance of a musical work was in 1847, when Bourget (a French composer) sued a café in which one of his works was performed. Two years later, he and two others established the Societé des Auteurs, Compositeures et Musique (SACEM) to administer public performance rights. SACEM is still the public performance society in France. Comparable organisations were set up in other countries as composers and authors came to recognise that their collective strength was needed if they were to administer and protect their rights.

INTERNATIONAL CONVENTIONS

In 1886, the countries most concerned about the use of copyright works of all kinds met in Switzerland. The idea was to produce an internationally accepted set of rules to govern international exploitation of copyright works and to produce a regime by which a citizen of any one country could be protected in another. Unless this could be achieved, copyright was doomed to be a parochial fascination governed by national laws with no coherent rules. Worse, international protection of copyright would vary enormously from country to country, making international commercial exploitation a nightmare.

The meeting resulted in the Berne Convention. The Convention formed the basis for international recognition and protection of copyright. It set a broad framework for member countries to enact national laws. In effect, the Convention prescribes what the national laws ought to achieve. If the local laws don't measure up, the country is ejected from the club and, once out of the club, its citizens' copyrights are not recognised by the remaining club members. The members are also required to give citizens of all member countries the same level of protection as the country gives to its own citizens.

The corollary of this internationalisation of copyright was the development of collection societies with international affiliations. The performance right collection societies were the first to set up affiliations with other collection societies. They agreed to apply broadly similar rules to their members and to collect royalties for members of affiliates.

CHARACTERISTICS OF COLLECTING SOCIETIES

Collecting societies have five common features. All societies:
- have machinery for the identification of copyright uses;
- have systems for the collection and distribution of income earned from the exploitation of copyrights;
- aim to advance the economic and creative interests of the owners that they represent; at the same time as they
- promote the efficiency of access by users of that copyright material; and
- fulfil their functions by means of collective administration.

COLLECTIVE ADMINISTRATION

An understanding of collective administration is essential to understanding the why and how of collecting societies.

It is an inherent feature of the system of copyright that it is based on the principle of granting exclusive rights to individual creators. For individual owners, it is often difficult to maximise the economic value of their rights and to protect those rights. The cost of doing so is often greater than the potential gain. Similarly, third parties wanting to use those rights must incur the trouble and expense of finding the appropriate rights owners, negotiating individual deals and administering and accounting to a plethora of such rights owners. The collective administration of copyright is often the most effective method of managing the rights, both for the owners of the rights and those who need access to them. Quite simply, collective administration is in the public interest.

For example, if music is to be publicly performed, it is reasonable to expect that the author of that music be rewarded for that use of his or her work. On the other hand, it is unreasonable to expect each person who wishes to play music in public to identify, find and negotiate licences with each of those rights owners.

We have now moved beyond questioning whether collective administration is in itself a good thing: it is essential to both rights owners and rights users. The important question is whether it is being carried out in a way that is economically effective and equitable to all parties - the owners, the users and the community in general.

This too, will change. As IT develops the capacity to capture digital uses and reproductions of copyright material, the need for collective administration diminishes. Rights owners will be more able to administer their own rights and materials without the need for those massive administrative overheads that are an essential part of a major collecting society in the atom-based world.

PRIMARY FUNCTIONS OF COLLECTING SOCIETIES

The main tasks of a collecting society are documentation, identification of use, collection and distribution. They are all enormously detailed procedures, time consuming and expensive to administer. It is the task of all collecting societies to tackle the challenge of administering their rights as efficiently as equity allows and as equitably as efficiency allows. This is the balance that determines whether a collective administration of rights is in the interests of the relevant rights owners. All societies have to make some compromises in the search for a balance between perfect process and cost efficiency.

Imagine the size of the documentation task that is required to properly document the hundreds of thousands of works which have a brief spark of commercial value and then remain forever in the 85% of works that are no longer income earning - the so-called dormant repertoire. Any system with administrative integrity must undertake the task but if it were to be truly efficient the collecting society would only expend its efforts on the 15% of its repertoire that is active. Of course it can't.

Another example of this is in the identification and distribution area. If every use of every work by every rights owner was perfectly reported and perfectly recorded, it might be feasible to avoid instances in which a disgruntled rights owner could complain that, 'I know my work was copied/performed/etc., but I didn't get any royalty. Something must be wrong with the collecting society!'

Until technology gives us this capability to capture all information, such processes will be imperfect. Until then, we will have to rely upon sampling techniques, approximation techniques; a balance between the absurd cost of obtaining perfect records and the aim of getting as much money to as many of the right people as possible.

Collection too, is an expensive and inherently inefficient aspect of collecting societies. If one could license just a limited number of users, the process would be easy. Similarly, if all licensees were fastidious in their self-reporting of uses, it would be easy. Instead, users quite understandably object to paying licence fees, or object to the quantum, or under-report their usage of copyright material, and all of this demands that the societies have an extensive obligation to the enforcement of their members' rights.

Indeed, one of the most common complaints about collecting societies seems to stem from the rights owner's lack of understanding of how his or her royalty cheque was arrived at. It is very simple when the transaction is a one-off licence. In such a case, you know that a negotiation has taken place and that a particular fee has been agreed upon. However, when the size of the licensing transaction is necessarily huge, such as licensing the television broadcast of music, it is economically inefficient to account to rights owners on a strict pay-for-use basis. All that one can reasonably expect is a process which is equally fair (or unfair) to all owners of the relevant rights. This demands that the process be statistically cogent.

Unfortunately, statistic-based schemes are difficult for the uninitiated to understand. They are also not particularly easy to describe with simplicity. For this reason, there is much adverse comment about the allocation processes used by societies that require the use of sampling techniques.

In 1994, the Federal Government appointed Shane Simpson to undertake the first major inquiry into Australian collecting societies. The brief included the task of investigating the operation, efficiency and equity of collecting societies. It made a number of recommendations, some of which have already been acted on, and others are still the subject of on-going government work. (Known as 'the Simpson Report' its full text can be read at www.dcita.gov.au/nsapi-text/?MIval=dca_dispdoc&ID=593.

AUSTRALIAN COLLECTION SOCIETIES

APRA

The Australasian Performing Right Association Pty Limited (APRA) was formed in 1926. Being the oldest collection society in Australia, it has acquired something of an elder statesman status in copyright matters. It was established because it had become clear, worldwide, that the new technologies of sound recording and wireless telegraphy were making it impossible for songwriters and composers to exercise control or gain reward from public performances (and public communications) of their works. Writers and publishers had already formed central clearinghouses to administer the performing right in the United States (1909) and the United Kingdom (1911), and, indeed, had done so much earlier in Europe. These had worked well, and so the model was adopted in Australia.

Its prime task is to license public performances and communications to the public (including broadcasts) of the works it controls, to collect the licence fees generated by those licences (and to enforce those licences where necessary) and to distribute the income to its members and affiliates.

MEMBERSHIP

APRA has more than 34 000 members. This has increased by 20% in just three years. It is affiliated to comparable societies in most other countries. APRA represents over 99% of all writers whose works are publicly performed. Most publishers are members too.

The eligibility requirements for membership are as follows.

- For writers: evidence of the public performance, broadcasting or recording of at least one composition.
- For publishers: evidence of bona fide music publishing activities - usually satisfied by proof of ownership or control of publishing rights in relation to at least 12 commercially recorded or published compositions.

INCOME AND PAYMENTS

In the 2005 financial year, APRA had gross revenue of $123.8 million. By far the biggest contribution to revenue is from television (40%), radio ($32%). The rest was made up of live (4%), cinema (3%), concerts (5%), mechanicals (13%) and clubs (3%). Online and ringtones earned $0.5 million during the period.

It is interesting to note that just fifteen years ago, foreign income was only $3.2 million. This was less than 10% of total income. In 2005, $17.1 million was earned from overseas (17% of total revenue). This is a dramatic indication of how the export value of Australian music increased during the decade.

Of this, APRA paid $107 million in royalties to its members. This sum is distributed according to very complex formulae but APRA does publish explanations of its Distribution Rules and Procedures on its website (www.apra.com.au).

COSTS
There are no joining or membership fees charged. It is a non-profit organisation. Its costs are deducted from the gross and the balance is distributed to the rights owners. In 2005, the cost to revenue percentage was 13%. This makes APRA one of the most cost-effective public performance collecting societies in the world.

LICENSING
APRA grants 'blanket' licences. These are licences giving the licensee permission to use any of the hundreds of thousands of works controlled by APRA.

The only area of public performance not licensed by APRA is so-called 'grand rights'. These are the rights used when works are performed in, say, an opera or a stage show. The presence of costumes is usually evidence of 'grand' use. To get these rights, the producer of the show has to negotiate the fee with the publisher representing the work.

The corollary of grand rights is, of course, 'small' rights - being concerts and the like, which APRA does license. Remember however that the APRA licence does not cover the use of music in 'tribute' shows. These too, must be separately licensed by the relevant music publisher.

IDENTIFICATION OF WORKS
Owner identification has two aspects: The registration by APRA of the title details provided by the copyright owner and the logging of performances by licensees.

REGISTRATION OF TITLE DETAILS
Members of the Association, and affiliated societies, provide the Association with information relating to the works that they have written or which they control. This information is essentially as follows:
- the title of the work;
- the duration of the work;
- an indication of whether the work is instrumental only or has lyrics;
- the names of the composer(s) and, if applicable, the lyricist(s) of the work;

- the publisher(s), if applicable, of the work;
- the proportions, in percentages, in which each party is to share in royalty allocations accruing to the work; and
- if known, and if applicable, the performer who has recorded the work.

Members generally provide this information online or by EDI. It is extremely important that you keep your registrations up to date.

These works are added to APRA's existing database of titles. This database currently consists of approximately 3.5m titles and 500,000 cue sheets on computer file.

When a music return, or log, is received from a licensee such as a radio station, the titles appearing in the log are matched against the title file database and a performance credit is entered against the work (depending, obviously, on the kind of performance involved). If the work cannot be identified it is referred to the Association's Research Department for investigation and, hopefully, identification.

LOGGING OF PERFORMANCES

Radio and television stations log the songs performed and report them to APRA. However, for live performances in venues such as hotels, restaurants and nightclubs, there is a self-reporting system: you have to provide the information to APRA yourselves. Quite simply, if you perform your own compositions live, you have to report it if you want to get paid by APRA. So too, do composers of music written or licensed to accompany advertisements on radio or television. Self-reporting is essential. No one else will do it for you. If you don't, APRA won't know that the performance occurred.

DON'T STOP THE MUSIC

In 1996 and 1997, APRA conducted a fierce compliance program. It sought to tell small business that the playing of music in public required a licence from APRA. Given that this was happening at the same time as the Phonographic Performance Company of Australia (PPCA) was focussing on small business, the sector felt that it was in a copyright blitzkrieg. The political fall-out was enormous.

Many of the complaints showed that there was little understanding of the requirements of the Copyright Act; others understood it but felt it was unreasonable. In particular, employers objected to having to get a licence just because their staff had had the radio on in places such as waiting rooms or garages (where the public might incidentally hear it too). It seemed a bit like taxing the family dog. The House of Representatives Committee on Legal and Constitutional Affairs held hearings throughout the country. Its report entitled 'Don't Stop the Music' was handed down in 1998.
(See: http://www.aph.gov.au/house/committee/.)

One of the key recommendations of the report was that APRA give complimentary licences to businesses that employed fewer than 20 people, where the performance was by way of a radio or television and was intended for the enjoyment of the staff rather than the customers or the general public. APRA has complied with the recommendation hardly surprising since it was APRA's proposal in the first place and much of the public heat has died away.

APRA, COMPETITION, CONSUMERS AND MONOPOLIES

In 1999 the Australian Competition Tribunal handed down its decision in a case regarding alleged anti-competitive conduct by APRA. It was the end of three and a half years of litigation.

As part of the ongoing battle between the APRA and the Federation of Australian Commercial Television Stations (FACTS) (now called Free Television Australia), FACTS made submissions to the ACCC arguing that APRA had a monopoly on the supply of performing rights in music. According to FACTS this monopoly gave rise to anti-competitive conduct as APRA's system of getting copyright assignments from its members, did not allow an APRA member to directly license a user.

APRA had suggested some amendments to their system to assuage FACTS' concerns and sought the authorisation of the ACCC of those amendments. The ACCC refused authorisation for certain aspects of APRA new operations including the arrangement under which composers and publishers assign their performing rights in musical works to APRA.

APRA appealed to the Australian Competition Tribunal. The Tribunal granted APRA an interim authorisation for its operations pending some minor alterations to APRA's rules. The Tribunal endorsed APRA's practices of obtaining assignments of copyright and the issue of blanket licences (one of the concerns of FACTS) noting that such practices were essential to APRA's operations.

The Tribunal, however, required that APRA introduce two new 'licence-back' system, an 'opt out system' whereby APRA members may obtain a non-exclusive licence of their works back from APRA for use of the work within Australia. Secondly, a dispute resolution system for small disputes as an alternative to the current system of applications to the Copyright Tribunal which was thought to be, in many cases, prohibitive. These have now been incorporated into APRA's procedures.

FARB AND THE COPYRIGHT

Also in 1999, there was a fiercely fought case in the Copyright Tribunal between APRA and the Federation of Australian Radio Broadcasters (now called Commercial Radio Australia). APRA sought an increase in the licence fee paid by radio broadcasters from the then current 2.66% of their gross advertising revenue (depending on the extent to which they broadcast music as a proportion of their airtime).

The Tribunal recognised that 'stations which make a high use of music have developed techniques and practices to focus (the) station's image with great precision...for these stations, their music is their defining feature'. Accordingly, it held that as of 1 January 2000, the top rate paid by commercial radio stations would increase to 3.5% of gross advertising revenue. Fees for the lower tier stations (such as talk-back) also increased.

Further, the Tribunal ordered that radio stations pay fees for the music actually broadcast during the period covered by the licence fee. Previously, it was calculated on the music broadcast during the APRA sample week. This change now permits the income to be distributed to rights owners more accurately.

All of this may sound dry and academic but if it is put another way: 'Songwriters get 30% more for the broadcast of their work', it sounds a lot more interesting!

MORE INFORMATION

If you want more information on APRA, go to its site at www.apra.com.au. It provides useful information on the publisher members; up-coming industry events; industry contacts; the licensing schemes; and the methods and payment timetables for distributions.

AMCOS

The Australasian Mechanical Copyright Owners Society Limited was established by Australian publishers to administer the collection and distribution of mechanical copyrights and fees. It was a subsidiary of the Australian Music Publishers Association Ltd. (AMPAL). AMCOS started its operations in January 1980. In 2004 the constitution of AMCOS was changed to permit writers to become direct members of AMCOS.

It is important to note that, unlike its associate collection societies in Europe, AMCOS does not act as a central collection body for the majority of mechanical copyright royalties paid by the major record companies.

As far as locally manufactured records are concerned, most publishers collect mechanical copyright fees directly from the major record companies. Small publishing organisations and independent owners may appoint AMCOS to collect the mechanicals on their behalf. This saves them having to set up an administration system themselves. Besides, if an obscure publisher (which the record companies don't know about) administers the rights, the chances of the record company finding the owner are pretty remote.

Imported records pose a considerable problem for most publishers, as the record companies do not always report mechanicals on a per title basis.

Accordingly, most publishers appoint AMCOS to collect mechanicals for imported records. Although the liberalisation of parallel import rules has meant that this function has somewhat shrunk, where mechanicals are payable on imported records, AMCOS collects the mechanicals and distributes them in the course of its annual distribution to owners.

FUNCTIONS

AMCOS performs a wide range of licensing functions.

- Licensing all record companies (except the 6 Majors) and individuals for the mechanical reproduction of members' works.
- Licensing of all record companies and individuals for the mechanical reproduction of works administered on behalf of affiliated, overseas societies.
- Music video licensing.
- Licensing production music.
- Licensing educational institutions for off-air copying of musical works (through Screenrights).
- Licensing educational institutions to photocopy print music.
- On-line and mobile licensing of music.

One of the most important developments for AMCOS has been the licensing of music content for on-line and mobile use. Most of these licences are offered in conjunction with an APRA licence (so that the user doesn't have to get seperate licences for the reproduction and for the communication.) Types of licensee include webcasters, download services, on-demand applications and portals.

MEMBERSHIP

It used to be true that only publishers could be members of AMCOS. This changed in 2004 when writers were admitted. Virtually all music publishers in Australasia are members of the Society as are a number of successful composers who are not signed to a publisher. There are currently 600 members.

AMCOS represents the works (or parts of works) controlled by its members, affiliated overseas Societies, and print publishers who have executed the Schools Photocopying authority.

INCOME

In 2005 AMCOS generated a gross income of $37.8 million. This was up more than $14 million from that collected in 2001. Of this, $34.2 million was earned from Australian sources and $3.6 million from its New Zealand operations.

COSTS

AMCOS does not charge joining fees or membership fees but deducts a set percentage from the gross revenue. Only AMCOS works on this set commission basis. (Worldwide, unlike performing rights societies that deduct their actual administration costs prior to distribution, mechanical rights societies traditionally deduct certain standard percentages.) Internationally, these administrative deductions average between 15% and 25%. In Australia the current standard rate is 10% (but for certain revenues streams increases to 17.5% where the member has fewer than 500 works. This means that AMCOS has one of the best ratios of administration costs to distributed sums. This is particularly impressive seeing that it is not permitted by its members to collect mechanical royalties that publishers receive direct from the major record companies.

Intersociety collections (including collections on behalf of APRA members) are charged at rates of 15% for mechanical usages and 20% for synchronisation licences only. This reflects the greater amount of administration required.

IDENTIFICATION OF WORKS AND USES

For a description of the mechanical licensing process, see page 200.

ADMINISTRATION

One of the major changes in the world of collecting societies has been that AMCOS has now ceased to administer its own affairs. In 1997 it closed its own offices and went under the administrative wing of APRA. This was a sensible move given that the beneficiaries of both organisations are similar and allowed cost savings to be made. Changes have been incremental but since April 1999, APRA fulfils most of AMCOS' licensing, accounting, distribution and administrative functions; AMCOS remains a separate company. The integration process is not likely to go much further: true merger would mean a complete rethinking of the APRA and AMCOS constitutions, stakeholders and payment principles. For more information, see the APRA website www.apra.com.au/corporate/default.asp.

ADMINISTERING THE COMMUNICATION RIGHT

AMCOS collects royalties in respect of mechanical reproduction of musical works whereas APRA collects income flowing from the public performance and communication rights in respect of those works.

Streaming music involves an exercise only of the communication right and APRA will administer and collect the income. However, the on-line download of a song involves an exercise of two rights: AMCOS' mechanical rights (which are exercised by the reproduction of the song on the computer's hard drive); and APRA's communication right (which is exercised by the on-line delivery of that work from the source to the end user).

In such circumstances, the societies will need to agree on how to administer the process to the benefit of their members, the users and the wider community. At the time of writing the licence rate for download services is 8% of retail (6.25% for AMCOS and 1.75% for APRA.) The significance of the split for APRA and AMCOS members is that APRA pays at least 50% of the net income directly to its members rather than to their publishers. The 8% rate is still the subject of registration and may yet end up in the Copyright Tribunal.

It is important to note that APRA/AMCOS license the Digital Service Provider (eg Telstra Big Pond Music or Apple iTunes) as opposed to continuing the traditional physical model of licensing the record label, as the label is no longer the manufacturer (of the download).

Ringtones have been licensed by AMCOS since 2001. Within 4 years this income is worth $4.5million per year. The AMCOS rate is 10% of retail plus a fixation fee of $10 for each work. APRA charges 1% for monophonic and polyphonic ringtones and 2% for phonographic ringtones (a.k.a. 'realtones'). All rates are subject to minimum fees.

PPCA

The Phonographic Performance Company of Australia Ltd was incorporated in 1969. The impetus for the Company was the Copyright Act 1968. This introduced broadcast and public performance rights in sound recordings. The Company was primarily established to license those rights and collect income from them.

PPCA also grants licences for sundry performance uses such as in-flight music and the like. In most cases, the record companies are happy to let PPCA look after licensing sundry uses such as these as, if they did the licensing themselves, the cost of the licence would make many projects uneconomic. Centralised licensing gives benefits of scale and helps keep the cost of creating and administering licences down.

MEMBERSHIP

PPCA is the only major collecting society that is a private company. Its shareholders are the major record companies. Its membership (as opposed to its shareholders) ranges from the major record companies, through to small Independents. Members must be the owners or licensees of the broadcast and public performance rights in protected sound recordings or music videos for the territory of Australia. Basically, any Australian owner of sound recording copyrights can and should join. Even if you are a small independent label, you should join - because unless you do, you will not be eligible for any PPCA payments.

COVERAGE

PPCA estimates that it represents copyright owners of over 95% of recordings. In a report by Price Waterhouse in 1993, it was estimated that about 7% of record business was not captured in ARIA statistics (which are also used by PPCA). It does not, however, collect on behalf of independent releases and that explains much of the differential.

INCOME AND DISTRIBUTION

In 2004, PPCA earned $12 million in licence fees. Of that, it distributed $8.8 million to members and spent $427,000 on anti-piracy. PPCA's full financial statements are available on its website at www.ppca.com.au). One of the catalysts for the Simpson Report back in 1994 was the Government disquiet that the costs incurred by the PPCA were too high in proportion to its income. What the report found was that one of the principal reasons for the apparently high costs to distribution ratio is that the income collected from licence fees is artificially low because of a quirk of government policy – the 1% ceiling.

Basically, the Copyright Act sets a ceiling of 1% (yes, just 1%) of the stations' gross income. That 1% is reduced by the proportion that 'protected' recordings represent of the total broadcast time from the station.

Of course, no station pays anything like 1% of its gross. The average is probably nearer 0.025%. Not much really, considering what would be left of most stations' programs if the music content were taken out. Even so, radio stations have traditionally defended the low royalty by emphasising the 'promotional' value of airplay, but this can hardly apply to stations with 'all gold' formats! Most of these tracks were hits a million years ago. Perhaps there is room for a graded scale, with a higher rate on older recordings, which might (though most programmers would pale at the thought) encourage broadcasters to feature new recordings.

In 1995, the Simpson Report found that there was no logical rationale for this protection. Broadcasters are quite tough and ugly enough to negotiate on their own behalf. They don't need legislative protection. However, at time of writing, the Government remains committed to maintaining the 1% ceiling. Naturally the radio industry continues to lobby hard to retain it and it does not take a great degree of cynicism to suggest that this anomaly is unlikely to be reformed except immediately after an election.

The relatively recent creation of the public performance copyright in sound recordings means that until a few years ago, PPCA had very little income at all. After all, its main source of income is from licensing broadcasters to play recordings that are copyright. The infamous pay for play boycotts in the mid-1970s were the first sign that this new copyright was being taken seriously by the broadcasters.

As noted elsewhere, recordings made or owned by nationals of countries that do not recognise this copyright (most notably, North America) are not granted that copyright here either, so there is a large gap in the repertoire that PPCA controls. Australian broadcasters tend to look to their industry compatriots in the United States rather than Europe, so it is not surprising that Australian broadcasters generally have no empathy for the idea of paying for broadcast rights, because it is an alien concept in the United States (at least in relation to recordings). This attitude has certainly hampered the rights being embraced in the way they have been by European broadcasters, who are accustomed to paying for broadcast rights. (See next section for payments to United States copyright owners.)

The pay for play boycotts arose when PPCA first sought to enforce the pay for play concept. Radio broadcasters retaliated by boycotting the records of several of the Majors and avoiding playing Australian or European recordings. (A similar boycott was applied by some television broadcasters around 1984, when pay for play was introduced for music videos.)

The situation was eventually resolved, though not satisfactorily as far as the record companies were concerned. They had to wait for the introduction of FM broadcasting in the late 1970s before they were able to try to introduce what they perceived as being a more equitable royalty rate. This rate was the subject of litigation in the landmark 'Triple M Decision' which set the formula that broadcasters apply when calculating the royalty payable in return for the right to broadcast copyright recordings. It is calculated as a percentage of the advertising revenue of the radio station.

UNITED STATES AND OTHER FOREIGN COPYRIGHT OWNERS

Even though a large proportion of the records played on Australian radio and television are by United States artists and companies, most of these do not receive royalties from PPCA.

Protection under our Copyright Act is extended to certain foreign recordings by the Copyright (International Protection) Regulations made under s. 184 of the Copyright Act. Under the regulations, **performance** and **broadcast** rights subsist in foreign sound recordings published in Australia only where:

(a) *the maker of the recording, when it was made, was a citizen of a Schedule 3 country;*

(b) *the maker was a resident in or incorporated in a Schedule 3 country; or*

(c) *the recording was made in a Schedule 3 country.*

Recordings made in many other countries (notably, the United States) also enjoy copyright protection, but that protection does not include a **performance** and **broadcast** right. It does, of course, include a **reproduction** right.

Protection follows if any of the above three platforms are satisfied. For instance:

- a recording made in Canada by a United States artist signed to a United States incorporated company is protected for broadcast and public performance in Australia; or
- a recording made in the United States by an Australian artist is protected in Australia.

It should be noted that the ultimate ownership of a company is irrelevant. So long as the company that makes the recording is incorporated in Australia or a Schedule 3 country, the requirement has been satisfied.

THE SCHEDULE 3 COUNTRIES AS AT 1 MARCH 2001 ARE:

Argentina, Austria, Bahamas, Bangladesh, Barbados, Bolivia, Brazil, Canada, Chile, Colombia, Costa Rica, Czech Republic, Denmark, Dominican Republic, Ecuador, Fiji, Finland, Germany, Greece, Guatemala, Guinea, Holy See, Honduras, Iceland, India, Ireland, Israel, Italy, Jamaica, Japan, Liechtenstein, Mauritius, Mexico, Netherlands, New Zealand, Norway, Pakistan, Panama, Paraguay, Philippines, Poland, Romania, Russian Federation, Slovakia, Spain, Sweden, Thailand, Turkey, United Kingdom, Uruguay and Venezuela.

DIRECT DISTRIBUTIONS TO ARTISTS

From 1994, instead of distributing the whole of the royalties to the record companies that might (or might not) distribute that income to performers, depending on their contracts with the artists, PPCA invited Australian recording artists to lodge returns, rather like APRA returns. PPCA now uses the APRA logs of performances and broadcasts of records to distribute the income to copyright owners.

When an artist is registered under the Artist Direct Distribution Scheme, 50% of the funds available for distribution in relation to a particular track got to the record label, 47.5% goes to the registered Australian artist, and 2.5% goes to the PPCA Performers' Trust Foundation which administers a small grants programs.

If the artist is not registered with PPCA, the funds are payable in respect of each track are sent to the relevant record company for distribution in accordance with the artist's record contract.

It is distributed by determining how often each recording has been broadcast/performed and the funds divided accordingly. The balance is paid to the copyright owner of the sound recording, to be divided in accordance with the relevant recording contracts (and no doubt, subject to the state of the recoupment position of an artist's advance account!). Application forms can be obtained from PPCA.

Artists must be the primary artists performing on a recording (so thus, paid session musicians cannot register). As at December 1993 there were 562 individual artists registered. There are now more than 1400.

There are no joining or membership fees and no set commission is charged. Administration costs are deducted from gross revenue.

THE FACTS CASE

For some years, PPCA had been attempting to obtain a proper fee from commercial TV stations for the broadcast use of sound recordings. In 1996 it began a Copyright Tribunal case so that a fee could be set. The Federation of Australian Commercial Television Stations (FACTS, now called Free Television Australia) argued that recording artists and record companies owning sound recordings do not have a broadcast right once the sound recording is synchronised into a film, TV program or video. The Tribunal referred the case to the Federal Court. The majority of the Federal Court agreed with the FACTS position and PPCA appealed to the High Court. In May 1999, the High Court handed down its judgment. The PPCA won.

The Copyright Act says that the 'broadcast of a sound recording is still a broadcast whether the sound recording is embodied in a film'. However, section 23 of the Act deems a 'sound track' not to be a sound recording. The TV stations argued that as soon as a sound recording is dubbed into a sound track it loses its identity as a sound recording and therefore, no fees are payable for the broadcast of the huge number of recordings used in TV programming.

Until this case, the TV stations had only paid a licence fee to PPCA for the broadcast of sound recordings behind test patterns. As a result of the High Court case, the Copyright Tribunal can now determine the proper fee that TV stations will pay for use of sound recordings.

PPCA's home page is at www.ppca.com.au. To read the judgment of the High Court in the FACTS case, see:
www.austlii.edu.au/au/cases/cth/high_ct/1998/39.html

ARBITRATION PROCEDURES

The PPCA licensing scheme provides an arbitration procedure (the Board of Review) to determine disputes between PPCA and its licensees. For example, in 1999 the Board of Review arbitrated a dispute between PPCA and five Melbourne nightclubs that were objecting to a fee increase and the way the fees were to be phased in. This is a very sensible mechanism as it is a much cheaper and faster process than taking the problem to the Copyright Tribunal.

SCREENRIGHTS

Screenrights was established in January 1990. (Until 1999 it was called the Audio-Visual Copyright Society.) Screenrights is the copyright collecting society approved by the Government to collect royalties from educational institutions such as schools, universities and technical colleges, when they copy programs from television or radio. (It also operates a similar service in New Zealand under the NZ Copyright Act.) It is also the society responsible for collecting payment for government copying from television.

As of September 2001, Screenrights has an additional function: It has been declared by the government to be the sole collecting society to collect copyright royalties for retransmission of free-to-air television programs by pay-TV services. In brief, the Copyright Act allows pay-TV services, and other retransmitters (but not webcasters), to retransmit free-to-air programs if they pay royalties to the declared society. Screenrights is that declared collecting society.

Retransmitters became liable to pay these royalties on 4 March 2001 when amendments to the Copyright Act made by the Copyright Amendment (Digital Agenda) Act 2000 came into effect. The rate of the royalties will be negotiated between Screenrights and the retransmitters. If they cannot agree, the issue can be referred to the Copyright Tribunal for determination.

The money that Screenrights collects is distributed on a non-profit basis to all relevant rights owners in programs that are identified as having been copied. This includes the rights owners in the copied film and the rights owners in any underlying works incorporated in the film (such as the music, the sound recordings, the script etc).

In 1999, Screenrights and the Vice Chancellors' Committee agreed on an important new procedure for administering the educational copying of broadcasts from radio, television, satellite and cable. This system is now based on a system of full record keeping. The full details of the system are provided at www.infonet.unsw.edu.au/admin/copyright/index.htm.

ROYALTIES COLLECTED AND COSTS

In 2004/5 Screenrights collected $21.4 million in royalties (up from $2.15 million in 1991) and declared a distribution pool of $17.41 million.

DISTRIBUTIONS TO OWNERS OF RIGHTS IN MUSICAL WORKS

Rights owners of musical works have always received an allocation of the money collected by Screenrights. APRA and AMCOS helped establish the organisation and both organisations have always been represented on the Screenrights board.

The allocation for musical works is distributed with the assistance of APRA: Screenrights notifies APRA of all copied titles and APRA researches these titles using its extensive database and identifies all of the rights owners in the copied music. The money allocated for musical rights is then distributed according to an internationally recognised scheme of allocation that takes into account factors such as the duration of the musical work, and its placement in the program (such as whether it is featured or background).

Where the rights owner is a member of AMCOS or APRA, payment is made to those collecting societies as an agent. (APRA acts as an agent for the collection of the royalties for local unpublished writers. Published works (both local and foreign) and unpublished foreign works are distributed through AMCOS.) They then distribute the money to the rights owners. This co-operation between societies means that considerable administrative overheads are saved.

DISTRIBUTIONS TO OWNERS OF RIGHTS IN SOUND RECORDINGS

When it was established, Screenrights did not provide for an allocation to rights owners of sound recordings.

However, in May 1998 this all changed. In the PPCA v. FACTS case, the High Court decided that, contrary to the understanding of the whole film and television industry, the separate copyright in the sound recording is not extinguished after it is incorporated into the soundtrack of a film. As a result of this decision, the owners of sound recordings are clearly entitled to share in the income collected by Screenrights. Consequently, Screenrights has amended its scheme of allocation to provide a share of the royalties collected for each program to be distributed to the owners of sound recordings.

The ownership of the copyright in the sound recordings is identified by PPCA.

FURTHER INFORMATION

Screenrights can be contacted at Level 3, 156 Military Road, Neutral Bay, NSW 2089, tel: (02) 9904 0133; fax: (02) 9904 0498; e-mail: info@screen.org; internet: www.screen.org.

CAL

Although not strictly related to the music business, the Copyright Agency Limited is an interesting example of efficient delegation of administrative responsibilities. CAL's primary function is to collect photocopying fees from schools and universities and distribute them to authors and book publishers. Although educational institutions photocopy sheet music and scores it would be very inefficient, both for rights owners and rights users, if music publishers were to set up a completely separate system to monitor such photocopying. Instead, because CAL is already in the business of monitoring the educational photocopy licence, CAL acts as the agent of AMCOS to monitor usage. The money is paid to AMCOS, which then distributes the revenue to its members. CAL's website is at www.copyright.com.au.

CHRISTIAN MUSIC COPYRIGHT COLLECTING COMPANIES

There are three agencies that have been established to collect royalties and grant licences in relation to church music. This is in spite of the fact that CAL offers a church music licence and that CAL licences are less expensive than its Christian competition. It is an interesting proof that where organisations see a niche, competition can follow. The societies are Christian Copyright Licensing Asia-Pacific Pty Limited, LicenSing (a division of the United States company MediaCom Inc), and Word of Life Pty Limited.

They act as agents, granting licences and collecting royalties on behalf of copyright owners, rather than collecting societies. (They do not take a licence or an assignment from the rights owners).

COPYRIGHT SOCIETIES CODE OF CONDUCT

The introduction of a voluntary code of conduct has been an important initiative to ensure good governance and transparency of collecting societies. The Code applies to all collecting societies. APRA was one of the strongest advocates of this oversight mechanism that sets out formal obligations of timeliness, efficiency, transparency and courtesy - all overseen by an annual compliance review by a former Federal Court judge. APRA has long been a leader in these matters but the formalisation of the process is a useful tool in several ways: It sets out basic principles with which collecting societies must comply; it provides fair mechanisms for dealing with criticisms and complaints; and provides for regular independent assessment of the governance standards achieved. Given the amount of money that is administered by the societies, and the importance of that income to the health of the industry, the implementation of the Code is a welcome innovation. Licensees will always argue the appropriate level of licence fees but at least, these days, there is little purpose in attacking the propriety of the collecting society.

INTERNATIONAL CO-ORDINATION
PUBLIC PERFORMANCE

APRA is just one of many public performance collecting societies around the world. The individual bodies belong to CISAC (the International Confederation of Authors and Composers, started in 1926) that acts as a co-ordinating body and lobby group. It meets regularly to keep its members' policies and rules consistent, to disseminate information between members and to represent its members' interests to legislators.

Members of CISAC act as collection agents for the affiliated societies. This is how an English composer can receive public performance income from Australia and vice versa.

Each collection body acts within its national copyright laws. This means a country's local practices will eventually have an effect on anyone receiving royalties from that territory. For example, in the 1930s the courts in the United States decided that ASCAP could not collect performance royalties from motion picture theatres, so alternative arrangements had to be made to cover this significant area of performance.

Also, some overseas societies apply different rules when distributing their royalties to members. In Britain, PRS (the Performing Right Society) splits the payout into twelfths and splits it eight-twelfths to the writer and four-twelfths to the publisher (although the writer and publisher could agree to vary that, so long as the writer gets at least six-twelfths). Most European societies use the same split.

There are various rules applied to splitting royalties where they are earned in a sub-publisher's territory. Usually, the local sub-publisher will get half (the publisher's share) and will pay the head publisher under its contract. The other half (the so-called writer's share) is paid to APRA (after any deduction for local arrangers and/or translators, who usually get two-twelfths each). APRA will then pay the writer.

If APRA receives income for which it has a publisher member, but the writer is not a member of APRA or any of the affiliates, APRA will pay the publisher its share and retain the writer's share for at least two distributions. If the writer is still not a member by then, the money is returned to the royalty pool to be shared in the next distribution.

Yes, it is complicated, but it works surprisingly well.

MECHANICAL COPYRIGHT

AMCOS recognises overseas copyright owners and collects on their behalf. The international body is Bureau International des Societes Gerant les Droits D'enregistrement et de Reproduction Mecanique (BIEM), which has representatives from most countries that recognise copyright. BIEM applies its rules in Europe, where most countries do not actually have a statutory rate. BIEM is also a negotiating body, frequently going head to head with the International Federation of the Phonographic Industry (IFPI), which represents record companies.

The equivalent of AMCOS in England is Mechanical Copyright Protection Society (MCPS). In the United States, mechanicals are collected by the Harry Fox Agency, or directly by the publishers themselves.

In Europe, the record companies do not account directly to the publishers for mechanical copyright royalties. Instead, they account to the mechanical copyright bodies, which in turn divide and distribute the income to their publisher-members. This means the societies are much more involved in the income flow and so wield more influence and power in their local industries than AMCOS does in Australia.

For example, the German collecting society Gesellschaft für Musikalische Aufführungs - und Mechanische Vervielfältigungsrechte (GEMA) collects mechanicals on virtually every record pressed in Germany, even (with a few exceptions) those which are exported. Centralised collection reduces the cost of administration but this is arguably rather less important now that computer power is so cheap. These days, even a small operation can easily afford a relatively sophisticated system to administer its mechanical copyright income.

BIEM members' practice of collecting mechanicals directly can cause complications where a sub-publisher tries to collect 100% of mechanicals on a work originating from a BIEM territory. This can happen in the United States and the United Kingdom especially, where American Mechanical Rights Association (AMRA) and MCPS respectively operate. It is common for local publishers to find that the local BIEM member is also applying to collect its member's share directly, so there is a conflict over who will collect. Naturally, the publisher wants to collect 100%, because this increases the amount it can retain and also helps it recoup advances made to the writer. This conflict has to be sorted out, but is time-consuming for all concerned and can even delay payment to the publisher until the split claim is resolved.

The application of local rules also means that, in some countries, mechanicals are collected where the records are pressed, whereas others collect wherever they are sold (the GEMA example noted above, is an example of collection in the place of manufacture, rather than of sale).

Life can get complicated in the heady world of international exploitation, which is why changing publishers can create a problem for any writer. All these collection societies have to alter their records to show the new publisher. Mistakes can happen, and before you know it, you are contributing to the 'Black Box' - that pool of unallocated and unclaimed money which publishers in Europe divide amongst themselves - because if they don't claim it, no one else will.

THE FUTURE ROLE OF COLLECTING SOCIETIES

The development of digital on-line delivery and digital rights management software which permits (and promotes) the on-line licensing of Intellectual Property, are all accumulating to give Australia's collecting societies great cause to re-evaluate their roles. They challenge the market power of collecting societies and indeed, challenge their very reason for existence.

On one hand, it is reasonable to argue that collecting societies will play a pivotal part in facilitating legitimate on-line music delivery. By acting as a central negotiating body for the rights they control, the task of negotiating rates, obtaining permissions, administering the uses, all can be made easier through the participation of a collecting society. On the other hand, many of the larger content companies are already saying that the on-line future will allow them to cut collecting societies out of the food chain entirely - or at least out of those parts of it that they can administer more profitable themselves.

Which is most likely? Probably both. To some extent the answer depends upon the development and deployment of rights management software that will permit the on-line licensing of intellectual property. Such software is already in its early stages of development and adoption. It will permit many of the transactions that are presently administered collectively by the societies, to be undertaken directly between the rights owner and the licensor (be it a retailer or the consumer.) In short, because the Majors already have huge IT capacity they are likely to do much of the job themselves.

As the large trans-national corporations move many of their digital rights licensing functions in-house, the only functions that they will leave with the societies are those which are the least profitable and the most expensive to administer. At the same time, the authors and the small companies that do not have such financial or administrative resources will continue to need the collecting societies. In other words, with the large companies excluding collecting societies from the profitable parts of the business, we will see the cost effectiveness of collecting societies decline as they are forced to maintain large administrative overheads in order to collect and distribute smaller and smaller revenues. Long term, it could be a gloomy picture for societies.

MULTI-FORMAT LICENSING

If ever there was an indictment of the collecting societies, it has been their failure to recognise the need of licensors in a multi-format media world, to license simply and cost-effectively the materials they require. For example, an increasing proportion of our teaching is now done on-line. It is commonplace for these teaching materials to include text, music, sound recordings, photographs, drawings and diagrams, video and film. How do our collecting societies meet these needs? How do they assist the authors and publishers of such materials to lawfully access copyright material and lawfully exploit them? They don't.

Each of the collecting societies is built around a narrow, right-specific, artform-specific activity. There has been no effort on the part of the societies to develop a system by which would-be licensors can go to one place for their multi-format licensing needs. It is an irony that the experts in collective administration have themselves been unable to get together to facilitate and administer the use of cross-format digital information.

The exception is Screenrights (because it was created to administer the rights of the various stakeholders in a film.) Unless the other, much larger societies can break out of their insularity and create a joint venture to facilitate such licensing, it will be the much smaller Screenrights that steals a march on all of them.

27
MERCHANDISING

THE DEVELOPMENT OF MERCHANDISING AS A HUGE
INCOME SOURCE IS ONE OF THE FEATURES OF THE
LAST DECADE IN THE ENTERTAINMENT BUSINESS.
NOT ONLY IS MERCHANDISE SOLD AT LIVE
PERFORMANCES (TOUR MERCHANDISING), IT IS NOW
SOLD THROUGH ORDINARY SHOPS (RETAIL
MERCHANDISING) IN QUANTITIES THAT MOST PEOPLE
WOULD NOT BELIEVE. THIS CHAPTER LOOKS AT THE
BASIC PRINCIPLES BEHIND MERCHANDISING AND
THEN DISCUSSES BOTH TOUR AND RETAIL
MERCHANDISING.

Merchandising is the exploitation of the rights in a name, image, object, design, or other thing, in association with an otherwise unrelated product or service. It works on two levels: it exploits and so makes the merchandised name, image or design valuable whilst, at the same time, it is intended to make profits through the sale of the associated products or services.

As an example, every sale of a Pokemon toy increases the overall value of the Pokemon trademarks, the rights in the Pokemon cartoons, the Pokemon clothing, the Pokemon franchises yet, at its simplest, the root of the transaction is about the sale of a simple toy.

In the entertainment industry, the term 'merchandising' is often used to refer to spin-off products. In the music industry, T-shirts and posters are the most common forms of spin-off products. In film, the soundtrack album is perhaps the most venerable example, although Walt Disney showed how film characters could give birth to products such as comics, books, toys, games and even wallpaper; spin-offs that would become even more valuable than the production in which the character was first presented. Each year, concert and theatre patrons purchase hundreds of thousands of glossy programs. Even in the visual arts, the advent of the so-called 'blockbuster' shows at national and state galleries have created a multi-million dollar business in spin-off merchandise which goes far beyond the traditional posters, postcards, books, replicas, badges, flags and so on.

In the music market, the biggest market for merchandising is still heavy metal and rock. However, musicians in all fields of music now merchandise - opera companies, string quartets, country bands, jazz groups. Everybody has at least a T-shirt available for sale. Kenny Rogers was reputed to be making more from selling T-shirts and hats at his concerts than he made from ticket sales. When Garth Brooks toured Australia he broke the merchandising record in almost every venue he played. In many venues he was averaging $15 per head.

AREAS OF MERCHANDISING

Merchandising in Australia is still in its infancy. Its potential to generate income is nowhere near fully exploited. The range of goods and its manner of promotion and sale, is still fairly primitive. The four most important areas of merchandising are:

TOUR MERCHANDISING

This is the most common form of merchandising in the Australian music industry. When the general public refers to merchandising, this is what they are thinking of. Although other areas of the entertainment industry have tackled more adventurous forms of merchandise, by far the biggest area of merchandising is still good ol' T-shirts, programs and posters sold at live performances.

RETAIL MERCHANDISING

This involves selling the concept to a retailer (for example, marketing and selling a range of clothing which carries the act's name, autograph or picture) and then licensing a wholesaler which, in turn, contracts with a manufacturer to make the products. Smaller retailers may choose to contract the manufacturer directly and cut out the wholesaler, but the larger ones will even specify the wholesalers with whom they prefer to deal.

As an example, a group such as the Spice Girls, who once upon a time had a large following in an easily definable market niche, may license a clothing manufacturer to make a line of clothing and use the group's name as the label for that product line. Usually, this kind of deal will also involve the artist agreeing to do a certain amount of promotion for the manufacturer and the retailers. This may include wearing the clothes on stage, appearances in magazine advertisements, point of sale photographs and so on. Such sales are based on a market identification of the product with the artist.

In Australia, the most notably successful groups to adopt retail merchandising have been groups such as Bananas in Pyjamas and Hi5, each of which markets to adjacent but definably different segments of the children's market. It's not for everyone: Why might "Elle", "Kylie" or "Delta" work as a clothing line whereas "Alex Lloyd" might not? No, the answer is not "it's just a gender thing" although it is true that young women are more likely to buy retail clothing merchandise.

MAIL ORDER
Music magazines, trade newspapers, television and radio advertisements are commonly used by mail order merchandisers but other possibilities are starting to be explored. Merchandisers in England have been successful in using inserts in record sleeves to market their goods. This form of marketing elicits an average 2% response with average £8 return. If your album sells 500,000 units, you can expect a return from merchandising of £80,000! Not bad for an insert in a product the fan has already purchased.

MARKETING AND WEB MERCHANDISING
About a thousand years ago (the mid 90s), Internet content was largely seen but not heard: Fine for selling porn but unsatisfying for music. Now it is so multimedia that nobody uses the word 'multimedia' anymore. We expect a website to fulfil many functions and do them in ways that attract and maintain our interest. Websites are no longer seen as digital billboards. They have become sophisticated tools for communicating with your audience, promoting your image and marketing your music products.

Don't think of your website as optional. Spend money on it. Give it creative time and energy. Your website can no longer be treated as the digital equivalent of a trestle table installed at the back of the venue. Originally seen as a place for selling peripheral product, the artist's website has become a central element of marketing and promotion. It is an opportunity to give those that don't know your music the opportunity to hear it; those that do know it, to buy it; those who were at the concert to be reminded how fantastic it was; those you weren't there to bemoan what they missed. The better websites give visitors the opportunity to stream grabs of the music, purchase it (either through downloads or on-line purchase of CDs), stream samples of live performances and sell tickets to your shows.

It is also an important tool for communicating cheaply but directly to your target audience. Make sure that it reflects your image, your professional personality and your skills. This is your only chance to control your web identity and, given the importance of the Internet in the way audiences investigate, find and acquire music, it is becoming essential to the business of the modern musician. Remember that your web presence is as close as most of your fans are ever going to get to you. So treat both them and yourself with respect and make the encounter as rich, rewarding and pleasurable as possible. If you and your music really are cheap, dumb and glib, your website should reflect that. If not...

SOME BASIC QUESTIONS

WHY MERCHANDISE?

There are two reasons to undertake merchandising - promotion and income. All too often we think only of the dollars that can be generated by the sale of merchandise and we forget that the promotional value of such goods is almost as important as the income it produces. A fan wearing one of your T-shirts is a walking, self-funding billboard.

The income aspect of merchandising remains the central focus of the deal. After all, if you sell a T-shirt for $30 at your concert and your royalty share is 30% (after GST is deducted) you will make $8.18. Compare how many records you would have to sell to clear $8 in record royalties!

WHEN TO MERCHANDISE?

There are no rules as to when you should start to merchandise. Most bands sign their first merchandising deal when they have recorded their first album and are about to undertake a major promotional tour.

It is often difficult to get tour support from record companies. This is not surprising, since the artists are usually asking for this money at a time they have just finished recording and the record company's investment in the recording is completely unrecouped. The merchandising advances can be an important alternative source of funding.

On the other hand, artists whose finances and popularity are driven by live performance, rather than record sales, find that merchandising is profitable as soon as they have a sufficiently large group of loyal fans.

HAVE YOU GOT THE RIGHTS?

The first thing you have to do is get expert advice as to who owns the material and whether any additional consents, approvals or clearances have to be obtained. This may include the artist who actually drew the work, a photographer, or a third party whose copyright has accidentally or deliberately been incorporated into the design. Failure to get all these can lead to you finding an injunction on your doorstep, ordering you to stop selling your merchandise.

For example, if you had an artist friend do the design for your record cover, did you get an assignment of rights from the artist? If not, you don't have any rights to merchandise or license! The graphic artist owns those rights because, as a general rule, the owner of copyright in a work of art is the artist who created it - even where he or she is commissioned to create the work. (For further discussion see Simpson, *The Visual Artist And The Law*, 2nd ed. Sydney: Law Book Co., 1994.)

If you get someone else to do artwork for you, make sure that you get a simple assignment from them. Remember, it must be in writing. Even a simple letter of confirmation will do.

If you want to use the image on your CD cover for merchandising purposes, make sure you (and not your record company), own the rights in the artwork. The Commissioning Letter at the end of this chapter will help you. If the record company owns it (and this will be clear from the recording contract), you have some negotiating to do.

Until you have secured your rights, there is little point trying to negotiate a deal with a merchandiser.

WHO NEGOTIATES?

All too often, merchandising agreements are negotiated by the artist's manager. This is particularly common with new acts trying to save on legal expenses. This 'saving' can turn out to be very expensive. Merchandising deals are much more complicated than just sorting out the length of the deal and the royalty rate. Anyone can do that.

It is essential that these agreements be fully negotiated by experienced lawyers who are familiar with the ramifications of the many different deal structures and can build into the agreement the necessary performance criteria and other protective clauses so you can gauge the merchandiser's effectiveness and get out of the deal if the merchandiser does not live up to its promises.

HOW DO WE ALLOCATE THE RIGHTS?

Unless the offer is too good to refuse, never hesitate to split up your merchandising between various companies. Choose the company for their speciality. Some are good at tour merchandising but not much else; others really only do T-shirts; a few are competent at retail merchandising. Almost no merchandisers excel in all areas.

The rule of thumb is simple: merchandising rights can be very valuable. Deal with companies who actually are in the business of merchandising. Deal with specialists. Ask for references. Only license the rights they can expertly exploit.

MERCHANDISING AND RECORD COMPANIES

One indication that there is a fortune to be made from merchandising is the fact that some of the Majors have established merchandising arms (or have simply bought into existing merchandising companies).

Accordingly, whereas record companies used to demand only the right to use the name and likeness of their artist for the purpose of promoting the artist, the artist's records and perhaps the record company itself, now some of them are attempting to make acquisition of merchandising rights a part of the record deal too.

These arrangements vary in size and scope. On the massive scale there is the Robbie Williams deal in which, in return for a massive advance, EMI acquired the right to participate in all of the artist's income streams. On the more mundane level is the demand by Sony/BMG that the artist pays the company 15% of merchandising and other deals introduced to the artist by the company, or Universal's requirement that the company acquire certain screen rights in respect of its artists.

This is a trend that will be resisted by recording artists and their advisers. Unless the advances are large and the marketing plans are sophisticated, there is a very real commercial advantage for artists to have their recording and merchandising deals in separate hands.

- No Australian record companies have effective merchandising divisions. This means that the record company that takes your merchandising rights will have to sub-license the rights to a 'real' merchandising company. This inevitably means that a third party will be taking a share of the profits. All that the record company is doing is what you could do yourself - getting someone else to do the job. The effect of this is that the record company takes a share of merchandising income but gives nothing in return.

- Such record companies will insist that your merchandising income be available to help recoup any unrecouped advances under the recording contract. It does not take much to work out why this is good for the company and bad for the artist. This can prove devastating because you are, in effect, being deprived of an alternative source of income to fund your touring.

- The record companies are rarely prepared to pay additional dollars for such rights.

Of course, the bottom line is that if you only have one record company interested in you, you will still do the deal even if the company does insist on taking your merchandising rights. However, it is not a good start to the relationship.

Even if the record company does not try to take all merchandising rights, it often demands that it own the copyright in all cover art. Recording artists should always get this negotiated out of their record contract. It means that if the artist wishes to produce merchandise using the cover art (and after all, this is going to be the most well-known image associated with the artists' name) they are going to have to pay the company for the right to use it.

The company will argue that 'If we're paying for it, we want to own it'. The response is simple enough; the artist should have the right to supply all cover art and own the rights to the material they supply. (Of course the company will need reasonable rights of approval of the work supplied.) This will only cost you a few hundred dollars but it means that you then hold the rights necessary to reproduce the image on your merchandise and thereby recoup your expenses many times over.

TOUR MERCHANDISING

Merchandising deals can be worth a lot of money and many acts have entered such agreements too soon, for too long and on terms that are quite unfair. The merchandising rights to your act are too valuable to be left to inexpert negotiation.

One recent act signed its merchandising away for a $10,000 advance: all rights, worldwide, for five years, and low royalties with no escalations. At the time, the inexperienced act and inexperienced management needed the money. They had big plans. When they had a number one record, they realised their mistake.

You must get expert advice before signing merchandising deals. The following are some of the factors that should be taken into account.

TERRITORY

The territory of the deal should only extend as far as the effective range of the merchandising company. None of the Australian companies are truly international in their scope so, in general, the territory should be restricted to Australia and New Zealand.

LENGTH OF A TOUR-MERCHANDISING DEAL

As mentioned above, to some extent, the length of the deal will be influenced by the size of the advance and the opportunity to recoup.

The period may be defined in many ways. A deal may be for a particular number of months, for one or more albums or for the length of a tour. Usually, the merchandiser will want a one-year deal with a number of options (exercisable at its discretion). It may also want your first-born child but that doesn't mean that it should get it.

Limiting the period, as much as is commercially viable, will usually be to your advantage. If you have an up-coming tour, the length of a tour is the artist's preferred option. If you are a super-group, you will be able to make the deal terminable at will (provided the advances are recouped or repaid), but if you are in this category you can afford to have somebody else read this book.

The 'album-tour cycle' is perhaps the most common term for a recording act. This means that the merchandising contract will last from the release of the album until the act starts recording the next album. There are four reasons for this structure being so popular.

1. Most acts undertake a heavy schedule of touring immediately after the release of the album to promote its sales. The act will supply the merchandiser with the artwork from the album and ensure that all designs used by the merchandiser are compatible with the total promotional push being given to the album. Thus, the merchandiser knows that it will have the maximum opportunity to sell its goods and the act knows that the merchandiser's efforts will provide valuable cross-promotion for the album.

2. The success of the album is an important measuring stick of the value of the merchandising deal. If it is a huge hit, the merchandising deal for the next album will be more favourable to the artist. If it flops, the merchandiser will not be stuck with a deal that is uneconomic.

3. By the end of the tour it will be clear to the act whether or not the merchandiser has been effective. If it has not lived up to its promises it will not get another term. The album-tour cycle gives the act the opportunity to evaluate performance.

4. There is nothing more annoying than having to change merchandising companies during the middle of a tour.

If there must be an option to extend the term, the fairest way of doing this is to structure it so that the artist is obliged, at the end of the tour cycle, to give the merchandiser the first option to negotiate for the new tour cycle. In this way the merchandiser has the opportunity to continue its development of products and strategies, while the artist ensures that the terms of the deal are regularly reviewed, to take into account any development in the artist's merchandising value. After all, if the artist's previous album was a smash hit, its merchandising value will be much greater than it was when the deal was negotiated before its tour and hit record.

EXTENSION FOR UNRECOUPMENT

You should never agree to a deal in which the term extends until recoupment of all outstanding advances. Advances are a calculated gamble for both parties, but no artist wants to be tied to an unsuccessful merchandiser. Cap the period of extension (if there must be one) and insist on the right (not the duty) to repay any unrecoupment should you want to bring the deal to an end even sooner. If you have had a $50,000 advance and the merchandiser has recouped $45,000, you don't want the term to extend for another year just because of $5,000. In such a case, the merchandiser would have done very well out of the deal even though it has not completely recouped, so you will usually find them very willing to negotiate a new deal when you go to repay the unrecouped balance.

Often the artist's buy-out right is subject to the company's right to match another offer. After all, you usually won't want to buy your way out of the deal unless there is another company offering you a better deal. The company will often insist that it should have the right to match that better offer but that if it chooses not to do so, the artist can then exercise its buy-out right.

ADVANCES FOR TOUR MERCHANDISING

With the increasing reluctance of record companies to fund tours, musicians have been looking to advances from merchandising companies to fund them.

Merchandise companies don't pay advances simply because they like risking their money, or because they want to support a tour. They do it to induce the act to sign with them and not another merchandiser. As with all advances, the starting point for determining the amount is calculated according to the merchandiser's best estimate of the potential income the act is likely to make from the deal, e.g. if the merchandising deal is to be for the period of a tour, the merchandiser will need to estimate how many people you are likely to draw in the tour. The calculation will take into account:

- What kind of an act is it?
- Are its fans likely to buy merchandise?
- What kind of merchandise?
- How many dates are booked?
- Which venues will be played?
- How big are the venues?
- How many seats are you going to sell?
- How much is each member of the audience likely to spend in merchandising dollars?
- What degree of record company support can be established?
- How good (artistically and technically) is the artwork?

Even with all this, the calculation of the advance is a matter of informed guesswork. Experienced merchandisers know what a particular type of act is likely to gross per head. The audience attending the performance of a popular rock act may spend about $3 to $4 per head on merchandise; the audience of a heavy metal act (who are the biggest spenders of merchandising dollars) may spend $6 to $7 per head; some freaks of marketing like Garth Brooks will double that every night; the audience at a chamber music concert is likely to spend only cents.

With this in mind, the merchandiser will estimate the number of people who will attend the concerts. To protect themselves, they will discount this figure so as to only take into account the paying audience (because those with complimentary tickets are notoriously miserly with their merchandising dollars. They probably got their T-shirt free as well!). They may then discount the figure further to take into account the nature and layout of the performance venues. (Open-air concerts often sell less because the merchandising outlets may not be as accessible or obvious as in closed venues.)

Once they have their estimate of heads, they multiply that number by the estimated dollar return per head. When you divide that figure by two and you have a rough idea of the advance.

To protect themselves further, merchandisers who are putting up a large advance will often build two further factors into a deal to protect themselves from being too badly burned. First, if the advance is really large, the merchandiser will demand a guarantee (e.g. if a figure is based on the tour selling 300,000 tickets and only 50,000 seats are sold, a portion of the advance may be repayable.)

Second, the size of the advance influences the term of the deal, because the merchandiser will need a reasonable period in which to recoup and make a profit. The bigger the advance, the longer the term.

TIMING OF ADVANCE PAYMENTS

Advances are usually paid according to a schedule. They are not paid all up front. An advance may be payable on signing, another at the beginning of the tour, a further advance after playing to so many thousand people and so on.

RECOUPABLE AND/OR REPAYABLE ADVANCES

Merchandising advances are always recoupable from income. You must make sure that, if your record company insists on acquiring your merchandising rights, no income from merchandising will be used to recoup your recording advances and expenses.

You should never have an obligation to repay unrecouped advances at the end of the term. Many agreements state that the term will continue until full recoupment. As discussed earlier, you should insist on a cap to that extension and the right to repay any unrecouped advances so that you can get out of the deal at the end of the term if you so wish.

Merchandisers believe that repayable guarantees provide some protection from miscalculation so that if the act fails, the merchandiser has a chance of getting its money back. The fact remains; if an act fails, usually there is no money to repay!

It is quite common for merchandising advances to be partly repayable and partly non-repayable. For example, there may be a non-recoupable signing-on fee, an initial advance that is recoupable but non-repayable and later advances that are recoupable but repayable. There are no rules. It all depends on your negotiating strength and skill.

THE SPLITS

In Australia and New Zealand, the share of tour merchandise paid to a mid-range artist is between 20% and 30%. Very established artists or those who have a current hit record may be in the 30% to 35% range and only the international super-groups can get 35% to 40%. After the tour, about 10% of retail is the mark (but more about this in the section entitled Retail Merchandising, which is coming up).

The merchandiser is usually reassured if you have a new album coming out because this means that the record company will be providing marketing support. Promotion to sell the record is likely to stimulate the sale of merchandise. This sort of information can work to improve your bargaining power.

THE ARTIST'S SHARE

There are two methods of paying the artist: a percentage of sales income or a set dollar amount per unit. The artist's percentages are usually paid on the gross retail sales less only GST and customs duty. Retail merchandising deals generally provide a set amount per unit when the duration of the deal is reasonably short and the range of goods is very limited; e.g. it may be used in a one-year agreement which licenses a company to produce posters of the artist. This works because posters sell for fairly standard prices, and the retail price is unlikely to change much in just one year.

In more complicated deals, where the term is longer or the range of goods is larger, a percentage is safer. After all, a percentage arrangement automatically takes factors such as inflation or unexpected mark-ups into account.

Assuming that you opt for a percentage deal, what are you really getting? A percentage of what? It may be based on wholesale or retail sales. It is also usually based on net sales. How is 'net' defined? What deductions will be permitted? These are not simple matters and your agreement must cover them all.

In retail merchandising (unlike tour merchandising), percentages are usually based on wholesale receipts. Accordingly, you make far less selling merchandise through retail outlets than you do from the performance venue. Just compare getting 30% of retail selling price of a T-shirt from a venue sale and 10% of the wholesale price from a retailer. The latter has to take into account the greater number of people involved, each one having their own overheads to recover.

Perhaps the question most often asked of an entertainment lawyer briefed to negotiate a merchandising deal is, 'What is the standard royalty?' The truth is that there are no 'standard royalties'. The rates vary enormously depending on the name and status of the artist, the advance structure, the guaranteed minimum royalty, as well as the type of product, territory and duration of the deal.

That said, retail licensing can be roughly divided into two categories: clothing; and everything else. The act's share of clothing sales is usually 10% to 12.5%. On everything else it is one step higher: 12.5% to 15%. Sometimes you may negotiate a couple of extra percentage points for the use of your own designs, as there will (if you have done your homework properly and secured all necessary assignments and approvals from the artist - see the Commissioning Letter at the end of this chapter) be lower costs involved in getting clearances to reproduce the artwork.

QUALITY CONTROL

You must make every effort to ensure the consistent quality of merchandising and the publicity relating to the sale of the merchandising. It may be very damaging to your reputation if the workmanship is shoddy or the publicity is tacky. Accordingly, you should have the right of prior approval over the nature of the goods, artwork, designs and manufacturing standard. You should sign-off on all samples.

Most merchandising companies understand the artist's need to retain creative and quality control over merchandise and are very willing to involve the artist in the process.

INVENTORY LEFTOVERS

Although a good merchandiser will not have much left over at the end of the contract period, what will happen to such material should be determined at the outset. Will it be sold or destroyed? If it is to be sold will it be for full price or junked? Will the company have a sell-off period? Can you buy-in any left over stock at junk prices?

ACCOUNTING AND PAYMENT

The licensee should agree to account to you at least monthly (if the term is yearly) or every week (if the term is for the duration of a tour). These accountings should show the sales made during that period and include an itemised list of the kinds and quantities and prices of articles sold.

Simultaneously with the supply of the accounts, the merchandiser should pay you the royalties due.

SALES EFFORTS

If you are an established artist you should insist on control over how the goods are to be sold. To do this you should require a marketing plan from the merchandiser. This needs to include a timetable setting out the dates on which various marketing methods will start and where, release dates of products, together with a cash-flow projection. This marketing plan should be subject to your approval.

There should also be an agreed style-guide, setting out the only permitted form, style and colours the merchandiser may use for the merchandise, together with any trade marks or other copyright notices that must be included on the goods. This is particularly important with retail merchandising, but only the biggest acts go to the trouble of style-guides for tour merchandise. Where there is no style-guide, you have to have the right to sign-off on all samples if you want to be able to ensure control of quality and use.

The contract will also specify that the merchandiser will make its best endeavours to market the goods and may stipulate various minimum standards. This may include an advertising campaign or other promotional efforts. If it does, the artist should have the right of prior approval.

Similarly, you will want control over where the goods are sold. Will sales be only from venues at which you are playing or will the distribution be wider? If it is wider, it is in your interests to consider which outlets would be in keeping with your public profile and limit the merchandiser to such outlets. The sales territory can cause problems if you have other merchandisers in place, e.g. if you have licensed various retailers to sell products, you may have promised them a certain degree of exclusivity. If so, you will have a duty to ensure that your tour merchandiser doesn't sell any inventory outside its authorised territory, otherwise it may be causing you to breach your agreement with the other merchandiser.

GROUP MEMBERS' OBLIGATIONS

It is very important that a group's partnership agreement deals with unrecouped advances. If anyone leaves the group while the merchandising advance is still unrecouped, he or she will have had the advantage of the advance but will not be contributing to the work that will recoup it. Will the leaving member have to pay back a share of the unrecouped balance? Some other means might be selected for achieving a fair result but whatever the procedure is to be, it must be worked out at the early stages - before the problem arises.

DOING YOUR OWN TOUR MERCHANDISING

You should not tie yourself to a merchandiser too early in your career. You will get minimal splits and minimum attention. Understandably, the merchandiser will give most attention to its more established, and thus more profitable, clients.

Instead, you should consider doing it yourself. Many less-established artists do their own. You can design the merchandise yourself or have a friend do it for you. You can hire vendors on an hourly rate or have fans, family or friends provide the sales team. Usually, the biggest problem is in scraping together the money to pay the manufacturer for the first order. Still, as the volumes are not likely to be great, the amount of money involved is not huge.

Once you've established the identity and extent of your market, you will be able to better judge your likely sales and may then be able to cash flow your orders from sales.

Because you have control of the whole process, you can ensure that the quality of the merchandise is high. This is most important. Your image will suffer if your merchandise falls to bits.

Best of all, you can keep your prices reasonable and still make more money because there is no middleman. You are both the wholesaler and the retailer!

Doing it yourself needs considerable administrative supervision. If you don't oversee it closely, you will incur a lot of expense and not make any money.

Treat your merchandising as a separate business from your other music work and deal with it as a separate profit centre. Keep books, keep invoices. Keep a record of all your deals, no matter how small. Don't forget to make sure that your GST obligations are met. After six months or so, you should examine the business and examine how it can be improved or whether it is worth continuing.

RETAIL MERCHANDISING

Retail merchandising has become very important to the music industry. This is a quite recent development; one that has occurred because both merchandisers and artists now realise that fans will buy music merchandise from traditional retail outlets as well as at performance venues.

You can either do deals directly with particular retail outlets or you can retain an agent to seek out and negotiate deals on your behalf. There are very few acts with sufficient administrative resources to put these deals together. Usually, it is more cost-effective to retain an agent who already has both a wide network of retailing contacts and an established supervision and administration system.

Most of the points discussed in relation to tour merchandising are relevant to retail merchandising and they won't be repeated here.

THE AGENT'S COMMISSION

The commission charged by licensing agents varies from agent to agent and act to act. The rate will be between 20% and 35% of the artist's gross receipts. So, if you license a poster manufacturer at 15%, on sales of 5,000 units at a retail price of $12 (+GST), the artist's royalty will be: 5,000 x $12 x 15% = $9,000. This will be paid to the agent which then deducts its (say) 30% ($2,700) and pays-through to the artist the remaining $6,300.

Remember that some agents would not recognise a conflict of interest if it hit them in the face. Some agents take a percentage from both the retailer and the act! This raises serious questions about whose agent they really are. Also, agents generally have long relationships with all the important retailers and particular record companies. If you are less than a super-star act, you may be dazzled and charmed by the agent, but remember; the deal the agent negotiates is never going to be so tough as to affect the agent's chances of doing more deals for other acts with that same retailer. As far as the agent is concerned, retailers last longer than acts.

THE AGENT'S ROLE

Assuming that you appoint a licensing agent, you will need to retain the right of approval over all sub-licensees, all deals and all products. The agent's job is to find, negotiate, make recommendations about and administer these deals. You will notice that it is not the agent's responsibility to enter the deals on your behalf! You would be asking for trouble if you duck your responsibility and leave the whole process to your agent. It may be less stressful to remain aloof from the responsibilities of decision-making, but it could be very costly.

You must also retain all the rights of approval discussed earlier. These must be spelled out in the licence agreement. Usually, your contract with the licensing agent will specify the matters that must be included in any sub-licensing deals.

Often, the agent's contract will have appended to it an approved licence agreement. This is the basic licence agreement that the artists have approved for use by the agent. It will contain all the essential protections such as approvals of artist photographs, merchandise types, designs and quality of product. Providing a standard form licence makes it easier for the agent to show the prospective retailer/manufacturer the general terms of the deal without having to get separate artist approvals for basic terms.

THE AGENT'S RIGHTS

In retail merchandising you must limit the goods licensed as narrowly as possible. You would not grant an exclusive licence to a manufacturer to make 'toys' featuring your name or likeness. You would specify a particular toy. Similarly with clothing, you would specify the range say; girls clothing (ages 14-19) or boys' shoes (sizes 3-8). This allows you to grant licences to other manufacturers to produce related but non-competing products that can make you additional income.

If the retailer wants a wide range of exclusivity it has to pay for it. It must also have the ability to produce, distribute and market that wide range of goods throughout the territory. If it does not, no juicy advance will make up for your loss of sales. Very few companies have market power in a wide range of goods. Find out what the company is really good at, and license it to do that task.

PROTECTION

There are five ways of minimising your exposure from the scourge of merchandise pirates:
- copyright;
- registration of designs;
- trademarks;
- the Trade Practices Act; and
- passing off.

These are complex areas of the law and you will need expert legal advice to navigate your way through them.

Let's assume that you have a distinctive and original piece of artwork that you want to use on your record cover and then merchandise. The artwork will probably be protected by copyright.

If the record is going to be released in the United States, it is worth registering the copyright there. You may also register it as a registered design and, in some cases, you might be justified in seeking further protection by registering it as a trademark as well.

Registration processes are quite expensive and you won't register a design or a trademark unless you are a major act with a serious opportunity for income from merchandising. Small acts will rely on the automatic protection that copyright provides.

If you are considering doing merchandising, get your legal advice early. Have your expert check that you have the right to do what you wish to do; that you own the necessary rights in the designs and objects that you wish to merchandise; that you have protected those rights as best you can.

Remember that merchandise piracy is a multimillion-dollar business in Australia. These parasites live off the name and reputation of others. They can do so because people are too often too busy, distracted, ignorant, or slack, to protect their own interests.

All too often, an artist who is the victim of a merchandise pirate finds that he or she cannot do anything because of insufficient care at the outset. Careful planning and expert advice are both essential before you start merchandising. Merchandising needs constant supervision and protection.

If you discover that someone is pirating your name and reputation by producing unauthorised merchandise, you must move quickly. Contact your music lawyer immediately. There are court orders procedures (called 'Anton Pillar' Orders) that allow for seizure of the pirate merchandise, which will allow you to get the merchandise off the street so it does not compete with your own, genuine products. Your lawyer will have to move very fast to prepare the documents, approach the court, get the necessary orders and then organise the raid on the merchandisers' operations. Speed is important, otherwise these fly-by-nighters will make their killing at your expense and disappear without trace.

For maximum efficiency, many of the major acts, anticipating that there will be bootleggers outside their concert venues, instruct their lawyers to draft the necessary documentation beforehand. If they are needed, they can move with maximum speed.

In March 1993, the lawyers for ACME, the company that held the exclusive merchandising rights for the Paul McCartney tour, made Australian legal history by obtaining a species of Anton Pillar order known as 'John Doe' Orders. 'John Doe' is the name used by the legal system where the party's true identity in not known. These orders allowed them to confiscate unauthorised merchandise being sold in the vicinity of the performance venue, without having to identify the bootleggers in the Court orders. The John Doe Orders also obliged the bootleggers to file an affidavit within 48 hours that disclosed their name, address, the amount and whereabouts of merchandise in their control or possession, and the names and addresses of their suppliers and manufacturers.

This swift and decisive weapon now makes it much easier to wage war on bootleggers. The legal costs are not cheap but given the amounts at stake, it has become a standard practice for many major touring artists.

COMMISSIONING LETTER FOR RECORD COVER ART

Dear   ,

Following our recent conversation, this is to confirm that I have
commissioned you to create original album cover art for me.
The basics of the agreement are:

The album: 'Stardust' by ....

Format of album: ....

Roughs: no. required:..

       date for delivery:..

Delivery date for final art: ....

Content: As agreed

Credit line: ....

Owner of copyright: ....

Owner of original artwork: ....

Fee (GST inclusive): $..........................payable upon delivery of finished art

Dated: ....

Signed:..
Commissioning Party

Signed:..
Artist

28
SPONSORSHIP AND PRODUCT ENDORSEMENT

THE ASSOCIATION OF AN ARTIST'S REPUTATION WITH A THIRD PARTY'S PRODUCT OR SERVICE IS NOW COMMONPLACE. IT PROVIDES AN IMPORTANT ADDITIONAL SOURCE OF FUNDING FOR THE ARTIST AND VERY VALUABLE PROMOTION BY ASSOCIATION FOR THE SPONSORS AND THEIR PRODUCTS. THIS CHAPTER EXAMINES WHY COMPANIES BECOME SPONSORS, HOW TO APPROACH COMPANIES FOR SPONSORSHIP AND SOME OF THE PROBLEMS TO LOOK OUT FOR WHEN WORKING WITH SPONSORS. A SHORT-FORM ENDORSEMENT PROPOSAL IS PROVIDED.

Names and reputations are valuable. In a marketing sense, they constitute your "brand". Whether you are a music hero or an ex-prime minister, your name and reputation is directly linked to your ability to make money.

The use of an artist's name and reputation to sell records is fundamental to the record business. These days, however, the income from performance, recording and publishing is only part of the financial repertoire of the successful musician.

One of the features of modern marketing and advertising is the exploitation of a celebrity's reputation to promote a third party's products or services. This takes two different forms: sponsorship and endorsement. Sponsorship usually involves the sponsor doing or providing something (usually old-fashioned money) to assist an organisation, event or artist and by that, gaining a commercial benefit by the association. By contrast, endorsement takes it one step further: It is an active promotion by the recipient of the company's products or services.

SPONSORSHIPS

Sponsorships have been commonplace in the classical music and theatrical fields for many years. They are now common in popular music also. This shift has occurred because marketing research has shown companies that their traditional avenue for sponsorship - sporting events - doesn't target women and children. Music does. Properly targeted, music sponsorship can get the company's message to a specific sex, age group and interest group.

This form of promotion by association has become an important and lucrative source of income for the many celebrities with a recognisable look or sound who are asked to hire their name, reputations, voices or faces to the promotion of products and services that have nothing to do with their own area of expertise or reputation. Do you remember all those famous Australians who lent their faces to Ansett's 'Absolutely' campaign - just weeks before the company went to the wall?

Both the sponsor and the sponsored, benefit from having a carefully drafted agreement between them, to protect their respective interests. A few words on the back of an envelope will not do. Those who are being sponsored have to make sure that their names and reputations are only being used in a manner and to the extent that is acceptable; the company needs to ensure that it is getting value for its money and that its brand name and corporate profile will not be endangered.

WHY COMPANIES BECOME SPONSORS

It is important to realise that companies do not usually involve themselves in sponsorships (or endorsements) because they think that the artist is talented or the event's objectives are worthwhile. They mostly do so because they have a product or service to promote and to sell or have a specific corporate objective to achieve. (Examples of the latter include companies who support an artist or an arts project to facilitate a corporate-to-corporate or a corporate-to-government relationship.) The longest lasting sponsorships are those that are most likely to enhance corporate objectives. Regrettably, philanthropy rarely has anything to do with it.

A company which is interested in providing sponsorship has a number of reasons for doing so and these follow.

IMAGE ESTABLISHMENT

Companies are often keen to be involved in a sponsorship either when they are new and establishing their profile in the marketplace, or when they have a new product or service that can be promoted by association with particular events, performances or broadcasts.

The classic example of this in the 1990s was the launch of the Optus telecommunications company and its competition to attract customers from Telstra. Its sponsorship of events (particularly those which have wide television audiences) was a spectacular exercise. The company is reputed to have spent approximately $65 million just promoting public recognition of its name.

IMAGE DEFINITION AND BRAND DEVELOPMENT

Associating its brandname products with your name and reputation gives the brand a certain image, one that clearly places it in a particular market and at the same time distinguishes it from its rivals. All experts in marketing emphasise that it is important that the image of the brandname must be clearly defined if the brand is to be marketed successfully. The sponsor company is using the artist's image to identify more clearly its own image and brands in the minds of potential purchasers.

For example, for many years Qantas has used "I Still Call Australia Home" with huge success to reinforce its image as the airline of first choice for Australian travellers.

Similarly, an insurance company might sponsor an event because it wants to be associated with the aspiration of the target audience. On the other hand, Coca-Cola used a star such as Elton John to endorse its product because his popularity crosses so many age groups. Anyone who likes Elton John (no matter what age) is a potential Coca-Cola buyer. In contrast, a computer company is likely to sponsor a performer or group that is associated with innovation and excellence.

IMAGE IMPROVEMENT

Some of the biggest corporate sponsors have supported the arts because it helps to improve their level of acceptance and the character of their profile in the community. The classic examples of this are the tobacco companies who, each year, spend many millions of dollars sponsoring sporting and cultural events. The mining companies are also useful examples. For the last 10 years, certain oil companies have been among the largest corporate sponsors of the arts, and this has helped change the community's general perception of them from rapacious multinationals to companies concerned for Australia and its quality of life. Similarly, Telstra's campaign featuring John Farnham associated it with an enormously popular, friendly, self-deprecatingly amusing entertainment icon. Who said, 'Can't buy me love'?

ASSOCIATION WITH EXCELLENCE

The Coca Cola-Elton John endorsement also provides an insight into another reason companies sponsor music; they benefit from association with excellence. Even if particular listeners don't like the music performed, if the artist has a proven record of popularity it can be assumed that it is, within its own genre, excellent.

In contrast, sometimes the sponsorship is very targeted rather than generic. The Australian Brandenburg Orchestra plays baroque and classical music that appeals to an audience of a particular demographic. Although the market is not large, it is well defined and the success with which the orchestra has combined excellence of performance with a mighty array of commercial sponsors is evident by visiting its website: See www.brandenburgorchestra.org.au.

One of the most common examples of sponsorship in the music business is the sponsorship given by instrument manufacturers. They are interested in having their instruments played in public by the best performers. The benefits of this link to excellence are obvious. The use of the instrument by the performer amounts to an indirect endorsement of the product. Les Paul (who is credited with inventing the electric guitar and who was one of the great innovators in recording technology) is a case in point. The Fender company was certainly not upset whenever Jimi Hendrix demolished one of their guitars. Notice how many album covers acknowledge support from instrument makers.

CLIENT AND STAFF RELATIONS

Never ever underestimate the importance that the company will attach to the opportunity that the sponsorship provides for entertaining and networking. The details of these opportunities may differ considerably between different genres of music. The genteel world of the symphony orchestra (which is very dependent on sponsorship because its overheads are so much greater than ticket sales can cover) provides many opportunities for networking. The boards and patrons of such organisations include many of the most powerful figures in the community and a major sponsorship will be attractive if it ensures social access (and thus potential business access) to this social circle, which is otherwise so hard to penetrate.

The company who sponsors a rock band will be looking for opportunities to improve staff or client relations by inviting them to concerts. They may also be interested in meeting the movers and shakers of the business (who inevitably are linked with the most successful acts) both for their personal and business needs.

Some of the best sponsorships are obtained from companies in which the CEO or owner has a personal love of the music. It is almost impossible to get major music sponsorship unless the principal decision maker has personal commitment. Identifying that person and pitching directly is almost always more effective than approaching the company through the well-trodden marketing door. You may end up talking to the marketing director but if you are doing so because the boss has provided the introduction, your proposal is given very serious consideration.

One of the little known success stories of recent years has been the 'Weekend Warriors': hundreds of (largely) men who used to play in a band or dreamed of doing so and who now have the time and money to do so as a hobby. Its fun, friendly, they can afford whatever instruments they want, it's pressure free and cheaper than a therapist. Many of the warriors are prepared to expand their personal involvement to a corporate support of younger, aspiring, musicians.

Once found and signed up, the challenge is to reinforce the pleasure that these decision makers get from their involvement with you and your music. There are lots of ways of doing this: invitations to shows, passes backstage, invitation to the after show party, playing a bracket at their company function or a private party, autographed posters and discs, even their own framed gold record for their office wall. The care and feeding of these pets is not something to be taken casually. The money you get from this source is not free. These decision makers know the value of money and expect you to recognise its value too.

THE RELATIONSHIP

For the company, sponsorship is not just about money. It is about relationships. Every successful sponsorship develops links between the humans behind the company and the humans associated with the music. Through those relationships, grow the personal and corporate profits that make for a successful sponsorship.

WHAT TO ASK FOR

What most acts or organisations are looking for is money. This may seem to be stating the obvious, but in fact it is so obvious that many acts look no further.

You must ask yourself, 'Why do I need this sponsorship?' There are usually only two possible answers: either the sponsorship will be underwriting the real costs of a project (usually directly related to a particular performance or tour); or it will be more in the nature of an artist's 'premium' (something that goes straight into the profit column in the accounts!).

If it is the latter motivation, it is money that you want. However, if your need is project-related, there are often more valuable things that the sponsor company can provide, e.g. when radio stations sponsor an event, they get their name over everything but, in return, provide the event with hugely expensive airtime that few artists or promoters could afford. This is a straightforward sponsorship deal, but no money changes hands. Both parties benefit from the association. Similar deals have been done with airlines, car companies, freight companies, communications companies, and even advertising agencies.

Sometimes the benefit that the artist seeks is not even so directly linked to the product of the sponsor. For example, if the group needs administrative resources, a large company with these capabilities already on staff may provide company staff, computer time, printing facilities, strategic advice and so on, in lieu of cash. This is more common in classical music than popular music but the principle remains true for all sponsorships. Look at the need and how best to fill it. Money is not necessarily the only or the best solution.

A MOMENT'S REFLECTION

Sponsorship is so hard to find that we often don't ask ourselves whether the particular corporate association will be good for the reputation of the artist or organisation. Remember that you are lending your reputation and image to the company; the association might benefit the company but will it benefit you in the long term?

Say you have a three-year sponsorship deal and in year two your sponsor is publicly associated with products that are made by children and women in Asia under appalling conditions or which cause brain tumours or birth defects. What if criminal charges are brought against the senior management of the company? All of these sorts of occurrences can alienate the artist's audience because the association is a two-way street.

Because of this, you should always have an exit clause in the event that the company reputation deteriorates in a way that may damage your reputation. Companies always include such parachute clauses; so should you. Image exchange and association is sometimes unforeseeable and not always favourable.

TOUR SPONSORSHIP

In analysing the attractiveness of a tour sponsorship, a company will consider the following factors.
- Name of the artist.
- Reputation of the artist.
- Demographic profile of the artist's fans in comparison with those of the company's target market.
- The number and style of venues.
- Number of people expected to attend the shows.
- Standard of management behind the artist and the tour.
- Cost of the sponsorship, including fees, expenses, bonuses.
- Indirect costs and associated expenditure (e.g. paid advertising support).
- Degree of exclusivity as sponsor.
- Means of product identification permitted.
- Degree of product endorsement involved.
- Available methods of spin-off publicity and promotion.

The detail that corporations insist upon when entering sponsorship and endorsement deals is not familiar to many in the music industry. Not for them, the old philosophy of 'throw them at the wall and if they stick, we'll make money'! The corporation will only spend its money on you if, after analysing the sorts of issues raised above, it thinks that by spending that money it will better achieve its corporate goals.

The amount of money that a sponsorship is worth to the company is influenced by:

- The degree of exclusivity;
- Whether the endorsement will be direct or indirect (or in other words the level of artist activity in company promotion);
- The means of identification that will be permitted; and
- The value that the company perceives in the association.

Once this is understood it is obvious that any proposal must spell out what the artist and the tour will physically provide for the company. For example:

- The right to hang banners and other signage bearing the corporate name, logo or product identification;
- The permitted areas of such signage;
- The inclusion of company name, logo and advertising in the program and on all printed material such as the tickets;
- The placement of such inclusions;
- The provision of tickets at reduced or no cost to company personnel/clients;
- The right to produce merchandise such as T-shirts, flags, etc. which will identify the artist with the corporate sponsor;
- Availability and preparedness of the artist to publicly acknowledge the sponsorship;
- The right to use the name and image of the artist in its own advertising and promotional material.

CONFLICT WITH VENUES

It is increasingly common for the major venues to have their own exclusive sponsorship deals with major companies. This can cause problems for artists using such venues, for the venue may insist that no competing sponsorships will be permitted. If the artist has already entered a sponsorship deal and cannot deliver its part of the bargain, nobody except the lawyers will be happy. To avoid these problems, make inquiries at the earliest stage possible to see if the venues that you intend to play do have such restrictions. Then you will know whether to find an alternative venue, negotiate an alternative means of promotion with your would-be sponsor, or pass up the opportunity of sponsorship altogether.

SPONSORSHIP OF RECORDS

Most of these sponsorships relate to either general overhead support for the artist or are directly related to particular performances or tours. It is unusual for a company to sponsor a record.

The exception to this, if it can be truly called sponsorship, is the company that issues a 'premium record' that is a record (frequently specifically compiled or re-packaged) that is intended to directly promote the sales of another product. For example, Philip Morris (the cigarette manufacturer) has produced many such records that it sells for a fraction of the usual retail price or uses as giveaways. It is just another variation on a master licensing deal. The record company gets a royalty for the reuse of the master recordings and the publishers collect mechanical royalties. This is perhaps not sponsorship in the true sense, as there is no attempt at developing a relationship between the artist and the company. Artists ought to make sure that the record companies' right to license premium records is strictly controlled, otherwise premiums can be just a way for companies to cash in on the reputation of the artist without taking into account the artist's needs or wishes.

This new variant on premiums is the sponsored download or ringtone. An example of this was the Fanta/Sony promotion "Sounds of Summer" in which consumers of Fanta could access a website that promoted Fanta and from there could choose from literally thousands of songs to use as their ringtone. Premiums are merely a way of promoting third party products through an association with music products. Their principal feature is that the third party product is the focus of the marketing intent, not the music. The music is not the subject of the promotion - it is the tool. This is the easiest way to distinguish between sponsorship and premiums.

DIRECT ENDORSEMENTS

When Britney Spears sings for Pepsi or Elton John sings for Coca-Cola, each is directly affixing his name and reputation to the product. They are endorsing it. Saying it is a Good Thing. The association with the company's product is direct and the amount of money paid to the artist reflects the perceived benefit of that association. It goes beyond mere sponsorship, which is a more passive relationship.

Celebrities have to be careful that they are not sued by disgruntled members of the public, who relied on their endorsement to buy goods that turn out to be less than satisfactory. Already in Australia there have been court cases in which celebrities have been sued for the faults of the companies and the products that they have endorsed.

THE ENDORSEMENT CONTRACT

In recent years, the complexity of endorsement contracts has increased in direct proportion to their importance as forms of product promotion and the monetary value of the deals.

Endorsement contracts must be negotiated and drafted with care. There is no standard deal. Every one reflects the needs of the individual act and sponsor. Musicians can be assured that the sponsorship or endorsement contract drafted by the company's lawyer will be calculated to further the interests of the company. It is not the company's duty to be even-handed.

As with all other important legal commitments entered, the contract should be read and negotiated by a lawyer who is familiar with such deals. You must be assured that your needs will be protected and that the corporate advantage sought by the company will be compatible with your own ethics and image. That said, many small-scale endorsement agreements never reach 'long form' contract stage. Many are done either by exchange of letters or Heads of Agreement. Using this style keeps it away from the complexity that may be introduced by the company's lawyers. On the other hand, its inherent vagueness is dangerous. Where the dollar value gets heavy, so too does the contract.

The following is an example of a proposal put to a clothing manufacturer who wished to have a recording artist wear the company's swim and surf clothes. As you will see, it is structured so as to provide a skeleton for use in the negotiation and, in turn, will form the basis of the next step, the Heads of Agreement:

ENDORSEMENT PROPOSAL

1. PARTIES:
   (a)
   (b)

2. TERM:
   (i) One year.
   (ii) Commencement date - upon execution of contract.
   (iii) Extensions available subject to further negotiations and mutual consent.

3. FEE:
   $30,000 per annum (+GST), payable in monthly instalments.

4. TERRITORY:
   Australia and New Zealand.

5. PRODUCT ENDORSEMENT:
   (i) Artist will wear Austracloth clothing and apparel in public appearances as and where she considers it appropriate.
   (ii) Surf and swimwear worn by the Artist will be exclusively by Austracloth.
   (iii) Artist will make best endeavours to have the Austracloth logo reproduced on Artist's records. (Please note that Extra Records has final right of approval on such endorsements.)
   (iv) Artist will include Austracloth apparel and promotional material in her guest D-J giveaway packages.

6. OPTIONAL DIRECT PROMOTIONAL ACTIVITY:
   (i) During the term, Austracloth may call upon Artist to be involved in the direct promotion and marketing of its products.
       (a) Television commercials: The fee for any such commercial will be $10,000. This fee includes a two-day, eight-hour day, photo-shoot.
       (b) Point-of-sale and/or press advertising: The fee for such services will be $10,000 per photo-shoot, each photo-shoot involving a maximum of two eight-hour days.
       (c) Personal and/or media appearances: Where the appearance is at the request of Austracloth, the fee will be $10,000 per day with a maximum of two such appearances in any one day.
   (ii) Time commitment:
       (a) Artist would be available for a maximum of four photo-shoots and ten days of personal and/or media appearances. Media appearances would be as mutually agreed.
       (b) All dates must be mutually acceptable.
   (iii) Exclusivity:
       If the fees paid to Artist for optional direct promotional activity on behalf of Austracloth exceeds $50,000, Artist will exclusively endorse Austracloth dance wear (in addition to her exclusive endorsement of Austracloth surf and swim wear).

(iv) Other matters:
  (a) Artist will have final right of approval of all photographs, artwork and storyboards which feature Artist's name or likeness.
  (b) No television commercial to be used by Austracloth after the expiration of the contract period in which it is produced.
  (c) No point-of-sale or press advertising to be used by Austracloth after the expiration of three months from the date of initial release and no such material to be used by Austracloth after the expiration of the contract.
  (d) Additional fees to be paid for each extra day that may be required for shooting of stills and/or commercials - $3,000.
  (e) Austracloth will meet all costs and expenses relating to the endorsement (for both Artist and her manager) including airfares, accommodation, taxi fares, make-up, wardrobe, etc.

7. **EXTRA RECORDS:**
  (i)   Artist is contractually bound to give priority in availability to Extra Records.
  (ii) All of Artist's contracts relating to merchandising or endorsements must be submitted to Extra Records for its approval. Artist undertakes to make best efforts to obtain that consent and provide evidence of that consent if required.
  (iii) This agreement is subject to Artist obtaining the written consent of Extra Records.

8. **TERMINATION**
  Either party may terminate the agreement if the other does anything or is involved in any controversy that that party believes may damage its reputation.

29
PHILANTHROPY

EVEN IF YOUR ORGANISATION RECEIVES
GOVERNMENT FUNDING, IT WILL HAVE TO FIND
ADDITIONAL SOURCES OF INCOME TO BALANCE THE
BUDGET. PHILANTHROPY IS ONE OF THEM.

Philanthropy is nothing more than giving money, goods, services or time to help others. It is different from sponsorship because sponsorship is an endorsement relationship. The return for philanthropists is much more subtle.

Off a rather low base, it appears that Australians are becoming increasingly generous. According to Philanthropy Australia, our philanthropic sector nationally amounts to roughly $5.4 billion a year. $3.5 billion of this comes from individual donations and $1.5 billion comes from businesses. (See www.philanthropy.org.au). This is nowhere near the per capita level of giving that occurs in the USA but the level of Australian philanthropy is likely to continue to increase as our baby boomers begin to inherit an estimated $60 billion from their parents.

There are many theories about what makes individuals and businesses give. Cynics may say that the donors are "doing it for the tax deduction" but such comments are ignorant or unfair: A donation of $10,000 still costs the donor the difference between the amount of the gift and the amount of the tax they would pay on that amount. They could choose to spend that money on something else. Similarly, if someone suggests that 'guilt' is a motivator ask, "Who would give money to a music organisation out of guilt?"

Individuals give money to an Arts organisation because they love what the company is trying to deliver and understand that the support of patrons is essential. It is a personal commitment to culture in general and the art form in particular. Companies are philanthropic for a more diverse set of reasons that range from the personal interest of a senior executive to measurable market benefits.

So how can your organisation reap the benefits of Australia's increasing generosity? How, as a donor, can you structure your activities so as to ensure that your gifts are effective? This chapter considers philanthropy from both the gift giver's and a gift receiver's perspective.

GIFT RECEIVERS

So you've read Chapter 3 of this book and established a not-for-profit organisation. You just lack... money! It is at this moment that you learn the most valuable lesson about philanthropy: your organisation's success depends largely upon its ability to establish and maintain relationships with generous individuals who share its vision.

ESTABLISHING RELATIONSHIPS

Board members of charitable organisations learn quickly that their performance is judged not only by reference to their skills, but also by their ability to give and raise money. As David Gonski (Chairman of the Australia Council for the Arts) aptly states: "You either give, get or get off!" (See: *Encouraging Wealthy Australians to be more Philanthropic. A Report for the Petre Foundation*, Tracey, D., Asia-Pacific Centre for Philanthropy and Social Investment Swinburne University, 2005, p15). Of course like all catch phrases it over-states the position but it makes the point that board members have an obligation to get the money that the organisation needs. Assuming that all the money is not going to come from the board members, it is up to the board to engage their circles of influence.

Like any networking, you start by identifying people you know and the people they know. See if your current group of friends, contacts and associates are interested in your organisation's purposes. Draw up lists of possible donors, work out how to approach them, polish the presentation - and ask. Many people are not very good at actually asking. They are too proud, shy or embarrassed. But unless you ask, you will never convert a supporter into a donor.

There are several organisations (such as Social Ventures Australia and Corporate Good Works) that assist in establishing such relationships. Some of these organisations charge for the service of matching donors with recipients. AdviceBank is free and manages short-term partnerships between business advisers and arts managers. These short-term partnerships can lead to long-term partnerships if managed with care.

SETTING UP AN ORGANISATION WITH TAX DEDUCTIBLE STATUS

DEDUCTIBLE GIFT RECIPIENT STATUS

Your donors will only be entitled to an income tax deduction if your organisation is a Deductible Gift Recipient (DGR). Gifts to a DGR are tax deductible. This is an advantage that you can offer your donor supporter.

To achieve DGR status, your organisation needs to be endorsed by the ATO. To be eligible for endorsement, your organisation must fall within one of the 30 general categories specified in the income tax law and set out in the DGR table available on the ATO website (www.ato.gov.au). The only DGRs that do not need to be endorsed are (i) those specifically listed by name in the income tax law or (ii) 'prescribed private funds' (discussed further below).

REGISTER OF CULTURAL ORGANISATIONS

One of the 30 categories of tax deductible organisations are cultural bodies that have been entered onto the Register of Cultural organisations (ROCO). This is the mechanism provided by the Federal Government for arts organisations seeking to obtain DGR status. Applications are made to the Department of Communications Information Technology and the Arts (DCITA) for listing on the ROCO. If you wish to make an application either write to DCITA or go to its website and get the Gift Pack. This provides a very easy to understand guide for making your application.

To be registered your organisation must meet the following eligibility criteria. It must:

- be a body corporate (i.e. either a company or an incorporated association), or a trust;
- promote literature, music, a performing art, a visual art, a craft, design, film, video, television, radio, community arts, Aboriginal arts or movable cultural heritage as its principal purpose;
- maintain a public fund (discussed further below) to receive gifts;
- use gifts made to the fund only in accordance with the principal purpose;
- not give any of its property, profits or financial surplus to its members, beneficiaries, controllers or owners. (This means that it must be non-profit-distributing. It can make a profit but those profits must go back into the organisation to further its purposes);
- agree to comply with any Government rules; and
- agree to participate in periodic reviews by DCITA in relation to the organisation's eligibility.

THE PUBLIC FUND

To demonstrate that your organisation has a public fund you need to be able to show that:

- you intend that the public will contribute to the fund and that you invite such contributions;
- members of the public contribute to the fund; and
- responsible members of the public participate in the administration of the fund. (This will be satisfied where the fund is administered or controlled by people who have a degree of responsibility in the community e.g. lawyers, doctors, clerics and other professional people satisfy this requirement.)

Your organisation's constitution is one of the key documents that DCITA will look to in assessing whether your organisation maintains an acceptable public fund. It is important that the organisation's constitution demonstrates that:

- the objects of the public fund fall within the cultural purposes requirements;
- the fund intends to invite and receive donations from the public;
- the public fund will be operated on a non-profit basis (no money is to be distributed to members or managers of the fund except as reimbursement for out-of-pocket expenses incurred on behalf of the fund or as proper remuneration for administrative services);
- the fund is managed by board members who have a degree of responsibility to the general community;
- gifts to the fund will be kept in a bank account that is separate from any other funds of the organisation (a separate bank account and clear accounting are essential); and
- if the organisation dissolves or winds-up, any money in the public fund will be transferred to another organisation with DGR status.

In addition, the organisation must be located in Australia, must have an Australian Business Number (ABN) and must undertake that it will notify the ATO if it ceases to be entitled to DGR endorsement.

It is important that donations are unconditional. In other words, if your organisation receives a donation, if it is to be tax deductible, it must not promise benefits. It can be for a specific purpose (such as to pay for the production of a CD or to support an education program) but you cannot offer free tickets or free drinks at the interval. Of course you can (and should) give acknowledgement of the gift (say in the program) but basically, all the donor gets in return for the donation is a receipt. That receipt should specify the amount of the gift, the name of your fund and your ABN.

INCOME TAX EXEMPT CHARITY STATUS

If you've successfully achieved the above, you should also consider applying for Income Tax Exempt Charity (ITEC) status. ITEC status means that any income your organisation earns is exempt from income tax and consequently that your organisation does not have to lodge income tax returns. For more information on ITEC status, see the ATO's website at www.ato.gov.au.

MAINTAINING RELATIONSHIPS

Understanding your donors and what they expect from you will set your organisation apart from the other 2,000 foundations and trusts in Australia. (See: Philanthropy Australia www.philanthropy.org.au). Set out below are a few tips on how you can make your donors feel appreciated:

- **Know your donors:** Engage your donors personally and learn as much about them as you can. Why are they donating? What is it that they want to achieve through their association with your organisation? Unless you understand this it will be impossible to satisfy their motivation and it will be difficult to translate them from a one-time donor into a regular supporter.
- **Explore the potential:** It is important to appreciate that while some donations may seem small, they may be large when viewed in proportion to your donor's wealth. However, sometimes small donors have the potential to be larger donors. If you create opportunities to get to know your donors you have a better chance of gauging whether the donor has the potential or inclination to become a larger donor.
- **It's more than money:** Potential donors may not be in a position to give money but may have goods, services, knowledge and expertise which may be as, if not more, valuable to your organisation.
- **Acknowledge your donors:** While you cannot give a benefit in exchange for a gift, there are other things you can do to make your gift givers feel appreciated. This may be done by a mention of thanks in the program and larger donors may even by thanked publicly at social events. There are many ways of showing gratitude.

    For example, you could make one of your larger donors a patron of your organisation. Orchestra Victoria acknowledged the Myer family's generosity by appointing family member Lady Southey as its patron. An even grander gesture might be to erect a statue of your gift giver! In May 2005, the Sydney Conservatorium of Music unveiled a bronze statue of George Henderson following his gift of $16 million (the most generous donation to the Australian arts in modern times).

Acknowledgement doesn't have to be that magnanimous – but it should reflect the size of the donation.

- **Keep them in the loop:** The 'no questions asked' days are over. Donors are becoming less content with simply handing over large sums of money and increasingly want to know how their money is being spent. You can really set your organisation apart from others by the quality and regularity of your communication with your donors. Let them know the difference their contribution has made to your organisation. Give them early information about events. Give them feedback after events. Make sure that they feel part of the process. Acknowledge that that their contribution has been significant to the success of the organisation. If you don't make them feel involved and special they will be less inclined to support you next year.

GIFT GIVERS

Philanthropists may be either individuals or companies.

INDIVIDUALS

Individual philanthropy in Australia has, for the most part, been left to a handful of very wealthy families. Without their support the classical music sector would collapse. That said, in Australia we do not have the tradition of individual patronage that is so evident in other cultures such as the USA. We may speculate as to why this is so but there is no doubt that the more favourable tax treatment of donors in the USA, for over a century, provided the basis for the tradition by which very wealthy individuals gave large amounts to the arts. This created its own social micro-climate of philanthropy.

In Australia, personal giving is driven by the desire to support the work of the organisation, not the tax deduction. However without the tax deduction there is a greater reluctance to give. As a nation we don't have a great tradition of honouring the generous. Indeed our tax system actively discourages it: Donors cannot expect to receive benefits from the donation. If there are benefits, it is no longer a 'gift' (because the donor is getting something in return) and it is therefore not tax deductible. A receipt, an acknowledgement and a warm inner glow, are all that the donor gets.

COMPANIES

Corporate philanthropy is also important. It is different from 'sponsorship'. It comes in several guises: Very few companies donate money just because it feels good. They must be able to justify the expenditure to their shareholders.

The philosophy of 'Corporate Social Responsibility' has entered the jargon of the boardroom and, albeit slowly, companies are realising that there is advantage in looking beyond the short-term balance sheet and being acknowledged by both staff and customers as a company that cares for and is involved in the community. The World Business Council for Sustainable Development defines corporate social responsibility as the continuing commitment by business to behave ethically and contribute to economic development while improving the quality of life of the workforce, their families and the local community and society at large.

More than goodwill, corporate community involvement or strategic corporate philanthropy, corporate social responsibility is a genuine attempt by a company to build meaningful relationships between the corporate sector and the rest of society. (See:http://www.corporate-responsibility.com.au; and http://www.ethics.org.au/).

Adopting Corporate Social Responsibility is not 'just' an ethical decision. It has been proven to have real benefits for the company and a number of Australia's largest and most influential companies have formally adopted this philosophy, not in a 'feel good' way but in a measurable, business-like way. (For example, see:
http://www.corporate-responsibility.com.au/PDFs/cri_results_2004.pdf).

These benefits are both external and internal. In Cavill + Co's 2004 study, Passion People, it was reported that 82% of responding staff would rather work for a company that supported good causes (http://www.cavill.com.au).

At the same time, Cause Related Marketing is taking off as businesses learn that companies aligning themselves with worthwhile causes are going to better differentiate themselves from their competitors. In the US in 1997, Coca-Cola donated 15 cents to Mothers Against Drunk Driving for every case of Coca-Cola bought during a 6-week promotion in more than 400 Wal-Mart stores. Coke sales in these stores increased 490% during the promotion. (See: http://www.causemarketingforum.com/page.asp?ID=345). Of course this isn't really philanthropy in the sense that it is driven by corporate self-interest but that, in itself, is no bad thing. Indeed, if it results in money flowing to the support of the arts, it is a good thing. If both parties are benefiting from the relationship, the relationship is more likely to last.

We are also becoming more creative in how we give. (For example, Sharegift is a free service that manages small gifts of shares that donors may wish to dispose of. See: www.sharegift.org.)

WORKPLACE GIVING

Tax reforms in August 2002 and January 2003 have led to increased workplace giving. More than 500 Australian businesses are participating in the workplace giving programs. (See the ABAF website at www.abaf.org.au.) For example, Ernst & Young, Mallesons and Diageo have workplace giving programs where:

- part of an employee's pay is donated by the employee as a gift to a DGR;
- the donation is matched by the employer; and
- the amount is donated pre-tax so that the individual's income is then taxed at a lower rate.

This mechanism has already proven to be an important source of philanthropic funds for cultural and social purposes, whilst having distinct and very real benefits to the environment of the workplace.

VOLUNTEERING

For many Australians, volunteering time and skills to a cause is more appealing than signing over a cheque. In the year 2000, there were approximately 4.4 million Australians who volunteered a total of 704 million hours to charities. (See the Philanthropy Australia website at www.philanthropy.org.au). Many music organisations depend on their volunteers. The benefit that these people get from the gift of their time and skills is completely non-financial: They get no pay; they get no tax deduction. Their return is the satisfaction of being part of the organisation and feeling that they are contributing to its aims and successes. So if you want to keep your volunteers you should develop a strategy to fulfil those needs. They should be properly trained to fulfil their tasks, have safe working conditions, be properly insured, regularly evaluated and appropriately acknowledged.

TAX CONSIDERATIONS FOR THE GIFT GIVER

If you wish to make a tax-effective donation in Australia, the ATO requires that your donation satisfies four conditions:

(a) It must be a gift (unqualified and voluntary).

The ATO won't allow a deduction for a payment that is not really a gift (i.e. where you get something in return, like raffle tickets).

(b) The recipient must be a DGR.

As discussed above, the recipient of the gift must be a DGR. You can find out whether a particular organisation has tax deductible status by calling the ATO on 13 28 61, or by searching the Australian Business Register at www.abr.business.gov.au.

(c) The donation must be an approved "gift type".

These include gifts of $2 or more; property valued at over $5,000; property donated within 12 months of purchase; trading stock; property under the Cultural Gifts Program such as indigenous arts, cultural artefacts, natural and scientific materials, film and social history pieces, paintings, manuscripts, books, antiques and jewellery. (For more information on the Cultural Gifts Program, see the ATO website at www.ato.gov.au). The ATO website specifies which gift types apply to each charity.

(d) The donation must comply with any relevant conditions imposed by legislation.

It is also important to remember the following:

- Make sure you keep records of your gifts to prepare your tax return.
- Tax deductions are claimed in the tax return for the income year in which your gift is made.
- The deduction for a gift cannot add to or create a tax loss (so it can't reduce your assessable income to below zero).
- In certain circumstances, you can elect to spread gift deductions over a period of up to five years. This includes gifts valued at over $5,000 and gifts made under the Cultural Gifts Program.
- The cost of valuing property for the purpose of making a gift is also deductible.
- When property is gifted there may be capital gains consequences. If the property you are gifting has increased in value since it was purchased the difference will be added to your assessable income. There are exceptions to this (testamentary gifts, cultural gifts and bequests are exempt from capital gains tax).

PRESCRIBED PRIVATE FUNDS

The introduction of Prescribed Private Funds (PPFs) in 1999 was designed to encourage greater corporate and personal philanthropy in Australia. Previous to these changes it was very difficult for individual philanthropists to set up a private foundation for philanthropic purposes. They had to comply with all the rules described above for Public Funds. People who wanted to do good things with their money were frustrated because they could not be a part of the decision making process as to how their own money would be spent. This was all changed by the introduction of the PPF. Now, businesses, families and individuals can set up their own private foundations and when they give to their foundation, they not only get a tax deduction, they can determine (within guidelines) which charities should benefit from their generosity.

The Government provides guidelines and a model trust deed to help establish the PPF. Funds that comply with the guidelines and the model trust deed provided in the *Income Tax Assessment Regulations 1997 (Cth)*, will be gift deductible entities under the *Income Tax Assessment Act 1997 (Cth)*. As at August 2005, there were 228 PPFs.

To qualify as a PPF:

- your fund must be established under a will or trust deed for the purpose of providing donations to DGRs;

- your fund must meet the public fund requirements (see above) but is not required to seek donations from the public; and
- your fund must meet certain integrity assurance measures.

Although the donor may be on the board of the PPF, the operation of the fund has to be monitored by a "Responsible Person" who can't be closely related to the founder or major donor. This person must be independent (not an employee or a relative). Often an accountant or legal adviser is assigned to be the fund's "Responsible Person". Their function is not to control which charities should receive donations from the fund but rather, that the fund operates in accordance with the regulations. The Responsible Person is responsible for overseeing the corporate governance of the fund.

PPFs cannot give money to individuals. They can only donate to organisations with DGR status. Because of this, some critics say that you might as well give the money directly to the DGR and not waste time on donating through your personal foundation. There is some truth in this but there are some real advantages in establishing the PPF.

(a) PPFs are relatively cheap to set up ($5,000-10,000 plus ongoing auditing fees).

(b) When the foundation is a family enterprise it has the potential to engender a tradition of philanthropy in the family; one that may continue from generation to generation. It makes philanthropy a shared family interest and characteristic. It encourages the younger generations to be giving as well as passing on basic business skills where the children are involved in the administration of the fund. (One of Australia's great philanthropic funds is that established and operated by the Myer family. Its motto is "Philanthropy is the glue that holds the family together".)

(c) There are also significant financial advantages in establishing a PPF. It allows you to build up a sizeable fund over a period of years whilst still claiming a tax deduction in the year of the gift. You give to the fund each year and allow it to build up until it reaches a capital base that can be substantial. That capital base is something that you agree with the ATO. Until that capital base is achieved, the money accumulates in the fund, income tax free, earning compound interest. No other mechanism allows you to do this. Once the agreed capital base is reached, the fund is only required to distribute amounts over the capital base amount. Accumulating and investing the trust fund money enables an initial donation to turn into something much greater.

30
MUSIC IN ADVERTISING

THE USE OF MUSIC IN ADVERTISING IS A VERY IMPORTANT SOURCE OF ANCILLARY INCOME TO COMPOSERS AND THEIR PUBLISHERS. THIS CHAPTER DISCUSSES THE THREE MAIN METHODS OF OBTAINING MUSIC FOR THESE PURPOSES: LICENSING ALREADY RECORDED MATERIAL, USING PRODUCTION MUSIC AND COMMISSIONING NEW WORKS.

It is generally accepted that this sector of the industry was born on New Years Eve 1928 when a local Minnesota radio station broadcast a little song asking 'Have You Tried Wheaties?'. The marketing and promotion business has for many years realised that the service or product that they wish to promote can be enhanced by association with music. Nowadays, almost all radio and television advertisements use music.

If you actively and critically listen to the music used in radio and television advertisements you will notice that advertisers use music with varying degrees of sophistication. Some advertisers use it as though it is an after-thought rather than an integral part of the communication process. Listen to the music that adds nothing to or even interferes with the purpose of the advertisement. In contrast, listen to the great uses of music: In these cases the music becomes the company's audio logo.

Many composers make their entire living (and a very good living too) writing music for radio and television advertisements and other corporate promotions. Others find that songs they have already released on record can enjoy a whole new financial life if they get used in an advertising campaign.

SOURCES OF MUSIC

Advertisers have a choice – they can use so-called 'production music' (sometimes called 'mood music' or 'library music'), commission a composer to write new music for the advertisement, or license particular tracks of material which have already been released on record.

COMMISSIONING ORIGINAL MUSIC

For many composers, their principal source of income is from the advertising industry. They are sometimes commissioned just to write the jingle theme but, more commonly these days, composers are commissioned to write the theme plus supply the fully leadered and cued sound recording of the music. The ready availability of compact, inexpensive recording equipment with high production quality allows composers to supply the complete product, to the financial benefit of both the composers and the commissioners.

In Australia, most jingle writers tend to be small but sophisticated operations that write and arrange the music in-house and also usually make the sound recordings on their own (often very sophisticated) equipment.

It is rare for lawyers to get involved in the negotiation of the commission agreement between the jingle writer and the advertising agency. Many of these agreements are still done verbally or with just a letter of confirmation. With many deals, particularly the smaller ones, there is no paperwork other than a standard form invoice. When an agency does use a written contract, it is usually perceived by the agency as being 'standard form', which really means only that it does not invite negotiation!

Many of the top jingle writers have developed their own standard contracts because many agencies have not taken the initiative to develop their own agreements. The composers find that if they submit their own simple agreement, the advertising agency is happy to use it. If this is possible, you can be sure that the agreement will be fairer to the composer than one that was drafted by the agency's lawyers!

Whether you are a large jingle house or an individual composer, there are two deal points that are always the most contentious: the budget and control of the rights.

THE RIGHTS

Whether the jingle writer will be able to retain any rights in the composition will depend on the relative negotiating power of the parties. At the end of the day, there are always more composers than there are advertisers.

It is common for the advertising agency/client to demand all rights in the jingle but there are no rules. Each jingle writer has to consider how much market power he or she has. The top writers can demand the retention of certain rights most of the time; the rest take the work on the best terms they can negotiate. The standard deal at the moment is a 24 month non-exclusive licence. However, some advertisers have started demanding an assignment of all rights. For that, they should expect to pay a 100% uplift.

If you are a jingle writer, you must remember that if you sign over all rights to the agency, you are losing all rights to future income from your work (other than performance income via APRA if you are a member). If the client uses the tune for 50 years (remember 'I Love Aeroplane Jelly'?) you will get no more for your work. If the client decides to rearrange the tune and reuse it in another form, the arranger will get paid but you will not. If the client decides to rework the tune, it has no obligation to use the original composer. The new composer who does the rewrite will get a fee, but you will not.

THE BUDGET

There are no rules for establishing the proper fee for writing a jingle. Every job will have different demands. This said, you must develop a standard budget sheet so that you can be sure that you will make the profit that you need from the job. After all, if you do too many jobs at a break-even or even at a loss in order to get the work, you are merely subsidising the advertiser. Worse, you will eventually go broke.

In Australia, the sources of a jingle writer's income are quite limited. Basically they are as follows:

DEMO FEES

Advertising agencies are notoriously insecure about their creative decisions. As a result, they often send out the brief to a number of jingle houses and get them to pitch their ideas. In return they offer nominal demo fees. These usually contain no margin for profit. The usual demo fee of $2,000 to $3,000 won't even pay the true overhead costs of producing the demo. Still, if you don't pitch, you are not in the race for the job.

Some agencies ask composers to do the demo 'on spec'. Avoid their kind invitation unless you are really desperate. There is no reason why you should subsidise the client's market research. Look at the car the advertising agency executive is driving and look at yours, and then ask yourself how much the agency is bleeding on behalf of its client.

CREATIVE FEES

The commission fee for an Australian commercial can vary from $1,000 to $15,000 for small jobs, to well over $50,000 for very large corporate campaigns with a large amount of music such as the Qantas campaign! There is no rule. The market is dependent on the status of the composer, his or her ability to negotiate, the size of the client advertiser and extent of the advertising campaign. In the United States a jingle house will pay-through about 25% (but up to 50%) of the creative fee to the hired composer. Here, because the jingle house is usually the composer's own business, this sort of division doesn't usually happen. The house keeps all.

The factors that you will take into account when deciding upon your creative fee will include the following:

- What is the market prominence of the advertiser?
- Is the ad going to be local, regional, national or international?
- What media will the advertisement be used in?
- What will be the length of the campaign?
- What is your usual rate for work of this sort?
- Are there any factors that should persuade you to raise or lower your usual remuneration for this work?

ARRANGING FEES

A freelance arranger will usually expect to be paid no less than the scale provided by the Arrangers' Guild. This scale is very modest and should be treated only as a minimum. Even when the arranging is done within the jingle house, a budget line should be included for this service.

In the United States a freelance arranger gets 30% to 40% of the arranging fee from the jingle house. In Australia we don't work on a percentage basis; it's a fee. While small jobs may be only around the $2,000 to $4,000 range, there is a trend with advertising agencies to purchase publishing rights for popular songs and have them re-recorded and/or re-arranged to suit their commercials. This sort of work is more and more common. The arranging fees then approximate original composed music because the agency will want production standards equivalent with modern pop music. This justifies a higher fee than 'mere' arranging.

SESSION FEES

If the composer is also expected to perform on the recording, it is only reasonable that he or she is paid for this work. This is different work from composing and it should be paid for separately. Session musicians are paid according to union scale on a per call basis. Again, these rates are minimums and established session musicians earn much more.

If you are a composer who is doing the whole project in-house, remember that your budget should include a line for session musicians. If you don't put this into the calculation you are basically performing for nothing. Why should you? If you use session musicians, don't forget to get the necessary clearances under the Performers' Protection legislation.

RESIDUALS

In the United States, successful jingle writers are very wealthy indeed. This is because the creative fee for writing the music is really the thin edge of the remuneration wedge. The real money is made out of residuals.

Negotiated by their union, singers get residuals for each use of their performance. For an advertisement in a big campaign this can amount to well over a hundred thousand dollars. Even small campaigns will net the singer $5,000 to $10,000 a year.

Accordingly, if you are the composer of a commercial in the United States, you will make very sure that, if your bargaining power permits, your contract will also state that you will be one of the singers used in the jingle. It is ironic that the creator of the jingle is paid less than the singer who merely dropped in for a call and performed it, but that just reflects the relative bargaining power of the unions representing composers and singers. Because of this, several composers write themselves into the deal as musicians (e.g. as guitarist or keyboard players) and often they'll be down as several (vocalist, guitar player, bass player AND keyboards!!!) The fees start looking really good then.

PUBLIC PERFORMANCE ROYALTIES

Jingle writers are eligible to receive income from APRA for the public performance of their work. Some years ago the radio and television stations were obliged to report all their jingles broadcasts. The only problem was that they didn't.

The payment of public performance royalties for the use of music in advertisements is a complex matter. In the past, APRA just paid a single jingle fee (of between $500 and $600) no matter how many times the jingle aired. Increasingly, as technology is allowing the capture of more sophisticated information, the fees are becoming more use-related. For example, in television uses:

- Music contained in station IDs and program promotions receives 15% of a full credit for each second of duration;
- Music contained in advertisements (including 'infomercials') and public service announcements receive 7.5% of a full credit for each second of duration;
- Music 'tags' included in television advertisements are, in the absence of a stated duration, paid at 5% of the total value of the commercial or, if the duration of the 'tag' is provided, that 'tag' is paid at the relevant percentage of 30 seconds.

(See: http://www.apra.com.au/general/all_about_royalties-television.asp).

At the moment, the broadcast of jingles by radio are still calculated by statistical sampling methods (principally because these uses are not reported electronically to APRA like most other broadcast music.) If a jingle is identified in the surveyed sample it will be subject to a 50% weighting (See: http://www.apra.com.au/general/all_about_royalties-radio.asp).

Now, the responsibility is on the jingle writer to report which stations are broadcasting their work. Each station must be reported by the writer (unless it is a State or nationwide campaign). The more stations you report, the more money you make. That said, the public performance income from jingles is not calculated merely on the frequency of play but upon the population base for each broadcast station, the time of day of broadcast and the revenue earned from that station. Small wonder that APRA's computer is known by the staff as 'Deep Thought'!

PRODUCTION MUSIC

Production music is basically a library of material composed and recorded especially for use in film. It is also referred to as library music or mood music. If you want 'love music', 'earthquake music', 'battle music' or whatever, there is production music available. Much of it is instrumental but it spans almost all musical categories.

Production music libraries are created and administered either by music publishers or by specialist production music suppliers (usually American, British or European). They either commission musicians to compose and record the material on the basis of a 50/50 split of income, or select works that are out of copyright and re-record the material so that they have no copyright obligation to third parties.

HOW LIBRARIES WORK

Production music libraries work in various ways. Production music is generally pre-recorded on compact disc and production houses buy or hire these so that they can use them as they need. (Remember that in this context, production houses include television and radio stations, advertising agencies, jingle houses, corporate and in-store video producers and so on.)

If the discs themselves are sold, the publisher usually only charges cost price (including import charges, transport costs, etc). Their intention is not to make money out of the discs, but rather from the use of the material on the discs. You own the discs but pay for the material you use. In contrast, some libraries sell sets of their compact discs of production music outright. With these, the purchase price (usually about $100 per disc) includes a pre-payment of all licence fees. You buy the disc and with it the right to unlimited use of the material, throughout the world and in perpetuity. A third variation is provided by production music libraries (usually based in the United States), which allow unlimited use of their material for a set annual fee.

Assuming that you are using a pay-for-play type library (for this is by far the most common) you will have a written licence agreement with the owner of the library. Some owners do their own administration and provide and administer their own licence agreements but most prefer to be represented in Australia through Australasian Mechanical Copyright Owners Society (AMCOS). The service provided by AMCOS is a cost-effective and simple one. The various music libraries grant AMCOS an exclusive licence to administer their mechanical rights licences and collect the fees resulting from usage. By combining in this way, the libraries using AMCOS enjoy the cost-benefit of sharing the administrative overhead that is involved in the licensing and collection process.

The producer of the soundtrack for the commercial selects the material he or she wants and only pays for the amount actually used. Within 28 days of using the music the production house must submit a completed cue sheet to AMCOS and pay the fees in accordance with the schedule of fees. AMCOS then pays through the fees (on a quarterly basis) to the publisher.

Some production houses use so much library music that the above system (where each use is individually reported) is too time-consuming. These users include radio stations, television stations and music-on-hold providers. These users can opt to pay a blanket annual licence fee. The annual fee is distributed to the relevant publishers according to the usage reports submitted by the companies to AMCOS.

The licence covers not only the right to reproduce the musical work but also includes the right to reproduce the sound recording which embodies that work.

Production music is further discussed in the Chapter 31, **Music in Film**.

LICENSING PRERECORDED AND RELEASED MATERIAL

The third means of obtaining music for use in advertising is the licensing of material that has already been released on records.

Recently there has been a great increase in the amount of licensing of standards or hit songs from the not very distant past. 'Up Up And Away' has obvious appeal for an airline commercial but most advertising agencies seem to shy away from using a song where the association between the words and the product is too obvious. Rather, they try to associate the feel and appeal of the original song with the new product. For example, there is no obvious association between jeans and Joe Cocker's song 'The Letter', but it was a hugely successful combination for Levi Strauss. It appealed to the Jack Kerouac instinct in young jeans buyers, as well as those who bought their first pair of jeans many sizes ago. Similarly, 'I Still Call Australia Home' has been a terrific success for Qantas. It has been the centrepiece of their television campaign for several years.

Some publishers license such songs themselves but others subcontract AMCOS to provide the administration of this process for them. As many composers these days have a clause in their publishing contracts which require the publisher to get the prior written consent of the writer before a work is licensed for advertising purposes, most publishers are very careful in granting such licences. The last thing they want is have an unhappy writer, let alone breach the publishing agreement and give the composer grounds for terminating it.

The fee for using a work that has already been released on record will depend on its success as a recorded work. If the song was a smash hit or has been recorded a number of times by various artists, the price will be high. If you want to use 'My Way' to advertise your particular service or product you can expect to pay royally for the commercial advantage of associating your business with such an international hit which has such an immediate recognition factor. Fees vary from $2,000 for a little-known local track to more than $500,000 for a runaway success that is to be used in a national and international campaign.

It must also be remembered that if you want to use the original sound recording (rather than re-record the work) you also have to get a licence from the owner of the copyright in the sound recording. Fees for such uses are usually about the same as those paid to the owner of the copyright in the song. Usually the owner of the copyright in the sound recording is the record company that made the record and it is usually the record company that negotiates and issues the licence. The fee will very much depend upon the artist whose version you want to use.

Use of recordings in soundtracks is generally discussed in Chapter 31, **Music in Film**.

31
MUSIC IN FILM

THE SOUNDTRACK IS AN INTEGRAL FACTOR IN THE AESTHETIC AND COMMERCIAL SUCCESS OF ANY FILM. THIS CHAPTER DISCUSSES THE THREE PRINCIPAL WAYS THAT FILM MUSIC IS OBTAINED: COMMISSIONING ORIGINAL MUSIC, USING PRODUCTION MUSIC AND THE LICENSING OF PRERECORDED AND RELEASED MATERIAL. THE COMMISSION CONTRACT IS DISCUSSED AND THE AGSC MODEL AGREEMENT IS PROVIDED, TOGETHER WITH A SHORT-FORM COMMISSION AGREEMENT FOR A LOW BUDGET FILM.

Musical accompaniment has been a feature of films from the beginning, but a single piano player with a sound effects box bears little relationship to the technical and legal complications associated with creating a film soundtrack for a modern film. Combining the two media – films and recordings – is a comparatively recent development.

Eugene A. Lauste made several short talkies between 1910 and 1914 before the Great War halted his efforts. The following decade was a period when every laboratory seemed to be trying to create a commercially viable synchronisation technology. There were two basic motion picture sound systems – sound-on-disc and sound-on-film. Edison Laboratories, Bell Laboratories, General Electric, Western Electric and J.T. Tykociner, all developed systems which managed the task with varying degrees of success.

Beside the fact that the sound quality of all of the systems was hard to love there was also great resistance from the theatre owners who resisted the expenditure of large amounts of money to equip the theatres with sound systems and from the producers who had large stocks of silent movies.

In 1923 the Rivoli Theater in New York exhibited one of the first programs of short de Forest Phonofilms, but the big breakthrough occurred on 6 August 1926 when 'Don Juan' opened in New York with the overture to Wagner's *Tannhauser* recorded by the New York Philharmonic. It didn't have dialogue, just music – the film composer's dream! But just a year later, the death of the silent movies was assured by the success of 'The Jazz Singer', starring Al Jolson. It was the first talkie – and from then on, screen composers had to put up with actors talking over the top of their work.

AND NOW TO THE PRESENT

Film production is a complex business and raising the capital to make a film is highly technical and fraught with peculiar problems. One of these, which affects those who compose and record music for films, is the insistence of producers on owning complete copyright ownership of all the copyright material included in any film. There are exceptions of course, but this is the industry's starting point. Many musicians and composers find this practice both odd and repugnant when they start in the industry. For many, this reaction does not alter even once they understand the reasons for the practice.

In many cases, the appropriation of all rights is forced upon producers by the demands of overseas (especially United States) distributors. They are (or pretend to be) reluctant to deal with films that come with 'strings' such as limitations on the way the film can be marketed, or exploited. It seems safe to assume that moral rights have never been a hot topic of conversation over the movie moguls' dinner tables. The idea of a copyright owner having some say in the way their work in a film is used (both in the film and in non-film exploitations) strikes at the very heart of the free enterprise system. Or something like that anyway.

When negotiating contracts for music in films you need to recognise these industry idiosyncrasies. Composers and soundtrack producers have to know what is possible and what is not.

SOURCES OF MUSIC

Most films these days have music. It is often fundamental to the atmosphere and impact of the visual image. The haunting panpipe musician in 'Picnic at Hanging Rock' is a perfect example of music complementing the story-line and images. In fact, the music was not especially commissioned. It was chosen at the last minute and licensed from a rather obscure record, yet it became identified with the film and undoubtedly was a factor in the film's success (as well as creating a whole new market for records of panpipes).

Some directors are quite specific in their requirements for music. They give precise descriptions and are constantly involved in its development. Others may just run off a video of the roughs, send it to whoever is responsible for the soundtrack and leave it to them to decide. Some producers such as Woody Allen are in the enviable position of being able to commission or license music (usually the latter), do an interim edit with the soundtrack in it, re-evaluate the film as a whole and re-shoot parts he or she does not like, then secure new music for the soundtrack. Pure luxury.

Film producers have several possible sources of soundtrack music and recordings.

- Production music (what used to be called Library Music) and sound-effects libraries.
- Licensed works and recordings.
- Specially commissioned works and recordings.

The decision about which to use will depend on the film's artistic requirements, the available money and the available time.

PRODUCTION MUSIC

Several of the large publishers have each created a repertoire of recordings that they refer to as library music or production music. Zomba Music, BMG and EMI probably have the biggest libraries. Recently, others have spotted the demand and have also created (or bought) libraries of recordings, particularly classical recordings that were in limited supply. These libraries have recorded music for inclusion (synchronisation) in the soundtracks of films and advertisements.

Music libraries have been a source of music for advertising agencies for many years. The libraries are able to grant non-exclusive licences relatively quickly and relatively cheaply compared with commissioned works and recordings. Of course, users have to take their chances that they will be able to find a piece of music suitable for their needs.

Generally, both the compositions and the recordings are assigned to the library. In this way, the copyright in the works and the recordings are always owned outright by the library, with the exception of the composer's public performance right, which remains with the composer (as required by APRA's rules). The publisher selects the repertoire and the composer pays for the production and markets the recordings. The publisher and composer/artist then share the mechanical and the performance income equally.

It is simple, cheap and profitable for all concerned. Unless his or her contract specifies otherwise, if production music is used behind a commercial, the composer will not get any additional fees from the library, even though that piece of music may be played thousands of times.

APRA AND PRODUCTION MUSIC

APRA logs the use of all kinds of music used by television and radio stations. Use of production music is measured in seconds: 1 point per second for TV; 1 point per 15 seconds for film. This calculation is made from the cue sheets provided by the production company or the composer as the case may be.

For advertisements, there is no cue sheet system and there are considerable problems in logging these uses. Although every advertising agency has a unique key number identifier, there is no uniformity between the numbers and it is presently impossible for APRA to link particular pieces of music with the key numbers. The process of keeping track of the uses is made relatively simple in the United Kingdom, where a universal numbering system has been adopted to identify each commercial. Here, however, key numbers are only mandatory for drug and alcohol advertisements. Although APRA continues to try to get both TV and radio stations to supply it with commercial broadcast information, for now, the system is dependent on self-reporting. This can be done on-line.

Presumably digital technology will provide an easy way of 'tagging' music, provided advertising agencies, broadcasters and APRA can formulate an industry standard. There are international initiatives afoot to do just that, although they are a long way from being put into practice.

AMCOS AND PRODUCTION MUSIC

Most production music for films is licensed through AMCOS. Clearance requests should be in writing, setting out the intended purpose to which the music will be put and the duration of the piece needed. AMCOS will process it and advise you of the licence fee, which will vary according to the duration of the music needed and the nature of the use. These libraries make money by being able to license all the recordings over and over, so exclusive licences are out of the question.

Sound effects are also available from libraries. Hollywood Edge, BBC and EMI (amongst others) have specially created boxed multiple sets of compact discs with hundreds of sound effects. These can be suitable for sampling and for creating sound envelopes in emulators. In most cases, the purchase price includes a licence to reproduce the sound effects, but read the label carefully and do not assume you can copy it unless you have made thorough inquiries. Better to do this than indulge in the all too frequent practice of sampling someone else's recording and risking an infringement action.

(For further discussion of Production Music see Chapter 30, **Music In Advertising**.)

LICENSING EXISTING RECORDINGS

If a filmmaker wants to synchronise an existing recording, at least two licences are needed: one from the owner of the recording and another from each owner of the musical work.

FINDING THE OWNER OF THE RIGHTS IN THE SOUND RECORDING

Directors seem to love obscure recordings. Unfortunately, old recordings usually have very tangled histories of ownership. Often it is a major effort just finding who the owner is, let alone trying to negotiate a licence. Companies go into liquidation and somehow the rights in the recordings get overlooked in the rush to sell off the assets. No doubt someone would know who bought the office furniture, but try tracking down a master tape and see what happens. Playing hunt-the-owner inevitably prolongs the licensing process and increases the cost of getting the licence, assuming the hunt is successful. That is one reason film makers should always have a few alternative tracks in the clearance pipeline, just in case there is a hitch with the first option.

It can even be a real task to find the owners of many quite recent recordings, if they are on obscure labels. Experienced music lawyers can help track down the owners and negotiate the necessary rights and the licence fees. There are also organisations, both in Australia and overseas, who assist filmmakers find licensors and negotiate licences. The actual licence itself should always be handled by a lawyer or a copyright licensing agent with experience in the area. It is far from simple.

There are also catalogues that can be consulted if an owner cannot be readily located. ARIA keeps a list of labels owned or controlled by its members, but this may not include really obscure recordings nor does it include labels without Australian representatives. The Record Industry Association of America and the British Museum also hold information on old and obscure recordings.

FINDING THE OWNER OF THE RIGHTS IN THE MUSIC

The owner of the rights in the musical work is usually a publisher. Identifying the work's publisher is usually fairly easy, but remember that different publishers may control the same work in different territories. Many songs have more than one publisher (referred to in Australia but not the US, as 'split publishing'). Assuming the film is going to be shown in more than one country, clearances have to be secured from all the publishers in all countries in which the film is to be released.

The fees publishers require for such licences vary with the publisher and the nature of the project. Small budget productions will usually be able to negotiate a single flat fee. It is a matter for negotiation.

WHERE NO OWNER CAN BE FOUND

If no owner can be found, even after exhaustive searches, the producer has to decide whether the music is so important it will still be used (and take the risk of a copyright owner springing out of the bushes after the film is released) or whether to use another piece of music. Proof of a comprehensive attempt to locate the owner will probably be a reasonable defence to a claim for flagrant copyright infringement, but who needs a claim like that in the first place? Better to use recordings whose owners can at least be found. (If the film has investors, distributors or insurers they will demand a full chain of title and the producer's solicitor has to provide a letter of assurance stating that all rights have been acquired.)

Many sound recordings are owned by an overseas entity and the clearance request will have to be referred to them, even if they have an Australian office or representative. Sometimes artists' permissions are also needed. This can prolong the approval process, especially in the case of classical recordings. It also makes the fees somewhat higher. It pays to shop around with recordings from different countries. The United Kingdom and Germany tend to be the dearest.

LICENCE FEES

The licence fee is entirely a matter for negotiation. It depends upon the fame of the work, nature of the rights wanted, the intended use and the scope of the territory. When in doubt as to what you actually need, get a quote for all rights (with each set of rights separately quoted) so you can select those you need immediately. The others can be secured later (the quote locks them in to that price), if the film's success justifies the additional expense.

As a general rule, the fee will increase in direct proportion to the status of the song (i.e. hits cost more than the rest) and whether the song is featured or background. The fee for foreground use of a little-known song may exceed that for background use of a standard.

CLEARANCE PROCEDURES

Clearance requests should always be in writing. Clearance requests for both the work and the recording should include:

- the proposed licensee's name;
- a very brief synopsis of the film and an indication of its budget;
- the producer and director and the production company;
- the name of the work(s) you want. Quote catalogue numbers and label names wherever possible, to make their task easier;
- the duration of music wanted in the soundtrack and the context in which it will be used;
- whether the use will be as background or foreground music;

- the territories where the film will be released; and
- the rights needed, such as:
    - (a) synchronisation
    - (b) theatrical performance
    - (c) home video
    - (d) broadcast (free to air television)
    - (e) cable/subscriber television
    - (f) any other unusual use.

Finally, never assume you have a licence until you actually see the piece of paper.

COMMISSIONED MUSIC

There are only a few composers in Australia who are able to make a reasonable living by writing exclusively for feature films and television mini-series. Nevertheless, there are still plenty of documentaries and made-for-television projects being made, all of which need music and a growing number of performers and composers are using screen composing as an adjunct to their other activities.

Where a film needs original music, the producer has to make decisions in ample time to have an appropriate budget built into the film's overall production budget and to leave enough time to commission a composer to complete the score and to have it recorded. There has to be enough time to allow the process to be completed in time for film editing. This is often the first time the visuals and the music actually meet. Unless there is enough time to fix any problems, there are likely to be some very unpleasant scenes and recriminations. This is why film music contracts always contain clauses to the effect that, as far as delivery dates are concerned, 'time is of the essence'. They aren't kidding.

As already mentioned, film producers generally insist on owning the copyrights in both the music and the sound recording they commission. They feel this is necessary, to have complete freedom to exploit the film. They frequently need to satisfy investors that the film's marketing and exploitation cannot be held hostage by various copyright owners.

If you do have reasonable bargaining power, you may be able to retain some rights. Because copyright can be divided any which-way, it should be possible to structure the deal in a way that gives the producer ownership of the parts it needs, and for you to retain the rest of the copyright not actually needed for the film.

In any event, all screen composers should be members of APRA. All screen commissioning contracts have a clause which excludes rights already assigned to APRA. This assures you of getting public performance royalties even though you have assigned all of your other rights. Just make sure that the contract also commits the producer to notifying you when a sale is made in a particular territory and the name of the film in that territory so that APRA can more readily identify the income.

COMPOSERS WITH PUBLISHING CONTRACTS

If you already have an exclusive writing agreement in place and you are offered a screen composing job, the first thing you should do is call your publisher.

Under your contract with the publisher, you will probably have undertaken to write exclusively for that publisher. If you were to contract with a film production company without your publisher's consent, you would almost certainly be breaching your publishing agreement. You will also have assigned or licensed exclusively to the publisher, the entire copyright in all your compositions as and when they are created. This means you would not be able to deliver any rights in the compositions to the film production company in any event!

Remember that advance you got when you did your publishing deal? That was in exchange for those rights. Besides, you need to work with your publisher if you want to get the job. Getting a film commission is hard enough without provoking a contract dispute with your publisher and the film producer.

Before gnashing your teeth and complaining about your publisher getting in the way – consider how your publisher could help you get a better deal. The publisher has more bargaining clout than most individual writers and may be part of a multinational publishing group which might be willing to help promote the film. It might be able to assist the producer to find secondary means of exploiting the soundtrack (e.g. release of the soundtrack as a record in its own right). Your publisher benefits from you being commissioned and from having your works recorded and exploited. There really is very little likelihood that a publisher will impede a reasonable deal. A good publisher will see it as an opportunity not to be missed.

Ultimately, the film producer must make the contract with the publisher, not you, because the publisher owns the rights. The publisher will negotiate the deal (in consultation with you) and collect any advances and fees. In turn, it will account to you in accordance with the terms of your publishing deal.

THE COMMISSION CONTRACT

Most production companies have their own film commissioning contracts which they will insist on using. Some are more satisfactory than others. As already mentioned, some items are negotiable. Some are not. Using the producer's contract is not a problem in itself, provided the end result is acceptable.

In any event, these contracts are usually too convoluted not to be handled by an expert, but you need to know how they work, and the reasons for the conditions they contain.

COMPOSING THE MUSIC AND MAKING THE SOUNDTRACK

The person who composes the music may not be the same person who makes the sound recording. It very much depends upon the kind of music and the scale of the production. Orchestral music will usually be recorded by the production company.

Smaller budget films, documentaries and television productions are more likely to have the same person composing the music and making the sound recording. This means the agreement will have to be a recording agreement as well as a music writing agreement.

Having to deal with these two rather different roles makes these agreements a bit unusual. Particular care is needed. All too many of these contracts contain confusion between rights in the musical works and rights in the sound recordings of those works.

The Australian Guild of Screen Composers has a standard contract it has approved as providing acceptable protection and rights to those making soundtracks. Contact details are at the end of this chapter. The Guild has kindly agreed to parts of its standard contract being reproduced below, with the commentary. This will help show the kind of clauses found in this type of agreement.

GENERAL TERMS

Following is a guide to the usual terms in the usual commission contract and what to look out for:

PARTIES

The commissioning party will be the film production company, which makes and owns the film. It will contract with you, as the writer, and/or with your publisher, for your services. Remember that unless you are dealing with a major film production company (or the Hollywood studios) most production companies are shelf companies with no other assets, no 'business' and no independent existence. How's that for a fair warning? In other words, know the party with whom you will be contracting, and try to get some guarantee that it will not just fold up leaving you as yet another unsecured creditor.

YOUR TASKS

You will be commissioned to:

- compose original music; and
- make adaptations of others' music as directed.

If you will also be making the recording, you will be commissioned to:

- select and engage musicians, studios, equipment and performers;
- obtain all clearances; and (perhaps)
- produce a sound recording, suitable for inclusion in the soundtrack of the film.

There will usually be a general requirement that you follow guidelines set by the director or someone nominated by the producer. You may be given discretion as to the nature of the music (although this will generally have been discussed at length before you were offered the contract).

If you are to deliver a sound recording, there will be a time limit by which it must be delivered in finished form, to enable the director and editors to assess the recording and to synchronise it with the visuals. The format in which sound recordings are to be delivered is usually prescribed too. Many producers want the multitracks as well as the mixed two-track master.

The quantity of music to be delivered will usually be defined by its place in the film (i.e. foreground, background, opening and end credits) and by duration. It is almost impossible to give a written definition of the desired music ('It must be good; it must be scary; it must be loud'), so the director usually retains the power to give ongoing instructions to the composer. Watch out for unreasonable directions. Not only could these cause delivery to be delayed but they can add significant costs which will not have been included in the original budget. Unexpected changes to the job description or to the tasks need to be considered carefully to see if they will adversely affect your ability to comply with the contract's terms.

If you are also making the sound recording, you will be responsible for getting clearances for the use of any music you use that you have not written, or to use excerpts or samples of others' sound recordings. This means writing clearance requests to all the appropriate publishers, wherever they may be and getting positive replies. If they demand fees, your budget has to include an allowance to cover them or you will be paying for them out of your profit margin.

You will also have to make sure you secure written consents under the performers protection part of the Copyright Act. Essentially, these consents are a written confirmation by each musician/performer that they consent to their performance being recorded and synchronised with visual images.

The standard contract of the Australian Guild of Screen Composers contains a Performers' Agreement and Consent that has to be signed by each and every performer and musician. The Consent includes the following:

> *I assign ... all rights I may have in relation to Sound Recordings (including my performances therein) made during the recording session referred to above ... including without limitation all rights arising pursuant to Part XIA of the Copyright Act 1968.*
>
> *I consent to the recording of my performances ... being used for the production of Sound Recordings and the use of (them) in all media ... including ... as part of the soundtrack of cinematographic films and on a soundtrack album.*
>
> *I waive all moral rights I may have in my performances recorded for inclusion in the Sound Recordings.*
>
> *I acknowledge that ... has the right to use, adapt, edit, mix, add to, subtract from, arrange, ... and combine the same with other performances ...*
>
> *I acknowledge that ... is the sole owner of the Sound Recordings and as the sole owner ... (is) exclusively entitled to exploit the Sound Recordings and to receive all proceeds from such exploitation.*

Unless signed consents can be provided for every musician, session singer, narrator and whatever, there is a risk that the film could be severely disrupted if an aggrieved performer sought to enforce their rights under the Copyright Act. If that happened, you, as the person responsible for getting the consents, would be liable for any losses the producers suffered as a result of your oversight. Be warned!

DELIVERY

When delivery dates are specified, these have to be met, or there will be a substantial penalty (and a reduction of the fee you would otherwise get), so you must allow yourself ample time to cover the seemingly inevitable hitches in production. For your own protection, always insist on inclusion of a clause that absolves you from liability in the event that delivery is delayed (or completely impossible) because of circumstances beyond your control (e.g. the multitrack disintegrates at the last moment – it has happened!). Prompt compliance is a two-way street. The producer has to provide the visuals as soon as possible, to give everyone a chance to start work.

The Guild contract includes a provision:

> *The Producer covenants ... to deliver the fine cut in accordance with the Music Production Timetable ... and to advise the Composer of any proposed changes to the Music Production Timetable and in particular any delays regarding the delivery of the fine cut.*

The Guild contract also provides for the composer to have 14 days to cure any default. In effect, if you do not meet a deadline you would have an additional 14 days. Some producers will resist a 'days to cure' provision because they are concerned that the production schedule may be disrupted. Late delivery of the soundtrack could lead to many people being unable to continue with their tasks, so the whole film's production timetable could be thrown out. On the other hand, the producer could agree to leave a 'days to cure' clause in and move the specified delivery dates forward by the same number of days.

COPYRIGHT OWNERSHIP OF MUSIC AND SOUND RECORDINGS

As already discussed, film production companies will usually want the copyright in the commissioned music to be assigned to it. Some companies will purport to take on the role of publisher and the agreement may include royalty provisions. If you're lucky, they may be comparable to those in a standard music publishing agreement. Other companies will offer a one-off payment in lieu of royalties. Always be careful of film producers who want to be your publisher. Most know nothing about publishing and do not have the infrastructure necessary to exploit and protect your works.

Naturally, once the works are assigned, you cannot use them again. They are the company's property. Beware of terms which attempt (inadvertently or quite deliberately) to affect your public performance income or which attempt to negate your right to receive mechanical copyright royalties on records and videos sold to the public. These mechanical royalties can be a valuable source of income if the soundtrack proves to be a hit. This may not be relevant, however, in some kinds of film or where the music is largely incidental or is background music which is unlikely to have large-scale commercial value.

Before doing any deal, join APRA. All assignments of copyrights have to be subject to rights already assigned, or to be assigned, to APRA. This protects your public performance rights.

Always be wary of clauses that involve you assigning all rights in any form of exploitation, even if not yet invented. If the producer insists on this being kept in, try to insist on a royalty mechanism of some kind. If the production company still exists in 40 years' time, you'll be thankful when the royalty cheque comes in. If the company's gone into the ether, at least you tried!

As far as the sound recording itself is concerned, under s.97(3) of the Copyright Act, where a person makes a sound recording for another person in return for 'valuable consideration' (e.g. a fee or a royalty), the latter is the copyright owner, unless there is an agreement to the contrary. To be on the safe side, the film's producers will include a clause assigning copyright in all recordings to the film's owner. Naturally this must be subject to the rights of any valid pre-existing copyright owners (e.g. the owners of any sound recordings licensed from third parties or your record company, if you happen to be under contract at the time).

If you do have to assign all the copyrights to the producer, you should always try to have any unused material (e.g. songs or recordings not included in the film's final cut) re-assigned to you. Alternatively, limit the assignment to works that are actually used in the film.

The right to issue soundtrack albums is a major area of concern in these contracts. Many producers will want an exclusive right to issue or license soundtrack albums. To do this may require the music to be substantially altered or even re-recorded. You should always have the first option to do this work. The payment for that extra work should be additional to that for delivering the film soundtrack. In most cases, you will be able to negotiate a royalty on soundtrack albums, in addition to the production fee. A royalty entitlement means you might be able to negotiate an advance, which is always useful.

YOUR FEES

If you are composing only, the fee will usually be a 'once and for all' payment for the rights in the music that you assign or license to the film company. The fee is a matter for negotiation. It will be affected by the film's music budget, your bargaining power, the use to be made of the music, the extent of your services, and the extent of any rights you manage to reserve (such as mechanical copyrights, pay television rights or whatever).

By preserving public performance income and mechanicals, you at least have a long-term opportunity to collect royalties in addition to the once-off fee from the film's producer.

If you are also making the recording you will need a budget to cover rehearsals, studio time, musicians and performers, tape, mixing and editing, duplication and all the other necessary steps. On top of that is your profit. Again, the amount you get will largely be determined by the film's music budget and your negotiating skills.

When you are to make the recording and the agreement gives the producer the right to make a soundtrack album, always insist on receiving a royalty on record sales. Soundtracks frequently attract a lower royalty than the usual recording contract, because the film's producers will want to keep a percentage of whatever royalty its licensee (the record company that releases the soundtrack album) pays for the licence.

Record royalties range from a miserable 5% of the dealer price (subject to the usual deductions – see the Chapter 23, **Record Royalties**) which is the kind of percentage a record producer might get, up to perhaps 15% of that base figure, if you are performing all the music too. The percentage you get is obviously influenced by the royalty rate the film producer can extract from the record company which is going to distribute the soundtrack album. The higher the film producer's royalty, the more they can afford to pay you.

PAYMENT SCHEDULES

If you are composing (and someone else is to make the recording), then your remuneration will usually be a fee, paid in instalments; often a third on commencement, a third on delivery of a certain amount of music and the balance on completion of your obligations.

If you are also making the recording, you will be spending money as you go, securing studios, musicians, etc. You need a cash flow during production or you will run out of money and anyway, who can guarantee that the film production company will have any money by the end of the job? The budget must set out a payment schedule related to the stages of production. It is essential to define exactly what has to be delivered and when, to ensure there is no ambiguity or uncertainty as to when you are entitled to each payment.

ARTISTIC CONTROL

This is always a difficult area because you are usually being commissioned to satisfy someone else's artistic judgment rather than produce something that only has to please you. The film's producers and the director will rarely guarantee to include all or any of your music in the final cut. That is their prerogative, so long as you get paid for all your work!

You should be present when your music is being synchronised. If this involves unusual travel or expenses, these should be reimbursed by the film's producer or built into the original budget. (The risk with the latter is that the additional cost is 'invisible' to the producer, so there is no incentive to keep the costs down. Better the additional costs be seen for what they are – additional to the fee for services.)

When the synchronisation is happening, the director will often ask for changes to the music and/or the recording. You should always have first option to make any changes. If you cannot do it, so be it, but at least you will not be surprised to see your music synched into the film after someone has taken a hatchet to your carefully produced work. Any additional time needed to effect the changes (which could be quite substantial) has to be paid for in addition to whatever was paid up to your delivery of the original music and/or recording. This can be calculated on an hourly rate plus disbursements or whatever suits everyone at the time.

You need assurances that once the release print has been made, the music will not subsequently be altered without your consent. You will be known by and identified with that music. Changes can have a dramatic and adverse effect. They could mean the difference between the start and the end of a wonderful career. If it's not your music which finally gets onto the film, make sure the world knows via the production credits.

MORAL RIGHTS

As you will remember from the discussion of Moral Rights in Chapter 8, the two main Moral Rights provided by the Copyright Act are the right of the composer to be acknowledged as the author of the work and the right of the author to control the way the work is altered. You cannot usually avoid these rights by obtaining a general waiver. However, because the production of a film is such a collaborative process, the Act provides that producers are permitted to obtain a general waiver of moral rights from composers who are contracted to provide soundtrack music. Provided the waiver is in writing, unlike other users of music, film producers are not obliged to specify the ways in which they acknowledge the composer or in which they may edit or alter the composition. Film producers can simply get a general waiver of these rights.

Accordingly, score commissioning contracts always contain a clause along the following lines: "The Composer waives his/her moral rights." This is not as harsh as it seems for all that it means is that the composer is waiving the statutory rights conferred by the Copyright Act. It does not mean that the composer cannot include contractual rights in the commissioning agreement. All good commissioning agreements will contain detailed provisions as to the credits that must be accorded to the composer in the credits of the film, as well as on the packaging of the DVD and any soundtrack album. Similarly, there will be clauses that describe the rights of the producer to alter and edit the music or to retain other composers as well as clauses that give the composer a right to be given first chance to make any changes that the producer believes necessary.

PRODUCTION CREDITS

Make sure there is an obligation on the producer to include your credits on all prints and in all promotional materials relating to the film, whenever any other principal credits are actually or customarily shown.

If you are required to provide biographical information, make sure its use is restricted to use in promoting the film and that only approved biographical material is used, otherwise unintentional distortions or inaccuracies can creep in which may be counterproductive for you.

CUE SHEETS

It is always the composer's job to ensure that full cue sheets are prepared. These are usually provided to the producer, who in turn ensures that these are filed with APRA and AMCOS. These collecting societies are currently developing an on-line cue sheet facility for programs and films, which will enable production companies, broadcasters and composers to enter music cue-sheets directly into the APRA database via the APRA website. Each electronically submitted cue-sheet will be allocated a unique identification number, which can be used by broadcasters for APRA and AMCOS reporting purposes. The on-line facility is expected to be operational during the first few months of 2002. When this system is up and running, composers would be well advised to take contractual responsibility for the filing of their own cue sheets. Then, the protection of their interests is in their own hands, rather than those of the producer or agency.

ACCOUNTING

Most films in Australia are produced by $2 companies. The companies are especially incorporated for a particular film. They have no other business or income-generating activities and tend to become dormant after a few years as the film gets to the end of its commercial life. This is one reason most deals here are done on a flat-fee rather than a royalty basis. At least there is a chance you will get something. You could grow gracefully old but impoverished waiting for royalties from a film production company that has gone into liquidation. Hollywood studios are a different matter. They tend to last.

Fortunately, royalties from public performance are paid directly to the composer, thus making your income stream independent of the production company's fortunes.

IF THINGS GO WRONG

If you are late in delivering the music or soundtrack and the delay arose because you were careless or otherwise irresponsible in some way, the producers will have the right to terminate the agreement, appoint another composer, sue you for any loss they suffer because of the delay and to make you return any money already paid to you under the contract. They will start to eye your goods and chattels hungrily. With good reason too.

Completion dates are sacrosanct in the film industry. Late completion can have terrible repercussions for the film's release and its chances of success, especially if it misses a key release period (such as the Christmas holiday season). This is why these contracts tend to be very particular about what happens if things go wrong. When you agree to delivery schedules, you have to be aware of the provisions and make sure you allow for any reasonably foreseeable delays.

AUSTRALIAN GUILD OF SCREEN COMPOSERS

Screen composers should belong to the Guild. It was established by screen composers for screen composers. The Guild can be contacted through its website at www.agsc.org.au.

It is a non-profit body which provides model contracts, runs seminars and workshops, makes submissions to Government on screen composers' behalf, lobbies Canberra, publishes a quarterly newsletter and generally provides a forum for composers to meet and exchange information. Screen composers everywhere should seriously consider joining, especially if new to the business. Copies of the model contract can be purchased from the Guild. (Please note that at the time of writing, the AGSC model still needed updating to take into account the GST and Moral Rights amendments. Before using it, these issues must be included.)

**AUSTRALIAN GUILD OF SCREEN COMPOSERS'
MODEL CONTRACT**

to compose music for synchronisation with film

THE DATE OF THIS AGREEMENT is:

THE PARTIES are:

1. ....of:...
(the "Composer")

2. ....of:...
(the "Producer").

RECITALS
A. The Producer is making a film/television/video production entitled

" ...." (the "Film").
B. The Composer has agreed to make his/her services available to the Producer to compose original musical works, to make musical arrangements and to produce a sound recording for synchronisation with the Film and has agreed to license certain rights in works composed by the Composer to the Producer on and subject to the terms and conditions of this Agreement.

THE TERMS:
1. COMPOSER'S DUTIES
1.1 The Composer covenants with the Producer as follows:
    (a) to compose original musical works (the "Original Music" which expression includes each and all parts of the works) all of which shall be suitable for incorporation by the Producer into the soundtrack of the Film as the background and incidental music for the Film for such duration as is specified in Schedule B;
    (b) to make original adaptations (the "Adapted Music") of any musical works and any lyrics not composed or written by the Composer but designated by the Producer (the "Designated Works");
    (c) to select and engage musicians, to contract for recording facilities, to conduct recording sessions and to do all things necessary to produce a master sound recording in the format specified in Schedule B (the "Master Sound Recording") of professional quality suitable for incorporation into the

soundtrack of the Film and acceptable for exploitation as part of the Film throughout the territories specified in Schedule B (the "Territory");

(d) that the Master Sound Recording shall consist of the following:

(i) an original performance of the Original Music (which may include a performance by the Composer); and

(ii) an original performance of any Adapted Music

(e) to obtain all necessary written clearances (in a form substantially similar to Schedule A) from all persons performing on the Master Sound Recording (the "Clearances");

(f) to consult with the Producer as and when reasonably required in connection with the Composer's duties and as reasonably required by the Producer for the purposes of making the Film;

(g) to ensure that the Master Recording is of a high technical standard which satisfies the reasonable requirements of the Composer and the Producer; and

(h) to comply with the Music Production Timetable agreed between the parties and set out in Schedule B.

2   ATTENDANCES

2.1 With the prior consent of the composer (which shall not be unreasonably withheld) the Producer's representative may attend any recording session for the Master Sound Recording.

2.2 The Producer agrees that the Composer shall be entitled to attend the synchronisation of the Master Sound Recording. If the Producer requires the attendance of the Composer, any reasonable travel and accommodation expenses thereby incurred by the Composer shall be at the expense of the Producer. No alterations, deletions or additions shall be made to the music soundtrack after or during such synchronisation without prior consultation with the Composer.

3.   GRANT OF RIGHTS

3.1 For the Budgeted Amount specified in Schedule B, the Composer as beneficial owner hereby grants to the Producer for the full term of copyright and throughout the Territory but subject to any prior rights vested in APRA and affiliated associations:

(a) the exclusive/non-exclusive* (*delete as applicable) right throughout the Territory to reproduce the Original Music and any Adapted Music in the Master Sound Recording and to incorporate the Master Sound Recording into the soundtrack of the Film and to copy the Film embodying and reproducing the Master Sound recording; and

(b) the exclusive/non-exclusive right* (*delete as above) throughout the Territory to reproduce, perform in public, broadcast or transmit to subscribers of a diffusion service, the Original Music and any Adapted Music by means of the production sale lease and hire of copies of the Film.

3.2 The Composer agrees and acknowledges that the Producer is the sole beneficial owner of only the synchronisation rights in the Master Sound Recording throughout the Territory. (Note that this agreement does not cover the right to make a sound-track album or other ancillary rights. These must be the subject of a separate specific agreement).

3.3 The parties agree that the copy of the tape embodying the Master Sound Recording and delivered by the Composer to the Producer, shall be at all times the absolute property of the Producer.

3.4 Nothing in this Agreement shall oblige the Producer to

(a) use the results of the Composer's services pursuant to this Agreement; or

(b) to make or exploit the Film.
(Subject to clauses 11 and 12 of this Agreement, nothing in this clause shall excuse the Producer from payment to the Composer of the Budgeted Amount).

3.5 All rights in the Original Music and any Adapted Music not expressly assigned or licensed to the Producer in this Agreement are reserved to the Composer.

4. MUSIC BUDGET

4.1 An amount described in Schedule B as the "Budgeted Amount" has been allocated by the Producer for the payment of the Music Expenses and the Composer agrees to carry out his/her duties pursuant to this Agreement to the best of his/her ability and for the Budgeted Amount.

4.2 The Music Expenses include all costs associated with the composition of the Original Music and any Adapted Music and the production and reproduction of the Master Sound Recording including but not limited to fees for the Composer and musicians, performers, engineers, producers, orchestrators, transportation of instruments, hire of studio and recording facilities, recording tape, transfer costs, copying of parts for musicians and the mixing and editing of the Master Sound Recording.

4.3 The Composer shall be solely responsible for the prompt payment of all Music Expenses from the Budgeted Amount and shall not engage or employ any person or incur any other expense on the Producer's account without its prior written consent.

4.4 The Producer shall be solely responsible for all costs associated with the acquisition of copyright and other similar rights from third parties in respect of the Designated Works.

4.5 In the event that the Music Expenses exceed the Budgeted Amount the Composer shall pay and bear from his/her own resources such excess costs unless s/he has first obtained the prior written consent of the Producer to such excess costs.

4.6 After delivery of the Master Sound Recording, the Producer shall be entitled to request the Composer to compose additional music or make major alterations to the musical work and Master Sound Recording ("the Altered Master"). All such additional expenses including the writing, scoring and recording costs shall be subject to a separate budget mutually agreed upon by both parties.

    (a) The Composer will (subject to any conflicting work commitments and subject to the parties having agreed the budget for such work) remain prepared to make such alterations as are requested by the Producer.

    (b) The Composer shall complete and deliver to the Producer the Altered Master in the recording formats as described in Schedule B upon such terms as are agreed between the Composer and the Producer, such agreement not to be unreasonably withheld.

5.   MUSIC CUE SHEETS

5.1 The Composer will complete a Music Cue Sheet setting out the nature, extent and exact timing of the Original Music and cues synchronised into the sound-track of the Film together with such other information as is customarily included in music cue sheets for such productions ("the Cue Sheet").

5.2 To enable the Composer to complete the Cue Sheet the Producer will on or before the Release Print Date specified in Schedule B, either:

    (a) deliver to the Composer a video copy of the release print of the Film, or

    (b) provide the Composer with reasonable access at reasonable times to a video copy of the release print of the Film and to equipment suitable for the purpose, at premises nominated for the purpose by the Producer

5.3 The Composer will use the video copy of the release print of the Film for the purpose of completing the Cue Sheet and will within the period of two (2) weeks after the date of such delivery or access (as the case may be) deliver the cue sheet to the Producer in triplicate.

5.4 The Producer warrants that it shall not make changes additions or deletions of any kind to the Master Sound Recording and cues that appear in the video copy of the release print of the Film without first notifying and obtaining the consent of the Composer (such consent not to be unreasonably withheld).

5.5 The Composer agrees to ensure that true copies of the Cue Sheet are forwarded to APRA and its Affiliates and for that purpose the Producer agrees to notify the Composer of all places and dates of first public screenings of the Film throughout the Territory.

6. PAYMENT OF REMUNERATION

6.1 Subject to the provisions of this Agreement the Producer shall as remuneration and as full consideration for all services rendered and for all rights granted to the Producer pay the Budgeted Amount outlined in Schedule B to the Composer according to the timetable provided in Schedule B.

6.2 The Producer shall supply the Composer with a VHS copy of the release print of the Film in stereo at no charge to the Composer.

7. WARRANTIES

7.1 The Composer warrants to the Producer that:

    (a) the Original Music will be his/her original work and the Adapted Music (if any) will be his/her original adaptation and the Composer will be the sole composer adaptor and/or writer thereof;

    (b) subject to the rights of APRA and similar associations throughout the world the Composer will be the absolute owner of the copyright of the Original Music and any Adapted Music;

    (c) the Clearances and Assignments will be valid and binding;

    (d) the reproduction of the Original Music and any Adapted Music will not infringe the copyright of any person;

    (e) the Composer is entitled to license all of the rights licensed hereunder; and

    (f) the Composer has not made, and will not make, any grant or assignment which will or might conflict with or impair the complete enjoyment of the rights and privileges granted to the Producer in this Agreement.

7.2 The Composer covenants that he/she will do all such acts and execute such documents as the Producer may require to vest in or confirm to the Producer or its successors in title or licensees the rights granted by this Agreement.

7.3 The warranties contained in clause 7.1 do not apply to any material taken directly by the Composer from the Designated Work by the Producer for adaptation or revision, but shall apply to any material the Composer may add to or interpolate into that Designated Work.

8. INDEMNITY

8.1 Each Party indemnifies the other and agrees to keep the other indemnified against all actions suits proceedings claims or demands made against it by reason of breach of any of the covenants or warranties in this Agreement and against all costs damages or expenses incurred in defending and/or settling (subject to any settlement being made with the prior written consent of the indemnifying party) any such actions suits proceedings claims or demands.

9. PRODUCTION COMPANY'S WARRANTY AND INDEMNITY

9.1 In respect of Designated Works, the Producer warrants to the Composer that it has or will have the right to incorporate those works into the Film and to exploit the Film and indemnifies the Composer against all actions suits proceedings claims or demands made against him/her in respect of Designated Works and against all costs damages and expenses incurred in defending and/or settling any such actions suits proceedings claims or demands.

10. CREDIT

10.1 The Producer covenants with the Composer to include (or cause the distributor to include) in all versions of the Film released for exhibition a full and appropriate credit. The credit shall be a single credit, in the form set out in Schedule B, shall follow that of the screenwriter and shall be of a size and duration equal to that accorded the screenwriter (if any). The Composer shall also be entitled to a similarly worded credit in all major paid advertising of the Film issued by or under the direct control of the Producer whenever both the individual producer and director receive a credit.

10.2 The credit provisions of clause 10.1 shall not apply to:

(a) group, list or teaser advertising, publicity or exploitation;

(b) advertising relating to the television exhibition to the Film;

(c) advertising or publicity specifically relating to any personnel concerned in the production of the Film;

(d) trailer or other advertising on the screen, radio or television;

(e) institutional or other advertising or publicity not relating primarily to the Film;

(f) so called "Award Ads" (including considerations nominations or congratulations for an Award) relating to any personnel concerned in the production of the Film; or

(g) advertising of less than six (6) column centimetres.

10.3 (a) Nothing contained in this Agreement with respect to position or size of type of the Composer's credit shall apply to advertising or publicity material in narrative form.

(b) If the title of the Film is used more than once in the same advertisement, i.e. a so-called "regular" use and a so-called "artwork" use (such as the weaving of the title as part of the background of the advertisement or a display or fanciful use thereof) any reference in the above credit provisions to the title of the Film shall be deemed to be a reference to the "regular" use of the title.

10.4 The Producer shall use its best endeavours to ensure that the distributors and broadcasters of the Film accord the Composer credit in accordance with this Agreement on all prints and major advertising issued by such distributors and broadcasters but the company shall not be liable for the neglect or default of any such distributor or broadcaster of the credit to which the Composer is entitled.

10.5 No casual failure to afford the Composer credit in accordance with this Agreement shall constitute a breach by the Producer and the Producer agrees to correct any such casual failure promptly upon notification.

10.6 Subject to 10.7 the Composer grants to the Producer the right and licence to use and publicise the Composer's name, photographs and biography in connection with the exploitation and advertising of the Film PROVIDED THAT nothing in this Agreement shall permit the Producer to hold out the Composer as directly endorsing any product or service without the Composer's prior consent. The Producer shall obtain the prior consent of the Composer to the photographs caricatures biographies and actual or simulated likeness to be used by the Producer, such consent not to be unreasonably withheld and, once given, shall be irrevocable.

10.7 The Composer reserves the right to remove his/her credit from the Film and associated publicity, at any time up to the completion of the release print.

11. SUSPENSION

11.1 The Producer shall be entitled by notice in writing to the Composer to suspend this engagement in any of the following events:

(a) if the Composer wilfully refuses or neglects to perform his/her obligations hereunder;

(b) if the Composer is incapacitated from rendering his/her services due to ill-health or other cause; or

(c) if production of the Film is delayed by any cause outside the direct control of the Producer including but not limited to fire, casualty, accident, riot, war, act of God, enemy action, strike, lock-out, labour conditions, judicial order or enactment or incapacity of any leading artist or key production personnel.

11.2 Suspension of the engagement shall have the following effects:

    (a) it will last as long as the event giving rise to it plus such further period not exceeding 21 days as may be reasonably required by the Producer to resume using the Composer's services or it will last until this Agreement is determined;

    (b) while it lasts, payment under this Agreement will cease to fall due;

    (c) the Composer shall not agree to render services to any person which might conflict with his/her services to the Producer when the suspension ends;

    (d) the Producer will remain entitled to all rights hereby granted to it; and

    (e) the term of this engagement will continue after the suspension ends (unless it ends by determination of this Agreement) for the length of time unexpired when the suspension began.

12. TERMINATION

12.1 The Producer shall be entitled by notice in writing to the Composer to terminate this engagement (whether or not the Producer has suspended the engagement for the same or another reason) in any of the following events:

    (a) if the Composer wilfully refuses or neglects to perform his/her obligations hereunder;

    (b) if the Composer is incapacitated from rendering his/her services due to ill-health, injury or otherwise for the consecutive or aggregate period of 21 days;

    (c) if the Composer is in breach of any material term or material condition of this Agreement; and

    (d) if production of the Film is delayed by any cause outside the direct control of the Producer including but not limited to fire, casualty, accident, riot, war, act of God, enemy action, strike, lock-out, labour conditions, judicial order or enactment or incapacity of any leading artist or key production personnel for a consecutive or aggregate period of 21 days.

12.2 The Producer may by notice in writing, be entitled at any time to terminate this engagement and replace the Composer with another composer.

12.3 In the event of non-payment by the Producer of the Budgeted Amount according to the Schedule Of Payments set out in Schedule B, the Composer may give written notice to the Producer of such non-payment and, if payment is not received within seven days of the service of such notice, the Composer may terminate the licence in the Master Sound Recording, the Original Music and any Adapted Music forthwith.

12.4 On termination of this engagement the Producer shall pay the remuneration due under this Agreement up to the date of the event giving rise to termination (or the beginning of any suspension preceding termination) and the next instalment (as per Schedule B).

12.5 On the expiration or sooner determination of this engagement:

    (a) each party will remain entitled to enforce any claim against the other party arising from any breach of this Agreement occurring before termination or expiration; and

    (b) each party will remain entitled to all rights hereby granted to it.

13 NOTICES

13.1 Any notice or request required by this Agreement to be given shall be in writing and delivered, telexed, faxed or sent by registered post to the intended recipient at the address shown in this Agreement. Notices or requests shall be deemed to have been received either when personally served or 3 days after having been sent.

14 INDULGENCES

14.1 No time or other indulgence granted by one party to another party shall be deemed to constitute a waiver of any of his or its rights hereunder unless expressed to do so in writing and signed by or on behalf of the party.

15. ASSIGNMENTS

15.1 The Producer may assign or license any or all of its rights and powers under this Agreement but shall remain liable to the Composer for its obligations and this Agreement shall bind and endure for the benefit of the parties and their respective successors administrators and assigns. The Producer shall notify the Composer of each such licence, disposal or dealing insofar as it affects the Composer. The Producer shall remain liable for the payment of all fees and royalties due to the Composer hereunder and any such licence disposal or other dealing shall be without prejudice to the rights of the Composer.

16. INDEPENDENT CONTRACTOR

16.1 It is acknowledged that the Composer is an independent contractor and not the employee or agent of the Producer.

17. GOVERNING LAW

17.1 The law of the Jurisdiction specified in Schedule B shall govern this Agreement and all disputes arising out of this Agreement shall be determined by the courts of that Jurisdiction.

18. INTERPRETATION

18.1 In the interpretation of this Agreement unless the context otherwise requires:

    (a) words and expressions are used as in the Copyright Act, 1968 (Cth);

    (b) clause headings shall be disregarded;

    (c) words importing the singular shall include the plural and vice versa;

    (d) words importing one gender shall include other genders;

    (e) all obligations undertaken by more than one party shall be deemed to be joint and several obligations;

    (f) all the Schedules annexed to this Agreement form part of this Agreement;

    (g) all warranties shall survive completion of this Agreement and shall be treated as conditions; and

    (h) the term "Film" includes trailers and commercial advertisements for the Film and all copies thereof.

19. SEVERABILITY

19.1 The intention of the parties is to create a binding agreement. If this Agreement shall be rendered invalid at any time by any one or more of the provisions contravening any statute, regulation, by-law or ordinance or contravening or offending any provision of law or equity, any such provisions shall to the necessary extent be read down or excised from this Agreement and the remainder of the clause shall remain in force.

20. VARIATION

20.1 This Agreement constitutes the whole agreement between the Parties and may be varied only in writing signed by all the parties.

Schedule A and B follow as part of this contract.

SCHEDULE A

TO: ....

RE: ....

I, ... acknowledge receipt of $..... as full payment for my contribution and performance of .... for the production and sound recording for use on the soundtrack and cinematograph films.

In the event that the sound recording is also used for the manufacture and sale of records, the above named Producer agrees to pay the sums which may be due for that use in accordance with the applicable award.

SIGNED: ....

DATED: ....

Schedule B follows as part of this contract.

SCHEDULE B

TERRITORIES: ....

DURATION OF ORIGINAL MUSIC: ....

THE BUDGETED AMOUNT: ....

SCHEDULE OF PAYMENTS:

(a) On execution of this Agreement..

(b) On delivery of the Master Sound Recording...........................

(c) Other ....

....

MUSIC PRODUCTION TIMETABLE:

(a) Delivery date of fine cut..

(b) Delivery date of Master Recording ....

(c) Other ....

....

(IF THE DATE FOR THE DELIVERY OF THE FINE CUT IS DELAYED FOR ANY REASON, THE DATE FOR THE DELIVERY OF THE SOUND RECORDING SHALL BE SUBJECT TO NEGOTIATION BETWEEN THE PARTIES TO DETERMINE A NEW DELIVERY DATE OF THE MASTER RECORDING).

RECORDING FORMAT OF MASTER SOUND RECORDING: ....

RELEASE PRINT DATE: ....

CREDIT:..

JURISDICTION OF THE AGREEMENT:

State: ....Country: ....

EXAMPLE OF A SHORT FORM COMMISSION AGREEMENT FOR LOW BUDGET FILM

MUSIC AND RECORDING COMMISSION AGREEMENT

DATE OF AGREEMENT:
THE PARTIES ARE:
1.   The company specified in **item 1** of the Schedule ("**Producer**").
2.   The person specified in **item 2** of the Schedule ("**Composer**") and if more than one person is named, then each will be bound jointly and severally.

PREAMBLE:
1.   The Producer is producing the film specified in **item 3** of the Schedule, ("**Film**").
2.   The Producer engages the Composer to compose original music score and to make, on the Producer's behalf, sound recordings of that score, suitable for inclusion in the sound track of the Film.

IT IS AGREED:
1.   The Composer will:
      (a)   Compose original music works suitable for synchronisation with the Film as specified in **item 4** of the Schedule ("**Music**");
      (b)   Select and engage musicians and/or conduct and/or perform in recording studios, leading to production of a master sound recording. This recording is to embody a performance of the Music in a format to be specified by the Producer, suitable for mixing down and incorporation into the soundtrack of the Film ("**Recording**"); and
      (c)   Supervise the mix down of the Recording if so requested by the Producer;
            (i)   Deliver the completed Music, Recording and music cue sheets within the fee specified in **item 5** of the Schedule ("**Fee**"); and
            (ii) Obtain the written consent of all persons who perform on the Recording ("**Performers' Consents**"). The Performers' Consents must be in the form of the example annexed to this agreement.
2.   In consideration of the Fee, which is to be paid to the Composer according to the timetable set out in **item 6**, the Composer hereby assigns to the Producer all rights (including all copyright) in the Music and in the Recording, throughout the World and without limitation. By way of example, these rights include the following:

(a) The exclusive right to synchronise and incorporate the Music and the Recording into film soundtracks, (including trailers and advertisements);

(b) The right in perpetuity to make copies of a film that embodies the Music and/or the Recording. Such copies may be made in any language and in any medium or format, whether now known or yet to be invented, for the purposes of communicating, distributing, broadcasting, selling, renting or otherwise exploiting such films;

(c) The right in perpetuity to permit the Music to be performed in public, whether by broadcast, transmission or any other means of communication to the public. These rights are however subject to any rights already vested in the Australian Performing Rights Association (A.P.R.A.) and its affiliated performing rights societies;

(d) To make adaptations of the Music or the Recording; and

(e) To make the Music and the Recording available to the public by any means and any medium whatsoever, whether now known or yet to be invented.

3. The Composer acknowledges that the Producer is and will be for all purposes the 'maker' as defined in the **Copyright Act** 1968 of the Recording and will own all copyright in it.

4. The Composer must deliver to the Producer, the Music, the Recording and the Performers' Consents, by the date specified in **item 7** of the Schedule ("**Delivery Date**"). Time is of the essence in relation to this clause.

5. The Composer warrants to the Producer that

(a) He/she has the right power and authority to enter and perform this Agreement;

(b) The Music is and will be original;

(c) Neither the Music nor the Recording will infringe any third party's rights;

(d) There have been (and will be) no dealings in relation to the copyright in either the Music or the Recording that may interfere with the Producer's rights granted herein.

(e) He/she has obtained all Performers' Consents (if applicable).

6. Provided that the Composer complies with the terms of this agreement, the Producer will ensure that the Composer receives a credit as composer of the Music as set out in **item 8** (the "**Credit**").

(a) the right to authorship credit is entirely governed by the terms of clauses 6 and 7;

(b) the Producer is entitled to adapt the Music and the Recording as it considers necessary for any purpose related to the Film; and

(c) the Producer has the so-called 'first publication right' in relation to the Recording and Music.

7. The Producer will use its best endeavours to ensure that all distributors and broadcasters of the Film give the Credit on all prints issued. The Producer will not, however, be liable for any neglect or default by such distributor or broadcaster where such neglect or default is not reasonably within the control of the Producer.

8. The Producer agrees to lodge a music cue sheet with APRA within 30 days of completion of the Film. The Producer will notify APRA of all places and dates of first public screenings throughout the World, within 90 days of each such screening provided that the Producer has such information.

9. The Composer acknowledges that he/she is an independent contractor and is not (and will not claim to be) the Producer's agent. The Composer promises that he/she is solely responsible for the payment of all taxes, worker's compensation, holiday pay and like responsibilities in respect of the Composer's services performed under this Agreement.

10. The Composer acknowledges that the Producer is not obliged to use all or any of the Music and/or the Recording.

11. In respect of his or her "moral rights", the Composer acknowledges that:

    (a) the right to authorship credit is entirely governed by the terms of clauses 6 and 7;

    (b) the Producer is entitled to adapt the Music and the Recording as it considers necessary for any purpose related to the Film; and

    (c) the Producer has the so-called 'first publication right' in relation to the Recording and Music.

12. The Producer undertakes to provide the Composer with one VHS copy of the Film for his/her private use.

13. The Composer agrees that the terms of this Agreement shall be subordinate to the terms of any completion guarantee and/or production investment agreements entered by the Production Company in respect of the Film or the production of the Film.

14. The Composer is solely responsible for and will attend to payment of income tax to the Australian Taxation Office in respect of the Fee(s) paid under this Agreement.

15. If any party becomes liable to pay GST (that party referred to here as the "**Supplier**") in relation to a Supply made under this Agreement to another party (the "**Recipient**"):

    (a) In addition to any amounts payable by the Recipient to the Supplier, the Recipient must pay the Supplier the GST payable on any Supply provided that the Supplier first provides the Recipient with a GST Tax Invoice for the amount of GST paid in relation to the Supply.

(b) The GST is payable at the same time as paying the amount on which the GST is calculated or the date on which the GST is payable, whichever is the earlier.

(c) "**GST Law**" is defined in the *A New Tax System (Goods and Services Tax) Act 1999 (Cth)*. "**GST**" means a tax, levy, duty, charge or deduction, together with any related additional tax, interest, penalty, fine or other damage, imposed by or under a GST Law. "**Tax Invoice**" and "**Supply**" are as defined in the GST Law.

(d) The Composer must provide a tax invoice to the Producer in respect of each taxable supply.

16. This Agreement is governed by and construed in accordance with the laws of the State of New South Wales. The parties unreservedly submit to the jurisdiction of the courts of New South Wales.

Agreed by the parties:

SIGNED by)
for and on behalf of the Producer in) ....
the presence of:)

....

SIGNED by)
the Composer) ....
in the presence of:)

....

SCHEDULE

item 1: Producer: ....

item 2: Composer: ....

item 3: Film: ....

    (i)   Name: ....

    (ii) Duration: ....

item 4: Music: ....

    (i)   Duration: ....

    (ii) Delivery Format: ....

item 5: Fee: ....

item 6: Payment Milestones: ....

item 7: Delivery Date: ....

    (i)   Music ....

    (ii) Recording and Performers' Consents ....

    (iii) Music Cue Sheets ....

item 8: Credit: ....

ANNEXURE 1

PERFORMER'S CONSENT

All performers, without exception, must sign this form
before recording of their performance commences.

The form in Annexure 2 must be signed by the Composer if he/she performs on
the recording.

Name Of Film:..

Name Of Performer:..

Address Of Performer:..

Fee:...

Producer:...

Composer:...

I confirm that I have been retained by the Composer to perform on a recording being made for purposes associated with (but not restricted to) the synchronisation with and exploitation of the Film. Without any limitation, the Producer may use the recording embodying my performance by any means and in any media whether now known or yet to be invented.

My Fee is the sole remuneration due to me. Once the Fee payable is paid, I will have no further claim in relation to the Recording or the Film for my services.

Name:..

Signature:...

Date: ....

ANNEXURE 2

COMPOSER'S CONSENT AS A PERFORMER

This form must be signed by the Composer if he/she performs on the recording

Name Of Composer: ....

Name Of Film: ....

Name Of Performer: ....

Address Of Performer: ....

Name Of Producer: ....

I confirm that I am a performer on a recording being made for purposes associated with (but not restricted to) the synchronisation with and exploitation of the Film. Without any limitation, the Producer may use the recording embodying my performance by any means and in any media whether now known or yet to be invented and use, adapt, edit, mix, add to, subtract from, arrange, and combine it with other performances.

The fee that I receive as Composer includes the remuneration due to me as a performer on the recording. Once that fee is paid, I will have no further claim in relation to my services.

Name: ....

Signature: ....

Date: ....

AN ENDNOTE

To conclude this chapter, it seems appropriate to include a practical note from a film composer who has paid his dues and had success. This little piece was in the AGSC newsletter and it is reproduced with kind permission of the author:

WHEN TO SAY NO TO WORK
The film composer's dilemma
By Guy Gross

I had been brought up on the 'never say no to work' attitude. And I really believed it was the best way to go. It certainly opened many doors and opportunities for me, and it is still the overriding advice I give new composers looking to break into the market. However over the past few years I've been reconsidering this choice.

True, it's now a bit easier, from a position of relative security and, with a reasonable track record behind me, but I still find myself thinking twice (if not thrice!).

ATTITUDE 1. 'Never say no to work'
This has certainly borne fruit for me. I can trace back my being asked to score The Adventures of Priscilla, Queen of the Desert to a really crappy documentary I did at Film Australia. The story goes like this: I was in the corridors of Film Australia (waiting for a $^1/_4$ inch to 35mm dub – remember that stuff?!) when someone came up and said 'Oh, you're the composer, aren't you?!'. To which I replied 'Well, I'm a composer…'. I went on to score a pretty bad (no budget) documentary for the person who thanked me for doing it.

The editing assistant on that no budget job found himself assisting another (this time only low budget) Film Australia documentary and their composer (no names mentioned) pulled out at the last minute. I think they thought it was a pretty bad documentary (it wasn't great!). So I was recommended by the assistant and came in at the eleventh hour and (never saying no to work) did the gig.

The lead editor on that doco found himself cutting a short film for a young director called Stephan Elliott and my name was mentioned as a 'classically trained up and comer'. One thing led to another and I eventually scored Stephan's first feature 'Frauds' and then went on to score 'The Adventures of Priscilla, Queen of the Desert'. All because of a no budget dog of a documentary that I didn't say no to.

ATTITUDE 2 'Only do quality jobs'
By this I mean jobs that fulfil high artistic and financial benchmarks. I have less experience in this (having rarely said no to work) but I do have a few friends and colleagues who work by this rule and I'm seeing its merits more and more. To me it's a very pragmatic question. Do I decline work that is not me or has compromised work conditions and wait (and maybe wait, and wait) till something that fits the bill comes along, if it ever does at all!? There's no doubt this is financially and professionally risky but it may pay off in the long term. It can certainly demonstrate great artistic integrity. But it can also give impressions of artistic snobbery. The tough question is this: is there enough work available for 'my niche' or do I have to extend myself artistically and professionally?

With all this in mind I have made a list of points I ask myself before accepting work. Not all jobs fulfil all these criteria but it's an interesting exercise to ask yourself.

1. IS IT A PROJECT THAT INTERESTS ME?
    It could be hard to get motivated to write music for 'the life of a dung beetle' if you're not into insects. Also, some jobs can last months. You might be OK about a short departure from your interests, but how will you feel over a long period of time?

2. DO I ENJOY WRITING THE STYLE OF MUSIC REQUIRED?
    Certainly it is appropriate to extend one's musical language, but there are limits. Would you really be happy doing a grungy electric guitar score if you're an Eastern European Folk Music expert? You've got to question the professionalism of the producers if they're asking you to score in a style you've never composed in. (See point 4) On the other hand, it's sometimes fun and challenging (and occasionally required) to throw yourself in the deep end and really stretch your musical self.

3. HAVE I BEEN GIVEN ENOUGH TIME TO DO A GOOD, STRESS-FREE JOB?
    This is a big one for me. I work to live. Not the other way around. There's only so far I'll go compromising my family life (and my health) for the industry. Though yes, sometimes pressure leads to great things. And sometimes 'ya gotta do what ya gotta do'. People are depending on you. It's a tough question in this '24/7' industry. The worst scenario is when the schedule is so tight you're forced to push through poor quality music.

4. IS THE REST OF THE TEAM PROFESSIONAL?
    I once heard a Hollywood composer say he'd never work on a job if he
    didn't respect the post audio team. At the time I thought he was a snob
    for that attitude but over time I can see some merit in this attitude.
    Unfortunately, there are still some wankers in this industry who live in
    the old school of 'effects versus music war'. It's a really stupid battle and
    a total drain on true creative story telling. I avoid them like the plague
    now (where I can). This point applies to all those involved in the
    production; from producer down. Or should I say up (just joking)?
    Always consider that an unprofessional team will make a simple job
    complex, and a complex job a nightmare.

5. IS THE BUDGET SUFFICIENT TO DECLINE OTHER WORK?
    I wish this question could be 'am I being paid what I'm worth?' but alas,
    we live in Australia. So we've got to be more pragmatic than that. Can I
    afford to do the gig, or should I be looking elsewhere for something
    better (perhaps opening a florist is a better option?) And yes, often you
    take what you can get ('Can I afford not to do this gig?'). But it should
    still be a consideration. If more of us fought for what we're worth, then
    we'd all be better off.
        It's an enlightening exercise to apply these questions to past jobs.
    Hindsight is a beautiful thing. It's amazingly obvious why the 'hell jobs'
    were such hell. They generally fell very short on my 5-point list.

I hope this gives you all food for thought.

Cheers,
Guy Gross

PS. I wrote this 5-point list for myself after scoring 'Welcome to Woop
    Woop'. (Also directed by Stephan Elliott). It was one of the worst
    experiences of my scoring career. It scored around 2 out of 5 on my list.
    (I loved the movie though.) And when you think about it, I also got
    that gig because of that dog of a documentary I did! Make of that what
    you will!

32
INSURANCE

INSURANCE IS ONE OF THOSE EXPENSES THAT
EVERYBODY RESENTS PAYING — UNTIL A
CATASTROPHE STRIKES. THEN, IT IS A BARGAIN. THIS
CHAPTER LOOKS AT SOME AREAS OF INSURANCE
THAT MUSICIANS AND THEIR MANAGERS SHOULD
CONSIDER WHEN IMPLEMENTING BASIC BUSINESS
PROTECTION.

INTRODUCTION

The music industry is a multimillion-dollar business, a fact that some insurance companies are finally starting to recognise. The music business, however, remains and is seen as a niche market by insurers and therefore the knowledge and expertise needed to properly underwrite the multitude of risks that face the industry is beyond all but a few specialists.

Most companies that have in the past offered cover to the music industry have done so by modifying existing non-entertainment insurance contracts. Good contracts must accurately reflect the needs of the client and not provide a merely piecemeal protection that ultimately reflects the limitations of the precedent document that was used. Patchwork arrangements are likely to result in only patchwork cover.

It can be difficult to assess exactly what policies are really needed and what is a reasonable premium for the cover offered. There are few bargains in insurance. All else being even, the more comprehensive the degree of cover, the higher the premium has to be.

Insurance brokers are in the business of finding the most appropriate policies for their clients. They know (or ought to know) about the competing policies and their comparative strengths and weaknesses. Insurance for professional musicians needs to be expertly arranged, and very few companies have the necessary experience in the entertainment industry. Probably the biggest is Aon Risk Services who have a specialist Entertainment Insurance Division, but you can refer to the *Australasian Music Industry Directory* for other names and contacts. Just check that they have the necessary experience!

As a general rule, if the insurance company is not particularly interested in selling musicians specialist services, it is not going to be very interested in a musician who makes a claim.

HOUSEHOLD CONTENTS

Musicians should not assume that their usual householder's contents policy will cover musical instruments and other equipment that they may have in the house. Indeed, many domestic policies expressly exclude musical instruments from the cover and most also exclude the instruments of a professional musician. Sometimes the company will agree to amend these policies so as to cover instruments but this is not automatic. Check thoroughly before assuming that the contents policy gives sufficient protection.

EQUIPMENT INSURANCE

Equipment can be very expensive. Most musicians and groups have thousands of dollars worth. It is here that the insurance dilemma is most evident – 'Can I afford to insure my gear? Can I afford not to?'

This becomes particularly important when equipment is bought on hire-purchase. Most companies providing hire-purchase facilities demand that the purchaser also takes out insurance on the goods. A few companies do not insist on insurance and this means that the repayments are slightly smaller. The saving is illusory. Musicians purchasing equipment on hire-purchase should always take out insurance on the gear because if it is stolen or destroyed the money will still be owed, but the musician will no longer have the equipment with which to earn the money necessary to meet the repayments. There are several fine Australian musicians who have had to abandon music and get a 'steady job' to repay the finance company.

As a very broad rule of thumb, equipment insurance will cost about 2% to 3% of the value of the insured property (plus stamp duty, GST, a small policy fee and in NSW, Victoria, WA and Tasmania a Fire Brigade Levy is applicable). This will provide cover against fire, malicious and accidental damage, theft from a securely locked vehicle, as well as burglary and theft from a venue/studio and place of storage. Only a few companies will cover flood damage and you should specifically ask about this if you require this cover. Similarly, only some policies will provide emergency-hire costs in the event of a claim.

However, the breadth of insurance cover is always negotiable, so if you decide that some aspects of this cover are not necessary, a narrower and therefore cheaper cover can be arranged. For example, if you restrict your cover to fire, burglary following forcible entry to buildings only, the cost of cover can reduce to about 1.6% (plus applicable government charges).

Ken Killen, who is the manager of Music & Entertainment Industry Insurances at Aon Risk Services, has a checklist (reproduced here with permission) that you should follow when shopping for musical equipment insurance:

1. Consult a well-established broker specialising in the music industry.
2. Ask for a copy of the policy terms and conditions.
3. Establish the events that are covered.
4. Establish the events that are not covered.
5. Ask if there are any special security requirements.
6. Find out the excess amount payable on claims.
7. Ask if the policy has a no claims discount scheme.
8. Check for any restrictions, e.g. whilst the equipment is in a motor vehicle.
9. Ask the premium cost.

TRAVEL INSURANCE

Travel is a feature of most musicians' lives. Distances are great but conditions are not. The value of the musician's baggage is often considerable, particularly when touring.

The strains of touring frequently affect one's health. In Australia, Medicare lessens the financial threat of large medical bills, but when touring overseas it makes good sense to take out health cover. The medical costs that flow from even non-serious illness or accident can dramatically drain the budget.

Travel insurance is relatively inexpensive and its protection worthwhile.

INCOME INSURANCE

Few musicians are in a position to afford income insurance and few of those who can afford it bother to insure. However, it can be useful because for most musicians income is dependent on live performance. By taking out income insurance the musician can lessen the financial risks.

There are two common approaches to income insurance.

INCOME PROTECTION INSURANCE

These policies guarantee renewal of cover each year until the age of 65 and pay weekly disability benefits up to the age of 65. This type of cover is the ideal and preferred option but would generally only be offered to musicians in PAYE full time employment (such as orchestra members or studio employees) as their weekly income is consistent and can be easily verified.

PERSONAL ACCIDENT AND ILLNESS INSURANCE

Whilst not ideal, this type of policy is generally all that is available to self-employed musicians.

Weekly benefits are averaged at 85% of the previous year's verifiable net income after expenses. A lump sum insured for permanent disability that arises from an accident is also included.

The main difference between this cover and income protection insurance is that renewal is not automatically guaranteed each year and payment of weekly benefits is limited to a maximum period of 52, 104 or 156 weeks depending on the option selected. So if a claimant becomes permanently disabled and can never perform again the weekly payments will cease once the benefit period is exhausted. There is generally an excess period of 14 days of disability before benefits commence.

This cover is relatively inexpensive and while not offering life-long protection, it will ease financial burdens following an accident or illness in the short term.

The premium is approximately the equivalent of 1.5 times the weekly benefit, per annum.

PUBLIC LIABILITY INSURANCE

Almost everyone involved in a musical performance, including the performers, manager, promoter and venue owner can be liable if members of the public, contracted service providers or the employees of others are injured.

This could arise if a member of the audience is hit by a bottle thrown by a drunk, injured in a fight, slips on the stairs and breaks a bone, gets a severe shock because of a technical fault in the equipment, or gets hit by pyrotechnics and so on. In one case a band was found liable when they accidentally triggered an electronically controlled stage extension into motion causing injury and personal property damage to members of the audience.

Injuries to members of the public can be expensive. In Australia, million-dollar verdicts are now commonplace for personal injury claims and an award of over seven million dollars has been made.

On most occasions the venue owner will have public liability insurance but it must be remembered that this protects the policyholder (the venue) and nobody else. If someone is injured he or she will probably sue everybody involved in the mounting of the performance, not just the venue. If the court awards damages against the venue and the musician, the venue's public liability cover will cover only the venue's liability, not the musician's.

Certainly, if the damage or injury is caused by the direct act or negligence of the musician (or crew), the venue will not come to the rescue. The venue (and its insurer) is running a business and if it can pass the buck, it will.

In general, the public liability cover is not expensive and all professional musicians must consider buying it.

NON-PERFORMANCE AND NON-APPEARANCE

This form of cover is principally of interest to promoters. Many occurrences may prevent a show going on: strikes, weather, equipment not arriving, a venue becoming unexpectedly unavailable and so on. (The failure to obtain necessary visas and permits is usually an 'exclusion'.)

If the performance does not proceed, the promoter will inevitably lose a lot of money – not just the chance of making a profit, but also the cold hard cash that has to be spent in preparing for the event. Certain artist fees, accommodation, travel, venue hire, printing, advertising, promotion and considerable administration costs will often still have to be paid, whether or not the show proceeds.

Non-appearance and non-performance cover is generally expensive (allow about 2% of budgeted expenses) but when many thousands (sometimes hundreds of thousands) of dollars are involved, it is usually treated as one of those overheads that the promoter cannot afford to do without.

EVENT INSURANCE

Any responsible promoter staging an event in front of a live audience will take out extensive insurance cover. That cover will be a combination of various types of cover discussed above. Ken Killen from Aon Risk Services has a checklist of the most common mistakes made by event organisers. It is gold dust for those starting out (and even those who have been just lucky up to now.)

COMMON INSURANCE MISTAKES IN EVENT INSURANCE

1. **Last minute action on insurance:** Arranging proper cover takes time. Don't leave it to the last moment. It's not like getting a cover note on your car.

2. **Budget for insurance increases:** Don't presume that premiums will cost the same as last year. Get your insurance quotes when you are putting the budget together.

3. **Lack of Expertise of Insurer:** Make sure that both your broker and your insurer are experienced in event insurance. Experience is essential. It is unlikely that the broker who arranged your house insurance is the right person to use.

4. **Describe Activities of Event Fully:** Describe the activities of the event fully and accurately to the insurance company. You have a duty of complete disclosure and if you make a claim it may be rejected if you have failed to be completely candid when taking out the policy. Describe exactly the event that you are staging.

5. **Provide Risk & Safety Procedures:** You must provide the insurance company with a complete description of the risk and safety control procedures. This demonstrates to the insurance company that you really do know what you are doing and that the possibility of a claim really is remote. (Since the tragic "Big Day Out" and the subsequent legal ramifications, this is at the front of the insurer's mind.)

6. **Be aware of Contract Implications:** Contractual arrangements that event managers make with venues, performers, subcontractors and hire companies can all affect your public liability insurance. Remember that public liability only covers the policyholder if the policyholder is held legally liable for a breach in their common law duty of care. This is particularly important because many venues require the event manager to take on a lot of the exposure that the event venue should be carrying.

   For example a lot of the venue contracts state that, *"the event management company will indemnify the venue against all claims, demands, arising out of the conduct of the event and occurring during the event period."*

   The effect of this is that if the venue is sued you as the event manager promise to make good the settlement of claims against the venue. Unfortunately for you, the insurance companies will not cover such an arrangement unless it is the event manager, event staff or volunteers that were negligent. It doesn't cover the actions of your sub-contractors (like the security firm you hired) and it doesn't protect you from situations in which injuries occur that are not due to your negligence and which would usually be the responsibility of the venue (such as legionnaires disease caught by an audience or team member.) If you have such a clause in your venue agreement you must inform the insurer.

7. **Participation Risks:** Often an insurance quote will be given for public liability that will exclude what are known as 'participation risks'. This may include victims of the 'mosh pit' or any situation in which members of the audience actually participate in the performance. The insurance will provide public liability coverage if any of the spectators are injured but exclude coverage of participants. (If the public liability cover cannot be extended to meet your needs you may need an additional form of insurance such as accident cover.)

8. **Disclaimers & Duty of Care:** Event organisers often get the participants to sign disclaimers. Disclaimers are great for discouraging claims against you but are unlikely to hold up in law. Despite the disclaimer, a common duty of care continues to apply.

9. **Adequate Insurance Coverage:** Have you enough cover? If you are dealing with a large event, the potential liability is truly enormous. The ten million dollar cover that many venues require may not be enough if there is a major disaster. Event managers should take out as much insurance as they can afford.

10. **Beware – all policies are not the same:** Don't go for the cheapest premium. Each company will offer a 'public liability policy' but each will have different terms and conditions. It is important to look closely to see how they affect your own particular circumstances. For example, some policies make the legal and other costs inclusive in the sum insured. Others will pay those costs over and above the sum insured. If you knew that two thirds of the money that your insurance company spent on claims last year went in legal and investigation costs and only one third went towards payouts – which policy would you look for?

FURTHER READING

(For further reading, see *The Arts Insurance Handbook, 2nd Edition*, Sydney: Arts Law Centre Of Australia, 2005.)

33
MUSIC LAWYERS

IF YOU HAVE ACHIEVED ANY LEVEL OF SUCCESS IN THE MUSIC BUSINESS, YOU KNOW THAT YOUR QUALITY OF LIFE IS GREATLY INFLUENCED BY THE QUALITY OF THOSE AROUND YOU WHO LOOK AFTER YOUR BUSINESS AFFAIRS. THESE DAYS, YOUR MUSIC LAWYER IS AN ESSENTIAL PART OF THAT TEAM. THIS CHAPTER IS INTENDED TO HELP YOU SELECT YOUR MUSIC LAWYER AND BETTER UNDERSTAND WHAT THEY DO, HOW THEY CHARGE, WHAT YOU EXPECT OF THEM AND WHAT THEY CAN EXPECT OF YOU.

CHOOSING YOUR MUSIC LAWYER

Not very many years ago, music lawyers were 'general practitioners'. We were trained to believe that if we were given the facts, we could find out the law and apply it. These days, things have changed. Although most lawyers still make their living from conveyancing, divorce, criminal law, wills and probate, the commercial lawyers have become much more specialised. There are now armies of besuited and neatly groomed men and women who wouldn't know a strata title from a decree absolute, or an arresting officer from an executor.

Among commercial lawyers there are a few who are all-rounders, but most find themselves doing one or two sorts of work more than others: taxation, bankruptcy and liquidations; mergers and acquisitions; banking and finance; insurance; superannuation; intellectual property; media and so on. These days, commercial lawyers are becoming more and more specialised both in their academic knowledge and in their business experience.

With this increased specialisation it is perhaps not surprising that there has been a change in the relationship between client and lawyer. We were taught at law school that it was our job to give legal advice and not commercial advice. Indeed, at one time it was considered unethical to advise whether or not a deal was a good one. That was for the client to decide upon alone and it was the lawyer's job to strap it up if the client decided to proceed.

These days, specialty-specific lawyers have become (for better or worse) an integral part of the commercial decision-making process. Of course, they still advise on the potential legal pitfalls of a deal but increasingly their advice is sought as to the terms of the deal. This makes sense because your specialist lawyer will probably have done many of these sorts of deals before and can therefore be expected to know not only how they work but also be familiar with the going market prices.

In some parts of the country there is a very strict prohibition on lawyers describing themselves as specialists, just as there are still very strict controls on the ability of lawyers to advertise their services to the public. Both of these restrictions are being relaxed to some degree but it is still difficult to find out which lawyers specialise in your area of need.

The best way to choose lawyers is to talk to people who have used them. Don't choose them for their smile or because they went to school with your sister or because they have a fabulously decorated office. You need someone you feel comfortable talking to, someone you feel able to trust and someone who is expert in your area of need.

No one lawyer can fulfil all of your legal needs. If your lawyer suggests otherwise, you need a new lawyer. Good lawyers will tell you when they do not have expertise in your area of need and will refer you to someone they know to be expert. It is only common sense that most lawyers have a wide range of contacts in their profession and if they don't know the right person, they probably know someone who does.

FINDING YOUR MUSIC LAWYER

Choosing your music lawyer is no easy task. These days, with the huge degree of speciality, not even all entertainment lawyers work in all areas of the entertainment industry. A film lawyer may hardly ever do record deals, another who does a lot of theatrical work may not have much experience in publishing and so on. Some are all rounders and others are more specialised.

The best way of choosing which entertainment lawyer to approach is by recommendation. Talk to your colleagues and contacts in the business. Find out who they use, what sort of work the lawyer has done for them and if they are happy with the service they have had. If the lawyer sounds right for you, ask a couple of other people for their opinions. Not only lawyers improve with experience. So do their clients!

Once you have selected your prospective lawyer, make an appointment to meet. If you intend this meeting to be an interview to make your mind up, make this clear when you make your appointment. Ask if you will be charged for the meet and greet time. Most charge for it. Some do not. If they do not, it is hardly fair to then use the time to ask for specific advice when you meet.

Remember that your music lawyer is not a designer accessory. You don't have to like his or her decor or hairstyle. That can be easily bought. You need a lawyer who is approachable, trustworthy and expert.

WHAT MUSIC LAWYERS DO
CONTRACT ANALYSIS, ADVICE AND NEGOTIATION
Your first meeting with your music lawyer will probably come about because you have been offered (or want to be offered) a recording, publishing or management contract. You are probably excited by the prospect that your career is about to enter a new phase. You want to sign but you don't know if the deal is a fair one.

You can almost guarantee that any contract you are offered can be improved by professional analysis and negotiation. Just remember that if your career is a failure, the terms of your contract probably won't matter. But if you are a success, a contract entered in your early days, in haste and without advice, will cause you grief.

No one can legitimately object to you taking a potential deal to your lawyer for advice. Most record companies and publishers will insist on it. Getting advice will not blow the deal. Music lawyers are in the business of making deals, not wrecking them!

As a general rule, don't sign any contract in the music business unless you get expert advice first. The document that seems straightforward to you may not be as benign as it looks. This is not the voice of paranoia. It is experience learned from hearing many clients over many years complaining about having entered deals that looked all right at the time. There are two reasons behind this advice. First, very few non-lawyers, particularly at the beginning of their careers, have the training to fully comprehend the legal (and thus professional) consequences of apparently simple contractual terms. Secondly, consider the old adage – 'A lawyer who does his own legal work has a fool for a client' (and a fool for a lawyer). It is very difficult to analyse a deal in which you are personally involved. Your conscious and subconscious desires and needs interfere with your judgment too easily.

When asked why they entered a deal without getting expert legal advice, many young musicians respond that they couldn't afford it. Remember that it will cost you less money in legal fees to get into a deal, than to fight your way out of one. It may be little solace but, if you can't afford to get proper advice, you probably can't afford to do the deal!

CONTRACT DRAFTING

One of the most important skills of any successful entertainment lawyer should be the ability to draft a tight and unambiguous contract. If they can do it succinctly and in reasonably simple English, so much the better.

Many clients seem to believe that their lawyer has a bundle of ready-made documents in the computer and that they simply press Button B and out comes the contract. If only it were so easy! Those same clients are then surprised at the amount they get charged for what, to them, seems like such a simple process.

Without doubt, your lawyer will have an extensive precedent base of earlier-prepared documents. These precedents are the backbone of the business. After all, no one wants to rethink and re-draft every document from scratch. It would waste time and would be very expensive for clients indeed. Although it may sound like lawyers making excuses, it is largely true that there is no such thing as a standard contract. Precedents are not standard contracts, they are models that you have shaped from other contracts and that you may use to create your next one.

No deal is the same. Why? Because no two parties are the same – either in personal or professional characteristics. The proof is simple: most music lawyers enjoy drafting agreements. If it were as straightforward as merely selecting the right precedent, it would soon become routine and boring. Instead, most are intrigued by the challenge of articulating the needs of the individual parties in such a way as to reflect accurately the practical needs and desires of their client.

GENERAL ADVICE

Many musicians who do not have a manager use their music lawyers to fulfil some of that role. They seek career advice, not just legal counsel. Because lawyers work so extensively in the industry they are generally well informed about the opportunities, the deals and the players. If the benefit of this is something your lawyer is prepared to offer (and is something you are prepared to pay for), so much the better.

Your lawyer will assist you with the structuring of your business and advise as to the other members that you may need on your team, such as a competent accountant experienced in the music industry to handle your financial affairs.

Because of their wide range of contacts in the industry, established music lawyers can be very helpful in sourcing a deal. This said, none of them really enjoy shopping demo tapes. Some will not do it at all (on the basis that it is not strictly a part of a lawyer's function). Of those that will agree to shop a deal for you, most will only agree if they really believe in the potential of the product.

You may be incredibly talented, but if you expect to use the reputation and contacts of your lawyer to promote your own commercial opportunity, you must realise that lawyers will expect to be paid for their efforts and the use of their reputations. Almost certainly, you will be asked to put some money into the firm's trust account before any shopping expedition will be undertaken.

WHAT LAWYERS COST

Like most specialists, entertainment lawyers are expensive (but then, so are good mechanics and anyone else who provides professional advice). In your first interview (or even when you make the first appointment) you should always ask about the basis upon which you will be charged. The methods of charging are fairly standard.

THE HOURLY RATE

Most Australian entertainment lawyers charge an hourly rate. At the time of writing this is generally between $350 and $550 an hour for partners. Employed solicitors cost less per hour than partners in the same firm. And don't forget, there is 10% GST to be added to the hourly rate.

Of course, not all of your money is going into your lawyer's pocket. The cost of buying and maintaining all the ancillary support (e.g. premises, staff, computer and communication equipment, etc.) will probably be running at 40% to 70% of gross billings and bad debts probably account for another 5% to 20%. In most practices, the 'hourly rate' includes all the support staff's time as well, so you do not get charged for secretaries' time as a separate item. It would be easy to bill it as a separate item, as some accountants do, but it is not usual practice for lawyers.

You should also ask how the hourly rate is calculated. Most lawyers divide up their working day into units of six minutes each. The unit is the minimum chargeable time for any work done on your behalf. This means that if you ring your lawyer for three minutes you will be charged one unit, if you talk for ten minutes you will be charged two units. It is not hard to work out that it is going to be cheaper to use someone who uses six-minute units rather than 10-minute or even 15-minute units!

Remember that you will be charged for all attention that you or your matter requires. All of the time that is taken up by you and your affairs is time that they cannot spend on some other client's paying work. If you communicate with your lawyer (whether in person, on the telephone, or by letter), expect to be charged. If your lawyer has to communicate to others on your behalf, expect to be charged. If your lawyer has to shop demos, attend meetings, negotiate, research, draft documents or travel, expect to be charged. Lawyers who use a time billing method have to keep very meticulous records of all of this because all they have to sell is their time.

On top of this you will be billed for all disbursements. These are any expenses incurred on your behalf. These will include filing fees, barristers fees, service agents' fees, travel costs, photocopying, faxes, postage, metered calls, couriers and the like.

ESTIMATES

You should always ask for an estimate of the likely cost to do the work that you want done. (In NSW, lawyers are obliged to do this in writing.) Remember that this can only be an estimate – an estimate is not a fixed quote. It is a guide based on the lawyer's experience of those particular types of deal. As the deal progresses, the individual circumstances of the transaction often mean that the estimate will need to be revised.

THE CAPPED FEE

Music lawyers are often asked to quote a capped fee, but few will work this way because they all know that if something that is completely out of the hands of the lawyer goes unexpectedly off-track, and it requires a huge amount of work to salvage, they will lose money on it. You don't have to be too bright to realise that, after a lawyer has been caught like this once, he or she is going to be gun-shy next time.

For this reason, when you demand a firm quote from your lawyer, realise that you are going to be paying a premium. There will be premium built into the quote to cover unforeseen contingencies. So, the down-side is that if everything goes very easily, you will have paid more than you would have had you used an hourly rate. On the other hand, you are secure in the knowledge that the amount is capped and that you can afford it. The all-in fee is a difficult gamble for both parties.

Capped fees are never used in litigation because, in anything more than the most banal cases, it is impossible to estimate accurately the twists and turns of the case and the tactics of your opponent. What looked hard may prove easy. What looked simple can turn into something like trench-warfare.

SUCCESS FEES

A few lawyers charge success fees. They charge an hourly rate but then charge an additional fee based on some predetermined indicator, such as the value of the advance on royalties. This is considered professionally unethical in some parts of the country but is permissible in others.

In day-to-day deals this is not recommended. There are a lot of very skilled music lawyers who will do the job for the hourly rate with the same degree of care and attention whether the advance is for twenty thousand or a million dollars.

PERCENTAGES

Although it is common practice in the United States, it is unusual in Australia for lawyers to work on a percentage basis. Indeed, in some States it is still illegal. Many lawyers in the United States will charge 10% (frequently more) of the particular deal's worth (e.g. advances) and many charge 5% of all gross income earned over the life of the deal!

The exception to this in Australia is in larger, corporate start-up transactions. In these situations it is increasingly common for the lawyer to be offered shares or options in the company in order to ensure an on-going relationship. It is a way of bonding the team from the outset and making sure that the key players share in the success that they help to build.

PAYING THE BILLS

The best way of souring your relationship with a lawyer is not to pay the bill. If you have a complaint about the bill, raise it as soon as possible after you receive it. You have every right to demand an itemised bill (unless you have agreed to an all-in fee). You will find that your lawyer is more than happy to discuss the bill, explain the charges and fix any errors. Some lawyers work on payment within 14 days and others within 30 days.

If you can't afford to pay you shouldn't have spent the money you didn't have or couldn't find. Don't just ignore the bill and hope that the lawyer will lose interest in it. Call and explain that (and why) you can't pay it all at once and try to work out a reasonable regular schedule of payments. The key words here are reasonable and regular. It is pointless paying off a bill of $6,000 at $50 a month. It'll take ten years! What's more, the loss of interest on the money and the cost of administering the account means that in such an arrangement the lawyer is losing more than you are paying!

If your lawyer does agree to a regular schedule of payments, walk over broken glass to make sure that you keep to the agreed schedule. Every music lawyer understands that a client's ability to pay sometimes lags behind the need to retain legal advice. If the lawyer has worked for you in good faith, you will keep that good faith by ensuring that your instalments arrive like clockwork. As soon as the lawyer has to chase you to make payments, you lose face and the lawyer loses interest in you.

COMMUNICATION

Keep in touch with your lawyer. Call, write, inform, discuss, then having made sure that you have got the advice you need, make your own decisions. Remember that lawyers are not blessed (or cursed) with telepathic powers. They can't help unless you involve them fully in your business dealing. The best money you will spend in a lawyer's office is getting into a deal; the worst is in trying to get out of a deal.

Although all of this communication costs you money, you can minimise the cost by making sure that you are as organised as possible. Instead of sitting in your lawyer's office and recounting the facts and having the lawyer laboriously write it all down in front of you, write out all the details before you come to the meeting. Preparation helps you get your money's worth.

CONFLICTS OF INTEREST

A lawyer has a legal and professional duty to disclose any conflict of interest. Having competing interests are in themselves neither illegal nor unethical. They may be unwise and they certainly can be abused, but the important thing is that they be disclosed. Only then is a client in a position to say, 'I need independent legal advice', or 'I don't mind if you work for both of us, but I'll remember that you do and take that into account when assessing your advice to me'.

All of the major music lawyers have both companies and talent on their client list. This can benefit the client because the lawyer will have a good understanding of the attitudes and needs of both parties. It also means that the lawyer's range of contacts in the industry will be useful in sourcing deals. Lawyers are often commercially attractive to new clients because of, rather than in spite of, their existing clients – and the consequent potential for deal-making.

For their part, companies like to know that their lawyers still act for talent because then they are more likely to be offered the first chance to sign the available talent.

Conflicts of interest are almost inevitable when the lawyer is the catalyst for the relationship between the parties. Imagine you are an established music lawyer. You are acting for a musician looking for a record deal. You also act for a record company. You call the A&R Manager or the Managing Director and tell them about your musician. They play the demo. They like it and want to do a deal. Another client, a film producer, tells you that she is looking for a composer to write and perform on the soundtrack of her next film; you believe that your musician client would be perfect for the job. You introduce the two of them and they decide to do a deal. The film producer wants a book done of her film. You act for a major publisher who you know is interested in this sort of project. You introduce them and they decide to do a deal. The musician now decides to get a publishing administration deal from a publisher. You act for a major publisher. You call them. They want it. Now the musician needs a publicist. Coincidentally you act for a couple of very good ones. You recommend them ... and so it goes on.

To some extent, particularly in sourcing deals, this capacity for conflict of interest makes a music lawyer particularly useful. However, beware. The sensible and ethical lawyer will always make it clear in such transactions that he or she is acting for only one party at a time and that the others are not only free to get independent legal advice but should actually do so. Whether or not they do is their business. Most lawyers will put that in writing so that they are protected if anything goes awry later.

CHANGING LAWYERS

If you are not happy with your lawyer you have every right to find another one. It is important that you are able to communicate with your lawyer and have faith in his or her skill. Once either of these is missing, you might as well change lawyers.

Although there is nothing stopping you simply going to another lawyer and asking them to arrange for the files to be passed over, it is preferable first to contact your lawyer and discuss the reasons for your displeasure. After all, there may be something quite simple that can be rectified if it is discussed. No relationship, personal or professional, is without its low moments. Most can be sorted out. In any event most lawyers appreciate the courtesy of being told why the change is being made. If the lawyer doesn't know why it happened, how can he or she improve the quality of service?

If you do change lawyers, your previous solicitor can (and probably will) hold on to your files until you pay your outstanding accounts with the firm. Swapping lawyers is not a way to avoid paying your bills.

FREE LEGAL ADVICE

This sounds too good to be true. Well, it is and it isn't, as you will see.

Australia is very fortunate in having services that provide a range of free legal advice to performers and artists of all kinds. Some services don't actually give advice, but they will direct you to someone who can. They are referral services rather than acting as lawyers. Others can provide initial contract and negotiating assistance. Their legal advisers are either in-house lawyers or panels of lawyers from legal firms who volunteer their time and expertise. Union members can also contact their union for assistance.

Of course, there are limits to how much these services can do for one person or artist. Unfortunately, most of these organisations are, to a greater or lesser extent, dependent upon government grants and in these stringent times, none receive sufficient funds to enable them to provide all the facilities needed to run a legal practice. This is why, ultimately, they are not a substitute for musicians retaining their own legal advisers.

CONTACTS

Arts Law Centre of Australia, The Gunnery, 43 Cowper Wharf Road, Woolloomooloo, NSW 2000, tel: (02) 9356 2566, toll free: 1800 221 457, fax: (02) 9358 6475, internet: www. artslaw.com.au

Arts Law Centre of Queensland, 4th Floor, 109 Edward Street, Brisbane, QLD 4000, tel: (07) 3211 3628, fax: (07) 3211 3758

Australian Copyright Council, 245 Chalmers Street, Redfern, NSW 2016, tel: (02) 9318 1788, fax: (02) 9698 1788, internet: www.copyright.org.au

34
INDUSTRY AWARDS

ALL MUSICIANS, EVEN IF THEY ARE NOT UNION
MEMBERS, ARE AFFECTED BY AWARDS, WHICH
SPECIFY MINIMUM TERMS AND CONDITIONS OF
ENGAGEMENT FOR ALL PERFORMERS AND
MUSICIANS COMING WITHIN THEIR SCOPE. ANYONE
WHO DOES LIVE OR SESSION WORK SHOULD KNOW
ABOUT INDUSTRIAL AWARDS.

The system of so-called 'awards' has operated in Australia for many years. Awards have been used in industry generally, to set minimum standards for conditions of employment.

Award conditions are established under the Industrial Relations system at Federal and State level and apply to anyone working in the particular industry that a specific award regulates. Federal awards apply throughout Australia. State awards only apply within the relevant State's borders and are usually intended to catch any activities which, for one reason or another, are not covered by Federal awards.

EMPLOYEE OR INDEPENDENT CONTRACTOR?

Awards govern the conditions applicable to employees. The relationship of 'employer and employee' is vital here – if the relationship is anything else, then no award applies. If someone is providing their services as an independent contractor then they are not employees. If they are not employees, then the terms of the award (which are minimum terms anyway) are irrelevant to the contractual relationship.

Awards cannot be 'written away' by the parties to an employment agreement. The best they can do is expressly deny that the relationship of employer–employee exists, and structure the agreement in such a way that a court, if reviewing the transaction, would be satisfied that the contract was for services, rather than of service.

The trick, though, is to determine whether, in any particular instance, the relationship is one in which the law deems the relationship of employer and employee despite the words used in any contract between them. There are many specialist texts which wrestle with the concept for pages but, in essence, the test the law applies is: 'What degree of control may potentially be exercised over the person providing their services?"

Often, this is not an easy question, particularly in an area such as the entertainment industry. Will an order (no matter how loudly given) make a bad singer sing well? Of course not, but the management of a venue can decide when and how the performance is to take place and what will be worn and so on. These are all signs of 'control' and will all be taken into account when trying to establish whether you are an employee or not. The more control indicators, the more likely you are to be deemed an employee for the purposes of the awards system.

In this context, 'employee' includes all people who receive payment in return for providing their labour, such as musicians, performing artists and professional athletes. Most live performances are deemed by Award to be made under contracts of employment, even if neither the management nor the performers have turned their minds to the question.

The courts will look at the whole transaction and all relevant surrounding circumstances, such as whether PAYG tax is deducted, whether overtime or other penalty rates are paid, how and when payments are made, and how long the services are to be provided. No one of these aspects is, in itself, conclusive but may indicate the true nature of the relationship.

UNIONS

Awards are administered by unions. The two main unions operating nationally in the entertainment and recording industries are the Media, Entertainment & Arts Alliance (MEAA) and the Musicians' Union of Australia (MUA).

The MUA is one of the oldest unions in Australia and is able to trace its origins back as far as the 1880s. It represents the interests of musicians from all areas of the music industry as well as vocalists who form an integral part of a group.

The MEAA arose from an amalgamation of several unions whose members worked in various parts of the media and entertainment industries. It represents virtually all performing arts other than instrumentalists and vocalists who are an integral part of a band.

Annual membership fees are modest and, on request, both unions will be happy to provide current fees and a full list of member services.

The MUA and the MEAA represent their members in industrial matters and operate a number of ancillary services for members, such as advice on contracts and assisting members in disputes with employers. They have lobbied strongly for many years to improve conditions for local performers. The unions have been heavily involved with the ongoing struggle to retain local content rules for television and radio programming, limits on foreign stars being imported to head local film and stage productions, and generally to further local employment opportunities.

They also have arrangements with third parties for discounted insurance and medical treatment and other services, as well as superannuation funds. These funds have become particularly important since the Superannuation Guarantee Act was introduced by the Federal Government, obliging all employers to contribute to superannuation for their employees.

Both unions have to deal with the fact that many performers (especially rock musicians) simply do not see themselves as employees under any circumstances. Many in the music business are either indifferent to the unions, or hostile to them. That attitude might change if they considered the ability of the American Federation of Musicians (AF of M) to improve its members' conditions in the United States (where, after all, unionism is often thought of as being only just this side of unpatriotic).

ENTERTAINMENT INDUSTRY AWARDS

The awards themselves are bulky documents, setting out minimum standards to be met in all employment conditions to which they apply. They go into great detail and are often quite complex. They are too bulky to be reproduced in full here, but if you really need copies of complete awards, they can be obtained from whichever Department in your State looks after industrial relations and safety. Federal Awards are available on the Internet at www.osiris.gov.au or www.airc.gov.au.

SESSION MUSICIANS

Session musicians and backing vocalists have a particular need to know about awards, as their remuneration is influenced by the prevailing minimum award provisions. Awards change from time to time, so you need to check with the MEAA or the MUA regularly, to ensure you have the most recent rates and conditions.

MAKING 'CAST' RECORDINGS OF SHOWS

Cast recordings of stage productions are unusual because there are specific award provisions affecting them.

They are also unusual because:

- some of the performers/actors may already be contracted to a record company while others are not; and
- the number of performers affects the way remuneration will be paid.

If a show's producers decide to make a cast recording, the relevant rights have to be secured to make and exploit the recording. This means the show's producers will contract the actors to attend recording sessions, or ask them to agree to the show being recorded during a performance, or the relevant record company will (with the producer's consent) conclude agreements with the actors directly.

The contract is usually fairly simple as it will be a once-off permission to record, rather than the exclusive services deal commonly used in the record industry. The agreement has to comply with the Performers Consent provisions of the Copyright Act and give the party making the recording all the rights it needs to exploit the recording.

Until recently, the rights to make cast recordings were usually secured in return for a lump-sum payment to the relevant actors whose performances were recorded and released on record. This course was chosen because the number of people to be contracted with is usually quite high, and the cost of having to negotiate perhaps 50 individual contracts made the exercise prohibitively expensive. Cast recordings are notorious for being indifferent sellers in this country. It takes many years for the average cast recording to break even, if it ever does that well.

Besides, if there is a large cast (say, 40 people), dividing the royalty up can lead to absurd results. A 2.5% share of the standard record royalty is almost too small to measure! By making a once-off payment that is a combined performance and royalty fee, each artist could get a measurable income from the project.

Nothing will deter a record company faster than the prospect of having to negotiate a multitude of agreements (each needing royalty accounting) and perhaps becoming embroiled in disputes over what 'stars' as opposed to 'extras' ought to receive. Most record companies will simply not bother with such projects as the returns are rarely there to justify the effort. Of course, there are always exceptions to any rule. 'Les Miserables' and the Australian 'Jesus Christ Superstar' cast recordings are two notable exceptions that sold particularly well, though no one could have predicted their success before they were released.

The Musicians' General Award requires that if a production is recorded, then the musicians must be paid the recording fee specified in the award as well as their fee for the live performance. The Copyright Act does give artists the right to refuse to have their performance recorded, but usually the agreement to record their performance will be part of the terms of the original employment contract.

Under the Actors (Theatrical) Award it is illegal (except for publicity purposes) to record a production, unless an agreement has been reached between the performers, the party making the recording and the MEAA. The MEAA stipulates that royalties are payable in addition to usual session/performance fees at the applicable rate, covering actual recording as well as rehearsal time. The MEAA has prepared a standard contract for cast recordings, which it generally insists on using as a condition for the union's approval to the recording going ahead.

35
KEEPING THE BOOKS

KEEPING A SIMPLE SET OF BOOKS AND RECORDS IS
ESSENTIAL FOR THE OPERATION OF ANY BUSINESS.
THAT OF THE MUSICIAN IS NO DIFFERENT. THIS
CHAPTER EXPLAINS WHAT RECORDS SHOULD BE
KEPT AND HOW THEY CAN BENEFIT YOU.

To most people, keeping books is a bore; this is why many musicians have managers and why managers must have the necessary business skills. Nevertheless, whether or not you have a manager, it is important that you have a working knowledge of what books and records to keep, their uses and above all, how to read and understand those books and records. If you do have a manager it is important that you can discuss financial matters with him or her and check that the records are being properly maintained. There are many well documented examples (e.g. The Beatles, Elton John) of disputes between managers and musicians that occurred because the musicians left all the financial matters to the manager's discretion.

Let's be blunt and unkind: Musicians, composers, managers, agents, independent record companies and publishers, publicists, retailers and promoters, are just running small businesses. It is very tempting to focus merely on the 'music' in 'music business'. Music is your passion but business is what allows you to live, pay rent, buy food and afford your chosen lifestyle. This is too important to delegate completely to a third party; it is your life and it is your responsibility. You don't have to do the books yourself but you should be actively involved in using them to plan your career and make strategic decisions. No one has the luxury of concentrating on the creative side of the business, to the exclusion of the financial side. This is one of the major reasons why many small businesses go broke.

The main reasons why it is essential for musicians to maintain proper books and records can be summarised as follows:

- to manage the collection, expenditure and investment of your money;
- to fulfil your taxation obligations;
- to do accurate tour budgeting and submissions for grants; and
- to borrow money.

MANAGING THE MONEY

The financial books and records show whether you are owed money (and thus what needs collecting), what you are spending your money on and indeed whether there is any money left to spend. Managing your financial affairs requires a degree of personal involvement. It is the difference between actively creating opportunities and passively letting things happen to you.

From the books and other records are produced profit and loss statements, balance sheets, taxation returns and tour budgets. These records are essential as a basis for prudent decision making. For example, at the end of a national tour, a band may know that, over all, the tour was a success but a detailed analysis of the financial records will reveal which States, cities or venues were profitable and which were not. Now the group has hard evidence on which it can base its next tour.

TAXATION

There are numerous tax deductions that can be claimed by musicians. Although the system is one of self-assessment, all deductions claimed must be backed up with evidence. The best evidence is a full set of receipts and ordered financial accounts. It should also be remembered that the onus of proof is on you, the taxpayer, to substantiate deductions. The Tax Commissioner frequently requires musicians to undergo desk audits to provide evidence of those deductions.

The tax laws require all persons carrying on a business to keep, for a period of five years, sufficient records of their income and expenditure to enable their assessable income and allowable deductions to be readily ascertained.

TOUR BUDGETS/GRANT APPLICATIONS

Books and records are useful for extracting information for preparation of tour budgets and submissions for subsidy or grants.

TOUR BUDGETS

A tour budget is an estimate of anticipated income and expenditure for a future tour. The tour budget may be based on income earned and expenditures incurred on similar tours in the past. These projections will show:

- whether the tour is likely to make a profit and how much;
- percentage attendance required to break even on the tour;
- itinerary of the tour – for example, it may be necessary to start a tour in the Eastern States and generate enough income there to pay for transport costs to, say, Western Australia; and
- timing of expenditure (e.g. deposits on venues).

SUBMISSIONS FOR SUBSIDIES OR GRANTS

The prime sources of subsidy are grants from State funding bodies, the Australia Council or tour support deals with the record company. In each case they will require budgets to be produced to justify the amounts sought. Each government funding source will have its own application forms; they will be long and detailed but must be completed accurately and fully, and submitted by the nominated closing date. Such grants must also be acquitted (i.e. you usually have to give a report showing how the money was actually spent). Record company funding is less bureaucratic in style but will still require a reasonable standard of detail.

BORROWING MONEY

Like any business, everyone in the music business will at some time need to borrow money. A lender looks at the following criteria when deciding whether to lend money:

- ability to repay the loan by making a profit;
- security; and
- financial history.

The books, if properly kept, will help to provide this information. The amount of detail required by the lender depends upon the size and purpose of the loan but would usually include the following:

- profit and loss statements for the past three years;
- taxation returns and assessments for the past three years;
- bank statements for the last 12–18 months;
- statement of assets and liabilities; and
- budgets – which show future income and expenditure and thus demonstrates to the lender the ability to repay the loan.

If you are able to produce the above information from the books and records, you will be able to demonstrate to the lender that you are running the business on a professional basis and have a proven track record. Without this track record, you won't get to square one with the lender.

BOOK KEEPING ESSENTIALS

Whether you are a new group starting out, an international rock group or a symphony orchestra, there are a number of essentials to the keeping of proper books and records. They include:

- a cash book (either manual or electronic);
- a petty cash book;
- periodical accounts;
- filing systems;
- GST paperwork – business activity statements (BAS); and
- an accountant.

Over the last ten years there have been several technological advances that have changed the way we do banking. For example, EFTPOS (electronic funds transfer at point of sale) cards, Internet banking, phone banking and credit cards linked to savings and home loan accounts. The basic principles of book keeping, however, have remained the same. Whether your records consist of cheque butts, deposit book entries, bank statements, or are contained within Internet banking records, does not matter. The most important thing is that you keep good records of all receipts, invoices and payments, so that you are aware of where your money is going – and can prove it was spent for business purposes.

CASH BOOK

A cash book is a record of all transactions that are made through your bank account. It is simply a matter of recording the details on a cheque butt, bank statement or deposit slip every time a transaction is made (e.g. a cheque or credit card payment when on tour for a motel room, airfare, or restaurant). There are now useful computer programs that allow you to enter all your data and 'reconcile' the accounts electronically, (e.g. Cashbook and MYOB). These programs, however, are based on the same fundamental bookkeeping principles outlined below. It is by no means compulsory that you buy an accounting computer program, but they do make it easier. You can complete your book keeping manually with the same result. The most important thing to remember is that you must keep a good 'paper trail' (whether using an electronic program or manual books).

The cash book is written up from cheque butts, deposit slips and credit card statements and is divided into two separate sections – receipts and payments.

RECEIPTS

When writing up the deposit slips into the cash book it is important to separate income (which may be taxable) from funds that are introduced either by way of loan or from one's own sources (which may not be taxable). A typical cash book summarising receipts might look like this.

CASH RECEIPTS								
DATE	DETAILS	BANK	CONCERT INCOME	ROYALTY INCOME	GRANTS	LOANS	SUNDRIES	GST
1/3/2006	Music Board of Australia Council	5,000			5,000			Y
3/3/2006	Concert – Ent. Centre	9,532	9,532					Y
4/3/2006	Concert – Opera House	5,850	5,850					Y
7/3/2006	Westpac Bank Loan	10,000				10,000		N

PAYMENTS

In the payments section of a cash book the following details will be recorded: date; details of cheque payment or credit card payment; cheque number; amount paid; category of expenditure.

The cash payment section of a cash book might look like the example opposite.

PETTY CASH BOOK

This book records all your other cash transactions and is commonly used when cheques or credit cards are not acceptable (e.g. payments for drinks, coffees, petrol, guitar strings, etc.)

If you just rely on memory when making cash purchases you are bound to forget some of them and this means missing out on tax deductions. Therefore, it is important to record these cash transactions on a regular basis: daily is recommended but at least once a week is essential.

While it is not always possible to obtain receipts for cash get them when possible, as further evidence to support the details included in the petty cash book.

PERIODICAL ACCOUNTS

These are usually called the profit and loss statement and the balance sheet. Basically, these are a summary of the cash book and petty cash book. This means adding up the bank totals for receipts and payments and summarising income and expense categories for a particular period.

These periodical accounts have to be done at least once a year for taxation purposes, but to obtain full benefit of them, they should be done on a more regular basis – quarterly is considered usual. The periodical accounts are your means of quantifying the profit or loss made for a particular period, a basic tool for future planning. Because of the importance of these, managers should provide periodical accounts at least quarterly, but many of the best do it monthly.

CASH PAYMENTS

DATE	DETAILS	REFERENCE	TOTAL	GST	MOTOR VEHICLE EXP	TRAVEL	ACCOM.	FOOD	WAGES	DRAWINGS	PETTY CASH
2006 March 1	BP Service Station	306001	156.10	Y	156.10						
March 2	Qantas	306002	600.00	Y		600.00					
March 3	Visa	306003	852.56	Y	40.00		420.00	392.56			
March 5	Dept of Motor Transport	306004	320.00	Y	320.00						
March 8	Cash	306005	300.00	Y						300.00	
March 9	Petty Cash	306006	150.00	N							150.00
March 10	Joe Doe	306007	250.00	Y					250.00		
March 10	Errol Ray	306008	250.00	Y					250.00		
March 10	Tom Mee	306009	250.00	N					250.00		

FILING SYSTEM

If the books, receipts and other financial records are to be useful then they should be filed for easy reference. There are various methods of arranging a filing system, but regardless of how it is done the system should have the following characteristics:

- easily show whether accounts have been paid or not;
- provide ready access to invoices, vouchers, bank statements, petty cash book, cash book, etc., via a central filing system (say a filing cabinet);
- provide ready access to different items of expenditure via an indexing system. The most common methods of indexing are the cheque number order and A–Z systems for paid accounts with separate files for 'legal', 'accountancy', 'insurance', 'bank statements' and so on.

GST PAPERWORK – BUSINESS ACTIVITY STATEMENTS (BAS)

The Goods and Services Tax brought with it additional bookkeeping responsibilities for businesses. If you are registered for GST, you must fill out a 'Business Activity Statement' (BAS) every three months and tell the ATO how much GST you have collected through sales (performances, royalties, sponsorships and the like), and how much GST you have paid. In order to do this you will need to keep meticulous records of your GST receipts and payments.

The BAS works by netting off the GST collected against the GST paid. If a business has paid out more GST in expenses than it has earned through GST, then the ATO will reimburse the business. If a business has earned more GST than it has paid out in GST, then the business will have to pay the balance to the ATO. The ATO will assess the BAS for each three-month period.

ROLE OF THE ACCOUNTANT

From the very beginning of your musical career you should retain specialised advice on bookkeeping needs. It is the accountant's role to customise a bookkeeping system to your requirements. Set up the system early so that it just becomes a natural way of doing things. Make sure that the accountant gives you a system that you understand and that is simple to use.

The accountant should also be able to advise you on a whole spectrum of financial matters including:

- types of structures to use – partnership, company, trust or sole trader;
- preparation of taxation returns and business activity statements;
- day-to-day advice such as workers' compensation obligations, financing, and tax deductions; and

- preparation of tour budgets, submissions for grants and periodical accounts.

CONCLUSION

Regardless of whether you maintain your own books and records or have a manager do it for you, and regardless of whether your records are kept manually or electronically, it is most important that you have a current understanding of your financial situation and responsibilities.

It is unwise for you to base professional decisions purely on artistic factors. An understanding of the financial aspects of your business will ensure that your decision-making processes are truly informed and based on real figures, not mere optimism.

36
TAXATION

AS THEY SAY, THERE ARE TWO THINGS YOU CAN
RELY ON: DEATH AND TAXES. WE SHALL LEAVE DEATH
ASIDE, AND IN THIS CHAPTER CONSIDER TAXES,
AND THE IMPORTANT ROLE 'TAX MANAGEMENT'
PLAYS IN RUNNING A SUCCESSFUL MUSIC BUSINESS.
REGARDLESS OF HOW BIG OR SMALL YOUR
BUSINESS, IT IS ESSENTIAL THAT YOU UNDERSTAND
THE BASICS OF HOW THE TAX SYSTEM WORKS AND
THAT YOU HAVE A GOOD KNOWLEDGE OF WHAT TAX
DEDUCTIONS YOU ARE ENTITLED TO CLAIM. THIS
CHAPTER AIMS TO GIVE YOU A BASIC
UNDERSTANDING OF THE TAXATION SYSTEM IN
AUSTRALIA AND TO ALERT YOU TO THE SPECIAL TAX
CONCESSIONS THAT APPLY TO MUSICIANS AND
SMALL BUSINESSES.

Many businesses lose out on hundreds and thousands of dollars each year, simply because they do not consider tax issues and investigate what deductions they can claim. It is too late to start thinking about it when the tax return is due. In order to claim the maximum tax deductions for your business, you will need to put good tax management practices into place from the start, to ensure you have kept all relevant receipts and documentation. Also fundamental is to get your business structure right in the first place (see Chapter 2, **Business Structures**), otherwise it could cost a fortune. It is important that you find a good accountant or tax specialist that you can call on and who understands your business.

The taxation system in Australia appears to be in a perpetual state of change. It seems no sooner has one got one's head around the workings of the present system, than a 'new tax system' is introduced, to undo all the good work. For this reason, it is important that you obtain up-to-date advice. This chapter is meant as a guide only. A good first port of call for further information is the website of the Australian Taxation Office, which can be found at: www.ato.gov.au. The ATO website provides good practical advice and current summaries of tax reforms and tax-related issues.

INTRODUCTION TO THE TAXATION SYSTEM IN AUSTRALIA

Taxes are collected by governments and in Australia we have three levels of government that exercise this authority.

- **Local Governments** (i.e. city and shire councils) collect fees and charges including charges for rates, advertising, and building;
- **State Governments** collect taxes such as payroll tax, stamp duties and land tax;
- **The Federal Government** collects taxes such as income tax (including capital gains tax and fringe benefits tax) and goods and services tax (GST) from individuals and companies.

In addition to being collectors of tax, each of the tiers of government 'redistributes' this wealth in the form of essential services, social security, subsidies, bounties and grants. The result of this collection and redistribution is a delicate balancing of not taking too much from the 'haves' and giving just enough to the 'have nots' in answer to political pressures.

TAXABLE INCOME AND ASSESSABLE INCOME

ASSESSABLE INCOME

Your assessable income is simply the sum total of all the income that you earn from your different income sources (e.g. income earned as a music teacher, income from live performances, from grants, or investments). Your assessable income is calculated before any deductions are taken out.

There are some rare sources of income that will not be included when you calculate your assessable income (e.g. certain prizes and scholarships), but generally speaking all income is assessable unless stated otherwise. Assessable income will include the following:

EMPLOYMENT

Many musicians take employment in order to supplement their income from live performance or composition. Whether they teach music in secondary schools, or make hamburgers and milk shakes is not important. The income therefrom is assessable.

BUSINESS INCOME

If you are running a business (see 'hobby or business' below) then all money earned by the business, or through the sale of the business, will be assessable.

PRIZES

Money given for music prizes will usually be assessable because the benefit received is an incident of the musician's vocation. Just as the cricketer of the year who wins a sports car must pay tax on his prize, so too must you if you are a professional musician and win a music competition.

BOUNTIES AND SUBSIDIES

Bounties and subsidies received in relation to a taxpayer's business are assessable. Thus, if a musician or composer receives a grant from the Australia Council towards the preparation of a work or, say, a standard six-month general grant, that money is assessable.

ROYALTIES

This is relevant to musicians who sell or license the right to use their music, copyrights or recordings. The income derived from these sorts of activities will be assessable.

GRATUITIES, BENEFITS AND BONUSES

Whether given in the form of money, meals, land, use of premises or otherwise, where a gratuity, benefit or bonus is given in relation to any employment of, or services rendered by, the recipient, that will be considered assessable income.

For example if a lawyer draws up a will in return for you performing at their wedding, that service should be accorded a monetary value and declared. Note: it is the value to the recipient that is assessable.

INCOME FROM CAPITAL GAINS

Income from 'capital gains' will generally be assessable. This is due to a form of tax known as 'capital gains tax'. Capital gains are profits that you make when you sell an asset for more than you bought it for. An asset is defined very broadly and includes any form of rights or property. It should be noted, however, that there are some exceptions: capital gains income (or capital gains profit) will not be assessable for the sale of the main residence of the taxpayer, or for assets (such as copyrights) created or acquired before 20 September 1985.

TAXABLE INCOME

Your **taxable income** is your *assessable income* minus all allowable tax deductions.

Taxable Income = Assessable Income – Allowable Deductions.

Example: Assume that your total income comprises $20,000 earned as a school music teacher and an additional $15,000 earned from live performances, your assessable income will be $35,000.

You may, however, be able to claim $2,000 dollars in tax deductions for money you have spent in the course of running your business as a performing musician (e.g. money spent on travel and transporting your instrument to live performances).

Your *taxable income*, therefore, will be your assessable income ($35,000) minus your allowable deductions ($2,000) which is $33,000.

Allowable deductions include all the deductions that the government will allow you to claim when calculating your taxable income. For further information on the various deductions you can claim, see the section entitled 'Deductions' below.

TAXABLE INCOME AND ASSESSABLE INCOME FOR OVERSEAS ARTISTS

The same rules apply to non-residents as to residents of Australia – that is,

Taxable Income = Assessable Income – Allowable Deductions.

Assessable income for overseas artists will only include income derived in Australia. Similarly, allowable deductions are those incurred in Australia in the earning of that income. This is so whether the taxpayer is an individual or a company.

TAX RATES FOR AUSTRALIAN RESIDENTS

Australian residents who earn less than $6,000 a year will not pay tax and in some circumstances, may not have to lodge a tax return. The tax rates for Australian residents (as at July 2001) are set out below.

To see how the tax rates work, go to the ATO site:
http://www.ato.gov.au/individuals/content.asp?doc=/content/12333.htm

Remember that if you are doing gigs, the promoter/venue has to take out Pay As You Go (PAYG) tax. (It used to be that the obligation to withhold tax from payments to individual performing artists only arose if the musician was an employee. Not so any more. Because the nature of the contractual arrangements varied so much and because it was often uncertain whether the performer was an employee or an independent contractor, the ATO brought in a regulation requiring that PAYG be withheld irrespective of whether the individual is an employee or independent contractor.

See http://ato.gov.au/content/downloads/n1023A-05-2005-w.pdf, which sets out the special regime for those working on a daily or hourly basis in the music industry. This is where you go to see what PAYG tax is payable in respect of your gigs.

TAX RATES FOR NON-AUSTRALIAN RESIDENTS

Non-Australian residents must pay tax from the first dollar that they earn in Australia. (For tax rates for non-Australian residents see http://www.ato.gov.au/individuals/content.asp?doc=/content/12333.htm).

LODGING YOUR TAX RETURN

DO I HAVE TO LODGE A TAX RETURN?

All Australian residents who earn over $6,000 within a financial year, and all non-residents who earn any income at all in Australia, must lodge a tax return. (The threshold rate of $6,000 applied at the time of writing).

If you are an Australian resident who earns **under** $6,000 in a financial year, you may have to lodge a tax return in some instances. There are a number of reasons why you may have to, including the following:

(a) If you received a Commonwealth of Australia government pension, allowance or payment.

(b) If you are a liable parent under a child support assessment.

(c) If you carried on a business.

(d) If you made a loss, or can claim a loss in a previous tax year.

(e) If you are a special professional covered by the income averaging provisions. These provisions apply to authors of literary, dramatic, musical or artistic works, inventors, performing artists, production associates and active sports persons. (See 'Income averaging for artists' below.)

(f) If you had amounts of tax withheld from income you received or earned.

(g) If you were required to lodge an activity statement under the pay as you go (PAYG) system and pay an instalment amount during the year and that amount has not been fully refunded to you.

(h) If you had amounts withheld from interest, because you did not quote a tax file number (TFN) or Australian Business Number (ABN) to the investment body.

(i) If you are under 18 years of age, and your income exceeded $643, and was not made up of salary or wages.

INDIVIDUALS

Individuals must lodge a tax return if their annual taxable income is over $6,000, or if any of the above reasons apply.

To help with the process, you can obtain resources from the Australian Taxation Office (the ATO) such as the 'TaxPack'. The TaxPack guide is designed to help individuals complete their tax return and provides detailed instructions and information. In addition, the ATO has introduced 'e-tax', an Internet lodgement facility that allows individual taxpayers to lodge their personal income tax return via the Internet. For further information see the ATO website (www.ato.gov.au).

PARTNERSHIPS

Partnerships per se are not taxed. The income is divided amongst each of the partners who then pay personal income tax on all earnings derived through the partnership. However, the partnership itself must lodge a partnership tax return and will need its own tax file number and ABN. The partnership's tax file number is used when it lodges its annual income tax return.

COMPANIES

All companies must lodge a tax return. Companies are taxed as a separate legal entity distinct from their shareholders. The company's net taxable income (that is, its total income less business expenses such as wages) is taxed at 30% (at the time of writing). There is no income tax free threshold for a company.

TRUSTS

All forms of trust, including deceased estates, discretionary and unit trusts must lodge a return. The trust's tax file number is used when the annual income tax return for the trust is lodged.

DEDUCTIONS

Generally, expenses incurred in deriving assessable income can be claimed as a deduction. It is important to make sure that you keep all your receipts, so that all deductions claimed can be substantiated. This may be bothersome, but you should accept the task as a necessary part of professional life. Receipts must be kept for five years.

For tax purposes, deductible expenses fall into two categories, 'capital expenses' and 'recurrent expenses'. The categorisation is important as it impacts on whether the deductions will be claimed as a lump sum deduction in one year, or whether the expenses will be depreciated (and claimed over a number of years). 'Capital expenses' and 'recurrent expenses' are explained in more detail below.

CAPITAL EXPENSES AND DEPRECIATION

Capital expenses relate to the cost of goods and materials bought for your music business. These might include: recording equipment, musical instruments or vehicles for the transport of equipment and group members.

For capital expenditure, deductions for the cost of the asset are spread over the useful life of the asset. This is known as **depreciation**. There are different ways to structure depreciation, discussed below. First, however, it is important to consider whether your business falls within the provisions of the 'Simplified Tax System'.

The **Simplified Tax System** (**STS**) was introduced from 1 July 2001. Businesses that fall within the STS can take advantage of special deductions and depreciation rates. You may be eligible to enter the STS for a year of income if the following apply:

1. You carry on a business in the relevant income year (for more information see the section entitled 'hobby or business' below); and

2. The STS annual turnover of your business for the year is less that $1 million; and

3. Your business has depreciating assets of less that $3 million at the end of that year.

   If you fall within the STS then the following will apply:
   - All depreciating assets costing less that $1,000 can be written off immediately;
   - You can pool all other assets and depreciate them as a single asset at the rate of 30%; and
   - All assets (excluding buildings) with an effective life of 25 years of more, can be pooled and depreciated at the rate of 5%.

   If you do not fall within the STS then the following will apply:
   - All depreciating assets costing less that $300 can be written off immediately;
   - All capital expenses costing less that $1,000 may be allocated to a pool and written off using a rate up to the four-year effective life diminishing value rate (the diminishing value method is explained below); and
   - For all other depreciating assets costing over $1,000, you may either 'self assess' their effective lives, or use the rate prescribed by the Tax Commissioner.

The table below sets out some of the effective lives prescribed by the Tax Commissioner for assets relevant to musicians.

Asset	Effective Life
Musical Instruments Associated portable equipment (including amplifiers, microphones, speakers, mixers and music stands)	6 and 2/3 years
Brass	10 years
Keyboard (acoustic)	10 years
Keyboard (electric)	5 years
Percussion	5 years
Stringed Instruments	10 years
Woodwind	10 years
Theatre equipment (Theatrical accessories – wigs, costumes, etc)	6 years

You can either structure your depreciation using the 'prime cost method' or the 'diminishing value method' depending on the percentage rate of deduction you want to claim in each year.

The Prime Cost Method means you receive a 'deductible allowance' at the same rate, (or dollar value) in each year until the remaining value of the asset is zero.

Example: If you were to buy a keyboard (acoustic) for $1,000 to use as part of your music business, the effective life would be 10 years. The price you paid for your keyboard would therefore be depreciated over 10 years. The rate of depreciation would therefore be:

$1,000 divided by 10 years = $100 a year

which would mean deductions at the rate of 10% of the purchase price each year for 10 years.

The **Diminishing Value Method** means you can claim a large deduction in the first few years, which reduces until the remaining value of the asset is zero. The diminishing value rate will be 150% of the prime cost rate for a particular item.

Example: The diminishing value rate is determined by looking at what the prime cost rate would be (the cost of the asset divided by the effective life) and then attributing a rate of 150%.

Therefore, if you were to buy the same keyboard for $1,000 to use as part of your music business, then using the 'diminishing value method', the keyboard would be depreciated at:

$1000 x 15% = $150 deduction for the first year
In the second year, the amount of the deduction for the first year must be reduced from the cost of the keyboard ($1,000 - $150 = $850) and then again calculated at the rate of 15%
$850 x 15% = $127.50 deduction for the second year
The process must then be repeated for each successive year, until the value of the asset is zero.

RECURRENT EXPENSES
Recurrent expenses are items that are fully deductible in the first year of income. For musicians and performers these include the following.

MATERIALS
The costs of all materials used for your work are generally deductible. The obvious examples include strings, sticks and skins, manuscript paper, pencils, erasers and so on.

REPAIRS
Expenditure incurred for repairs to premises, plant, machinery, implements, utensils or articles used for the purpose of producing income may be deductible. For example, deductions could be claimed for repairs to instruments, repairs to a practice studio (rented or owned), repairs to an amplifier or music stand.

COMMISSIONS
You may deduct the amount of commission paid to your agent. This is clearly a sum expended in producing assessable income.

BANK CHARGES
Bank fees charged on business accounts are deductible.

LEGAL AND ACCOUNTING EXPENSES
These are deductible if they are incurred in deriving assessable income. This includes the expenses relating to: legal expenses; borrowing money (including legal fees, procuration fees, stamp duties, valuation fees, survey fees, etc.); discharging a mortgage (if the property is wholly used to produce assessable income, the whole amount is deductible. If not, an apportionment must be made); preparing lease documents; matters of copyright, designs; trademark and patents (including the costs of grant, registration, or extension). Some legal fees, however (such as those incurred in the purchase of an investment property), are capital expenses.

SUBSCRIPTIONS AND BOOKS
Subscriptions to work-related periodicals and magazines are deductible. As a general rule the cost of relevant books is deductible if under $50. Books over that value would be depreciated annually.

CARTAGE
The costs of transporting your instrument (and other equipment required for a performance) will be deductible.

CLEANING
Few musicians are able to afford the luxury of employing someone to clean their practice studio (if they have one) and instruments, but if cleaners are employed, those expenses are deductible. In any event, the cost of the cleaning materials and agents is deductible. Similarly, the costs of cleaning 'special' clothes used in the production of income are deductible.

CONFERENCES AND CONVENTIONS
Like doctors, lawyers and other notorious conventioneers, musicians may claim the expenses incurred in attending professionally relevant conventions and conferences. If you go to MIDEM or South By Southwest, the trip is deductible. (If you extend the trip and take a holiday, you must apportion your expenses between the two purposes. Keep a travel diary of all appointments and expenses and keep ALL receipts.)

DISCOUNTS
The amount of any discount, in the form of a rebate given in the fee for performance, will be deductible. For example, if you choose to perform at a function and agree to give a 20% discount off your normal performance fees, the amount of that discount will be deductible.

HIRE, RENT OR LEASE
Rental of any rehearsal space, the hiring of any motor vehicles or equipment and any lease payments on motor vehicles etc., are fully deductible where used solely for business purposes. These expenses may be apportioned where the items are both for business and personal use.

INSURANCE PREMIUMS
The premiums paid for insurance against accident, loss of income, damage to or theft of instruments and damage to rehearsal studios are all deductible.

INTEREST
When money is borrowed to produce assessable income or to buy an asset that is to be used in the earning of income, the interest is deductible.

Example: the interest on moneys borrowed to purchase an instrument, to set up a recording studio or rehearsal room, purchase an amplifier, or to buy any materials such as strings, would be deductible. A distinction must be drawn between interest payments and principal repayments. The former is deductible whereas the latter is not. If you are able to claim this deduction, it is recommended that you ask the lending institution for a statement that will show how much interest has been paid. This statement will help substantiate the claim.

LIGHTING AND POWER
These costs are deductible, but where utility usage is both for private and professional purposes, an apportionment must be made.

POSTAGE AND OTHER MAILING COSTS
The postage costs incurred in sending letters, performance invitations, accounts, recordings, music, and even instruments, are all deductible.

RENTAL OF RECORDING STUDIO AND REHEARSAL SPACE
Rental costs are clearly deductible, but if the space is also used for domestic accommodation, an apportionment must be made.

SALARIES OR WAGES PAID TO EMPLOYEES AND ASSISTANTS
These are deductible. Examples include book-keeping and secretarial assistants, employment of other musicians, sound engineers or composers.

STATIONERY
The costs of stationery, pens and pencils, paper clips, ink, manuscript paper, music folders, briefcases and the like are deductible.

TELEPHONE
Telephone accounts (including rental and call charges) are deductible. Where the musician does not also have a dedicated business line, an apportionment will be necessary between private and business use.

TRAVELLING AND ACCOMMODATION
The costs incurred in travelling between one's home and place of work are not generally deductible, unless the musician is obliged to transport bulky instruments and equipment to and from the place of performance. A full deduction may be allowable where the transport cost is primarily attributable to the transport of equipment rather than personal transport.

Travel costs (including transportation costs such as bus, taxi or plane fares and petrol costs, as well as related expenses such as the money spent on food and accommodation during the trip) may be allowable deductions for musicians where they:

- accept a casual engagement requiring absence from home;
- are on tour (i.e. travelling from place to place and absent from home); and
- are on a long-term engagement (usually less than six months) in one place but requiring absence from their home.

There are specific rules associated with what travel and accommodation expenses can be claimed. The ATO's TaxPack is a useful guide and sets out the rules relating to travel expenses and what evidence you need to be able to claim these expenses. For further information see the ATO website (www.ato.gov.au).

PARKING FEES, BRIDGE AND ROAD TOLLS
You can claim a deduction for these costs only if the travel was for work – for example, between your employer's studio and a performance venue. You cannot claim a deduction for these costs for travel to and from work.

HAIRDRESSING
You can claim a deduction for the cost of a particular hairstyle if it is required for a role or costume.

MAKEUP
Where the makeup or cleanser is used exclusively for stage appearances, a full deduction is allowed.

CLOTHING AND DRY CLEANING
Any special clothing used exclusively for performance will be an allowable deduction in full. Dry cleaning and laundry charges will also be allowed for performance clothing.

LESSONS AND MASTER CLASSES
Where lessons are taken to maintain acting, singing, dancing or other skills related to your business, their cost may be deductible. However, such costs will only be deductible if the classes are to help you obtain work-related specific skills.

PUBLICITY
The costs of promotion, advertising, photographs, stationery, postage etc. are fully deductible.

PAYMENT OF ROYALTIES
Royalties and fees paid for a licence to use copyright material are fully deductible.

ANSWERING MACHINES, MOBILE PHONES, PAGERS AND OTHER TELECOMMUNICATIONS EQUIPMENT

You can only claim a deduction for the work-related part of the rental cost or depreciation on the purchase price of these items.

PROFESSIONAL LIBRARY

You can claim a deduction for the work-related part of the depreciation on a professional library that includes books, tapes, compact discs, records and videos containing reference material directly relevant to your income earning activities.

DISKS, TAPES AND CASSETTES

You can claim a deduction for the work-related part of the cost of audio and video tapes and compact discs – for example, tapes used for rehearsal.

HOBBY OR BUSINESS?

WHAT IS A BUSINESS?

The next section may appear long and tortuous but it is extremely important. If you are in music as a hobby, your income will not be taxable but you won't be able to claim your expenses. (They will almost certainly be more than your income.) On the other hand, you may be working in the music industry - as a business not a hobby – and not be making a profit. Many working in the music industry make a loss from their music work and the only way that they survive is by having two jobs: instrumentalist/lecturer, composer/barista, etc. In this situation, you want to be able to off-set your music business losses against your income from the other sources.

To do this you must establish that although your music industry activity is loss making, it is being carried on as a 'business' – not a hobby. There are many factors that may indicate that a 'business' is being carried on. None of them is determinative. Whether a business is being carried on is based on the overall impression gained after looking at the activity as a whole and the intention of the taxpayer undertaking it. General factors indicating a 'business' include:

- Whether the activity has a significant commercial purpose or character; this indicator comprises many aspects of the other indicators;
- Whether the taxpayer has more than just an intention to engage in business;
- Whether the taxpayer has a purpose of profit as well as a prospect of profit from the activity;
- Whether there is repetition and regularity of the activity;

- Whether the activity is of the same kind and carried on in a similar manner to that of the ordinary trade in that line of business;
- Whether the activity is planned, organised and carried on in a businesslike manner such that it is directed at making a profit;
- The size, scale and permanency of the activity; and
- Whether the activity is better described as a hobby or a form of recreation activity.

In 2005 the ATO introduced a Ruling (TR 2005/1) that revolutionised the tax position of many working in the arts and entertainment business: The Ruling is set out in full on the ATO website but the following sections are intended to provide a summary of some its main points: See: http://law.ato.gov.au/atolaw/view.htm?DocID=TXR%2FTR20051%2FNAT%2FATO%2F00005.

At long last, the ATO recognised that because of the nature of arts activity, arts businesses typically have different characteristics to those found in other businesses. By this ruling the ATO has recognised that many professionals working in the music business supplement their music industry income with income from other sources, especially in the early stages of their careers. The music activity may lose money but it is no less a business because of that.

The Ruling provides many factors that may indicate you are carrying on a music business – not just a hobby:

- The practice of skills in the manner and for the time required to maintain a high professional standard;
- Musical activity conducted with sufficient regularity to demonstrate a commitment to engage in a business, not just indulge a hobby or pastime;
- Regular participation in activities designed to promote their music work, build their reputation as a musician, to find or create markets for that work; and
- Activities of the same kind and carried on in the manner characteristic of the relevant industry

    For this indicator you look at the various characteristics of others working in the industry. These business indicators may include:
- Industry and peer recognition;
- Qualifications (or equivalent experience) typical of those in the relevant industry sector. (In some sectors of the arts industry formal qualifications are the norm. In others, especially in new and emerging types of art, it would be less usual for an artist to have any formal qualifications);
- Public recognition (for example, is the taxpayer described as such in

the media? Is their opinion as a musician sought by the public? Is their music used by others as examples for teaching purposes?);

- Meeting the eligibility and selection criteria for grants, awards and professional opportunities (for example, residencies) open to others in the music industry;
- Appointment to a position being contingent on the person's status in the music industry (for example, being offered a position as a composer in residence; where a teaching position is based on the employee's status as a professional musician; being appointed as a member of relevant boards or committees);
- Membership of professional associations, including unions (such as MEAA or the Musicians' Union) that are dedicated to serving the professional needs and interests of musicians?
- Reputation building in a manner consistent with others in the relevant industry sector;
- Methods of application and time commitment to activity consistent with others in the relevant industry sector; and
- Obtaining the advice or services of an agent, manager, legal or financial adviser.

SIGNIFICANT COMMERCIAL PURPOSE OR CHARACTER

Just saying that you have the intention to be in business, is not enough. In determining whether an activity has a significant commercial purpose or character, one must really look to all the other business indicators.

INTENTION OF THE TAXPAYER

What identifies you as a professional rather than an enthusiastic amateur is your intention to carry on as a business that which others frequently pursue merely as a pastime. It is assessed objectively: Is your decision to commercially exploit your skills reflected in your overt and planned activities.

The fact that the activity is one that others may do on a non-commercial basis will not deprive the activity of a commercial purpose or character if you can demonstrate an intention to carry on that activity as a business. Whether or not you possess the relevant intention, will usually be determined by a consideration of the objective factors set out below.

PROFIT MOTIVE

This indicator refers to your intention to profit from the activity, by looking at your activities objectively. It is not enough for you merely to say so.

The fact that you are prepared to make losses to realise a business ambition can be consistent with carrying on a business. This is the case even when the prospects of turning a profit may be slim, or the fact that you also enjoy or even are passionate about the activity (for example, a musician who is also an instrument collector.)

Many businesses make losses, especially in the short term. Some make losses over several years. They are still businesses so long as they have an intention and expectation, on objective grounds, that their activities would eventually become profitable. The ATO acknowledges that in the case of an arts business, which is a notoriously high-risk commercial activity where there is more variability between the cost of creating the art and its commercial value, it may often be difficult to assess whether a profit motive exists solely from whether a profit has in fact been made by the activity. Therefore, whether you are engaged in the following kinds of activities will be relevant in ascertaining whether you have a genuine intention to profit from your arts activities:

- Endeavouring to bring your musical work or services to relevant markets;
- Creating or enhancing industry contacts;
- Offering your musical services or skills for a fee to the public;
- Offering expert musical services through commission or consultancy;
- Related income seeking activities including applying for grants, awards, patronage, commissions, and so on;
- Undertaking activities designed to raise your profile (or that of your music) in the music industry;
- Entering music competitions, residencies and award events;
- Undertaking research into the proposed music business and consultation of music experts or business advisers prior to and during the activity; and
- Reputation-building as part of an overall intention to make a profit.

It will be a question of fact in each case whether the available evidence points to the activity being pursued with profit making in mind. If you are driven solely by the personal enjoyment and satisfaction you derive from your art, you are not carrying on a business.

REPETITION AND REGULARITY

The ATO requires that the activity should be conducted on a regular basis overall. There must also be repetition, usually not in the sense of producing identical output, but rather in the repeated application of musical skills to different pieces of work or performances. (Note however that being in business is not the same as just being 'busy'.)

Constant activity is not required to prove that you are carrying on a business. Indeed, it is accepted that musicians may for financial reasons engage in other types of non-arts related work, which may be periodically or simultaneously interspersed with their arts activities.

ORGANISATION IN A BUSINESSLIKE MANNER AND THE USE OF SYSTEM

Although the actual creation of art may be the product of intuition and inspiration, professional arts activity can still be carried on in a systematic and organised manner in accordance with ordinary commercial principles. Whether an arts activity is being carried on in a businesslike manner will be demonstrated by the presence of factors such as:

- Good record keeping of sales, expenses, invoices, receipts and accounts;
- Presence of formal, written contracts to record agreements to supply work or services;
- Evidence of a body of work that demonstrates a record in the particular field;
- Use of an accountant, lawyer, business manager, agent or other appropriate source of commercial expertise;
- Membership of a recognised organisation or professional association;
- Presence of a written business plan (that is, a written description of the intended future direction of the business and how that future direction will be realised), perhaps developed in consultation with the taxpayer's accountant or manager;
- Maintaining insurance in respect of their arts products or performances for public liability where their work is being distributed or performed;
- Advice from professional artists who have succeeded in their industry sector;
- Keeping relevant qualifications and skills up to date (for example, through taking relevant courses, subscription to journals, attendance at conferences);
- Systematic and researched attempts to bring the art work to suitable markets; and
- Use of traditional business structures (like companies, trusts or partnerships). Lack of use of such a structure however is merely neutral in deciding whether a music activity is being carried on as a business, as many professional music businesses are carried on as sole traders.

SIZE OR SCALE OF ACTIVITY

As most professional musicians carry on their business as sole traders, this will necessarily limit the size or scale of their activities. Small is fine. Indeed, the Ruling recognises that scale and irregularity of activity may be characteristic of the type of artistic pursuit in question, even when carried on as a business. Whether an arts activity is being carried on with sufficient size and scale so as to constitute a business may be demonstrated by the following:

- The activity and output is beyond what is needed to meet the personal needs of the artist; and
- The volume of output is sufficient to enable the taxpayer to be regularly bringing their work to suitable markets.

The courts have also recognised that the nature of some businesses may be such that periods of business activity 'may be intermittent with long intervals of quiescence in between'. This observation is especially pertinent in the arts, for the following reasons:

- Most musicians supplement their arts-related income with income from other sources and those other sources may be time-demanding;
- Many musicians will have periods of perceived commercial inactivity while they are engaged in the creative process; and
- In order to maintain the high professional standards required of a professional musician, many must devote substantial time to the maintenance and development of their skills and experience. For example, by attending workshops, a master class or undertaking a residency.

Therefore, the fact that a musician may have some periods of perceived relative inactivity will not (by itself) preclude a finding that he or she is carrying on a business throughout the whole period, including periods of relative inactivity.

The Ruling also recognises that artists may apply their artistic skills across a range of related activities during their professional life. For example, an actor may take a part in a musical if that is the kind of work that is available, or a musician may spend part of their time tutoring private students rather than performing. However, this diverse application of artistic skill may also be driven by the need for creative stimulation and individual development over the course of their career. For example, you may begin your career as an actor and gradually evolve into a musician.

Therefore, in considering whether you are carrying on a business, it is acknowledged that you may engage in a variety of arts-related activities, none of which, when viewed in isolation, would be of sufficient scale to amount to the carrying on of a business. However, the same activities viewed as a whole may present a cohesive picture of an artist diligently exploiting their skills in a variety of ways so as to amount to the carrying on of a business.

NOT A HOBBY OR RECREATION

The pursuit of a hobby (or recreational pursuit, or pastime), is not the carrying on of a business for taxation purposes. As noted above, money derived from the pursuit of a hobby is not regarded as income and therefore is not assessable... even though the operations may be fairly substantial.

Similarly, expenses incurred in relation to a hobby activity, or recreational pursuit, or pastime, are not allowable deductions. However it is recognised that a hobby, and so on, can sometimes turn into a business - a taxpayer may enjoy what they do and still be carrying on a business. What distinguishes the professional from the hobbyist is an intention (objectively determined), to carry on as a business that others undertake merely for personal enjoyment, coupled with activities that implement the taxpayer's intention to carry on a business.

SOME INDICATORS OF A TAXPAYER ENGAGED ONLY IN THE PURSUIT OF A HOBBY OR RECREATION INCLUDE:

- It is evident, as determined on an objective basis, that the taxpayer does not intend to make a profit from the activity;
- Losses are incurred because the dominant motive for engaging in the activity is personal pleasure, rather than the taxpayer also being driven by the desire to commercially exploit their artistic skills;
- There is no plan in place to demonstrate how the taxpayer intends to make a profit from their music;
- Performances are mostly to friends and relatives, not to the general public; and
- The taxpayer does not intend to carry on a business, but rather intends to pursue a hobby or engage in a form of recreation (as shown by the absence of the other business indicators discussed above).

EXAMPLES

CARRYING ON A BUSINESS

Alicia is a musician and teaches students regularly at her home in a room specially set up for students. She advertises under the name 'Music made easy with Alicia' in the Yellow Pages as well as in local newspapers and school newsletters. She teaches the children of friends and also teaches students who have seen her advertisements. Alicia teaches music in order to make a profit and covers all expenses incurred as a result of her teaching. Whether or not she makes a profit, Alicia would most likely be considered to be 'carrying on a business' and could claim all advertising and other expenses associated with running the business as tax deductions.

CONDUCTING A HOBBY

Jim plays the trumpet. He performs at weddings but only when asked to by family or friends. He does not intend to increase the number of weddings at which he performs and only charges a small fee, which would barely cover his costs. Jim's trumpet performance would be considered a hobby and Jim would therefore not include the amounts received at the weddings, in his income tax return. Consequently, Jim cannot claim any expenditure incurred in relation to his hobby against any other income he earns.

REGISTERING YOUR BUSINESS: GST, ABN, TAX FILE NUMBERS AND PAYG WITHHOLDING TAX

THE ABN

The Australian Business Number (ABN) is the identifying number that businesses use when dealing with other businesses. In the course of business, you generally need to quote your ABN on your invoices or other documents relating to supplies that you make to other businesses, to avoid having tax withheld from payments to you. You will also need to use your ABN in certain dealings with the ATO and other areas of government. If you're registered for GST, it is important that you put your ABN on your invoices and head them 'tax invoice'.

REGISTERING FOR AN ABN

All music businesses, whether set up as an association, a freelance contractor, a company or a partnership, must obtain an ABN if they are involved in 'carrying on an enterprise'. You can obtain an ABN even if you don't register for GST. All Corporations Act companies are automatically entitled to an ABN, while other entities must meet certain criteria in order to be entitled. You can register electronically at the ATO website located at www.ato.gov.au, or obtain a registration application from the ATO.

THE AUSTRALIAN COMPANY NUMBER AND THE ABN

Companies incorporated in Australia are regulated by the Australian Securities and Investments Commission. On forming a company you are issued with an Australian Company Number (ACN). When a company registers for an ABN, the number issued by the Australian Business Registrar will be its ACN, with two check digits at the beginning. For example, if your ACN is 999 888 777, then your ABN will generally add two digits at the beginning of the ACN and so may appear as 21 999 888 777. The ABN will eventually replace your ACN or Australian Registered Body Number (ARBN), but will not replace your tax file number.

Companies don't have to quote both the ABN and ACN on documents.

Under the Corporations Act, a company is required to show its ACN on all public documents and negotiable instruments. However, following amendments to the Corporations Regulations, companies with an ABN can use the ABN in place of their ACN, on the condition that:

- the ABN includes the company's ACN as the last nine digits; and
- the company quotes the ABN in the same way it quoted its ACN.

It is a good idea to put your ABN on your business stationery, especially your invoices. Other businesses will need this information so they don't withhold tax from payments to you. If you are registered for GST, other businesses will also need your ABN to claim input tax credits for GST included in the price of goods and services you supply.

In addition to all this, you will need to complete a Business Activity Statement (BAS) which must be submitted to the ATO.

WHAT IS GST?

GST is a goods and services tax that was introduced on 1 July 2000. This requires businesses to add 10% of the normal sales price of goods or services to their invoices and fees. GST is called a consumer tax because consumers pay it at the time they pay for goods or services.

> **Example:** Jane is a violinist and runs a wedding music business called 'Weddings by Jane Pty Ltd'. She performs at weddings for a fee of $150 an hour. If Jane performs for 2 hours, the final bill to the client will be:
>
> | | |
> |---|---|
> | $150 x 2 (hours) | $300.00 |
> | GST (+ 10% of $300) | $ 30.00 |
> | **Total bill inclusive of GST** | **$330.00** |
>
> Jane gives a tax invoice to the client that shows the actual fee for the services delivered, together with the GST charged. The client pays $330 and Jane then has to send $30 GST to the ATO. The consumer of the service has paid the tax; the provider of the service has collected the tax and remitted it to the ATO; the world is smiling. Well, it's not quite that simple.

GST PAPERWORK

If you are a registered business, you must fill out a 'Business Activity Statement' (BAS) every 3 months and tell the ATO how much GST you have collected through sales, and how much you have paid out in expenses.

The BAS is like a tax return in many ways. If a business has paid out more GST in expenses than it has collected in GST, then the ATO will reimburse the business. If a business has earned more GST than it has paid out in GST, then the business will have to pay the balance to the ATO. The ATO will assess the BAS for each three-month period.

Example: Lets take our previous example of Weddings by Jane Pty Ltd. Assume that at the end of a three-month period, Jane has worked 120 hours and has earned a total of $19,800, of which $1,800 has been paid to account for GST.

Performance fees	$150 x 120 (hours) =	$18,000.00
(not including GST)		
GST on her performance fees:	$18,000 x 10% =	$1,800.00
Total Income (inclusive of GST):		**$19,800.00**

Jane has also paid GST to the sum of $1,000 in costs associated with running the business (e.g. GST paid on sheet music and as part of the service fees she paid to have her violin repaired).

Jane must fill out a Business Activity Statement at the end of the three-month period. This will account for all the GST she has been paid ($1,800) and will also account for the GST she has had to pay in running the business ($1,000). Jane will therefore owe the ATO $800 GST for that three-month period, being the difference between what she paid out for GST and the amount of GST that she has collected during the period.

REGISTERING FOR GST

You *must* register for GST if:

- you are an entity carrying on an enterprise – (if you are in business and not a hobby you probably meet this requirement); and
- your annual turnover is at or above the registration turnover threshold of $50,000.

You may *choose* to register if your turnover is below the $50,000 turnover threshold.

WHAT ARE THE BENEFITS OF GST REGISTRATION?

You should consider registering your business for GST even if your turnover is below the $50,000 threshold. By registering for GST you are entitled to claim input tax credits for the GST included in the price paid for things you acquire and the GST paid on importations, if they are for use in your business. If you are not registered you cannot claim input tax credits, so your business costs could be higher than those of your competitors.

OBTAINING A TAX FILE NUMBER

Partnerships, companies and trusts need their own tax file number. You obtain a business tax file number at the same time as you register the business for an ABN, using the same application form. Sole traders use their own tax file number in dealings with the ATO.

REGISTERING FOR PAYG WITHHOLDING

If you make payments from which withholding is required (for example, wages to employees or payments to businesses that do not quote an ABN), you must register with the ATO before you first withhold. You can register for PAYG withholding by either completing a form (which can be sent to the ATO in paper or electronic form) or by contacting the ATO. If you are applying for an ABN, you can use the same form to register for PAYG withholding.

REGISTERING FOR FRINGE BENEFITS TAX

If you are an employer and provide fringe benefits to your employees, the ATO requires that you register for fringe benefits tax (FBT). Fringe benefits are all the non-monetary benefits that are provided to employees, such as a car. This is accountant territory.

PERSONAL SERVICES INCOME

On 1 July 2000, a new measure took effect regarding the taxation of personal services income. If you earn personal services income, your available deductions are limited. If you channel your income through a company, partnership or trust (called a 'personal services entity'), this entity must treat the income as your personal income for tax purposes. The entity may also have pay as you go (PAYG) obligations regarding the income.

DOES THIS AFFECT YOU?

You will be affected by the measure only to the extent that your income, or the income of any other business entity, is your personal services income – that is, income that is mainly a reward for, or the result of, your personal efforts or skills. Income is not personal services income if it is mainly:
- for supplying or selling goods;
- for granting a right to use property; or
- generated by an income-producing asset, such as a truck.

Your personal services income will not be affected by the measure if you are conducting a 'personal services business', either on your own or through a company, partnership or trust.

There are complicated tests used in determining whether your income is 'personal services income'. This is a very significant change to the way personal service companies have had to pay tax and really means that if you are using a company structure, you should be using an accountant or at least retaining one to check your procedures.

CARRYING FORWARD LOSSES

A musician may work for many years without making a profit. Then along comes the successful recording deal, publicity, and the musician becomes 'established' and the profits start rolling in. Anyway, that is the theory.

Perhaps, however, the scenario is slightly different. Perhaps the musician takes two or three years to prepare before each recording agreement. During those years, considerable losses are incurred but during the year of the recording deal, the artist makes a considerable profit.

The tax system allows losses to be carried forward indefinitely, providing that you were carrying on a business when you incurred the losses. For example, if a singer–songwriter accumulates $30,000 losses over 2005, 2006 and 2007 and then signs three major deals and earns an income of $55,000 in 2008, the accumulated losses from previous years may be brought forward and set off against the later profit.

This facility is insufficiently utilised by most artists. In order to take advantage of it, simple but detailed accounts must be maintained, because the taxpayer must be able to prove that he or she was carrying on a business during the loss period, and be able to prove the accumulated losses when the monetary windfall eventually occurs. The keeping of financial records may be a chore, but the alternative is considerably worse. If the losses cannot be brought forward, the taxpayer will have to pay ordinary income tax on the assessable income.

ABNORMAL RECEIPTS

From the sale of a copyright, the grant of a licence in a copyright, advances on royalties and prize monies, a musician may receive an abnormal sum. When tax is taken into account, the benefit from the payment may be virtually illusory. In an attempt to mitigate these harsh effects, a concessional rate of tax is applied to income that includes such abnormal receipts.

The Act provides a special formula for making this computation. It is complicated; the province of accountants, not musicians. It is, however, important to keep it in mind, to keep good records, and to obtain advice from an accountant or a tax specialist.

INCOME AVERAGING FOR SPECIAL PROFESSIONALS

Artists, composers, performers and writers may take advantage of special 'income averaging' concessional tax treatment if they fall within the definition of a 'special professional' and certain other provisions apply.

Income averaging allows special professionals whose income may vary wildly from year to year to reduce the devastating taxation effect of having a successful year. The provisions will only apply to individuals who are Australian residents at some time during the income year.

If you are an artist, composer or writer you will only be considered a 'special professional' if the following apply:

(i) You are engaged or commissioned to produce one or more specified works; and

(ii) Successive engagements or commissions do not result in continuous employment over a substantial period of time.

If you are a performer, to be considered a 'special professional', you must use intellectual, artistic, musical, physical or other personal skills in the presence of an audience or perform or appear in a film, on a tape or disc or in a television or radio broadcast.

The provisions in the Act for calculation of assessment of the eligible income are complicated and an accountant or tax specialist familiar with the provisions should be consulted.

TAX PLANNING AND BUSINESS STRUCTURES

There are many factors that must be taken into account when deciding on a business structure. One important factor will be the tax implications. Listed below, are some of the basic tax advantages of the different structures.

PARTNERSHIPS

Partners in a partnership pay tax on the income they earn as part of their personal income tax. One advantage of a partnership structure is 'income splitting'.

Example: A musician who enters into a bona fide partnership with a spouse (or friend) may 'split' the income earned by the partnership. In the hands of two individuals, the tax paid on $15,000 is:

	Musician	*Spouse*
Gross Income	$7,500	$7,500
Tax (2001 rates)	(7,500 – 6,000) x 0.25	(7,500 – 6,000) x 0.25
	= 375	= 375
Net Income	$7,125	$7,125
Total tax for partners:	$ 750.00	
Total Net Income	**$14,250**	

However, an individual would have paid:

Gross Income	$15,000
Total tax	$ 2,250 (15,000 – 6,000 x 0.25)
Total Net Income	**$ 12,750**

So you can see that a partnership arrangement can save money and minimise tax payments for all involved in the business.

COMPANIES

A company has a legal identity distinct from those who control it. It can sue, be sued, hire, fire, enter contracts – and pay tax. It has traditionally been a way of splitting income and maximising deductions.

The current rate of company tax is 30 per cent. However, it must be remembered that companies pay tax from the first dollar of income earned.

Furthermore, where the company is a sham, that is, the company is really the musician, then a contract between the hirer and musician may be deemed to be personal and any income generated will be assessable in the musician's personal income.

TRUSTS

Trusts can be of three types: discretionary, fixed and unit. Each has a trustee who assumes responsibility and makes decisions.

Discretionary trusts allow the trustee to make decisions as to income distribution, whereas fixed and unit trusts set a date and rate of payments to trust beneficiaries.

A trust allows a musician to therefore take advantage of 'income splitting' (as explained above) yet retain control as trustee.

SUPERANNUATION

Private superannuation or one provided by an employer is a means of 'forced saving' for which tax benefits are received.

TAX ISSUES FOR OVERSEAS ARTISTS

Non-residents pay personal income tax from the first dollar of income. Non-resident corporations pay company tax at 30 per cent from the first dollar of income.

INCOME FROM ENGAGEMENTS

All income derived by a non-resident from performance in Australia is assessable as are fees for interviews etc.

INCOME FROM ROYALTIES

Where an Australian is paying a royalty to an overseas artist, that person (or company) must report to the Taxation Commissioner the amount of the royalty and retain from that payment the amount required by Australian law. Generally the rate is 15 per cent. Where only royalty income is derived by an overseas resident, a tax return need not be lodged. Where other revenue is earned as well, a tax return must be submitted showing all (non-royalty) income and deductions.

DOUBLE TAX TREATY

In all cases the existence of a double tax treaty should be checked. Double tax treaties prevent non-resident overseas artists who earn income in Australia from having to pay tax in Australia as well as in the overseas country in which they are a resident. The treaty rules in which country the tax is to be paid, and ensures that the other country will give a credit for that tax paid.

CHOOSING A TAX OR ACCOUNTING PROFESSIONAL

Accountants are not licensed by the government, although it is necessary for tax agents and company auditors to be registered. Two professional bodies regulate the accounting profession – The Institute of Chartered Accountants and the Australian Society of Accountants. The profession is quite complex and subject to specialisation.

Make sure that you choose a member of one of these professional bodies as their expertise is backed by their membership of the professional body. Just as importantly, make sure that your accountant is experienced in handling music industry clients. As you can see from this chapter, there are many issues that require that specialist knowledge.

37

GETTING THE INTERNATIONAL DEAL

THIS CHAPTER GIVES SOME HINTS FOR THOSE
WHO LIKE PLANE AND BUS TRAVEL. IT'S NOT FOR
EVERYONE — BUT FOR THOSE WHO HAVE THE RIGHT
INGREDIENTS, IT IS FULFILLING AND ENRICHING. FOR
THE REST, IT IS JUST FRUSTRATING AND EXHAUSTING.

At some time or another, most professional musicians, dream of having an
international career. Indeed, it is perhaps inevitable that in an age when local
styles are so dominated by American and European influences that musicians
are tempted to think that they might as well try to launch themselves in a
larger market than Australia can offer. If they are going to struggle here, they
might as well struggle in Los Angeles or London where the prize for success
is so much larger.

To have this ambition is understandable but bringing it to realisation is
extraordinarily difficult. Because the market is so large, the competition is
proportionally large. 'Coals to Newcastle' is nothing compared to taking rock,
jazz or R&B to the United States.

Quite simply, there is no easy recipe for overseas success. It happens rarely
and when it does, it is due to a range of factors and events, few of which could
have been predicted. That said, there are some lessons that can be learned
from those who have made it.

TALENT — THE STARTING POINT

Success is not just a question of talent. There are thousands of talented people
who don't manage to have a national career let alone an international one.
Success demands a quiver of characteristics of which talent is but one.

Many artists are enormously gifted but don't have sufficient faith in that talent. Others lack the ability to gauge their abilities and realistically mould their opportunities to their own talents and character.

Some don't have the emotional strength to withstand the psychological stress that is inherent in continuously having to deal with the expectations of others and rely on others. Others can't bear the weight of success and the darkness of frequent disappointment. Some simply can't cope with the difficulty of maintaining strong interpersonal relationships in the face of the loneliness and isolation that is inherent in every artist who is stretching out to establish an international reputation.

Frequently, artists don't have support from a talented and loyal team that will help to establish the networks; negotiate the deals; protect them from the wolves; support and encourage them when they need it; and tell them 'no' when they need a reality check. No one gets international recognition through his or her own, solitary effort. You need a healthy ego to realise that you can't do it yourself and that if you have success, you haven't done it yourself. You are part of a team of talented people, each of whom deserves and needs respect and recognition of their role in the overall success.

One of the essential aspects of success is marketing and promoting the talent. Talent is the flour in a cook's cupboard. Every cook has flour. It has little value in itself. However, what it is mixed with, what is done with it and the appropriateness of why and when and for whom it is prepared, all contribute to the success of the cook. If the cook wishes to extend his or her reputation beyond their circle of family and friends, their skills must be marketed and promoted; they must be 'sold'.

There are several very good books on how to market and promote your talent. That is not my subject in this chapter. That said, unless you find a way to convince those in control of the market that you have that something extra that can be transformed into an internationally marketable product, you should be satisfied with the local market and not castigate yourself for recognising where your attributes are best suited. Happiness is not something that is found in other people's expectations.

When looking to establish an overseas market, finding the appropriate way to market an act in a non-familiar territory is difficult. It's hard to get noticed by decision-makers and it's even harder to get noticed by the public. What works in Australia, with all the benefits of playing on your home ground, doesn't necessarily work when playing in New York or Berlin.

Perhaps the biggest issue is whether there is a market at all, for what you have to offer. What is it that you have that is different from what is already locally available in the overseas territory?

If you want an example of this, consider John Farnham and Jimmy Barnes. These are two of the most successful Australian recording artists of all time. Neither has an international career. Neither will. They are truly products of a local culture – and no lesser for it. The fact is that neither of these artists offers anything that is not already available in any major city in the United States. Sometimes, being an Australian provides a little touch of the exotic but if you are performing essentially American material to an American market, it is no surprise that there is enormous local competition.

Then there is 'presence'. You don't get overseas acceptance by staying in Fitzroy or Darlinghurst and running your international career by remote control. If you want to become one the biggest recording stars in Europe you have to be in Europe. You have to be available to do interviews and meetings; to go onto a television or radio program without notice to fill in for someone else who cancelled at the last moment; to make a guest appearance with someone that you met just last week at an industry party. You have to be there.

The degree to which this is important obviously varies between music genres. It is neither possible nor appropriate for a symphony orchestra to relocate to another country. It is almost essential for a musician working in popular music, jazz and some genres of classical music. In any event those who are really working a lot overseas, find that constant plane travel from Australia is simply too expensive, too tiring and too patchwork.

Finally, there is the factor of cultural awareness. Many artists try to break into foreign markets with scant understanding of the culture of the people to which they are intending to sell their product. This may not be a big factor if you already have an international reputation and you are touring on the strength of an already proven major success. But if you are trying to open up a new market for an act that has no reputation outside Australia, it pays to be humble enough to know some basics of language and acceptable codes of behaviour, communications and relationships. (For example, in France one would need to understand the significance of the use of 'tu' rather than 'vous' in conversation. Coming from a country like Australia in which everyone seems able to address people that they have just met, irrespective of their status, by their first name, it is important to appreciate that in other cultures, such familiarity does indeed breed contempt.)

CONTACTS

No matter if you have the qualities discussed above, you won't launch an international career without contacts.

Very few artists at an early stage in their career have the necessary contacts to launch outside Australia. To take this big step, they have to use the contacts of others.

The primary sources of contacts are:
- colleagues in the business who have been there before you;
- lawyers;
- managers; and
- agents.

Colleagues are free, the others are sources that you have to buy.

COLLEAGUES

The network of the entertainment industry is extensive. In this field, the classic six degrees of separation is probably three too many. One word from a colleague in the right ear can do more for your overseas career opportunities than all the show-reels, demos and brochures in the world!

Use these personal contacts respectfully, but do use them. Just remember that whilst people can be very generous with their contacts, they were hard won and they will be rightfully protective of them. If they aren't absolutely sure that you have what it takes or they fear that you may abuse the generosity in any way, you will get lots of smiles and assurances but no meaningful assistance.

LAWYERS

One of the traditional ways of accessing overseas networks is to pay a lawyer to help you do it. Top lawyers can:
- get the phone picked up;
- get you an appointment;
- ensure that the contract is fair – given your stage of development; and
- help you get a good agent/business manager.

Note – they do not guarantee to get a deal!

All top Australian entertainment lawyers have wide networks of competent and connected lawyers in various fields of the industry and in most territories. If they think that the artist has what it takes, they **might** make an introduction to some of their colleagues.

Overseas lawyers charge a lot. Expertise and contacts don't come cheap. Remember that when you are using lawyers to help you in your career, you are using the resources that they have spent their professional life building up. Many overseas lawyers charge double the rate of local Australian lawyers and when you take into account the exchange rate, the bill can cause a tremble around the lower lip.

In the United States, some will charge on a commission basis (usually 10% of all advances or 5% of gross income), some will do it on an hourly rate basis; and some charge both. In the United Kingdom the usual approach is still the hourly rate. Everything is negotiable – but only if you have some leverage. (If you have that kind of leverage, your lawyer probably helped you get it, so you don't argue much!)

Another problem is that top lawyers are busy with top clients. They are hard to retain because their services are so much in demand. None of them will take you on unless you have a personal recommendation from someone that they trust, such as another client or your local lawyer.

Still, being represented by a young blood in the star lawyer's firm is often just as good. The name of a top law firm brings a certain gravitas to your affairs and it can be better to be represented by someone on the way up and who is still hungry to establish themselves rather than someone who is in the same firm but has too many star clients to be available for you.

A respected lawyer from a respected firm can make all the difference in obtaining overseas deals and in closing them quickly on fair terms.

Finally, remember that all top lawyers in the business have to deal with conflicts of interest. Such conflicts are not, of themselves, a problem. Many times, it is why you chose that lawyer in the first place! The problem arises only when the conflict is undisclosed. No lawyer is going to act for both parties at the same time but he or she may well have acted, at some time or other, for the party with which you want to make contact. After all, in every field in the arts and entertainment industry there are only a limited number of star artists and star companies. Each of those fields has its star lawyers.

So, what will local lawyers look for in artists who want to retain them to access their brain and their networks?

- Is there real international talent evident from the demo, the clip, the show-reel?
- Is the quality of the production of those materials of the highest artistic and technical standard?
- Is quality and creativity evident in the design and packaging of demo and promo material?
- Does the artist have the support of talented and experienced management?
- What is their chance of success?
- Do they have personality?
- Is their live act ready for a critical overseas audience?
- Are they likeable and enjoyable to work with?
- Are they going to pay the bill?

These are also the sorts of subjective decisions that companies make when considering long-term relationships with artists. The business is based on relationships.

To have a career, you need a capacity to form relationships and exhibit loyalty to those who work with you and thus make them want to commit themselves to your goals.

Relationships involve mutual respect and for this reason, the so-called 'dreaded artistic temperament' is not something that lawyers see in their successful clients. Those who reach success demand quality service and they deserve it! The most difficult clients are usually those who are 'wannabes' – they haven't yet made it but feel that they should already enjoy the trappings of the stars. They tend not to last long because they create just too much friction. Quite simply, they fail the relationship test.

MANAGERS

Few Australian managers have the experience of breaking an artist internationally. Those that do are much sought after and usually their books are full. Paradoxically, most Australian managers will insist on signing their artists for the world, even though they do not have overseas experience, skills or contacts.

Accordingly, it is important that the management agreement provides a very clear mechanism to ensure that the artist will have consent over the appointment of any co-managers or personal managers. Many agreements even specify that the artist can require the manager to appoint a co-manager in a particular overseas territory.

Agreements should also protect the artist from suffering additional commissions where an overseas co-manager is appointed. This is a case where the local manager will have to take a cut in commission and negotiate a lower rate with the co-manager in the overseas territory so that the artist does not unfairly carry the burden of the manager's inability to deliver his or her services on a worldwide basis.

Artists seeking to break overseas need highly experienced management in each relevant territory. Few have experience in more than one country. Often the artist will be best having one manager in Australia, another in the United States and another in the United Kingdom or Europe. Where that is the case, they will be well advised to make one of those managers responsible for over-all co-ordination.

Managers who take on responsibility for more than one territory must be prepared to travel. International careers demand constant attention. There aren't many international managers with a wonderful family life, but they do know the first names of a lot of flight attendants.

AGENTS

The first step in building an overseas career is to get a good agent in the territory.

In each area of the music sector, the word 'agent' means something slightly different. Performing artists have agents to book their performances; composers and producers have agents too. Their functions vary in detail but can all be brought down to a simple proposition: an agent is someone who has a commercial interest in selling your artistic product to those who may not yet know that they want to buy it.

A good agent has a contacts list to die for. They know the market; who the players are; who is right for any particular talent; and how best to pitch the talent. They not only know their target on a first-name basis, they probably had lunch together on Thursday.

There are the huge companies like William Morris that have large specialist departments, and small but influential agencies with one or two staff. With agencies, size definitely doesn't matter. It depends on the attributes and the commitment of the human who takes responsibility for your career.

Finding the right agent is a matter of research. Who are the really active agents working in your field, in the territory that you want to penetrate? Which of them represents your kind of talent? Then you have to work out how best to pitch yourself to them. That's the hard part.

WHERE TO BASE THE BUSINESS

One common question asked by artists is, 'Should I set up an overseas company in a tax haven?'. Generally, this is a question that the lawyer will duck because it is really one for the accountants.

If your business is based in Australia, it doesn't matter where the money is earned; tax will be payable. You have to move your residence and your whole business to the tax haven. That is why so many artists are based in countries such as Ireland or Monaco. If you want to live off the money in Australia, you will be liable to pay Australian tax even if the money is earned offshore.

There aren't many avenues for tax minimisation these days and those that do exist are usually closed off sooner rather than later. International tax schemes are expensive to set up and to maintain and are just not worth it unless you have vast success.

The most sensible advice is to pay a competent accountant with knowledge of the business and who has experience in dealing with royalty income and overseas receipts. There are not a lot of them. This accountant will make sure that you are not paying more than you should. Some structures are better than others – just don't try to be too clever. Many artists have had their career wrecked by seeking and taking tax advice that was too slick by half. Tax schemes are like pornography: if it seems too good to be true, it probably is.

38
THE ART OF THE DEAL

THE MUSIC INDUSTRY IS DEAL DRIVEN. EVERY DOLLAR EARNED IS A PRODUCT OF THE NEGOTIATION OF A CONTRACT. GOOD NEGOTIATORS ACHIEVE BETTER DEALS FOR THEIR CLIENTS. ACCORDINGLY, NEGOTIATION SKILLS ARE ESSENTIAL TO SUCCESS IN THE BUSINESS. THIS CHAPTER PROVIDES THE PERSONAL INSIGHTS OF A DEALMAKER.

To end this book it seems appropriate to give some insights into deal making. These observations are personal and subjective. They reveal just one approach to the deal-making process. They may not suit everyone. It is just one approach – but one that has been proven to work.

A DEAL IS A RELATIONSHIP

Most truly lucrative deals in the music industry are long term. They are not just contracts. They are relationships.

This is important to acknowledge when negotiating the deal. Anyone can read a contract and comment on it but a good dealmaker recognises that a deal is not just about royalty rates and advances. It is also the basis of the on-going relationship of the parties and therefore, the negotiation will often require complex exploration and documentation of the personal, creative and commercial needs and expectations of the parties.

In this context, the contract is the process for defining a relationship. It's the guidance system for the artistic and commercial deliverables. Looked at this way, it is the basis of an enduring association of mutual benefit.

There are whole books on deal making. This chapter is going to focus on just three aspects of the process:

- the background intelligence;
- techniques of the negotiation; and
- the content of the deal.

THE BACKGROUND INTELLIGENCE

When approaching a new deal, the dealmaker asks the following questions.

WHAT ARE THE PARTIES' CREATIVE NEEDS AND EXPECTATIONS?

ARTISTIC CONTROL OVER MATERIAL

Who is going to have artistic control over material written or performed? For example, some musicians are content to give the other party say in the style or content of material; others are adamant that this is absolutely their exclusive domain. The reality check questions might be:

"Are you the focus? Is this really your project? Are you creating something as an expression of your own identity and one your own initiative or are you doing it as part of a collaborative process of which your contribution is but a part?"

Compare the needs of a musician making a record with one recording an advertisement; or a composer of a film score with the composer of a string quartet. In each of these situations the importance of creative control is quite different.

CONTROL OVER ARTISTIC PROCESS

Process is usually less contentious than content. For example in recording agreements, issues like selection of producer, engineer, studio, recording timetable and so on, can usually be settled reasonably quickly. Both the record company and the artist need to be assured that they are going to get a record that has the sound and the quality expected. Different studios have different characteristics; different producers create different soundscapes.

Some recording artists also insist on producing their own material; others can't or don't want to. At one end of the spectrum you have the 'I do it all myself' approach and at the other, you have the 'I just turn up and put down my track' approach. If you want to produce, you have to convince the company that you are capable of the task so that it will be prepared to risk its investment in this way. If you don't have production experience, it will be essential that the negotiator finds a mechanism by which your creative needs can be matched with the record company's commercial need for reassurance. It isn't easy.

ARTISTIC SUPPORT

Not many artists are good at everything in the creative process. Who is? Accordingly, it is sensible to find out what support the artist may need. For example, many songwriters have a gift for melody but do not have the skills necessary to arrange that melody. They are going to need a top arranger to turn the simple melody into a hit.

Sometimes the support needed is not, in itself, artistic. For example, if an artist has young children to look after, it will be essential to ensure that the deal recognises that these obligations will interfere with the availability of the artist unless child-minding or some other provision is made. Similarly if the band is still school age it may be necessary to arrange a tutor to tour with the group (as in the early days of Silverchair.) Unless the deal recognises any conflicting obligations faced by the artist, and deals with those conflicts, it is not establishing the framework for a mutually successful long-term relationship: It won't work. Such arrangements are easier to negotiate with Majors than with Independents. Majors have the resources to do it; with independents, it is sometimes possible but always more difficult.

Are the people in the target company likely to recognise and honour the artist's needs? This is a subjective assessment based on instinct and experience. After all, companies are made up of people. Some people in the business are known to be caring and supportive of their artists. Others burn them. No negotiator can change the character of the key players on the other side and if you are negotiating the only deal on the table, you won't have the luxury of choice.

WHAT ARE THE CLIENT'S COMMERCIAL NEEDS?

Different clients have different commercial needs. A Major will be able to provide advances to permit the purchase of equipment, living allowances and tour support. It will certainly have greater marketing and promotion muscle. It has overseas offices that promise the possibility of international exposure. However, not all artists want or are suited to a Major. Some prefer or are more suited to a small independent company where the freedoms may be greater and the relationships more personal.

Issues such as tour support and marketing budget are often much negotiated but are very hard to get into a contract in concrete terms. So much depends on the circumstances that exist at the time the record is released or the tour is undertaken.

For this reason, it is important to try to gauge whether the people in the company are likely to recognise and honour these needs. In some deals you know from previous experience that the A&R manager or the Managing Director can be trusted to follow through, irrespective of the actual words on the contract. With others, you know that if it isn't in black and white, it isn't going to be delivered.

WILL THE ARTIST HAVE THE PERSONAL SUPPORT NECESSARY TO BE SUCCESSFUL?

No one can do it alone. Everyone needs strong, loyal and skilled support. The rarity of such support is one of the reasons that so few artists become successful.

You need to have your own support system (such as your management) but every artist needs his or her recording company to provide huge personal, financial and administrative commitment.

Is there anyone in the company who cares? Who will look after your interests in the corporate sandpit? In the publishing company, the professional manager, or in the record company, the A&R manager, will be hugely important to your well-being. You must have someone within the company that thinks that you are absolutely terrific and who will go in to bat for you when times get tough. (Just remember that in six months your champion will probably move to another company. Your contract is a lot longer than theirs.)

WHAT ARE THE COMPANY'S COMMERCIAL NEEDS?

Every good negotiator tries to make it as easy as possible for the other side to say 'yes'. To do this, you have to think about how requests are framed. In order to do this, it helps to understand how the other side thinks and works. This requires that you understand something of the company's internal mechanisms and what is happening within the company. What does it need? What are its priorities? How far is the company's negotiator allowed to go in order to achieve those ends?

Often, the difference between getting your request agreed to and having it rejected, is whether or not it is administratively or commercially practicable. Is it doable? For example, you can argue all day to have a Major publisher provide quarterly accounting but, unless you have extraordinary muscle, you will never achieve it. The custom in the publishing industry is for half-yearly accounting and all the systems are set up that way. No company is going to change its whole way of operating just for you.

That is not to say that you have to accept it every time the business affairs manager rejects your request with the mantra, 'It is not company policy'. Sometimes the company does have a policy that is absolutely immovable and you might as well accept it and move on. Other times, the 'company policy' line is just the resort of the greedy or the intellectually lazy. With experience, you get a feel for which is which.

WHAT DO OTHER ARTISTS OF THE SAME GENRE, AND A SIMILAR LEVEL OF SUCCESS, RECEIVE?

You often hear that an international star has just signed a deal worth tens of millions of dollars. Even the most ambitious Australian act knows that it is unlikely to match these figures. But what is a reasonable expectation? There is no easy answer. What a new and unproven artist or writer can realistically expect is very different from what can be achieved for someone who has a track record of success. Because a star is someone who has the capacity to earn money for both sides of the deal, it is always easier to negotiate for a star than for a newcomer.

There is one situation when the absence of track record doesn't matter. In fact its just the opposite: It's when there is a rumour going round the industry that a new, unsigned act is truly fabulous and that the blood of three or four A&R directors has been observed in the water.

Genre is also important. The publishing contract for a popular music composer will look very different from a classical composer. The merchandising deal for a jazz musician ('I'd like to see that!') would be a lot less interesting than that for a touring top-ten artist.

UNDERSTAND NEGOTIATION DISCIPLINE

Discipline is essential to a successful negotiation. All too often, many significant deal points have already been conceded by the artist or the manager before the lawyer gets a chance to negotiate them. If you are going to hire an experienced music lawyer to represent you (and why wouldn't you?) don't talk business; talk music.

Discussing the commercial aspects of the deal with the other side, before bringing in the expert, does not save legal fees. It will probably cost even more, as the negotiator will almost certainly have to try to regain some of the points that you have given away. Premature discussion about the deal can cost you a lot of money over many years. Stick to what you are good at. There is a great expression that says it all: 'Don't hire a dog and bark yourself'!

Even when the negotiation is getting down to the wire and the nerves are being sorely tested, discipline must remain firm. For example, a company executive might hint that your lawyer is going in too hard and may even give the impression that this may be endangering the deal. This is a common and banal ploy – but one that is often successful. The inexperienced artist, desperate to get the deal, may well concede all sorts of points to the company in the fear that the negotiator is inept or ruining the relationship with the company. The experienced artist will simply make it politely clear that such commercial matters are in the hands of the negotiator, deftly steer the conversation back to artistic issues, and then report back to the negotiator so that he or she knows exactly what has been said. Negotiation requires team loyalty. Remember who is on your side. Don't be rattled; the company executive is just trying to get the best deal possible for the company.

If you really do fear that your negotiator is threatening the deal, discuss your concerns 'off-line'. The company should not be a part of that discussion. It is a matter for your team to resolve. Don't flag your concerns to the other side. Think of the analogy of a football team – if you have a problem with one of the members of the team, you don't ask the other side's coach how your player is going and how he should play. You thrash it out behind closed doors. A wise player will listen to criticism and modify his or her technique or behaviour as necessary.

TECHNIQUES OF THE NEGOTIATION

Every negotiator has a personal approach to negotiating. For some, it seems to be an exercise in water torture in which every point is tackled again and again until either the point is conceded or the deal is blown to pieces. For others, it is an exercise in ego exposure. There is another, more productive, way to do it.

1. **ALWAYS START WITH A DEAL MEMO – NOT A FULL CONTRACT**

   If you are approaching a large deal, the points will be complex and inter-relating. For this reason, it is easier to get an overall picture of the deal if the deal points are first set out in summary form without all of the distraction of the legalese that will bind those points together. Although the final agreement may be several centimetres thick, the principal points can usually be set out in a couple of pages. These provide a focus for the negotiation.

2. **FOCUS ON THE IMPORTANT COMMERCIAL POINTS**

   When you do get the full-length contract, don't try to redraft it – none is perfect – focus on the deal points and the traps for the unwary. If you are not careful you will win all the grammatical corrections and lose all the commercial points.

3. **HAVE A GOOD REASON FOR EVERY REQUEST**

   The essence of successful, long-term deal making is reason and common sense. If you can make the other side understand that your request is reasonable, you are more likely than not going to get the concession.

For this reason, bold ambit claims are rarely effective. If both sides know that the claim is indefensible, what is the point of making it? This approach is more about ego than about achieving a commercial outcome.

4. SPEAK WITH ONE VOICE

Remember the warnings given above: Always let the negotiator talk the business.

This is not just a matter of effectiveness. It is essential to maintaining the relationship between the parties themselves. This relationship should always remain positive. If anyone has to be a pain, let it be the negotiator.

5. ASK FOR ALL YOUR CHANGES IN A BLOCK

Try to put your requests to the other side in a block. Don't keep asking for changes that haven't been raised before. The negotiation process is not an endurance test and the other side will be rightfully irritated if you keep revisiting points that they think have already been settled.

This is not to say that deal points cannot be revisited. Often, points that you have already agreed upon will be revisited because of issues arising from the negotiation of later deal points. After all, it is a bargaining process.

6. DON'T PROMISE WHAT YOU CAN'T DELIVER

This is a business where your word is important. As a dealmaker, you get to know who you can trust, and who you can't. If you give an undertaking, you should crawl over broken glass to deliver on your promise.

It's a small world. The word gets around. If you can't be sure of delivering something, don't promise it.

7. NEVER LOSE YOUR TEMPER UNLESS YOU MEAN TO

Remember, as the lawyer in 'Prizzi's Honour' said when the Mafia Don's son was kidnapped: 'This isn't personal. It's only business'.

Negotiation is an exercise in control. If you lose your temper, the other side wins. It's that simple.

8. NEGOTIATION IS NO PLACE TO HAVE EGO NEEDS

Too many negotiators have their ego on the table. Negotiators should have a strong ego, but they should check on it in the shower in the morning, get dressed, and then leave it in their pocket when they leave home.

All too often we forget that someone who seems to have what we call a 'big ego', in fact is demonstrating that they have a 'weak ego'.

9. SHOULD YOU DO THE DEAL OR SHOULD YOU WALK?

At the end of the day, there are limits to every deal. Where is the line in the sand?

The negotiator's job is to facilitate deals, not to bust them. If the other side won't vary unconscionable terms, no lawyer will ever stand in the way of their client doing the deal – that must always be the client's absolute decision.

That said, there are some situations in which the lawyer may well give a client advice NOT to proceed with a deal. If the client still wants to go ahead, the lawyer will facilitate that wish. But in those circumstances the lawyer will feel more like a pall-bearer than a personal trainer. These are unhealthy deals and will usually die.

After all, if the contract is not reasonably fair to both sides, it will never work. If either party feels ripped off, or grows disillusioned with the deal, it's over – it will never work. Only the lawyers will win.

The best deal is not the richest; it's the one that demonstrates a mutual commitment to succeed. Instead, too often, testosterone and ego dominate the negotiation process. They are both destructive in this situation. It's much better to concentrate on how best to maximise the commercial value of the music in a way that both parties will benefit.

CONTENT OF THE DEAL
THE MYTH OF THE GRAND ADVANCE

You often hear people say that if you negotiate a huge advance, the company has to make you successful because it is the only way that it will earn back the advance. This just isn't right. When things go pear-shaped, the fact that there is a large unrecouped balance is more likely to make the company negative about an act rather than more determined. The unrecouped balance sits on the balance sheet as a reminder that the company executive made a mistake. Accordingly, it is likely to write-off the loss and get on with other acts who are more likely to make money. There is always a point when the company says, enough is enough, swallows the embarrassment and bails out.

Big advances are usually illusions. Sometimes, they are marketing tools; sometimes they are just crutches for limp egos. Remember, advances are only an early payment of your own money. That's not so special. Think about what you need it for; how you are going to use it; how you are going to make it work.

If you are a success, you are better off getting a smaller advance and setting that off against higher royalties or other deal points. If you are going to fail, get as big an advance as you can. It's all you will ever get.

The best approach is to build a deal that recognises the present but provides for the future. It is often cleverest to make a deal cheap for the other side to get into and yet ensures that if there is success, both share in the upside. Once you are successful you will be able to negotiate large advances and large shares of the income stream. David Bowie, Robbie Williams and others of that commercial stature have been able to lever their businesses in really innovative ways: Success provides a greater range of financial options.

UNDERSTAND HOW THE DEAL WORKS

As discussed earlier in the chapter, the contract has to embody the needs and expectations of both parties. The contract is the formal expression of those matters – so you should understand how they will be implemented.

DEFINING THE UNKNOWN

A contract is a document that tries to guess the future. It is doomed to fail if it is viewed as a stable, concrete, thing. It has to be viewed as a work in progress. It is sometimes useful to build into its mechanisms the capacity to re-evaluate the value of the deal in light of the new technologies, the new levels of success and other factors that are unforeseeable at the time it is entered.

For example, how are we supposed to negotiate a fair royalty rate for a new and evolving technology? Any negotiator knows how difficult this is. Until the industry has experience with the true costs of a medium, the actual sales that are achieved and so on, it is impossible to define these sorts of things. Rather, the parties have to develop mechanisms for achieving a fair result later, when they have more information.

DISPUTE RESOLUTION

It is invaluable to build into long-term deals a mechanism for dispute resolution. There is nothing more corrosive to a relationship than the powerful side simply adopting a take it or leave it attitude, or the parties heading off to court. Both are commercially disastrous. You need a circuit breaker. These days there are several mediation and arbitration agencies that provide a comparatively fast and inexpensive alternative to the courts.

RENEGOTIATION

All deals are potentially renegotiable. The only two questions are: What are you prepared to give in return for what you want? Does the other side want what you are prepared to offer?

Both parties must recognise that deals will flex depending on the degree of success being achieved. Quite simply, a gold record gives the artist an edge. A large unrecouped balance gives the company the edge.

CONCLUSION

Long-term deals are like marriage: they are easy to get into and hard to get out of. The likelihood of long-term success in the relationship is enhanced if, at the outset, the parties discuss their mutual needs and expectations and come to a better understanding both of themselves and of the other party.

Even where that occurs, it must be recognised that the contract is just the start of the process: there will be good times and hard times and the only way through, will require good communication, loyalty and mutual respect.

INDEX

A&M 178, 332, 349, 388
  Napster and 291–292
ABC 326, 334
  music clips archives 468
ABN see Australian business number (ABN)
Accommodation
  taxation deductions 629–630
  touring 133, 152
Accountants 617–618, 645
Accounting see also Book keeping, Budgets
  accounts department 265–266
  copyright 167
  expenses 627
  group recording contracts 425
  label deals 391–392
  master licence deals 414–415
  mechanical licence process 202
  pressing and distributing deals 402–403
  publishing contracts 265–266
  royalties 443–444
  soundtracks, original 565
  tour merchandising 514
Accounts department 215
  accounting 265–266
  record company 345
AC/DC 178, 321
ACN see Australian company number (ACN)
Adaptations 188–189
  arrangements 223–224
Administration deals 253
  advances 253
  copyright ownership 253
  covers 254–255
  duration 253
  income splits 253–254
Advances 237–238
  administration deals 253
  managers' 104
  master licence deals 414
  myths 660–661
  non-recoupable deals 427–428
  producers' 460
  recording costs and 105
  recoupment 239–240
    groups 425
  single-song assignment 229
  tour merchandising 511–512
    payments, timing of 512
    recoupable and/or repayable 512
Advertising 146–147, 542
  commissioning original music 543
    rights 543–544
  jingles 207, 543
    arranging fees 545
    budget 544
    creative fees 544–545
    demo fees 544

public performance royalties 546–547
  residuals 546
  session fees 545
music, licensing 195–196, 205, 443
production music 543, 547, 553
  libraries 547–548
secondary exploitation 378–379
TV record sales 439–440
AdviceBank 533
AEG Telefinken 274
Aerosmith 388
Agents 78–79, 131, 135–136
  agency agreements, written 82–84
  bonds 122
  booking agreements 85–86, 131
    authority to make 81
  conflicts of interest 78–79
  controlling 114–115, 123–124
  definition 116–117
  employment offers, dealing with 81
  fees and commissions 82, 119, 137–140
  function 79–80, 131
  government report (NSW 1989) 79
  international 652
  interstate 123
  letter of intent 137
  licences 118–119
  managers as 107
  merchandising
    commission 516–517
    rights 517
    role 517
  performance deposits and fees 81–82
  powers and authorities 80–82
  promoters, distinguished 131
  records, keeping 121
  representation authority 80
  trust accounts 120–121
  venue consultants 78, 87–88
    controlling 114–115, 123–124
    definition 117–118
    fees 120
    licences 118–119
Agreements
  agency 82–84
  booking 81, 85–86
  publishing see Publishing contracts
  service 38–39
  shareholder 25, 38
Air Supply 321, 328
Allans 198
Allen, Woody 551
Alpert, Herb 388
AMCOS see Australian Mechanical Copyright
    Owners Society (AMCOS)
American Federation of Musicians 381–382, 608
American Mechanical Rights Association (AMRA)
    500

AMPAL see Australian Music Publishers Association
   Ltd (AMPAL)
AMPEX 274
The Angels 328
Anonymous works
   copyright, duration of 165
AOL 297
   Time Warner and 324, 328, 331, 334
Aon Risk Services 590, 591, 593
APRA see Australasian Performing Right Association
   (APRA)
Arena, Tina 322
ARIA see Australian Record Industry Association
   (ARIA)
Arranging music
   copyright issues 223–224
   jingle writing 545
Art department 341–342
Artist and repertoire department (A & R) 339–340
   producers, as 454
Artist roster 346
Artists
   American Federation of Musicians 381–382
   control see Creative control
   family support 655, 656
   image 352, 376
   label deals
      advantages 393–394
      points to watch 394
   merchandising, share of
      retail 513
      tour 513–514
   minimum delivery commitments 370
   producers, relationships with 457–458
   'services', definition 361–363
   support for 655, 656
   websites 505
Arts Law Centre of Australia 41
Artwork
   copyright 380
   cover 380
      commissioning letter 520
   master licence deals 406, 407
   merchandising 506–507
   protection 518
   royalty deductions 434
Asylum Records 332, 388
Atlantic Records 332, 388
Atomic Pop.com 297
Audience numbers 141
Audio and video tape 274–275
Audio Fidelity 273
Audiovisual see Music clips
Audition recordings
   mechanical income 200
Australasian Music Industry Directory
   agents and promoters 135
   distributors 396
   insurance brokers 590
   names 22
   record companies 346
   venues 126

Australasian Performing Right Association (APRA)
   40, 187, 206, 209, 484, 488
   anti-competitive conduct 487
   code of conduct 498
   compliance program 486–487
   cue sheets, filing 564–565
   identification of works 485–486
   income and payments 484–485, 490–491
   licensing 485
   membership 484, 556, 561
      costs 485
   production music 552–553
   public performance and broadcasting rights
      196–197, 497
      logging performances 486
   registration
      co-writers 222
      title deeds to works 485–486
   royalty splits 259–260, 499
   tracing performances 208
Australian artists
   international success 321–322
Australian Brandenburg Orchestra 523–524
Australian Broadcasting Corporation see ABC
Australian business number (ABN) 33, 88, 130, 535,
   638–639
Australian company number (ACN) 638–639
Australian Copyright Council 41
Australian Crawl 328
Australian Guild of Screen Composers (AGSC) 41,
   558, 566
   model contract 567–578
   Performers' Agreement and Consent 559
Australian Mechanical Copyright Owners Society
   (AMCOS) 40, 187, 193, 194, 202, 209, 305, 306,
   411
   administration 490
      communication right 490–491
   commissions 490
   cue sheets, filing 564–565
   establishment 488–489
   foreign copyright 500–501
   functions 488
   identification of works and uses 490
   income 489
   membership 489
      costs 490
   production music 548, 553
Australian Music Publishers Association Ltd
   (AMPAL) 187, 488
Australian Music Retailers Association 317
Australian record business
   budget record companies 337
   competition
      domestic 317
      international 319
   distance, problems of 319
   distributors 336
   EMI and 328, 334
   growth 314–317
   history 314, 319–320
      1960s 320
      1970s 320–321

1980s 321
1990s 322
2000s 322–323
Independents 325, 335–336
Majors 325–334
profit 318–319
record clubs 337–338
tele-marketers 336–337
United States, comparison with 314
vertical integration 323–325
Warner and 334
The Australian Record Company (ARC) 329–330
Australian Record Industry Association (ARIA) 187, 554
catalogue, using 346
sales statistics 315–316, 435
Author see also Composer
copyright ownership 159
joint authorship 165, 219–220
Awards, employment see Employment
Bacharach, Burt 191
Bachelor Girl 224
'Back slappers' 62
Background music
mechanical income 200
Backing vocals
sampling 180
Bananas in Pyjamas 334, 504
'Bandstand' 320
Bank charges 627
Bankruptcy 31
Bardeen, John 274
Bargaining power 126
employers, dealing with 126–127
Barnes, Jimmy 192, 322, 648
Basie, Count 329
BBC
production music 553
Beach Boys 443, 454–455
Beastie Boys 176
The Beatles 178, 320, 321, 328, 349, 457
Beethoven, Ludvig von 157
Belafonte, Harry 330
Bell, Alexander Graham 329
Bell Laboratories 272, 274, 550
Benefits
assessable income 621
Berlin, Irving 270
Berliner, Emil 271, 330
Berne Convention 155, 158, 172, 481
Bertelsmann Group 297, 325, 330
Beyonce 146
BIEM see Bureau International des Sociétés Gerant les Droits D'enregistrement et de Reproduction Mecanique (BIEM)
Big Days Out 145
Bigpond Music 297
Biscayne Partners Pty Ltd 112
BitTorrent 284, 294
Block, Harvey 111
Blogs 284
BMG 292, 297, 325, 328, 330–331, 508
Napster 292–293, 330–331

production music 552
Board
assignment of responsibilities 58
caring for your 57
checklist 73–77
conspiracies 63–64
decision making 58–59
delegation 60
legal responsibilities 65–73
limits, setting 59
new members 57–58
policy, defining 58–59
problem members 61–64
back slappers 62
bullies 62
celebrities and socialites 62
conflicts of interest 64, 68–69
diary afflicted members 64
ghosts 61–62
lifers 63
martyrs 63
secret agents 63–64
sleepers 62
talkers 64
purpose 53
selecting the 44, 53–56
skills matrix 56
statutory duties 65
strategy, setting 58–59
Bonuses
assessable income 621
Book keeping 611–612, 618 see also Accounting, Budgets
accountant, role of 617–618
borrowing money 613
essentials 614–618
filing system 617
losses, carrying forward 642
periodical accounts 615
receipts 614–615
abnormal 642
taxation see Taxation
Booking agreements 85–86
agents 81
Boscobel Productions Ltd 97
Bourget 480
Bowie, David 320
Braithwaite, Daryl 92–93, 110
Brand recognition 298, 521
Brattain, Walter 274
Brazin 298
Broadcasting
digital 287–288
music clips 476
retransmission by pay-TV services 496
rights 196–197, 485–487, 491
direct distribution to artists 494–495
royalties 441–442
Bronfman, Edgar Jr 334
Brooks, Garth 504
Budget records 337
royalties 440–441
Budgets see also Accounting, Book keeping

event insurance 594
jingle writing 544
music clips 469–470, 475, 477–478
overages, responsibility for 464
recording 372
touring 133–134, 612–613
'Bullies' 62
Bureau International des Sociétés Gerant les Droits D'enregistrement et de Reproduction Mecanique (BIEM) 500
Business
carrying on 637
definition 631–633
elements 633–635
hobby, distinguished 631–638
registration 638–641
size or scale of activity 635–637
where to base 652
Business activity statements (BAS) 617
Business affairs department 341
Business name registration 23
Business structures 30
companies 36–39
groups 32, 419–420
major record companies 326–327
not-for-profit organisations 40–41
partnership 32–36, 93–94, 420
protecting names 23–25
solo, working 30–31
trusts 39
Byrnes, Ed 324
Byron Bay Blues Festival 145
CAAMA 40
CAL see Copyright Agency Ltd (CAL)
Cancellation
performances 152
Capital gains income 621
Carmina Burana 174, 193
Cartage 628
Caruso 330
Cassettes
budget and mid-price 440
DAT format 277, 280
packaging deductions 435–436
sales statistics 436
'Cast' recordings 609–610
Catering 150
CBS Records 329–330, 333, 334, 340, 368
CDM Ltd 26
CDNow 297
CD-R 278
CD-ROM 277–278, 280
CDs 277–278, 299, 321, 330, 435
budget and mid-price 440
packaging deductions 436
CDV 282
'Celebrities and socialites' 62
Chambers, Kasey 328
Chappell Music Publishing 332, 333
Charles, Ray 146
Cher 191, 352
Chrysalis Music 328
Cinemas

licence fees 206
CISAC see International Confederation of Authors and Composers (CISAC)
Clapton, Eric 374
Cleaning 628
Clips see Music clips
Clothing 630
Cocker, Joe 192, 548
Code of Ethics 115
Cold Chisel 421
Cold Play 286
Cole, Nat King 304
Collecting societies 196, 305, 480
characteristics 481
Christian music 498
code of conduct 498–499
collective administration 481–482
functions 482–484
future role 501–502
government inquiry 483
international 499–501
multi-format licensing 502
Collective works
copyright ownership 219–220
Columbia Phonograph Co 271, 329–330
Co-managers 96
Commercial Radio Australia
APRA, conflict with 487–488
Commissions
agents 82, 119, 137–140
merchandising 516–517
AMCOS 490
booking agents' 107
lawyers 650
managers 103–104
exclusions 104–107
regulation of fees 119–120
termination of agreement, following 108–109
sub-publisher 260–261
taxation 627
Communication to the public
copyright and 155–156, 206
music publication 188
royalty splits 259–260
income 196–197, 490–491
licensing users 206–207
websites 505
Como, Perry 330
Companies 36–39 see also Business structures
contracts 39
formation of 37–38
liability 37
limited by guarantee 50
advantages 50
directors, duties of 66–69
disadvantages 51
formation of company 51
name of group, protecting 25
not-for-profit organisations see Not-for-profit organisations
objects 37
philanthropy 537–538
proprietary 36

service agreements 38–39
shareholder agreements 38
taxation 624
   planning 644
trusts 39
Competition
   copyright and 182
   Ergas Report 183–184
Complaints Committee 122–123
Composer
   controlled composition clauses 448
   copyright ownership 159, 464–465
   jingle writers 543–544
   original soundtracks 557
      contract 557–585
   producer as co-composer 464
   single-song assignment 228–229
   writer-for-hire agreements 227–228
Composition
   co-writing 217–225
Computers 280–281 see also Internet, Technology
Concerts
   films 469
   royalties, payment of 207
   tracing performances 208
Conferences and conventions 628
Confidentiality
   managers 102–103
Conflicts of interest
   agents 78 79
   directors 68–69
   lawyers 603–604
   managers 94
Contacts 350, 649
Contracts
   companies and 39
   endorsement 529–531
   lawyers, role of 598–599
   managers and artists 92–93, 98–99, 110
      enforcement 110–111
   performance terms
      enforcement 129–130
      negotiating 127–129
   producers 456
      job description 456
      parties 457
      services required 457–458
      termination 465–466
   soundtracks, original 557–565
      accounting 565
      artistic control 563
      copyright ownership 561–562
      cue sheets 564–565
      delivery dates 560–561, 565
      fees 562
      model contract 567–578
      moral rights 564
      parties 558
      payment schedule 563
      production credits 564
      services required 559–560
Contracts (recording) 357–358
   A & R, working with 372

budget 372
   creative development 373
   disputes 372–373
   'satisfactory record', interpretation 373–374
'all media' contracts 362
artist
   artistic control 371
   minimum delivery commitments 370
   'services', definition 361–363
assignment 382–383
breaking 424
costs 376
   funding record production 376–377
   recouping 378
cover art 380
definitions 365–366
delays and interruptions 368
   liability 368
distribution see Distribution
duration 366
   contract years 366
   options 366–367
   'wake-up' clauses 367
exclusivity 361
expectations of parties
   artist 645–655, 657
   client 655–656
getting a contract 349
   creating awareness 350
   demos 352–355
   knowing someone 350, 649
   live work 351
   professional image 352
   publicity stunts 352
   talent shows 355
groups 418–419
   accounting 425
   changes to group 423–424
   elements 419
   ill or absent members 426
   liability, individual and group 420–421
   liaison with record company 422–423
   parties 420
   professional name 421–422
   recoupment 425
   royalties 425
   solo careers by members 421, 422, 424
guest appearances 362
indemnities 383–384
Internet and web site control 365
key issues 360
lawyers, role of 598–599
leaving member clauses 424
moral rights 381
music clips 474–475
   budget 475
   creative control 475
   director, choice of 476–477
   packaging deductions 476
   parties 476
   royalties 475–476
negotiations 355–356, 657–660
   group contracts 422–423

notice, giving 384–385
oral agreements 358–359
other media, working in 363–365
overseas releases 369
ownership of recordings 159–163, 379–380
producers' 456–458, 465–466
publicity and image 376
purpose 358
record company, commitment of 370–371
release commitment 374
    artist delay 374
    control of releases 375
    disputes 375
    record company delay 374
remixing rights 381
re-recording, restrictions 380–381
secondary exploitation 378–379
services, contract for 361
    artist's 'services', definition 361–363
studio work 362–363
suspension clauses 368
territory, concept of 368–369
warranties 383
written
    heads of agreement 359
    inducement letters 359–360
    informal deal memos 359
Co-operatives 49–50
    Register of Co-operative Societies 50
Copyright 153, 185
    accounting and inspection 167
    artwork 380
    assignment of 165–166, 256–257
        re-assignment 268
        royalty caps and reductions 449–450
    automatic protection 157–158
    basic terms 166–168
    collective work 220
    communication to the public 155–156, 196–197, 206–209
        royalty splits 259–260
    competition and 182
        Ergas Report 183–184
    covers 255
    creative control 167, 301
    department 215
    disputes 168, 201
    duration 166, 174–175
        anonymous works 165
        films 165
        joint authorship, works of 165
        literary works 164
        musical works 164
        pseudonymous works 165
        published editions 164
        sound recordings 164
    enforcement 167
    exclusivity 167
    fair dealing 169
    free trade agreement with US 156
    home copying 169
    importance of 153–154
    insubstantial portion, use of 168–169

international conventions 155, 158, 172, 481
    master licence deals 404
    'material form' 157
    merchandising 518
    misconceptions 154
    moral rights 172
        attribution 173
        duration 174–175
        false attribution, protection against 173–174
        infringements 175–176
        integrity 174
        waiver 175, 176
    non-copyright rights, protection of 170–171, 178
    ownership
        administration deals 253
        co-writers 219–221
        foreign 493–494
        master licence deals 405
        music clips 474
        musical works 159, 497
        performers 163–164, 171–172
        prerecorded material 554–555
        published editions 164
        sound recordings 159–163, 379–380, 497
        soundtracks, original 556, 561–562
    parallel importing 180–185
    parties 166
    permissions 162
    producers' 225
        masters 464
        works composed by third parties 464–465
        works composed with artist 464
    publishing see Publishing
    record producers 225
    registering 157–159
    reproduction 157, 168–169
    reversion of 268
    rights 155, 166
        licensing 166, 191
    sampling 176–180
    single-song assignment 228–229
    source 154–155
    statutory licences 191, 201
    technology and 276–277, 281, 302–4, 312
        controlled access, promoting 304–306
        income collection 307
        management of copyright 304
        policing copyright 306–307
    termination 167
    transactions 165
    what is covered? 155
    writer-for-hire agreements 227–228
Copyright Agency Ltd (CAL) 498
Coronet label 329
Corporate Good Works 533
Corporate social responsibility 537–538
Cosby, Bill 332
Cover art 380
Covers 191–193
    administration deals 254–255
    Australian record business, history 319–320
    royalty splits 258–259
Co-writing 217

accidental 226
additional writers 225–226
APRA registration 222
arranging 223–224
contractual obligations 222–223
control 221
copyright ownership 219–221
  collective works 220
  joint works 220–221
documentation 218–219
partnerships 219
record producers 225
royalties, splitting 222
translating 224–225
CRA 187
Crazy Frog 286–287
Cream 421
Creative control
  artistic process, over 654
  clauses 266–267, 371, 373
  creative development 373
  digital age 301
  material, over 654
  music clips 475
  producers 457, 458
  soundtrack, original 563
Creative services manager 211–212
Credits, production 564
Crosby, Stills and Nash 388
Cue sheets 564–565
Cultural Gifts Program 539–540
Cultural organisations see Not-for-profit
  organisations
Dance parties
  licences for 206
DAT cassette format 277, 280
David, Hal 191
Davies, Ray 97
DCC 277, 282
  royalties and 299, 437
de Forest Phonofilms 550
de Martinville, Leon Scott 271
Deal
  art of the 653–662
  content 660–661
  international 646–652
  negotiation 657–658
    techniques 658–660
  relationship, as 653, 662
  understanding the 661
'Debasing' original works 193
Debts
  liability for 69–71
Decca 273, 332
Deep Purple 27
Def American 387
Defective records 430
Deletions 430–431
Demo recordings 352–355
  jingles 544
  lawyers forwarding 352, 599
  mechanical income 200
Denmark Productions Ltd 97

Department of Communications Information
  Technology and the Arts (DCITA) 534
Deposits
  agents, collected by 81–82
'Diary afflicted' board members 64
Digital technology 275–279
  artistic control 301
  broadcast 287–288
  collecting societies, role of 501–502
  copyright and 289, 302–307
  digital object identifiers (DOIs) 305–306
  downloads see Downloads
  internet see Internet
  on-line delivery 282–283, 312–313, 323
    cost savings 299
    department (record company) 345
    future developments 308–311
    sales figures 314–315
  royalties and 298–301
Digital World Services 331
Dion, Celine 191
Dire Straits 321
Directors
  conflicts of interest 68–69
  duties of 66–69
    disclosure 68
    honesty 68
    information, use of 68
    position, use of 68
    reasonable care and diligence 68
  liability 69–71
Diskjockey.com 297
Disputes
  A & R, working with 372–373
  copyright 168, 201
  name 25–27
  release 375
  resolution 661
Distribution
  digital see Downloads
  income 198–200, 208
  label deals 386–394
  master licence deals 404–416
  pressing and distributing deals 394–403
  record distributors 336
    role 398
    selecting 396
  record rental 417
Dolby, Ray 275
Dolphy, Eric 189
Donations
  non-profit organisations 42
Double tax treaty 645
Downloads 279, 289, 323
  artistic control 301
  business, changing 295–298
  collecting societies, role of 501–502
  'content, access, price', importance of 298
  copyright, future of 302–304
    controlled access, promoting 304–306
    income collection 307
    management of copyright 304
    policing copyright 306–307

EMI 294, 295–296, 328
file sharing 294
history 290–291
legal 294–295, 323
MP3 279, 283–284, 290, 323
Napster 284, 290, 291–292, 294, 297
on-line music 281–283, 294, 312–313, 323
post Napster 292–293
ring-tones 28, 285–287
royalties and 299–301
Dreamworks 388
Dressing rooms 149–150
The Drifters 27
Dumas, Alexandre 480
Dusty, Slim 328
DVDs 278–279, 282, 323
DVD-Audio 279
music clips 467, 471–472
sales statistics 317
Dylan, Bob 308, 329, 340
The Eagles 178
The Easybeats 320
ECM labels 387
Edison, Thomas 271, 272
Edison Laboratories 550
Education and training 630
Educational recordings
mechanical income 200
Electronic age 272–275
Electronic percussion 321
Elektra Records 332, 388
Elliot, Stephen 586
EMI 272, 325, 328, 331, 334, 508
downloads 294, 295–296
production music 552, 553
Employment
agents, negotiation by 81
employee awards 606–607
employers, dealing with 126–127
income 620
independent contractors 606–607
industry awards 606, 608
Actors (Theatrical) Award 610
Musicians' General Award 610
payroll services 87–88
performer as employee
copyright issues 163
recording contracts, distinguished 361
session musicians 608
terms 81, 127–128
unions 607–608
wages, taxation and 629
eMusic.com 290
Engagements
confirmation of 85–86, 128
managers, duty to procure 101
Entertainment Industry Act 1989 (NSW)
Complaints Committee, establishment 122–123
purpose 115, 123–124
regulatory role 114–115
Entertainment Industry Interim Council (EIIC) 115, 122
Equipment

taxation deductions 627–631
Ergas Report 183–184
Events 145
Exclusivity
copyright 167
managers 96
master licence deals 404
record contracts 361
Exploitation 186
Fair dealing 169
The Falls Festival 145
Farben, I.G. 274
Farnham, John 191, 192, 322, 330, 523, 648
Fast Tracks Kiosks 298
Featuradio Sound Productions 329
Federation of Australian Commercial Television
Stations (FACTS)
APRA, conflict with 487
PPCA, conflict with 495, 497
Federation of Australian Radio Broadcasters (FARB)
APRA, conflict with 487–488
Fees
agents' 82, 119
lawyers 600–602
managers' 119–120
performance 81–82
four walls deal 139–140
net participation deals 139
payment of 140–141
percentage of gross or net 138
percentage of gross or net, fee against 138–139
set fee 137
staggered percentage of gross 139
producers' 458
payment, timing of 459
per master 459
total recording package 459
soundtrack, original 562
payment schedule 563
venue consultants' 120
Festival (company) 325, 326, 332, 333, 335, 388
Festivals 145
classical music 40
Fibre optics 282, 303
The Fifth Dimension 27
Film 550–551
concert films 469
copyright 172, 551
duration of 165
lump sum payments 444
record contracts and 364
soundtracks see Soundtracks
sources of music 551–552
synchronisation 194–195, 204–205
royalties 442–443, 462
Financial planning
managers 101–102
not-for-profit organisations 44
touring 133–135
The Firm (Jimmy Page) 27
Fitzgerald, Ella 454
Five Platters Inc 26–27
Flat records 271–272

Fleetwood, Mick 26
Fleetwood Mac 26
Format exceptions 431
Founder syndrome 45
Frampton, Peter 97
Franklin, Aretha 329
'Free goods' 430, 437
   royalty deductions 447, 450
Free Television Australia
   APRA, conflict with 487
   PPCA, conflict with 495
Free trade agreement with US
   copyright issues 156
Free TV Australia 187
Funicello, Annette 324
Geffen, David 388
Geffen Records 388
General Electric 550
Genesis 27
Gershwin 191
Gesellschaft für Musikalische Aufführungs - und
   Mechanische Vervielfältigungsrechte (GEMA)
   500
GetMusic 330
'Ghosts' 61–62
Gifts see Philanthropy
'The Glen Miller Story' 468
Gnutella 284
Goffin and King 191
Goldmark, Peter 273
Gonski, David 533
Goodrem, Delta 330
Goods and services tax (GST) 620, 639 see also
   Taxation
   paperwork 617, 639–640
   pressing and distribution deals 402, 403
   pricing 432–433, 434
   publishing income 264–265
   registration 640
   royalties 434
Grand rights 485
   income earned from 207–208
Grants
   applications 613
   assessable income 621
   non-profit organisations 42
Gratis copies 430
Gratuities
   assessable income 621
Grokster 284, 292, 294
Gross, Guy 586
Groups
   decision making 423
   dynamics 419
   members leaving 424
   merchandising 515
   new members 423–424
   recording contracts 418–419
      accounting 425
      changes to group 423–424
      ill or absent members 426
      liability, individual and group 420–421
      liaison with record company 422–423

      parties 420
      professional name 421–422
      recoupment 425
      royalties 425
   solo careers by members 421
      first option rights 424
      group name, using 422
   structures 32, 419–420
GST see Goods and services tax (GST)
Gudinski, Michael 325, 335, 388
Guns N' Roses 388
Hairdressing 630
Hal Leonard 198
Hammond, John 329, 340
Harmonia Mundi 387
Harris, Rolf 320
Harry Fox Agency 446, 500
Heads of agreement 359, 529–531
Henderson, George 536
Henley, Don 388
Hi5 504
Hi-fi 273
Higgins, Missy 328
HMV
   Fast Tracks Kiosks 298
'Hoadley's Battle of the Sounds' 320
Hobby
   business, distinguished 631–638
Holiday, Billie 329
Hollywood Edge 553
Home copying 169
The House of Blues (HOB) 284
Houston, Whitney 191, 192
Human resources
   not-for-profit organisations 44
Image
   definition 523
   establishment 522–523
   improvement 523
   publicity and 352, 376
Imitation
   sound-alikes 27–28
Implementation Act see United States Free Trade
   Agreement Implementation Act 2004
Income see also Royalties
   administration deals 253–254
   advertising 195–196, 205, 207
   assessable 620–621
   averaging 642–643
   calculation and collection 198–200
      Internet copyright 307
   communication to the public 206–207
      royalty splits 259–260
   distribution 198–200, 208
   grand rights, exception for 207–208
   GST 264–265
      pressing and distribution deals 402, 403
   mechanical 188, 190
      covers 191–193
      mechanical royalties 190–191, 199–200, 263–264
   overseas 209
      net receipts 261–262
      source, at 262–263

sub-publisher's commission 260–261
payments, timing of 209
personal services 641
print 188, 189–190
public performance 188, 208
self-reporting 208–209
sheet music, from 189–190, 198–199
    royalty splits 259
sources 189
sundry 197–198
synchronisation 188, 194, 204, 207
    original soundtrack material 194–195, 204–205
    prerecorded material 195, 205, 548–549, 555
    production music 194, 204, 547–548, 552–553
    royalties 442–443, 462
    tracing performances 208
Incorporated association 47–49
    advantages 48
    disadvantages 48–49
    formation of 49
    management committee, duties of 65–66
INDECS project 305
Indemnities 383
Inducement letters 359–360
Industry awards see Employment
Inertia 336
Informal deal memos 359
Infringement of moral rights
    defences 175–176
    remedies 175
Insurance 589–590
    equipment 590–591
    event 593–595
    household contents 590
    income 591
        accident and illness insurance 592
        protection insurance 592
    performance 151–152, 593
    public liability 592–593
    taxation deductions 628
    travel 591
Integrity
    managers 102–103
International Confederation of Authors and
    Composers (CISAC) 499
International Creative Management 78
International deals 646–652
International Federation of the Phonographic
    Industry (IFPI) 294, 314
International Standard Recording Code (ISRC) 406
Internet 281–282
    'communication to the public' 155–156
    copyright 154
    downloads see Downloads
    legal regulation 302
    merchandising 505
    record contracts and 365
    royalties 298–301
    webcasting 284–285
InterTrust 306
INXS 321, 322, 349
iPods 279, 286, 323

Isley Brothers 330
iTunes 294, 297, 323
J.T. Tykociner 550
Jackson, Janet 176
Jackson, Mahalia 329
Jackson, Michael 146, 321, 449
    'Thriller' album 470
Jamster 286
'The Jazz Singer' 468
Jet 328
Jingles 207, 543–544
    arranging fees 545
    budget 544
    creative fees 544–545
    demo fees 544
    public performance royalties 546–547
    residuals 546
    session fees 545
John, Elton 146, 220, 349, 388, 523, 528
John Doe orders 519
Johnson, Eldridge 330
Joint authorship
    copyright 219–220
    duration of 165
Jolson, Al 330
Jukeboxes
    income from 206
    video 206, 471
Kazaa 284, 293, 294
Kelly, Paul 157, 328
Kemp, Gary 221
Kernaghan, Lee 334
Killen, Ken 591, 593
Kinks 97
Kinney Corporation 332
Kiss 376
Kitt, Eartha 330
Label
    definition 387
    identity 389–390
    ownership 387
Label deals 386
    accounts, keeping 391–392
    artists
        advantages 393–394
        points to watch 394
    cross recoupable deals 390
    funding 390, 394
    manufacture and distribution 394
    negotiating 389
    promotion 394
    purpose 388–389
    release guarantee 389
    rights
        audit 393
        granting 390–391
        reversion 392
    royalties 393
    territory 392–393
Lambert, Thomas 271–272
Lasers 275
Lauste, Eugene A. 550

Lawyers 596
  advice
    contract 598
    free 604
    general 599–600
  changing 604
  communication 602–603
  conflicts of interest 603–604
  contact information 605
  contract analysis, advice, negotiation 598, 657
  cost 600
    capped fees 601
    estimates 601
    hourly rate 600–601
    percentages 602
    success fees 601
  demo tapes, forwarding 352, 599
  endorsement contracts 529
  finding and choosing 596–598
  label deals 391
  master licence deals 408, 411
  merchandising protection 518
  payment 602
  pressing and distribution deals 397
  recording contracts 361, 366
Led Zeppelin 149
Legal expenses 627
Leiber and Stoller 191, 214
Letter of intent 137
Levy, Alain 295
Licences
  advertising, music used for 195–196, 205
  APRA 485
  broadcasting see Broadcasting
  commissioned material 194–195, 204–205, 556
  entertainment industry representatives 118–119
  fees
    producers sharing in 462
  licensing manager 212
  prerecorded and released material 195, 205,
    548–549, 555
  production music 194, 204, 543, 547–548, 552–553
  publishing deals, common clauses 256–257
'Lifers' 63
Lighting and power 629
Limewire 284
Literary works
  copyright, duration of 164
Little River Band 27, 321, 328
Live performance see Performing live
Lopez, Trini 332
Lump sum payments 444–445
Lurch (Adams Family) 324
Lyrics
  controlled composition clauses 448
  copyright 153, 159
McCartney, Paul 519
Macquarie label 329
McVie, John 26
Mailing costs 629
Makeup 630
Managers
  advances 104

artists, and 89, 97, 112
  financial relationship 93–94
  legal relationship 92–93
bonds 122
booking agents, as 107
co-managers 96
commission 103–104
  exclusions 104–107
  regulation of fees 119–120
contracts 92–93, 98–99
  agreement checklist 113
  enforcement 110–111
  termination 108–109
controlling 114–115, 123–124
definition 117
exclusivity 96
functions and obligations 99–100
  business management 101–102
  confidentiality 102–103
  engagements, procuring 101
  hard work 102–103
  integrity 102–103
group member, as 93–94
group recording contracts, negotiating 422–423
historical reputation 89
international 651
interstate 123
licences 118–119
management, scope of 94–95
merchandising expenses 107
performance costs 105–107
personal 97
powers 109–110
publishers, liaison with 211
qualifications 90–91
record contracts, getting 350, 354
  groups, for 422–423
recording costs 104–105
records, keeping 121
separate business, as 94
termination of agreement
  remuneration following 108–109
territory 97–98
tour support 107
trust accounts 120–121
when do you need? 91–92
Managing director (publishing) 211
Marketing see also Advertising, Public relations
  department (record company) 343, 347
  label deals 394
  master licence deals 411
  merchandising see Merchandising
  name, importance of 21
  not-for-profit organisations 77
  pressing and distribution deals 399
    promotional copies 400
  promotional materials 145–146
    music clips 468
  talent 647
Markie, Biz 178
Martin, George 457
'Martyrs' 63
Master licence deals 404

accounting 414–415
advances 414
artwork 406, 407
delivery of masters 410
duration 408
exclusivity 404
jurisdictional clauses 415–416
licensed rights 405–406, 409
master recordings 404, 406
  format 406
mechanical copyright fees 411–412
packaging 406, 410
parties 405
production costs 406–407, 410
promotion 411
proof of copyright 405
royalties 412–413
sub-licensing 409
termination 415
territory 407–408
withholding tax 416
Masters 404, 406
copyright
  producers' 464
format 406
MC Hammer 177
MCA 325, 332
MCPS see Mechanical Copyright Protection Society
  (MCPS)
MCY.com 284
MEAA see Media, Entertainment and Arts Alliance
  (MEAA)
Mechanical age 270–272
Mechanical Copyright Protection Society (MCPS)
  500
Mechanical income 188, 190, 446
covers 191–193
foreign copyright 500–501
master licence deals 411–412
mechanical royalties 190–191, 199–200
  Canada 263–264
  USA 263–264
payments, timing of 209
pressing and distribution deals 401
royalty caps and reductions 445–446
  controlled compositions 448
  examples 451–453
  'first use' rights 449–450
  'free goods' 447, 450
  North America 446–447
  pro rata rates 450
  publisher 449–450
  'records sold' 447–448
  retention and offset clauses 450
  three quarter rate 448
  videos 450
synchronisation see Synchronisation
video 450
Mechanical licence process 200–201
accounting 202
claims 201
controlled composition clauses 204
financial results 203

notice, issuing prescribed 201
payment 201–202
reporting the use 201
retentions 202
  sale-or-return 203
  standard wholesale 203
returns 202, 430
United Kingdom 203
United States 203
Media, Entertainment and Arts Alliance (MEAA)
  607–608, 610
Membership fees
non-profit organisations 42
Merchandising 147, 503–504
agent
  commission 516–517
  rights 517
  role 517
agreements, negotiation of 507
copyright 153
expenses, managers and 107
mail order 505
marketing see Marketing, Public relations
protection 518–519
purpose 506
record companies 507–509
retail 504–505, 516–517
rights 506–507
  allocation 507
soundtracks 503
sundry income 197–198
tour 504, 509
  accounting 514
  advances 511–513
  artist's share 513–514
  do it yourself 515–516
  duration of deal 509–510
  groups, obligations of members 515
  leftovers 514
  marketing plan 514–515
  payment 514
  quality control 514
  splits 513
  territory 509
  unrecoupment 510–511
web 505
when to? 506
Mercury 332
Mersey Sound 320
Michael, George 424
Michaelson, Scott 112
Midnight Oil 321, 322
Mid-price records
royalties 440–441
Miller, Mitch 329
Mingus 189
MiniDisc 277
royalties and 299, 437
Minogue, Kylie 146, 192, 322, 352
Mitchell, Joni 388
Mobile phones 288
ringtones see Ringtones
Money

book keeping see Book keeping
borrowing 613
cash book 614
grant applications 613
interest 628–629
managing 612
petty cash book 615
royalties see Royalties
taxation see Taxation
Moral rights 172
attribution 173
duration 174–175
false attribution, protection against 173–174
infringements
defences 175–176
remedies 175
integrity 174
remixing 381
soundtrack, original 564
waiver 175, 176
Morpheus 284
Moss, Jerry 388
Mousketeers 324
MP3 279, 283–284, 290, 323
MP3.com 290
MTV 470
MUA see Musicians' Union of Australia (MUA)
Mulcahy, Russell 477
Mushroom Records 325, 326, 333–334, 335, 388
Music clips 321, 323, 467, 479
budgets 469–470, 477–478
clearances 479
commissioning 474
concert films 469
copyright ownership 474
music in clips 474
delivery dates 479
DVDs 467, 471–472
future formats 472–473
history 468
producers 473
contracts 476–479
promotional tool 468
recording contracts 474–476
budget 475
creative control 475
packaging deductions 476
royalties 475–476
recoupment 429
rights, ownership of 478–479
royalties
caps and reductions 450
producers' 462
storyboard 477
telecasting 472
television 468, 469
video jukeboxes 206, 471
video sales 471
Music Council of Australia 40
Music Industry Advisory Council (MIAC) 171
Music publishing see Publishing
Music Sales 198
Music videos 321

Musica Viva 40
Musical styles
diversification 322
Musical works
attribution, right of 173
false attribution, protection against 173
copyright
duration 164, 174–175
ownership 159
Musicians' Union of Australia (MUA) 607–608
Musicmaker.com 297
MusicNet 331
MyPlay 331
Name
disputes 25–27
group recording contracts and 421–422
protecting 23–25
business name registration 23
company and shareholder agreements 25
legislative protection 28–29
partnerships 24–25
trade marks 23–24
search 22–23
selecting 21–29
solo career using group name 422
sound-alikes 27–28
protection from 28–29
using 146–147
value 21, 421
what's in a? 25–27
Napster 284, 290, 291–292, 294, 297, 330
post Napster 292–293
Natural justice 65
Negativland 178
Negotiation
deal 657–660
employment 81
lawyer, role of 598, 657
merchandising agreements 507
recording contracts 355–356
group contracts 422–423
renegotiation 661
techniques 658–660
New Edition 27
Not-for-profit organisations 40–41
board see Board
classical music groups 40
communication channels 59
company limited by guarantee 50–51, 66–69
co-operatives 49–50
cultural organisations, register of (ROCO) 52, 534
deductible gift recipient status 534
directors see Directors
establishing 41, 43
board, selecting the 44, 53–56
implementation strategy, defining 44
objects, defining 43–44, 73–74
excluded persons 71–72
financial planning 44, 75–76
funding, sources of 42–43, 76
establishing relationships 533–534
human resources 44
incorporated associations 47–49, 66

management 53–60, 74–75
marketing 77
non-profit, definition 42
prohibited persons 71–72
public relations 77
structure, selecting 45–52
trusts 51–52, 72–73
unincorporated non-profit groups 46–47, 65–66
Notice, giving 384–385
Okamura, Professor 274
O'Neill, Sharon 368
Oracle Distribution 336
Oral agreements 358–359
O'Sullivan, Gilbert 178
Override royalties 363
Overseas artists
taxation 622, 645
Overseas income 209
net receipts 261–262
source, at 262–263
sub-publisher's commission 260–261
Overstocks 430–431
P2P networks 284
Paananen, Vesa-Matti 285
Pacific Records 329
Packaging
company policy 435
master licence deals 406, 410
royalty deductions 434–435
cassettes 435–436
CDs 436
music clips 476
vinyl records 435
Page, Larry 97
Page One 111
Paley, William 329
Parallel importing 180–181, 184–185
competition policy 182
Ergas Report 183–184
protection, removal of 322
sound recordings 181
Partnership 32–36, 420
checklist 33–36
co-writers 219
manager as part of 93–94
protecting group name 24–25
taxation 624
planning 643–644
Parton, Dolly 192
Passing off 518
Payroll services 87–88
Performance
copyright 153, 154, 159
moral rights, duration of 175
non-copyright rights, protection of 170–171
costs
managers and 105–107
fees
agents, collected by 81–82
income 188
rights 196–197
royalties 441–442
jingle writing 546–547

tracing 208
logging 486
Performers
attribution, right of 173
false attribution, protection against 173–174
consent form 171
copyright ownership 159, 163–164, 171–172
definition 160
employees, as 163
non-copyright rights, protection of 170–171, 178
Performers' Protection clearance 464
Performing live 125, 351
audience numbers 141
bargaining power 126
booking confirmation 128
cancelling contracted performances 152
catering 150
complimentary tickets 142–143
contracting performances 135
dressing rooms 149–150
employers, dealing with 126–127
fees 206
four walls deal 139–140
net participation deals 139
payment of 140–141
percentage of gross or net 138
percentage of gross or net, fee against 138–139
set fee 137
staggered percentage of gross 139
festivals and events 145
insurance 151–152, 592–593
event insurance 593–595
travel insurance 591
performance details 148
performers, rights of see Performers
permits and consents 151
photographers 150–151
power requirements 149
publicity 145–147
creating public awareness 351
recording the performance 150
royalties 206–207
splits 259–260, 499
security arrangements 148
set up 147–148
staging 148–149
starting out 125–126
support acts 143–144
buying in 145
taxation 130
terms
enforcement 129–130
negotiating 127–129
ticket prices 141
ticket sales 142
touring see Touring
Performing Right Society (PRS) 499
Perkins, Carl 191
Permits and consents
performance 151
Personal managers 96
Peter, Paul and Mary 332
Petersen, Paul 323

Petty cash book 615
Phantom/MGM Distribution 336
Philanthropy 532–533
   acknowledgment of donors 536–537
   assessable income 621
   companies 537–538
   establishing relationships 533
   individuals 537
   maintaining relationships 536–537
   taxation issues 534–536, 539–541
   volunteering 539
   workplace giving 538–539
Philips 274, 276, 325, 330, 332, 333
   digital compact cassette (DCC) 277
Phonograph 158
Phonographic Performance Company of Australia
      Ltd (PPCA) 413, 442, 486
   arbitration 495–496
   coverage 492
   direct distribution to artists 494–495
   FACTS, conflict with 495, 497
   foreign copyright owners 493–494
   functions 491
   income and distribution 492–493
   membership 491–492
   pay for play boycotts 493
Photographers
   live performances 150–151
Piano roll 270
Pink 146
Pink Floyd 27
Pirate music
   downloads see Downloads
Pitney, Gene 454
The Platters 26–27
The Police 321, 349, 421
PolyGram 295, 325, 332, 333–334, 388
Pop Mechanix 25–26
Popular culture (Australia)
   1960s 320
   1970s 320
Popular Mechanics 25–26
Porter, Cole 191, 270
Power requirements 149
PPCA see Phonographic Performance Company of
      Australia Ltd (PPCA) see PPCA
Premiums
   mechanical income 200
   royalties 440
   sponsorship 528
Prerecorded material 195, 205, 548–549, 553
   clearance procedures 555–556
   licence fees 555
   music, ownership of 554
   no owner found 555
   sound recording, ownership of 554
Presley, Elvis 191, 330
Pressing and distributing deals 394–395
   accounting 402–403
   advantages 395
   deductions 402
   distribution 400
      fees 401–402

distributor
   role 398
   selecting a 396
   expenses 396–397
   funding 395, 397
   manufacturing 398–399
   master licence deals, distinguished 394, 395–396
   ownership 399
   promotion 399
      promotional copies 400
   stock control 399, 403
   termination 403
   trading terms 401
   who does what? 397–398
Pricing
   GST and 432–433, 434
   published price to dealers (PPD) 432
      calculation 432–433
   recommended retail price (RRP) 431–432
      royalty calculation 432
   wholesale 432
Print income 188, 189–190
   calculation, collection and distribution 198–199
   print licences 198
Print music 213
   sales 213–214
Prior, John 220–221
Prizes
   income from 620–621
Producers 454–455
   administrative and financial control 457–458
   budget overages, responsibility for 464
   contracts 456
      job description 456
      parties 457
      services required 457–458
      termination 465–466
   copyright 225
      masters 464
      works composed by third parties 464–465
      works composed with artist 464
   creative control 457, 458
   fees 458
      advances 460
      payment, timing of 459
      per master 459
      recoupment 460
      share of licence fees 462
      total recording package 459
   remixing 465
   royalties 444, 455, 459–462
      A-side protection 463
      pro-rata calculations 463
      rates 460
      reductions 462
      timing of payment 460, 461–462
      video 462
      who will pay? 460–461
   selecting a producer 458
   third party 455–456
Producers (film)
   music clips 469, 473
Product endorsement see also Sponsorship

contracts 529–531
direct endorsement 528
Production department 342–343
Production music 194, 204, 543, 547
libraries 547–548, 552
Profit motive 633–634
Promoters 135–136
agents, distinguished 131
attitudes 136–137
letter of intent 137
remuneration 137–140
seeking 135
Promotion see Marketing, Public relations
PRS see Performing Right Society (PRS)
Pseudonymous works
copyright, duration of 165
Public funds 535
prescribed 540–541
Public relations see also Marketing, Promotion,
Sponsorship
'all media' contracts 362
artist name and reputation, using 146–147
brand recognition 298, 521
creating awareness 350
guest appearances 362
interviews 145
knowing someone 350
music clips 468
name, importance of 21
not-for-profit organisations 77
press releases 146
professional image 352, 376
promotional give-aways 430
royalty reductions 447, 450
publicity stunts 352
record company, using 146
record contracts 376
taxation deductions 630
Publicity stunts 352
Publishing 186–187, 210
accounts department 215
accounting 265–266
agreements 192
business affairs department 214–215
contracts see Publishing contracts
copyright 153, 154, 187
duration 164
ownership 164
copyright department 215
creative services manager 211–212
income 187
sources 189–198
Internet 296
licensing manager 212
managing director 211
overseas 209
net receipts 261–262
source, at 262–263
sub-publisher's commission 260–261
pluggers 214
'publication', meaning of 157
publisher, role of 187
rights 188, 189

adaptation 188–189
communication to the public 188
reproduction 188
royalties 97
caps and reductions 449–450
self-publishing 252
transcribers 212–213
warehousing 216
Publishing contracts
accounting 265–266
administration deals 253–255
advances 237–238
recoupment 239–240
assignment of copyright 165–166, 256–257
re-assignment 268
creative control clauses 266–267
duration 235–237
licences 256–257
obligations of publisher 257–258
productivity commitment 240
publisher's warranties 268
retention period 236–237
reversion of copyright 268
sample 241–252
single-song assignment 228–229
specific-works agreements 229–235
split deals 238–239
writer-for-hire agreements 227–228
writer's warranties 267
Puff Daddy 177
Pye 273
Radio 272, 274
digital 287–288
royalties, payment of 207
community radio 207
narrowcast radio 207
tracing performances 208
Radio Corporation of America (RCA) 330
Rajon 336, 337
Rajon, Buck 26
RealNetworks 331
Receipts 614–615
Record clubs 337–338
royalties 438–439
Record companies
accounts department 345
art department 341–342
artist and repertoire department (A & R)
339–340
budget 372
creative development 373
disputes 372–373
producers, as 454
'satisfactory record', interpretation 373–374
Australian see Australian record business
budget 337
business, changing the way they do 295–298
business affairs department 341
choosing 346–348
competition 317
downloads, fighting 291–294
'hot' 346–347
Independents 325, 335–336

Majors 325–326
  head office 327
  local 334
  multinational 327–334
  structures 326–327
marketing and promotions department 343, 347
merchandising 507–509
on-line department 345
production department 342–343
relationships with 347–348
sales representatives 344
shares in 445
stock control 342–343
technology, alliances with 296
warehouse department 344
Record producers
  copyright 225
Record shops
  Fast Tracks Kiosks 298
Recording
  budget 372
  contracts see Contracts (recording)
  costs
    managers and 104–105
  digital technology 275–279
  early recordings 270–271
  electric 272–273
  flat records 271–272
  hi-fi 273
  live performance 150
  portable 275
  royalties 97, 104
  sound see Sound recordings
Recoupable deals 377, 429
  groups 425
  producers 460
Reeves, Alan 273
Register of Cultural Organisations (ROCO) 52, 534
Releases
  artist delay 374
  control of releases 375
  disputes 375
  guarantee 389
  overseas 369
  record company delay 374
  secondary 378
  singles versus albums 370–371
Remixes
  producers and 465
  rights 381
Rentals
  record 417
  taxation deductions, 628, 629
Repairs 627
Representation
  agents, by 80
Reprise Records 332
Reproduction 157
  home copying 169
  insubstantial portion, use of 168–169
  music publication rights 188
Reputation see also Public relations
  artist name and, using 146–147

brand recognition 298, 521
  importance of 54
Retail merchandising 504–505, 516
  agent
    commission 516–517
    rights 517
    role 517
Retentions 202
  sale-or-return 203
  standard wholesale 203
Retransmission
  copyright royalties 496
Richard, Cliff 328
Riddle, Nelson 454
Rights
  advertising music, original 543–544
  audit 393
  copyright 155, 166
    licensing 166, 191
  label deals
    granting 390–391
    reversion 392
  master licence deals 405–406, 409, 413
  merchandising 506–507
    allocation 507
  moral see Moral rights
  music clips, ownership of 478–479
  non-copyright, protection of 170–171, 178
  public performance and broadcasting 196–197,
    485–487, 491
  record companies
    first option on soloists leaving groups 424
  remixing 381
Ringtones 285–287, 528
  mechanical income 200, 491
  sound-alike recordings 28
Rivoli Theatre 550
Robert Stigwood Organisation 332, 388
Rodeo Records 329
Rogers, Kenny 504
Rogers and Hammerstein 191
Royalties 97, 427 see also Income
  accounting 443–444
  accounts department 345
  alternatives 444
  assessable income 621
  base 431–432
    calculating 433, 476
  broadcast 441–442
  caps and reductions 445–453
    producers' 462
  'cast' recordings 609–610
  covers, administration deals for 254
  cross recoupable deals 390
  DCCs 299, 437
  deductions 433
    arbitrary 437
    artwork 434
    delivery charges 434
    double 437–438
    GST 434
    new technology 436–437
    packaging 434–436

deletions 430–431
format exceptions 431
gratis copies for promotion 430
label deals 393
lump sum payments 444–445
master licence deals 412–413
mechanical see Mechanical income
MiniDiscs 299, 437
music clips 475–476
net sales 429–431
non-recoupable 377, 427–428
override 363
overstocks 430–431
pricing and
    published price to dealers (PPD) 432–433
    recommended retail price (RRP) 431–432
producers' 444, 455, 459–460
    A-side protection 463
    pro-rata calculations 463
    rates 460
    reductions 462
    share of licence fees 462
    timing of payment 460, 461–462
    video royalties 462
    who will pay? 460–461
rates 431
record contracts 376–377
    groups 425
recoupable 377, 429
    groups 425
returns 202, 430
sales by unusual marketing methods 438–441
secondary exploitation 378–379
shares, as 445
single-song assignment 229
soundtrack, original 562
    payment schedule 563
splits 238–239, 258, 499
    administration deals 253–254
    covers 258–259
    co-writers 222
    sheet writing 259
synchronisation fees 442–443
    producers sharing 462
    royalty splits 258–259
taxation 630
technology and 298–301
video 450, 462
SACD 279
SACEM see Societé des Auteurs, Compositeures et
    Musique (SACEM)
Sales
    deletions 430
    first 431
    gratis copies for promotion 430
    mechanicals on 'records sold' 447–448
    merchandising see Merchandising
    music videos and DVDs 471–472
    net sales 429–431
    published price to dealers (PPD) 432
        calculation 432–433
    recommended retail price (RRP) 431–432
        royalty calculation 432

record clubs 438–439
returns 202, 430
statistics 315–316, 435
    cassettes 436
    DVDs 317
Sales representatives 344
Sam and Dave 27
Sampling 176–179
    backing vocals 180
    payment for 179–180
Sanity
    Fast Tracks Kiosks 298
Savage Garden 97, 322
Scour 290
Screenrights 496, 502
    costs 496
    retransmission by pay-TV services 496
    royalties collected 496
        musical works 497
        sound recordings 497
Seagram Co 332
Sebastian, Guy 192
'Secret agents' 63–64
Security arrangements 148
The Seekers 320, 328
Self-publishing 252
Self-reporting 208–209
Session musicians
    industry awards 608
    payment 381, 444
        jingle writing 545
Set up 147–148
Seven Arts 332
Sex Pistols 321
SFX Entertainment 284
The Shadows 328
Sharegift 538
Shareholder agreements 25, 38
Shares
    royalties paid as 445
Sharman Networks 293
Sheet music 213
    income from 189–190
        calculation 198–199
        collection 198–199
        distribution 198–199
        royalty splits 259
    print licences 198
    sales 213–214
Sheldon, Zelda 220–221
Shock Records 326, 336
Silverchair 322, 655
Simpson Music 180
Sinatra, Frank 191, 332
Singer-songwriter
    publishing terms 192
Single-song assignment 228–229
Singles versus albums 370–371
Skills matrix 56
'Sleepers' 62
The Smiths 33
Social Ventures Australia 533
Societé des Auteurs, Compositeures et Musique

(SACEM) 480
Societé des Gens de Lettres 480
Soloists 30–31
Sonart 336
Songwriter
  publishing terms 192
Sony 276, 325, 328–330, 334, 424, 508
  MiniDisc 277
Sound recordings
  'cast' recordings 609–610
  commissioned music 558
  copyright 153, 154, 158, 497, 554
    compensation 163
    duration 164, 175
    ownership 159–163
    performances 156, 159, 173–174
    recordings made prior to 1 January 2005
    161–163
  parallel importing 181, 182
  permissions 162
Soundtracks see also Film
  commissioning 194–195, 204–205, 556—557
    composers with publishing contracts 557
    contract 557–578
    when to say no to work 586–588
  credits, production 564
  master licence deals 409
  merchandising 503
  prerecorded material 195, 205, 548–549, 553
    clearance procedures 555–556
    licence fees 555
    music, ownership of 554
    no owner found 555
    sound recording, ownership of 554
  production music 194, 204, 547, 552–553
    libraries 547–548
  role and importance 550–551
  secondary exploitation 378–379
Spandau Ballet 221
Spears, Britney 146, 528
Spendour in the Grass 145
Sponsorship 521–522, 526
  conflict with venues 527
  exit clause 526
  product endorsement see Product endorsement
  reasons for 522
    association with excellence 523–524
    brand development 523
    client and staff relations 524–525
    image definition 523
    image establishment 522–523
    image improvement 523
  records, of 528
  relationship, nature of 525
  tour 526–527
  what to ask for 525–526
Springsteen, Bruce 340
Stage productions
  'cast' recordings 609–610
Staging 148–149
Statement of objectives 43–44
Status Quo 422
Stevens, Connie 324

Sting 224
Stock control
  pressing and distribution deals 399, 403
  record companies 342–343
Subscriptions 628
Subsidies
  assessable income 621
Superannuation 644
Support acts 143–144
  buying in 145
Synchronisation ('synch') income 188, 194
  creative control clauses 266–267
  master licence deals 413
  music in music clips 474
  original soundtrack material 194–195
    commissioning costs 204–205, 562–563
  prerecorded material 195, 205, 548–549, 553
    clearance procedures 555–556
    licence fees 555
    music, ownership of 554
    no owner found 555
    sound recording, ownership of 554
  production music 194, 204, 547, 552–553
    libraries 547–548
  royalties 442–443
    producers' 462
    splits 258–259
Take That 421
Talent 646–648
Talent shows 355
'Talkers' 64
Taupin, Bernie 220
Taxation 612, 619
  assessable income 620–621
  Australian system 620
  business
    activity statements (BAS) 617
    nature of 631–638
    registration 638–641
    structures 31, 37–38
  capital expenses 624
  deductible gift recipient status 534
  deductions 624
    recurrent expenses 627–631
  depreciation 624
  discounts 628
  fringe benefits, registration 641
  GST see Goods and services tax (GST)
  income averaging 642–643
  income tax exempt charity status (ITEC) 536
  intention of taxpayer 633–635
  label deals 391
  losses, carrying forward 642
  overseas artists 622, 645
  PAYG 622
    registration 641
  payroll services 87–88
  performing live 130
  personal services income 641
  philanthropy 534–536, 539–541
  planning 643
  rates
    Australian residents 622

non-Australian residents 622
receipts 614–615
abnormal 642
recurrent expenses 627–631
returns
companies 624
individuals 623
partnerships 624
requirement to lodge 623
trusts 624
Simplified Tax System (STS) 625–627
tax file number, obtaining 640
taxable income 621–622
overseas artists 622, 645
TVA (France) 434
VAT (UK) 434
withholding
master licence deals 416
Technology 269–270
copy protection information 280
copyright problems 276–277, 289, 302–307
culture and 303, 312
digital see Digital technology
royalty deductions for new 436–437
Telecasting 472
Tele-marketers 336–337
Television
music clips 468, 469
record contracts and 364
royalties, payment of 207
community television 207
narrowcast television 207
subscription services 207
synchronisation 194–195, 204–205
royalties 442–443, 462
tracing performances 208
Territory
copyright 167
label deals 392–393
managers 97–98
master licence deals 407–408
parallel importing and 181
record contracts 368–369
tour merchandising 509
where to base the business 652
Tickets
complimentary 142–143
prices 141
sales 142
Tijuana Brass 388
Time Life 337
Time Warner 324, 331, 334
Tiny Tim 352
Touring 97, 131–132 see also Performing live
accommodation 133, 152
agents
promoters, distinguished 131
using 135–140
budget preparation 133–134, 612–613
funding 135
merchandising 504
accounting 514
advances 511–513

artist's share 513–514
do it yourself 515–516
duration of deal 509–510
groups, obligations of members 515
leftovers 514
marketing plan 514–515
payment 514
quality control 514
splits 513
territory 509
unrecoupment 510–511
planning 132–133
promoters
agents, distinguished 131
using 135–140
publicity 145–147
sponsorship 526–527
support managers 107
Trademarks
labels 387
merchandising 518
name 23–24
Trading terms 401
Transistor, invention of 274
Translating music
copyright issues 224–225
Travel
insurance 591
taxation deductions 629–630
touring see Touring
Trusts 39
discretionary 39
not-for-profit organisations 51–52
taxation 624
planning 644
trustees, duties of 72–73
unit 39
TVA 434
U2 178
UMG 288, 330
Unincorporated non-profit group 46
advantages 46
committee members, duties of 65–66
disadvantages 46–47
formation of 47
Unions 607–608
United States Free Trade Agreement
Implementation Act 2004 156, 159, 160, 163,
170, 172
United States Gramophone Company 271
Universal Copyright Convention (UCC) 158
Universal Music 324, 325, 331–332, 388, 508
Universal Music Mobile 288
Valance, Holly 112
Vanilla Ice 177
VAT 434
Vega, Susan 178
Venue consultants 78, 87
controlling 114–115, 123–124
definition 117–118
fees, regulation of 120
licences 118–119
payroll services 87–88

Venues
  performance fees and 137–140
  searching for 126–127
  sponsorship, conflicting deals 527
  webcasting 284–285
Verve 177, 332, 387
Victor Talking Machine Company 330
Video clips see Music clips
Video tape 274–275
The Vines 212
Vinyl 271–272, 276
  packaging deductions 435
Virgin 328
  Fast Tracks Kiosks 298
Virgin Megastores 297
Vivendi Universal 288, 324, 332
Volunteering 539
Walt Disney 324
Warehousing 216
  overstocks 430–431
  pressing and distribution deals 399–400
  record companies 344
Warlow, Anthony 192
Warner Brothers 324, 332
Warner Music 325, 326, 332–334, 388
Warner/Chappell 198, 332, 333
Warranties
  publishers 268
  record contracts 383
  writer's 267
WEA 388
Webcasting 284–285
'Weekend Warriors' 524–525
Western Electric 550
Wham 421
Whitesnake 388
The Wiggles 334
William Morris Agency 78, 652
Williams, Robbie 286–287, 508
Winsoar, James 285
WIPO Performances and Phonograms Treaty
  (1996) 172
Workplace giving 538–539
Writer-for-hire agreements 227–228
Yahoo Music 297
You Am I 212
Young, John Paul 318
Young, Neil 388
Zappa, Frank 360
Zoomba Music 552

ABOUT THE AUTHOR

SHANE SIMPSON is one of the leading advisors and deal-makers in the Australian music industry. He is a principal of Simpsons Solicitors, a firm specialising in intellectual property, the arts, entertainment and the media. He is a consultant to governments, NGO's, institutions and major corporations, both nationally and internationally.

A long time ago, in a place far away, he was a professional musician.

He has written or edited numerous books most of which deal with the relationship of law to cultural and intellectual property. He was the founder of the Arts Law Centre of Australia. He headed the Federal Government Inquiry into "Copyright Collecting Societies in Australia". He has been on the board of many of Australia's most important cultural companies and philanthropic foundations.